THE TRUTH ABOUT FOREVER & LOCK AND KEY

ALSO BY SARAH DESSEN

Along for the Ride
Dreamland
Just Listen
Keeping the Moon
Lock and Key
The Moon and More
Once and for All
Saint Anything
Someone Like You
That Summer
This Lullaby
The Truth About Forever
What Happened to Goodbye

SARAH DESSEN

THE TRUTH ABOUT FOREVER
&
LOCK AND KEY

PENGUIN BOOKS

PENGUIN BOOKS
An imprint of Penguin Random House LLC, New York

The Truth About Forever first published in the United States of America by Viking,
an imprint of Penguin Random House LLC, 2004
First paperback edition published by Speak, an imprint of Penguin Group (USA) LLC, 2006
Lock and Key first published in the United States of America by Viking,
an imprint of Penguin Random House LLC, 2008
First paperback edition published by Speak, an imprint of Penguin Group (USA) LLC, 2009
This omnibus edition published by Penguin Books,
an imprint of Penguin Random House LLC, 2022

Visit us online at penguinrandomhouse.com.

This edition ISBN 9780593527665

Printed in the United States of America

1 3 5 7 9 10 8 6 4 2

LSCH

THE TRUTH ABOUT FOREVER

For Jay, as ever, and for my cousins

who, like me, know by heart the view
of the river and the bay,
the complex rules of Beckon,
and all the ways you Can't Get to Heaven

to name you all would be a book in itself:
you know who you are.

Chapter One

Jason was going to Brain Camp. It had another name, a real name, but that's what everyone called it.

"Okay," he said, wedging a final pair of socks along the edge of his suitcase. "The list. One more time."

I picked up the piece of paper beside me. "Pens," I said. "Notebooks. Phone card. Camera battery. Vitamins."

His fingers moved across the contents of the bag, finding and identifying each item. Check and double-check. With Jason, it was always about being sure.

"Calculator." I continued, "Laptop. . . ."

"Stop," he said, putting up his hand. He walked over to his desk, unzipping the slim black bag there, then nodded at me. "Skip down to list number two."

I scanned down the page, found the words LAPTOP (CASE), and cleared my throat. "Blank CDs," I said. "Surge protector. Headphones. . . ."

By the time we'd covered that, then finished the main list—stopping to cover two other sub-headings, TOILETRIES and MISCELLANEOUS—Jason seemed pretty much convinced he had everything. Which did not, however, stop him from continuing to circle the room, mumbling to himself. It took a lot of work to be perfect. If you didn't want to break a sweat, there was no point in even bothering.

Jason knew perfect. Unlike most people, for him it wasn't some distant horizon. For Jason, perfect was just over the next hill, close enough to make out the landscape. And it wasn't a place he would just visit. He was going to live there.

He was the all-state math champ, head of the debate team, holder of the highest GPA in the history of our high school (he'd been taking AP classes since seventh grade, college sections since tenth), student council president two years running, responsible for an innovative school recycling program now implemented in districts around the country, fluent in Spanish and French. But it wasn't just about academics. Jason was also a vegan and had spent the past summer building houses for Habitat for Humanity. He practiced yoga, visited his grandmother in her rest home every other Sunday, and had a pen pal from Nigeria he'd been corresponding with since he was eight years old. Anything he did, he did well.

A lot of people might find this annoying, even loathsome. But not me. He was just what I needed.

I had known this from the first day we met, in English class sophomore year. We'd been put into groups to do an assignment on *Macbeth*, me and Jason and a girl named Amy Richmond who, after we pulled our desks together, promptly announced she was "no good at this Shakespeare crap" and put her head down on her backpack. A second later, she was sound asleep.

Jason just looked at her. "Well," he said, opening his textbook, "I guess we should get started."

This was right after everything happened, and I was in a silent phase. Words weren't coming to me well; in fact I had trouble even recognizing them sometimes, entire sentences seeming like they were another language, or backwards, as my eyes moved across them. Just printing my own name on the top of a page a few days previously, I'd second-guessed the letters and their order, not even sure of that anymore.

So of course *Macbeth* had totally mystified me. I'd spent the entire weekend struggling with the antiquated language and weird names of the characters, unable to even figure out the most basic aspects of the story. I opened my book, staring down at the lines of dialogue: *Had I but died an hour before this chance/I had liv'd a blessed time; for, from this instant,/ there's nothing serious in mortality:/all is but toys.*

Nope, I thought. Nothing.

Lucky for me, Jason, who was not about to leave his grade in someone else's hands, was used to taking control of group work. So he opened his notebook to a clean page, pulled out a pen, and uncapped it. "First," he said to me, "let's just get down the basic themes of the play. Then we can figure out what to write about."

I nodded. All around us I could hear our classmates chattering, the tired voice of our English teacher, Mr. Sonnenberg, telling us again to please settle down.

Jason skipped down a few lines on his page. *Murder*, I watched him write. His handwriting was clean, block-style, and he moved across the page quickly. *Power. Marriage. Revenge. Prophecy. Politics.* It seemed like he could go on forever, but then he stopped and looked at me. "What else?" he asked.

I glanced back down at my book, as if somehow, the words there would suddenly form together into something coherent. I could feel Jason looking at me, not unkindly, just waiting for me to contribute.

"I don't . . ." I said finally, then stopped, the words sticking.

I swallowed, then started over. "I don't understand it. Actually."

I was sure, hearing this, he'd shoot me the same look he'd given Amy Richmond. But Jason surprised me, putting down his pen. "Which part?"

"Any of it," I said, and when he didn't roll his eyes as I'd been expecting, I added, "I mean, I know there's a murder plot and I know there's an invasion but the rest . . . I don't know. It's totally confusing."

"Look," he said, picking up his pen again. "It's not as complicated as you think. The key to really understanding is to start with the prophecy about what's going to happen . . . see, here. . . ." He started flipping pages in his book, still talking, and pointed out a passage to me. Then he read it aloud, and as his finger moved across the words it was like he changed them, magic, and suddenly they made sense.

And I felt comfort. Finally. All I'd wanted for so long was for someone to explain everything that had happened to me in this same way. To label it neatly on a page: this leads to this leads to this. I knew, deep down, it was more complicated than that, but watching Jason, I was hopeful. He took the mess that was *Macbeth* and fixed it, and I had to wonder if he might, in some small way, be able to do the same for me. So I moved myself closer to him, and I'd been there ever since.

Now, he zipped up his laptop case and put it on the bed with the rest of his stuff. "Okay," he said, taking one last glance around the room. "Let's go."

His mom and dad were already in their Volvo when we came outside. Mr. Talbot got out, opened the trunk, and he and Jason took a few minutes getting everything situated. As I got in the backseat and put on my seatbelt, Mrs. Talbot turned around and smiled at me. She was a botanist, her husband a chemist, both of them professors. They were so scholarly that every time I saw either of them without a book in their hands they looked weird to me, as if they were missing their noses, or their elbows.

I tried not to think about this as she said, "So, Macy. What are you going to do until August without Jason?"

"I don't know," I said. I was working at the library, taking over Jason's job at the information desk, but other than that, the next eight weeks were just looming ahead, empty. While I had a few friends from student council, most had gone away for the summer themselves, to Europe or camp. To be honest, Jason's and my relationship was pretty time consuming: between yoga classes and student government stuff, not to mention all the causes we dealt with, there just hadn't been much time for anyone else. Besides, Jason got easily frustrated with people, so I'd been hesitant to invite new people out with us. If they were slow, or lazy in any way, he lost patience fast, and it was just easier to hang out with him, or with his friends, who could keep up with him. I'd never really thought about this as a bad thing, actually. It was just how we were.

On the way to the airport, Jason and his dad discussed some elections that had just happened in Europe; his mom fretted about construction traffic; and I sat there, looking at the inch between Jason's knee and mine and wondering why I didn't try to move closer to him. This wasn't new. He hadn't even kissed me until our third date, and now, after a year and a half, we still hadn't discussed going all the way. At the time we met, someone just hugging me still felt like too much to bear. I didn't want anyone to get too close. So this had been all I wanted, a boy who understood how I felt. Now, though, I sometimes wished for more.

At the airport, we said good-bye at the gate. His parents hugged him, then discreetly walked across the waiting room to stand at the window there, looking out at the runway and the big stretch of blue sky that hung over it. I put my arms around Jason, breathing in his smell—sport stick deodorant and acne cleanser—deeply, so I'd get enough to last me awhile.

"I'm going to miss you," I told him. "So much."

"It's only eight weeks," he said.

He kissed me on the forehead. Then, quickly, so quickly I didn't even have time to react, on the lips. He leaned back and looked at me, tightening his arms around my waist.

"I'll email you," he said, and kissed me on the forehead again. As they called his flight and he disappeared down the hallway to the plane, I stood with the Talbots and watched him go, feeling a tug in my chest. It was going to be a long summer. I'd wanted a real kiss, something to remember, but I'd long ago learned not to be picky in farewells. They weren't guaranteed or promised. You were lucky, more than blessed, if you got a good-bye at all.

My dad died. And I was there.

This was how people knew me. Not as Macy Queen, daughter of Deborah, who built pretty houses in brand new cul-de-sacs. Or as sister of Caroline, who'd had just about the most beautiful wedding anyone had ever seen at the Lakeview Inn the previous summer. Not even as the one-time holder of the record for the fifty-yard dash, middle school division. Nope. I was Macy Queen, who'd woken up the day after Christmas and gone outside to see her father splayed out at the end of the road, a stranger pumping away at his broad chest. I saw my dad die. That was who I was now.

When people first heard this, or saw me and remembered it, they always made that face. The one with the sad look, accompanied by the cock of the head to the side and the softening of the chin—*oh my goodness, you poor thing*. While it was usually well intentioned, to me it was just a reaction of muscles and tendons that meant nothing. Nothing at all. I hated that face. I saw it everywhere.

The first time was at the hospital. I was sitting in a plastic chair by the drink machine when my mother walked out of the small waiting room, the one off the main one. I already knew this was where they took people to tell them the really bad news: that their wait was over, their person was dead. In fact, I'd just watched another family make this progression, the ten or so steps and the turn of a corner, crossing over from hopeful to hopeless. As my mother—now the latter—came toward me, I knew. And behind her there was this plump nurse holding a chart, and she saw me standing there in my track pants and baggy sweatshirt, my old smelly running shoes, and she made the face. *Oh, poor dear*. Then though, I had no idea how it would follow me.

I saw The Face at the funeral, everywhere. It was the common mask on the people clumped on the steps, sitting quietly murmuring in the pews, shooting me sideways looks that I could feel, even as I kept my head down, my eyes on the solid black of my tights, the scuffs on my shoe. Beside me, my sister Caroline sobbed: through the service, as we walked down the aisle, in the limo, at the cemetery, at the reception afterward. She cried so much it seemed wrong for me to, even if I could have. For anyone else to join in was just overkill.

I hated that I was in this situation, I hated that my dad was gone, I hated that I'd been lazy and sleepy and had waved him off when he'd come into my room that morning, wearing his smelly Waccamaw 5K shirt, leaning down to my ear to whisper, *Macy, wake up. I'll give you a head start. Come on, you know the first few steps are the hardest part.* I hated that it had been not two or three but five minutes later that I changed my mind, getting up to dig out my track pants and lace my shoes. I hated that I wasn't faster on those three-tenths of a mile, that by the time I got to him he was already gone, unable to hear my voice, see my face, so that I could say all the things I wanted to. I might have been the girl whose dad died, the girl who was there, and everyone might have known it. Like so much else, I could not control that. But the fact that I was angry and scared, that was my secret to keep. They didn't get to have that, too. It was all mine.

When I got home from the Talbots', there was a box on the porch. As soon as I leaned over and saw the return address, I knew what it was.

"Mom?" My voice bounced down the empty front hall as I came inside, bumping the door shut behind me. In the dining room, I could see fliers stacked around several floral arrangements, everything all set for the cocktail reception my mother was hosting that night. The newest phase of her neighborhood, luxury townhouses, was just starting construction, and she had sales to make. Which meant she was in full-out schmooze mode, a fact made clear by the sign over the mantel featuring her smiling face and her slogan: *Queen Homes—Let Us Build Your Castle.*

I put the box on the kitchen island, right in the center, then walked to the fridge and poured myself a glass of orange juice. I drank all of it down, rinsed the cup, and put it in the dishwasher. But it didn't matter how I busied myself. The entire time, I was aware of the box perched there waiting for me. There was nothing to do but just get it over with.

I pulled a pair of scissors out of the island drawer, then drew them across the top of the box, splitting the line of tight brown packing tape. The return address, like all the others, was Waterville, Maine.

Dear Mr. Queen,

As one of our most valued EZ Products customers, please find enclosed our latest innovation for your perusal. We feel assured that you'll find it will become as important and time-saving a part of your daily life as the many other products you've purchased from us over the years. If, however, for some reason you're not completely satisfied, return it within thirty days and your account will not be charged.

Thank you again for your patronage. If you have any questions, please feel free to contact our friendly customer service staff at the number below. It's for people like you that we work to make daily life better, more productive, and most of all, easy. It's not just a name: it's a promise.

Most cordially,
Walter F. Tempest
President, EZ Products

I scooped out Styrofoam peanuts, piling them neatly next to the box, until I found the package inside. It had two pictures on the front. In the first one, a woman was standing at a kitchen counter with about twenty rolls of tinfoil and waxed paper stacked up in front of her. She had a frustrated expression on her face, like she was about two breaths away from some sort of breakdown. In the picture beside it, the woman was at the same counter. Gone were the boxes, replaced instead by a plastic console that was attached to the wall. From it, she was pulling some plastic wrap, now sporting the beatific look usually associated with madonnas or people on heavy medication.

Are you tired of dealing with the mess of so many kinds of foil and wrap? Sick of fumbling through messy drawers or cabinets? Get the Neat Wrap and you'll have what you need within easy reach. With convenient slots for sandwich and freezer bags, tinfoil and waxed paper, you'll never have to dig through a drawer again. It's all there, right at your fingertips!

I put the box down, running my finger over the edge. It's funny what it takes to miss someone. A packed funeral, endless sympathy cards, a reception full of murmuring voices, I could handle. But every time a box came from Maine, it broke my heart.

My dad loved this stuff: he was a sucker for anything that

claimed to make life simpler. This, mixed with a tendency to insomnia, was a lethal combination. He'd be downstairs, going over contracts or firing off emails late into the night, with the TV on in the background, and then an infomercial would come on. He'd be sucked in immediately, first by the happy, forced banter between the host and the gadget designer, then by the demonstration, followed by the bonus gifts, just for ordering Right Now, by which point he was already digging out his credit card with one hand as he dialed with the other.

"I'm telling you," he'd say to me, all jazzed up with that pre-purchase enthusiasm, "that's what I call an *innovation*!"

And to him, it was: the Jumbo Holiday Greeting Card Pack he bought for my mother (which covered every holiday from Kwanzaa to Solstice, with not a single Christmas card), and the plastic contraption that looked like a small bear trap and promised the perfect French Twist, which we later had to cut out of my hair. Never mind that the rest of us had long ago soured on EZ Products: my father was not dissuaded by our cynicism. He loved the *potential*, the possibility that there, in his eager hands, was the answer to one of life's questions. Not "Why are we here?" or "Is there a God?" These were queries people had been circling for eons. But if the question was, "Does there exist a toothbrush that also functions as a mouthwash dispenser?" the answer was clear: Yes. Oh, yes.

"Come look at this!" he'd say, with an enthusiasm that, while not exactly contagious, was totally endearing. That was the thing about my dad. He could make anything seem like a good time. "See," he'd explain, putting the coasters cut from sponges/talking pocket memo recorder/coffeemaker with remote-control on-off switch in front of you, "this is a great idea.

I mean, most people wouldn't even think you could come up with something like this!"

Out of necessity, if nothing else, I'd perfected my reaction—a wow-look-at-that face, paired with an enthusiastic nod—at a young age. My sister, the drama queen, could not even work up a good fake smile, instead just shaking her head and saying, "Oh, Dad, why do you buy all that crap, anyway?" As for my mother, she tried to be a good sport, putting away her top-end coffeemaker for the new remote-controlled one, at least until we realized—after waking up to the smell of coffee at three A.M.—that it was getting interference from the baby monitor next door and brewing spontaneously. She even tolerated the tissue dispenser he installed on the visor of her BMW (*Never risk an accident reaching for a Kleenex again!*), even when it dislodged while she was on the highway, bonking her on the forehead and almost hurling her into oncoming traffic.

When my dad died, we all reacted in different ways. My sister seemed to take on our cumulative emotional reaction: she cried so much she seemed to be shriveling right in front of our eyes. I sat quiet, silent, angry, refusing to grieve, because it seemed like to do so would be giving everyone what they wanted. My mother began to organize.

Two days after the funeral, she was moving through the house with a buzzing intensity, the energy coming off of her palpable enough to set your teeth chattering. I stood in my bedroom door, watching as she ripped through our linen closet, tossing out all the nubby washcloths and old twin sheets that fit beds we'd long ago given away. In the kitchen, anything that didn't have a match—the lone jelly jar glass, one freebie plate commemorating Christmas at Cracker Barrel—was tossed, clanking and breaking its way into the trash bag she dragged behind her from room to room, until it was too full to budge. Nothing was safe. I came home from school one day to find that my closet had been organized, rifled through, clothes I hadn't worn in a while just gone. It was becoming clear to me that I shouldn't bother to get too attached to anything. Turn your back and you lose it. Just like that.

The EZ stuff was among the last to go. On a Saturday morning, about a week after the funeral, she was up at six A.M., piling things in the driveway for Goodwill. By nine, she'd emptied out most of the garage: the old treadmill, lawn chairs, and boxes of never-used Christmas ornaments. As much as I'd been worried about her as she went on this tear, I was even more concerned about what would happen when she was all done, and the only mess left was us.

I walked across the grass to the driveway, sidestepping a stack of unopened paint cans. "All of this is going?" I asked, as she bent down over a box of stuffed animals.

"Yes," she said. "If you want to claim anything, better do it now."

I looked across these various artifacts of my childhood. A pink bike with a white seat, a broken plastic sled, some life jackets from the boat we'd sold years ago. None of it meant anything, and all of it was important. I had no idea what to take.

Then I saw the EZ box. At the top, balled up and stuffed in the corner, was the self-heating hand towel my dad had considered a Miracle of Science only a few weeks earlier. I picked it up carefully, squeezing the thin fabric between my fingers.

"Oh, Macy." My mother, the stuffed animal box in her arms, frowned at me. A giraffe I vaguely remembered as belonging to my sister was poking out the top. "You don't want that stuff, honey. It's junk."

"I know," I said, looking down at the towel.

The Goodwill guys showed up then, beeping the horn as they pulled into the driveway. My mother waved them in, then walked over to point out the various piles. As they conferred, I wondered how many times a day they went to people's houses to take things away—if it was different when it was after a death, or if junk was junk, and they couldn't even tell.

"Make sure you get it all," my mother called over her shoulder as she started across the grass. The two guys went over to the treadmill, each of them picking up an end. "I have a donation . . . just let me get my checkbook."

As she went inside I stood there for a second, the guys loading up things from all around me. They were making a last trip for the Christmas tree when one of them, a shorter guy with red hair, nodded toward the box at my feet.

"That, too?" he asked.

I was about to tell him yes. Then I looked down at the towel and the box with all the other crap in it, and remembered how excited my dad was when each of them arrived, how I could always hear him coming down the hallway, pausing by the dining room, the den, the kitchen, just looking for someone to share his new discovery with. I was always so happy when it was me.

"No," I said as I leaned over and picked up the box. "This one's mine."

I took it up to my room, then dragged the desk chair over to my closet and climbed up. There was a panel above the top shelf that opened up into the attic, and I slid it open and pushed the box into the darkness.

With my dad gone, we had assumed our relationship with EZ Products was over. But then, about a month after the funeral, another package showed up, a combination pen/pocket stapler. We figured he'd ordered it right before the heart attack, his final purchase—until the next month, when a decorative rock/sprinkler arrived. When my mother called to complain, the customer service person apologized profusely. Because of my father's high buying volume, she explained, he had been bumped up to Gold Circle level, which meant that he received a new product every month to peruse, no obligation to buy. They'd take him off the list, absolutely, no problem.

But still the stuff kept coming, every month, just like clockwork, even after we canceled the credit card they had on file. I had my own theory on this, one I shared, like so much else, with no one. My dad had died the day after Christmas, when all the gifts had already been put into use or away. He'd given my mom a diamond bracelet, my sister a mountain bike, but when it was my turn, he'd given me a sweater, a couple of CDs, and an I.O.U. written on gold paper in his messy scrawl. *More to come*, it had said, and he'd nodded as I read the words, reassuring me. *Soon.* "It's late, but it's special," he'd said to me. "You'll love it."

I knew this was true. I would love it, because my dad just *knew* me, knew what made me happy. My mother claimed that when I was little I cried anytime my dad was out of my sight, that I was often inconsolable if anyone but he made my favorite meal, the bright orange macaroni-and-cheese mix they sold at the grocery store three for a dollar. But it was more than just emotional stuff. Sometimes, I swear, it was like we were on the same wavelength. Even that last day, when he'd given up trying to rouse me from bed, I'd sat up those five minutes later as if something had summoned me. Maybe, by then, his chest was already hurting. I'd never know.

In those first few days after he was gone, I kept thinking back to that I.O.U., wondering what it was he'd picked out for me. And even though I was pretty sure it wasn't an EZ Product, it felt strangely soothing when the things from Waterville, Maine, kept arriving, as though some part of him was still reaching out to me, keeping his promise.

So each time my mother tossed the boxes, I'd fish them out and bring them upstairs to add to my collection. I never used any of the products, choosing instead to just believe the breathless claims on the boxes. There were a lot of ways to remember my dad. But I thought he would have especially liked that.

Chapter Two

My mother had called me once ("Macy, honey, people are starting to arrive") and then twice ("Macy? Honey?") but still I was in front of the mirror, parting and reparting my hair. No matter how many times I swiped at it with my comb, it still didn't look right.

Once, I didn't care so much about appearances. I knew the basics: that I was somewhat short for my age, with a round face, brown eyes, and faint freckles across my nose that had been prominent, but now you had to lean in close to see. I had blonde hair that got lighter in the summer time, slightly green if I swam too much, which didn't bother me since I was a total track rat, the kind of girl to whom the word *hairstyle* was defined as always having a ponytail elastic on her wrist. I'd never cared about how my body or I looked—what mattered was what it could do and how fast it could go. But part of my new perfect act was my appearance. If I wanted people to see me as calm and collected, together, I had to look the part.

It took work. Now, my hair had to be just right, lying flat in all the right places. If my skin was not cooperating, I bargained with it, applying concealer and a slight layer of foundation, smoothing out all the red marks and dark circles. I could spend a full half hour getting the shadowing just right on my eyes, curling and recurling my eyelashes, making sure each was lifted and separated as the mascara wand moved over them, darkening, thickening. I moisturized. I flossed. I stood up straight. I was fine.

"Macy?" My mother's voice, firm and cheery, floated up the stairs. I pulled the comb through my hair, then stepped back from the mirror, letting it fall into the part again. Finally: perfect. And just in time.

When I came downstairs, my mother was standing by the door, greeting a couple who was just coming in with her selling smile: confident but not off-putting, welcoming but not kiss-ass. Like me, my mother put great stock in her appearance. In real estate, as in high school, it could make or break you.

"There you are," she said, turning around as I came down the stairs. "I was getting worried."

"Hair issues," I told her, as another couple came up the front walk. "What can I do?"

She glanced into the living room, where a group of people were peering at a design of the new townhouses that was tacked up on the wall. My mother always had these cocktail parties when she needed to sell, believing the best way to assure people she could build their dream house was to show off her own. It was a good gimmick, even if it did mean having strangers traipsing through our downstairs.

"If you make sure the caterers have what they need," she said to me now, "that would be great. And if it looks like we're running low on brochures, go out and get another box from the garage." She paused to smile at a couple as they crossed the foyer. "Oh," she said, "and if anyone looks like they're looking for a bathroom—"

"Point them toward it graciously and with the utmost subtlety," I finished. Bathroom detail/directions were, in fact, my specialty.

"Good girl," she said, as a woman in a pantsuit came up the walk. "Welcome!" my mother called out, pushing the door open wider. "I'm Deborah Queen. Please come in. I'm so glad you could make it!"

My mother didn't know this person, of course. But part of selling was treating everyone like a familiar face.

"Well, I just love the neighborhood," the woman said as she stepped over the threshold. "I noticed you were putting up some new townhouses, so I thought I'd . . ."

"Let me show you a floor plan. Did you see that all the units come with two-car garages? You know, a lot of people don't even realize how much difference a heated garage can make."

And with that, my mother was off and running. Hard to believe that once schmoozing was as painful to her as multiple root canals. But when you had to do something, you had to do it. And eventually, if you were lucky, you did it well.

Queen Homes, which my dad had started right out of college as a one-man trim carpenter operation, already had a good business reputation when he met my mother. Actually, he hired her. She was fresh out of college with an accounting degree, and his finances were a shambles. She'd come in, waded through his paperwork and receipts (many of which were on bar napkins and matchbooks), handled a close call with the IRS (he'd "forgotten" about his taxes a few years earlier), and gotten him into the black again. Somewhere in the midst of all of it, they fell in love. They were the perfect business team: he was all charm and fun and everyone's favorite guy to buy a beer. My mother was happy busying herself with file folders and The Bigger Picture. Together, they were unstoppable.

Wildflower Ridge, our neighborhood, had been my mother's vision. They'd done small subdivisions and spec houses, but this would be an entire neighborhood, with houses and townhouses and apartments, a little business district, everything all enclosed and fitted around a common green space. A return to communities, my mother had said. The wave of the future.

My dad wasn't sold at first. But he was getting older, and his body was tired. This way he could move into a supervisory position and let someone else swing the hammers. So he agreed. Two months later, they were breaking ground on the first house: ours.

They worked in tandem, my parents, meeting potential clients at the model home. My dad would run through the basic spiel, tweaking it depending on what sort of people they were: he played up his Southern charm for Northerners, talked NASCAR and barbeque with locals. He was knowledgeable, trustworthy. Of course you wanted him to build your house. Hell, you wanted him to be your best friend. Then, the hard selling done, my mom would move in with the technical stuff like covenants, specifications, and prices. The houses sold like crazy. It was everything my mother said it would be. Until it wasn't.

I knew she blamed herself for his death, thought that maybe it was the added stress of Wildflower Ridge that taxed my dad's heart, and if she hadn't pushed him to expand so much everything would have been different. This was our common ground, the secret we shared but never spoke aloud. I should have been with him; she should have left him alone. Shoulda, coulda, woulda. It's so easy in the past tense.

But here in the present, my mother and I had no choice but to move ahead. We worked hard, me at school, her at outselling all the other builders. We parted our hair cleanly and stood up straight, greeting company—and the world—with the smiles we practiced in the quiet of our now-too-big dream house full of mirrors that showed the smiles back. But under it all, our grief remained. Sometimes she took more of it, sometimes I did. But always, it was there.

I'd just finished directing an irate woman with a red-wine stain on her shirt to the powder room—one of the catering staff had apparently bumped into her, splashing her cabernet across her outfit—when I noticed the stack of fliers on the foyer table was looking a bit low. Grateful for any excuse to escape, I slipped outside.

I went down the front walk, cutting around the caterer's van in the driveway. The sun had just gone down, the sky pink and orange behind the line of trees that separated us from the apartments one phase over. Summer was just starting. Once that had meant early track practice and long afternoons at the pool perfecting my backflip. This summer, though, I was working.

Jason had been at the library information desk since he was fifteen, long enough to secure a reputation as the Guy Who Knew Everything. Patrons of the Lakeview Branch had gotten accustomed to him doing everything from finding that obscure book on Catherine the Great to fixing the library computers when they crashed. They loved him for the same reason I did: he had all the answers. He also had a cult following, particularly among his co-workers, who were both girls and both brilliant. They'd never taken kindly to me as Jason's girlfriend, seeing as how, in their eyes, I wasn't even close to their intellectual level, much less his. I'd had a feeling that their acceptance of me as a sudden co-worker wouldn't be much warmer, and I was right.

During my training, they snickered as he taught me the intricate ins and outs of the library search system, rolled their eyes in tandem when I asked a question about the card catalog. Jason had hardly noticed, and when I pointed it out to him, he got impatient, as if I was wasting his time. That's not what you should be worrying about, he said. Not knowing how to reference the tri-county library database quickly in the event of a system crash: now *that* would be a problem.

He was right, of course. He was always right. But I still wasn't looking forward to it.

Once I got to the garage, I went to the shelves where my mom kept her work stuff, moving a stack of FOR SALE and MODEL OPEN signs aside to pull out another box of fliers. The front door of the house was open, and I could hear voices drifting over, party sounds, laughing, and glasses clinking. I hoisted up the box and cut off the overhead light. Then I headed back to the party and bathroom duty.

I was passing the garbage cans when someone jumped out at me from the bushes.

"Gotcha!"

I shrieked and dropped the box, which hit the ground with a thunk, spilling fliers sideways down the driveway. Say what you will, but you're never prepared for the surprise attack. It defines the very meaning of taking your breath away: I was gasping.

For a second, it was very quiet. A car drove by.

"Bert?" A voice came from down the driveway, by the catering van. "What are you doing?"

Beside me, a bush rustled. "I'm . . ." a voice said hesitantly—and much more quietly—from somewhere within it. "I'm scaring *you*. Aren't I?"

I heard footsteps, and a second later could make out a guy in a white shirt and black pants walking toward me up the driveway. He had a serving platter tucked under his arm. As he got closer he squinted, making me out in the semi-dark.

"Nope. Not me," he said. Now that he was right in front of me, I could see that he was tall and had brown hair that was a little bit too long. He was also strikingly handsome, with the sort of sculpted cheekbones and angular features that you couldn't help but notice, even if you did have a boyfriend. To me he said, "You okay?"

I nodded. My heart was still racing, but I was recovering.

He stood there, studying the bush, then stuck his hand right into its center. A second later, he pulled another guy, this one shorter and chunkier but dressed identically, out through the foliage. He had the same dark eyes and hair, but looked younger. His face was bright red.

"Bert," the older guy said, sighing, as he let his hand drop. "Honestly."

"You have to understand," this Bert said to me, solemnly, "I'm down in a big way."

"Just apologize," the older guy said.

"I'm very sorry," Bert said. He reached up and picked a pine needle out of his hair. "I, um, thought you were someone else."

"It's okay," I told him.

The older guy nudged him, then nodded toward the fliers.

"Oh, right," Bert said, dropping down to his knees. He started to pick them up, his fingers scratching the pavement, as the other guy walked a bit down the driveway, picking up the ones that had slid there.

"That was a good one, too," Bert was muttering as I squatted down beside him to help. "Almost had him. Almost."

The light outside the kitchen door popped on, and suddenly it was very bright. A second later the door swung open.

"What in the world is going on out here?" I turned to see a woman in a red apron, with black curly hair piled on top of her head, standing at the top of the stairs. She was pregnant, and was squinting out into the dark with a curious, although somewhat impatient, expression. "Where is that platter I asked for?"

"Right here," the older guy called out as he came back up the driveway, a bunch of my fliers now stacked neatly upon the platter. He handed them to me.

"Thanks," I said.

"No problem." Then he took the stairs two at a time, handing the platter to the woman, as Bert crawled under the deck for the last few fliers that had landed there.

"Marvelous," she said. "Now, Wes, get back to the bar, will you? The more they drink, the less they'll notice how long the food is taking."

"Sure thing," the guy said, ducking through the doorway and disappearing into the kitchen.

The woman ran her hand over her belly, distracted, then looked back out into the dark. "Bert?" she called out loudly. "Where—"

"Right here," Bert said, from under the deck.

She turned around, then stuck her head over the side of the rail. "Are you on the ground?"

"Yes."

"What are you *doing*?"

"Nothing," Bert mumbled.

"Well," the woman said, "when you're done with that, I've got crab cakes cooling with your name on them. So get your butt in here, please, okay?"

"Okay," he said. "I'm coming."

The woman went back inside, and a second later I heard her yelling something about mini-biscuits. Bert came out from under the deck, organizing the fliers he was holding into a stack, then handed them to me.

"I'm really sorry," he said. "It's just this stupid thing."

"It's fine," I told him, as he picked another leaf out of his hair. "It was an accident."

He looked at me, his expression serious. "There are," he said, "no accidents."

For a second I just stared at him. He had a chubby face and a wide nose, and his hair was thick and too short, like it had been cut at home. He was watching me so intently, as if he wanted to be sure I understood, that it took me a second to look away.

"Bert!" the woman yelled from inside. "Crab cakes!"

"Right," he said, snapping out of it. Then he backed up to the stairs and started up them quickly. When he got to the top, he glanced back down at me. "But I am sorry," he said, saying the words that I'd heard so much in the last year and a half that they hardly carried meaning anymore. Although I had a feeling he meant it. Weird. "I'm sorry," he said again. And then he was gone.

—✳—

When I got inside, my mother was deep in some conversation about zoning with a couple of contractors. I refreshed the fliers, then directed a man who was a bit stumbly and holding a glass of wine he probably didn't need to the bathroom. I was scanning the living room for stray empty glasses when there was a loud crash from the kitchen.

Everything in the front of the house stopped. Conversation. Motion. The very air. Or so it felt.

"It's fine!" a voice called out, upbeat and cheerful, from the other side of the door. "Carry on as you were!"

There was a slight surprised murmur from the assembled crowd, some laughter, and then slowly the conversation built again. My mother smiled her way across the room, then put a hand on the small of my back, easing me toward the foyer.

"That's a spill on a client, not enough appetizers, and a crash," she said, her voice level. "I'm not happy. Could you go and convey that, please?"

"Right," I said. "I'm on it."

When I came through the kitchen door, the first thing I did was step on something that mushed, in a wet sort of way, under my foot. Then I noticed that the floor was littered with small round objects, some at a standstill, some rolling slowly to the four corners of the room. A little girl in pigtails, who looked to be about two or three, was standing by the sink, fingers in her mouth and wide eyed as several of the marblelike objects moved past her.

"Well." I looked over to see the pregnant woman standing by the stove, an empty cookie sheet in her hands. She sighed. "I guess that's it for the meatballs."

I picked up my foot to examine it, stepping aside just in time to keep from getting hit by the door as it swung open. Bert, now leafless and looking somewhat composed, breezed in carrying a tray filled with wadded-up napkins and empty glasses. "Delia," he said to the woman, "we need more crab cakes."

"And I need a sedative," she replied in a tired voice, stretching her back, "but you can't have everything. Take the cheese puffs and tell them we're traying the crab cakes up right now."

"Are we?" Bert asked, passing the toddler, who smiled widely, reaching out for him with her spitty fingers. He sidestepped her, heading for the counter, and, unhappy, she plopped down into a sitting position and promptly started wailing.

"Not exactly at this moment, no," Delia said, crossing the room. "I'm speaking futuristically."

"Is that a word?" Bert asked her.

"Just take the cheese puffs," she said as she picked up the little girl. "Oh, Lucy, please God okay, just hold back the hysterics for another hour, I'm begging you." She looked down at her shoe. "Oh no, I just stepped in a meatball. Where's Monica?"

"Here," a girl's voice said from the other side of the side door.

Delia made an exasperated face. "Put out that cigarette and get in here, *now*. Find a broom and get up these meatballs . . . and we need to get some more of these cheese puffs in, and Bert needs . . . what else did you need?"

"Crab cakes," Bert said. "Futuristically speaking. And Wes needs ice."

"In the oven, ready any second," she said, shooting him a look as she walked over to the broom closet, toddler on her hip, and rummaged around for a second before pulling out a dustpan. "The crab cakes, not the ice. Lucy, please, don't slobber on Mommy. . . . And the ice is . . . oh, shit, I don't know where the ice is. Where did we put the bags we bought?"

"Cooler," a tall girl said as she came inside, letting the door slam behind her. She had long honey-blonde hair and was slouching as she ambled over to the oven. She pulled it open, a couple of inches at a time, then glanced inside before shutting it again and making her way over to the island, still moving at a snail's pace. "Done," she announced.

"Then please *take* them out and *put* them on a tray, Monica," Delia snapped, shifting the toddler to her other hip. She started scooping up the meatballs into the dustpan as Monica made her way back to the oven, pausing entirely too long to pick up a pot holder on her way.

"I'll just wait for the crab cakes," Bert said. "It's only—"

Delia stood up and glared at him. It was quiet for a second, but something told me this was not my opening. I stayed put, scraping meatball off my shoe.

"Right," he said quickly. "Cheese puffs. Here I go. We need more servers, by the way. People are grabbing at me like you wouldn't believe."

"Monica, get back out there," Delia said as the tall girl ambled back over, a tray of sizzling crab cakes in her hand. Putting down the dustpan, Delia moved to the island, grabbing a spatula, and began, with one hand, to load crab cakes onto the plate at lightning speed. "Now."

"But—"

"I know what I said," Delia shot back, slapping a stack of napkins onto the edge of the tray, "but this is an emergency situation, and I have to put you back in, even if it is against my better judgment. Just walk slowly and *look* where you're going, and be careful with liquids, please God I'm begging you, okay?"

This last part, I was already beginning to recognize, was a mantra of sorts for her, as if by stringing all these words together, one of them might stick.

"Okay," Monica said, tucking her hair behind her ear. She picked up the tray, adjusted it on her hand, and headed off around the corner, taking her time. Delia watched her go, shaking her head, then turned her attention back to the meatballs, scooping the few remaining into the dustpan and chucking them into the garbage can. Her daughter was still sniffling, and she was talking to her, softly, as she walked to a metal cart by the side door, pulling out a tray covered with Saran Wrap. As she crossed the room she balanced it precariously on her free hand, her walk becoming a slight waddle. I had never seen anyone so in need of help in my life.

"What else, what else," she said as she reached the island, sliding the tray there. "What else did we need?" She pressed a hand to her forehead, closing her eyes.

"Ice," I said, and she turned around and looked at me.

"Ice," she repeated. Then she smiled. "Thanks. Who are you?"

"Macy. This is my mom's house."

Her expression changed, but only slightly. I had a feeling she knew what was coming.

I took a breath. "She wanted me to come and check that everything's all right. And to convey that she's—"

"Incredibly pissed," she finished for me, nodding.

"Well, not *pissed*."

Just then, there was a splashing crash from the next room,

followed by another short silence. Delia glanced over at the door, just as the toddler started wailing again.

"Now?" she said to me.

"Well . . . yes," I said. Actually, I was betting this was an understatement. "Now, she's probably pissed."

"Oh, dear." She put a hand on her face, shaking her head. "This is a disaster."

I wasn't sure what to say. I felt nervous enough just watching all this: I couldn't imagine being responsible for it.

"Well," she said, after a second, "in a way, it's good. We know where we stand. Now things can only get better. Right?"

I didn't say anything, which probably didn't inspire much confidence. Just then, the oven timer went off with a cheerful *bing!* noise. "Okay," she said suddenly, as if this had signaled a call to action. "Macy. Can you answer a question?"

"Sure," I said.

"How are you with a spatula?"

This hadn't been what I was expecting. "Pretty good," I said finally.

"Wonderful," she said. "Come here."

Fifteen minutes later, I'd figured out the rhythm. It was like baking cookies, but accelerated: lay out cheese puffs/crab cakes on cookie sheet in neat rows, put in oven, remove other pan from oven, pile onto tray, send out. And repeat.

"Perfect," Delia said, watching me as she laid out mini-toasts at twice my speed and more neatly. "You could have a bright future in catering, my dear, if such a thing even exists."

I smiled at this as Monica, the slothlike girl, eased through the door, carrying a tray laden with napkins. After her second spill she'd been restricted to carrying only solids, a status further amended to just trash and empty glasses once she'd bumped into the banister and sent half a tray of cheese puffs down the front of some man's shirt. You'd think moving slowly would make someone less accident prone. Clearly, Monica was bucking this logic.

"How's it going out there?" Delia asked her, glancing over at her daughter, Lucy, who was now asleep in her car seat on the kitchen table. Frankly, Delia had astounded me. After acknowledging the hopelessness of her situation, she had immediately righted it, putting in two more trays of canapés, getting the ice from the cooler, and soothing her daughter to sleep, all in about three minutes. Like her mantra of Oh-please-God-I'm-begging-you-okay; she just did all she could, and eventually something just worked. It was impressive.

"Fine," Monica reported flatly, shuffling over to the garbage can, where, after pausing for a second, she began to clear off her tray, one item at a time.

Delia rolled her eyes as I slid another tray into the oven. "We're not always like this," she told me, opening another package of cheese puffs. "I swear. We are usually the model of professionalism and efficiency."

Monica, hearing this, snorted. Delia shot her a look.

"But," she continued, "my babysitter flaked on me tonight, and then one of my servers had other plans, and then, well, then the world just turned on me. You know that feeling?"

I nodded. You have no idea, I thought. Out loud I said, "Yeah. I do."

"Macy! There you are!" I looked up to see my mother standing by the kitchen doorway. "Is everything okay back here?"

This question, while posed to me, was really for Delia, and I could tell she knew it: she busied herself laying out cheese puffs, now at triple speed. Behind her, Monica had finally cleared her tray and was dragging herself across the room, the tray bumping against her knee.

"Yes," I said. "I was just asking Delia about how to make crab cakes."

As she came toward us, my mother was running a hand through her hair, which meant she was preparing herself for some sort of confrontation. Delia must have sensed this, too, as she picked up a dish towel, wiping her hands, and turned to face my mother, a calm expression on her face.

"The food is getting rave reviews," my mother began in a voice that made it clear a *but* was to follow, "but—"

"Mrs. Queen." Delia took a deep breath, which she then let out, placing her hand on her chest. "Please. You don't have to say anything more."

I opened up another tray of crab cakes, keeping my head down.

"I am so deeply sorry for our disorganized beginning tonight," Delia continued. "I found out I was understaffed at the last minute, but that's no excuse. I'd like to forgo your remaining balance in the hopes that you might consider us again for another one of your events."

The meaningful silence that followed this speech held for a full five seconds, until it was broken by Bert bursting back through the door. "Need more biscuits!" he said. "They're going like hotcakes!"

"Bert," Delia said, forcing a smile for my mother's sake, "you don't have to bellow. We're right here."

"Sorry," Bert said.

"Here." I handed him the tray I'd just finished and took his empty one. "There should be crab cakes in the next few minutes, too."

"Thanks," he said. Then he recognized me. "Hey," he said. "You work here now?"

"Um, no." I put the empty tray down in front of me. "Not really."

I glanced over at my mother. Between Delia's heartfelt "sorry" and my exchange with Bert, I could see she was struggling to keep up. "Well," she said finally, turning her attention back to Delia, "I appreciate your apology, and that seems like fair compensation. The food *is* wonderful."

"Thank you so much," Delia said. "I really appreciate it."

Just then there was a burst of laughter from the living room, happy party noise, and my mother glanced toward it, as if reassured. "Well," she said, "I suppose I should get back to my guests." She started out of the room, then paused by the fridge. "Macy?" she said.

"Yes?"

"When you're done in here, I could use you. Okay?"

"Sure," I said, grabbing a pot holder and heading over to the oven to check on the crab cakes. "I'll be there in a sec."

"She's been wonderful, by the way," Delia told her. "I told her if she needs work, I'll hire her in a second."

"That's so nice of you," my mother said. "Macy's actually working at the library this summer."

"Wow," Delia said. "That's great."

"It's just at the information desk," I told her, opening the oven door. "Answering questions and stuff."

"Ah," Delia said. "A girl with all the answers."

"That's Macy." My mother smiled. "She's a very bright girl."

I didn't know what to say to this—what could you say to this?—so I just reached in for the crab cakes, focusing on that. When my mother left the kitchen, Delia came over, pot holder in hand, and took the tray as I slid it out of the oven. "You've been a great help," she said, "really. But you'd better go out there with your mom."

"No, it's fine," I said. "She won't even notice I'm not there."

Delia smiled. "Maybe not. But you should go anyway."

I stepped back, out of the way, as she carried the tray over to the island. In her car seat, Lucy shifted slightly, mumbling to herself, then fell quiet again.

"So the library, huh?" she said, picking up her spatula. "That's cool."

"It's just for the summer," I told her. "I'm filling in for someone."

She started lifting crab cakes off the cookie sheet, arranging them on a tray. "Well, if it doesn't work out, I'm in the book. I could always use someone who can take directions and walk in a straight line."

As if to punctuate this, Monica slunk back in, blowing her bangs out of her face.

"Catering is an insane job, though," Delia said. "I don't know why you'd want to do it, when you have a peaceful, normal job. But if for some reason you're craving chaos, call me. Okay?"

Bert came back in, breezing between us, his tray now empty. "Crab cakes!" he bellowed. "Keep 'em coming!"

"Bert," Delia said, wincing, "I'm *right here*."

I walked back to the door, stepping aside as Monica ambled

past me, yawning widely. Bert stood by impatiently, waiting for his tray, while Delia asked Monica to God, please, try and pick up the pace a little, I'm begging you. They'd forgotten about me already, it seemed. But for some reason, I wanted to answer her anyway. "Yeah," I said, out loud, hoping she could hear me. "Okay."

The last person at the party, a slightly tipsy, very loud man in a golf sweater, left around nine-thirty. My mother locked the door behind him, took off her shoes, and, after kissing my forehead and thanking me, headed off to her office to assemble packets for people who had signed the YES! I WANT MORE INFO sheet she'd had on the front hall table. Contacts were everything, I'd learned. You had to get to people fast, or they'd slip away.

Thinking this, I went up to my room and checked my email. Jason had written me, as promised, but it was mostly about things that he wanted to remind me of concerning the info desk (make sure to keep track of all copier keys, they are *very expensive* to replace) or other things I was handling for him while he was away (remember, on Saturday, to send out the email to the Foreign Culture group about the featured speaker who is coming in to give that talk in August). At the very end, he said he was too tired to write more and he'd be in touch in a couple of days. Then just his name, no "love." Not that I'd been expecting it. Jason wasn't the type for displays of affection, either verbal or not. He was disgusted by couples that made out in the hallways between classes, and got annoyed at even the slightest sappy moments in movies. But I knew that he cared about me: he just conveyed it more subtly, as concise with expressing this emotion as he was with everything else. It was in the way he'd put his hand on the small of my back, for instance, or how he'd smile at me when I said something that surprised him. Once I might have wanted more, but I'd come around to his way of thinking in the time we'd been together. And we were together, all the time. So he didn't have to do anything to prove how he felt about me. Like so much else, I should just know.

But this *was* the first time we were going to be apart for more than a weekend since we'd gotten together, and I was beginning to realize that the small reassurances I got in person would not transfer over to email. But he loved me, and I knew that. I'd just have to remember it now.

After I logged off, I opened my window and crawled out onto the roof, sitting against one of the shutters with my knees pulled up to my chest. I'd been out there for a little while, looking at the stars, when I heard voices coming up from the driveway. A car door shut, then another. Peering over the edge, I saw a few people moving around the Wish Catering van as they packed up the last of their things.

". . . this *other* planet, that's moving within the same trajectory as Earth. It's only a matter of time before it hits us. I mean, they don't talk about these things on the news. But that doesn't mean it's not *happening*."

It was Bert talking. I recognized his voice, a bit high-pitched and anxious, before I made him out, standing by the back of the van. He was talking to someone who was sitting on the bumper smoking a cigarette, the tip of which was bright and red in the murky dark.

"Ummm-hmmm," the person said slowly. Had to be Monica. "Really."

"Bert, give it a rest," another voice said, and Wes, the older guy, walked up, sliding something into the back of the van. I'd hardly seen him that night, as he'd worked the bar in the den.

"I'm just trying to help her be informed!" Bert said indignantly. "This is serious stuff, Wes. Just because *you* prefer to stay in the dark—"

"Are we ready to go?" Delia came down the driveway, her voice uneven, Lucy on her hip. She had the car seat dangling from one hand, and Wes walked up and took it from her. From where I was sitting, I could make out clearly the top of his head, the white of his shirt. Then, as if sensing this, he leaned his head back, glancing up. I slid back against the wall.

"Did we get paid?" Bert asked.

"Had to comp half," she said. "The price of chaos. Probably should bother me, but frankly, I'm too pregnant and exhausted to care. Who has the keys?"

"I do," Bert said. "I'll drive."

The silence that followed was long enough to make me want to peer over the edge of the roof again, but I stopped myself.

"I don't think so," Delia said finally.

"Don't even," Monica added.

"What?" Bert said. "Come on! I've had my permit for a year! I'm taking the test in a week! And I have to have some more practice before I get the Bertmobile."

"You have," Wes said, his voice low, "to stop calling it that."

"Bert," Delia said, sighing, "normally, I would love for you to drive. But it's been a long night and right now I just want to get home, okay? Next time, it's all you. But for now, just let your brother drive. Okay?"

Another silence. Someone coughed.

"Fine," Bert said. "Just fine."

I heard a car door slam, then another. I leaned back over to see Wes and Bert still standing at the back of the van. Bert was kicking at the ground, clearly sulking, while Wes stood by impassively.

"It's not a big deal," he said to Bert after a minute, pulling a hand through his hair. Now I knew for sure that they were brothers. They looked even more alike to me, although the similarities—skin tone, dark hair, dark eyes—were distributed on starkly different builds.

"I never get to drive," Bert told him. "Never. Even lazy Monotone got to last week, but never me. Never."

"You will," Wes said. "Next week you'll have your own car, and you can drive whenever you want. But don't push this issue now, man. It's late."

Bert stuffed his hands in his pockets. "Whatever," he said, and started around the van, shuffling his feet. Wes followed him, clapping a hand on his back. "You know that girl who was in the kitchen tonight, helping Delia?" Bert asked.

I froze.

"Yeah," Wes answered. "The one you leaped out at?"

"Anyway," Bert said loudly, "don't you know who she is?"

"No."

Bert pulled open the back door. "Yeah, you do. Her dad—"

I waited. I knew what was coming, but still, I had to hear the words that would follow. The ones that defined me, set me apart.

"—was the coach when we used to run in that kids' league, back in elementary school," Bert finished. "The Lakeview Zips. Remember?"

Wes opened the back door for Bert. "Oh yeah," he said. "Coach Joe, right?"

Right, I thought, and felt a pang in my chest.

"Coach Joe," Bert repeated, as he shut his door. "He was a nice guy."

I watched Wes walk to the driver's door and pull it open. He stood there for a second, taking a final look around, before climbing in and shutting the door behind him. I had to admit, I was surprised. I'd gotten so used to being known as the girl whose dad died, I sometimes forgot that I'd had a life before that.

I moved back into the shadows by my window as the engine started up and the van bumped down the driveway, brake lights flashing as it turned out onto the street. There was a big wishbone painted on the side, thick black paint strokes, and from a distance it looked like a Chinese character, striking even if you didn't know, really, what it meant. I kept my eye on it, following it down through the neighborhood, over the hill, down to the stop sign, until it was gone.

Chapter Three

I couldn't sleep.

I was starting my job at the library the next day, and I had that night-before-the-first-day-of-school feeling, all jumpy and nervous. But then again, I'd never been much of a sleeper. That was the weird thing about that morning when my dad came in to get me. I'd been out. Sound asleep.

Since then, I had almost a fear of sleeping, sure that something bad would happen if I ever allowed myself to be fully unconscious, even for a second. As a result, I only allowed myself to barely doze off. When I did sleep enough to dream, it was always about running.

My dad loved to run. He'd had me and my sister doing it from a young age with the Lakeview Zips, and later he was always dragging us to the 5Ks he ran, signing us up for the kids' division. I remember my first race, when I was six, standing there at the starting line a few rows back, with nothing at my eye level but shoulders and necks. I was short for my age, and Caroline had of course pushed her way to the front, stating clearly that at ten-almost-eleven, she didn't belong in back with the babies. The starting gun popped and everyone pushed forward, the thumping of sneakers against asphalt suddenly deafening, and at first it was like I was carried along with it, my feet seeming hardly to touch the ground. The people on the sides of the street were a blur, faces blowing by: all I could focus on was the ponytail of the girl in front of me, tied with a blue grosgrain ribbon. Some big boy bumped me hard from the back, passing, and I had a cramp in my side by the second length, but then I heard my dad.

"Macy! Good girl! Keep it up, you're doing great!"

I knew by the time I was eight years old that I was fast, faster than the kids I was running with. I knew even before I started to pass the bigger kids in the first length, even before I won my first race, then every race. When I was really going, the wind whistling in my ears, I was sure that if I wanted to, it was only another burst of breath, one more push, and I could fly.

By then it was just me running. My sister had lost interest around seventh grade, when she discovered her best event was not, as we'd all thought, the hundred meters, but in fact flirting with the boy's track team afterwards. She still liked to run, but didn't much see the point anymore if she didn't have someone chasing after her.

So it was me and my dad who went to meets, who woke up early to do our standard five-mile loop, who compared T-band strains and bad-knee horror stories over icepacks and PowerBars on Saturday mornings. It was the best thing we had in common, the one part of him that was all mine. Which was why, that morning, I should have been with him.

From that morning on, running changed for me. It didn't matter how good my times were, what records I'd planned to break just days before. There was one time I would never beat, so I quit.

By altering the familiar route that took me past the intersection of Willow and McKinley whenever I went out, and looping one extra block instead, I'd been able to avoid the place where everything had happened: it was that easy, really, to never drive past it again. My friends from the track team were a bit harder. They'd stuck close to me, loyal, at the funeral and the days afterwards, and while they were disappointed when the coach told them I'd quit, they were even more hurt when I started to avoid them in the halls. Nobody seemed to understand that the only person I could count on not to bring up my dad, not to feel sorry for me, or make The Face—other than my mother—was me. So I narrowed my world, cutting out everyone who'd known me or who tried to befriend me. It was the only thing I knew to do.

I packed up all my trophies and ribbons, piling them neatly into boxes. It was like that part of my life, my running life, was just gone. It was almost too easy, for something I once thought had meant everything.

So now I only ran in my dreams. In them, there was always something awful about to happen, or there was something I'd forgotten, and my legs felt like jelly, not strong enough to hold me. Whatever else varied, the ending was the same, a finish line I could never reach, no matter how many miles I put behind me.

"Oh, right." Bethany looked up at me through her slim, wire-framed glasses. "You're starting today."

I just stood there, holding my purse, suddenly entirely too aware of the nail I'd broken as I unfastened my seat belt in the parking lot. I'd put so much time into getting dressed for this first day, ironing my shirt, making my hair part perfectly straight, redoing my lipstick twice. Now, though, my nail, ripped across the top, jagged, seemed to defeat everything, even as I tucked it into my palm, hiding it.

Bethany pushed back her chair and stood up. "You can sit on the end, I guess," she said, reaching over to unlatch the knee-high door between us and holding it open as I stepped through. "Not in the red chair, that's Amanda's. The one next to it."

"Thanks," I said. I walked over, pulling the chair from the desk, then sat down, stowing my purse at my feet. A second later I heard the door squeak open again and Amanda, Bethany's best friend and the student council secretary, came in. She was a tall girl with long hair she always wore in a neat braid that hung halfway down her back. It looked so perfect that during long meetings, when my mind wandered from the official agenda, I'd sometimes wondered if she slept in it, or if it was like a clip-on tie, easily removed at the end of the day.

"Hello, Macy," she said coolly, taking a seat in her red chair. She had perfect posture, shoulders back, chin up. Maybe the braid helped, I thought. "I forgot you were starting today."

"Um, yeah," I said. They both looked at me, and I was distinctly aware of that *um*, so base, hanging in the air between us. I said, more clearly, "Yes."

If I was working toward perfect—working being the operative word—these girls had already reached it and made maintaining it look effortless. Bethany was a redhead with short hair she wore tucked behind her ears, and had small freckled hands with the nails cut straight across. I'd sat beside her in English, and had always been transfixed when I saw her taking notes: her print was like a typewriter, each letter exact. She was quiet and always composed, while Amanda was more talkative, with a cultured accent she'd picked up from her early years in Paris, where her family had lived while her father did graduate work at the Sorbonne. I'd never seen either of them sporting a shirt with a stain on it, or even a wrinkle. They never used anything but proper English. They were the female Jasons.

"Well, it's been really slow so far this summer," Amanda said to me now, smoothing her hands over her skirt. She had long, pale white legs. "I hope there's enough for you to do."

I didn't know what to say to that, so I just smiled my fine-just-fine smile again and turned back to the wall that my desk area faced. Behind me, I could hear them start talking, their voices low and soothing. They were saying something about an art exhibit. I looked at the clock. It was 9:05. Five hours, fifty-five minutes to go.

By noon, I'd answered only one question, and it concerned the location of the bathroom. (So it wasn't just in my house. Anywhere, I looked like I knew about the toilet, if nothing else.) There'd been a fair amount of activity at the desk: a problem with the copy machine, some inquiries into an obscure periodical, even someone with a question about the online encyclopedia that Jason had specifically trained me to handle. But even if Amanda or Bethany was helping someone else and the person came right to me, one of them jumped up, saying, "I'll be with you in just a second," in a tone that made it clear asking me would be a waste of time. The first few times this happened, I'd figured they were just letting me get my feet under me. After awhile, though, it was obvious. In their minds, I didn't belong there.

At noon, Amanda put a sign on the desk that said WILL RETURN AT 1:00 and drew a bagel in a Ziploc bag from her purse.

Bethany followed suit, retrieving an apple and a gingko biloba bar from the drawer next to her.

"We'd invite you to join us," Amanda said, "but we're drilling for our Kaplan class. So just be back here in an hour, okay?"

"I can stay, if you want," I said. "And then take my lunch at one, so there's someone here."

They both just looked at me, as if I'd suggested I could explain quantum physics while juggling bowling pins.

"No," Amanda said, turning to walk out from behind the desk. "This is better."

Then they disappeared into a back room, so I picked up my purse and went outside, walking past the parking lot to a bench by the fountain. I took out the peanut butter and jelly sandwich I'd brought, then laid it in my lap and took a few deep breaths. For some reason, I was suddenly sure that I was about to cry.

I sat on the bench for an hour. Then I threw out my sandwich and went back inside. Even though it was 12:55, Bethany and Amanda were already back at the desk, which made me seem late. As I navigated a path between their chairs to get to my seat, I could feel them looking at me.

The afternoon dragged. The library was mostly empty, and I suddenly felt like I could hear everything: the buzzing of the fluorescent lights over my head, the squeak of Bethany's chair as she shifted position, the tappety-tap of the online card catalog station just around the corner. I was used to quiet, but this felt sterile, lonely. I could have been working for my mom, or even flipping crab cakes with a spatula, and I wondered if I'd made the wrong choice. But this was what I had agreed to.

At three o'clock, I pushed my chair back and stood up, then

opened my mouth to say my first words in over two hours. "I guess I'll see you guys tomorrow."

Amanda turned her head, her braid sliding over her shoulder. She'd been reading some thick book on the history of Italy, licking her finger with each turn of a page. I knew this because I'd heard her, every single time.

"Oh, right," she said, as Bethany gave me a forced smile. "See you tomorrow."

I could feel their gazes right around my shoulder blades as I crossed the reading room and pushed through the glass doors. There, suddenly, was the noise of the world: a car passing, someone laughing in the park across the street, the distant drone of a plane. One day down, I told myself. And only a summer to go.

"Well," my mother said, handing me the salad bowl, "if you were supposed to love it, they wouldn't call it work. Right?"

"I guess," I said.

"It'll get better," she said, in the confident way of someone who has no idea, none at all. "And it's great experience. That's what really matters."

By now, I'd been at the library for three days, and things were not improving. I knew that I was doing this for Jason, that it was important to him, but Bethany and Amanda seemed to be pooling their considerable IQs in a single-minded effort to completely demoralize me.

I was trying to keep my emails to Jason upbeat and reassuring, but after day two, I couldn't help but vent a little bit about Bethany and Amanda and the way they'd been treating me. That was even before another dressing down in front of a patron, this time from Bethany, who felt compelled to point out—twice—that, to her trained ear, I'd mispronounced Albert Camus' name while directing a sullen summer school student to the French literature section.

"Cam-oo," she'd said, holding her mouth in that pursed, French way.

"Cam-oo," I repeated. I knew I'd said it right and wasn't sure why I was letting her correct me. But I was.

"No, no." She lifted up her chin again, then fluttered her fingers near her mouth. "Cam-ooo."

I just looked at her, knowing now that no matter how many times I said it, even if I trotted Albert himself up to give it a shot, it wouldn't matter. "Okay," I said. "Thanks."

"No problem," she said, swiveling in her stupid chair, back to Amanda, who smiled at her, shaking her head, before going back to what she was doing.

So it was no wonder that when I got home that day, I was cheered, greatly, to see that Jason had written me back. *He* knew how impossible those girls were; he would understand. A little reassurance, I thought, opening it with a double-click. Just what I needed.

After I scanned the first two lines, though, it was clear that my self-esteem and general emotional well-being were, to Jason anyway, secondary. *After your last email*, he wrote, *I'm concerned that you're not putting your full attention into the job. Two full paragraphs about the info desk, but you didn't answer the questions I asked you: did the new set of* Scientific Monthly Anthologies *come in? Have you been able to access the tri-country database with my password?* Then, after a couple of reminders about other things it was crucial I attend to, this: *If you're having problems with Bethany and Amanda, you should address them directly. There's no place in a working environment for these interpersonal issues.* He didn't sound like my boyfriend as much as middle management. Clearly I was on my own.

"Honey?"

I looked up. Across the table, my mother was looking at me with a concerned expression, her fork poised over her plate. We always ate at the dining room table, even though it was just the two of us. It was part of the ritual, as was the rule that she fixed the entrée, I did the salad or vegetable, and we lit the candles, for ambiance. Also we ate at six sharp, and afterwards she rinsed the dishes and loaded them in the dishwasher, while I wiped down the counters and packed up leftovers. When we'd been four instead of two, Caroline and my dad had represented the sloppy, easygoing faction. With them gone, my mother and I kept things neat and organized. I could spot a crumb on the countertop from a mile off, and so could she.

"Yes?" I said.

"Are you okay?"

As I did every time she asked this, I wished I could answer her honestly. There was so much I wanted to tell my mother, like how much I missed my dad, how much I still thought about him. But I'd been doing so well, as far as everyone was concerned, for so long, that it seemed like it would be a failure of some sort to admit otherwise. As with so much else, I'd missed my chance.

I'd never really allowed myself to mourn, just jumped from shocked to fine-just-fine, skipping everything in between. But now, I wished I had sobbed for my dad Caroline-style, straight from the gut. I wished that in the days after the funeral, when our house was filled with relatives and too many casseroles and everyone had spent the days grouped around the kitchen table, coming and going, eating and telling great stories about my dad, I'd joined in instead of standing in the doorway, holding myself back, shaking my head whenever anyone saw me and offered to pull out a chair. More than anything, though, I wished I'd walked into my mother's open arms the few times she'd tried to pull me close, and pressed my face to her chest, letting my sad heart find solace there. But I hadn't. I wanted to be a help to her, not a burden, so I held back. And after a while, she stopped offering. She thought I was beyond that, when in fact I needed it now more than ever.

My dad had always been the more affectionate of the two of them, known for his tight-to-the-point-of-crushing bear hugs, the way he'd ruffle my hair as he passed by. It was part of his way of filling a room. I always felt close to him, even when there was a distance between us. My mom and I just weren't that effusive. As with Jason, I knew she loved me, even if the signs were subtle: a pat on my shoulder as she passed; her hand smoothing down my hair; the way she always seemed to be able to tell, with one glance, when I was tired or hungry. But sometimes I longed for that sense of someone pulling me close, feeling another heartbeat against mine, even though I'd often squirmed when my dad grabbed hold and threatened to squeeze the life out of me. It was another thing I never thought I'd miss, but did.

"I'm just tired," I told my mother now. She smiled, nodding: this she understood. "Tomorrow will be better."

"That's right," she replied, with certainty. I wondered if hers was an act, too, or if she really believed this. It was so hard to tell. "Of course it will."

—✳—

After dinner, I went up to my room and, after a few false starts and a fair amount of deleting, composed what I thought was a heartfelt yet not too cloying email to Jason. I answered all his questions about the job, and attached, as requested, a copy of the school recycling initiatives he'd implemented, which he wanted to show someone he'd met at camp. Then, and only then, did I allow myself to cross from the administrative to the personal.

I know it may seem petty to you, all this info desk drama, I wrote. *But I guess I just really miss you, and I'm lonely, and it's hard to go to a place where you're so spectacularly unwelcome. I'll just be really happy when you're home.*

This, I told myself, was the equivalent of touching his shoulder, or resting my knee against his as we watched TV. When you only had words, you had to make up for things, say what you might not need to otherwise. In fact, I felt so sure of this, I took it a step further, closing with *I love you, Macy.* Then I hit the send button before I had a chance to change my mind.

With that done, I walked over to my window, pushing it open, and crawled outside. It had rained earlier, one of those quick summer storms, and everything was still dripping and cool. I sat on the sill, propping my bare feet on the shingles. It was the best view, from my roof. You could see all Wildflower Ridge, and even beyond, to the lights of the Lakeview Mall and the university bell tower in the distance. In our old house, my bedroom had been distinct for a different reason. It had the only window that faced the street and a tree with branches close enough to step onto. Because of this, it got a lot of use. Not from me, but from Caroline.

She was wild. There was no other word for it. From seventh grade on, when she went, in my mother's words, "boy crazy," keeping Caroline under control was a constant battle. There were groundings. Phone restrictions. Cuttings off of allowance, driving privileges. Locks on the liquor cabinet. Sniff tests at the front door. These were played out, in high dramatic form, over dinners and breakfasts, in stomping of feet and raising of voices across living rooms and kitchens. But other transgressions and offenses were more secret. Private. Only I was witness to those, always at night, usually from the comfort of my own bed.

I'd be half sleeping, and my bedroom door would creak open, then close quickly. I'd hear the pat-pat of bare feet across the floor, then hear her drop her shoes on the carpet. Next, I'd feel the slight weight as she stepped up onto my bed.

"Macy," she'd whisper, softly but firmly. "Quiet. Okay?"

She'd step over my head, then hoist herself up on the sill that ran over my bed, slowly pushing open the window.

"You're going to get in trouble," I'd whisper.

She'd stick her feet out the window. "Hand me my shoes," she'd say, and when I did she'd toss them out onto the grass, where I'd hear them land with a distant, muted *thunk*.

"Caroline."

She'd turn and look at me. "Shut it behind me, don't lock it, I'll be back in an hour. Sweet dreams, I love you." And then she'd disappear off to the left, where I'd hear her easing herself down the oak tree, branch by branch. When I sat up to shut the window she was usually crossing the lawn, her footsteps leaving dark spots in the grass, shoes tucked under her arm. By the stop sign a block down, a car was always waiting.

It was always more than an hour, sometimes several, before

she appeared on the other side of the window, pushing it back up and tumbling in on top of me. All businesslike in the leaving, my sister was usually sloppy and sentimental, smelling of beer and sweet smoke, upon her return. She was often so sleepy she didn't even want to go back to her own room, instead just pushing her way under my blankets, shoes still on, makeup smearing my pillowcases. Sometimes she was crying, but she would never tell me why. Instead she'd just fall asleep beside me, and I'd doze in fits and spells before shaking her awake as the sun was rising and pushing her back to her own room, so she wouldn't be discovered. Then I'd crawl back into bed, smelling her all around me, and tell myself that next time, I would lock that window. But I never did.

By the time we moved to Wildflower Ridge, Caroline was in college. She was still going out all the time, sometimes way late, but my parents had given up trying to stop her. Instead, in exchange for her living at home while she attended the local university and waited tables at the country club, they required only that she keep her GPA above a 3.0 and make her entrances and exits as quietly as possible. She didn't need to use my window, which was a good thing, because in the new house there was not a tree nearby and the drop was a lot farther.

After my dad died, she sometimes didn't come home at all. My mind had raced with awful possibilities, picturing her dead on the highway, but the truth was actually much more innocuous. By then, she'd already fallen hard for Wally from Raleigh, the once-divorced up-and-coming lawyer ten years her senior she'd been seeing for awhile. She'd kept him, like so much else, secret from our parents, but after the funeral things got more serious, and before long, he asked her to marry him. All of this took longer than it sounds, summing it up. But at the time it seemed fast, really fast. One day Caroline was tumbling in my window; the next I was standing at the front of a church, all too aware of my uncle Mike walking her down the aisle toward Wally.

People made their comments, of course, about Caroline just needing a father figure, and how she was too young, getting married right after graduation. But she adored Wally, anyone could see that, and the quick nature of the wedding planning made it that much more of a happy distraction for all of us that spring. Plus, and best of all, their shared conviction that this had to be the Best Wedding Ever finally gave Caroline and my mother a solid common ground, and they'd gotten along pretty well ever since.

So after all that rebellion in her teens, my sister turned out to be surprisingly efficient, bagging a college diploma and a husband all within the same month. Now, as Mrs. Wally Thurber, she lived in Atlanta, in a big house on a cul-de-sac where you could hear a highway roaring twenty-four hours a day. It was climate controlled, with a top-of-the-line thermostat system. She never had to open a window for anything.

As for me, I wasn't much for sneaking out, first because I was a jock and always had early practice, and then because Jason and I just didn't do stuff like that. I could only imagine how he'd react if I asked him to pick me up at midnight at the stop sign. Why? he'd say. Nothing would be open, I have yoga in the morning, God, Macy, honestly. And so on. He'd be right, of course. The sneaking out, the partying, all those long nights doing God-knows-what, were Caroline things. She'd taken them with her when she left, and there was no place for them here now. At least in my mind.

"Macy," she'd say whenever she called and found me home on a Friday night, "what are you doing? Why aren't you out?" When I'd tell her I was studying, or doing some work for school, she'd exhale so loudly I'd have to hold the phone away from my ear. "You're young! Go out and live, for God sakes! There's time for all that later!"

My sister, unlike most of her new friends in the garden club and Junior League, did not gloss over her wild past, maintaining instead that it had been crucial to her development as a person. In her view, my own development in this area was entirely too slow-going, if not completely arrested.

"I'm fine," I'd tell her, like I always did.

"I know you are, that's the problem. You're a *teenager*, Macy," she'd say, as if I weren't aware of this or something. "You're supposed to be hormonal and crazy and emotional and wild. This is the best time of your life! You should be living it!"

So I'd swear that I was going out the next night, and she'd tell me she loved me, and then I'd hang up and go back to my SAT book, or my ironing, or the paper that wasn't due for another two weeks. Or sometimes I'd crawl out onto the roof and remember her wild days and wonder if I really was missing something. Probably not.

But the roof was still a nice sitting spot, at any rate. Even if my adventures in the outside world, my God-knows-what, started and ended there.

—✳—

Work, despite my mother's assurances, did not improve. In fact, I'd come to realize that the cold treatment I'd received initially was actually Bethany and Amanda being *nice*. Now they hardly spoke to me at all, while keeping me as idle as possible.

By Friday, I'd had enough silence to last a lifetime. Which was too bad for me, because my mother was down at the coast for a weekend developer meet-and-greet conference. I had the entire house, every silent inch of it, to myself for two full days.

She'd invited me to come along, offering the opportunity to lie on the beach or by the pool, all that fun summer beach stuff. But we both knew I'd say no, and I did. It was just one more thing that reminded me of my dad.

We had a house at the beach, in a little town called Colby that was just over the bridge. It was a true summer house, with shutters that creaked when the wind blew hard, and a front porch that was always covered in the thinnest layer of sand. While we all went down for the big summer weekends, it was mostly my dad's place. He'd bought it before he met my mom, and all the bachelor touches pretty much remained. There was a dartboard on the pantry door, a moose head over the fireplace, and the utensil drawer held everything my dad considered crucial to get by: a beer opener, a spatula, and a sharp fillet knife. Half the time the stove was on the fritz, not that my dad even noticed unless my mom was there. As long as the grill was gassed up and working, he was happy.

It was his fishing shack, the place he took his buddies to catch red drum in October, mahimahi in April, bluefin tuna in December. My dad always came home with a hangover, a coolerful of fish already cleaned, and a sunburn despite the SPF 45 my mom always packed for him. He loved every minute of it.

I wasn't allowed on these trips—they were, traditionally, estrogen-free—but he often took me down on other weekends, when he needed to work on the house or just felt like getting away. We'd cast off from the beach or take out his boat, play checkers by the fire, and go to this hole-in-the-wall place called the Last Chance, where the waitresses knew him by name and the hamburgers were the best I'd ever tasted. More than our old house, or our Wildflower Ridge place, the beach shack *was* my dad. I knew if he was haunting any place, it would be there, and for that reason I'd stayed away.

None of us had been down, in fact, since he died. His old Chevy truck was still there, locked in the garage, and the spare key it was always my job to fish out from the conch shell under the back porch had probably not been touched either. I knew my mom would probably sell the house and the truck eventually, but she hadn't yet.

So on Friday afternoon, I came home to find the house completely and totally quiet. This would be good, I told myself. I had a lot of stuff I wanted to get done over the weekend: emails to send out, research on colleges to do, and my closet had gotten really cluttered. Maybe this would be the perfect time to organize my winter sweaters and get some stuff to the thrift shop. Still, the silence was a bit much, so I walked over and turned on the TV, then went upstairs to my room to the radio, flipping past the music channels until I landed on a station where someone was blathering on about science innovations in our century. Even with all those voices going, though, I was acutely aware that I was alone.

Luckily, I got proof otherwise when I checked my email and

there was one from Jason. By the second line, though, I knew a bad week had just gotten much, much worse.

Macy,

I've taken some time before writing back, because I wanted to be clear and sure of what I was going to say. It's been a concern of mine for awhile that we've been getting too serious, and since I've been gone I've been thinking hard about our respective needs and whether our relationship is capable of filling them. I care about you, but your increasing dependency on me—made evident from the closing of your last email—has forced me to really think about what level of commitment I can make to our relationship. I care about you very much, but this upcoming senior year is crucial in terms of my ideological and academic goals, and I cannot take on a more serious commitment. I will have to be very focused, as I'm sure you will be, as well. In view of all these things, I think it's best for us to take a break from our relationship, and each other, until I return at the end of the summer. It will give us both time to think, so that in August we'll know better whether we want the same things, or if it's best to sever our ties and make this separation permanent.

I'm sure you can agree with what I've said here: it just makes sense. I think it's the best solution for both of us.

I read it through once, then, still in shock, again. This isn't happening, I thought.

But it was. The world was still turning: if I needed proof,

there was the radio across the room, from which I could hear headlines. A war in some Baltic country. Stocks down. Some TV star arrested. And there I sat, staring at the flickering screen, at these words. Words that, like the first ones Jason had read to me from *Macbeth*, were slowly starting to make awful sense.

A break. I knew what that meant: it was what happened right before something was officially and finally broken. Finished. Regardless of the language, it was most likely I was out, all for saying *I love you*. I'd thought we'd said as much to each other in the last few months, even if we never said it aloud. Clearly I'd been wrong.

I could feel my sudden aloneness in my gut, like a punch, and I sat back in my chair, dropping my hands from the keyboard, now aware of how empty the room, the house, the neighborhood, the world, was all around me. It was like being on the other side of a frame and seeing the camera pull back, showing me growing smaller, smaller, smaller still until I was just a speck, a spot, gone.

I had to get out of there. So I got in my car and drove.

And it helped. I don't know why, but it did. I wound through Wildflower Ridge, cresting the hills and circling the ground that had just been broken for the newest phase, then ventured farther, onto the main road and toward the mall. I drove in silence, since every song on the radio was either someone shrieking (not good for my nerves) or someone wailing about lost love (not good, period). In the quiet I'd been able to calm down as I focused on the sound of the engine, of gears shifting, brakes slowing, all things that, at least for now, were working just as they were supposed to.

On my way back, traffic was thick, everyone out for their Friday night. At stoplights I looked at the cars around me, taking in families with kids in car seats, probably headed home from dinner, and college girls in club makeup, blasting the radio and dangling cigarettes out their open windows. In the middle lane, surrounded by all these strangers, it seemed even more awful that I was going back to an empty house, up to my room to face my computer screen and Jason's email. I could just see him typing it out at his laptop, so methodical, somewhere between condensing the notes he'd taken that day and logging on to his environmental action Listservs. To him, I was a commitment that had become more of a burden than an asset, and his time was just too precious to waste. Not that I had to worry about that. From now on, clearly, I would have plenty of time on my hands.

As I approached the next intersection, I saw the wishbone.

Same bold black strokes, same white van. It was passing in front of me now, and I could see Delia driving, someone else in the passenger seat. I watched them move across the intersection, bumping over the slight dip in the middle. WISH, it said on the back, two letters on each door.

I am not a spontaneous person. But when you're alone in the world, really alone, you have no choice but to be open to suggestions. Those four letters, like the ones that I'd written to Jason, had many meanings and no guarantees. Still, as the van turned onto a side street, I read that WISH again. It seemed as good a time as any to believe, so when my light dropped to green and I could go, I put myself in gear and followed them.

Chapter Four

“So I say, I *know* that you’re not insulting my outfit. I mean, I can take a lot—already have taken a lot—but I won’t tolerate that. You’re my sister. You know. A girl has got to draw the line somewhere, right?”

Okay, I thought. Maybe this was a bad idea.

After almost turning back three times, two drive-bys, and one final burst of courage, I was standing in front of McKimmon House, a mansion in the historical district. In front of me was the Wish Catering van, now parked crookedly against the curb, the back doors flung open to reveal several racks of serving pans, blocks of packaged napkins, and a couple of dented rolling carts. Inside, I could hear a girl’s voice.

“So I do it: I draw the line. Which means, in the end, that I have to walk, like, two miles in my new platform sandals, which gave me blisters you would not believe,” she continued, her voice ringing out over the quiet of the street. “I mean, we’re talking deserted roads, no cars passing, and all I could think was—grab those spoons, no, not those, the other ones, right there—that this has got to officially be the worst first date *ever*. You know?”

I took a step backwards, retreating. What had I been thinking, anyway? I started to turn back to my car, thinking at least it wasn’t too late to change my mind.

Just then, though, a girl walked to the open doors of the van and saw me. She was small, with a mass of blonde ringlets spilling down her back, and with one look, I just knew it was she I'd heard. It was what she had on that made it obvious: a short, shiny black skirt, a white blouse with a plunging neck, tied at the waist, and thigh-high black boots with a thick heel. She had on bright red lipstick, and her skin, pale and white, was glittering in the glow of the streetlight behind me.

"Hey," she said, seeing me, then turned her back and grabbed a pile of dishtowels before hopping out of the van.

"Hi," I said. There was more I was going to say, entire words, maybe even a sentence. But for some reason I just froze, as if I'd gotten this far and now could go no further.

She didn't seem to notice, was too busy grabbing more stuff out of the van while humming under her breath. When she turned around and saw me still standing there, she said, "You lost or something?"

Again I was stuck for an answer. But this time, it was for a different reason. Her face, which before had been shadowed in the van, was now in the full light, and my eyes were immediately drawn to two scars: one, faint and curving along her jaw line, like an underscore of her mouth, and the other by her right temple, snaking down to her ear. She also had bright blue eyes and rings on every finger, and smelled like watermelon bubblegum, but these were things I noticed later. The scars, at first, were all I could see.

Stop staring, I told myself, horrified at my behavior. The girl, for her part, didn't even seem to notice, or be bothered. She was just waiting, patiently, for an answer.

"Um," I said finally, forcing the words out, "I was looking for Delia?"

The front door of the van slammed shut, and a second later Monica, the slow girl from my mother's party, appeared. She was carrying a cutting board, which, by the expression of weariness on her face, must have weighed about a hundred pounds. She blew her long bangs out of her face as she shuffled along the curb, taking her time.

The blonde girl glanced at her. "Serving forks, too, Monotone, okay?"

Monica stopped, then turned herself around slowly—a sort of human three-point turn—and disappeared back behind the van at the same snail's pace.

"Delia's up at the house, in the kitchen," the girl said to me now, shifting the towels to her other arm. "It's at the top of the drive, around back."

"Oh," I said, as Monica reappeared, now carrying the cutting board and a few large forks. "Thanks."

I started over to the driveway, getting about five feet before she called after me.

"If you're headed up there anyway," she said, "would you please please please take something with you? We're running late—and it's kind of my fault, if you want the whole truth—so you'd be really helping me out. If you don't mind."

"Sure," I said. I came back down the driveway, passing Monica, who was muttering to herself, along the way. At the back of the van, the blonde girl had pulled out two of the wheeled carts and was piling foil pans onto them, one right after another. When she was done she stuck the towels on top of one, then rolled the other over to me.

"This way," she said, and I followed her, pushing my cart, to the bottom of the driveway. There we stopped, looking up. It was steep, really steep. We could see Monica still climbing it, about halfway up: it looked like she was walking into the wind.

The girl looked at me, then at the driveway again. I kept noticing her scars, then trying not to, which seemed to make it all that more obvious. "God," she said, sighing as she pushed her hair out of her face, "doesn't it seem, sometimes, that the whole damn world's uphill?"

"Yeah," I said, thinking about everything that had already happened to me that night. "It sure does."

She turned her head and looked at me, then smiled: it changed her whole face, like a spark lighting into a flame, everything brightening, and for a second I lost track of the scars altogether. "Oh well," she said, leaning over her cart and tightening her fingers around its handle. "At least we know the way back will be easy. Come on."

Her name was Kristy Palmetto.

We introduced ourselves about halfway up the hill, when we stopped, wheezing, to catch our breath. "Macy?" she'd said. "Like the store?"

"Yes," I replied. "It's a family name, actually."

"I like it," she said. "I intend to change my name as soon as I get to a place where nobody knows me, you know, where I can reinvent myself. I've always wanted to do that. I think I want to be a Veronique. Or maybe Blanca. Something with flair, you know. Anybody can be a Kristy."

Maybe, I thought, as she started to push her cart again. But even five minutes into our friendship, I knew that this Kristy was different.

As we came up to the side door it opened, and Delia stuck

her head out. She had on a red Wish Catering apron and there was a spot of flour on her cheek. "Are those the ham biscuits? Or the shrimp and grits?"

"The biscuits," Kristy said, pushing her cart up against the side of house and gesturing for me to do the same. "Or the shrimp."

Delia just looked at her.

"It's definitely one or the other," Kristy said. "Definitely."

Delia sighed, then came out and started peering into the various pans on the carts.

Kristy leaned against the wall, crossing her arms over her chest. "That hill is a killer," she said to Delia. "We've got to get the van up here or we'll never get everything in on time."

"If we'd left when we were supposed to," Delia said, lifting the lid of one pan, "we could have."

"I said I was sorry!" Kristy said. To me she added, "I was having a fashion crisis. Nothing looked good. Nothing! Don't you hate it when that happens?"

"And anyway," Delia continued, ignoring this tangent, "they have strict rules about service vehicles up here by the garden. The grass is apparently very fragile."

"So are my lungs," Kristy said. "And if we do it fast, they'll never notice."

Monica appeared in the open door, holding a cookie sheet. "Mushrooms?" she asked.

"Meatballs," Delia said, without looking up. "Put three trays in, get another three ready."

Monica turned her body slowly, glancing at the oven behind her. Then she looked at Delia again. "Meatballs," she repeated, like it was a foreign word.

"Monica, you do this every weekend," Delia said. "Try to retain some knowledge, please God I'm begging you."

"She retains knowledge," Kristy said, a little defensively. "She's just mad at me for holding us up, and that's how she expresses it. She's not good at being forthright about her emotions, you know that."

"Then go help her, please," Delia said in a tired voice. "With the meatballs, not her emotions. Okay?"

"Okay," Kristy said cheerfully, pulling open the door and going inside.

Delia put her hand on the small of her back and looked at me. "Hi," she said, sounding a little surprised. "It's Macy, right?"

"Yes," I said. "I know this is probably a bad time—"

"It's always a bad time," Delia said with a smile. "It's a bad business. But I chose it, so I can't really complain. What can I do for you?"

"I just wondered," I said, then stopped. I felt stupid now for holding her up, when so much else was going on. Maybe she had just been being nice when she'd said she would hire me. But then again, I was already here. I'd climbed that hill. The worst she could do was send me back down. "I just wondered," I said again, "if the offer still stood. About the job."

Before Delia could answer, Kristy reappeared in the doorway. "Meatballs are in," she said. "Can I get the van now?"

Delia looked down the driveway, then shot a glance in the front window of the house. "Can *you*? No," she said.

"It's just one hill." Kristy rolled her eyes. To me she said, "I'm a terrible driver. But the fact that I admit it, shouldn't that count for something?"

"No," Delia said. She looked down the driveway, then at the

house, as if weighing the pros and cons, before digging into the pocket of her apron to pull out some keys. "Once it's up here, unload fast," she said to Kristy. "And if anyone starts freaking, pretend you had no idea about the rules."

"What rules?" Kristy said, reaching for the keys.

Delia shifted them out of her reach, holding them out to me instead. "And Macy drives. Period. No argument."

"Fine," Kristy said. "Let's just do it, okay?"

She turned on her heel and started down the driveway, bouncing a bit with each step. Even from a distance, you couldn't help but watch her: maybe it was the boots or the hair or the short skirt, but somehow to me it was something else. Something so electric, alive, that I recognized it instantly, if only because it was so lacking in myself.

Delia was watching her, too, a resigned expression on her face, before turning her attention back to me. "If you want a job, it's yours," she said, dropping the keys into my hand. "Payday's every other Friday, and you'll usually know your schedule a week in advance. You'll want to invest in a few pairs of black pants and some white shirts, if you don't have a few already, and we don't work on Mondays. There's probably more you need to know but we're off to a rocky start here, so I'll fill you in later. Okay?"

"Sounds good," I said.

Kristy, already halfway down the driveway, turned her head and looked up at us. "Hey, Macy!" she yelled. "Let's go!"

Delia shook her head, pulling the screen door open. "Which is to say," she said to me, "welcome aboard."

At the library, I'd had two weeks of training. Here, it was two minutes.

"What's most important," Kristy said to me, as we stood side by side at the counter, piling mini ham biscuits onto trays, "is that you identify what you're carrying and keep all crumpled-up napkins off your tray. No one will pick up anything and stick it in their mouth if it's next to a dirty napkin."

I nodded, and she continued.

"Here's what you need to remember," she continued, as Delia bustled past behind us, putting down another sheet of meatballs. "You don't exist. Just hold out your tray, smile, say, 'Ham biscuits with Dijon mustard,' and move on. Try to be invisible."

"Right," I said.

"What she means," Delia clarified from the stove, "is that as a server, it's your job to blend in and make the partygoer's experience as enjoyable as possible. You are not attending the event: you are facilitating it."

Kristy handed me the tray of ham biscuits, plunking down a stack of napkins on its edge. This close to her, I still found my eyes wandering to her scars, but slowly I was getting used to them, my eyes drawn now and then to other things: the glitter on her skin, the two tiny silver hoops in each of her ears. "Work the edge of the room first. If you cross paths with a gobbler, pause for only a second, then smile and keep moving, even if they're reaching after you."

"Gobbler?" I said.

"That's someone who will clear your whole tray if you let them. Here's the rule: two and move. When they reach for a third, you're gone."

"Two and move," I said. "Right."

"If they don't let you move on," she continued, "then they cross over to grabber status, which is completely out-of-line behavior. Then you are wholly within your rights to stomp on their foot."

"No," Delia said, over her shoulder. "Actually, you're not. Just excuse yourself as politely as possible, and get out of arm's reach."

Kristy looked at me, shaking her head. "Stomp them," she said, under her breath. "Really."

The kitchen was bustling, Delia moving from the huge stove to the counter, Monica unwrapping one foil tray after another, revealing the salmon, steaks, whipped potatoes. There was a crackling energy in the air, as if everything was on a higher speed than normal, the total opposite of the info desk. If I'd wanted something other than silence, I'd surely found it. In spades.

"If there are old people," Kristy said now, glancing at the door, "make sure you go to them, especially if they're sitting down. People notice when Grandma's starving. Watch the room, keep an eye on who's eating and who's not. If you've done a full walk of the room and the goat cheese currant stuffed celery sticks aren't finding any takers, don't keep walking around."

"Goat cheese currant?" I said.

Kristy nodded gravely.

"It was just one time, one job!" Delia hissed from behind us. "I wish you all would just let that go. God!"

"If something sucks," Kristy said, "it sucks. When in doubt, grab some meatballs and get back out there. *Everybody* loves meatballs."

"What time is it?" Delia asked, as the oven shut with a bang. "Is it seven?"

"Six forty-five," Kristy told her, tucking a piece of hair behind her ear. "We need to get out there."

I picked up my tray, then stood still while Kristy adjusted one biscuit that was close to falling off the edge. "You ready?" she asked me.

I nodded.

She pushed the door open with one hand, and some people standing nearby waiting for drinks at the bar turned and looked at us, their eyes moving immediately to the food. Invisible, I thought. After all the attention of the last year or so, I was pretty sure I could get used to that. So I lifted my tray up, squared my shoulders, and headed in.

Thirty minutes later, I'd discovered a few things. First, everybody does love meatballs. Second, most gobblers position themselves right by the door, where they have first dibs on anything you bring out, and if you try to sidestep them, they quickly move into grabber mode, although I'd yet to have to stomp anyone. And it's true: you are invisible. They'll say anything with you standing there. Anything.

I now knew that Molly and Roger, the bride and groom, had lived together for three years, a fact that one gobbler relative was sure contributed to the recent death of the family matriarch. Because of some bachelorette party incident, Molly and her maid of honor weren't currently speaking, and the father of the groom, who was supposed to be on the wagon, was sneaking martinis in the bathroom. And, oh yeah, the napkins were wrong. All wrong.

"I'm not sure I understand," I heard Delia saying as I came

back into the kitchen for a last round of goat cheese toasts. She was standing by the counter, where she and Monica were getting ready to start preparing the dinner salads, and next to her was the bride, Molly, and her mother.

"They're not right!" Molly said, her voice high pitched and wavery. She was a pretty girl, plump and blonde, and had spent the entire party, from what I could tell, standing by the bar with a pinched expression while people took turns squeezing her shoulder and making soothing it's-okay noises. The groom was outside smoking cigars, had been all night. Molly said, "They were supposed to say *Molly and Roger*, then the date, then underneath that, *Forever*."

Delia glanced around her. "I'm sorry, I don't have one here . . . but don't they say that? I'm almost positive the one I saw did."

Molly's mother took a gulp of the mixed drink in her hand, shaking her head. Kristy pushed back through the door, dumping a bunch of napkins on her tray, then stopped when she saw the confab by the counter.

"What's going on?" she said. Molly's mother was staring at the scars, I noticed. When Kristy glanced over at her, she looked away, though, fast. If Kristy noticed or was bothered, it didn't show. She just put her tray down, tucking a piece of hair behind her ear.

"Napkin problems," I told her now.

Molly choked back a sob. "They don't say *Forever*. They say *Forever* . . ." She trailed off, waving her hand. "With that dot-dot-dot thing."

"Dot dot dot?" Delia said, confused.

"You know, that thing, the three periods, that you use when you leave something open-ended, unfinished. It's a—" She paused, scrunching up her face. "You know! That thing!"

"An ellipsis," I offered, from the across the room.

They all looked at me. I felt my face turn red.

"Ellipsis?" Delia repeated.

"It's three periods," I told her, but she still looked confused, so I added, "You use it to make a transition. Also, it's used to show a thought trailing off. Especially in dialogue."

"Wow," Kristy said from beside me. "Go Macy."

"Exactly!" Molly said, pointing at me. "It doesn't say *Molly and Roger, Forever*. It says *Molly and Roger, Forever . . . dot dot dot*!" She punctuated these with a jab of her finger. "Like maybe it's forever, maybe it's not."

"Well," Kristy said under her breath to me, "it is a *marriage*, isn't it?"

Molly had pulled out a Kleenex from somewhere and was dabbing her face, taking little sobby breaths. "You know," I said to her, trying to help, "I don't think anyone would think that an ellipsis represents doubt or anything. I think it's more, you know, hinting at the future. What lies ahead."

Molly blinked at me, her face flushed. Then she burst into tears.

"Oh, man," Kristy said.

"I'm sorry," I said quickly. "I didn't mean—"

"It's not about the forever," her mother told me, sliding her arm over her daughter's shoulders.

"It's all about the forever!" Molly wailed. But then her mother was steering her out of the kitchen, murmuring to her softly. We watched her go, all of us quiet. I felt completely and totally responsible. Clearly, this had not been the moment to show off my grammar prowess.

Delia wiped a hand over her face, shaking her head. "Good Lord," she said, once they were out of earshot. She looked at us. "What should we do?"

Nobody said anything for a second. Then Kristy put down her tray. "We should," she announced, definitively, "make salads." She started over to the counter, where she began unstacking plates. Monica pulled the bowl of greens closer, picking up some tongs, and they got to work.

I looked back over at the door, feeling terrible. Who knew three dots could make such a difference? Like everything else, a love or a wish or whatever, it was all in the way you read it.

"Macy." I glanced up. Kristy was watching me. She said, "It's okay. It's not your fault."

And maybe it wasn't. But that was the problem with having the answers. It was only after you gave them that you realized they sometimes weren't what people wanted to hear.

"All in all," Delia said three hours later, as we slid the last cart, now loaded down with serving utensils and empty coolers, into the van, "that was not entirely disastrous. In fact, I'd even go so far as to say it was half decent."

"There was that thing with the steaks," Kristy said, referring to a panicked moment right after we distributed the salads, when Delia realized half the fillets were still in the van and, therefore, ice cold.

"Oh, right. I forgot about that." Delia sighed. "Well, at least it's over. Next time, everything will go smoothly. Like a well-oiled machine."

Even I, as the newbie, knew this was unlikely. All night

there'd been one little problem after another, disasters arising, culminating, and then somehow getting solved, all at whiplash speed. I was so used to controlling the unexpected at all costs that I'd felt my stress level rising and falling, reacting constantly. For everyone else, though, this seemed perfectly normal. They honestly seemed to believe that things would just work out. And the weirdest thing was, they *did*. Somehow. Eventually. Although even when I was standing right there I couldn't say how.

Now Kristy reached into the back of the van, pulling out a fringed black purse. "Hate to say it," she said, "but I give the marriage a year, tops. There's cold feet, and then there's oh-God-don't-do-it. That girl was *freaking*."

Monica, sitting on the bumper, offered what I now knew to be one of her three default phrases, "Mmm-hmmm." The other two were "Better quit" and "Don't even," both said with a slow, drawled delivery, the words running together into one: "Bettaquit" and "Donneven." I didn't know who had christened her Monotone, but they were right on the money.

"When you get home," Delia said to me, running her hands over her pregnant belly once and then resting her spread fingers there, "soak that in cold water and some Shout. It should come out."

I looked down at my shirt and the stain there I'd completely forgotten about. "Oh, right," I said. "I'll do that."

About halfway through dinner, some overeager groomsman, leaping up to make a toast, had spilled a full glass of cabernet on me. I'd already learned about gobblers and grabbers: at that moment, I got a full tutorial on gropers. He'd pawed me for about five minutes while attempting to dab the stain out, resulting in me getting arguably more action than I ever had from Jason.

Jason. As I thought his name, I felt a pull in my gut and realized that for the last three hours or so, I'd forgotten all about our break, my new on-hold girlfriend status. But it had happened, was still happening. I'd just been too busy to notice.

A car turned onto the road, its headlights swinging across us, then approaching slowly, very slowly. As it crept closer, I squinted at it. It wasn't a car but more like some sort of van, painted white with gray splotches here and there. Finally it reached us, the driver easing over to the curb carefully before cutting off the engine. A second later, a head popped out of the window.

"Ladies," a voice came, deep and formal, "witness the Bertmobile."

For a second, no one said anything. Then Delia gasped.

"Oh, my God," Kristy said. "You've got to be joking."

The driver's side door swung open with a loud creak, and Bert hopped out. "What?" he said.

"I thought you were getting Uncle Henry's car," Delia said, taking a few steps toward him as Wes climbed out of the passenger door. "Wasn't that the plan?"

"Changed my mind," Bert said, jingling his keys. In a striped shirt with a collar, khaki pants with a leather belt, and loafers, he looked as if he was dressed up for something.

"Why?" Delia asked. She walked up to the Bertmobile, her head cocked to the side. A second later, she took a step back, putting her hands on her hips. "Wait," she said slowly. "Is this an—"

"Vehicle that makes a statement?" Bert said. "Yes. Yes it is."

"—ambulance?" she finished, her voice incredulous. "It is, isn't it?"

"No way," Kristy said, laughing. "Bert, only you would think you could get action in a car where people have *died.*"

"Where did you get this?" Delia said. "Is it even legal to drive?"

Wes, now standing by the front bumper, just shook his head in a don't-even-ask kind of way. Now that I looked closer at the Bertmobile, I could in fact make out the faintest trace of an A and part of an M on the front grille.

"I bought it from that auto salvage lot by the airport," Bert said. You would have thought it was a new-model Porsche by the way he was beaming at it. "The guy there got it from a town auction. Isn't that the *coolest*?"

Delia looked at Wes. "What happened to Uncle Henry's Cutlass?"

"I tried to stop him," Wes told her. "But you know how he is. He insisted. And it *is* his money."

"You can't make a statement with a Cutlass!" Bert said.

"Bert," Kristy said, "*you* can't make a statement, period. I mean, what are you *wearing*? Didn't I tell you not to dress like someone's dad? God. Is that shirt polyester?"

Bert, hardly bothered by this or any of her other remarks, glanced down at his shirt, brushing a hand over the front pocket. "Poly-*blend*," he said. "Ladies like a well-dressed man."

Kristy just rolled her eyes, while Wes ran a hand over his face. Monica, from behind me, said, "Donneven."

"It's an ambulance," Delia said flatly, as if saying it aloud might get her used to the idea.

"A former ambulance," Bert corrected her. "It's got history. It's got personality. It's got—"

"Final sale status," Wes said. "He can't take it back. When he drove it off the lot, that was it."

Delia sighed, shaking her head.

"It's what I wanted," Bert said. It was quiet for a second: no one, it seemed, had an argument for this.

Finally Delia walked over and put her arms around Bert, pulling him close to her. "Well, happy birthday, little man," she said, ruffling his hair. "I can't believe you're already sixteen. It makes me feel *old*."

"You're not old," he said.

"Old enough to remember the day you were born," she said, pulling back from him and brushing his hair out of his face. "Your mom was so happy. She said you were her wish come true."

Bert looked down quickly, turning his keys in his fingers. Delia leaned close to him, then whispered something I couldn't hear, and he nodded. When he looked up again, his face was flushed, and for a second, I saw something in his face I recognized, something familiar. But then he turned his head, and just like that, it was gone.

"Did you guys officially meet Macy?" Delia asked, nodding at me. "Macy, these are my nephews, Bert and Wes."

"We met the other night," I said.

"Bert sprung at her from behind some garbage cans," Wes added.

"God, are you two still doing that?" Kristy said. "It's so stupid."

"I only did it because I'm down," Bert said, shooting me an apologetic look. "By three!"

"All I'm saying," Kristy said, pulling a nail file out of her purse, "is that the next person who leaps out at me from behind a door is getting a punch in the gut. I don't care if you're down or not."

"Mmm-hmmm," Monica agreed.

"I thought she was Wes," Bert grumbled. "And I wouldn't jump out from behind a door anyway. That's basic. We're way beyond that."

"Are you?" Kristy asked, but Bert acted like he didn't hear her. To me she said, "It's this stupid gotcha thing, they've been doing it for weeks now. Leaping out at each other and us, scaring the hell out of everyone."

"It's a game of wits," Bert said to me.

"Half-wits," Kristy added.

"There's nothing," Bert said, reverently, "like a good gotcha."

Delia, yawning, put a hand over her mouth, shaking her head. "Well, I hate to break this up, but I'm going home," she announced. "Old pregnant ladies have to be in bed by midnight. It's the rule."

"Come on!" Bert said, sweeping his hand across the ambulance's hood. "The night is young! The Bertmobile needs *christening*!"

"We're going to ride around in an ambulance?" Kristy said.

"It's got all the amenities!" Bert told her. "It's just like a car. It's *better* than a car!"

"Does it have a CD player?" she asked him.

"Actually—"

"No," Wes told her. "But it does have a broken intercom system."

"Oh, well, then," she said, waving her hand. "I'm sold."

Bert shot her a look, annoyed, but she smiled at him, squeezing his arm as she started over to the Bertmobile. Monica stood up and followed her, and they went around to the back, pulling open the rear doors.

"Have a fun night," Delia called after them. "Don't drive too fast, Bert, you hear?"

This was greeted with uproarious laughter from everyone but Wes—who looked like he would have laughed but was trying not to—and Bert, who just ignored it as he walked over to the driver's side door.

"Wes," Delia called out, "can you come here for a sec?"

Wes started over toward her, but I was in the way, and we did that weird thing where both of us went to one side, then the other, in tandem. During this awkward dance I noticed he was even better looking up close than from a distance—with those dark eyes, long lashes, hair curling just over his collar, his jeans low on his hips—and he had a tattoo on his arm, something Celtic-looking that poked out from under the sleeve of his T-shirt.

Finally I stopped moving, and he was able to get past me. "Sorry about that," he said, smiling, and I felt myself flush for some reason as I watched him disappear around the side of the van.

"Where are we supposed to sit?" I could hear Kristy asking from the back of the Bertmobile. "Oh, Jesus, is that a gurney?"

"No," Bert said. "It's where the gurney used to be. That's just a cot I put in until I find something more comfortable."

"A cot?" Kristy said. "Bert, you're *entirely* too confident about this car's potential. Really."

"Just get in, will you?" Bert snapped. "My birthday is ticking away. Ticking!"

Wes was walking back to the Bertmobile as I dug out my keys and started toward my car, passing the van on my way.

"Have a good night," he said to me, and I nodded, my tongue fumbling for a response, but once I realized that saying the same thing back would have been fine—God, what was wrong with me?—it was too late, and he was already getting into the Bertmobile.

As I passed the van, Delia was in the driver's seat fastening her seat belt. "You did great, Macy," she said. "Just great."

"Thanks."

She grabbed a pen off the dashboard, then reached into her pocket and pulled out a crumpled napkin. "Here," she said, writing something on it, "this is my number. Give me a call on Monday and I'll let you know when I can use you next. Okay?"

"Okay," I said, taking the napkin and folding it. "Thanks again. I had a really good time."

"Yeah?" She smiled at me, surprised. "I'm glad. Drive safe, you hear?"

I nodded, and she cranked the engine, then pulled away from the curb, beeping the horn as she turned the corner.

I'd just unlocked my door when the Bertmobile pulled up beside me. Kristy was leaning forward from the backseat, hand on the radio: I could hear the dial moving across stations, from static to pop songs to some thumping techno bass beat. She looked across Wes, who was digging in the glove compartment, right at me.

"Hey," she said, "you want to come out with us?"

"Oh, no," I said. "I really have to go—"

Kristy twisted the dial again, and the beginning of a pop song blasted out, someone shrieking *"Baaaaby!"* at full melodic throttle. Bert and Wes both winced.

"—home," I finished.

Kristy turned down the volume, but not much. "Are you sure?" she said. "I mean, do you really want to pass this up? How often do you get to ride in an ambulance?"

One time too many, I thought.

"It's a refurbished ambulance," Bert grumbled.

"Whatever," Kristy said. To me she added, "Come on, live a little."

"No, I'd better go," I said. "But thanks."

Kristy shrugged. "Okay," she told me. "Next time, though, okay?"

"Right," I said. "Sure."

I stood there and watched them, noting how carefully Bert turned around in the opposite driveway, the way Wes lifted one hand to wave as they pulled away. Maybe in another life, I might have been able to take a chance, to jump into the back of an ambulance and not remember the time I'd done it before. But risk hadn't been working out for me lately; I needed only to go home and see my computer screen to know that. So I did what I always did these days, the right thing. But before I did, I glanced in my side mirror, catching one last look at the Bertmobile as it turned a far corner. Then, once they were gone, I started my engine and headed home.

Chapter Five

Dear Jason,

I received your email, and I have to say I was surprised to learn that you felt I'd been

Dear Jason,

I received your email, and I can't help but feel that maybe you should have let me know if you felt our relationship was

Dear Jason,

I received your email, and I can't believe you'd do this to me when all I did was say I love you, which is something most people who've been together can

No, no, I thought, and definitely, no.

It was Monday morning, and even with two full days to craft a response to Jason's email, I had nothing. The main problem was that what he'd written to me was so cold, so lacking in emotion, that each time I started to reply, I tried to use the same tone. But I couldn't. No matter how carefully I worked at it, by the time I finished all I could see was the raw sadness in the lines as I scanned them, all my failings and flaws cropping up in the spaces between the words. So finally, I decided that the best response—the safest—was none at all. Since I hadn't heard from him, I assumed he'd accepted my silence as agreement. It was probably just what he wanted anyway.

As I drove to the library to begin another week at the info desk, I got stuck behind an ambulance at a stoplight, which made me think, as I had pretty frequently since Friday, about Wish Catering. I'd already had to confess about my new job to my mother, after she found my wine-stained shirt in the laundry room soaking in Shout. That's what I get for following instructions.

"But honey," she said, her voice more questioning than disapproving, but it was early yet, "you already have a job."

"I know," I said, as she took another doubtful look at the shirt, eyeing the stain, "but I bumped into Delia on Friday at the supermarket, and she was all frazzled and short-handed, so I offered to help her out. It just kind of happened." This last part, at least, was true.

She shut the washer, then turned and looked at me, crossing her arms over her chest. "I just think," she said, "that you might get overwhelmed. Your library job is a lot of responsibility. Jason is trusting you to really give it your full attention."

This would have been, in any other world, the perfect time to tell my mother about Jason's decision and our break. But I didn't. I knew my mother thought of me as the good daughter, the one she could depend on to be as driven and focused as she was. For some reason, I was sure that Jason's breaking up with me would make me less than that in her eyes. It was bad enough that *I* assumed I wasn't up to Jason's standards. Even worse would be for her to think so.

"Catering is just a once in a while thing," I said now. "It's not a distraction. I might not even do it again. It was just . . . for fun."

"Fun?" she said. Her voice was so surprised, as if I'd told her that driving nails into my arms was, also, just that enjoyable. "I would think it would be horrible, having to be on your feet all the time and waiting on people . . . plus, well, that woman just seemed so disorganized. I'd go crazy."

"Oh," I said, "that was just when they were here. On Friday night, they were totally different."

"They were?"

I nodded. Another lie. But my mother would never have understood why, in some small way, the mayhem of Delia's business would appeal to me. I wasn't even sure I could explain it myself. All I knew was that the rest of the weekend had been a stark contrast to those few hours on Friday night. During the days, I'd done all the things I was supposed to: I went to yoga class, did laundry, cleaned my bathroom, and tried to compose an email to Jason. I ate lunch and dinner at the same time both days, using the same plate, bowl, and glass, washing them after each meal and stacking them neatly in the dish rack, and went to bed by eleven, even though I rarely fell asleep, if at all, before two. For forty-eight hours, I spoke to no one but a couple of telemarketers. It was so quiet that I kept finding myself sitting at the kitchen table listening to my own breathing, as if in all this order and cleanliness I needed that to prove I was alive.

"Well, we'll just see how it goes, okay?" my mother had said as I reached over and turned on the washer. The water started gurgling, tackling the wine stain. "The library job is still your first priority. Right?"

"Right," I agreed, and that was that.

Now, however, as I walked in to begin my second week of

work—even though our shifts began at nine, and it was only eight-fifty, Bethany and Amanda were, naturally, already there and in place in their chairs—I felt a sense of inescapable dread. Maybe it was the silence. Or the stillness. Or the way Amanda raised her head and looked at me as I approached, her brow furrowing.

"Oh, Macy," she said, with the same slightly surprised tone she'd used every day I'd showed up, "I wondered if you would make it in today . . . considering."

I knew what she meant, of course. Jason wasn't one to spill secrets, but there were a couple of other people from our high school at Brain Camp, one of whom, a guy named Rob who squinted all the time, was good friends with both Amanda and Jason. Whatever way it had gone, clearly this break wasn't just my secret anymore. Now, it was Information, and as they were with everything else, Bethany and Amanda were suddenly experts.

"Considering," Amanda said, repeating the word slowly as if, by not rising to the bait, I must not have heard her, "what happened with you and Jason."

I turned so I was facing her. "It's just a break. And it has nothing to do with my job."

"Maybe so," she said, as Bethany put a pen to her lips. "We were just concerned it might, you know, affect your performance."

"No," I said. "It won't." And then I turned back to my computer screen. I could see their faces reflected there, the way Amanda shook her head in a she's-so-pathetic way, how Bethany pursed her lips, silently agreeing, before slowly swiveling back to face forward.

And so began my longest day yet. I didn't do much of anything, other than answer an all-time high of two questions (one from a man who stumbled in, unshaven and stinking of liquor, to ask about a job opening, and another from a six-year-old concerning how to find Mickey Mouse's address, both of which were, at least in Bethany and Amanda's opinion, not worth their time, but fully suited to mine). All this made it more than clear that last week, I'd been an annoyance to be tolerated. Now I was one easily, and rightfully, ignored.

It was just after dinner and I was following routine, wiping down the kitchen countertops, when the phone rang. I didn't even reach for it, assuming it was a client calling for my mother. But then I heard her office door open.

"Macy? It's for you."

The first thing I heard when I picked up the kitchen phone was someone sobbing, in that blubbering, gaspy kind of way.

"Oh, Lucy, honey, please," I heard a voice saying over it. "You only do this when I'm on the phone, why is that? Hmmm? Why—"

"Hello?" I said.

"Macy, hi, it's Delia." The crying started up again fresh, climbing to a full-out wail. "Oh, Lucy, sweetie, please God I'm begging you, just let Mommy talk for five seconds. . . . Look, here's your bunny, see?"

I just sat there holding the phone, as the crying subsided to sniffling, then to hiccuping, then stopped altogether.

"Macy," she said, "I am so sorry. Are you still there?"

"Yes," I told her.

She sighed, that world-weary exhale I already associated

with her, even though we hardly knew each other. "The reason I'm calling," she began, "is that I'm kind of in a bind and I could use an extra pair of hands. I've got this big luncheon thing tomorrow, and currently I'm about two hundred finger sandwiches behind. Can you help me out?"

"Tonight?" I said, glancing at the clock on the stove. It was 7:05, the time when I usually went upstairs to check my email, then brushed and flossed my teeth before reviewing a few pages of my SAT word book so that I wouldn't feel too guilty about camping out in front of the TV until I was tired enough to try sleeping.

"I know it's short notice, but everyone else already had plans," Delia said now, and I heard her running water. "So don't feel bad about saying no. . . . It was just a shot in the dark, you know. I dug out your mom's business card and thought I'd at least try to woo you over here."

"Well," I said, and the no, I can't, I'm sorry, was perched right there on my tongue, so close to my saying it that I could feel my lips forming the words. But then I looked around our silent, perfectly clean kitchen. It was summer, early evening. Once this had been my favorite time of year, my favorite time of night. When the fireflies came out, and the heat cooled. How had I forgotten that?

". . . don't know why you'd want to spend a few hours up to your elbows in watercress and cream cheese," Delia was saying in my ear as I snapped to, back to reality. "Unless you just had nothing else to do."

"I don't," I said suddenly, surprising myself. "I mean, nothing that can't wait."

"Really?" she said. "Wonderful. Oh, God. You're saving my

life! Here, let me give you directions. Now, it's kind of a ways out, but I'll pay you from right now, so your driving time will be on the clock."

As I picked a pen out of the jar by the phone, pulling a notepad closer to me, I had a sudden pang of worry thinking about this deviation from my routine. But this was just one night, one chance to vary and see where it took me. The fireflies were probably already out: maybe it wasn't just a season or a time but a whole world I'd forgotten. I'd never know until I stepped out into it. So I did.

Delia's directions were like Delia: clear in places, completely frazzled in others. The first part was easy. I'd taken the main road through town then past the city limits, where the scenery turned from new subdivisions and office buildings to smaller farmhouses to big stretches of pasture and dairy lands, plus cows. It was the turn off of that road, however—which led to Delia's street—where I got stuck. Or lost. Or both. It just wasn't *there*, period, no matter how many times I drove up and down looking for it. Which became sort of embarrassing, as there was a produce stand I kept driving by—its sign, painted in bright red, said, TOMATOES FRESH FLOWERS PIES—where an older woman was sitting in a lawn chair, a large flashlight in her lap, reading a paperback book. The third time I passed her, she put the book down and watched me. The fourth, she got involved.

"You lost, sugar?" she called out as I crept past, scanning the scenery for the turnoff—"It's a narrow dirt road, blink and you'll miss it," Delia had said—wondering if this was some sort of induction process for new employees or something, like hazing or catering boot camp. I stopped my car, then backed up slowly. By the time I reached the stand, the woman had gotten out of her chair and was coming to bend down into my passenger window. She looked to be in her early fifties, maybe, with graying hair pulled back at her neck, and was wearing jeans and a white tank top, with a shirt tied around her ample waist. She still had the paperback in her hand, and I glanced at the title: *The Choice*, by Barbara Starr. There was a shirtless man on the cover, a woman in a tight dress pressed against him. Her place was held with a nail file.

"I'm looking for Sweetbud Drive," I said. "It's supposed to be off this road, but I can't—"

"Right there," she said, turning and pointing to a gravel strip to the right of the produce stand, so narrow it looked more like a driveway than a real street. "Not your fault you missed it, the sign got stolen again last night. Bunch of damn potheads, I swear." She indicated a spot on the other side of the drive where, in fact, there was a metal pole, no sign attached. "And that's the *fourth* time this year. Now nobody can find my house until the DOT gets someone out here to replace it."

"Oh," I said. "That's terrible."

"Well," she replied, switching her paperback to the other hand, "maybe not terrible. But it sure is inconvenient. Like life isn't complicated enough. You should at least be able to follow the *signs*." She stood up, stretching. "Oh, and on your way, watch out for the big hole. It's right past the sculpture, and it's a doozy. Stick to the left." Then she patted my hood, smiled at me, and walked back to her lawn chair.

"Thank you," I called out after her, and she waved at me over her shoulder. I turned around in the road and started down Sweetbud Drive, mindful that somewhere up ahead there was both a sculpture and a big hole. I saw the sculpture first.

It was on the side of the narrow drive, in a clearing between two trees. Made of rusted metal, it was huge—at least six feet across—shaped like an open hand. It was encircled by a piece of rebar with a bicycle chain woven around its edges, like some sort of garland. In the palm of the hand, a heart shape had been cut out, and a smaller heart, painted bright red, hung within it, spinning slightly in the breeze that was blowing. I just sat there, my car barely crunching over the gravel, and stared at it. I couldn't help but think I had seen that design somewhere before.

And then I hit the hole.

Clunk! went my front left wheel, disappearing into it entirely. O-kay, I thought, as my entire car tilted to one side, *this* must be why she called it a doozy.

I was sitting there, trying to think of a way I could get myself out somehow and save the embarrassment of having to make such an entrance, when I looked up ahead and saw someone walking toward me from a house at the end of the road. It was just getting dark, so at first it was hard to make them out. Only when he was right in front of my wildly slanting front bumper did I realize it was Wes.

"Whatever you do," he called out, "don't try and reverse out of it. That only makes it worse." Then, as he got closer, he looked at me and started slightly. I wasn't sure who he'd been expecting, but obviously it was a surprise seeing me. "Hey," he said.

"Hi." I swallowed. "I'm, um—"

"Stuck," he finished. He disappeared for a second, ducking down to examine the hole and my tire within it. Leaning out my window, at the odd angle I was, I found myself almost level with the top of his head. A second later, when he looked up at me, we were face-to-face, and again, even under these circumstances, I was struck by how good looking he was, in that accidental, doesn't-even-know-it kind of way. Which only made it worse. Or better. Or whatever. "Yup," he said, as if there'd been any doubt, "you're in there, all right."

"I was warned, too," I told him, as he stood up. "I just saw that sculpture, and I got distracted."

"The sculpture?" He looked at it, then at me. "Oh, right. Because you know it."

"What?" I said.

He blinked, seeming confused, then shook his head. "Nothing. I just thought maybe, um, you'd seen it before, or something. There are a few around town."

"No, I haven't," I said. The breeze had stopped blowing now, and in the stillness the heart was just there in the center of the hand, suspended. "It's amazing, though."

I heard a door slam off to my right and glanced over to see Delia standing on the front porch of a white house, her arms crossed over her chest. "Macy?" she called out. "Is that you? Oh, God, I forgot to tell you about the hole. Hold on, we'll get you out. I'm such an idiot. Just let me call Wes."

"I'm on it," Wes yelled back, and she put a hand on her chest, relieved, then sat down on the steps. Then, to me, he added, "Hold tight. I'll be back in a second."

I sat there, watching as he jogged down the street, disappearing into the yard of the house at the very end. A minute later an engine started up, and a Ford pickup truck pulled out to face me, then drove down the side of the road, bumping over the occasional tree root. Wes drove past me, then backed up until his back bumper was about a foot from mine. I heard a few clanks and clunks as he attached something to my car. Then I watched in my side mirror as he walked back up to me, his white T-shirt bright in the dark.

"The trick," he said, leaning into my window, "is to get the angle just right." He reached over, putting his hands on my steering wheel, and twisted it slightly. "Like that," he said. "Okay?"

"Okay," I said, putting my hands where his had been.

"Have you out in a sec," he said. He walked back to the truck, got in, and put it in gear. I sat there, hands locked where he'd said to keep them, and waited.

The trucked revved, then moved forward, and for a second, nothing happened. But then, suddenly, I was moving. Rising. Up and out, bit by bit, until, in my headlights, I could see the hole emerging in front of me, now empty. And it was huge. More like a crater, like something you'd see on the moon. A doozy, indeed.

Once I was back on level ground, Wes hopped out of the truck, undoing the tow rope. "You're fine now," he called from somewhere near my bumper. "Just keep to the left. *Way* left."

I stuck my head out the window. "Thank you," I said. "Really."

He shrugged. "No problem. I do it all the time. Just pulled out the FedEx guy yesterday." He tossed the tow rope into the truck bed, where it landed with a thunk. "He was not happy."

"It's a big hole," I said, taking another look at it.

"It's a monster." He ran a hand through his hair, and I saw the tattoo on his arm again, but he was too far away for me to make it out. "We need to fill it, but we never will."

"Why not?"

He glanced over to Delia's house. I could now see her coming down the walk. She had on a long skirt and a red T-shirt, her feet bare. "It's a family thing," he said. "Some people believe everything happens for a reason. Even massive holes."

"But you don't," I said.

"Nope," he said. He looked over my car at the hole, studying it for a second. I was watching him, not even aware of it until he glanced at me. "Anyway," he said, as I focused back on my steering wheel, "I'll see you around."

"Thanks again," I said, shifting into first.

"No problem. Just remember: left."

"Way left," I told him, and he nodded, then knocked the side of my bumper, *rap-rap*, and started back to the truck. As he climbed in, I turned my wheel and eased around the hole, then drove the fifty feet or so to Delia's driveway, where she was waiting for me. Right as I reached to open my door, Wes's truck blurred past in my rearview mirror: I could see him in silhouette, his face illuminated by the dashboard lights. Then he disappeared behind a row of trees, gravel crunching, and was gone.

"The thing about Wes," Delia said to me, unwrapping another package of turkey, "is that he thinks he can fix anything. And if he can't fix it, he can at least do something with the pieces of what's broken."

"That's bad?" I asked, dipping my spreader back into the huge, industrial-size jar of mayonnaise on the table in front of me.

"Not bad," she said. "Just—different."

We were in Delia's garage, which served as Wish Catering central. It was outfitted with two industrial-size ovens, a large fridge, and several stainless-steel tables, all of which were piled with cutting boards and various utensils. We were sitting on opposite sides of one of the tables, assembling sandwiches. The garage door was open, and outside I could hear crickets chirping.

"The way I see it," she continued, "is that some things are just meant to be the way they are."

"Like the hole," I said, remembering how he'd glanced at her, saying this.

She put down the turkey she was holding and looked at me. "I know what he told you," she said. "He said that I was the reason the hole was still there, and that if I'd just let him fill it we wouldn't have the postman pissed off to the point of sabotaging our mail, and I wouldn't be facing yet another bill from Lakeview Tire for some poor client who busted their Goodyear out there."

"No," I said slowly, spreading the mayonnaise in a thin layer on the bread in front of me, "he said that some people believe everything happens for a reason. And some people, well, don't."

She thought for a second. "It's not that I believe everything happens for a reason," she said. "It's just that . . . I just think that some things are meant to be broken. Imperfect. Chaotic. It's the universe's way of providing contrast, you know? There have to be a few holes in the road. It's how life *is*."

We were quiet for a second. Outside, the very last of the sunset, fading pink, was disappearing behind the trees.

"Still," I said, putting another slice of bread on the one in front of me, "it *is* a big hole."

"It's a huge hole," she conceded, reaching for the mayonnaise. "But that's kind of the point. I mean, I don't want to fix it because to me, it's not broken. It's just here, and I work around it. It's the same reason I refuse to trade in my car, even though, for some reason, the A/C won't work when I have the radio on. I just choose: music, or cold air. It's not that big of a deal."

"The A/C won't work when the radio is on?" I asked. "That's so weird."

"I know." She pulled out three more slices of bread, putting mayonnaise, then lettuce, on them assembly-line style. "On a bigger scale, it's the reason that I won't hire a partner to help me with the catering, even though it's been chaos on wheels with Wish gone. Yes, things are sort of disorganized. And sure, it would be nice to not feel like we're close to disaster every second."

I started another sandwich, listening.

"But if everything was always smooth and perfect," she continued, "you'd get too used to that, you know? You have to have a little bit of disorganization now and then. Otherwise, you'll never really enjoy it when things go right. I know you think I'm a flake. Everyone does."

"I don't," I assured her, but she shook her head, not believing me.

"It's okay. I mean, I can't tell you how many times I've caught Wes out there with someone from the gravel place, secretly trying to fill that hole." She put another row of bread down. "And Pete, my husband, he's tried twice to lure me to the car dealership to trade in my old thing for a new car. And as far as the business, well . . . I don't know. They leave me alone on that. Because of Wish. Which is so funny, because if she was here, and saw how things are . . . she'd flip out. She was the most organized person in the *world*."

"Wish," I said, reaching for the mayonnaise. "That's such a cool name."

She looked up at me, smiling. "It is, isn't it? Her real name was Melissa. But when I was little, I mispronounced it all the time, you know, Ma-wish-a. Eventually, it just got shortened to Wish, and everyone started calling her that. She never minded. I mean, it fit her." She picked up the knife at her elbow, then carefully sliced the sandwiches into halves, then fourths, before stacking them onto the tray beside us. "This was her baby, this business. After she and the boys' dad divorced, and he moved up North, it was like her new start, and she ran it like a well-oiled machine. But then she got sick. . . . Breast cancer. She was only thirty-nine when she died."

It felt so weird, to be on the other side, where you were the one expected to offer condolences, not receive them. I wanted my "sorry" to sound genuine, because it was. That was the hard thing about grief, and the grieving. They spoke another language, and the words we knew always fell short of what we wanted them to say.

"I'm so sorry, Delia," I told her. "Really."

She looked up at me, a piece of bread in one hand. "Thank you," she said, then placed it on the table in front of her. "I am, too." Then she smiled at me sadly, and started to assemble another sandwich. I did the same, and neither of us said anything for a few minutes. The silence wasn't like the ones I'd known lately, though: it wasn't empty as much as chosen. There's a entirely different feel to quiet when you're with someone else, and at any moment it could be broken. Like the difference between a pause and an ending.

"You know what happens when someone dies?" Delia said suddenly, startling me a bit. I kept putting together my sandwich, though, not answering: I knew there was more. "It's like, everything and everyone refracts, each person having a different reaction. Like me and Wes. After the divorce, he fell in with this bad crowd, got arrested, she hardly knew what to do with him. But then, when she got sick, he changed. Now he's totally different, how he's so protective of Bert and focused on his welding and the pieces he makes. It's his way of handling it."

"Wes does welding?" I asked, and then, suddenly, I thought of the sculpture. "Did he do—"

"The heart in hand," she finished for me. "Yeah. He did. Pretty incredible, huh?"

"It is," I said. "I had no idea. I was talking about it with him and he didn't even tell me."

"Well, he'll never brag on it," she said, pulling the mayonnaise over to her. "That's how he is. His mom was the same way. Quiet and incredible. I really envy that."

I watched her as she cut another two sandwiches down, the knife clapping against the cutting board. "I don't know," I said. "You seem to be pretty incredible. Running this business with a baby, and another on the way."

"Nah." She smiled. "I'm not. When Wish died, it just knocked the wind out of me. Truly. It's like that stupid thing Bert and Wes do, the leaping out thing, trying to scare each other: it was the biggest gotcha in the world." She looked down at the sandwiches. "I'd just assumed she'd be okay. It had never occurred to me she might actually just be . . . gone. You know?"

I nodded, just barely. I felt bad that I didn't tell her about my dad, chime in with what I knew, how well I knew it. With Delia, though, I wasn't that girl, the one whose dad had died. I wasn't anybody. And I liked that. It was selfish but true.

"And then she was," Delia said, her hand on the bread bag. "Gone. Gotcha. And suddenly I had these two boys to take care of, plus a newborn of my own. It was just this huge loss, this huge *gap*, you know."

"I know," I said softly.

"Some people," she said, and I wasn't even sure she'd heard me, "they can just move on, you know, mourn and cry and be done with it. Or at least seem to be. But for me . . . I don't know. I didn't want to fix it, to forget. It wasn't something that was broken. It's just . . . something that happened. And like that hole, I'm just finding ways, every day, of working around it. Respecting and remembering and getting on at the same time. You know?"

I nodded, but I didn't know. I'd chosen instead to just change my route, go miles out of the way, as if avoiding it would make it go away once and for all. I envied Delia. At least she knew what she was up against. Maybe that's what you got when you stood over your grief, facing it finally. A sense of its depths, its area, the distance across, and the way over or around it, whichever you chose in the end.

Chapter Six

"Okay," Wes said under his breath. "Watch and learn."

"Right," I said.

We were at the Lakeview Inn, finishing up appetizers for a retirement party, and Wes and I were in the coat closet, where he was teaching me the art of the gotcha. I'd been sent by a woman to hang up her wrap and found him there, perfectly positioned and silent, lying in wait.

"Wes?" I'd said, and he'd slid a finger to his lips, gesturing for me to come closer with his other hand. Which I'd done, unthinkingly, even as I felt that same fluttering in my stomach I always felt when I was around Wes. Even when we weren't in an enclosed, small space together. Goodness.

In the next room, I could hear the party: the clinking of forks against plates, voices trilling in laughter, strains of the piped-in violin music that the Lakeview Inn had played at my sister's wedding as well.

"Okay," Wes said, his voice so low I would have leaned closer to hear him if we weren't already about as close as we could get. "It's all in the timing."

An overcoat that smelled like perfume was hanging in my face: I pushed it aside as quietly as possible.

"Not now," Wes was whispering. "Not now . . . not now . . ."

Then I heard it: footsteps. Muttering. Had to be Bert.

"Okay . . ." he said, and then he was moving, standing up, going forward, "now. *Gotcha!*"

Bert's shriek, which was high pitched to the point of ear-splitting, was accompanied by him flailing backwards and losing his footing, then crashing into the wall behind him. "God!" he said, his face turning red, then redder as he saw me. I couldn't really blame him: there was no way to be splayed on the floor and still look dignified. He said, sputtering, "That was—"

"Number six," Wes finished for him. "By my count."

Bert got to his feet, glaring at us. "I'm going to get you so good," he said darkly, pointing a finger at Wes, then at me, then back at Wes. "Just you wait."

"Leave her out of it," Wes told him. "I was just demonstrating."

"Oh no," Bert said. "She's part of it now. She's one of us. No more coddling for you, Macy."

"Bert, you've already jumped out at her," Wes pointed out.

"It's *on*!" Bert shouted, ignoring this. Then he stalked down the hallway, again muttering, and disappeared into the main room, letting the door bang shut behind him. Wes watched him go, hardly bothered. In fact, he was smiling.

"Nice work," I told him, as we started down the hallway to the kitchen.

"It's nothing," he said. "With enough practice, you too can pull a good gotcha someday."

"Frankly," I said, "I'm a little curious about the derivation of all this."

"Derivation?"

"How it started."

"I know what it means," he said. For a second I was horrified, thinking I'd offended him, but he grinned at me. "It's just such an SAT word. I'm impressed."

"I'm working on my verbal," I explained.

"I can tell," he said, nodding at one of the Lakeview Inn valets as he passed. "Truthfully, it's just this dumb thing we started about a year ago. It pretty much came from us living alone in the house after my mom died. It was really quiet, so it was easy to sneak around."

I nodded as if I understood this, although I couldn't really picture myself leaping out at my mother from behind a door or potted plant, no matter how perfect the opportunity. "I see," I said.

"Plus," Wes continued, "there's just something fun, every once in a while, about getting the shit scared out of you. You know?"

This time I didn't nod or agree. I could do without scares, planned or unplanned, for awhile. "Must be a guy thing," I said.

He shrugged, pushing the kitchen door open for me. "Maybe," he said.

As we walked in, Delia was standing in the center of the room, hands pressed to her chest. Just by the look on her face, I knew something was wrong.

"Wait a second," she said. "Everyone freeze."

We did. Even Kristy, who normally ignored most directives, stopped what she was doing, a cheese biscuit dangling in midair over her tray.

"Where," Delia said slowly, taking a look around the room, "are the hams?"

Silence. Then Kristy said, her voice low, "Uh-oh."

"Don't say that!" Delia moved down the counter, hands suddenly flailing as she pulled all of the cardboard boxes we'd lugged in closer to her, peering into each of them. "They have to be here! They have to be! We have a *system* now!"

And we did. But it was new, only implemented since the night before, when, en route to a cocktail party, it became apparent that no one had packed the glasses. After doubling back and arriving late, Delia had used her current pregnancy insomnia to compile a set of checklists covering everything from appetizers to napkins. We were each given one, for which we were wholly responsible. I was in charge of utensils. If we were lacking tongs, it was all on me.

"This is not happening," Delia said now, plunging her hands into a small box on the kitchen island hardly big enough for half a ham, let alone the six we were missing. "I remember, they were in the garage, on the side table, all ready to go. I *saw* them."

On the other side of the kitchen door, I could hear voices rising: it was getting more crowded, which meant soon they'd be expecting dinner. Our menu was cheese biscuits and goat cheese toasts to start, followed by green bean casserole, rice pilaf, rosemary dill rolls, and ham. It was a special request. Apparently, these were pork people.

"Okay, okay, let's just calm down," Delia said, although rustling through the plastic bags full of uncooked rolls with a panicked expression, she seemed like the only one really close to losing it. "Let's retrace our steps. Who was on what?"

"I was on appetizers, and they're all here," Kristy said, as Bert came through the swinging door from the main room, an empty tray in his hand. "Bert. Were you on ham?"

"No. Paper products and serving platters," he said, holding

the one in his hand up as proof. "Why? Are we missing something?"

"No," Delia said firmly. "We're not."

"Monica was on ice," Kristy said, continuing the count. "Macy was utensils, and Wes was glasses and champagne. Which means that the ham belonged to—" She stopped abruptly. "Oh. Delia."

"What?" Delia said, jerking her head out of a box filled with loaves of bread. "No, wait, I don't think so. I was on—"

We all waited. It was, after all, her system.

"Main course," she finished.

"Uh-oh," Bert said.

"Oh God!" Delia slapped a hand to her forehead. "I did have the hams on the side table, and I remember being worried that we might forget them, so while we were packing the van I put them—"

Again, we all waited.

"On the back of my car," Delia finished, placing her palm square in the middle of her forehead. "Oh, my God," she whispered, as if the truth, so horrible, might deafen us all, "they're still at the house. On my *car*."

"Uh-oh," Bert said again. He was right: it was a full thirty minutes away, and these people were expecting their ham in ten.

Delia leaned back against the stove. "This," she said, "is awful."

For a minute, no one said anything. It was a silence I'd grown to expect when things like this happened, the few seconds as we accepted, en masse, the crashing realization that we were, in fact, screwed.

Then, as always, Delia pushed on. "Okay," she said, "here's what we're going to do. . . ."

So far, I'd done three jobs with Wish since that first one, including a cocktail, a brunch, and a fiftieth-anniversary party. At each, there was one moment—an old man pinching my butt as I passed with scones; the moment Kristy and I collided and her tray bonked me in the nose, showering salmon and crudités down my shirt; the time when Bert had hit me with another gotcha, jumping out from behind a coat rack and sending the stacks of plates I was carrying, as well as my blood pressure, skyrocketing—when I wondered what in the world I'd been thinking taking this on. At the end of the night, though, when it was all over, I felt something strange, a weird calmness. Almost a peace. It was like those few hours of craziness relaxed something held tight in me, if only for a little while.

Most of all, though, it was fun. Even if I was still learning things, like to duck when Kristy yelled, "Incoming!" meaning she had to get something—a pack of napkins, some tongs, a tray—across a room so quickly that only throwing it would suffice, or never to stand in front of swinging doors, ever, as Bert always pushed them open with too much gusto, without taking into consideration that there might be anything on the other side. I learned that Delia hummed when she was nervous, usually "American Pie," and that Monica never got nervous at all, was in fact capable of eating shrimp or crab cakes, hardly bothered, when the rest of us were in total panic mode. And I learned that I could always count on Wes for a raised eyebrow, an under-the-breath sarcastic remark, or just a sympathetic look when I found myself in a bind: no matter where I was in the room, or what was happening, I could look over at the bar and feel that someone, at least, was on my side. It was the total opposite of how I felt at the library, or how I felt anywhere else, for that matter. Which was probably why I liked it.

But then, after the job was over and the van packed up to go home, after we'd stood around while Delia got paid, everyone laughing and trading stories about grabbers and gobblers and grandmas, the buzz of rushing around would wear off. As I'd begin to remember that I had to be at the library the next morning, I could feel myself starting to cross back to my real life, bit by bit.

"Macy," Kristy would say, as we put the last of the night's supplies back in Delia's garage, "you coming out with us tonight?"

She always extended the invitation, even though I said no every time. Which I appreciated. It's nice to have options, even if you can't take them.

"I can't," I'd tell her. "I'm busy."

"Okay," she'd say, shrugging. "Maybe next time."

It went like that, our own little routine, until one night when she squinted at me, curious. "What do you do every night, anyway?" she'd asked.

"Just, you know, stuff for school," I'd told her.

"Donneven," Monica said, shaking her head.

"I'm prepping for the SATs," I said, "and I work another job in the mornings."

Kristy rolled her eyes. "It's *summertime*," she told me. "I mean, I know you're a smarty-pants, but don't you ever take a break? Life is long, you know."

Maybe, I thought. Or maybe not. Out loud I said, "I just really, you know, have a lot of work to do."

"Okay," she'd said. "Have fun. Study for me, while you're at it. God knows I need it."

So while at home I was still fine-just-fine Macy, wiping up sink splatters immediately and ironing my clothes as soon as they got out of the dryer, the nights when I arrived home from catering, I was someone else, a girl with her hair mussed, a stained shirt, smelling of whatever had been spilled or smeared on me. It was like Cinderella in reverse: if I was a princess for my daylight hours, at night I let myself and my composure go, just until the stroke of midnight, when I turned back to princess again, just in time.

The ham disaster was, like all the others, eventually averted. Wes ran to the gourmet grocery where Delia was owed a favor, and Kristy and I just kept walking through with more appetizers, deflecting all queries about when dinner was being served with a bat of the eyelashes and a smile (her idea, of course). When the ham was finally served—forty-five minutes late—it was a hit, and everyone went home happy.

It was ten-thirty by the time I finally pulled into Wildflower Ridge, my headlights swinging across the town common and into our cul-de-sac, where I saw my house, my mailbox, everything as usual, and then something else.

My dad's truck.

It was in the driveway, right where he'd always parked, in front of the garage, left-hand side. I pulled up behind it, sitting there for a second. It *was* his, no question: I would have known it anywhere. Same rusty bumper, same EAT . . . SLEEP . . . FISH bumper sticker, same chrome toolbox with the dent in the middle from where he'd dropped his chainsaw a few years earlier. I got out of my car and walked up to it, reaching out my finger to touch the license plate. For some reason I was surprised that it didn't just vanish, like a bubble bursting, the minute I made contact. That was the way ghosts were supposed to be, after all.

But the metal handle felt real as I pulled open the driver's side door, my heart beating fast in my chest. Immediately, I could smell that familiar mix of old leather, cigar smoke, and the lingering scent of ocean and sand you carry back with you from the beach that you always wish would last, but never does.

I loved that truck. It was the place my dad and I spent more time together than anywhere else, me on the passenger side, feet balanced on the dashboard, him with one elbow out the window, tapping the roof along with the beat on the radio. We went out early Saturday mornings to get biscuits and drive around checking on job sites, drove home from meets in the dark, me curled up in that perfect spot between the seat and window where I always fell asleep instantly. The air conditioner hadn't worked for as long as I'd been alive, and the heat cranked enough to dehydrate you within minutes, but it didn't matter. Like the beach house, the truck was dilapidated, familiar, with its own unique charm: it *was* my dad. And now it was back.

I eased the door shut, then went up to the front door of my house. It was unlocked, and as I stepped inside, kicking off my shoes as I always did, I could feel something beneath my feet. I crouched down, running my finger over the hardwood: it was sand.

"Hello?" I said, then listened to my voice bounce around our high ceilings back to me. Afterwards, nothing but silence.

My mother was at the sales office, had been there since five. I knew this because she'd left a message around ten on my cell phone, telling me. Which meant that either sometime in the last five hours my father's truck had driven itself from the coast, or there was another explanation.

I went back down the hallway and looked up to the second floor. My bedroom door, which I always left closed to keep it either cooler or warmer, was open.

I wasn't sure what to think as I climbed the stairs, remembering how many times I'd wished my dad would just turn up at the house one day, this whole thing one big misunderstanding we could all laugh about together. If only.

When I got to my room, I stopped in the open door and noticed, relieved, everything familiar: my computer, my closed closet door, my window. There was the SAT book on my bedside table, my shoes lined up by the wastebasket. All as it should be. But then I looked at the bed and saw the dark head against my pillow. Of course my father wasn't back. But Caroline was.

She'd just stopped in for a visit. But already, she was making waves.

"Caroline," my mother said. Her voice, once polite, then stern, was now bordering on snappy. "I'm not discussing this. This is not the place or time."

"Maybe this isn't the place," Caroline told her, helping herself to another breadstick. "But Mom, really. It's time."

It was Monday, and we were all at Bella Luna, a fancy little bistro near the library. For once, I wasn't eating lunch alone, instead taking my hour with my mother and sister. Now, though,

I was realizing maybe I would have preferred to eat my regular sandwich on a bench alone, as it became increasingly clear that my sister had come with An Agenda.

"I just think," she said now, glancing at our waitress as she passed, "that it's not what Dad would have wanted. He loved that house. And it's sitting there, rotting. You should see all the sand in the living room, and the way the steps to the beach are sagging. It's horrible. Have you even been down to check on it since he died?"

I watched my mother's face as she heard this, the way, despite her best efforts, she reacted to the various breaches of the conduct we'd long ago agreed on concerning my father and how he was mentioned. My mother and I preferred to focus on the future: this was the past. But my sister didn't see it that way. From the minute she'd arrived—driving his truck because her Lexus had blown a gasket while at the beach—it was like she'd brought him with her as well.

"The beach house is the least of my concerns, Caroline," my mother said now, as our waitress passed by again with a frazzled expression. We'd been waiting for our entrees for over twenty minutes. "I'm doing this new phase of townhouses, and the zoning has been extremely difficult. . . ."

"I know," Caroline said. "I understand how hard it has been for you. For both of you."

"I don't think you do." My mother put her hand on her water glass but didn't pick it up or take a sip. "Otherwise you would understand that this isn't something I want to talk about right now."

My sister sat back in her chair, twisting her wedding ring around her finger. "Mom," she said finally, "I'm not trying to upset you. I'm just saying that it's been a year and a half . . . and maybe it's time to move on. Dad would have wanted you to be happier than this. I know it."

"I thought this was about the beach house," my mother said stiffly.

"It is," Caroline said. "But it's also about living. You can't hide behind work forever, you know. I mean, when was the last time you and Macy took a vacation or did something nice for yourselves?"

"I was at the coast just a couple of weeks ago."

"For work," Caroline said. "You work late into the night, you get up early in the morning, you don't do anything but think about the development. Macy never goes out with friends, she spends all her time holed up studying, and she's not going to be seventeen forever—"

"I'm fine," I said.

My sister looked at me, her face softening. "I know you are," she said. "But I just worry about you. I feel like you're missing out on something you won't be able to get back later."

"Not everyone needs a social life like you had, Caroline," my mother said. "Macy's focused on school, and her grades are excellent. She has a wonderful boyfriend. Just because she's not out drinking beer at two in the morning doesn't mean she isn't living a full life."

"I'm not saying her life isn't full," Caroline said. "I just think she's awfully young to be so serious about everything."

"I'm fine," I said again, louder this time. They both looked at me. "I am," I said.

"All I'm saying is that you both could use a little more fun in your lives," Caroline said. "Which is why I think we should fix up the beach house and all go down there for a few weeks in August. Wally's working this big case all summer, he's gone all the time, so I can really devote myself to this project. And then, when it's finished, we'll all go down there together, like old times. It'll be the perfect way to end the summer."

"I'm not talking about this now," my mother said, as the waitress, now red-faced, passed by again. "Excuse me," my mother said, too sharply, and the girl jumped. "We've been waiting for our food for over twenty minutes."

"It will be right out," the girl said automatically, and then scurried toward the kitchen. I glanced at my watch: five minutes until one. I knew that Bethany and Amanda were most likely in their chairs already, the clock behind them counting down the seconds until they finally had something legitimate to hold against me.

My mother was focusing on some distant point across the restaurant, her face completely composed. Looking at her in the light falling across our table, I realized that she looked tired, older than she was. I couldn't remember the last time I'd seen her really smile, or laugh a big belly laugh like she always did when my dad made one of his stupid jokes. No one else ever laughed—they were more groan inducing than anything else—but my mother always thought they were hysterical.

"When I first got to the beach house," Caroline said, as my mother kept her eyes locked on that distant spot, "I just sat in the driveway and sobbed. It was like losing him all over again, I swear."

I watched my mother swallow, saw her shoulders rise, then fall, as she took a breath.

"But then," my sister continued, her voice soft, "I went inside and remembered how much he loved that stupid moose head over the fireplace, even though it smells like a hundred old socks. I remembered you trying to cook dinner on that stove top with only one burner, having to alternate pans every five minutes just to make macaroni and cheese and frozen peas, because you swore we wouldn't eat fish one more night if it killed you."

My mother lifted up her hand to her chin, pressing two fingertips there, and I felt a pang in my chest. Stop it, I wanted to say to Caroline, but I couldn't even form the words. I was listening, too. Remembering.

"And that stupid grill that he loved so much, even though it was a total fire hazard," Caroline continued, looking at me now. "Remember how he always used to store stuff in it, like that Frisbee or the spare keys, and then forget and turn it on and set them on fire? Do you know there are still, like, five blackened keys sitting at the bottom of that thing?"

I nodded, but that was all I could manage. Even that, actually, was hard.

"I haven't meant to let the house go," my mother said suddenly, startling me. "It's just been one more thing to deal with. . . . I've had too much happening here." It can't be that easy, I thought, to get her to talk about this. To bring her closer to the one thing that I'd circled with her, deliberately avoiding, for months now. "I just—"

"It needs some new shingles," Caroline told her, speaking slowly, carefully. "I talked to the guy next door, Rudy? He's a carpenter. He walked through with me. It needs basic stuff, a stove, a screen door, and those steps fixed. Plus a coat of paint in and out wouldn't hurt."

"I don't know," my mother said, and I watched as Caroline

put her hand on my mother's, their fingers intertwining, Caroline's purposefully, my mother's responding seemingly without thinking. This reaching out to my mom was another thing I'd been working up to, never quite getting the nerve, but she made it look simple. "It's just so much to think about."

"I know," my sister said, in that flat-honest way she had always been able to say anything. "But I love you, and I'll help you. Okay?"

My mother blinked, then blinked again. It was the closest I'd seen her come to crying in over a year.

"Caroline," I said, because I felt like I had to, someone had to.

"It's okay," she said to me, as if she was sure. No question. I envied her that, too. "It's all going to be okay."

Even though I scarfed down my linguini pesto in record time and ran the two blocks back to the library, it was one-twenty by the time I got back to work. Amanda, seated in her chair with her arms crossed over her chest, narrowed her eyes at me as I let myself behind the desk and, as I always did, battled around their thrones to reach my crummy little station in the back.

"Lunch ends at one," she said, enunciating each word carefully as if my tardiness was due to a basic lack of comprehension. Beside her, Bethany smiled, just barely, before lifting a hand to cover her mouth.

"I know, I'm sorry," I said. "It was unavoidable."

"Nothing is unavoidable," she said snippily before turning back to her computer monitor. I felt my face turn red, that deep burning kind of shame, as I sat down.

Then, about a year and half too late, it hit me. I was never going to be perfect. And what had all my efforts gotten me, really, in the end? A boyfriend who pushed me away the minute I cracked, making the mistake of being human. Great grades that would still never be good enough for girls who Knew Everything. A quiet, still life, free of any risks, and so many sleepless nights to spend within it, my heart heavy, keeping secrets my sister had empowered herself by telling. This life was fleeting, and I was still searching for the way I wanted to spend it that would make me happy, full, okay again. I didn't know what it was, not yet. But something told me I wouldn't find it here.

So a few days later, back at Delia's after working a late-afternoon bridal shower (in a log-cabin lodge, no less, very woody) and encountering another disaster of sorts (soda water dispenser explosion during toasts), I'd made it through another day with Wish that was pretty much like all the others. Until now.

"Hey, Macy," Kristy said, wiping something off the hem of her black fringed skirt, part of the gypsy look she was sporting, "You coming out with us tonight?"

It was our routine now, how she always asked me. As much part of the schedule as everything in my other life was, dependable, just like clockwork. We both knew our parts. But this time, I left the script, took that leap, and improvised.

"Yeah," I said. "I am."

"Cool," she said, smiling at me as she hitched her purse over her shoulder. The weird thing was how she didn't even seem surprised. Like she knew, somehow, that eventually I'd come around. "Come on."

Chapter Seven

"Oh, man," Kristy said, carefully guiding another section of my hair over the roller, "Just wait. This is going to be *great*."

Personally, I wasn't so sure. If I'd known that going out with Kristy meant subjecting myself to a makeover, I probably would have thought twice before saying yes. Now, though, it was too late.

I'd had my first reservations when she'd insisted I shed my work clothes and put on a pair of jeans she was absolutely sure would fit me (she was right) and a tank top that she swore would not show off too much cleavage (she was wrong). Of course, I couldn't really verify either of these things completely, as the only objective view was the mirror on the back of the closet door, which was now facing the wall so that, in her words, I wouldn't see myself until I was "done." All I had to go on was Monica, who was sitting in a chair in the corner of the room, smoking a cigarette she had dangling out the window and making occasional ummm-hmm noises whenever Kristy needed a second opinion.

Clearly, this was a different sort of Friday night than I was used to. But then, everything was different here.

Kristy and Monica's house wasn't a house at all but a trailer, although, as we approached it, Kristy explained that she preferred to call it a "doublewide," as there was less redneck association with that moniker. To me, it looked like something out of a fairy tale, a small structure painted cobalt blue with a big sprawling garden beside it. There her grandmother Stella, whom I'd met the night I was lost, grew the flowers and produce she sold at her stand and to local restaurants. I'd seen lots of gardens before, even fancy ones in my neighborhood. But this one was incredible.

Green and lush, it grew up and around the doublewide, making the structure, with its bright cobalt color and red door, look like one more exotic bloom. Along the front, sunflowers moved lazily in the breeze, brushing a side window: beneath them were a row of rosebushes, their perfumelike scent permeating the air. From there, the greenery spread sideways. I saw a collection of cacti, all different shapes and sizes, poking out from between two pear trees. There were blueberry bushes beside zinnias and daisies and coneflowers, woolly lamb's ear up against bright purple lilies and red hot pokers. Instead of set rows, the plots were laid out along narrow paths, circling and encircling. Bamboo framed a row of flowering trees, which led into one small garden plot with tiny lettuces poking up through the dirt, followed by pecan trees next to geraniums, and beside them a huge clump of purple irises. And then there was the smell: of fruit and flowers, fresh dirt and earthworms. It was incredible, and I found myself just breathing it in, the smell lingering on me long after we'd gone inside.

Now Kristy slid another bobby pin over a curler, smoothing with her hand to catch a stray piece of hair that was hanging over my eyes.

"You know," I said, warily, "I'm not really a big hair person."

"Oh, God, me neither." She picked up another roller. "But

this is going to be wavy, not big. Just trust me, okay? I'm really good with hair. It was, like, an obsession with me when I was bald."

Because she was behind me, fussing with the rollers, I couldn't see her face as she said this. I had no idea if her expression was flippant or grave or what. I looked at Monica, who was flipping through a magazine, not even listening. Finally I said, "You were bald?"

"Yup. When I was twelve. I had to have a bunch of surgeries, including one on the back of my head, so they had to shave all my hair off," she said, brushing out a few of the loose tendrils around my face. "I was in a car accident. That's how I got my scars."

"Oh," I said, and suddenly I was worried I had been staring at them too much, or she wouldn't have brought it up. "I didn't—"

"I know," she said easily, hardly bothered. "But it's hard to miss them, right? Usually people ask, but you didn't. Still, I figured you were probably wondering. You'd be surprised how many people just walk right up and ask, point-blank, like they're asking what time it is."

"That's rude," I said.

"Mmm-hmm," Monica agreed, stubbing her cigarette out in the windowsill.

Kristy shrugged. "Really, I kind of prefer it. I mean, it's better than just staring and acting like you're not. Kids are the best. They'll just look right at me and say, "What's wrong with your face?" I like that. Get it out in the open. I mean, shit, it's not like it isn't anyway. That's one reason why I dress up so much, you know, because people are already staring. Might as well give them a show. You know?"

I nodded, still processing all this.

"Anyway," Kristy continued, doing another roller, "it happened when I was twelve. My mom was on one of her benders, taking me to school, and she ran off the road and hit this fence, and then a tree. They had to cut me out of the car. Monica, of course, was smart enough to have the chicken pox so she didn't have to go to school that day."

"Donneven," Monica said.

"She feels guilty," Kristy explained. "It's a sister thing."

I looked at Monica, who was wearing her normal impassive expression as she examined her fingernails. She didn't look like she felt particularly bad to me, but then again so far I'd only seen her with one expression, a sort of tired blankness. I figured maybe it was like a Rorschach inkblot: you saw in it whatever you needed or wanted to.

"Besides the scars on my face," Kristy was saying, "there's also one on my lower back, from the fusion, and a big nasty one on my butt from the skin graft. Plus there are a couple on my scalp, but you can't see those since my hair grew back."

"God," I said. "That's horrible."

She picked up another curler. "I did not like being bald, I can tell you that much. I mean, there's only so much you can do with a hat or a scarf, you know? Not that I didn't try. The day my hair started to come in for real, I cried I was so happy. Now I can't bring myself to cut it more than just a tiny bit every few months. I *relish* my hair now."

"It is really nice," I told her. "Your hair, I mean."

"Thanks," she said. "I'm telling you, I think I appreciate it more than most people. I never complain about a bad hair day, that's for sure."

She climbed off the bed, tucking the hairbrush in her pocket before crouching down in front of me to secure a few loose wisps of hair with a bobby pin. "Okay," she said, "you're almost set, so let's see. . . . Monotone."

"Nuh-uh," Monica said, sounding surprisingly adamant.

"Oh, come on! If you'd just let me try something, for once, you'd see that—"

"Donneven."

"*Monica.*"

Monica shook her head slowly. "Bettaquit," she warned.

Kristy sighed, shaking her head. "She refuses to take fashion risks," she said, as if this was a true tragedy. Turning back to her sister, she held up her hands in a visualize-this sort of way. "Look. I've got one word for you." She paused, for dramatic effect. "Pleather."

In response to this, Monica got up and started toward the door, shaking her head.

"Fine," Kristy said, shrugging, as Monica went down the hallway, grabbing her purse off the floor by the door, "just wear what you have on, like you always do. But you won't be dynamic!"

The front door slammed shut, responding to this, but Kristy hardly seemed bothered, instead just walking back to her closet and standing in front of it, her hands on her hips. Looking out the window beside me, I could see Monica start up the driveway, altogether undynamically, and as usual, exceptionally slowly.

Kristy bent down, pulling a pair of scuffed penny loafers out from under the hanging clothes and tossing them to me. "Now, I know what you're thinking," she said, as I looked down at them. "But penny loafers are entirely underrated. You'll see.

And we can do your cleavage with this great bronzer—I think it's in the bathroom."

And then she was gone, pulling open the bedroom door and heading down the hallway, still muttering to herself. My head felt heavy under the rollers, my neck straining as I looked down at the tank top she'd given me to wear. The straps had tiny threads of glitter woven throughout, and the neckline plunged much farther than anything I owned. It was way too dressy to go with the jeans, which were faded, the cuffs rolled up and frayed at the ankle; a heart was drawn on the knee in ballpoint pen. Looking at it, the solid blackness at its center, the crooked left edge, not quite right, all I could think was that these weren't my clothes, this wasn't who I was. I'd been acting out against Bethany and Amanda, but I was the one who would really pay if this went all wrong.

I have to get out of here, I thought, and stood up, pulling one of the curlers by my temple loose and dropping it on the bed. A single corkscrew curl dropped down over my eyes and I stared at it, surprised, as it dangled in my field of vision, the smallest part of me transformed. But I was leaving. I was.

My watch said 6:15. If I left now, I could get home in time to be back on my schedule as if I'd never strayed from it. I'd tell Kristy my mom had called me on my phone, saying she needed me, and that I was sorry, maybe another time.

I stood up, pulling another curler out, then another, dropping them on the bed as I hurriedly slung my purse over my shoulder. I was almost to the door when Kristy came back down the hallway, a small compact in her hands.

"This stuff is great," she said. "It's like an instant tan, and we'll just put it—"

"I've just realized," I said, plunging right in to my excuses, "I really think—"

She looked up at me then, her eyes widening. "Oh, God, I totally agree," she said, nodding. "I didn't see it before, but yeah, you're absolutely right."

"What?"

"About your hair," she said, as she came into the room. I found myself backing up until I bumped against the bed again. Kristy reached past me, grabbing a white shirt that was lying on one of the pillows and, before I could stop her, she'd slid my arm inside one sleeve. I was too distracted to protest.

"My hair?" I said, as she eased my other arm in, then grabbed the shirttails, knotting them loosely around my waist. "What?"

She reached up, spreading her fingers and pulling them through my hair, stretching out the curls. "I was going to brush it out, but you're right, it looks better like that, all tousled. It's great. See?"

And then she walked over to the closet door, pushing it shut, and I saw myself.

Yes, the jeans were faded and frayed, the heart on the leg crooked, too dark. But they fit me really well: they could have been mine. And the tank top was a bit much, glittering in so many places from the overhead light, but the shirt over it toned it down, giving only glimpses here and there. The shoes, which had looked dorky when I put them on, somehow went with the jeans, which hit in such a way that they showed a thin sliver of my ankle. And my hair, without the clear, even part that I worked so hard for every morning, drawing a comb down the center with mathematical precision, was loose and falling over my shoulders, softening my features. None of it should have worked together. But somehow, it did.

"See? I told you," Kristy said from behind me, where she was standing smiling, proud of her handiwork, as I just stared, seeing the familiar in all these changes. How weird it was that so many bits and pieces, all diverse, could make something whole. Something with potential. "Perfect."

It took Kristy considerably longer to assemble her own look, a retro sixties outfit consisting of white go-go boots, a pink shirt, and a short skirt. By the time we finally went out to meet Bert, he'd been waiting for us in the doublewide's driveway for almost a half hour.

"It's about time," he snapped as we came up to the ambulance. "I've been waiting forever."

"Does twenty minutes constitute forever now?" Kristy asked.

"It does when you're stuck out here waiting for someone who is selfish, ungrateful, and thinks the whole world revolves around her," Bert said, then cranked up the music he was playing—a woman wailing, loud and dramatic—ensuring that any retort to this would be drowned out entirely.

Kristy tossed her purse inside the ambulance, then grabbed hold of the side of the door, pulling herself up. The music was still going, reaching some sort of climax, with a lot of thundering guitars. "Bert," she yelled, "can you *please* turn that down?"

"No," he yelled back.

"Pink Floyd. It's my punishment, he knows how much I hate it," she explained to me. To Bert she said, "Then can you at least turn on the lights back here for a second? Macy can't see anything."

A second later, the fluorescent light over her head flickered, buzzed, and then came on, bathing everything in a gray, sallow light. It was so hospital-like I felt the nervousness that had been simmering in my stomach since we'd left the house—ambulance phobia—begin to build. "See, he'll do it for *you*," she said. She stuck out her hand to me. "Here, just grab on and hoist yourself up. You can do it. It's not as bad as it looks."

I reached up and took her hand, surprised at her strength as she pulled me up, and the next thing I knew I was standing inside the ambulance, ducking the low ceiling, hearing the buzz of that light in my ear. There was now an old brown plaid sofa against one wall, and a small table wedged between it and the back of the driver's seat. Like a traveling living room, I thought, as Kristy clambered around it, grabbing her purse on the way, and slid into the passenger seat. I sat down on the couch.

"Bert, please turn that down," Kristy yelled over the music, which was now pounding in my ears. He ignored her, turning his head to look out the window. "Bert. Bert!"

Finally, as the shrieking was reached a crescendo, Bert reached over, hitting the volume button. And suddenly, it was quiet. Except for a slow, knocking sound. *Thunk. Thunk. Thunk.*

I realized suddenly that the sound was coming from the back doors, so I got up, pushing them open. Monica, a cigarette poking out of one side of her mouth, looked up at me.

"Hand," she said.

"Put that out first," Bert said, watching her in the rearview mirror. "You know there's no smoking in the Bertmobile."

Monica took one final drag, dropped the cigarette to the ground, and stepped on it. She stuck her hand out again, and I hoisted her up, the way Kristy had done for me. Once in, she collapsed on the couch, as if that small activity had taken just about everything she had.

"Can we go now, please?" Bert asked as I pulled the doors shut. Up in the passenger seat, Kristy was messing with the radio, the wailing woman now replaced by a boppy pop beat. "Or would you like another moment or two to make me insane?"

Kristy rolled her eyes. "Where's Wes?"

"He's meeting us there. If we ever *get* there." He pointed, annoyed, at the digital clock on the dashboard, which said 7:37. "Look at that! The night is just ticking away. Ticking!"

"For God sakes, it's early," Kristy said. "We've got plenty of time."

Which, I soon found out, was a good thing. We'd need it, with Bert behind the wheel.

He was a slow driver. More than slow, he was also incredibly cautious, a driver's ed teacher's dream. He paused for green lights, came to full stops before railroad crossings that hadn't seen trains in years, and obeyed the speed limit religiously, sometimes even dropping below it. And all the while, he had both hands on the wheel in the ten-and-two position, watching the road like a hawk, prepared for any and all obstacles or hazards.

So it seemed like ages later that we finally turned off the main road and onto a gravel one, then began driving on grass, over small rises and dips, toward an area where several cars were parked, encircling a clearing with a few wooden picnic tables in the center. People were sitting at them, on them, grouped all around, and there were several flashlights scattered across the surfaces of the tables, sending beams of light in all directions. Bert backed in, so we were facing the tables, then cut the engine.

"Finally," Kristy said, unbuckling her seat belt with a flourish.

"You could have walked," Bert told her.

"I feel like we did," she said. Then she pushed her door open, and I heard voices nearby, someone laughing. "I'm going to get a beer. Anybody else want one?"

"Me," Monica said, standing up and pushing open the back doors. She eased herself out with a pained expression, then started across the grass.

"Macy?" Kristy asked.

"Oh, no thanks," I said. "I'm fine."

"Okay." She climbed out the front door, letting it fall shut behind her. "Be right back."

I watched them cross into the clearing and walk past one of the picnic tables to a keg that was under some nearby trees. Two guys were standing by it, and one of them, who was tall with a shock of red hair, immediately went to work getting Kristy a beer, eyeing her appreciatively as he did so. Monica was standing by with a bored expression, while the redhead's friend shot her sideways looks, working up to saying something.

Bert was sitting on the back bumper of the ambulance, scanning the crowd, and I joined him, letting my feet dangle down. Most of the faces here were new to me, which made sense, since this was more of a Talbert High crowd, while I went to Jackson, on the other side of town. Still, I did recognize a few people I knew from school. I wondered if any of them knew me.

I looked across the clearing then, and saw Wes. He was standing with a group of guys around an old Mustang, talking, and seeing him I felt that same sort of lurch in my stomach as I had the first night I'd met him, and the night he'd pulled me out of the hole, and just about every time we'd crossed paths since. I couldn't explain it, had never felt it before: it was completely out of my control. So idiotic, I thought, and yet there I was again, staring.

After a minute or two he broke off from the group and started across the clearing. While I was making a pointed effort not to watch him—or, okay, not watch him the entire time—it was hard not to notice, as I took a quick glance around the circle, that I was not alone in my observations. I counted at least three other girls doing the same thing. I wondered if they felt as stupid as I did. Probably not.

"Hey," he said. "What took you guys so long?"

Bert rolled his eyes, nodding toward Kristy, who was now coming back toward us with Monica. "What do you think?"

"I heard that," she said. "You know, it takes time to look like this. You can't just throw this sort of outfit together."

Bert narrowed his eyes, looking at her. "No?"

Ignoring this, she said, "A fat lot of good it's doing me here, though. There aren't any good prospects."

"What about that guy at the keg?" Bert asked.

"Please." She sighed. "Can't a girl have high standards? I don't want an *ordinary* boy."

There was bout of laughter from the jeep parked beside us, and a second later a blonde girl in a halter top suddenly stumbled over. "Hey," she said, pointing at me. "I know you. Don't I know you?"

"Um, I'm not sure," I said, but I did know her. It was Rachel Newcomb: we'd run middle school track together. We hadn't spoken in years.

"I do, I do," she said, snapping her fingers, hardly seeming to notice everyone else looking on. Kristy raised her eyebrows.

"You know me, Rachel," Bert said quickly. "Bert? I tutored you last summer at the Kaplan center, in math?"

Rachel looked at him briefly, then turned her attention back to me. "Oh shit, I know! We used to run together, right? In middle school? And now you date that guy, the one who's always yelling at us about bicycling!"

It took me a second.

"Recycling?" I said.

"Right!" She clapped her hands. "That's it!"

There was hysterical laughter from the jeep, followed by someone yelling, "Rachel, you're so freaking stupid!"

Rachel, hardly bothered, plopped herself down between me and Bert. "God," she said, tipping her head back and laughing, "remember how much fun we used to have at meets? And you, shit, you were *fast*. Weren't you?"

"Not really," I said, instinctively reaching to smooth my hair before realizing it wasn't even parted. I could feel Kristy watching me, listening to this.

"You were!" she poked Bert in the arm. "You should have seen her. She was so fast, like she could . . ."

There was an awkward silence as we all waited for whatever verb was coming.

". . . fly," Rachel finished, and I heard Kristy snort. "Like she had freaking wings, you know? She won everything. You know, the only way anyone else ever got to win anything was when you quit."

"Well," I said, willing her to get up and move on, before she said anything else. Whatever anonymity I'd enjoyed so far this summer had been based on everyone from Wish not being from my school and therefore not knowing anything about me. I had been a clean slate, and now here was Rachel Newcomb, scribbling out my secrets for everyone to see.

"We were the Running Rovers," Rachel was saying to Monica now, slurring slightly. "I always thought that name was so dumb, you know? It made us sound like dogs. Go Rovers! Woof! Woof!"

"Good God," Kristy said, to no one in particular. Still, I felt my face burn, and that was even before I glanced up to see Wes looking at me.

"Look," Rachel said, slapping a hand on my knee. "I want you to know something, okay?"

Even though I knew what was coming—how, I have no idea—I could think of no way to stop her. All I could do was stand off to the side and watch everything fall apart.

"And what I want you to know is," she said earnestly, as if this was private and we didn't have an audience, "that I don't care what anyone says, *I* don't think you're all weird since that thing happened with your dad. I mean, that was messed up that you were there. Most people couldn't handle that, you know? Seeing someone die like that."

I just sat there, looking at her: at her flushed face, the sloshy cup of beer in her hand, the white of her tan line that was visible, just barely, beneath the straps of her halter top. I could not bring myself to look at the others. So much for my fairy tale, however brief, my luxury of scars that didn't show. Somewhere, I was sure I could hear a clock chiming.

"Rachel!" someone yelled from the next car over. "Get over here or we're leaving you!"

"Oh, gotta go!" Rachel stood up, flipping her long hair over her shoulder. "I'm going," she said, redundantly. "But I meant what I said, okay? Remember that. Remember what I said. Okay?"

I couldn't even nod or say a word. Rachel stumbled off to the jeep, where she was greeted with more laughter and a few bicycling jokes. Then someone turned up the radio, some Van Morrison song, and they all started singing along, off-key.

It was one of those moments that you wish you could just disappear, every particle in you shrinking. But that, I knew, was impossible. There was always an After. So I lifted my head, and looked at Kristy, seeing Bert watching me, Wes's and Monica's faces in my peripheral vision. Then I took a breath, to say what, I didn't know. But before I could, Kristy had walked over and sat down beside me.

"That girl," she said, wrapping her hand around mine, "is as dumb as a bag of hammers."

"No kidding," Bert said softly, and when I looked at him I saw not The Face, but instead a good-humored sort of disgust, not directed at me, not about me at all.

Kristy leaned across me, saying, "Wasn't she the one you had to explain the concept of odd numbers to during that summer math tutoring thing you did?"

Bert nodded. "Twice," he said.

"Moron."

"Mmm-hmm," Monica said, nodding.

Kristy rolled her eyes, then took a sip of her beer. Her palm felt warm against mine, and I realized how long it had been since anyone had held my hand. I looked at Wes, remembering his sculpture, the heart cut into the palm. He was looking at me, just as I'd thought he would be, but like Bert's, his look was not what I expected. No pity, no sadness: nothing had changed. I realized all those times I'd felt people stare at me, their faces had been pictures, abstracts. None of them were mirrors, able to reflect back the expression I thought only I wore, the feelings only I felt. Until now, this moment, as our eyes met. If there was a way to recognize something you'd never seen but still knew by heart, I felt it as I looked at his face. Finally, someone understood.

"Still," Kristy said wistfully, "I did like her halter top. I have a black skirt that would look just *great* with that."

We just sat there for a second, none of us talking. In the middle of the clearing, someone was playing with a flashlight, the beam moving across the trees overhead, showing bits and pieces of branches and leaves, a glimpse here and there, then darkness again. I knew that in the last few minutes everything had changed. I'd tried to hold myself apart, showing only what I wanted, doling out bits and pieces of who I was. But that only works for so long. Eventually, even the smallest fragments can't help but make a whole.

An hour later, we were in the back of the Bertmobile on the couch, being honest. It might have been the beer.

I was not a drinker, never had been. But after what had happened with Rachel, I'd felt shaken enough to agree when Kristy offered to go get me a very small beer, which I was, she assured me, under absolutely no obligation to drink. After a few sips, we'd started talking about boys, and it just went from there.

"Here's the thing," she said, crossing one white boot over the other. "My last boyfriend left me for dead out in the middle of nowhere. It's not like that should be so hard to improve upon. I want a nice boy. You know?"

It was strange to me to be sitting there as if the whole thing with Rachel had never happened. But after we'd sat there for just a second, Wes said he had someone he had to find who had promised him some rebar; Bert tagged along; and Kristy, Monica, and I moved onto the couch to discuss other things. My secret, released, did not hover over like a dark cloud. Instead, it dissipated, grew fainter, until it seemed, if not forgotten, left behind for the time being.

"What I really would like," Kristy said now, pulling me back to the present conversation, "is a smart boy. I'm sick of guys who can't even remember my name, much less spell it. Someone really focused and brainy. That's what I want."

"No, you don't," I said, taking another sip of my beer. Only when I swallowed did I realize they were both looking at me, waiting for me to elaborate. "I had a boyfriend like that," I explained. "Or have. Or sort of have."

"Oh, those are the worst," she said sympathetically, nodding.

I was confused. "What are?"

"Sort-of boyfriends." She sighed. "You know, they sort of like you, then they sort of don't. The only thing they're absolutely sure of is that they want to get into your pants. I *hate* that."

"Mmm-hmm," Monica agreed adamantly.

"Actually," I said, "it's not like that, exactly. We're more sort of not together, and not broken up. We're on a break."

"A break," Kristy repeated, sounding out the word as if it was foreign, one she'd never heard before. "Meaning . . ." She moved her hand in a motion that meant I was supposed to jump in, anytime now.

"Meaning," I told her, "that there were some concerns about us not wanting the same things, not having the same expectations. So we've agreed to not be in contact until the end of the summer, and then we're going to see where we stand."

She and Monica contemplated this for a moment. "That," Kristy said finally, "is just so very mature."

"Well, that's Jason," I told her. "It was his idea, really."

"How long has this break been going on?" she asked.

I thought for a second. "Since the night I met you," I told her, and her eyes widened, surprised. "He'd just emailed me about it, like, an hour earlier."

"That is so funny," she said, "because that night, I was picking up on something, like you had a boyfriend or were in some sort of situation." She pointed at Monica. "Didn't I say that, that night?"

"Mmm-hmm," Monica said.

"You just looked . . ." she said, searching for the word, "*taken*, you know? Plus you hardly reacted to Wes. I mean, you did a little, but nothing like most girls. It was a little swoon. Not a *sa-woon*, you know?"

I said, "Sa-woon?"

"Oh, come on," she said, shaking her head. "Even a blind girl could tell he's amazing."

Beside me, Monica sighed wistfully in agreement.

"So why haven't you gone out with him?" I asked her.

"Can't," she said flatly. "He's too much like family. I mean, after the accident, when my mom flaked out and took off to find herself and we came to live with Stella, I was crazy for him. We both were."

"Bettaquit," Monica said darkly.

"It's still a sore subject," Kristy explained, while Monica turned her head, exhaling. "Anyway, I did everything I could to get his attention, but he'd just gotten back from Myers School then, was still dealing with his mom dying and all that. So he had a lot on his mind. At least I told myself that's why he could resist me."

"Myers School?" I said.

Kristy nodded. "Yeah. It's a reform school."

I knew this. Jason had tutored out there, and I'd often ridden along with him, then sat in the car doing homework while he went inside. Delia had said Wes had gotten arrested: I supposed this was the punishment. Maybe he'd even been there those days, as I sat in the car, looking up at the loops of barbed wire along the fence, while cars whizzed by on the highway behind me.

"Okay," Kristy said, tapping her foot to the music, "tell us about the sort-of boyfriend."

"Oh," I said, "we've been dating for a year and a half."

I took a sip of my beer, thinking this would suffice. But they were sitting there, expectant, waiting for more. Oh, well, I thought. Here goes nothing.

"He went away for the summer," I continued, "and a couple of weeks after he left, he decided maybe it was better that we take this break. I was really upset about it. I still am, actually."

"So he found someone else," Kristy said, clarifying.

"No, it's not like that," I said. "He's at Brain Camp."

"Huh?" Monica asked.

"Brain Camp," I repeated. "It's like a smart-kid thing."

"Then he found someone else at Brain Camp," Kristy said.

"No, it's not about someone else."

"Then what is it about?"

It just seemed wrong to be sitting here discussing this. Plus I was embarrassed enough by what had happened, what I'd done to freak him out, so embarrassed I hadn't even told my mother, whom I should have been able to tell anything. I could only imagine what these girls would think.

"Well," I said, "a lot of things."

Another expectant pause.

I took a breath. "Basically, it came down to the fact that I ended an email by saying I loved him, which is, you know, big, and it made him uncomfortable. And he felt that I wasn't focused enough on my job at the library. There's probably more, but that's the main stuff."

They both just looked at me. Then Monica said, "Donneven."

"Wait a second." Kristy sat up against the edge of the couch, as if she needed her full height, small though it was, to say what was coming next. "You've been dating for a year and a half and you can't tell the guy you love him?"

"It's complicated," I said, taking a sip of my beer.

"And," she continued, "he broke up with you because he didn't think you were focused enough on your job performance?"

"The library," I said, "is very important to him."

"Is he ninety years old?"

I looked down at my beer. "You don't understand," I said. "He's been, like, my life for the last year and a half. He's made me a better person."

This quieted her down, at least temporarily. I ran my finger around the rim of my cup.

"How?" she said finally.

"Well," I began, "he's perfect, you know? Great in school,

smart, all these achievements. He can do anything. And when I was with him, it was like, good for me. It made me better, too."

"Until . . ." she said.

"Until," I said, "I let him down. I pushed too hard, I got too attached. He has high standards."

"And you don't," she said.

"Of course I do."

Monica exhaled, shaking her head. "Nuh-*uh*," she said adamantly.

"Sure doesn't seem like it," Kristy said, seconding this. She took a sip of her beer, never taking her eyes off of me.

"Why not?" I asked.

"Listen to yourself," she said. "God! Are you actually going to sit there and say he was justified in dumping you because you dared to get attached to him after a year and a half? Or because you didn't take some stupid job at the library as seriously as he thought you should?"

I knew this was, pretty much, what I'd just said. But somehow it sounded different now, coming from her.

"Look," she said, as I struggled with this, trying to work it out, "I don't know you that well. I'll admit that. But what I see is a girl any guy, especially some library nerd who's off at Cranium Camp—"

"Brain Camp," I muttered.

"—would totally want to hear say she loved him. You're smart, you're gorgeous, you're a good person. I mean, what makes him such a catch, anyway? Who is he to judge?"

"He's Jason," I said, for lack of a better argument.

"Well, he's a fuckhead." She sucked down the rest of her beer. "And if I were you, I'd be glad to be rid of him. Because anyone that can make you feel that bad about yourself is toxic, you know?"

"He doesn't make me feel bad about myself," I said, knowing even as my lips formed the words this was exactly what he did. Or what I let him do. It was hard to say.

"What you need," Kristy said, "what you *deserve*, is a guy who adores you for what you are. Who doesn't see you as a project, but a *prize*. You know?"

"I'm no prize," I said, shaking my head.

"Yes," she said, and she sounded so sure it startled me: like she could be so positive while hardly knowing me at all. "You *are*. What sucks is how you can't even see it."

I turned my head, looking back out at the clearing. It seemed no matter where I turned, someone was telling me to change.

Kristy reached over and put her hand on mine, holding it there until I had to look up at her. "I'm not picking on you."

"No?" I said.

She shook her head. "Look. We both know life is short, Macy. Too short to waste a single second with anyone who doesn't appreciate and value you. "

"You said the other day life was long," I shot back. "Which is it?"

"It's both," she said, shrugging. "It all depends on how you choose to live it. It's like forever, always changing."

"Nothing can be two opposite things at once," I said. "It's impossible."

"No," she replied, squeezing my hand, "what's impossible is that we actually think it could be anything *other* than that. Look, when I was in the hospital, right after the accident, they thought I was going to die. I was really fucked up, big time."

"Uh-huh," Monica said, looking at her sister.

"Then," Kristy continued, nodding at her, "life was very short, literally. But now that I'm better, it seems so long I have to squint to see even the edges of it. It's all in the view, Macy. That's what I mean about forever, too. For any one of us our forever could end in an hour, or a hundred years from now. You can never know for sure, so you'd better make every second count."

Monica, lighting another cigarette, nodded. "Mmm-hmm," she said.

"What you have to decide," Kristy said to me, leaning forward, "is how you want your life to be. If your forever was ending tomorrow, would this be how you'd want to have spent it?" It seemed like it was a choice I had already made. I'd spent the last year and a half with Jason, shaping my life to fit his, doing what I had to in order to make sure I had a place in his perfect world, where things made sense. But it hadn't worked.

"Listen," Kristy said, "the truth is, nothing is guaranteed. You know that more than anybody." She looked at me hard, making sure I knew what she meant. I did. "So don't be afraid. Be *alive*."

But then, I couldn't imagine, after everything that had happened, how you could live and not constantly be worrying about the dangers all around you. Especially when you'd already gotten the scare of your life.

"It's the same thing," I told her.

"What is?"

"Being afraid and being alive."

"No," she said slowly, and now it was as if she was speaking a language she knew at first I wouldn't understand, the very words, not to mention the concept, being foreign to me. "Macy, no. It's not."

It's not, I repeated in my head, and looking back later, it seemed to me that was the moment everything really changed. When I said these words, not even aloud, and in doing so made my own wish: that for me this could somehow, someday, really be true.

A little bit later Kristy and Monica headed off to the keg again, but I stayed behind, sitting on the back bumper of the ambulance. I was feeling a bit woozy from the small amount of beer I'd had, not to mention everything Kristy had said. Too much to contemplate even under the best of conditions, now it was close to impossible.

I looked up after a few minutes to see Wes coming toward me from across the clearing. He had a bunch of metal rods under his arm—the rebar he'd been promised, I assumed. I just sat there watching him approach, his slow loping gait, and wondered what it would be like if he was coming to see me, coming to be with me. It wasn't what I thought when I saw Jason; that was more a reassurance. With him in sight, I could always get my bearings. If anything, Wes was the opposite. One look, and I had no idea what I was doing.

"Hey," he said as he got closer, and I made myself look up at him, as if surprised, oh look, there you are. Which worked fine, until he sat down next to me, and again I felt that looseness, something inside me coming undone. He put the rods down beside him. "Where is everybody?"

"The keg," I said, nodding toward it.

"Oh. Right."

Talk about forever: the next silent minute seemed to go on for that and longer. I had a picture of a school clock in my mind, those final seconds of the hour when the minute hand just trembles, as if willing itself to jump to the twelve. Say something, I told myself, sneaking a glance at Wes. He hardly seemed to be noticing this lapse, instead just watching the crowd in the middle of the clearing, his arms hanging loosely at his sides. Once again I could see the very bottom of the tattoo on his upper arm. Kristy had told me to live, whatever that meant in all its variations, and her words were still resonating. Oh well, I thought, here goes.

"So what is that?" I asked him, forcing the words out, then immediately realized I was looking at him, not at his arm, so this question could concern just about anything. He raised his eyebrows, confused, and I added—face flushing, God help me—"Your tattoo, I mean. I've never been able to see what it is."

This full sentence, an inquiry to boot, seemed to me on par with Helen Keller finally signing W-A-T-E-R. I mean, really.

"Oh," he said, pushing up his shirtsleeve. "It's just this design. You saw it that first day you came out to Delia's, right?"

I felt myself nodding, but truthfully I was just staring at the black, thick lines of the design, now fully revealed: the heart in the hand. This one was, of course, smaller, and contained within a circle bordered by a tribal pattern, but otherwise it was the same. The flat palm, fingers extended, the red heart in its center.

"Right," I said. Like the first time I'd seen it, I couldn't help think that it was familiar, something pricking my subconscious, as weird as that sounded. "Does it mean something?"

"Sort of." He looked down at his arm. "It's something my mom used to draw for me when I was a kid."

"Really."

"Yeah. She had this whole thing about the hand and the heart, how they were connected." He ran a finger over the bright red of the heart, then looked at me. "You know, feeling and action are always linked, one can't exist without the other. It's sort of a hippie thing. She was into that stuff."

"I like it," I said. "I mean, the idea of it. It makes sense."

He looked down at the tattoo again. "After she died I started tinkering with it, you know, with the welding. This one has the circle, the one on the road has the barbed wire. They're all different, but with the same basic idea."

"Like a series," I said.

"I guess," he said. "Mostly I'm just trying to get it right, whatever that means."

I looked across the clearing, catching a sudden glimpse of Kristy as she moved through the crowd, blonde head bobbing.

"It's hard to do," I said.

Wes looked at me. "What is?"

I swallowed, not sure why I'd said this out loud. "Get it right."

He must think I'm so stupid, I thought, vowing to keep my mouth shut from now on. But he just picked up one of the rods he'd carried over, turning it in his hands. "Yeah," he said, after a second. "It is."

Kristy was now almost to the keg. I could see her saying something to Monica, her head thrown back as she laughed.

"I'm sorry about your mom," I said to Wes. I didn't even think before saying this, the connotation, what it would or wouldn't convey. It just came out, all on its own.

"I'm sorry about your dad," he replied. We were both looking straight ahead. "I remember him from coaching the Lakeview Zips, when I was a kid. He was great."

I felt something catch in my throat, a sudden surge of sadness that caught me unaware, almost taking my breath away. That was the thing. You never got used to it, the idea of someone being gone. Just when you think it's reconciled, accepted, someone points it out to you and it just hits you all over again, that shocking.

"So," he said suddenly, "why'd you stop?"

"Stop what?" I said.

"Running."

I stared down into my empty cup. "I don't know," I said, even as that winter day flashed in my mind again. "I just wasn't into it anymore."

Across the clearing, I could see Kristy talking to a tall blond guy who was gesturing, telling some kind of elaborate story. She kept having to lean back, dodging his flailing fingers.

"How fast were you?" Wes asked me.

I said, "Not that fast."

"You mean you couldn't . . . fly?" he said, smiling at me.

Stupid Rachel, I thought. "No," I said, a flush creeping up my neck, "I couldn't fly."

"What was your best time for the mile?"

"Why?" I said.

"Just wondering," he said, turning the rod in his hands. "I mean, I run. So I'm curious."

"I don't remember," I said.

"Oh, come on, tell me," he said, bumping my shoulder with his. I cannot believe this, I thought. "I can take it."

Kristy was glancing over at us now, even as finger guy was still talking. She raised her eyebrow at me, then turned back to face him.

"Okay, fine," I said. "My best was five minutes, five seconds."

He just looked at me. "Oh," he said finally.

"What? What's yours?"

He coughed, turning his head. "Never mind."

"Oh, see," I said, "that's not fair."

"It's more than five-five," he told me, leaning back on his hands. "Let's leave it at that."

"That was years ago," I said. "Now I probably couldn't even do a half a mile in that time."

"I bet you could." He held the rod up, squinting at it. "I bet," he said, "you'd be faster than you think. Though maybe not fast enough to fly."

I felt myself smile, then bit it back. "You could outrun me easily, I bet."

"Well," he said, "maybe someday, we'll find out."

Oh, my God, I thought, and I knew I should say something, anything. But now Kristy, Bert, and Monica were walking toward us, and I missed my chance.

"Twenty minutes to curfew," Bert announced as he got closer, looking at his watch. "We need to go."

"Oh, my God," Kristy said, "you might actually have to go over twenty-five to get us home in time."

Bert made a face at her, then walked to the driver's side door, opening it. Monica climbed up into the ambulance, plopping herself on the couch, and I followed her, with Kristy right behind me.

"What were you two talking about?" she whispered as Wes pulled the doors shut.

"Nothing," I said. "Running."

"You should have seen your face," she said, her breath hot in my ear. "Sa-woooon."

Chapter Eight

"Okay," Caroline said, pushing a button on the camera and then coming over to sit next to my mother. "Here we go."

It was Saturday morning. My sister had arrived the night before, having spent the day in Colby meeting with the carpenter about the renovations and repairs to the beach house. This was familiar ground to her, as she'd already done her own house, plus the place she and Wally had in the mountains. Decorating, she claimed, was her calling, ever since one of her college art professors told her she had a "good eye," a compliment that she took to mean she was entitled to redo not only her own house but also anyone else's.

So although my mother was just barely on board—which was itself miraculous, in my opinion—Caroline was moving full steam ahead, showing up with not only most of her extensive library on home decorating but also pictures she'd taken with Wally's digital camera, so she could walk us though the suggested changes with visual aides.

"These things are a real lifesaver when you're doing long-distance remodeling," she explained as she hooked the camera up to the TV. "I don't know what we ever did without them."

She pushed a button, and the screen went black. Then, just like that, the beach house appeared. It was the front view, the way it looked if you had your back to the ocean. There was the deck, with its one rickety wooden bench. There were the stairs that led over the dunes. There was the old gas grill, beneath the kitchen window. It had been so long since I'd seen it, but still I felt a lurch in my stomach at how familiar it was. It seemed entirely possible that if you leaned in closer, peering in the back window, you'd see my dad on the couch reading the paper and turning his head to look as you called his name.

My mother was just staring at it, holding her coffee cup with both hands, and I wondered again if she was going to be able to handle this. But then I looked at my sister, and she was watching my mom, too. After a second she said, very carefully, "So this is the way it looks now. You can see that the roof is sagging a bit. That's from the last big storm."

My mother nodded. But she didn't say anything.

"It needs to be braced, and we have to replace some shingles as well. The carpenter was saying as long as we're shoring it up we might want to consider adding a skylight, or something . . . since the living room gets so little light from those front windows. You know how much you always complained about that."

I remembered. My mother was forever turning on lights in the living room, complaining it was like a dungeon. ("All the better for naps!" my father would claim, just before falling asleep on the couch with his mouth open.) She preferred to spend her time in the front bedroom, which had a big window. Plus the moose gave her the creeps. I wondered what she was thinking now. It was hard for her; it was hard for me, too. But I kept remembering everything Kristy had said two nights before, about not being afraid, and how if I'd come home when I got scared, I would have missed everything that had happened.

"But I've never dealt with skylights," Caroline said. "I don't know how much they run, or if they're even worth the trouble."

"It depends on the brand," my mother said, her eyes on the screen. "And the size. It varies."

I had to hand it to my sister. For all her pushing, she knew what she was doing. Take one small step—show the picture, which she knew would be hard for my mother—and pair it with something she'd feel entirely sure about: work.

It went the same way for the next half hour, as Caroline carefully guided us through the beach house, room by room. At first it was all I could do to swallow over the lump in my throat when I saw the view from the deck of the ocean, or the room with the bunk beds where I always slept. Even worse were the pictures of the main bedroom, where a pair of my dad's beat-up running shoes was still parked against the wall by the door.

But slowly, carefully, Caroline kept bringing us back. For every sharp intake of breath, every moment I was sure I couldn't bear it, there was a question, something logical to grab onto. I'm thinking maybe glass blocks in place of that window in the bathroom, she'd say, what do you think? Or, see how the linoleum's coming up in the kitchen? I found some great blue tile I think we could replace it with. Or would tile be too expensive? And each time, my mother would reply, grabbing the answer as if it was a life preserver in a choppy sea. Once she had her breath back, they'd move on.

When the slideshow was over, I left them in the living room discussing skylights and went to pull my laundry out of the dryer so I could iron something for the info desk the next day. I was almost done when my mother appeared in the doorway, leaning against it with her arms crossed over her chest.

"Well," she said, "your sister sure seems to have found herself a project, hasn't she?"

"Where is she?"

"Out in her car. She's got some swatches she wants to show me." She sighed, running her hand over the edge of the door frame. "Apparently, corduroy upholstery is all the rage these days."

I smiled, smoothing a crease out of the pants I was holding. "She is an expert at this," I said. "You know what a great job she did with her place, and the mountain house."

"I know." She was quiet for a second, watching as I folded a shirt and put it in the basket at my feet. "But I can't help but think it's a lot of money and work for such an old house. Your father always said the foundation would probably go in a few years. . . . I just wonder if it's worth it."

I pulled Kristy's jeans out of the dryer and folded them. The black heart on the knee was just as dark as ever. "It might be fun," I said, picking my words carefully. "To have a place to go again."

"I don't know." She pulled a hand through her hair. "I wonder if it would be easier, if the foundation might be flawed, to just take it down. Then we'd have the lot and could start over."

I was bent over, peering into the dryer to pull out the last things in there, and for a second I just froze. Minutes ago, I'd gotten my first look at the beach house in over a year. To think that it, like so much else, might one day just be gone—I couldn't even imagine. "I don't know," I said. "I bet the foundation's not that bad."

"Mom?" Caroline called from the living room. "I've got the swatches. . . . Where are you?"

"Coming," my mother said over her shoulder. "It was just an idea," she added, more quietly, to me. "Just a thought."

It shouldn't have surprised me, really. My mother trafficked in new houses, so of course the idea of everything being perfect and pristine, even better than before, would appeal to her. It was the dream she sold every day. She had to believe in it.

"Is that new?" she asked me suddenly.

"Is what new?"

She nodded at the tank top I'd just finished folding. "I haven't seen it before."

Of course she hadn't: it was Kristy's, and here, in the bright light of the laundry room, I knew it looked even more unlike something I'd wear than it had when I'd first agreed to put it on. You could plainly see the glittery design on the straps, and it was clear it was lower cut than my mother was most likely comfortable with. In Kristy's room, in Kristy's world, it was about as shocking as a plain white T-shirt. But here, it was completely out of place.

"Oh, this isn't mine," I said. "I just, um, borrowed it from a friend."

"Really?" She looked at it again, trying to picture, I was sure, one of my student council friends sporting such a thing. "Who?"

Kristy's face immediately popped into my mind, with her wide smile, the scars, those big blue eyes. If the tank top was enough to cause my mother concern, I could only imagine how Kristy, in one of her full outfits, would go over, not to mention any of my other Wish friends. It seemed simpler, and smarter, to just say, "This girl I work with. I spilled some salad dressing on my shirt last night so she lent me this, to drive home in."

"Oh," she said. It wasn't that she sounded relieved, but clearly, this was an acceptable explanation. "Well. That was nice."

"Yeah," I said, as she left the doorway, heading to the kitchen, where my sister and her swatches were waiting. "It was."

I left them downstairs, my mother listening dubiously as Caroline explained about how corduroy wasn't just for overalls anymore, and went up to my room, putting my laundry basket on the bed. After I'd stacked all my T-shirts, shorts, and jeans in the bureau, and laid out my info desk clothes for the week to be ironed, the only things left were Kristy's jeans and the tank top. I went to put them on my desk, where I'd be sure to see them the next time I was leaving for work and could return them, but then, at the last minute, I stopped myself, running the thin, glittery strap of the tank top between my thumb and forefinger. It was so different from anything of mine, it was no wonder my mother had noticed it instantly. That was why I should have returned it immediately. And that was why, instead, I slipped it into my bottom drawer, out of sight, and kept it.

On Sunday, my sister was cooking dinner, and she needed arugula. I wasn't entirely sure what that was. But I still got recruited to go look for it with her.

We'd just started down the second aisle of the farmer's market, my sister deep into an explanation of the difference between lettuce and arugula, when suddenly, there was Wes. Yikes, I thought, my hand immediately going to my hair, which I hadn't bothered to wash (so unlike me, but Caroline, convinced there was going to be some mass rush on exotic greens, had insisted we leave right after breakfast), then to my clothes—an old Lakeview Mall 5K T-shirt, shorts, and flip-flops—which I'd thrown on without considering the fact I might see anyone I knew, much less Wes. It was one thing for him to see me catering, when, even if I was in disarray, at least I wasn't alone. Here, in broad daylight, though, all my old anxieties came rushing back.

". . . not to be confused with field greens," Caroline was saying, "which are an entirely different thing altogether."

He was at the very end of the row, with a bunch of sculptures set up all around him, talking to a woman in a big floppy hat, who was holding her checkbook. Looking more closely, I saw one big piece, which was sporting a SOLD sign, as well as several smaller ones. They were all whirligigs, a part of each spinning in one direction or another in the breeze.

I took a sudden left, finding myself facing a table full of pound cakes and crocheted pot holders, as Caroline kept walking, still talking about various types of greens. It took her a second to realize I'd ditched her, and she doubled back looking annoyed.

"Macy," she said, entirely too loudly, at least to my ears, "what are you doing?"

"Nothing." I picked up one of the pot holders. "Look, aren't these nice?"

She looked at the pot holder—which was orange and spangled and not nice at all—then at me. "Okay," she said. "Tell me what's going on."

I glanced back down at Wes, hoping he'd gone to look for arugula too, or had maybe gone to help the woman get the sculpture to her car. But no. Now, in fact, he was looking our way.

My way, to be exact. The woman with the floppy hat was gone, and he was just standing there, watching me. He lifted his hand and waved, and I felt my face flush as I put the pot holder back with its hideous brethren.

"Macy, what on earth is wrong with you? Are you okay?" Caroline squinted at me from behind her entirely too expensive designer sunglasses, then turned her head to see what, exactly, had made me turn bright red. I watched her gaze move across the tables of fresh corn, goat cheese, and hammocks, until, finally: "Oh."

I knew what she was thinking, could hear Kristy's voice in my head: *Sa-wooon.*

"Do you know that guy?" she asked me, still staring.

"Sort of," I said. Now that we'd all seen each other, there was no amount of pot holders, or hammocks, that could save me. Thinking this, I took Caroline by the elbow. "Come on."

As we got closer, I looked at the sculptures and realized there were no heart in hands on display. Instead, I noticed another theme: angels and halos. The smaller pieces were all stick figures made of various bits of metal and steel, with gears for faces and tiny nails for fingers and toes. Above the heads of each was a sculpted circle, each decorated in a different way. One was dotted with squares of different colored glass, another had long framing nails twisting off in all directions, an angel Medusa. On the large sculpture with the SOLD sign, barbed wire was threaded around the halo, much the same as on the sculpture on Sweetbud Drive, and I thought of the Myers School again, the way the wire there had curved the same way around the fence, roped like ribbon.

"Hey," Wes said as we came up. "I thought that was you."

"Hi," I said.

"These are amazing," Caroline said, reaching out her hand to the large sculpture and running a finger along the edges of the gear that made up its midsection. "I just love this medium."

"Thanks," Wes said. "It's all from the junkyard."

"This is Wes," I said, as she walked around the sculpture, still examining it. "Wes, this is my sister, Caroline."

"Nice to meet you," Caroline said in her socialite voice, extending her hand. They shook hands, and she went back to circling the sculpture, taking off her sunglasses and leaning in closer. "What's great about this," she said, as if we were in a museum and she was leading the tour, "is the contrast. It's a real juxtaposition between subject matter and materials."

Wes looked at me, raising his eyebrows, and I just shook my head, knowing better than to stop my sister when she was on a roll. Especially about art, which had been her major in college.

"See, it's one thing to do angels," she said to me, while Wes looked on, "but what's crucial here is how the medium spells out the concept. Angels, by definition, are supposed to be perfect. So by building them out of rusty pieces, and discards and scraps, the artist is making a statement about the fallibility of even the most ideal creatures."

"Wow," I said to Wes, as she moved on to the smaller pieces, still murmuring to herself. "I'm impressed."

"Me, too," he replied. "I had no idea. I just couldn't afford new materials when I started."

I laughed, surprising myself, then was surprised even more—no, shocked—when he smiled at me, a heartbreaker's smile, and for a second I was just in the moment: me and Wes, surrounded by all those angels, in the sunshine, on a Sunday.

"Oh, wow," Caroline called out, shaking me back to attention, "is this sheet metal you used here? For the face?"

Wes looked over to where she was squatting in front of a figure with a halo studded with bottle caps. "That's an old Coke sign," he told her. "I found it at the dump."

"A Coke sign!" she said, awed. "And the bottle caps . . . it's the inevitable commingling of commerce and religion. I love that!"

Wes just nodded: a fast learner, he already knew to just go along with her. "Right," he said. Then, in a lower voice to me he added, "Just liked the Coke sign, actually."

"Of course you did," I said.

A breeze blew over us then, and some of the halos on the smaller pieces began to spin again. A small one behind us was decorated with jingle bells, their ringing like a whistling in the air. As I bent down closer to it, the bells whizzing past, I saw the one behind it, which was turning more slowly. It was a smaller angel with a halo studded with flat stones. As I touched one as it turned, though, I realized it wasn't a stone but something else that I couldn't place at first.

"What is this?" I asked him.

"Sea glass," Wes said, bending down beside me. "See the shapes? No rough edges."

"Oh, right," I said. "That's so cool."

"It's hard to find," he said. The breeze was dying down, and he reached out and spun the halo a bit with one finger, sending the light refracting through the glass again. He was so close to me, our knees were almost touching. "I bought that collection at a flea market, for, like, two bucks. I wasn't sure what I was going to use it for, then, but it seemed too good a thing to pass up."

"It's beautiful," I said, and it was. When the halo got going fast, the glass all blurred, the colors mingling. Like the ocean, I thought, and looked at that angel's face. Her eyes were washers, her mouth a tiny key, the kind I'd once had for my diary. I hadn't noticed that before.

"You want it?"

"I couldn't," I said.

"Sure you can. I'm offering." He reached over and picked it up, brushing his fingers over the angel's tinny toes. "Here."

"Wes. I can't."

"You can. You'll pay me back somehow."

"How?"

He thought for a second. "Someday, you'll agree to run that mile with me. And then we'll know for sure whether you can kick my ass."

"I'd rather pay you for it," I said, as I reached into my back pocket for my wallet. "How much?"

"Macy, I was kidding. I know you could kick my ass." He looked at me, smiling. Sa-woon, I thought. "Look. Just take it."

I was about to protest again, but then I stopped myself. Maybe for once I should just let something happen, I thought. I looked down at the angel in his hand, at those sparkling bits of glass. I did want it. I didn't know why, couldn't explain it if I had to. But I did.

"Okay," I said. "But I am paying you back somehow, sometime."

"Sure." He handed it to me. "Whatever you want."

Caroline was coming back over to us now, picking her way through the smaller sculptures and stopping to examine each one. She had her purse open, her phone to her ear. ". . . no, it's more like a yard art thing, but I just think it would look great on the back porch of the mountain house, right by that rock garden I've been working on. Oh, you should just see these. They're so much better than those iron herons they sell at Attache Gardens for hundreds of dollars. Well, I know you liked those, honey, but these are better. They are."

"Iron herons?" Wes said to me.

"She lives in Atlanta," I told him, as if this explained everything.

"Okay, honey, I'm going. I'll talk to you later. Love you, bye!" She snapped the phone shut, then dropped it into her purse before slinging it back over her shoulder. "All right," she said to Wes, "let's talk prices."

I hung back, holding my angel, as they walked through the various pieces, Caroline stopping the negotiations every so often to explain the meaning of this or that piece as Wes stood by politely, listening. By the time it was all over she'd bought three angels, including the Coke bottle cap one, and had gotten Wes's number to set up an appointment for her to come see the bigger pieces he had out at his workshop.

"A steal," she said, ripping her sizeable check out of her checkbook and handing it to him. "Really. You should be charging more."

"Maybe if I show someplace else," he told her, folding the check and sticking it in his front pocket, "but it's hard to get pricey when you have baked goods on either side of you."

"You will show someplace else," she told him, picking up two of her angels. "It's only a matter of time." She looked at her watch. "Oh, Macy, we have to run. I told Mom we'd be home for lunch so we could look at the rest of those color swatches."

Something told me my mother, who that morning had picked out windows and a skylight with about as much enjoyment as someone getting a root canal, would not be broken up to miss that conversation. But I figured it wasn't worth pointing that out to Caroline, who was already distracted checking out another angel with a thumbtack halo, which she'd somehow missed earlier. "Well," I said to Wes, "thank you again."

"No problem," he said, glancing over at my sister. "Thanks for the business."

"That's not me," I told him. "It's all her."

"Still," he said. "Thanks anyway."

"Excuse me," a woman by the big sculpture called out, her voice shrill, "do you have others like this?"

Wes looked over. "I should go, I guess."

"Go," I said. "I'll see you later."

"Yeah. See you around."

I stood there watching as he walked over to the woman, nodding as she asked her questions, then looked down at the angel in my arms, running a finger over the smooth sea glass dotting her halo.

"Ready?" Caroline said from behind me.

"Yeah," I said. "I'm ready."

Chapter Nine

"Now this," Delia said to me, her voice low, "*really* makes me nervous."

Looking out from the kitchen, I could only nod in agreement. But while Delia was referring to the fact that we were in a house where delicate antiques crowded just about every level surface and Monica had just been sent out with a trayful of full wineglasses, for me it was something else entirely. Namely the fact that a mere two feet from the door in which we were standing, in prime grabber location, were Jason's parents.

Since we'd arrived I'd been in the kitchen with Wes, shelling shrimp as fast as humanly possible because Delia, distracted by another crisis involving the ovens not lighting, had forgotten to get it done earlier. Suddenly, I'd heard a trilling laugh I recognized. As Kristy pushed through from the living room, her tray picked clean of the biscuits she'd walked out with only minutes earlier, I saw Mrs. Talbot. And as the door swept shut, I was almost certain she saw me.

"Unbelievable," Wes said.

"What?" For a second I thought he meant Mrs. Talbot.

"Look at that." I followed his gaze, realizing he meant the shrimp in my hands, as well as the pile in front of me, which was twice the size of his. "How are you doing those so fast?"

"I'm not," I said, sliding the shrimp out of the shell and dropping it on my pile.

He just looked at me, then down at the one he was holding. "I've been watching you," he said, "and while I've been working on this one, you've done five. At least."

I picked up another one, ripped the legs off, then slid off the shell in one piece, dropping the shrimp onto my pile.

"Six," he said. "This is getting embarrassing. How'd you learn to do that?"

Starting another one, I said, "My dad. In the summers, we used to buy a couple of pounds of shrimp to steam and eat for dinner. He loved shrimp, and he was super fast. So if you wanted to eat, you had to keep up." I dropped the shrimp onto my pile. "It was a Darwinian thing."

He finally finished the one in his hand, putting it on the pile. "In my house," he said, "it was the opposite. You did everything you could to keep from eating."

"Why?"

"After the divorce," he said, picking up another one and, eyeing how I was doing it, ripping all the legs off at once, "my mom got into natural foods. Part of the whole cleanse your life, cleanse your body thing. Or something. No more hamburgers, no more hot dogs. It was lentil loaf and tofu salad, and that was a good day."

"My dad was the total opposite," I told him, starting another one. "He was a firm believer in the all-meat diet. To him, chicken was a vegetable."

"I wish," he said.

"Shrimp! I need shrimp!" Delia hissed from behind us. I

scooped the pile in front of me onto a plate, then ran to the sink, rinsing them quickly and patting them dry as she hurriedly piled toothpicks, napkins, and cocktail sauce onto a platter.

"Those biscuits are going fast," Kristy reported as she came back through the door, balancing her tray on her upturned palm. Today, she was in her most striking outfit yet: a black leather skirt and motorcycle boots paired with a loose white peasant blouse. Her hair was held back at the back of her head with a pair of red chopsticks. "That crowd is all professor types, and they're so weird that way, ultra polite but really grabby at the same time. Like they say, 'Oh, my, doesn't that look tasty,' and then clean out your whole tray."

"Two and move," I said.

"Don't I know it." She blew a piece of hair out of her face. "It's just work, is all I'm saying."

There was a crash from the other room, just as Delia handed off the shrimp tray. We all froze.

"Shit," Delia said. "I mean, shoot. No, actually, I mean shit. I really do."

Kristy eased open the door a tiny bit. "It wasn't anything of theirs," she reported, and I saw Delia visibly relax. "But a couple of wineglasses bit it on the carpet."

"Red or white?" Delia asked.

"Ummm," Kristy said. "Looks like red."

"Shit," Delia said again, crossing the room to the plastic Tupperware container she always brought with us. "And Bert would pick today to have other plans."

I looked at Wes quizzically, and he said, "Bert's a whiz with stains. He can get anything out of anything."

"Really," I said.

"Oh yeah." Wes nodded, slowly de-shelling another shrimp. "He's a legend."

Delia yanked a bottle of carpet cleaner and a rag out of the container. "And how are you?" she asked me, handing them to me.

"How am I what?"

"At getting out stains."

I looked down at the rag and cleaner in my hands, as Kristy pushed out the door.

"Um," I said. Through the still open door, I could see Monica down on the floor, slowly picking up pieces of broken glass as the hostess of the party stood by, watching. "I'm not—"

"Good," Delia said, pushing me through the door. "Go to it!" She'd given me such a nudge I actually stumbled over the threshold: luckily, I was able to catch myself right before doing a face plant into a nearby end table. I caught my breath, then crossed the room over to Monica, who'd made what looked like very little headway in the cleaning up effort.

"Hey," I said, starting to kneel down beside her. "You okay?"

"Mmm-hmmm," she said. But then she stood up, wiping her hands on her apron and starting across the floor to the kitchen, leaving me and the tray behind her. So much for teamwork, I thought, as I dropped the cloth and cleaner beside me and began to pick up the broken glass as fast as I could. I'd just gotten what I hoped was all of it and begun spraying the carpet when I heard a voice.

"Macy? Is that you?"

For a second, I just kept spraying, as if doing so long enough might remove not only the stain, but me and this entire situation as well. After I gave the carpet a good dousing, though, it was clear I had no choice but to look up.

"Hi," I said to Mrs. Talbot, who was standing over me holding a napkin piled with shrimp. "How are you?"

"We're well," she said, glancing a bit hesitantly over at Mr. Talbot, who was helping himself to shrimp from Kristy's tray as she tried, unsuccessfully, to move on. "Are you . . . working here?"

Even though I knew this was a valid question, the fact that I was wearing a Wish Catering apron, holding a rag, and on my knees on the carpet fighting a stain made me wonder if Mrs. Talbot was really all that smart after all. "Yes," I said, tucking a piece of hair behind my ear. "I, um, just started."

"But you're still at the information desk," she said, suddenly serious, and I could see Jason in her features, this automatic concern that all be As It Should. "Aren't you?"

I nodded. "I'm just doing this occasionally," I said. "For extra money."

"Oh." She glanced over again at Mr. Talbot, who was standing in place chewing, his napkin piled with what, to my eye, looked like a lot more than two shrimp. "Well. That's wonderful."

I ducked my head back down, and after a second a woman came up to her, asking about some research trip, and thankfully, they moved on. I'd been dousing, then patting, then dousing for a good five minutes when a pair of motorcycle boots appeared right at my eye level, foot tapping.

"You know," Kristy said, her voice low, "it doesn't look so good for you to be on the floor like this."

"There's a stain," I said. "And Monica just abandoned me to deal with it."

She squatted down across from me, moving her knees to one side in a surprisingly ladylike way. "It's very hard for her," she said to me, her voice serious. "She's self-conscious about her clumsiness, so a lot of the times rather than acknowledge it she just shuts down. It's a defense mechanism. You know, she's very emotional, Monica. She really is."

As she said this, Monica pushed through the door from the kitchen, carrying a trayful of goat cheese toasts. She started across the room, her face flat and expressionless, walking right past us without even a glance.

"See?" Kristy said. "She's *upset*."

"Macy," a man's voice boomed from over our heads. "Hello down there!"

Kristy and I both looked up at the same time. It was Mr. Talbot, of course, and he was smiling widely, although I assumed it had more to do with Kristy's shrimp tray than us reuniting. As she and I both stood, he proved me right by immediately reaching for one and popping it into his mouth.

"Hi, Mr. Talbot," I said, as Kristy looked on, annoyed. "It's good to see you."

"And you," he replied. "Martha tells me you've taken on this job in addition to your library work. That's very ambitious of you. I know Jason finds the information desk to be a full-time commitment."

"Oh, well," I said, bending down to retrieve my cleaner and rag, as the stain looked, miraculously, like it was actually fading, "I'm sure for him, it is."

Mr. Talbot, reaching for another shrimp, raised his eyebrows.

"I mean," I said, quickly, as Kristy switched her tray to the other hand, "that Jason just gives such a big commitment to everything. He's very, you know, focused."

"Ah, yes, he really is," he said, nodding. Then he lowered his voice, adding, "I'm so glad that you understand that, considering the decision he had to make recently about your relationship." He dabbed his lips with a napkin. "I mean, he is fond of you. But Jason just has so much on his plate. He has to be very careful not to get distracted from his goals."

I just stood there, wondering how, exactly, he expected me to react to this. I was a distraction from his goals? I felt my face flush.

"At any rate," Mr. Talbot continued, "I know he hopes, as we do, that you two can work things out once he returns."

And with that, he started to reach for another shrimp. But as his fingers neared the edge of the tray, zeroing in, Kristy yanked it away with such force that a couple actually slid off the other side and hit the carpet, *thud thud*. Mr. Talbot looked confused. Then he looked at the shrimp on the floor, as if actually wondering if the two-second rule applied here.

"So sorry," Kristy said smoothly, turning on her heel, "but we're on goal to get out another round of appetizers, and we can't allow ourselves to be distracted."

"Kristy," I hissed.

"Come on," she said, and then she was starting across the floor, and there was really nothing I could think of to do but follow her. Which I did, not looking back, although whether it was to save my pride or save myself the sight of Mr. Talbot eating shrimp off the floor, I wasn't sure.

Kristy knocked the kitchen door open, walked to the opposite counter, and put down her tray with a bang. Wes and Delia, who were arranging more wineglasses on two platters, looked up at us.

"You are not going to believe," she said, "what just went down out there."

"Did something else break or spill?" Delia asked. "God! What is going on today?"

"No," Kristy said. Looking at her, I realized that I was upset, even hurt: but Kristy, she was *pissed.* "Do you know who's out there?"

Delia looked at the door. "Monica?"

"No. Macy's jerkwad boyfriend's father. And do you know what he did out there, in front of God and me and everybody?"

This time, neither Wes nor Delia offered any theories, instead just looking at me, then back at Kristy. Outside, I heard Mrs. Talbot trilling again.

"He said," she said, "that his stupid asshole son put their relationship on hold because she wasn't in line with his *goals.*"

Delia raised her eyebrows. I had no idea what Wes's reaction was, as I was making a concentrated effort not to look at him.

"And then," Kristy continued, reaching full throttle, "he ate half my shrimp plate. He insults my friend—to her face!—and then tries to go for shrimp. I wanted to sock him."

"But," Delia said carefully, "you didn't. Right?"

"No," Kristy replied, as Delia visibly relaxed again, "but I did cut him off. He's on crustacean restriction, from here on out. He tries another grab, he's getting a foot stomp."

"Oh, don't do that," Delia said, as I concentrated on a spot on the opposite wall, still trying to calm myself from the various shames that had been thrown my way in the last few minutes, "please God I'm begging you. Can't you just avoid him?"

"It's the principle of the thing," Kristy replied, piling more shrimp on her tray by the handful, "and no, I can't."

The door swung open again, and Monica ambled in, blowing her bangs out of her face. "Shrimp," she said flatly, looking at Kristy.

"I'm sure they do," she shot back, plunking another container of cocktail sauce and some napkins onto her tray. "Bastards."

"Kristy," Delia said, but she was already pushing back out the door, her tray on her palm, rising to shoulder level. As it swung shut, Delia looked around, somewhat desperately, then picked up a tray of filled wineglasses, lifting it carefully with both hands.

"Just to be on the safe side," she said, nudging the door open with her toe and glancing out at the living room, where I could see Kristy zipping past a group of people who were reaching, in vain, for her shrimp, "I'm going to make a pass around the room and keep an eye on her. Wes, grab that other tray of glasses. Monica, get another trayful of toasts out here. And Macy—"

I turned and looked at her, glad to have something else to focus on.

"I'm sorry," she said, and smiled at me so kindly I felt like it was a third shame, the biggest of all, even though I knew that wasn't how she intended it. Still, I felt something hurt in my heart as the door swung shut again, as if all the inadequacies I'd felt since Jason's email were no longer hidden away inside me but were as clear on my face as if they were written there.

After Delia left, the room seemed to feel smaller. Monica was slowly moving toasts onto her tray, while Wes finished pouring the wine behind me. I could see out the kitchen door to the garden and the road beyond it, and for a second I considered just pushing it open and walking out, could almost feel the grass under my feet, the sun on my face as I just left this behind.

Monica picked up her tray, then brushed past me and out the door. As it swung open, I heard a second of party noises and voices, and then it was quiet again. When I turned around to look at Wes he was already lifting his tray, arranging the glasses on it, clearly more concerned with keeping them balanced than with my various shortcomings. But then he looked at me.

"Hey," he said, and I felt some part of me brace, preparing for what came next, "are you—"

"I'm fine," I told him, my easy, knee-jerk answer. "It was nothing, just some stupid thing somebody said."

"—gonna be able to grab that other tray?" he finished.

Then we both shut up, abruptly: it was one of those moments when you're not sure what to respond to first, like a conversational photo finish where you're still waiting for the judges to weigh in.

"Yeah." I nodded at the tray behind him. "Go ahead, I'm right behind you."

"All right," he said. And then, for one second, he looked at me, as if maybe he should say more. But he didn't. He just walked to the door, pushing it open with his free hand. "I'll see you out there."

As he disappeared into the living room I caught another quick, slicing glimpse of the party, not enough to see much, but then I didn't have to, really. I knew Kristy was probably exacting the revenge she thought I was due, while Delia moved right behind her, making apologies and smoothing rough edges. Monica was most likely following her own path, either oblivious or deeply emotionally invested, depending on what you believed, while Wes worked the perimeter, always keeping an eye on everything. There was a whole other world out there, the Talbots' world, where I didn't belong now, if I ever had. But it was okay not to fit in everywhere, as long as you did somewhere. So I picked up my tray, careful to keep it level, and pushed through the door to join my friends.

"Delia," Kristy said, "just go, would you please? Everything's fine."

Delia shook her head, pressing one finger to her temple. "I'm forgetting something, I just know it. What is it?"

Her husband, Pete, who was standing by his car with his keys in hand, said patiently, "Is it that our dinner reservations were for ten minutes ago?"

"No," she snapped, shooting him a look. "It's something else. God, think, Delia. *Think.*"

Beside me, Kristy yawned, then looked at her watch. It was eight-thirty and, finally done with the academic cocktail party, we were amassed in the client's driveway, waiting to leave. We'd been all ready to go, and then Delia had that feeling.

"You know what I mean," she said now, snapping her fingers, as if that action might cause some sort of molecular shift that would jog her memory. "When you just know you're forgetting something?"

"Are you sure it's not a pregnancy thing?" Kristy asked.

Delia glared at her. "Yes," she said. "I'm sure."

We all exchanged looks. The closer Delia got to her due date, the angrier she became when anyone attributed anything—loss of memory, mood swings, her conviction that every room was always too hot, even when everyone else's teeth were chattering—to her condition.

"Honey," Pete said gently, tentatively reaching to put his hand on her arm, "our sitter is costing us ten bucks an hour. Can we please go to dinner? Please?"

Delia closed her eyes, still trying to remember, then shook her head. "Fine," she said, and with that one word, everyone began to scatter, Pete opening the door to their car, Kristy digging out her own keys, Wes starting toward the van, "but then I'll remember in five minutes, and it will be too late."

She was still muttering as she eased herself into the passenger seat of Pete's car, then pulled the seat belt across her belly, struggling to make it reach. As I got into the van with Wes, I watched them pull out of the driveway, then start down the road. I wondered, as they reached the stop sign there, if she'd already remembered. Probably.

"When is that baby due?" Kristy called out as she and Monica pulled up beside us. About fifteen minutes earlier, when the van was packed and we'd been paid, she'd disappeared for a few minutes into the garage, emerging in an entirely different outfit: a short denim skirt, a blouse with ribboned sleeves, and high-heeled platform sandals, her hair held up in a high ponytail. Not only was she versatile, I'd marveled as she did a little spin, showing it off, but quick. Clark Kent becoming Superman had nothing on her, and he didn't even have to worry about hair.

"July tenth," Wes told her, cranking the van's engine.

"Which leaves us," she said, squinting as she attempted to do the math for a second before giving up, "entirely too long before she gets normal again."

"Three weeks," I said.

"Exactly." She sighed, checking her reflection in the mirror. "Anyway, so listen. This party is in Lakeview. Take a right on Hillcrest, left on Willow, house at the end of the cul-de-sac. We'll see you guys there. Hey, and Macy?"

"Yeah?"

She leaned farther out the window, as if we were sharing a confidence, even though there was a fair amount of space, not to mention Wes, between us. "I have it on good authority," she said, her voice low, "that there will be extraordinary boys there. You know what I mean?"

Wes, beside me, was fiddling with his visor. "Um, no," I said.

"Don't worry." She put her car in gear, then pointed at me. "By the end of the night, you will. See you there!" And then, in a cloud of dust, the radio blasting, she was gone, hardly slowing for the stop sign at the end of the road.

"Well," Wes said, as we pulled out of the driveway with slightly less velocity, "to the party, then. Right?"

"Sure."

I tried, for the first five minutes or so of the drive, to come up with a witty conversation starter. Topics, from the inane to slightly promising, flitted through my brain as we moved along the quiet, mostly deserted country roads. Finally, when I couldn't stand the silence anymore, I opened my mouth, not even knowing what I was going to say.

"So," I began, but that was as far as I got. And, as it turned out, as far as we got.

The engine, which had been humming along merrily up until that point, suddenly began to cough. Then lurch. Then moan.

And then: nothing. We were stopped dead in the middle of the road.

For a second, neither of us said anything. A bird flew by overhead, its shadow moving across the windshield.

"So," Wes said, as if picking up where I'd left off, "*that's* what Delia forgot."

I looked at him. "What?"

He lifted his finger, pointing at the gas gauge, which was flat on the *E*. Empty. "Gas," he said.

"Gas," I repeated, and in my mind, I could hear Delia's voice, echoing this, finally remembering with a palm slapped to her forehead. *Gas.*

Wes already had his door open and was getting out, letting it fall shut behind him. I did the same, then walked around the van to the deserted road, looking both ways.

I'd heard people talk about being in the middle of nowhere, but it had always been an exaggeration. Now, though, as I took in the flat pastureland on either side of us, it seemed completely appropriate. No cars were in sight. I couldn't even see any houses anywhere nearby. The only light was from the moon, full and yellow, halfway up the sky.

"How far," I said, "would you say it is to the nearest gas station?"

Wes squinted back the way we'd come, then turned and looked ahead, as if gathering facts for a scientific guess. "No idea," he said finally. "Guess we'll find out, though."

We pushed the van over to the side of the road, then rolled up the windows and locked it. Everything sounded loud in the quiet: our footsteps, the door shutting, the owl that hooted overhead, making me jump. I stood in the middle of the road while Wes did a last check of the van, then walked over, his hands in his pockets, to join me.

"Okay," he said, "now we decide. Left or right?"

I looked one way, then the other. "Left," I said, and we started walking.

"Green beans," Wes said.

"Spaghetti," I replied.

He thought for a second, and in the quiet, all I could hear was our footsteps. "Ice cream," he said.

"Manicotti."

"What's with all the *I* words?" he said, tipping his head back and staring up at the sky. "God."

"I told you," I said. "I've played this game before."

He was quiet for a minute, thinking. We'd been walking for about twenty minutes, and not one car had passed. I had my cell phone with me, but Kristy wasn't picking up, Bert wasn't home, and my mother was at a meeting, so we were pretty much on our own, at least for the time being. After going along in silence for a little while, Wes had suggested that we play a game, if only to make the time pass faster. It was too dark for I Spy, so I suggested Last Letter, First Letter, which he'd never heard of. I even let him pick the category, food, but he was still struggling.

"Instant breakfast," he said finally.

"That's not food."

"Sure it is."

"Nope. It's a drink."

He looked at me. "Are you seriously getting competitive about this?"

"No," I said, sliding my hands in my pockets. A breeze blew over us, and I heard the leaves on the trees nearby rustling. "But it is a drink, not a food. That's all I'm saying."

"You're a rule person," he said.

"My sister was a cheater. It sort of became necessary."

"She cheated at this game?"

"She cheated at *everything*," I said. "When we played Monopoly, she always insisted on being banker, then helped herself to multiple loans and 'service fees' for every real estate transaction. I was, like, ten or eleven before I played at someone else's house and they told me you couldn't do that."

He laughed, the sound seeming loud in all the quiet. I felt myself smiling, remembering.

"During staring contests," I said, "she always blinked. *Always*. But then she'd swear up and down she hadn't, and make you go again, and again. And when we played Truth, she lied. Blatantly."

"Truth?" he said, glancing over his shoulder as something—another owl, I hoped—hooted behind us. "What's that?"

I looked at him. "You never played Truth, either?" I asked. "God, what did you guys do on long car trips?"

"We," he said, "discussed politics and current events and engaged in scintillating discourse."

"Oh."

"I'm kidding," he said, smiling. "We usually read comics and beat the crap out of each other until my dad threatened to pull over and 'settle things once and for all.' Then, when it was just my mom, we sang folk songs."

"You sang folk songs," I said, clarifying. Somehow I couldn't picture this.

"I didn't have a choice. It was like the lentil loaf, no other options." He sighed. "I know the entire Woody Guthrie catalog."

"Sing something for me," I said, nudging him with my elbow. "You *know* you want to."

"No," he said flatly.

"Come on. I bet you have a lovely singing voice."

"I don't."

"Wes," I said, my voice serious.

"Macy," he replied, equally serious. "No."

For a minute we walked in silence. Far, far off in the distance, I saw headlights, but a second later they turned off in another direction, disappearing. Wes exhaled, shaking his head, and I wondered how far we'd walked already.

"Okay, so Truth," he said. "How do you play?"

"Is this because you can't think up another *I* food?" I asked.

"No," he said indignantly. Then, "Maybe. How do you play?"

"We can't play Truth," I told him, as we crested a small hill, and a fence began on one side of the road.

"Why not?"

"Because," I said, "it can get really ugly."

"How so?"

"It just can. You have to tell the truth, even if you don't want to."

"I can handle that," he said.

"You can't even think of an *I* food," I said.

"Can you?"

"Ice milk," I said. "Italian sausage."

"Okay, fine. Point proved. Now tell me how to play."

"All right," I said. "But you asked for it."

He just looked at me. Okay, I thought. Here we go.

"In Truth," I said, "there are no rules other than you have to tell the truth."

"How do you win?" he asked.

"That," I said, "is such a boy question."

"What, girls don't like to win?" He snorted. "Please. *You're* the one who got all rule driven on me claiming Instant Breakfast isn't a food."

"It's not," I told him. "It's a beverage."

He rolled his eyes. I can't believe this, I thought. A week or two ago putting a full sentence together in front of Wes was a challenge. Now we were arguing about liquids.

"Okay," he said, "back to Truth. You were saying?"

I took in a breath. "To win, one person has to refuse to answer a question," I said. "So, for example, let's say I ask you a question and you don't answer it. Then you get to ask me a question, and if I answer it, I win."

"But that's too simple," he said. "What if I ask you something easy?"

"You wouldn't," I told him. "It has to be a really hard question, because you don't want me to win."

"Ahhh," he said, nodding. Then, after mulling it for a second he said, "Man. This is diabolical."

"It's a girl's game," I explained, tilting my head back and looking up at the stars. "Always good for a little drama at the slumber party. I told you, you don't want to play."

"No. I do." He squared his shoulders. "I can handle it."

"You think?"

"Yup. Hit me."

I thought for a second. We were walking down the center yellow line of the road, the moonlight slanting across us. "Okay," I said. "What's your favorite color?"

He looked at me. "Don't coddle," he said. "It's insulting."

"I'm trying to ease you in," I said.

"Don't ease. Ask something real."

I rolled my eyes. "Okay," I said. And then, without even really thinking about it, I said, "Why'd you get sent to Myers School?"

For a second, he was quiet, and I was sure I'd overstepped. But then he said, "I broke into a house. With a couple of guys I used to hang out with. We didn't take anything, just drank a couple of beers, but a neighbor saw us and called the cops. We ran but they caught us."

"Why'd you do that?"

"What, run?"

"No," I said, although I had to admit I was curious about that, too. "Break in."

He shrugged. "I don't know. These guys I was friends with, they'd done it a couple of times, but I never had before. I was there, so I went along." He ran a hand through his hair. "It was my first offense, my only offense, but the county was on this whole thing where they were punishing right off, to scare you out of doing more, so I got sent away. Six months, let out after four."

"My boyfriend," I said, then, feeling the need to correct myself, added, "sort-of boyfriend, he used to tutor there."

"Really."

I nodded. "Yup."

"So what's the deal with that," he asked. "The boyfriend."

"What?"

"I get to ask a question now," he said. "That's how the game goes, correct?"

"Um," I said. "Yes. I guess."

He waved his hand at me in a take-it-away sort of motion. Great, I thought, scanning the horizon for headlights. No such luck.

"I'm waiting," Wes said. "Does this mean you pass?"

"No," I snapped. "I mean, no. I'm answering. I'm just collecting my response."

Another few seconds passed.

"Is there a time limit for this?" he asked. I shot him a look. "Just wondering."

"Fine," I said, taking a breath. "We've been dating for about a year and a half. And he's just, you know, a genius. Really smart, and driven. He went away for the summer, and I was just, you know, being a little too clingy or something I guess, and it sort of freaked him out. He's very independent."

"Define clingy," he said.

"You don't know what clingy is?"

"I know what it means to me," he said. "But it's different for different people."

"Well," I said, then stopped, not sure how to explain. "First, he was upset that I wasn't taking my job, which had been his job, more seriously. And then, I said I loved him in an email, and that made him a little skittish."

"Skittish?"

"Do you need a definition of that, too?" I said.

"Nope. Know it." He tipped his head back, looking up at the

moon. "So things went sour because you said those three words, and because you weren't as serious about the library as he wanted you to be."

"Right," I said. Again, it sounded stupid, but of course everything does when you're just getting the bare bones facts, only the basics, without—and then it hit me. "Wait," I said. I stopped walking. "I never said anything about the library."

"Yeah, you did," he said. "You—"

"Nope." I was sure of it. "I didn't."

For a second we just stood there.

"Kristy," I said finally.

"Not exactly. I just heard you guys talking that night, out at the clearing."

I started walking again. "Well, now you've heard it twice. Although I think you should be penalized in some way, because you asked a question you already knew the answer to, and that is totally against the rules."

"I thought the only rule was you had to tell the truth."

I made a face at him. "Okay, so there are two rules."

He snorted. "Next you'll tell me there are service charges, too."

"What is your problem?" I asked.

"All I'm saying," he said, shrugging, "is that I vote that the second one be done away with."

"You don't get to *vote*," I said. "This is an established game."

"Clearly it isn't." He was so freaking stubborn, or so I was noticing. "You seem to be making up rules as you go."

"I am not," I said indignantly. He just looked at me, obviously not believing this, so I said, "Fine. If you're proposing a rule change, you have to at least present a case for it."

"That is so student council," he said with a laugh.

I was pretty sure this was an insult. "I'm waiting," I told him.

"You should be allowed to occasionally ask a question you know the answer to," he said, as I reflected how it was so like a guy to change the rules when he'd only just started playing, "so that you can be sure the other person is telling the truth."

And then we both saw it: headlights, in the distance. They came closer, even closer, and then finally swung left, disappearing down a side road. So close, and yet so far.

Wes sighed, shaking his head, then looked at me. "Okay, forget it," he said. "I drop my case. We tell the truth, or else. Okay?"

I nodded. "Fine with me."

"Go ahead then," he said. "It's your turn."

I thought for a second, really wanting to come up with something good. Finally I said, "Okay, fair's fair. What was the story with your last girlfriend?"

"My last girlfriend," he said, "or the girlfriend I have now?"

I had to admit I was surprised. Not just surprised, I realized, gauging the sudden drop in my stomach, but disappointed. But only for a second. Of course a boy like him had a girlfriend.

"The current girlfriend," I said. "What's the story there?"

"Well," he said. "To begin with, she's incarcerated."

I looked at him. "You're dating a prisoner?"

"Rehab." He said this so easily, the way I'd told people Jason was at Brain Camp, as if it was just that normal. "I met her at Myers. She was in for shoplifting, but since then she got busted with some pot, so now she's at Evergreen Care Center. At least until her dad's insurance runs out."

"What's her name?"

"Becky."

Becky. Becky the shoplifting pothead, I thought, and then immediately told myself I was being petty. "So it's serious," I said.

He shrugged. "She's been in and out of trouble for the last year, so we've hardly gotten to see each other. She says she hates for me to see her at Evergreen, so we're sort of waiting until she gets out to see what happens."

"And when's that?" I asked.

"End of the summer." He kicked at a rock, sending it skittering across the pavement. "Until then, everything's just sort of on hold."

"That's me, too," I said. "We're supposed to get together in August, when we'll know better whether we want the same things, or if it's best to make this break permanent."

He winced, listening to this. "That sounds verbatim."

I sighed. "It is. Right off the email he sent me."

"Ouch."

"I know."

So there we were, me and Wes, still walking, in the dark, on a break. It was weird, I thought, how much you could have in common with someone and, from a distance, never even know it. That first night at my mom's he'd just been a good-looking boy, one I figured I'd never see again. I wondered what he'd thought of me.

"Okay," he said, as we started up a hill lined by trees, "my turn."

I slid my hands in my pockets. "Okay, shoot."

"Why'd you really stop running?"

I felt myself take in a breath, like this had hit me in my gut: it was that unexpected. Questions about Jason I could handle, but this was something else. Something more. But we were playing Truth, and so far he'd played fair. It was dark and quiet, and we were alone. And suddenly, I found myself answering.

"The morning my dad died," I said, keeping my eyes on the road ahead, "he came into my room to wake me up for a run, and I was sleepy and lazy, so I waved him off and told him to go without me."

This was the first time, ever, that I'd told this story aloud. I couldn't even believe I was doing it.

"A few minutes later, though, I changed my mind." I stopped, swallowing. I didn't have to do this. I could pass, and if I lost, no big deal. But for some reason I kept going. "So I got up and went to catch up with him. I knew the route he'd take, it was the same one we always did. Out our neighborhood, a right on Willow, then another right onto McKinley."

Wes wasn't saying anything, but I knew he was listening. I could just tell.

"I was a little less than halfway into that first mile when I came over this ridge and saw him. He was lying on the sidewalk."

I felt him look at me, but I knew if I turned to face him I'd stop. So I just kept talking. My footsteps, our footsteps, were so steady. Keep going, I thought. Keep going.

"At first," I said, "it didn't even compute, you know? I mean, my mind couldn't put it together, even though it was right in front of my face."

The words kept coming, almost too fast, tumbling over my tongue like they'd been held back for so long that now, finally free, nothing could stop them. Not even me.

"I started running faster. I mean, faster than I ever had. It was adrenaline, I guess. I'd never run that fast in my life. Never."

All I could hear were our footsteps. And the quiet dark. And my voice.

"There was this man," I went on. "He was just some random guy who'd been on his way to the store, and he'd stopped and was trying to give my dad CPR. But by the time I got to him, he'd already given up. The ambulance came, and we went to the hospital. But it was too late."

And then it was done. Over. I could feel my breath coming quickly, through my teeth, and for a second I felt unsteady, as if with this story no longer held so closely against me, I'd lost my footing. Grief can be a burden, but also an anchor. You get used to the weight, to how it holds you to a place.

"Macy," he said quietly.

"Don't," I said, because I knew what came next, some form of "I'm sorry," and I didn't want to hear it, especially now, especially from him. "Please. Just—"

And then, suddenly, there was light. Bright yellow light, rising over the other side of the hill, splashing across us: instantly, we had shadows. We were both squinting, Wes raising one hand to shield his eyes. The car had a rumbling engine, and it seemed like it took forever to pull up beside us and slow to a stop.

"Hey." A man's voice came from behind the wheel. After all the brightness, I couldn't make out his face. "You kids need a ride someplace? What you doing out here?"

"Ran out of gas," Wes told him. "Where's the nearest station?"

The man jerked his thumb in the opposite direction. "About three miles that way. Where'd you break down?"

"About two miles that way," Wes told him.

"Well, get in then," he said, reaching to unlock the back

door. "I'll run you up there. You about scared me to death, though, walking out here in the dark. Thought you were deer or something."

Wes pulled open the door for me, holding it as I climbed in, then sliding in beside me. The car smelled like cigar smoke and motor oil, and as the man began to drive I could make out his profile: he had white hair and a crook nose, and drove slowly, almost as slowly as Bert. It was amazing we hadn't seen him coming. He'd just appeared, as if he'd dropped out of the sky or something.

As I leaned back against the seat, my heart felt like it was shaking: I couldn't believe what I'd just done. There was no way to take the story back, folding it neatly into the place I'd kept it all this time. No matter what else happened, from here on out, I would always remember Wes, because with this telling, he'd become part of that story, of my story, too.

"That you?" the man asked, glancing back at us in the rearview mirror as we passed the Wish van.

"Yes, sir," Wes replied.

"Well, you had no way to know, I guess," he said, and I wasn't sure what he meant until about a minute later, when we crested a hill, took a corner, and there was a gas station, all lit up. The neon sign in the window said, almost cheerfully, OPEN. "Had no idea how close you were."

"No," Wes said. "I guess we didn't."

As we pulled up to the station I turned to look at him, to say something, but he was already pushing open the door and getting out of the car, walking around to the trunk, where the man had a gas can. I sat there, the fluorescent light flickering overhead, as the man went inside to buy cigarettes and Wes pumped gas, his back to me, eyes on the numbers as they clicked higher and higher.

I turned my head and saw he was looking at me. In this, my first true glimpse of his face in over an hour, I braced myself for what I might see. After all, with Jason, anytime I'd opened up, he'd pulled back. I was prepared, even expecting it to happen again.

But as I looked at Wes, I saw only those same familiar features, even more so now, that same half-smile. He motioned for me to roll down the window.

"Hey," he said.

"Hey."

I waited. What came next? I wondered. What words would he say to try and make this better? "I thought of one," he said.

For a second, I just blinked at him. "What?"

"Iceberg lettuce," he said. Then he added, quickly, "And don't say it's not a food, because it is. I'm willing to fight you on it."

I smiled. "No fight," I told him. "It's a keeper."

The pump stopped then, and he hung the hose back up, screwing the top on the gas can. "Need anything?" he asked, and when I shook my head, he started toward the store.

I heard a buzzing under my feet: my phone. I unzipped my purse and pulled it out, hitting the Talk button as I raised it to my ear. "Hel—"

"Where *are* you?" Kristy demanded. I could hear party noises behind her, music and loud voices. "Do you know how worried we are? Monica's about sick, she's almost inconsolable—"

"We ran out of gas," I told her, switching the phone to my

other ear. "I left you a message. We were stuck out in the middle of nowhere."

"Message? I didn't get any—" A pause as, presumably, she actually checked for the first time. "Oh. Well. God! Where are you? Are you okay?"

"We're fine. We got a ride and we're getting gas for the van right now."

"Well, thank goodness." I heard her cover up the phone and relay this information to Monica, who, upset or not, I imagined would receive it with her same flat, bored expression. Then Kristy came back on. "Look, I gotta tell you, if I were you guys, I'd just go straight home. This party is a bust. And I was totally misled. There are *nothing* but ordinary boys here."

I turned and looked into the gas station, where Wes was now paying, as the man who'd driven us looked on. "That's too bad," I said.

"It's okay, though," she assured me. "Someday I'll show you an extraordinary boy, Macy. They do exist. You just have to believe me."

"Don't worry," I said. "I do."

Chapter Ten

My mother was stressed.

Truthfully, my mother was *always* stressed. I couldn't remember the last time I'd seen her actually relax and sit still in a way that made it obvious she wasn't already thinking about the next six things she had to do, and maybe the six after that. Once, she'd been a pro at decompressing, loved to sit on the back deck of the beach house in one of our splintery Adirondack chairs for hours at a time, staring at the ocean. She never had a book or the paper or anything else to distract her. Just the horizon, but it kept her attention, her gaze unwavering. Maybe it was the absence of thought that she loved about being out there, the world narrowing to just the pounding of the waves as the water moved in and out.

Everything about Wildflower Ridge led back to my mom. The original proposal for the development, the floor plans for each phase, the landscaping, the community organization; every decision was hers. So I was used to her cell phone joining us for dinner every night, sitting on the third place mat, accustomed to her being at the model home office late into the night, entirely unsurprised when I came home to find contractors, local business owners, or prospective home buyers sitting in our living room listening to a spiel about what makes Wildflower Ridge special.

Her current project was the townhouses, and for my mother they were especially important. She'd taken a risk by going for luxury, adding all kinds of fancy accoutrements like heated garages, marble bathrooms, balconies, and high-end appliances, all for the discerning, affluent professional. But just as she began building, the economy took a slide: there were layoffs, the stock market plummeted, and suddenly everyone was tentative with their dollars, especially when it came to real estate. Since she'd already started, she had no choice but to keep going, but her nervousness had driven her to work harder at making contacts and sales. Considering how many of her waking hours (i.e., all of them) were devoted to this already, it seemed close to impossible. Hence stress. Lots of it.

"I'm fine," she said to Caroline one morning a couple of days after my late night with Wes, as the three of us sat at the kitchen table. My sister was spending most of her time shuttling between her house in Atlanta, making sure Wally was eating enough vegetables while he battled some corporation in his law case, and the coast, where she conferred with the carpenter, dickered over fabric and paint chips, and, by the looks of the receipts I'd seen, bought up most of the inventory at Home Depot. In between, she'd taken to dropping in to show us pictures of the progress, ask for our opinions on decorating decisions, and tell my mother, repeatedly, that she needed to relax and take a vacation. Yeah, right.

"Mom," she said now, as I took a bite of cereal, "you're not fine. Are you even sleeping?"

"Of course I am," my mother said, shuffling through some papers. "I sleep like a baby."

That is, if she was sleeping at all. More than once lately I'd come downstairs at two or three A.M. only to see her in her office, still in her work clothes, typing away, or leaving voice-mail messages for her contractors or subs. I didn't know when she went to bed, but by the next morning when I was getting up for work she was always in the kitchen, showered and dressed in new clothes, already talking on her cell phone.

"I just want to be sure that when the house is done, you'll commit to this vacation," my sister said now, opening one of her beach-house folders and sorting through some photographs. "It looks like it's going to be August, probably the second week."

"Anytime after the seventh is fine," my mother said, moving her coffee cup aside to make a note on something with the pencil in her hand. "That's the gala for the opening of the town-houses."

"You're having a gala?" I said.

"Well, it's a reception," she told me, picking up her cell phone, then putting it down, "but I'm planning for it to be nicer and bigger than the sales events we've had here before. I'm renting a tent, and I've found this fantastic French caterer. . . . Oh, that reminds me, I've *got* to call about the kitchen faucets if I want to change them from ruby to diamond class."

And then she was up, pushing back her chair and starting across the kitchen, still muttering to herself. How she'd gotten from caterers to faucets was hard to say, but it was hard keeping up with her these days.

"So the eighth?" Caroline called after her. "Of August? I can write that down, it's firm?"

My mother, halfway through the door, turned her head. "The eighth," she said, nodding, "firm. Absolutely."

Caroline smiled, pleased with herself, as my mother disappeared down the hallway. She picked up her folder, tapping it on the tabletop to straighten its contents, then put it down in front of her again. "So it's set," she said. "The eighth to the fifteenth, we're officially on vacation."

I put my spoon down in my now empty bowl, finally realizing why this date had been ringing a bell in my head. It was the day after Jason was returning from Brain Camp: by then I'd know whether we were together or really over. But now it was only the end of June. The townhouses still needed windows, fixtures, landscaping. The beach house was going to be painted, the floors sanded, the new décor installed under my sister's watchful eye. The new would be new, the old, new again. What I'd be, on a break, broken, or otherwise, I had no idea. Luckily for all of us, though, we still had time.

Wes and I were friends now. And really, no one was more surprised than me.

Initially, the only thing we shared, other than working for Wish, was that we both had lost a parent. This was a lot to have in common, but it wasn't just about that anymore, either. The truth was, since our night stranded together, I felt comfortable around Wes. When I was with him, I didn't have to be perfect, or even try for perfect. He already knew my secrets, the things I'd kept hidden from everyone else, so I could just be myself. Which shouldn't have been such a big deal. But it was.

"Okay," he said to me one night, as we sat on the back deck rail at a party in the Arbors, a neighborhood just down from my own, "what's *that* about?"

I followed his gaze to the open sliding glass door that led

into the kitchen, where three girls I recognized from my school—the sort of girls who hung out in the parking lot after late bell, wearing sunglasses and cupping their hidden cigarettes against their palms—were staring at us. Or more specifically, at me.

"Well," I said, taking a sip of the beer I was holding, "I think they're just surprised to see me here."

"Really."

I nodded, putting my beer back on the rail. Inside, over the girls' heads, I could see Kristy, Bert, and Monica playing quarters at a long oak table in the dining room, the fancy centerpiece of which had been pushed aside and was now piled high with beer cans. More often than not at parties lately, I ended up sitting with Wes off to the side, while Kristy and everyone else trolled for extraordinary boys, or in Bert's case, desperate freshman girls. While they tried their luck and bemoaned the prospects, we on-a-break types just sat and shot the breeze, watching the party unfold around us.

"And they're surprised to see you here because . . ." Wes said, nodding at a guy in a baseball hat who passed by, saying his name.

"Because," I said, "they think I'm Miss Perfect."

"You?" he said, sounding so surprised I felt obligated to shoot him a look. "I mean, ah, I see."

I picked up my beer, taking another sip. "Shut up," I said.

"No seriously, this is interesting," he said, as the girls moved out onto the deck, disappearing behind a clump of people waiting in line at the keg. "Perfect as in . . ."

"Goody-goody," I said, "by association. Jason would never be here."

"No?"

"God, no."

Wes considered this for a second, as I noted at least six different girls around the deck checking him out. As much as I was getting used to this happening whenever I was with him, it was still a little unnerving. I'd lost count of how many dirty looks I'd gotten just by sitting next to him. We're not like that, I wanted to say to the girls who stared at me, slit-eyed, their eyes following me whenever I went to the bathroom or to find Kristy, waiting for me to be far enough away to move in. By now, though, I could spot who was and wasn't his type a mile off. The girl in the tight black dress and red lipstick, leaning against the keg? Nope. The one in the denim skirt and black T with the tan? Maybe. The one who kept licking her lips? Ugh. No. No. No.

"Let's say Jason was here," he said now. "What would he be doing?"

I considered this. "Probably complaining about the smoke," I said, "and getting very concerned about whether all these cans are going to be properly recycled. What about Becky?"

He thought for a second, pulling a hand through his hair. In the dining room, I could hear Kristy laughing loudly. "Passed out someplace. Or behind the bushes sneaking a smoke that she'd deny to me later."

"Ah," I said.

"Ah."

The girl in the tight black dress was passing by us now, eyeing Wes and walking entirely too slowly. "Hi," she said, and he nodded at her but didn't reply. Knew it, I thought.

"Honestly," I said.

"What?"

"Come on. You have to admit it's sort of ridiculous."

"What is?"

Now that I had to define it, I found myself struggling for the right words. "You know," I said, then figured Kristy had really summed it up best. "The sa-woon."

"The what?"

"Wes, come on," I said. "Are you seriously not aware of how girls stare at you?"

He rolled his eyes, leaning back on his palms. "Let's get back to the idea of you being perfect."

"Seriously. What's it like?"

"Being perfect? I wouldn't know."

"Not being perfect." I sighed. "Being . . ."

As I tried to come up with something, he flicked a bug off his arm.

". . . gorgeous," I finished. Two weeks earlier, this would have mortified me: I could just see myself bursting into flames from the shame. But now, I only felt a slight twinge as I took another sip of my beer and waited for him to answer.

"Again," he said, as the parking lot girls passed by, eyeing both of us, "I wouldn't know. You tell me."

"Donneven," I said, in my best Monica imitation, and he laughed. "We're not talking about me."

"We could be," he said, as I watched Bert take note of a group of what looked like ninth graders who had just come into the living room.

"I'm not gorgeous," I said.

"Sure you are."

I just shook my head, knowing this was him evading the

question. "You," I said, "have this whole tall, dark stranger thing going on. Not to mention the tortured artist bit."

"Bit?"

"You know what I mean."

He shook his head, clearly discounting this description. "And you," he said, "have that whole blonde, cool and collected, perfect smart girl thing going on."

"You're the boy all the girls want to rebel with," I said.

"You," he replied, "are the unattainable girl in homeroom who never gives a guy the time of day."

There was a blast of music from inside, a thump of bass beat, then quiet again.

"I'm not perfect," I said. "Not even close."

"I'm not tortured. Unless you count this conversation."

"Okay." I picked up my beer. "What do *you* want to talk about?"

"How about," he said, "that we've got an ongoing game of Truth to get back to?"

"How about," I said, as a guy from my English class stumbled by, looking sort of queasy, "not. I can't handle Truth tonight."

"You're only saying that," he said, "because it's my turn."

"It isn't. It's mine."

"It's—"

I said, "I asked you about Myers School, then you asked me about Jason. I countered with a question about Becky, and you asked me about running. Two rounds, my turn."

"See, *this* is why I don't hang out with smart girls," he said. Then he rubbed his hands together, psyching himself up, while I rolled my eyes. "Okay, go ahead. I'm ready."

"All right," I said, tucking a piece of hair behind my ear. "What's it like to always have girls swooning over you?"

He turned and looked at me. "Macy."

"You're the one who wanted to play."

He didn't say anything for a minute, and I wondered if he was going to pass. Too competitive, I thought, and I was right. "I don't know," he said. "It's not something I notice, if it's even happening."

"The name of the game," I told him, "is *Truth.*"

He turned and looked at me, annoyed. "Fine. It's weird. I mean, it's not like it counts or anything. They don't know me by looking, nobody does. It's totally surface. It's not real."

"Tell that to her," I said, nodding at the girl in the far corner, who was still ogling him.

"Funny," he muttered, making it a point to look away. "Is it my turn yet?"

"No, I have a follow-up question."

"Is that legal?"

"Yes," I said, with authority. Now I was Caroline, making up my own rules. "Okay, so if that's not real, what is? What counts, to you?"

He thought for a second, then said, "I don't know. Just because someone's pretty doesn't mean she's decent. Or vice versa. I'm not into appearances. I like flaws, I think they make things interesting."

I wasn't sure what answer I'd expected. But this wasn't it. For a second, I just sat there, letting it sink in.

"You know," I said finally, "saying stuff like that would make girls even crazier for you. Now you're cute *and* somewhat more attainable. If you were appealing before, now you're off the charts."

"I don't want to be off the charts," he said, rolling his eyes. "I do, however, want to be off this subject."

"Fine," I said. "Go ahead, it's your turn."

Inside, I could see Kristy chatting up some guy with dreadlocks, while Monica sat beside her, looking bored. Bert, for his part, was eyeballing the girl with the quarter, who, by my count, had now missed the cup six times in a row.

"Why is being perfect so important to you?"

I felt myself blink. "It's not," I said.

He narrowed his eyes at me. "What's this game called again?"

"That's the truth," I said. "I don't care that much about being perfect."

"Seems like you do."

"How do you figure?"

He shrugged. "Every time you've mentioned your boyfriend, you've said he was."

"Well, he is," I said. "But I'm not. That was part of the problem."

"Macy, come on." He looked at me. "I mean, what's perfect, anyway?"

I shook my head, lifting my beer to my lips. It was empty, but I needed something to do. "It's not about being perfect, really. It's about . . . I don't know. Being in control."

"Explain," he said, and I sighed.

"I don't know if I can," I told him. I glanced back at the dining room, looking for Kristy, a distraction, but she and Monica and Bert were gone, the table now deserted. "When my dad died, it was like everything felt really shaky, you know? And trying to be the best I could be, it gave me something to focus on. If I could just do everything right, then I was safe."

I couldn't believe I was saying this, not here, at a party packed with classmates and strangers. In fact, I couldn't imagine saying it anywhere, really, except in my own head, where it somehow made sense.

"That sucks, though," Wes said finally, his voice low. "You're just setting yourself up to fail, because you'll never get everything perfect."

"Says who?"

He just looked at me. "The world," he said, gesturing all around us, as if this party, this deck encompassed it all. "The universe. There's just no way. And why would you want everything to be perfect, anyway?"

"I don't want everything to be perfect," I said. Just me, I thought. Somehow. "I just want—"

"Curfew," I heard from beside me, and I looked up to see Monica standing there, blowing her bangs out of her face. She gestured to her watch, then to the kitchen, where I could see Bert and Kristy waiting for us.

"Saved by the bell," Wes said, hopping down off the rail. I slid down too, taking my time, my last three words still hovering in my mind. Here was a boy who liked flaws, who saw them not as failings but as strengths. Who knew such a person could even exist, or what would have happened if we'd found each other under different circumstances? Maybe in a perfect world. But not in this one.

—✳—

Oh, how I hated the info desk.

Before, it had been bad. Boring. Stifling. So quiet I was sure, if I listened hard enough, I could hear the blood moving through my veins, the plates of the earth shifting, time literally passing. Even if my day was going well, all it took was pushing open the doors of the library for everything to just stop. Sink. And stay that way for the full six hours I was stuck there.

One day, I was crossing to the periodical room, carrying a stack of moldy old *Nature* magazines. I'd just passed one of the stacks when I heard it.

"Gotcha!"

I jumped, startled. Not scared, since it had been more of a whisper, a low-key gotcha, which made sense once I stopped and leaned back, craning my neck, and saw Kristy. She was dressed in a white pleather skirt, a pink short-sleeved fuzzy sweater, and her white go-go boots, her hair pulled up high on her head. She was also wearing sunglasses, huge white ones, and carrying a fringed purse. She looked like she should be at the rodeo. Or maybe dancing in a cage. But not in fiction A-P, which is where she was.

"Hey!" she said, entirely too loudly: a man at the next shelf, whose arms were full of books, peered through at us. "How's it going?"

"What are you doing here?" I asked her, shifting the magazines to my other arm.

"Monica needed intellectual stimulation," she said, nodding across the library, where I could see Monica, chewing gum and looking exhausted, examining some books in nonfiction. "She's a total bookworm, inhales them. I'm more of a magazine gal myself, but I came along to see how you spent your days."

I glanced over at the info desk, where I could see Bethany on the phone, typing away at her keyboard. Amanda was beside her, looking at us. Or, to be more specific, at Kristy. "Well," I said, "this is it."

"Who's the braid?" she asked me, pushing her sunglasses up onto her head and staring back at Amanda, who was not dissuaded. I wondered if she thought we couldn't see her or something.

"That's Amanda," I said.

"Right." Kristy raised an eyebrow. "She's quite the starer, isn't she?"

"Apparently so."

Kristy crossed her eyes at Amanda, who seemed taken aback, quickly dipping her head down and opening a book in front of her. "I have to say, though, I'm digging that twin set. Is it merino wool?"

"I have no idea."

"I bet it is." She hitched her purse up on her shoulder. "So look, Monica and I are going to that new wrap place for lunch. You want to come?"

"Wrap place?" I asked. Now Bethany was off the phone, and she and Amanda had their heads together, talking. Every once in a while one of them would look up at us, then say something to the other.

"Yeah. It's at the mall. They'll put, like, anything in a tortilla for you. I mean, within reason. Can you come?"

I glanced at the clock. It was 11:45. "I don't know," I said, as Amanda pushed back from the info desk in her chair, sliding sideways, her eyes still on me, "I probably shouldn't."

"Why not? You do *get* lunch, don't you?"

"Well, yeah."

"And you have to eat, right?"

"I guess so," I said.

"So what's the problem?" she asked.

"It's complicated," I told her. "They don't like it when I take lunch."

"Who doesn't?"

I nodded toward Amanda and Bethany.

"And you care about that because . . ." Kristy said slowly.

"They intimidate me," I said. "I'm a loser. I don't know, pick one."

Kristy narrowed her eyes. "Intimidated?" she said. "Really?"

I fiddled with the magazines, embarrassed I'd even admitted this. "It's complicated."

"I just don't understand," she said, shaking her head. "I mean, they're so . . . unhappy. Why would they intimidate you?"

"They're not unhappy," I said.

"They're totally miserable!" She looked at them, saw them staring, and shook her head. "Look at them. Really. Look. Look right now."

"Kristy."

"Look." She reached up, cupping her fingers around my chin, and turned my head. Bethany and Amanda stared back at us. "Can't you see it? They're all milky and uptight-looking. I mean, I like a twin set as much as the next person, but you don't have to wear it like you have a stick up your ass. Clearly all the smarts in the world don't translate to good fashion sense. And God, what's with the staring?" She cleared her throat. "What,"

she repeated, her voice carrying easily across the room, "is with the staring. Huh?"

Bethany's face flushed, while Amanda's mouth opened, then shut again.

"Shh," someone said from the next row over.

"Oh, you shush," Kristy said, dropping her hand from my chin. "Macy," she said, her voice serious, "if that's ideal, they can have it. Right?"

Hearing this, I had no idea what to say.

"Then it's decided," Kristy said. "You'll take lunch, because you're human and you're hungry and most of all, you are not intimidated. We'll meet you outside at . . . what, noon? Is that when you get off?"

"Yeah," I said. Monica was walking across the library toward the front door now, a couple of books under her arm. "At noon."

"Cool. We'll see you in fifteen minutes." She glanced around again before leaning in closer to me, her voice softening. "I mean, you have to get out of here, right? Even if it's just for an hour. Too much time in a place like this could really do a person some damage. I mean, look what it's done to *them.*"

But I was thinking about what it had done to me. Being here, miserable, day after day. In so many ways, I was realizing, the info desk was a lot like my life had been before Wish and Kristy and Wes. Something to be endured, never enjoyed.

"I'll see you outside," she said to me, dropping her sunglasses back down to her face. Then she squeezed my arm and started toward the front doors. As she passed underneath the huge central skylight, the sun hit her, and for a second, it was like she was sparkling, the light catching her hair and glinting off, winking. I saw it. Bethany and Amanda did, too. So when I came back from lunch an hour later and walked up to the info desk to find them waiting for me, chairs aligned perfectly, it didn't bother me that they asked, haughtily, if I'd enjoyed lunch with my "friends" in such a way that I could hear the quotation marks. I didn't care that they snickered when I answered yes, or spoke in hushed tones. Because now, I didn't care what they thought. It wasn't new, this realization that I would never be like them. What was different now was that I was glad.

Chapter Eleven

"You know," I said, for what had to be the hundredth time since I'd gotten to Kristy's house two hours earlier, "I just think maybe I'll go home."

"Macy." Kristy turned around from the mirror, where she was examining the side view of her outfit: a short red skirt, a black strappy tank, and a pair of sandals that could only be described as ankle breakers. "I told you, there's no commitment for you here. It's just a bunch of us going out, not a big deal."

This was her latest version of the night's events. Every time I objected, it got more and more suspiciously innocuous. The basic gist was that Monica and Kristy had met a couple of guys at a day catering job while I'd been at the library who were, while not extraordinary, in Kristy's words, "promising." Both the guys worked delivering pizzas, so they could only meet up after curfew, which meant we had to wait until Stella dozed off in front of the TV, then sneak out. I'd gotten recruited that afternoon after we'd worked a job, when Kristy invited me over to spend the night. It wasn't until I was already there, under the impression we were actually going to stay in, that I'd been informed that the guys were bringing a third and had asked Kristy and Monica to do the same.

"I told you," I said, "I'm not interested—"

Monica, who was sitting by the window, about to light a cigarette, turned her head. “Now,” she said, nodding out the screen at something I couldn’t see. Kristy immediately moved over to stand behind her chair, bending down to peer out as well, waving her hand to indicate I should come join them.

“What is it?” I said, looking over Monica’s head. It was barely getting dark, and all I could see was the end of the sunset and the side of Stella’s garden, several rows of lettuce and some daylilies, with a path running between them.

“Just wait,” Kristy told me, her voice a whisper. “It happens every night, right about this time.”

I expected to see a bird, or maybe some unusual flower that only bloomed at dusk. Instead, after a second of staring, I heard something. A *thump, thump, thump* noise that was so familiar, and yet I couldn’t quite place it. But I knew it. It was—

“Mmm-hmmm,” Monica murmured, just as Wes came into view on the path. He was running, his pace quick and steady. He was in shorts, his shirt off, staring ahead as he passed. His back was tan and gleaming with sweat.

Beside me, I heard Kristy sigh, a long one that lasted all the way until he disappeared through a row of trees and around a turn, where I could see his own house in the distance. “Good God,” she said finally, fanning her face with her hand, “I’ve seen it a million times, but it just never gets old. Never.”

“Come on,” I said, as Monica nodded, seconding this. “It’s *Wes*.”

“Exactly.” Kristy turned and walked back to the mirror, bending in to inspect her cleavage. “I mean, there aren’t a lot of benefits to living out here in the middle of nowhere. But that is definitely one of them.”

I shook my head, exasperated, as I went over and sat down

on the bed. Monica lit her cigarette, reaching up to dangle it halfway out the window, the smoke curling up past the panes.

"Is that why you are being so difficult about tonight?" Kristy asked as she flopped down beside me, glancing through the open doorway down the hall at Stella. An hour earlier, when she'd settled in front of the TV, she'd begun dozing immediately. Now, by the looks of it, she'd moved on to full snooze.

"What?"

She nodded toward the window. "Our Wesley. I know you guys have some sort of weird thing going on, with that game you play and everything—"

"It's called a friendship," I said. "And no, it has nothing to do with that. I told you, I'm on a break. I'm not interested in hanging out with some new guy."

"Unless it's Wes," she said, clarifying.

I just looked at her. "That's different. He's in a relationship, too, so it's not weird or anything."

Her eyes widened. "Oh, my God!" she said, slapping a hand over her mouth. "I *totally* get it now."

"Get what?"

She didn't answer me. Instead, she leaned over the bed, rummaging beneath it for a few seconds. I could hear things clanking against each other—what did she have down there?—and glanced at Monica, who just exhaled, shrugging. Then Kristy lifted up her head.

"You and Wes," she said, triumphant, "are just like *this*."

She was holding a book, a paperback romance. The title, emblazoned in gold across the cover, was *Forbidden*, and the picture beneath it was of a man in a pirate outfit, eye patch and all, clutching a small, extremely busty woman to his chest. In the background, there was a deserted island surrounded by blue water.

"We're pirates?" I said.

She tapped the book with one fingernail. "This story," she said, "is all about two people who can't be together because of other circumstances. But secretly, they pine and lust for each other constantly, the very fact that their love is forbidden fueling their shared passion."

"Did you just make that up?"

"No," she said, flipping the book over to read the back cover. "It's right here! And it's totally you and Wes. You can't be together, which is exactly why you want to be. And why you can't admit it to us, because that would make it less secret and thus less passionate."

I rolled my eyes. Monica, across the room, said, "Hmmm," as if all of this actually made sense.

Kristy put the book on the bed between us. "I have to admit," she said wistfully, crossing her arms over her chest, "an unrequited love is so much better than a real one. I mean, it's perfect."

"Nothing's perfect," I said.

"Nothing *real*," she replied. "But as long as something is never even started, you never have to worry about it ending. It has endless potential." She sighed, the same way she'd sighed at seeing Wes running by without a shirt: with emphasis, and at length. "So romantic. No wonder you don't want to go out with Sherman."

I was distracted, thinking about what she'd said, until she got to this last part. "Sherman?" I said.

She nodded. "That's John and Craig's friend. He's visiting from Shreveport."

"Sherman from Shreveport?" I said. "This is the guy you're determined I go out with?"

"You can't judge a book by its cover!" she snapped. When I slid my eyes toward *Forbidden*, she grabbed it up, shoving it back under the bed. "You know what I mean. Sherman might be very nice."

"I'm sure he is," I said. "But I'm not interested."

She just looked at me. "Of course not," she said finally. "Why would you be, when you have your very own sexy, misunderstood pirate Silus Branchburg Turlock to pine for?"

"Who?"

"Oh, just forget it," she said, getting up and stomping out of the room. A second later the bathroom door swung shut with a bang. I looked at Monica, who was staring out the window, her face impassive as always.

"Sherman." Saying it aloud, it sounded even more ludicrous. "From Shreveport."

"Donneven?" she said slowly, exhaling.

"Exactly."

And so it was that at ten-fifteen, when John and Craig and Sherman from Shreveport pulled into the driveway, headlights flashing just once before going dark again, I crept outside, following Kristy down the stairs. Stella didn't stir as Monica eased the door shut behind us, then started over to the car, the guy in the passenger seat climbing out to meet her. Kristy waved at the driver, who waved back, then turned to me. There was someone else in the backseat, but I couldn't make out a face: just a form, leaning against the window.

"Last chance to change your mind," she said to me, her voice low.

"Sorry," I told her. "Maybe another time."

She shook her head, clearly not buying this, then pushed her purse up her arm. "Your loss," she said, but she squeezed my arm as she started over to the car. "Call me tomorrow."

"I'll do that," I said.

As she got closer, the guy driving smiled at her, then opened the back door. "Watch out for Sherman," he said as she started to get inside. "He started his night a few hours ago, and now he's already out."

"What?" Kristy said.

"Don't worry," the guy told her, getting back behind the wheel. "We think he puked up everything he had in him already. So you should be okay."

Kristy looked at the slumped body beside her, then at me, and I raised my eyebrows. She shrugged before pulling the door shut and waving to me as the car slowly backed out of the driveway and up to the road, the engine chugging softly.

Which left me alone in the quiet of Stella's garden. I was about to get into my car, then changed my mind, dropping my purse through my open window and instead starting down through the sunflowers and into the thick of the dark, fragrant foliage.

Everything in the garden felt so *alive.* From the bright white flowers that reached out like trailing fingers from dipping branches overhead all the way down to the short, squat berry bushes that lined the trail like stones, it was like you could feel everything growing, right before your eyes. I kept walking, taking in clumps of zinnias, petunias, a cluster of rosebushes, their bases flecked with white speckles of eggshells. I could see the roof of the doublewide over to my right, the road to my left, but the garden seemed thick enough to have pushed them back even farther on the periphery, as if once you entered it moved in to surround you, crowding up close to hold you there.

I could see something else up ahead, something metallic, catching the moonlight: there was a clearing around it, rimmed by bobbing rambler roses. Stepping through them, I found myself at the back of a sculpture. It was a woman; her arms were outstretched to the side, palms facing the sky, and lying across them were slim pieces of pipe, the ends curving downwards. I moved around it and stood in its shadow, looking up at the figure's head, which was also covered in the thin, twisted pipes, and crowned with a garland made of the same. Of course this was one of Wes's, that much was obvious. But there was something different, something I couldn't quite put my finger on. Then, I realized that the sculpture's hair and those bits of pipe it was holding all ended in a washer bisected by a tiny piece of metal: every one was a flower. Looking at it from the top, where the moonlight illuminated those curling pipes, to the bottom, where the sculpture's feet met the ground, I finally got it that this was Stella, the entire figure showing the evolution of that thick, loamy dirt moving through her hands to emerge in bloom after bloom after bloom.

"Macy?"

It was the gotcha of all gotchas. The gotcha of all *time*, even. Which somewhat justified the shriek that came out of my mouth, the way my heart leaped in my chest, and how these two events then repeated themselves when a flock of tiny sparrows, startled by my startling, burst forth from the sculpture's base and flew in dizzy circles, rising over the rosebushes and disappearing into the dark.

"Oh," I said, swallowing, "my God."

"Wow," Wes said. He was standing by the path, his hands in his pockets. "You really *screamed.*"

"You scared the shit out of me!" I said. "What are you doing out here, lurking around in the dark?"

"I wasn't lurking," he said. "I've been calling your name for five minutes at least, ever since you walked in here."

"You have not."

"I really have been," he said.

"You have not," I said. "You snuck up and got your big gotcha and now you're just so happy."

"No," he replied slowly, as if I were a toddler having a totally unjustified tantrum, "I was on my way out and I saw you dropping your purse through the window. I called your name. You didn't hear me."

I looked down at the ground, my heart calming now. And then a breeze gusted up over us, the flowers behind Wes leaning one way, then the other. I heard a whirring noise above me and looked up at the sculpture. As the wind blew, the curved flowers in the figure's hands began spinning, first slowly, then faster, as the garland on her head began to do the same.

Wes and I just stood there, watching it, until the wind died down again. "You really scared me," I said to Wes, almost embarrassed now.

"I didn't mean to."

"I know."

Everything was settling back to how it had been: my heart, the flowers in the figure's hand and her garland, even the sparrows, which were now clustered on the rosebushes behind me, waiting to come back home. I started back over to the path, Wes holding aside one trailing branch so I could step through.

"Let me make it up to you," he said, as he fell in step behind me.

"You don't have to," I said.

"I know I don't have to. I want to. And I know just the way."

I turned back and looked at him. "Yeah?" I asked.

He nodded. "Come on."

Apologies come in all shapes and sizes. You can give diamonds, candy, flowers, or just your deepest heartfelt sentiment. Never before, though, had I gotten a pencil that smelled like syrup. But I had to admit, it worked.

"Okay," I said. "You're forgiven."

We were at the World of Waffles, which was located in a small, orange building right off the highway. I'd driven by it a million times, but it had never occurred to me to actually stop there. Maybe it was the rows of eighteen-wheelers that were always parked in the lot, or the old, faded sign with its black letters spelling out Y'ALL COME ON. But now I found myself here, just before eleven on a Saturday night, holding my peace offering, a pencil decorated with waffles, scented with maple, that Wes had purchased for me at the gift shop for $1.79.

The waitress came up as I lifted my menu off the sticky table, pulling a pen out of her apron. "Hey there, sugar," she said to Wes. She looked to be about my mother's age, and was wearing thick support hose and nurses' shoes with squeaky soles. "The usual?"

"Sure," he said, sliding his menu to the edge of the table. "Thanks."

"And you?" she asked me.

"A waffle and a side of hash browns," I told her, and put my menu on top of his. The only people in there other than us were an old man reading a newspaper and drinking endless cups of coffee and a group of drunken college students who kept laughing loudly and playing Tammy Wynette over and over on the jukebox.

I picked up my pencil, sniffing it. "Admit it," Wes said, "you can't believe you've gotten this far in life without one of those."

"What I can't believe," I said, putting it back down on the table, "is that you're *known* at this place. When did you start coming here?"

He sat back in the booth, running his finger along the edge of the napkin under his knife and fork. "After my mom died. I wasn't sleeping much, and this is open all night. It was better than just driving around. Now I'm sort of used to it. When I need inspiration, I always come here."

"Inspiration," I repeated, glancing around.

"Yeah," Wes said, emphatically, as if it was obvious I wasn't convinced. "When I'm working on a piece, and I'm kind of stuck, I'll come here and sit for awhile. Usually by the time I finish my waffle I've figured it out. Or at least started to."

"What about that piece in the garden?" I said. "What did that come from?"

He thought for a second. "That one's different," he said. "I mean, I made it specifically for someone."

"Stella."

"Yeah." He smiled. "She made the biggest fuss over it. It was to thank her, because she was really good to Bert and me when my mom was sick. Especially Bert. It was the least I could do."

"It's really something," I told him, and he shrugged, that way

I already recognized, the way he always did when you tried to compliment him. "All of your pieces have the whirligig thing going on. What's that about?"

"Look at you, getting all meaning driven on me," he said. "Next you'll be telling me that piece is representative of the complex relationship between agriculture and women."

I narrowed my eyes at him. "I am not my sister," I said. "I just wondered, that's all."

He shrugged. "I don't know. The first stuff I did at Myers was just basic, you know, static. But then, once I did the heart-in-hand stuff, I got interested in how things moving made a piece look different, and how that changes the subject. How it makes it seem, you know, alive."

I thought back to how I'd felt as I started into Stella's garden earlier that night, that tangible, ripe feeling of everything around you somehow breathing as you did. "I can see that," I said.

"What were you doing out there, anyway?" he asked. Across the restaurant, the jukebox finally fell silent.

"I don't know," I said. "Ever since the first day Kristy brought me there, it's sort of fascinated me."

"It's pretty incredible," he said, sipping his water. The heart in hand on his upper arm slid into view, then disappeared again.

"It is," I said, running my finger down the edge of the table. "Plus, it's so different from anything at my house, where everything is just so organized and new. I like the chaos in it."

"When Bert was a kid," Wes said, sitting back in his seat and smiling, "he got lost in that garden, trying to take the shortcut back from the road. We could all hear him screaming like he was stranded in the jungle, but really he was about two feet from the edge of the yard. He just lost his bearings."

"Poor Bert," I said.

"He survived." He slid his glass in a circle on the table. "He's tougher than he seems. When my mom died, we were all most worried about him, since he was only thirteen. They were really close. He was the one who was there when she found out about the cancer. I was off at Myers. But Bert was a real trooper. He stuck by her, even during the bad parts."

"That must have been hard for you," I said. "Being away and all."

"I was back home by the time things really got bad. But still, I hated being locked up when they needed me, all because of some stupid thing I'd done. By the time I got out, all I knew was that I never wanted to feel like that again. Whatever else happened, to Bert or anyone, I was going to be there."

The waitress was approaching the table now, a plate in each hand. On cue my stomach grumbled, even though I hadn't thought I was hungry. She deposited the plates with a clank, gave us each a quick second to ask for something else, and then shuffled off again.

"Now, see," Wes said, nodding at my plate, "this is going to blow your mind."

I looked at him. "It's a waffle, not the second coming."

"Don't be so sure. You haven't tasted it yet."

I spread some butter on my waffle, then doused it with syrup before cutting off a small bite. Wes watched as I put it in my mouth. He hadn't even started his yet, as if first, he wanted to hear my verdict. Which was, pretty good. Damn good, actually.

"Knew it," he said, as if he'd read my mind. "Maybe not the second coming, but a religious experience of sorts."

I was on my second bite now, and tempted to totally agree

with this. Then I remembered something, and smiled.

"What?" he said.

I looked down at my plate. "What you just said, that's so funny. It reminded me of something my dad always used to say."

He popped a piece of waffle in his mouth, waiting for me to go on.

"We never went to church," I explained, "even though my mother always thought we should, and she was always feeling guilty about it. But my dad loved to cook big breakfasts on Sunday. He said that was his form of worship, and the kitchen was his church, his offering eggs and bacon and biscuits and . . ."

"Waffles," Wes finished for me.

I nodded, feeling a lump rise in my throat. How embarrassing, I thought, to suddenly be on the verge of tears at a truck stop waffle house with Tammy Wynette in the background. But then I thought how my dad would have loved this place, probably even loved Tammy Wynette, and the lump just grew bigger.

"My mom," Wes said suddenly, spearing another piece of his own waffle, "was the one who first brought me here. We used to stop on the way back from Greensboro, where my grandmother lived. Even during the health-food phase, it was a sort of ritual. This was the only place she'd ever eat something totally unhealthy. She'd get the Belgian waffle with whipped cream and strawberries and eat every bit of it. Then she'd complain the entire way home about how sick she felt."

I smiled, taking a sip of my water. The lump was going away now. "Isn't it weird," I said, "the way you remember things, when someone's gone?"

"What do you mean?"

I ate another piece of waffle. "When my dad first died, all I could think about was that day. It's taken me so long to be able to think back to before that, to everything else."

Wes was nodding before I even finished. "It's even worse when someone's sick for a long time," he said. "You forget they were ever healthy, ever okay. It's like there was never a time when you weren't waiting for something awful to happen."

"But there was," I said. "I mean, it's only been in the last few months that I've started remembering all this good stuff, funny stuff about my dad. I can't believe I ever forgot it in the first place."

"You didn't forget," Wes said, taking a sip of his water. "You just couldn't remember right then. But now you're ready to, so you can."

I thought about this as I finished off my waffle. "It was hard, too, I think, because after my dad died my mom kind of freaked and cleaned out all his stuff. I mean, she threw out just about everything. So in a way it was like he'd never been there at all."

"At my house," Wes said, "it's the total opposite. My mom is, like, everywhere. Delia packed a lot of her stuff into boxes, but she got so emotional she couldn't do it all. One of her coats is still in the hall closet. A pair of her shoes is still in the garage, beside the lawn mower. And I'm always finding her lists. They're everywhere."

"Lists?" I said.

"Yeah." He looked down at the table, smiling slightly. "She was a total control freak. She made lists for everything: what she had to do the next day, goals for the year, shopping, calls she had to return. Then she'd just stuff them somewhere and forget about them. They'll probably be turning up for years."

"That must be sort of weird," I said, and then, realizing this didn't sound right, added, "or, you know, good. Maybe."

"It's a little of both." He sat back in the booth, tossing his napkin on his now empty plate. "It freaks Bert out, but I kind of like it. I went through this thing where I was sure they meant something, you know? If I found one, I'd sit down with it and try to decipher it. Like picking up dry cleaning or calling Aunt Sylvia is some sort of message from beyond." He shrugged, embarrassed.

"I know," I said. "I did the same thing."

He raised his eyebrows. "Really."

I couldn't believe I was about to tell him this. But then the words were just coming. "My dad was, like, addicted to those gadgets they sell on late-night TV. He was always ordering them, things like that doormat with the sensor that lets you know when someone's about to—"

"The Welcome Helper," he finished for me.

"You know it?"

"No." He smiled. "Yes, of course. Everyone's seen that freaking commercial, right?"

"My dad bought all that stuff," I told him. "He couldn't help himself. It was like an addiction."

"I've always wanted to order that coin machine that sorts things automatically," he said wistfully.

"Got it," I told him.

"No way."

I nodded. "Anyway, after he died, the company kept sending them. I mean, every month a new one shows up. But for awhile,

I was convinced it meant something. Like my dad was somehow getting them to me, like they were supposed to mean something."

"Well," Wes said now, "you never know. Maybe they do."

I looked at him. "Do what?"

"Mean something," he said.

I looked out the window, where car lights were blurring past distantly on the highway. It was after midnight, and I wondered where so many people were going. "I keep them," I said softly, "just in case. I can't bear to throw them out. You know?"

"Yeah," he said. "I know."

We stayed there for another hour. In that time, customers came and went all around us. We saw families with sleeping babies, truckers stopping in before the next leg, one young couple who sat in the booth across from us with a map spread out between them, tracing with their fingers the route that would take them to wherever they were going next. All the while, Wes and I just sat there, talking about anything and everything. I couldn't remember the last time I'd talked so much, really talked. Maybe I never had.

Still, I beat Kristy to Stella's by about ten minutes. I'd just waved good-bye to Wes and slipped inside, past where Stella was still sleeping, when the guys dropped her and Monica off in the driveway. By the time she got to her room, carrying her shoes, I'd already spread the sleeping bag she'd pulled out for me earlier on the floor next to her bed and changed into my pajamas. She looked entirely unsurprised to see me.

"Good night?" I asked, as she pulled off her skirt and top, exchanging them for a T-shirt and a pair of boxer shorts.

"No." She sat down on the bed, pulled a container of cold

cream out of the bedside table, and began smearing it all over her face. When it was half covered, she said, "Let me just say this: Sherman, even though he was passed out the entire time, was the best of the lot."

"Ouch."

She nodded, screwing the cap back on the container. "Those boys *wished* they were even ordinary. I mean, it's so disappointing. What's worse than ordinary? I feel like I'm working backwards now."

"Oh, that's not true," I told her. "It was just one bad night."

"Maybe so." She stood up and went to the door. "But a girl could lose heart in this world. That's all I'm saying, you know?"

As she went to the bathroom to wash her face, I stretched out on the sleeping bag. If I looked up through the window behind me, I could see the garden and the moon above it. Soon, though, I was too tired to do even that, instead just closing my eyes, only aware of Kristy returning by the sound of the door sliding shut and the loud sigh she emitted as she crawled into her bed.

"It just sucks," she said, yawning, "when a night is over and you have not one damn thing to show for it. Don't you hate that?"

"Yeah," I said. "I do."

She harrumphed again, turning over and fluffing her pillow. "Good night, Macy," she said after a second of quiet. Her voice sounded sleepy. "Sweet dreams."

"You too. Good night."

A minute later I could hear her breathing grow steady: she fell asleep that fast. I just lay there for a few minutes, staring up at that moon behind my head, then reached beside the sleeping bag for my purse, rummaging around until I found what I was looking for. Then, in the dark, I wrapped my fingers more tightly around what I had to show for my evening—a pencil that smelled like sugar and syrup. In the morning, when I woke up with the sun spilling over me, it was still in my hand.

"Macy? Is that you?"

I put my shoes down on the bottom step of the landing, laying my purse beside them. My mother was usually up first thing on weekend mornings, leaving soon after for the model home to greet potential homeowners. Now, though, it was almost ten, and I could see her in the recliner by the window, drinking a cup of coffee and reading a real estate magazine. She looked idle and still, which she never was. Ever. So she had to be waiting for me.

"Um, yeah," I said. As I walked across the foyer, I instinctively tucked in my shirt, then reached up to smooth my hair, running a finger down the part. "Kristy made breakfast, so I stayed longer than I planned. What are you doing home?"

"Oh, I just decided to take an hour or so to get caught up here." She put her magazine on the table beside her. "Plus I just feel like it's been ages since we've had a chance to talk. Come sit down, tell me what's going on."

I had a flashback, suddenly, to being at the top of the stairs and watching Caroline come down after a night out, then have to make her way to the living room, where my mom was always waiting to begin a "discussion." It was always a bit tense, that feeling of certain friction to come in the air. Kind of like this.

I came over and sat down on the couch. The sunlight was slanting through the window, bright and piercing, and in it I felt especially exposed, as if every little flaw, from my mussed hair to my chipped toenail polish, was especially noticeable. I wanted to scoot over to the chair or the ottoman, but thought this would attract even more attention. So I stayed where I was.

"So," my mother said, "how was work yesterday?"

"Good." She was looking at me, waiting for more, so I said, "Fun. It was a prewedding thing, which means everyone's either all hung over from the rehearsal dinner or freaking out about last-minute details. This time, it was both. So it was a little crazy. And then, you know, we had this whole thing with the crepes catching on fire, but that really wasn't our fault. Entirely."

My mother was looking at me with an expression of polite but detached interest, as if I were describing the culture of a foreign country she would never visit in a million years. "Well," she said, "you certainly have been putting in a lot of hours catering lately."

"Not that many," I said. Then, realizing I sounded defensive—did I sound defensive?—I added, "I mean, it's just been busy the last couple of weeks because Delia's booked a lot of jobs before the baby comes. Pretty soon I won't have anything to do, probably."

My mother slid the magazine off her lap and onto the couch. "You'll still have the info desk, though," she said. "Right?"

"Oh, yeah, right," I said, too quickly. "I mean, yes. Of course."

A pause. Too long of a pause for my taste.

"So how is the library?" she said finally. "You hardly mention it anymore."

"It's okay. Just, you know, the same." This was definitely the truth. My days at the library had not improved at all in the last few weeks. The difference was it just bothered me less. I put in my time, avoided Bethany and Amanda as much as possible, and got out of there the minute the big hand hit three. "It's work. If it was fun, they'd call it fun, right?"

She smiled, nodding. Uh-oh, I thought. I just knew there was something coming. I was right.

"I was out for a lunch meeting yesterday, and I saw Mrs. Talbot," she said now. "She told me that Jason is really enjoying the Scholars' Retreat he's on this summer."

"Really," I replied, reaching up to smooth my part again.

"She also said," she continued, crossing her legs, "that Jason told her you two are taking a break from your relationship for the summer."

Oh, great, I thought. "Um, yeah," I said. "I mean, yes."

For a second, it was so quiet I could hear the refrigerator humming. I remembered these awkward pauses from Caroline's homecomings, as well. It was now, in the empty spaces between accusations and defenses, that I had always wondered what, exactly, was happening.

"I was surprised," she said finally, "that you didn't mention it to me. She said this happened weeks ago."

"Well, it *is* just a break," I told her, trying to make my voice sound cheery, confident. "We're going to talk as soon as he gets back. We both just thought for now it was the best thing to do."

My mother put her hands in her lap, folding them around each other, and leaned forward slightly. I knew that stance. I'd seen it at a million sales cocktails. She was moving in. "I have to say, Macy," she began, and I felt something inside me start to deflate slightly, "that I'm a little bit concerned about you right now."

"Concerned?" I said.

She nodded, keeping her eyes on me. "You've been out an awful lot of nights lately with your new friends. You're working so many hours catering that I fear you're not giving your full attention to the library job, which is your most important commitment in terms of your college transcript."

"I haven't missed a single day there," I told her.

"I know you haven't. I'm just . . ." she trailed off, glancing out the window. Now the sun was on her face, and I could immediately make out tiny lines around her eyes, how tired she looked. Not for the first time, I felt a stab of worry, totally overreacting I knew, that maybe she was pushing herself too hard. I hadn't noticed with my dad. Neither of us had. "This coming year is so *important* for you, in terms of college and your future. It's crucial that you do well on your SATs and are focused on your classes. Remember how you told me you wanted to be working toward preparing for those goals this summer?"

"I am," I said. "I've been studying my words and taking practice tests online."

Another glance out the window. Then she said, "You've also been spending nights out with your friend Christine—"

"Kristy," I said.

"—as well as a bunch of other new friends I haven't met and don't know." She looked down at her hands, folding and unfolding them in her lap. "And then I hear this about you and Jason. I just wonder why you didn't feel like you could tell me about that."

"It's just a break," I said, "and besides, Jason doesn't have anything to do with my goals. They're totally separate things."

"Are they, though?" she asked. "When you were with Jason, you were home more. Studying more. Now I hardly see you, and

I can't help but wonder if the two are connected somehow."

I couldn't argue with that. In the last few weeks, I *had* changed. But in my mind, those changes had been for the better: I was finally getting over things, stepping out of the careful box I'd drawn around myself all those months ago. It was a good thing, I thought. Until now.

"Macy," she said, her voice softening. "All I'm saying is that I want to be sure your priorities are straight. You've worked so hard to get where you are. I don't want you to lose that."

Again, I could agree with this. But while for her it meant how I'd pushed myself to be perfect, gotten good grades, scored the smart boyfriend, and recovered from my loss to be composed, together, fine just fine, for me, it worked in reverse. I'd been through so much, falling short again and again, and only recently had found a place where who I was, right now, was enough.

This was always the problem with my mother and me, I suddenly realized. There were so many things we thought we agreed on, but anything can have two meanings. Like sides of a coin, it just matters how it falls.

"I don't want that either," I said.

"Good. Then we're on the same page. That's all I wanted to be sure of." She smiled, then squeezed my hand as she stood up, our accepted sign of affection. As she started toward her office, I headed for the stairs and my room. I was halfway there when she called after me.

"Honey?"

I turned around. She was standing at her office door, her hand on the knob. "Yes?"

"I just want you to know," she said, "that you can talk to me about things. Like Jason. I want you to feel like you can share things with me. Okay?"

I nodded. "Okay."

As I climbed the stairs, I knew that my mother had already moved on to the next challenge, this issue now filed under Resolved. But for me, it wasn't that simple. Of course she'd think I could tell her anything: she was my mother. In truth, though, I couldn't. I'd been wanting to talk to her for over a year about what was bothering me. I'd wanted to reach out to her, hold her close, tell her I was worried about her, but I couldn't do that either. So it was just a formality, what we'd just agreed on, a contract I'd signed without reading the fine print. But I knew what it said. That I could be imperfect, but only so much. Human, but only within limits. And honest, to her or to myself, never.

When I got to my room, I found a shopping bag sitting in the center of my bed with a note propped up against it. I recognized the loopy, flowing script even from a distance: Caroline.

Hi Macy,

Sorry I missed you. I'll be back in a couple of days, hopefully with a good progress report of the renovation. I forgot when I was here last time to drop this off for you. I found it in the bedroom closet of the beach house the last time I was there, when I was cleaning stuff out. I'm not sure what it is (didn't want to open it) but I thought you should have it. I'll see you soon.

It was signed with a row of *X*s and *O*s, as well as a smiley face. I sat down on the bed next to the bag, opening the top. I took one glance, then shut it, quick.

Oh, God, I thought.

In that one glimpse, I'd seen two things. Wrapping paper—gold, with some pattern—and a white card with my name written on it. In another hand I recognized, would know anywhere. My dad's.

More to come, the card he'd given me that Christmas Day, the last day I'd had with him, had said. *Soon*. So my missing present wasn't an EZ gift after all, but this.

I reached to open the bag, then stopped myself. As much as I wanted to, I couldn't unwrap it now, I realized, because no matter what it was, it would disappoint me. All this time it wasn't a gift I'd wanted: it was a sign. So maybe it was best to let this, of all things, have endless potential.

I pulled my chair over to the closet, took the bag, and pushed it up and over next to the box with the EZ products. Whatever it was, it had waited a long time to find me. A little bit longer wouldn't make that much of a difference.

Chapter Twelve

"Whose turn is it to ask?"

"Yours," Wes said to me.

"Are you sure?"

He nodded, cranking the van's engine. "Go ahead."

I sat back in my seat, tucking one foot underneath me as we pulled out of Delia's driveway and started down Sweetbud Road. We'd won the toss, which meant we got to go wash the van, while Bert and Kristy were stuck making crab cakes. "Okay," I said, "what's your biggest fear?"

As always, he took a second to think about his answer. "Clowns," he said.

"Clowns."

"Yup."

I just looked at him.

"What?" he said, glancing over at me.

"That is not a real answer," I told him.

"Says who?"

"Says me. I meant a real *fear*, like of failure, of death, of regret. Like that. Something that keeps you awake nights, questioning your very existence."

He thought for a second. "Clowns."

I rolled my eyes. "Please."

"That's my answer." He slowed down, edging carefully

around the hole. I glanced at the heart in hand, which was still, shimmering in the heat. "I don't like clowns. They scare the shit out of me, ever since I went to the circus as a kid and one popped a balloon right in my face."

"Stop it," I said, smiling.

"I wish I could."

We were at the end of the road now, a cloud of dust settling all around us.

"Clowns," I repeated. "Really?"

He nodded. "Are you going to accept it as my answer, or not?"

"Is it the truth?"

"Yeah. It is."

"Fine," I said. "Then it's your turn."

I knew a lot about Wes now. That he'd gotten his first kiss from a girl in sixth grade named Willa Patrick. That he thought his ears were too big for his head. And that he hated jazz, wasabi, and the smell of patchouli. And clowns.

The game we'd begun the night we were stranded was ongoing: whenever we found ourselves alone, driving to a job or prepping silverware or just hanging out, we picked it up automatically where we'd left off the last time. When everyone else from Wish was around, there was noise and drama and laughter and chaos. But times like these, it was just me, Wes, and the truth.

When I'd first started playing Truth, back in my slumber party days, it had always made me nervous. Wes was right in saying it was diabolical: the questions asked were always personal or embarrassing, preferably both. Often, playing with my friends or sister, I'd choose to pass on a question and lose rather than have to confess I was madly in love with my math teacher. As I got older, the games were even more brutal, with questions revolving around boys and crushes and How Far You'd Gone. But with Wes, Truth was different. He'd asked me the hardest question first, so all that followed were easier. Or somewhat easier.

"What," he asked me one day, as we walked through Milton's Market looking for paper towels, "is the grossest thing that's ever happened to you?"

"Ew," I said, shooting him a look. "Is this really necessary?"

"Answer or pass," he told me, sliding his hands in his pockets.

He knew I wouldn't pass. He wouldn't either. We were both totally competitive, but really, there was more to it than that, at least for me. I liked this way of getting to know him, these random facts and details, each one like a puzzle piece I examined carefully, figuring out how it fit in with the rest. If either of us won, it would all be over. So I had to keep answering.

"Fifth grade," I said, as we turned onto the paper product aisle. "It was December, and this woman came in to talk to us about Hanukkah. I remember she gave us gelt."

"That's the gross part?"

"No," I said, shooting him a look. "I'm getting to it." Being so economical with his own words, Wes was always prodding me to hurry up and get to the point, to which I responded by padding my story that much more. It was all part of the game. "Her name was Mrs. Felton, Barbara Felton's mom. Anyway, so we got gelt, we were talking about the menorah. Everything was fine."

We were at the paper towels now. Wes pulled an eight-pack

off the shelf, tucking it under his arm, then handed me another one, and we started toward the registers.

"Then," I said, "my teacher, Mrs. Whitehead, comes up to Norma Piskill, who's sitting beside me, and asks if she's okay. And Norma says yes, although looking at her, I notice she's a little green."

"Uh-oh," he said, making a face.

"Exactly." I sighed. "So the next thing I know, Norma Piskill is trying to get up, but she doesn't make it. Instead, she pukes all over me. And then, as I'm standing there dripping, she does it again."

"Yuck."

"You asked," I said cheerfully.

"I did," he agreed, as we got in line. "Your turn."

"Right." I thought for a second. "What do you worry about most?"

As always, he paused, considering this. From vomit to deep introspection: this was how Truth worked. You either went with it, or you didn't. "Bert," he said flatly, after a second.

"Bert," I repeated.

He nodded. "I just feel responsible for him, you know? I mean, it's a big brother thing. But also with my mom gone. . . . She never said so but I know she was counting on me to take care of him. And he's so . . ."

"So what?" I asked as the cashier scanned the towels.

He shrugged. "So . . . Bert. You know? He's intense. Takes everything really seriously, like with all his Armageddon stuff. A lot of people his age, you know, they just don't *get* him. Everything he feels, he feels strongly. Too strongly, sometimes. I think he freaks people out."

"He's not that bad," I said, as he handed the cashier a twenty and got change. "He's just . . ." And now I was at a loss, unable to find the right word.

"Bert," he finished for me.

"Exactly."

And so it went. Question by question, answer by answer. Everyone else thought we were weird, but I was starting to wonder how I'd ever gotten to know anyone any other way. If anything, the game made you realize how little you knew about people. After only a few weeks, I knew what Wes worried about, what embarrassed him most, his greatest disappointment. I couldn't be sure of any of these things when it came to my mother, or Caroline, or Jason, and knew they'd be equally stymied if asked about me.

"I just think it's weird," Kristy said to me after walking up on us a couple of times, only to catch the tail end of Wes detailing some seventh-grade trauma or me explaining why I thought my neck was strange-looking. "I mean, Truth or Dare, that I understand. But this is just talking."

"Exactly," I said. "Anyone can do a dare."

"I don't know about *that*," she said darkly. "Everyone knew if you were smart, you always picked Truth over Dare. That way you could at least lie, if you had to."

I just looked at her.

"What?" she said. She rolled her eyes. "I wouldn't lie to you. I'm talking about cutthroat slumber party ethics. Nobody tells the truth all the time."

"You do in this game," I said.

"Maybe *you* do. But how do you know he is?"

"I don't know," I told her. "I just do."

And I did. It was why I liked being with Wes so much, that summer. He was the one person I could count on, unequivocally, to say exactly what he meant, no hedging around. He had no idea, I was sure, how much I appreciated it.

"Macy!"

I turned around, and there was Bert, standing at the top of his driveway in an undershirt and a pair of dress pants. There was a piece of tissue stuck to his chin and another on his temple, both clearly shaving injuries, and he looked desperate. "Can you come here for a second?"

"Sure," I said, starting across the road. When I got within a few feet of him, I could smell his cologne. One step closer, and every step after that, it was all I could smell, which was saying something, considering I'd spent the last hour helping Delia peel garlic to make hummus and was pretty fragrant myself. "What's going on?"

He turned around and started down the driveway toward his house, walking at such a fast, frenzied pace that I found myself struggling to keep up with him. "I have an important engagement," he said over his shoulder, "and Kristy was supposed to help me get ready. She *promised.* But she and Monica had to take Stella to deliver bouquets, and she's not back yet."

"Engagement?" I asked.

"It's my Armageddon club social. A *big* deal." He looked at me pointedly, as if to emphasize this. "It only happens once a year."

"Right," I said. As we walked up the steps to his front door, I watched as one of the pieces of tissue dislodged from his face, taking flight over his head and disappearing somewhere behind us. On the bright side, at least with us moving, I couldn't smell the cologne. As much.

I'd never been inside Wes and Bert's house before. From the road, all you could see was that it was wood, cozy and cabinlike, but I was surprised, as I followed Bert in, by how open and bright it was. The living room was big, with beams across the ceiling and skylights, the furniture modern and comfortable looking. The kitchen ran against the back wall, and there were plants all along the counter, many of them leaning toward one large window above the sink. Also there was art everywhere: abstract paintings on the walls, several ceramic pieces, and two of Wes's smaller sculptures on display on either side of the fireplace. I'd expected it to look, well, like two teenaged guys lived there, with pizza boxes piled up on the counter and half-filled glasses cluttering every surface, but it was surprisingly neat.

"What's at issue here," Bert said as we headed down the hallway, passing a closed door and another bedroom along the way, "is dots or stripes. What do you think?"

He pushed open the door to his bedroom, going inside, but once I hit the threshold I just stood there, staring. Not at the two button-up shirts he was now holding out to me, but at the huge poster behind him, which took up the entire wall. It said, simply, ATTENTION:ARMAGEDDON and featured a graphic image of a blue earth being shattered to bits. The rest of the room was decorated the same way, with posters proclaiming THE END IS NEARER THAN YOU THINK and one that said simply MEGA TSUNAMI: ONE WAVE, TOTAL ANNIHILATION. The remaining wall space was taken up by shelves, all of which were packed with books featuring similar titles.

"Stripes," Bert said, shaking one shirt at me, "or dots. Stripes or dots. Which one?"

"Well," I said, still totally distracted, "I think—"

Just then the door behind me opened, and Wes emerged from the bathroom, hair wet, rubbing his face with a towel. He had on jeans and no shirt, which, frankly, was almost as distracting as the mega-tsunami. Or even more so. He started to wave hello to me, then stopped. And sniffed. Twice.

"Bert," he said, wincing, "what did I tell you about cologne?"

"I'm hardly wearing any," Bert said, as Wes put a hand over his nose, disputing this. He held up the shirts again, clearly willing to take all opinions. "Wes, which should I wear? First impressions are important, you know."

Wes's voice was muffled, through his hand. "My point exactly. Were you going for overpowering?"

Bert ignored this, turning back to me. "Macy. *Please*. Stripes or dots?"

As always, I found myself feeling a kind of affection for Bert, in his weird bedroom, wearing his nerdy undershirt, one piece of tissue still stuck to his face. "The stripes," I told him. "They're more grown-up looking."

"Thank you." He dropped the polka-dotted shirt on the bed, slipping on the other one and buttoning it quickly. Turning to face himself in the mirror, he said, "That's what I thought, too."

"Are you wearing a tie?" Wes asked him, walking back into the bathroom and tossing the towel over the shower rod.

"Should I?"

I said, "What kind of impression are you going for?"

Bert thought for a second. "Mature. Intelligent. Handsome."

"Overpowering," Wes added.

"Then yes," I told Bert, who was now scowling. "Wear a tie."

As Bert pulled open his closet door and began rummaging around, I turned to look at Wes, who'd walked into his own room and was now pulling on a gray T-shirt. Unlike Bert's, Wes's walls were bare, the only furnishings a futon against one wall, a milk crate stacked with books, and a bureau with a mirror hanging over it. There was a black-and-white picture of a girl taped to the mirror, but I couldn't make out her face.

"The thing about the Armageddon social," Bert said to me now, as I turned around to see him struggling to knot a blue tie, "is that it's the one time of the year EOWs from all over the state get together."

"EOWs?" I asked, watching him loop the tie, start a knot, and then yank it too tight before dismantling it and starting over.

"End-of-worlders," he explained, trying another knot. This time, the front came out way too long, almost hanging to his belt buckle. "It's a great opportunity to learn about new theories and trade research tips with like-minded enthusiasts." He looked down at the tie. "God! Why is this so hard? Do you know how to do this?"

"Not really," I said. My father had never been the formal type, and Jason, who wore ties often, could do one with his eyes closed, so I'd had no reason to learn.

"Kristy promised she would help me," he muttered, yanking on the tie, which only made the front go longer. His face was getting red. "She *promised*."

"Calm down," Wes said, stepping around me into the room and walking up to Bert. He untangled the tie, smoothing the ends. "Stand still." Then Bert and I both stood and watched as, with one cross, a twist, and a yank, he tied the knot perfectly.

"Wow," Bert said, looking down at it as Wes stepped back, examining his handiwork. "When did you learn that?"

"When I had to go to court," Wes told him. He reached up, plucking the piece of tissue off his brother's face, then straightened the tie again. "Do you have enough money?"

Bert snorted. "I prebought my ticket way back in March. There's a chicken dinner and dessert. It's all paid for."

Wes pulled out his wallet and slid out a twenty, tucking it into Bert's pocket. "No more cologne, okay?"

"Okay," Bert said, looking down at the tie again. The phone rang and he picked up a cordless from the bed. "Hello? Hey, Richard. Yeah, me too. . . . Um, striped shirt. Blue tie. Poly-blend slacks. My good shoes. What about you?"

Wes stepped back into the hallway, shaking his head, and went into his room. I leaned against the doorjamb, taking another look at its sparse furnishings. "So," I said, "I see you're a minimalist."

"I'm not into clutter," he replied, opening the closet and pulling out something, "if that's what you mean. If you don't see it here, I don't need it."

I stepped inside, then walked over to his bureau, leaning in to look at the girl in the picture. I knew I was probably being nosy, but I couldn't help myself. "So, is this Becky?"

He turned around, glancing over at me. "No. Becky's skinny, angular. That's my mom."

Wish was beautiful. That's what I thought first. And in this picture, young, maybe her late teens or early twenties. I immediately recognized Bert's round face in her features, and Delia's dark curly hair and wide smile. But more than anything, she reminded me of Wes. Maybe it was the way she was not looking at the camera but instead just beyond it, half-smiling, nothing posed or forced about her. She was sitting on the edge of a fountain, her hands resting easily in her lap. You could see water glittering behind her.

"She looks like you," I said.

He came up behind me, a box in his hand, and then we were both framed in the mirror, peering in. "You think?"

"Yeah," I said. "I do."

Bert came out of his room, walking quickly, a lint roller in one hand. "I'd better go," he said. "I want to be there right when the doors open."

"You're taking the roller?" Wes asked him.

"There's always the possibility of car lint," Bert told him, sticking it in his front pocket. "So I look okay?"

"You look great," I told him, and he smiled at me, genuinely pleased.

"I'm staying at Richard's tonight, so we can recap," Bert said, pulling the door open. "I'll see you tomorrow, okay?"

Wes nodded. "Have fun."

Bert disappeared down the hallway, and seconds later I heard the front door slam. Wes grabbed his keys and wallet off the bureau, shifting the box he was carrying to his other arm, and we started toward the living room, me taking one last look at Wish before he shut the door behind us.

"I should go, too, I guess," I said, as we came into the living room. Again, I was struck by how cozy it was, unlike my house, which, with its high ceilings and huge rooms, always seemed to feel empty.

"Don't tell me," he said. "You're going to the Armageddon social, too?"

"How'd you guess?"

"Just a hunch."

I made a face. "No, I'll actually be studying. Doing laundry. I don't know, I might get really out of hand and iron some clothes. With *starch*."

"Uh-oh," he said. "Now you're talking crazy."

He pulled the door open and I stepped outside, stopping on the stairs as he locked it. "Okay, fine, Mr. Excitement. What's your plan?"

"Well," he said, holding up the box in his hand, "I have to drop by this party in Lakeview and give a friend of mine these car parts I found at the salvage yard."

"A party *and* car parts?" I said. "Don't hurt yourself, now."

"I'll try not to."

I smiled at him, digging my own keys out of my pocket.

"You want to ride along?"

I was sort of surprised that he asked me. And even more surprised how quickly I answered, no hesitation, as if this had been what I'd been planning to do all along. "Sure."

The party was big and in full swing by the time we pulled up twenty minutes later. As we walked up to the front door, dodging people grouped along the driveway and front lawn, I was, as always, aware of the fact that we were being stared at. Or that Wes was. He hardly seemed to notice, but I wondered how he'd ever gotten used to it.

Once inside, I'd barely crossed the threshold when someone grabbed my arm. Someone in a denim miniskirt, cowboy boots, and a hot pink bustier. One guess.

"Oh, my God," Kristy hissed in my ear, yanking me sideways to the bottom of the stairs. "I *knew* it! What are you doing? Macy, you'd better start talking. Now."

Wes had stopped in the middle of the foyer and was looking around for me. When he finally spotted me and saw I was with Kristy, he mouthed he'd be right back, then disappeared down the hallway past a clump of cheerleaders, who watched him go with wistful expressions. Not that I could focus on this, as Kristy was about to break my arm.

"Will you stop?" I asked her, wrenching myself out of her grip. "I think you sprained something."

"I can't believe," she said indignantly, not even hearing this, "that you and Wes are out on a date and you didn't even tell me. What does this say about our friendship? Where is the *trust*, Macy?"

I felt someone bump my other side and looked over to see Monica, a bottled water in one hand, looking out at the crowd in the living room with a bored expression.

"Did you see who Macy is *with*?" Kristy said to her.

"Mmm-hmm," Monica said.

"I am not *with* him," I said, rubbing my elbow. "He needed to drop something off, I was over there helping Bert get ready for the Armageddon social, and he just—"

"Oh, shit!" Kristy put a hand to her mouth, her eyes wide. "I forgot about the social. God, please tell me he didn't wear that polka-dot shirt."

"He didn't," I told her, and she visibly relaxed. "Stripes."

"Tie?"

I nodded. "The blue one."

"Good." She took a sip of the beer she was holding, then pointed a finger at me. "Now, let's get back to you and Wes. Do you swear there's nothing going on?"

"God, calm down," I said. She was still looking at me, as if this was not an acceptable answer. I added, "I swear."

"All right then," she said, nodding toward the dining room, where I could see a bunch of guys gathered around the table. "Prove it."

"Prove it?" I said, but she was already dragging me down into the foyer, across the living room, and into the dining room, plopping me down in a chair, and perching herself on the arm. Monica, true to form, arrived about thirty seconds later, looking winded. Not that Kristy seemed to notice. Clearly she was on a mission.

"Macy," she said, gesturing down the table to a heavyset guy in a baseball cap, another in an orange shirt, and, at the end, a hippie-looking type with blue eyes and a ponytail, "this is John, Donald, and Philip."

"Hi," I said, and they all said hello in return.

"Macy's currently sort of between relationships," Kristy explained, "and I am trying, *trying*, to show her that there is a whole world of possibilities out there."

Everyone was looking at me, and I felt my face redden. I wondered when Wes was coming back.

"These guys," Kristy continued, gesturing around the table, "are totally undateable. But they're really nice."

"The fact that we're undateable, however," John, the one in the baseball hat, said to me, "did not stop her from dating all of us."

"That's how I know!" she said, and they all laughed. Donald handed her a quarter and she bounced, missing, and drank. "Look," she said to me, "I'm going to go do a preliminary sweep. When I come back, I'll walk you through and introduce you to some prospects. Okay?"

"Kristy," I said, but she was already walking away, patting John on the head as she passed him.

"Your turn," he said, nodding at me.

I picked up the quarter. While I'd seen this game played before, I'd never tried it myself. I bounced the quarter like Kristy had, and it landed in the cup with a splash, which was good. I thought. "What happens now?" I asked Philip.

He swallowed. "You pick someone to drink."

I looked around the table, then pointed at John, who raised his cup, toasting me.

"Your turn again," Philip said.

"Oh." I bounced the quarter again: again, it went in.

"Watch out!" Donald said. "She's on fire!"

Just barely: with my third bounce, I missed. Philip indicated that I should drink, which I did, and pushed the quarter on to John. "Oh well," I said. "It was fun while it lasted." He made it, of course, and pointed at me.

"Bottoms up," he said, so I drank again.

And again. And again. The next twenty minutes or so passed quickly—or at least it seemed that way—as I missed just about every bounce I took *and* was picked to drink whenever anyone else landed one in. Dateable or not, these guys were ruthless. Which meant that by the time Wes slid into the seat beside me, things were seeming a little fuzzy. To say the least.

"Hey," he said. "Thought you were lost."

"Not lost," I told him. "Kidnapped. And now, a colossal failure at quarters. Did you find your friend?"

He shook his head. "He's not here. You about ready to go?"

"Beyond ready," I said. "In fact, I think I'm a little—"

"Macy." I turned around to see Kristy, hands on hips, looking determined. "It's time to do this."

"Do what?" Wes asked, and I was wondering the same thing, having totally forgotten our earlier conversation. Not that it mattered, as she already had me on my feet, stumbling slightly, and was dragging me full force into the kitchen. Oh, right, I thought. Prospects.

"You know," I said. "I don't think I'm really—"

"Five minutes," she said firmly. "That's all I'm asking."

Fifteen minutes later, I found myself still in the kitchen, which was now packed with people, talking to a football player who was named either Hank or Frank: it had been too loud to make it out exactly. I'd been trying to extract myself, but between the crowd pressed all around me and Kristy watching like a hawk as she talked to her own prospect, it was kind of hard. Plus I was feeling a bit unsteady. Make that a lot unsteady.

"Don't you date Jason Talbot?" he said to me, shouting to be heard over the music that was blasting from a nearby stereo.

"Well," I began, pushing a piece of hair out of my face.

"What?" he yelled.

I said, "Actually, we're—"

He shook his head, cupping a hand behind his ear. "What?"

"No," I said loudly, leaning in closer to him and almost losing my balance. "No. I don't."

Just then, someone bumped me from behind, pushing me into Hank/Frank. "Sorry," I said, starting to step back, but he put his hands on my waist. I felt dizzy and strange, too hot, entirely too hot.

"Careful there," he said, smiling at me again. I looked down at his hands, spread over my hips: they were big and hammy. Yuck. "You okay?"

"I'm fine," I said, trying to step back again. But he moved with me, sliding his arms farther around my waist. "I think I need some air," I said.

"I'll come with you," he said, and Kristy turned her head, looking at me.

"Macy?" she said.

"She's fine," Hank/Frank said.

"You know," I said to Kristy, but I lost sight of her as a tall girl with a pierced nose stepped between us, "I think we should—"

"Me too," Hank/Frank said. I could feel his fingers brushing under my shirt, touching my bare skin. I felt a chill, and not the good kind. He leaned in closer to me, his lips touching my ear just slightly, and said, "Hey, let's go somewhere."

I looked for Kristy again, but she was gone, nowhere I could see. Now I was feeling totally woozy as Hank/Frank leaned into my ear again, his voice saying something, but the music was loud, the beat pounding in my ears.

"Wait," I said, trying to pull back from him.

"Shhh, calm down," he said, moving his hands up my back. I yanked away from him, too hard, then stumbled backwards, losing my balance. I could feel myself falling fast, into the space behind me, even as I tried to right myself. And then, suddenly, there was someone there.

Someone who put his hands on my elbows, steadying me, pulling me back to my feet. The hands were cool on my hot skin, and I could just feel this presence behind me, solid, like a wall. Something to lean on, strong enough to hold me.

I turned my head. It was Wes.

"There you are," he said, as Hank/Frank looked on, annoyed. "You about ready to go?"

I nodded. I could feel his stomach against my back, and without even thinking about it I felt myself leaning back into him. His hands were still cupping my elbows, and even though I knew this was weird, that I'd never do it any other time, I just stayed where I was, pressed against him.

"Hey," Hank/Frank said to me, but Wes had already started through the crowd. There were so many people, so much to navigate, and as the distance fluctuated between us his hand kept slipping, down my arm to my wrist. And maybe he was going to let go as people pressed in on all sides, but all I could think was how when nothing made sense and hadn't for ages, you just have to grab onto anything you feel sure of. So as I felt his fingers loosening around my wrist, I just wrapped my own around them, tight, and held on.

The instant we walked out the front door, someone yelled Wes's name, loud. It startled me, startled both of us, and I dropped his hand quickly.

"Where you been, Baker?" some guy in a baseball hat, leaning against a Land Rover, was yelling. "You got that carburetor for me?"

"Yeah," Wes yelled back. "One second."

"Sorry," I said to him as he turned and looked at me. "I just, it was so hot in there, and he—"

He put his hands on my shoulders, easing me down so I was

sitting on the steps. "Wait here," he said. "I'll be right back. Okay?"

I nodded, and he started across the grass toward the Rover. I took in a deep breath, which just made me feel dizzier, then cupped my head in my hands. A second later, I had the feeling that I was being watched. When I turned my head, I saw Monica.

She was standing just to my right, smoking a cigarette, the bottle of water tucked under her arm. I knew well she was not the type to creep up or move fast, which meant she'd seen us come out. Seen us holding hands. Seen everything.

She put her cigarette to her lips, taking a big drag, and kept her eyes on me, steady. Accusingly.

"It's not what you think," I said. "There was this guy in there. . . . Wes rescued me. I grabbed *his* hand, just to get out."

She exhaled slowly, the smoke curling up and rising between us.

"It was just one of those things," I said. "You know, that just happen. You don't think or plan. You just do it."

I waited for her to dispute this with a "Donneven," or maybe an "Mmm-hmm," meant sarcastically, of course. But she didn't say a word. She just stared at me, indecipherable as ever.

"Okay," Wes said, walking up, "let's get out of here." Then he saw Monica and nodded at her. "Hey. What's going on?"

Monica took another drag in reply, then turned her attention back to me.

I stood up, tilting slightly, and then righted myself, not without effort. "You okay?" Wes asked.

"I'm fine," I said. He headed down the walk toward the truck, and I followed. At the bottom of the steps, I turned back to Monica. "Bye," I told her. "I'll see you tomorrow, okay?"

"Mmm-hmm," she answered. I could feel her still watching me, as I walked away.

"If you could change one thing about yourself," Wes asked me, "what would it be?"

"How about everything I did between leaving your house and right now?" I said.

He shook his head. "I told you, it wasn't that bad," he said.

"You didn't have some football player pawing you," I pointed out.

"No," he said, "you're right about that."

I sat back against the side of the truck, stretching my legs out in front of me. Once we left the party, Wes had stopped at the Quik Zip, where I'd bought a big bottled water and some aspirin. Then he drove me back to my house, rebuffing my half-hearted protests by promising to get me back to my car the next morning. Once there, I'd expected him to just drop me off, but instead ever since, we'd been sitting in my driveway, watching fireflies flit around the streetlights and telling Truths.

But not the one about why I'd grabbed his hand. Everything had been such a blur, so hot and crazy, that there were moments I wondered if I'd imagined the whole thing. But then I'd remember Monica, her flat skeptical look, and know it had happened. I kept thinking about Jason, how weird he'd always been about physical contact, how reaching out for him was always like taking a chance, making a wish. With Wes, it had come naturally, no thinking.

"I wouldn't be so afraid," I said now. Wes, watching a firefly bob past, turned to look at me. "If I could change anything about myself. That's what it would be."

"Afraid," he repeated. Once again, I was reminded how much I liked that he never judged, in face or in tone, always giving me a chance to say more, if I wanted to. "Of . . ."

"Of doing things that aren't planned or laid out in advance for me," I said. "I'd be more impulsive, not always thinking about consequences."

He thought about this for a second. "Give me an example."

I took a sip of my water, then set it down beside me. "Like with my mother. There's so much I want to say to her, but I don't know how she'll react. So I just don't."

"Like what?" he asked. "What do you want to say?"

I ran my finger down the tailgate, tracing the edge. "It's not as much what I'd say, but what I'd do." I stopped, shaking my head. "Forget it. Let's move on."

"Are you passing?" he asked.

"I answered the question!" I said.

He shook his head. "Only the first part."

"That was not a two-part question," I said.

"It is now."

"You know you're not allowed to do that," I said. When we'd started, the only rule was you had to tell the truth, period. Still, ever since, we'd been bickering over various addendums. There had been a couple of arguments about the content of questions, one or two concerning the completeness of answers, and too many to count about whose turn it was. This, too, was part of the game. It was considerably harder to play by the rules, though, when you were making them up as you went along.

He looked at me, shaking his head. "Come on, just answer," he said, nudging my arm with his.

I exhaled loudly, leaning back on my palms. "Okay," I said, "I'd just . . . if I could, I'd just walk up to my mother and say whatever I felt like saying, right at that moment. Maybe I'd tell her how much I miss my dad. Or how I worry about her. I don't know what. Maybe it sounds stupid, but for once, I'd just let her know exactly how I feel, without thinking first. Okay?"

It wasn't the first time I'd felt a wave of embarrassment pass over me in giving an answer, but this was more raw and real, and I was grateful for the near-dark for whatever it could hide of my expression. For a minute, neither of us said anything, and I wondered again how it was possible that I could confess so much to a boy I'd only known for half a summer.

"That's not stupid," he said finally. I picked at the tailgate, keeping my head down. "It's not."

I felt that weird tickle in my throat and swallowed over it. "I know. But just talking about anything emotional is hard for her. For us. It's like she prefers we just not do that anymore."

I swallowed again, then took a deep breath. I could feel him watching me.

"Do you really think she feels that way?" he asked.

"I have no real way of knowing. We don't talk about it. We don't talk about anything. That's the problem." I ran my finger around the edge of my water. "That's my problem, actually. I don't talk to anybody about what's going on in my head, because I'm afraid they might not be able to take it."

"What about this?" he asked, waving his hand between us. "Isn't this talking?"

I smiled. "This is Truth," I said. "It's different."

He pulled a hand through his hair. "I don't know. The vomit story alone was *huge*."

"Enough with the vomit story," I said, exasperated. "Please God I'm begging you."

"The point is," he continued, ignoring this, "that you've told me a lot playing this game. And while some of it might be weird, or heavy, or downright gross—"

"Wes."

"—it's nothing I couldn't handle." He was looking at me now, his face serious. "So you should remember that, when you're thinking about what other people can deal with. Maybe it's not so bad."

"Maybe," I said. "Or maybe you're just really extraordinary."

As this came out, it was like someone else had said it. I just heard the words, even agreed with them, and a second later realized it was my voice. Oh, my God, I thought. This is what happens when you don't think and just do.

We sat there, looking at each other. It was warm out, the fireflies sparkling around us, and he was close to me, his knee and mine only inches apart. I had a flash of how his hand had felt earlier, his fingers closing over mine, and for one crazy second I thought that everything could change, right now, if only I could let it. If he'd been any other boy, and this was any other world, I would have kissed him. Nothing would have stopped me.

"Okay," I said, too quickly, "my turn."

He blinked at me, as if he'd forgotten we were even playing. So he'd felt it, too.

"Right," he said, nodding. "Go ahead. Hit me."

I took in a breath. "What's the one thing you'd do," I asked, "if you could do anything?"

As always, he took a second to think, staring straight ahead out at the clearing. I had no idea what he'd say, but then I never did. Maybe he'd reply that he wished he could see his mom again, or suddenly be granted X-ray vision, or orchestrate world peace. I don't know what I was expecting. But it wasn't what I got.

"Pass," he said.

For a second I was sure I'd heard wrong. "What?"

He cleared his throat. "I said, I pass."

"Why?"

He turned his head and looked at me. "Because."

"Because why?"

"Because I just do."

"You know what this means, right?" I said, and he nodded. "You know how the game works?"

"You have to answer whatever question I ask next," he said. "And if you do, you win."

"Exactly." I sat up straighter, bracing myself. "Okay. Go ahead."

He drew in a breath, and I waited, ready. But all he said was, "No."

"No?" I said, incredulous. "What do you mean, no?"

"I mean," he repeated, as if I were slow, "no."

"You have to ask a question," I told him.

"Not immediately," he replied, flicking a bug off his arm. "For a question this important, a question that carries the outcome of the game, you can take as long as you want."

I could not believe this. "Says who?"

"Says the rules."

"We have more than covered the rules," I told him. "That is *not* one of them."

"I'm making an amendment," he explained.

I was truly stumped. In fact, everything that had happened

in the last five minutes, from me calling him extraordinary, to that one moment I felt something shift, to this, felt like some sort of out-of-body experience.

"Okay, fine," I said. "But you can't just take forever."

"I don't need that long," he said.

"How long?"

"Considerably less than forever." I waited. Finally he said, "Maybe a week. You can't bug me about it, either. That will nullify the entire thing. It has to just happen when it happens."

"Another new rule," I said clarifying.

He nodded. "Yup."

I just looked at him, still processing this, when suddenly there was a burst of light from the other end of the street as a car came over the hill. We both squinted, and I put my hand to my face, then lowered it as I realized it was my mother. She was on the phone—of course—and didn't seem to see us at first as she passed, pulling into the driveway and up to the garage. It was only when she got out of the car, the phone still between her ear and shoulder, that she looked over at us, squinting slightly.

"Macy?" she said. "Is that you?"

"Yes," I replied. "I'm coming in, right now."

She went back to her conversation, still walking, but not before taking another glance at me and at Wes's truck before climbing the stairs, finding her keys, and letting herself inside. A second later, the foyer light came on, followed by the ones in the kitchen and back hall as she moved toward her office.

"Well," I said to Wes, hopping down from the tailgate. "Thanks for a truly exciting evening. Even if you *are* leaving me hanging."

"I think you can handle it," he said as he walked around to the driver's side, climbing behind the wheel.

"All I'm saying," I said, "is that when this is all over, I'm going to submit, like, twenty amendments. You won't even recognize the rules once I'm done with them."

He laughed out loud, shaking his head, and I felt myself smile. What I wouldn't have admitted to him, not then, maybe not ever, was that I was actually happy to have to wait awhile. The game had become important to me. I didn't want it to end at all, much less right that second. Not that he had to know that. Especially since he hadn't asked.

"You know," I told him, "after all this buildup, it had better be a good question."

"Don't worry," he said, sounding sure of himself, as always. "It will be."

Chapter Thirteen

"Goodness," my mother said, tracing her finger down one side of the picture on the table in front of her. "It's really coming along."

My sister beamed. "Isn't it? The plumber's coming tomorrow to install the new toilet, and the skylights are in. We've just got to decide on paint colors and then they can start on the walls. It's going to be just *gorgeous*."

I'd never thought it was possible for someone to be so enthusiastic about going over paint chips that, to my eye anyway, looked exactly alike. But Caroline had completely thrown herself into the beach house project. And while there were new window treatments and skylights, the moose head was still over the fireplace (although it had been cleaned by a professional—hard to believe someone actually *did* such things for a living), and the same splintery Adirondack chairs remained on the back deck, where they'd be joined by a new wrought-iron bench and a row of decorative flowerpots. All the things we loved about the beach house, she said, would still be there. It was, she said, what my dad would have wanted.

"What I'm thinking," Caroline said now, as my mother moved on to another picture, squinting at it, "is that once the kitchen is all painted, I can do some tiling along the molding. Kind of a southwestern look, with different patterns. I have it in here somewhere, hold on."

I watched my mother as she looked through the latest round of pictures, picking up one showing the new sliding glass doors to examine it more closely. I could tell her mind was wandering to other houses, other paint chips, other fixtures: the ones in the townhouses, which were progressing on a parallel timeline to Caroline's project. I knew that to her, the beach house was distant, past, while her projects were present and future, close enough to see from the top of our driveway, rising up over the next hill. Maybe you could go backwards and forwards at the same time, but it wasn't easy. You had to want to. My sister, her mind dancing with images of plantation shutters and smooth blue kitchen tiles, might not have been able to see this. But I could. I only hoped that eventually, my mother would come around.

A few nights later, I worked a fiftieth birthday party with Wish in the neighborhood right next to Wildflower Ridge. They picked me up on their way there, and afterwards, dropping me off, Delia asked a favor.

"I *so* have to pee," she said. "Would it be all right if I came in for a second?"

"Sure," I said.

"Delia!" Bert said, looking at his watch. "We're in a hurry here!"

"And I'm pregnant and about to pee all over myself," she replied, opening her door and swinging one leg out. "I'll only be a second."

But a second, to Bert, was too long. All night he'd been obsessing about how he needed to be home by ten at the very latest in order to see *Update: Armageddon*, a show that covered, in his words, "all the latest doings in doomsday theory." But the party had run long, and even though we'd rushed as much as we could, time was clearly running out, not only for the world, but for Bert as well.

"I'm coming, too," Kristy said now, unlocking the side door. "Every time I tried to use the bathroom at that party someone was in it."

"My show comes on in five minutes!" Bert said.

"Bert," Wes said, pointing at the dashboard clock, which said 9:54, "it's over. You're not going to make it."

"Update: it's too late," Kristy added.

Bert glared at both of them, then slumped in his seat, looking out the window. For a second it was quiet, except for Delia grunting as she lowered herself onto the grass by the sidewalk. I looked at my dark house, looming up in front of us: my mother was at an overnight meeting in Greensboro, not due back until morning.

"You can come in and watch it here," I said. "I mean, if you want to."

"Really?" Bert looked at me, surprised. "You mean it?"

"Macy," Kristy moaned, knocking me with her elbow, "what are you *thinking*?"

"She's thinking that she's kind and considerate," Bert said as he quickly slid down the seat to the open door, "unlike some people I could mention."

"I'm sorry," Delia said, putting her hand on my arm, "but I'm really bordering on emergency status with my bladder here."

"Oh, right," I said. "Come on, it's just inside."

"So we're all going in?" Wes asked, cutting the engine.

"Yep," Kristy said. "Looks that way."

As we approached the front steps, Delia waddling, Kristy eyeing the house, with Bert and Wes and Monica bringing up the rear, I told myself that even if my mother had been home, I could have done this, invited my friends in. But the truth was, ever since her talk with me about concerns for my priorities, I'd stopped talking about my job at Wish, or Kristy, or anything related to either. It just seemed smarter, as well as safer.

I unlocked the front door, then pointed Delia to the powder room. She moved across the foyer faster than I'd seen her go in weeks, the door shutting swiftly behind her. "Oh, sweet Jesus," we heard her say. Kristy laughed, the sound sudden and loud, bouncing off the high ceiling above us, and we all looked up at once, following it.

"See," Bert said to her, "I told you this place was huge."

"It's a palace." Kristy peered in the dining room, eyeing my sister's wedding portrait, which was hanging over the sideboard. "How many bedrooms are there?"

"I don't know, five?" I said, walking to the bottom of the stairs and glancing up at the second floor. There were no lights on, and the rest of the house was dark.

"Is the TV this way?" Bert asked me, poking his head into the living room. Wes reached up and popped him on the back of his head, reminding him of his manners. "I mean, is it okay if I find the TV?"

"It's in here," I said, starting down the hallway to the kitchen, hitting light switches as I came upon them. I pointed to the right, to the family room. "The remote should be on the table."

"Thanks," Bert said, crossing quickly to the couch. "Oh, wow, this TV is *huge*!" Monica followed him, flopping down on the leather recliner, and a second later I heard the set click on.

I walked into the kitchen, pulling open the fridge. "Does anybody want anything to drink?"

"Do you have Dr Pepper?" Bert called out. I saw Wes shoot him a look. "I mean, no thanks."

Kristy smiled, running her finger along the top of the island. "Look at this, it's so cool. Like it has little diamonds in it. What's this called?"

"I don't know," I said.

"Corian," Wes told her, peering over her shoulder.

"Everything here is so *nice*," Kristy said emphatically, looking around the kitchen. "If Stella ever gets her fill of me, I'm moving in with Macy. She's got five bedrooms. I'd even sleep in that powder room. I bet it's nicer than my whole doublewide."

"It's not," I said.

From the living room, I could hear an announcer on the TV, speaking in a deep, important-sounding voice: "This is the future. This is our fate. This is *Update: Armageddon.*"

"Come on you guys, it's on!" Bert yelled.

"Bert, use your inside voice," Kristy told him, turning on her stool to look out the sliding glass doors at the backyard. "Wow! Monica, are you seeing this deck out here? And the pool?"

"Umm-hmm," Monica replied.

"Monica loves pools," Kristy told me. "She's like a freaking fish, you can't get her out of the water. Me, I'm more of a lie-by-the-pool-drinking-something-with-an-umbrella-in-it kind of girl."

I took a few cans of Coke out of the fridge, then pulled some glasses out of the cabinet, filling them with ice. Kristy was now flipping through a *Southern Living* my sister had left behind during her last stay, while Wes stood at the back glass doors, checking out the backyard. With the noise from the TV, and everyone there, I was suddenly aware of how quiet and still my house was normally. Just the addition of so many people breathing gave it a totally different feel, some sort of palpable energy that was never there otherwise.

"I," Delia announced as she came down the hallway, her flip-flops smacking the tile floor, "feel *so* much better. Never would I have imagined that peeing could make me so happy."

From the TV, the announcer bellowed, "What do you think will bring . . . the *end of the world*?"

"From the looks of it," Kristy said, flipping a page, "I'd put my money on this room decorated entirely in gingham. I mean, it's just hideous."

"Macy?"

I jumped, startled. It was my mother, pulling a gotcha all her own. As I turned around, my heart thumping in my chest, I saw her standing in the open archway that led to the hallway to her office, file folder in hand. She'd been here the entire time.

"Mom," I said, too quickly. "Hi."

"Hi," she replied, but she wasn't looking at me, her eyes instead moving across the room to take in Bert and Monica in front of the TV, Wes by the back doors, Delia making her way over to the couch and, finally, Kristy, her head still bent over the magazine. "I thought I heard voices."

"We just got here." I watched as she came into the room, sliding the file onto the counter. "I invited everyone in to watch this show. I hope that's okay."

"Of course it is," she said. Her voice sounded up, cheery, forced. Fake. "I've been wanting to meet your new friends."

Hearing this, Kristy lifted up her head, sitting up straighter. "Kristy Palmetto," she said, sticking out her hand.

My mother, businesswoman that she was, reached for the hand first. Then she took her first good look at Kristy's face and saw the scars. "Oh . . . hello," she said, stumbling slightly on the second word. She recovered quickly, though, as I knew she would, and the next thing she said was smooth, absolutely not affected. "I've heard a lot about you from Macy. It's so nice to meet you."

"You have a beautiful home," Kristy told her. She patted the island. "I especially love this Coreal."

"Corian," Wes corrected from behind her.

"Right." Kristy smiled at my mother, who was doing that thing where you try to look everywhere but where your eyes are drawn naturally. Luckily, Kristy, in her black velvet shirt and short skirt, wearing full makeup, with her hair piled up on her head, offered plenty of other options. "It's just gorgeous. Anyway, I told Macy if she's not careful I'm moving in here. I heard you have extra bedrooms."

My mother laughed politely, then glanced at me. I smiled, noting how forced it felt, like my lips weren't covering my teeth enough. This was the way I always used to smile, I thought. When I had to work at it.

"Mom," I said, nodding toward Wes as he turned around from the glass doors, "this is Wes."

"Hi," Wes said.

"And you know Delia," I said, gesturing to where she was sitting on the couch.

"Of course! How are you?" my mother said.

"Very pregnant," Delia called back, smiling. "But other than that, fine."

"She's due any second," I explained, and when my mother looked slightly alarmed I added, "I mean, any day. And that's Bert, and next to him is Monica."

"Hello," my mother called out, as Bert and Monica waved hello, "nice to meet you."

"Have you heard," the announcer on the TV bellowed, "the Big Buzz?"

"Bert really wanted to watch this show," I explained. "It's, um, about theories."

"Crackpot theories," Kristy said.

"These are backed up by science!" Bert yelled.

"Bert," Wes said, walking over to the living room, "inside voice."

"By science," Bert repeated, more quietly. "The end of the world is no joke. It's not a matter of if. It's *when*."

I looked at my mother. Something told me that the expression on her face—confusion, curiosity, maybe even shock—was not unlike the one I probably had the first day I'd been introduced to these people. But seeing it there, I had a feeling this wasn't necessarily a good thing.

"Macy," she said to me after a second, "can I talk to you in my office for a moment?"

"Um, sure," I said.

"Can you believe this?" Kristy asked me, holding up the magazine to show me a living room full of wicker furniture. "Have you ever seen a more uncomfortable looking couch?"

I shook my head, then followed my mother down the short hallway to her office. She shut the door behind us, then crossed to her desk and stood behind it. "It's after ten," she said, her voice low. "Don't you think it's a little late to have people over?"

"Bert really wanted to see this show," I said. "It's only a half hour. Plus, I thought you were at that meeting."

"You have to work in the morning, Macy," she said, as if I didn't know this. "And we've got a big day tomorrow as well, with the Fourth of July picnic, and you working the welcome booth. It's not a good night for company."

"I'm sorry," I said. "They'll be gone soon."

She looked down at her desk, riffling through some papers, but her disapproval was palpable. I could feel it all around me, settling, taste it in the air.

There was a burst of laughter from the living room, and I glanced at the door. "I should go back out there," I said. "I don't want to seem rude."

She nodded, running a hand through her hair. I stood up and started toward the door.

"What happened to Kristy?" she asked, just as I was about to push it open.

I had a flash of Kristy, just moments earlier, extending her hand to my mother so cheerfully. "She was in a car accident when she was eleven."

"Poor thing," she said, shaking her head as she pulled a pencil out of the holder on her desk. "It's must be just horrible for her."

"Why do you say that?" I asked. Truthfully, I hardly noticed Kristy's scars at all anymore. They were just part of her face, part of who she was. Her outfits garnered more of my attention, maybe because they at least were always changing.

She looked at me. "Well," she said, "only because of the disfigurement. It's hard enough being that age, without a handicap to deal with."

"She's not handicapped, Mom," I said. "She just has a few scars."

"It's just so unfortunate." She sighed, picking up a folder, moving it to the other side of the desk. "She'd be a pretty girl, otherwise."

Then she started writing, opening the folder and jotting something down. Like I was already gone, this was the end of it, there could be no rebuttal, no other side. Of course Kristy wasn't beautiful: her flaws were right there, where anyone could see. Of course we were over my dad's passing: just look around, we were successful, good in school, fine just fine. I'd never spoken up to say otherwise, so I had no one to blame but myself.

Thinking this, I went back into the kitchen, where I found Wes now sitting next to Kristy, both of them looking at *Southern Living*.

"See, this stuff isn't nearly as good as yours," Kristy was saying, pointing at a page. "I mean, what is that supposed to be, anyway?"

"An iron heron," he said, glancing at me. "I think."

"A what?" Kristy said, squinting at it again.

"No way," I said, coming over to look for myself. Sure enough, there was an iron heron, just like my sister had been talking about.

"They're big in Atlanta," Wes explained to Kristy.

"Huge," I said.

Kristy looked at him, then at me. "Whatever," she said,

nodding, as she pushed her chair out and hopped down. "I'm going to find out about that Big Buzz."

I watched her as she walked into the living room, flopping down in our overstuffed chair. She ran her hands over the arms, settling in, then looked up at the ceiling before directing her attention to the TV.

Wes, across from me, turned a page of the magazine. "Everything okay with your mom?" he asked, not looking up.

"Yeah," I said, glancing down at one of the iron herons. "I'm not getting the appeal of those," I said.

He pointed at the picture. "See, first, they're very clean and simple looking. People like that. Second, they have the wildlife thing going for them, so they fit in well with a garden. And thirdly," he turned the page, indicating another picture, "the artist takes himself, and the herons, very seriously. So that gives them a certain cachet as well."

I looked at the artist. He was a tall guy with white hair pulled back in a ponytail, striking a pensive pose by a reflecting pond. *To me*, one of the quotes below it read, *my herons represent the fragility of life and destiny*. "Ugh," I said. "If that's taking your work seriously, he can have it. "

"Exactly."

"Just wait, though," I said. "Someday you'll be in *Southern Living*, with a picture just like that, talking about the deep true meaning of your work."

"Unlikely," he said. "I don't think they pick people who got their start by being arrested and getting sent to reform school."

"Maybe that could be your angle," I suggested. He made a face at me. "And anyway, what kind of attitude is that?" I asked.

"A realistic one," he told me, shutting the magazine.

"You," I said, poking him, "need a little positivity."

"And you," he said, "need to stop poking me."

I laughed, then heard something behind me and turned around. It was my mother again, standing in the doorway. How long had she been there, I wondered, but one look at the expression on her face—stern, chin set, clearly not happy—answered this question.

"Macy," she said, her voice level, "could you hand me that folder on the counter, please."

I walked over to the counter by the fridge, feeling her watching me. Wes, who couldn't help but pick up on the sudden tension in the air, started toward the living room. As he got close, Kristy moved over in the big chair, making room, and he slid in beside her.

"A reverberation," the announcer was saying from the living room, "that would cause a domino effect among the population, causing people to slowly go insane from the constant, unknown droning."

"You can go crazy from vibrations?" Kristy said.

"Oh, yeah," Bert said. "You can go crazy from anything."

". . . a natural phenomenon," the announcer was saying, "or perhaps a tool used by extraterrestrials, who may communicate using sounds beyond our comprehension?"

"Interesting," Delia murmured, rubbing her stomach.

"Mmm-hmm," Monica echoed.

I picked up the folder and brought it to my mother. She stepped out into the darkness of the hallway, giving me a look that meant I should follow.

"Macy," she said, "did I just hear that boy say he's been arrested?"

"It was a long time ago," I said. "And—"

"Macy!" Kristy called out. "You're going to miss the mega-hunami!"

"Tsunami," Bert said.

"Whatever," she said. "It's the mega part that matters, anyway."

But I could barely hear this. I was just watching my mother, the way she was staring at them, her judgment so clear on her face. From Delia's chaotic business practices to Kristy's scars to Wes's past, it was clear they were far from flawless.

"He's the boy you were with the other night, correct?" she asked.

"What?" I asked.

She looked at me, her face stern, as if I was talking back, which I wasn't. "The other night," she repeated, enunciating the words, "when I came home and you were outside with someone. In a truck. Was that him?"

"Um," I said, "yeah, I guess it was. He just gave me a ride." And here I'd thought she'd hardly noticed us. But now, as I watched her looking at Wes, I knew this was one more thing she would hold against me. "It's not what you think. He's a nice guy, Mom."

"When the show is over," she said, as if I hadn't even said this, "they leave. Understood?"

I nodded, and she stuck the folder under her arm as I headed back through the kitchen, toward the living room. I was almost there when I heard her call after me.

"I forgot to tell you," she said, her voice loud and clear. "Jason called. He's going to be in town for the weekend."

"He did?" I said. "He is?"

"His grandmother's taken ill, apparently," she said. "So he's coming down for the weekend. He said to tell you he gets in around noon, and he'll see you at the library."

I just stood there, trying to process this information, as she turned and headed back to her office. Jason was coming home. And of course my mother had felt it necessary to announce this out loud, in front of everyone—especially Wes—while so much of our other business had been conducted in private. She'd told me she wanted me back on track: this was one way of nudging me there.

When I walked into the living room, the announcer on the TV was talking about the mega-tsunami, describing in detail how all it would take was one volcano blowing to set off the chain reaction of events that would end with that big wave crashing over our extended coastline. What other proof, I thought, did you need that life was short. That volcano could already be rumbling, magma bubbling up, pressure building to an inevitable, irrevocable burst.

Kristy scooted over on the wide arm of the oversized chair, making a space for me between herself and Wes, who was studying the screen intently. He didn't say anything as I sat down, and I wondered if he'd heard my mother say Jason was coming home. Not that it mattered. We were just friends, after all.

"Everything okay?" Kristy asked me, and I nodded, my eyes on the TV, which was showing a computer simulation of the mega-wave. There was the volcano blowing, there was the land falling into the ocean, all of these events that led up to this one, huge After as the wave rose up and began to move across the ocean, crossing the space between Africa and where we were. All I could think was that right there, in every passing second, was the future winding itself down. Never would forever, with all its meanings, be so clear and distinct as in the true, guaranteed end of the world.

Chapter Fourteen

The next day, I woke up in the mother of all bad moods. I'd tossed and turned all night, having one bad dream after another. But the last one was the worst.

In it, I'd been walking down the sidewalk outside of the library during my lunch break, carrying my sandwich, and a car pulled up beside me, beeping its horn. When I turned my head, I saw my dad was behind the wheel. He motioned for me to get in, but when I reached for the door handle the car suddenly lurched forward, tires squealing. My dad kept looking back at me, and I could tell that he was scared, but there was nothing I could do as it headed into the intersection, which was filling up with cars from all directions. In my dream, I started to run, and it felt so real: the little catch I always felt in my ankle right after a start, that certain feeling that I'd never get my pace right. Each time I got close to my dad, he'd slip out of my reach, and everything I grabbed thinking it was the car or a part of the car slipped through my hands.

I woke up gasping, my sheets tangled around my legs. Unfurling them slowly, I could feel my pulse banging in my wrist as I struggled to calm down. Not a good start, I thought.

My mother was on the phone as I came into the kitchen, dealing with some last-minute details for the Wildflower Ridge Independence Day Picnic and Parade she'd been planning for weeks now. After my shift at the library, which was open special holiday hours until one, I was supposed to be there at the neighborhood information table, to smile and answer any and all questions. Even if I had gotten a good night's sleep—or any sleep at all—it would have been a long day. Now, with Jason and everything else still to get through before that even began, it felt like there was no way for it to be anything but positively endless.

I was sitting at the kitchen table, forcing down some cheese grits and trying not to think about it, when my mother hung up the phone and came over to sit beside me, her coffee in hand. "So," she said, "I think we should talk about last night."

I put my spoon down in my bowl. "Okay," I said.

She took a breath. "I've already conveyed to you—"

And then the phone rang. She got up, pushing out her chair, and crossed the kitchen, picking it up on the second ring.

"Deborah Queen," she said. She listened for a second, turning her back to me. "Yes. Oh, wonderful. Yes. Three-thirty at the latest, please. Thanks so much." She hung up the phone, jotting something down, then came back over to her chair. "Sorry about that," she said, picking up her coffee cup and taking a sip. "As I was saying, we've already discussed my unhappiness with some recent changes I've noticed in you. And last night, it seemed that some of my concerns were well founded."

"Mom," I said. "You don't—"

There was a shrill ringing sound from her purse, which was on the island: her cell phone. She turned around, digging it out, then pushed a button, pressing it to her ear. "Deborah Queen. Oh, Marilyn, hello! No, it's a perfect time. Let me just run and get those figures for you." She held up her finger, signaling for me to stay put, then got up, disappearing down the hallway to her office. It was bad enough to be having to have this conversation; the fact that it was getting dragged out was excruciating. By the time she returned and hung up, I'd washed out my bowl and put it in the dishwasher.

"The bottom line is," she said, sitting down again and picking right up where we'd left off, "that I don't want you hanging around with those people outside of work."

Maybe it was that I was tired. Or the fact that she couldn't even commit to this conversation without interruptions. But whatever the reason, what I said next surprised us both.

"Why?"

It was just one word. But with it, I'd taken a stand against my mother, albeit small, for the first time in as long as I could remember.

"Macy," she said, speaking slowly, "that boy has been *arrested*. I don't want you out riding around with someone like that, out at all hours—"

The phone rang again, and she started to push herself up out of her chair, then stopped. It rang again, then once more, before falling silent.

"Honey, look," she said, her voice tired. "I know what can happen when someone falls into a bad crowd. I've already been through this before, with your sister."

"That's not fair," I said. "I haven't done anything wrong."

"This isn't about punishment," she said. "It's about prevention."

Like what was happening to me was a forest fire, or a contagious disease. I turned my head, looking out the window at the backyard, where the grass was shimmering, wet under the bright sun.

"You have to realize, Macy," she said, her voice low. "The choices you make now, the people you surround yourself with, they all have the potential to affect your life, even who you are, forever. Do you understand what I'm saying?"

In fact, I knew this to be true now more than ever before. With just a few weeks of being friends with Kristy, and more importantly, Wes, I had changed. They'd helped me to see there was more to the world than just the things that scared me. So they *had* affected me. Just not in the ways she was afraid of.

"I do understand," I said, wanting to explain this, "but—"

"Good," she said, just as the phone rang again. "I'm glad we see eye to eye."

And then she was up. Walking to the phone, picking it up, already moving on. "Deborah Queen," she said. "Harry. Hello. Yes, I was just thinking that I needed to consult you about . . ."

She walked down the hallway, still talking, as I just sat there, in the sudden quiet of the kitchen. Everyone else could get through to my mother: all they had to do was dial a number and wait for her to pick up. If only, I thought, it was that easy for me.

When I went to leave for work, I found myself blocked in by a van that was filled with folding chairs. I went back inside, pulling my mother away from another phone call, only to find out some salesman had taken the keys home with him after parking it there.

"I'll drive you," she said, grabbing her purse off the counter. "Let's go."

Silences are amplified by small spaces, we found out once we were not only in the car but stuck in a traffic jam, with other annoyed commuters blocking us in on all sides. Maybe my mother had no idea I was upset with her. Until we'd gotten in the car, I hadn't really realized it either, but now, with each passing second, I could feel myself getting angrier. She'd taken my dad's stuff from me, his memories. Now she wanted to take my friends, too. The least I could do was fight back.

"Honey, you look tired," she said, after we'd been sitting in silence for a few minutes. I'd felt her glancing at me, but hadn't looked back. "Did you not sleep well?"

My *I'm fine* was poised on my lips, about to come automatically. But then, I stopped myself. I'm not fine, I thought. So instead I said, "No. I didn't. I had bad dreams."

Behind us, someone honked.

"Really," she said. "What about?"

"Actually," I said, "Dad."

I was watching her carefully as I said this, saw her fingers, curled around the steering wheel, pulse white at the tips, then relax. I had that twinge in my stomach, like I was doing something wrong.

"Really," she said, not taking her eyes off the road as the traffic began to pick up.

"Yeah," I said slowly. "It was scary. He was driving this car, and—"

"Your room was probably too hot," she said, reaching forward and adjusting her vent. "And you do have an awful lot of blankets on your bed. Whenever you get hot, you have nightmares."

I knew what this was: a conversational nudge, her way of easing me back between the lines.

"It's weird," I made myself say, "because right after he died, I had a lot of dreams about him, but I haven't lately. Which is why last night was so disturbing. He was in trouble, and I couldn't save him. It scared me."

These four sentences, blurted out too fast, were the most I had said to my mother about my dad since he died. The very fact they had been spoken, were able to bridge the gap from my mind to the open air, was akin to a miracle, and I waited for what would come next, partly scared, partly exhilarated.

My mother took in a breath, and I curled my fingers into my palms.

"Well," she said finally, "it was only a dream."

And that was it. All this buildup to a great leap, and I didn't fall or fly. Instead I found myself back on the edge of the cliff, blinking, wondering if I'd ever jumped at all. It's not supposed to be like this, I thought. My mother was looking straight ahead, her eyes focused on the road.

As she pulled up to the library, I got my purse and opened the door, feeling the already thick heat hit my face as I stepped out onto the curb.

"Can you find a way home?" she asked me. "Or should I pick you up?"

"I'll get a ride," I said.

"If I don't hear from you," she told me, "be at the Commons at six sharp. Okay?"

I nodded, then shut my door. As she drove off, I just stood there watching her go, realizing how similar my dream had been to this, me standing in this exact spot, a car moving away. Like I'd never woken up at all, and soon I'd open my eyes to another morning, another way of all this happening. But as my mother pulled out onto the street, she wasn't looking back at me scared, or needing me. She was fine. Just fine.

—✳—

I walked into the library at exactly 9:12. Bethany and Amanda both looked up from the info desk. Bethany turned her head slightly, eyeing the clock over her head, then looked back at me.

"There was a big traffic jam on Cloverdale," I said, pushing open the swinging door and immediately whacking my knee on the back of her chair. I waited for her to slide sideways, so I could pass, but she didn't, so I had to step around her, which put me in a direct line with Amanda's chair. Of course.

"I come that way," she said coolly, pushing herself a bit more in my path, the wheels squeaking. "I didn't hit any holdups this morning."

I moved around her, having to sidestep the garbage can in the process, and put my bag on the floor next to my seat, which was piled high with periodicals. I moved them onto the table beside my computer, then sat down. I had been putting up with this for weeks. Weeks. Why? Because I had an obligation? To whom? Not to Jason, who'd shed his commitment to me as easily as a second, ill-fitting skin. And certainly not my mother, who, for all the time I'd suffered here, still thought I wasn't dedicated enough.

It just wasn't worth it. Not even close.

Clearly, I wasn't the only one who'd been alerted to Jason's homecoming visit. All morning long, Bethany and Amanda bustled and chattered as they updated the database and organized the invoices for all the periodicals that had come in during his absence. I, however, was exiled to the back room to organize mildewed magazines. I had about two full hours to think about Jason and what I would say to him once he arrived. But as much as I tried to focus on formulating a plan, my mind kept slipping back to Wish and Wes and everything that had happened in the last few weeks. The night Jason had announced our break, all I could think about was how to fix things between us. But now, I wasn't sure what I wanted.

After the magazines were done, I sat facing the wall outside my window, knowing that the time was ticking down to his arriving. Any minute now, I kept thinking, that door will open and something will happen. I just didn't know what.

Beside me, Amanda and Bethany were busy practicing their conversational French for a school club trip they were taking at the end of the summer. All those guttural sounds on top of my anxious mood were about to drive me crazy. Which was probably why, when they finally, abruptly, shut up, I noticed.

Oh, God, I thought. Here we go. One moment Amanda was saying something about the Champs Élysées, and the next, they were both staring at the library's front entrance, speechless.

I looked up, already picturing Jason in my mind. But it wasn't him. It was Wes.

He'd just come in and was standing by the front door, looking around as if getting his bearings. Then he saw me and started toward the desk with that slow, loping walk that I knew so well.

As he approached, I could hear the wheels of Bethany and Amanda's chairs moving; they were pushing up closer, arranging their postures. But he came right to me.

"Hey," he said.

I had never been so happy to see anyone in my entire life. "Hey."

"So look," he began, leaning over the desk, "I was—"

"Excuse me?" Bethany said. Her voice was loud, even.

Wes turned and looked at her. As he did so, I watched his profile, his arm, that little bit of the heart in hand peeking out from his sleeve.

"We can help you over here," Bethany said to him. "Did you have a question?"

"Um, sort of," Wes said, glancing at me, a mild smile on his face. "But—"

"I can answer it," Bethany said solidly, so confidently. Amanda, beside her, nodded, seconding this.

"Really, it's fine," he said, then looked at me again. He raised his eyebrows, and I just shrugged. "Okay, so—"

"She's only a trainee, she won't know the answer," Bethany told him, pushing her chair over closer to where he was, her voice too loud, bossy even. "It's better if you ask me. Or ask us."

Then, and only then, did I see the tiniest flicker of annoyance on Wes's face. "You know," Wes said, "I think she'll know it."

"She won't. Ask me."

Now it wasn't just a flicker. Wes looked at me, narrowing his eyes, and for a second I just stared back. Whatever happens, I thought, happens. For the first time, time at the info desk was flying.

"Okay," he said slowly, moving down the counter. He leaned on his elbows, closer to Bethany, and she sat up even straighter, readying herself, like someone on *Jeopardy!* awaiting the Daily Double. "So here's my question."

Amanda picked up a pen, as if there might be a written portion.

"Last night," Wes said, his voice serious, "when the supplies were being packed up, what happened to the big tongs?"

The sick part was that Bethany, for a second, looked as if

she was actually flipping through her mental Rolodex for the answer. I watched her swallow, then purse her lips. "Well," she said. But that was all.

I could feel myself smiling. A real smile.

Wes looked at Amanda. "Do you know?"

Amanda shook her head slowly.

"All right," he said, turning back to look at me. "Better ask the trainee, then. Macy?"

I could feel Amanda and Bethany looking at me. "They're in the bottom of that cart with the broken back wheel, under the aprons," I said. "There wasn't room for them with the other serving stuff."

Wes smiled at me. "Oh," he said, shaking his head like this was just so obvious. "Of *course.*"

I could hear wheels squeaking as Bethany and Amanda pushed themselves farther down the counter. Wes watched them go, hardly bothered, then leaned over the counter and looked down at me.

"Nice co-workers," he said under his breath.

"Oh, yeah," I said, not as quietly. "They hate me."

The chairs stopped moving. Silence. Oh, well, I thought. It's not like it was a secret.

"So anyway," I asked him. "What's going on?"

"Typical Wish chaos," he said, running a hand through his hair. "Delia's freaking out because one of the coolers broke last night and everything in it's gone bad. Kristy and Monica are at the beach, so now she and Bert and I have to make five more gallons of potato salad on the fly *and* work this job with just three of us. Then, I'm on my way back from a mayonnaise run when Delia calls up, hysterical, saying we have no tongs and I should come here and ask you." He took a deep breath, then said, "So how's your day so far?"

"Don't ask," I said.

"Has the boyfriend shown up yet?"

So he did hear, I thought. I shook my head. "Nope. Not yet."

"Well, just think, it could be worse," he said. "You could be having to make potato salad. Just imagine being up to your elbows in mayonnaise."

I made a face. He was right, this wasn't a pretty picture.

"The point is, we could really use you," Wes said, running a hand over the counter between us. "It's too bad you can't get out of here."

A moment passed, during which all I could hear was the silence of the library. The ticking of the clock. The slight squeak of Bethany's chair. And after everything that had happened, from the first day until the last five minutes, that was the last straw.

"Well," I said. "Maybe I can."

I turned around and looked at Bethany and Amanda, who were pretending to be huddled over some periodical while listening to every word we were saying. "Hey," I called out, and they looked up, in tandem, like a creature with two heads. "You know, I think I'm going to go."

A moment passed as this sunk in.

Amanda's eyes widened. "But you don't get off for another hour," she said.

"Your shift," Bethany added, "ends at one."

"Well," I said, picking up my purse. "Something tells me you're not really going to miss me."

I stood up and pushed in my chair. Wes was watching me,

curious, his hands in his pockets, as I took one last look around my pitiful little workstation. This could be a big mistake, I thought, but it was already happening. I was not a girl with all the information, but I knew one thing. If this was my forever, I didn't want to spend another second of it here.

"If you leave now," Bethany said under her breath, "you can't come back."

"You're right," I told her. And I was so glad that she was. Right, that is. "I can't."

I started to walk toward the swinging door, but, as usual, her chair was in my way. And beyond that was Amanda's. It had been so hard to come in here that first day, and every day since. I figured that by now, I'd earned a clear path out.

So I picked up my purse and tossed it over the desk. It hit the carpet with a thud, right by Wes's feet. Then, in a fashion my sister the rebel would have appreciated, I hoisted myself up, throwing one leg over, and jumped the counter, while Bethany and Amanda watched, stunned.

"Wow," Wes said, raising his eyebrows as I picked up my purse. "Nice dismount."

"Thanks," I said.

"Macy," Bethany hissed at me. "What are you *doing*?"

But I didn't answer her, didn't even look back as we started across the library, everyone staring, to the exit. This felt right. Not just leaving, but how I was doing it. Without regret, without second guessing. And with Wes right there, holding the door open for me as I walked out into the light.

Chapter Fifteen

Lucy picked up a crayon, gripping it in her short, chubby fingers. When she put it to the paper she pressed hard, as if only by doing so would the color transfer. "Tree," she announced, as a squiggle emerged, stretching from one end of the paper to the other.

"Tree," I repeated, glancing at Wes. Even now, a full hour after I'd jumped the info desk, he was still looking at me the way he had the entire ride back to Sweetbud Drive, with an expression that was half impressed, half outright incredulous. "Stop it," I said to him.

"Sorry." He shrugged, as if this would help him to shake it, once and for all. "I just can't get that visual out of my head. It was—"

"Crazy," I finished for him, as Lucy, sitting between us on Wes's side porch, exhaled loudly before picking up another crayon.

"More like kick-ass," he said. "I mean, that's the way I've always wanted to quit jobs but never had the nerve, you know?"

"It wasn't kick-ass," I said, embarrassed.

"Maybe not to you."

Truthfully, for me, it just hadn't sunk in yet. I knew that across town something bigger than the mega-tsunami had hit and was already reverberating, sending shockwaves that would eventually ripple out to meet me. I could just see Jason at the library, listening with that same incredulous expression, as my desk leap was described, in SAT verbal perfect words, by Amanda and Bethany. He was probably already calling my cell phone to demand an explanation, which was why I'd turned it off, deciding to give myself at least until six, when I had to meet my mother, to try not to think about what happened next. For now, I just wanted to do something else. Like color.

Thinking this, I glanced at Lucy again. When we'd come back with the mayonnaise, Delia had been beyond frazzled, frantically boiling huge kettles of water while she and Bert chopped a small mountain of potatoes in the garage. Lucy, hot and bored, was underfoot, and Delia had handed her off to us, asking us to just entertain her until it was time to start mixing everything up. Now I watched as she pushed one of her tight black curls out of her face and pressed an orange crayon to the paper, zigzagging across it. "Cow," she said, with authority.

"Cow," I said.

A breeze blew over the porch then, ruffling the trees, and suddenly there was a flash, something glinting around the side of the house, that I caught out of the corner of my eye. I leaned back on my palms, craning my neck, and saw that in the side yard there were several angels, big and small, as well as a few works in progress: large pieces of rebar twisted and sculpted, a couple of whirligigs that were still only gigs, missing their moving parts. Behind them, lining the fence, was what looked like a small salvage yard, pile after pile of pieces of pipe, metal car parts and hardware, gears in every size from enormous to small enough to fit in the palm of your hand.

"So," I said, nodding toward that side of the house, "that's where the magic happens."

"It's not magic," he replied, watching Lucy scribble orange all across the top of the page.

"Maybe not to you," I said, as he made his modest face. "Can I see?"

As we came around the corner of the porch, Lucy, who was toddling along ahead of us, immediately ran down the stairs and toward a large piece that was made up of hubcaps attached to a twisted center pipe. "Push! Push!" she demanded, slapping at one of the lower parts with her hand.

"Say please," Wes told her. When she did, he gave one of the top hubcaps a big push, and the entire piece began spinning, some of the circles rising up, while others moved down, all of it circular, catching the light again and again. Lucy stepped back, watching entranced and silent until it slowed a couple of minutes later, then creaked to a stop.

"More!" she said. She was so excited she was hopping up and down. "Wes, more!"

Wes looked at me. "This," he said dryly, "can go on for hours." But he pushed it again anyway.

"Wes?" Delia's voice carried over the trees. "Can you come over here? I need something heavy lifted."

"I *said* I can do it," I heard Bert protest. "I'm stronger than I look!"

"Wes?" Delia called again. Poor Bert, I thought.

"Coming," Wes replied. To me he said, "You okay with her for a minute?" When I nodded, he headed around the side of the house. Lucy watched him go, and I wondered if she was going to start screaming. But instead she began walking across the yard with what for a two-year-old seemed like a strong sense of purpose.

When I finally caught up with her, she was at the back fence. Looking over her shoulder, I saw a row of three small heart-in-hand sculptures, miniatures of the one by the side of the road. Each one was slightly different: in the first, the heart had a zigzag across it, like it was broken. In another, the edges of the heart were jagged, pointy, and sharp looking. My favorite was the one on the very end, where the heart in the center of the palm had another, smaller, hand cut into its center, reminding me of the little nesting dolls I'd had as a kid. All the sculptures were especially rusted and dirty: clearly they'd been there for awhile before Lucy pushed aside the grass covering them.

Now, she turned her head and looked at me. "Hands," she said.

"Hands," I repeated. I watched as she took her small hand and pressed it to the hand in the first sculpture, her fingers overlapping the rusted ones, the pale, smoothness of her skin contrasting with the dark, ragged metal. Then she glanced back at me and I did the same, pressing my hand to the one beside it.

I felt a shadow fall over us and looked up to see Wes coming back across the yard, with Delia beside him. Lucy turned her head and, seeing her mother, scrambled to her feet and darted across the grass, hurling herself at Delia's knees. Delia looked down at her, shaking her head, and pulled her fingers through Lucy's dark curls.

"What are you guys doing?" Wes asked me.

"She was showing me these," I told him, nodding toward the sculptures. "I never knew you made small ones."

"Just for a little while," he said, dismissively. "They never really caught on."

"So," I said, standing up, "is it time for potato duty?"

"Nope," Wes told me. "False alarm."

"Really?"

Delia pressed Lucy against her legs. "It's the strangest thing," she said, shaking her head. "Right as we're about to start boiling all those potatoes, I get this phone call from the client. Turns out that they don't want potato salad after all, that they'd rather do coleslaw and macaroni and cheese, which we have plenty of, instead."

"I tried to tell her," Wes said, "that this is a *good* thing."

"Of course it is," I told her. "Why wouldn't it be?"

She smoothed her hand over Lucy's head. "It's just . . . weird. I don't know. It makes me suspicious."

Wes just looked at her. "You know, sometimes things do go the way they're supposed to. It's not unheard of."

"It is for us," Delia said with a sigh. "Anyway, now we at least we have plenty of time to get ready. Which I guess, you know, is good." She still didn't sound convinced.

"Don't worry," Wes said, as we started back toward her house. "I'm sure disaster will strike any minute now."

Delia reached down, taking Lucy's hand. "Yeah," she said, seeming encouraged. "You're probably right."

As we packed for the job, though, things kept happening. Or, more accurately, *not* happening. Whereas we usually had to cram all the carts in and hope they'd fit, for some reason this time Delia had managed to organize the items in the coolers so economically that we were able to take one less, so everything went in easily, with even (gasp!) room left over. The best round serving platter, which had been missing for weeks, suddenly turned up in the garage, behind one of the freezers. And, most amazing of all, instead of racing down Sweetbud Road already late, we finished with time to spare and actually found ourselves having to kill time instead of scramble for it. It was a little weird, I had to admit.

Delia and I ended up on the front steps fanning ourselves, while Bert and Wes milled around the garage, packing the last few things. "So," she said, leaning back on her hands in an effort to get comfortable. "I heard you quit your job."

I glanced at Wes, who was passing by with a box of napkins. "Couldn't help it," he said. "It's just too good not to tell."

"Maybe you should tell my mom, then," I said, pulling my hair back behind my neck.

"No thanks," he said, before disappearing back into the garage.

"You really think she'll be mad?" Delia asked me. "From what you've said about that job, you were miserable there."

"I was," I said. "But to her, it's not about that. It's about the fact that I made a commitment."

"Ah."

"And that this job would look good on my transcript."

"I see."

"And," I finished, "it fits right in with what she wants me to be."

"Which is?"

I ran the fabric of my shirt between my thumb and forefinger, remembering our conversation that morning, as well as the one the night before. "Perfect," I said.

Delia shook her head. "Come on," she said, waving her hand as if brushing this very thought aside, "I'm sure she doesn't want that."

"Why wouldn't she?" I asked.

"Well, for starters, because it's impossible." She leaned back again, shifting her weight a little bit. "And secondly, because she's your mother. And mothers, of all people, are the least likely to care about such things."

"Yeah, right," I said glumly.

"I'm serious." She stretched her feet out in front of her, smoothing her hands over her belly. "I know something about this, okay? All I care about for Lucy, and Wes and Bert, is that they be happy. Healthy. And good people, you know? I'm not perfect, not by a long shot. So why would I expect them to be?"

"My mom's not like that," I told her, shaking my head.

"Okay," she said. "Then what *is* she like?"

I sat there for a second, considering this, surprised, as the seconds passed, that the answer didn't come more easily. "She works too much," I began, then stopped. "I mean, since my dad died she's had to carry the whole business. There's always so much to do, I worry about her. A lot."

Delia didn't say anything. I could feel her watching me.

"And I think she works so much because she can be in control of it, you know?" I said. She nodded. "It makes her feel, I don't know, safe."

"I can understand that," Delia said softly. "Losing someone can make you feel very out of control. Totally so."

"I know," I said. "But it's not really fair. Like, after my dad died, I wanted to be okay for her. So I was. Even when I had to fake it. But now, when I really do feel okay, she's not happy with me. Because I'm not perfect anymore."

"Grieving doesn't make you imperfect," Delia said quietly, as Bert came back out to the van, adjusting one of the carts inside. "It makes you human. We all deal with things differently, Macy. Your mom is missing your dad in her own way, every day. Maybe you should ask her about it."

"I can't," I said. "I can't even bring him up. I tried this morning for the first time in ages, and she just shut down."

"Then try again." She moved closer to me, putting an arm around my shoulder. "Look, everyone mourns at their own pace. Maybe you're just a little bit ahead of her, but she'll get to you eventually. The important thing is that you keep trying to talk to each other, even if it's difficult at first. It gets easier. I promise."

I felt so tired all of a sudden that I just relaxed into her shoulder, leaning my head there. She smoothed her hand over my hair, saying nothing. "Thank you," I said.

"Oh, sweetie," she replied, her voice vibrating under my cheek. "You're so welcome."

We sat there like that, not talking, for a good minute or two. Then, from the garage, we heard it.

"*Gotcha!*"

It was Bert who shrieked in response to this. I knew it instantly.

Delia sighed loudly. "Honestly," she said.

"That's ten," I heard Wes say, and Bert grumbled something I couldn't make out in return. "And counting."

Once we got to the party, our good-luck trend continued. It seemed at first that we were off to a normal start, when we arrived to find that the large gas grills Delia had ordered from her equipment company would not, no matter how many times Wes tried, ignite with any sort of flame.

"Oh, my God!" she was hissing at me as people started arriving. "This is a cookout. A *cookout*. You have to cook outside. It's part of the definition!"

"Delia, just—"

And then, suddenly, there was a *whoosh*, and we had fire. It turned out that the gas tanks just hadn't been hooked up. No problem.

Then, about an hour later, as I was doing a last round of appetizers before the grilled items came out, Bert noticed that we'd only brought one case of hamburger patties instead of two, which left us about, oh, a hundred or so short.

"Okay," Delia said, putting her hands to her face, "God, just let me think . . . think . . ."

"What's wrong?" Wes said as he passed through, picking up more ginger ale for the bar.

"We didn't bring enough hamburgers," I told him. To Delia I said, "Look, it's fine, most people probably won't even—"

"Three cases isn't enough?" Wes said.

Delia took her hands off her face. "There were supposed to be two," she said, speaking slowly.

"You said three," he told her. "I remember."

"I said two," she said, sounding out the words carefully.

"I don't think so."

"Two!" Delia held up two fingers, waving them in the air. "Two boxes is what I said."

"But there *are* three," he told her, speaking equally slowly. "One in the first cart, two in the cooler. Go check. They're there."

I did, and they were. Not only were we not scrambling for beef, we had a surplus. And that wasn't all. Bert and I almost collided and spilled condiments all over each other, but I was able to step aside at the last second, disaster averted. The ice cream scoopers were nowhere to be found, until they magically appeared, in the drawer beneath where they were supposed to be. And so on.

"I'm telling you," Delia said to me later, as we stood in the back of the kitchen, surveying the yard, which was full of happy, well-fed people enjoying food, beverage, and each other's company without incident, "this just makes me *very* nervous."

"Delia," I said, watching as Wes poured a glass of wine for a woman in a strappy sundress who was gesturing grandly, talking to him. He was just nodding, in an oh-sure-absolutely way, as if what she was saying was fascinating. As he bent down to scoop ice though, out of her sight, I saw him roll his eyes.

"I know, I know." She chewed on her pinkie nail. "It's just so weird. Everything is going too well."

"Maybe you've just earned it," I offered. "You know, the cumulative effect of all those bad nights."

"Maybe," she said. "I just wish we'd have one little mishap. It would be reassuring."

The weirdest thing was, I could see her point. Once, this sort of night had been all I aspired to, everything going like clockwork, just perfect. But now it was a little eerie. Not to mention, well, boring.

I couldn't help but think, though, as the hour crept from four to four-thirty to five, that maybe this was a trend that could work in my favor. After all, in about a half hour I'd get dropped off at the Commons, where I'd have to face my mother and explain quitting the info desk. The closer it got, the more nervous I became. Each time my stomach jumped, though, I reminded myself of what Delia had said to me, about how it might be hard to tell my mother how I really felt, but I had to try anyway. It wouldn't be easy, but it was a start. And like my dad always said, the first step is always the hardest.

I was mulling over this as I stood by the buffet, spatula in hand, when a hand blurred across my vision. "Hello?" Wes said, as I blinked, looking at him. "Man, where were you?"

"The land of truth and consequences," I said, poking at the vegetarian option (grilled marinated peppers and spicy black-bean burgers) which had, so far, had no takers. "Less than an hour before everything hits the fan."

"Ah, right," he said, eyeing the veggie burgers disdainfully, "Jason."

"Not Jason," I said. "God. He's the least of my problems. My *mother*."

"Oh." He nodded. "Right."

"I haven't even thought about Jason," I told him, using the spatula to stack the burgers so that maybe they'd look more appetizing. "I mean, I was dreading seeing him at the library, because that was not going to be a good scene. But now . . . now, everything's different. I mean, we're . . ."

Wes waited, not saying anything, as I searched for the right word. A woman passed by, eyeing the peppers before loading up from the next pan, which was full of steaks.

"Over," I finished, realizing this myself just as I said it. I could only imagine Jason's response to me quitting the info desk: he'd never want me back now, and that, I realized, was just fine with me. "It's over," I said again, testing how I felt as my mouth formed the word. Okay, actually. "We're over."

"Wow," Wes said slowly. "Are you—"

"Excuse me, are these vegetarian?" I looked up to see a short, squat woman in a bright print dress, holding a plateful of potato chips. She had on thick, wire-rimmed glasses, which clearly were not strong enough for her to make out the sign that said VEGETARIAN ENTRÉE.

"Yes," I said. "They are."

"Are you sure?"

I nodded, then scooped up one of the burgers and put it on her plate. She squinted down at it, then moved on. To Wes I said, "What were you—"

"Lady at the corner table wants a white wine spritzer," Bert reported as he passed by with a trayful of crumpled napkins and empty cups. "Pronto!"

Wes started around the table, glancing back at me. "Um, nothing," he said. "I'll tell you later."

As he went back to the bar, Delia moved down the table, rearranging the items in the pans. "It is just so weird," she said, taking in the black-bean burgers, "because I meant to bring more of those, and forgot them. I was so worried we wouldn't have enough!"

"Nope," I said, waving off a fly that was buzzing over them. "Plenty."

"See, again," she said, sighing. "Too good. Too good! I don't like this. I need a sense of balance. I never thought I'd admit this, but I need *chaos*."

Just as we were leaving, she got her wish.

It happened as we were packing the last of our stuff into the van. Wes and I were pushing in the carts, and Delia was at the top of the driveway, getting her check from the client, who was so entirely happy with her catering experience that she was paying full price *and* adding a bonus, which was another first. So all was great, wonderful: perfect. And then I heard a shriek.

It wasn't Delia. Nope. It was the client, reacting to the fact that Delia's water had just broken. The baby was on its way.

Chapter Sixteen

"Are you okay?"

I nodded. "I'm fine. Fine."

This was my mantra, the thing I kept saying in my mind. Actually, though, I wasn't entirely certain. All I knew for sure was that I was at the hospital: everything beyond that, like the last time I'd been here, was a bit of a blur.

After the initial shock of the water breaking, we'd done what we did best: gathered our wits, got a plan, and went into action. It wasn't until we'd piled into the van and were on our way to the hospital, Delia beside me, my hand gripped in hers, that I'd glanced at the clock on the dashboard. It was five forty-five, which meant that in fifteen minutes, I was supposed to be meeting my mother at the Commons. Considering how things were going, this should have been my biggest concern. But instead, my mind kept drifting back to another ride, not so long ago.

Then, I'd been holding a hand, too. My father's, though, had been limp, my fingers doing all the work to hold our palms to each other. Instead of Bert, who was breathing loudly through his nose while Delia waved him off, annoyed, there'd been a paramedic across from me, his hands moving swiftly to attach an oxygen mask and prepare the defibrillator. And instead of the wind whooshing past from Wes's open window, and Delia on her cell phone calmly making arrangements with Pete and the babysitter, there had been an eerie, scary silence, punctuated only by the sound of my heart beating in my ears. Then, a life was ending. Here, one was about to begin. I didn't believe in signs. But it was hard to ignore the fact that someone, somewhere, might have wanted me to go through this again and see there was another outcome.

The memories were everywhere. When we pulled up at the curb, it was in the same spot. Entering emergency, the doors made that same smooth *swish* noise. Even the smell was the same, that inexplicable mix of disinfectant and florals. For a second, I'd thought for sure I couldn't do it, and found myself hanging back. But then Wes turned back and looked at me, offering the same question he'd been asking ever since. I'd nodded, then fallen in beside him. He was pushing Delia in a wheelchair and she was taking deep, slow breaths, so I did, too. When we got on the elevator and the doors slid shut, I finally relaxed and felt myself rise.

What I felt now was a different kind of scared. For the past two and a half hours, I'd sat on the bench in the hallway a few feet down from Delia's room, watching as doctors and nurses first ambled in and out, as if there were a million years before anything really happened, then started moving more quickly, and even more so, and then suddenly, everything was a commotion. Machines were beeping, voices calling out pages overhead, the floor beneath my feet reverberating as a doctor jogged down the hallway, his stethoscope thumping against his chest.

In my opinion, everyone else was entirely too calm. Especially Wes, who, when he wasn't asking if I was all right, was eating one of the many snack foods he kept disappearing to buy from the vending machine downstairs. Now, as he unwrapped a package of little chocolate doughnuts, offering me one, I shook my head.

"I don't see how you can turn down a chocolate doughnut," he said, popping one into his mouth. From Delia's doorway, I was sure I heard a groan or a moan, followed by Pete's voice, soothing.

"I don't see how you can *eat*," I replied, as a nurse emerged from the room, her arms full of some sort of linens, and started down the hallway toward the desk.

He chewed for a second, then swallowed. "This could go on for ages," he said, as Bert, who was sitting on his other side, jerked awake from the nap he'd been taking for the last half hour, blinking. "You have to keep your strength up."

"What time is it?" Bert asked sleepily, rubbing his eyes.

Wes handed him a doughnut. "Almost seven," he said.

I felt my stomach do a flip-flop, although I wasn't sure it was from hearing that I was now officially an hour late to meet my mother, or from the shriek that came from Delia's room, this one loud and extended enough that we all looked at the slightly open door until it abruptly stopped. In the quiet that followed, I pushed myself to my feet.

"Macy?" Wes said.

"I'm fine," I said, knowing that was his next question. "I'm just going to call my mom."

I'd left my cell phone in the van, so I walked to the line of pay phones, digging some change out of my pocket. The first time, the line was busy and I hung up and tried again. Still busy. I pushed open a door that led outside to a small patio, where I sat for a few minutes, looking at the sky, which was slowly growing darker. It was perfect fireworks weather. Then I went back inside and called again, getting the solid busy beep once more. This time, I held on for her voicemail, then cleared my throat and tried to explain.

"It's me," I said, "I know you're probably worried, and I'm really sorry. I was on my way to meet you but Delia went into labor so now I'm at the hospital. I have to wait until someone can drive me, but I'll get there as soon as I can. I'm sorry, again. I'll see you soon."

There, I thought as I hung up the phone. Done. I knew it wouldn't solve everything, or even anything. But I'd deal with that when the time came.

When I came back to the bench where Wes and Bert and I had been sitting, it was empty. In fact, there was nobody in the hallway at all, or at the nurses' station, and for a second I just stood there, feeling totally creeped out. Then Wes stuck his head out of Delia's room. He was grinning.

"Hey," he said. "Come see."

He held the door for me as I stepped inside. Delia was sitting up in the bed, the sheets gathered around her midsection. Her face was flushed, and in her arms was this tiny little thing with dark hair. Pete was sitting on her right, his arm over her shoulders, and they were both looking down at the baby. The room was so quiet, but in a good way. By the window, even Bert, pessimist of pessimists, was smiling.

Then Delia looked up and saw me. "Hey," she said softly, waving me over. "Come say hello." As I came around the bed, she shifted her arms, so the baby was closer to me. "Look. Isn't she beautiful?"

Up close, the baby looked even smaller: her eyes were

closed, and she was making these little snuffly noises, like she was dreaming about something amazing. "She's perfect," I said, and for once, it was the exact right word to use.

Delia trailed her finger over the baby's cheek. "We're calling her Avery," she said. "It's Pete's mom's name. Avery Melissa."

"I like it," I said.

I stared down at the baby's face, her little nose, the tiny nails on her tiny fingers, and suddenly it all came back to me: getting here, the walk across the lobby, how scared I'd been remembering everything about being with my dad. I could feel it rushing over me and I wanted to block it out, but I steeled myself, tightening my fingers into my palms. Avery's eyes were open now, and they were dark and clear. As she looked at me, I wondered what it was like for the world to be so new, everything a first. Today I hadn't had that luxury: each thing that happened since the moment we pulled up was an echo of something else.

Now I watched Delia study her daughter, smiling and slightly teary, and I had a flash of my own mother, all those months ago, walking out of the waiting room downstairs toward me. More than anything I'd wanted to see something in her expression that gave me hope, but there was nothing. Just the same overwhelming sadness and shock, reflected back at me. That had been when this all began, the shift between us, everything changing.

I felt something ache in my chest, and suddenly I knew I was going to cry. For me, for my mother. For what we'd had taken from us, but also for what we'd given up willingly. So much of a life. And so much of each other.

I swallowed, hard, then backed away from the bed. "I, um,"

I said, and I could feel Wes watching me, "I need to go try my mom again."

"Tell her I couldn't have done it without you," Delia said. "You were a real pro."

I nodded, barely hearing this, as Delia bent her head back over the baby, smoothing the blanket around her head.

"Macy," Wes said as I moved past him, out into the hallway.

"It's just," I said, swallowing again. "I . . . need to talk to my mom. I mean, she's worried probably, and she's wondering where I am."

"Okay," he said. "Sure."

Suddenly I just missed my mother—who once stared at the ocean, who laughed huge belly laughs—so much it was like a pain, something throbbing. I gulped down some air. "So I'll just do that," I said to Wes. "Call my mom. And I'll be back."

He nodded. "All right."

I crossed my arms over my chest as I started toward the elevators, walking quickly, struggling to stay calm, even as tears began to sting my eyes. I could feel my heart beating as I ducked around the next corner to an empty alcove. I barely made it before I was sobbing, hands pressed to my face as the tears just flowed, tumbling over my fingers.

I don't know how long I was there before Wes came. It could have been seconds, or minutes, or hours. He said my name and I wanted to collect myself, but I just couldn't.

When he first put his arms around me, it was tentative, like maybe he expected I'd pull away. When I didn't, he moved in closer, his hands smoothing over my shoulders, and in my mind I saw myself retreating a million times when people tried to do this same thing: my sister or my mother, pulling back and into myself, tucking everything out of sight, where only I knew where to find it. This time, though, I gave in. I let Wes pull me against him, pressing my head against his chest, where I could feel his heart beating, steady and true. I felt someone pass by, looking at us, but to them I was just another person crying in a hospital. I couldn't believe it had taken me this long to finally understand. Delia was right: it was fine, okay, expected. This was what you were supposed to do. And it happened all the time.

We caught the last of the fireworks, the biggest and best, as we walked to the Wish van in the hospital parking deck. As they burst overhead, Wes and Bert and I all stopped to look up at them, the whiz and pop as they shot upwards, and the trailing, winding sparks that fell afterwards. Avery was lucky, I thought. She'd always have a party on her birthday.

After everything that had happened, I'd thought that maybe things would be weird between Wes and me when I finally emerged from the ladies room, having splashed my face with cold water in an attempt to compose myself somehow. But as usual, he surprised me, walking me back to Delia's room to say our good-byes as if nothing really out of the ordinary had happened. And maybe it hadn't.

When we turned into Wildflower Ridge, he pulled up at the far edge of the Commons, a decent distance from the picnic and fireworks area, as if he knew I'd need a little bit of a walk to get my head together and prepare myself for the next challenge. In the backseat, Bert was asleep, snoring with his mouth open.

Before I opened my door and hopped out, I eased my purse from under his elbow, careful not to wake him.

Wes got out too, stretching his arms over his head as he came to meet me in front of the van. Looking more closely, I could see the party was breaking up, people gathering their blankets and strollers and dogs, chatting with each other as they rounded up the children who weren't already sleeping in arms or over shoulders.

"So," Wes said, "what are you doing tomorrow?"

I smiled, shaking my head. "No idea. You?"

"Not much. Got a few errands to take care of in the afternoon. I'm thinking about running in the morning, maybe trying that loop in this neighborhood."

"Really," I said. "Are you going to ask me *the* question? Maybe shout it from the street?"

"Maybe," he said, smiling. "You never know. So you'd better be ready. I'll probably pass by around nine or so. I'll be the one moving really slowly."

"Okay," I said. "I'll keep an eye out."

He started back to the driver's side. "Have a good night."

"You too," I said. "And thanks."

Once he was gone, I took a deep breath, then started across the Commons to find my mother. There was so much I wanted to say to her, and for once I wouldn't overthink, instead just letting the words come. Delia had convinced me that my mother only wanted me to be happy. It was up to me to show her that I was now, and why.

After picking my way through the crowd, dodging little kids and various dogs, I spotted my mother talking to Mrs. Burcock, the president of the homeowner's association. I watched her as she listened, waving now and then at people passing by. The night had clearly been a success, and she seemed relaxed as I walked up to stand beside her. She turned and glanced at me, smiling, then redirected her attention back to what Mrs. Burcock was saying.

". . . and bring it up at the meeting next week. I just really think a pooper-scoop rule would improve things for everyone, especially out here on the Commons."

"Absolutely," my mother replied. "Let's bring it to the table and see how everyone responds."

"Well, Macy," Mrs. Burcock said to me. She was an older woman with a prim haircut. "Did you have a good evening?"

"I did," I said. I could feel my mother watching me. "Did you?"

"Oh, it was just wonderful. We'll have to start planning next year, right, Deborah?"

My mother laughed. "Starting tomorrow," she said. "First thing."

Mrs. Burcock smiled, then waved and started across the Commons toward her house. My mother and I stood there for a second, not talking, as more neighbors passed on either side of us.

"So," I said. "Did you get my message?"

She turned her head and looked at me, and I saw, in that one moment, that she was mad. Beyond mad. Furious. I couldn't believe I'd missed it before.

"Not now," she said, her lips hardly moving as she formed the words.

"What?"

"We are not," she said, and this time I could hear, clearly, the absolute rigidness in her voice, "going to discuss this now."

"Great event, Deborah!" A man in khakis and a golf shirt called out as he passed us, a couple of kids in tow.

"Thanks, Ron," my mother replied, smiling. "Glad you enjoyed it!"

"Mom, it wasn't my fault," I said. I took a breath: this wasn't how I wanted this to go. "Delia went into labor, and I couldn't—"

"Macy." Never before had I flinched at the sound of my own name. But I did now. Big time. "I want you to go home, get changed, and get into bed. We'll discuss this later."

"Mom," I said. "Just let me explain, you don't understand. Tonight was—"

"Go." When I didn't, she just stared at me, then said, *"Now."*

And then she turned her back and walked away. Just walked away from me, her posture straight, crossing over to where her employees were waiting for her. I watched her as she listened to them, giving her full attention, nodding, all the things she hadn't, for even one second, done for me.

I walked home, still in shock, and went up to my room. As I passed my mirror I stopped, seeing my shirt was untucked, my jeans had a barbeque sauce stain on them, my hair and face were all mussed and wild from crying. I looked different, absolutely: even if I hadn't been able to explain it, all that had happened showed on my face, where my mother had seen it, instantly. *Get changed*, she said, which was ironic, because all I'd wanted to tell her was that I already had.

I was so screwed.

It wasn't just that I hadn't showed up for the picnic. It was also the fact that Jason, arriving at the info desk to find I'd quit, had immediately called my cell phone, then my house. Not finding me available, he discussed the situation with my mother, who had been trying to reach me ever since. I'd forgotten to turn my phone back on, then left it in the van, never checking it afterwards. Until late that night, when I finally pulled it out of my bag. I had ten messages.

Put plainly, I was in big trouble. Luckily, I had someone around who knew that area, could recognize the landmarks, and knew the best road out.

"When you first get down there, just let her talk," Caroline said. She'd been unlucky enough to stop in that morning en route from the beach house, walking right into this maelstrom. Now we were in the bathroom, where I was devoting twice as much time as usual to brushing my teeth as I attempted to put off the inevitable. "Sit and listen. Don't nod. Oh, and don't smile. That really makes her mad."

I rinsed, then spit. "Right."

"You have to apologize, but don't do it right off, because it seems really ungenuine. Let her blow it out of her system, and then say you're sorry. Don't make excuses, unless you have a really valid one. Do you?"

"I was at the *hospital*," I said, picking up the bottle of mouthwash. If I was going down, at least I'd have nice breath. "My friend was giving birth."

"Was there not a phone there?" she asked.

"I called her!" I said.

"An *hour* after you were supposed to be at the picnic," she pointed out.

"God, Caroline. Whose side are you on?"

"Yours! That's why I'm helping you, can't you see?" She sighed impatiently. "The phone thing is so basic, she'll go to that right off. Don't even try to make an excuse; there isn't one. You can always find a phone. *Always*."

I took in a mouthful of Listerine, then glared at her.

"Tears help," she continued, leaning against the doorjamb and examining her fingernails, "but only if they're real. The fake cry only makes her more angry. Basically, you just have to ride it out. She's always really harsh at first, but once she starts talking she calms down."

"I'm not going to cry," I told her, spitting.

"And, oh, whatever you do," she said, "don't interrupt her. That's, like, *lethal*."

She'd barely finished this sentence when my mother's voice came from the bottom of the stairs. "Macy?" she said. "Could you come down here, please."

It wasn't a question. I looked at Caroline, who was biting her lip, as if experiencing some sort of post-traumatic flashback.

"It's okay," she said. "Take a deep breath. Remember everything I told you. And now"—she put her hands on my shoulders, squeezing them as she turned me around—"go."

I went. My mother who was waiting at the kitchen table, already dressed in her work clothes, did not look up until I sat down. Uh-oh, I thought. I put my hands on the table, folding them over each other in what I hoped was a submissive pose, and waited.

"I'm extremely disappointed in you," she said, her voice level. "*Extremely*."

I felt this. In my gut, which burned. In my palms, which were sweating. It was what I had worked to avoid for so long. Now it was crashing over me like a wave, and all I could do was swim up toward the surface and hope there was air there.

"Macy," she said now, and I felt myself blinking. "What happened last night was unacceptable."

"I'm sorry," I blurted, too early, but I couldn't help it. I hated how my voice sounded, shaky, not like me. The night before I'd been so brave, ready to say all and everything. Now, all I could do was sit there.

"There are going to be some changes," she said, her voice louder now. "I can't count on you to make them, so I will."

I wondered fleetingly if my sister was sitting on the steps, knees pulled to her chest, as I had been so many times, hearing her addressed this way.

"You will not be catering anymore. Period."

I felt a "but" rising in my throat, then bit it back. Ride it out, Caroline had said, the worst is always first. And Delia was going to be out of commission for awhile anyway. "Okay," I said.

"Instead," she said, dropping her hand to the arm of her chair, "you'll be working for me, at the model home, handing out brochures and greeting clients. Monday through Saturday, nine to five."

Saturday? I thought. But of course. It was the busiest day, as far as walk-in traffic went. And all the better to keep me under her thumb. I took a breath, holding it in my mouth, then let it out.

"I don't want you seeing your friends from catering," she continued. "All of the issues I have with your behavior—staying out late, showing less concern about your commitments—began when you took that job."

I kept looking at her, trying to remember everything I'd felt the night before, that sudden welling of emotion that had made me miss her so much. But each time I did, I just saw her steely, professional façade, and I wondered how I could have been so mistaken.

"From now until school starts, I want you in by eight every night," she continued. "That way, we can be sure that you'll be home and rested enough to focus on preparing for the school year."

"Eight?" I said.

She leveled her gaze at me, and I saw my sister was right. Interruptions were lethal. "It could be seven," she said. "If you'd prefer."

I looked down at my hands, silent, shaking my head. All around us the house was so quiet, as if it, too, was just waiting for this to be over.

"You have half a summer left," she said to me, as I studied my thumbnail, the tiny lines running along it. "It's up to you how it goes. Do you understand?"

I nodded, again. When she didn't say anything for a minute I looked up to see her watching me, waiting for a real answer. "Yes," I said. "I understand."

"Good." She pushed back her chair and stood up, smoothing her skirt. As she passed behind me, she said, "I'll see you at the model home in an hour."

I just sat there, listening to her heels clack across the kitchen, then go mute as she hit the carpet, heading to her office. I stayed in place as she gathered her briefcase, then called out a good-bye to Caroline as she left, the door shutting with a quiet thud behind her.

A few seconds later I heard my sister come down the stairs. "That," she said, "was pretty bad."

"I can't see my friends," I said. "I can't do anything."

"She'll ease up," she told me, glancing toward the door. She didn't sound entirely convinced, though. "Hopefully."

But she wouldn't. I knew that already. My mother and I had an understanding: we worked together to be as much in control of our shared world as possible. I was supposed to be her other half, carrying my share of the weight. In the last few weeks, I'd tried to shed it, and doing so sent everything off kilter. So of course she would pull me tighter, keeping me in my place, because doing so meant she would always be sure, somehow, of her own.

I went up to my room and sat down on my bed, listening to the sounds of the neighborhood: a lawn mower, someone's sprinkler whirring, kids riding their bikes in a nearby cul-de-sac. And then, later, the sound of footsteps coming down the sidewalk. I looked at my watch: it was 9:05. The footsteps approached, getting louder and louder, and then slowed as they passed my house. I peered under my shade, and sure enough, it was Wes. He was still moving, but slowly, as if maybe he was hoping I'd come out and join him, or at least wave hello. Maybe he might have even asked that question. But I didn't do anything. I couldn't. I just sat there, as the rest of my summer began to sink in, and a second later, he picked up the pace and moved on.

Chapter Seventeen

It was Tuesday night, six-fifteen on the nose. My mother and I were having dinner and making conversation. Now that we worked together, this was even easier, since we always had something safe to talk about.

"I think we're going to see a real upswing in the townhouse sales this week," she said to me as she helped herself to more bread. She offered me the bowl, but I shook my head. "The interest has been higher lately, don't you think?"

When my punishment had first started, I'd sulked openly, making sure my mother knew how much I disagreed with what she'd done to me. Pretty soon I'd figured out this didn't help my case, though, so I'd progressed to the cold but polite stage, which meant I answered when addressed, but offered no more than the most basic of responses.

"There have been a lot of walk-ins," I said.

"There really have." She picked up her fork. "We'll just have to see, I guess."

By the time we finished eating, I'd have about an hour and a half before curfew. If I didn't go out to yoga class or to the bookstore to browse and drink a mocha (basically the only two allowed options for my "free" time), I'd watch TV or get my clothes ready for work the next day, or just sit on my bed, the window open beside me, and study my SAT word book. It was weird how if I flipped back enough pages, I could see the way I'd carefully made notes, earlier in the summer, next to the harder words, or underlined their prefixes or suffixes neatly. I couldn't even remember doing that now: it was like it was another person, some other girl.

Once, this had been the life I'd wanted. Even chosen. Now, though, I couldn't believe that there had been a time when this kind of monotony and silence, this most narrow of existences, had been preferable. Then again, once, I'd never known anything else.

"Caroline should be coming into town again next week," my mother said, putting her fork down and wiping her mouth with a napkin.

"Thursday, I think," I replied.

"We'll have to plan to have dinner, so we can all catch up."

I took a sip of my water. "Sure."

My mother had to know I was unhappy. But it didn't matter: all she cared about was that I was her Macy again, the one she'd come to depend on, always within earshot or reach. I came to work early, sat up straight at my desk and endured the monotony of answering phones and greeting potential homebuyers with a smile on my face. After dinner, I spent my hour and a half of free time alone, doing accepted activities. When I came home afterwards, my mother would be waiting for me, sticking her head out of her office to verify that, yes, I was just where I was supposed to be. And I was. I was also miserable.

"This salad," she said now, taking a sip from her wine glass, "is just wonderful."

"Thanks," I told her. "The chicken's good, too."

"It is, isn't it?"

Around us, the house was dark and quiet. Empty.

"Yes," I said. "It really is."

I missed Kristy. I missed Delia. But most of all, I missed Wes.

He'd called the first night of my punishment, my cell phone buzzing as I sat on my bed, contemplating the rest of my summer, which now seemed to stretch out ahead of me, endless and flat. I'd been feeling sorry for myself all day, but it really kicked into overdrive the minute I punched the TALK button and heard his voice.

"Hey," he said. "How's it going?"

"Don't ask."

He did though, as I knew he would, just as I knew he would listen, making sympathetic noises, as I outlined my restrictive curfew and the very real possibility that I might not see him again, ever. I didn't go so far as to tell him that he and everyone else from Wish were off limits, although I had a feeling he probably knew that, too.

"You'll be okay," he said. "It could be worse."

"How?"

The only noise was the buzzing of the line as he considered this. "Could be forever," he said finally.

"It's until the end of the summer," I said. "It *is* forever."

"Nah. It just seems like it now, because it's the first day. You'll see. It'll go fast."

This was easy for him to say. While my life had slowed to a near stop, Wes's was now busier than ever. When he wasn't working on sculptures to keep up with increasing demand, he was driving to garden art places to drop off pieces and take new orders. At night, he was working the job he'd taken delivering for A la Carte, a store that specialized in high-end, restaurant-quality dinner entrees brought right to your door. Most of our conversations lately had taken place while he was en route to one delivery or another. While I sat in my room, staring out the window, he was constantly in motion, crisscrossing town with bags of chicken parmigiana and shrimp scampi riding shotgun beside him. I was always happy to hear his voice. But it wasn't the same.

We didn't talk about our Truth game, other than to agree to keep it on hold until we got to see each other face-to-face. Sometimes, at night, when I sat out on my roof alone, I'd run over the questions and answers we'd traded back and forth in my head. For some weird reason, I was afraid I might forget them otherwise, like they were vocabulary words or something else I had to study to keep close at hand.

Kristy had been in touch as well, calling to extend invitations to come over and sunbathe, or go to parties (she knew I was grounded, but like "free time" for my mother, this was clearly a flexible term for her), or just to talk about her new boyfriend. His name was Baxter, and they'd met cute, when he stopped by the produce stand while she was sitting in for Stella one day. He'd talked to her for over an hour, then, besotted, bought an entire bushel of cucumbers. This was clearly extraordinary, or at least, notable, and now she was busy much of the time, too. That was the thing about being on the inside: the world was just going on, even when it seemed like time for you had stopped for good.

I was bored. Sad. Lonely. It was only a matter of time before I cracked.

I'd had a long day at the model home, stapling Welcome

packets and listening to my mother give her sales spiel to six different prospective clients. It was the same thing I'd done the day before, and the day before that. Which was bad enough even before you factored in that I'd eat the same dinner (chicken and salad) with the same person (my mother) at the same time (six sharp), then fill the hours before bedtime the same way (yoga and studying). With all of this combined, the monotony hit lethal levels. So it was no wonder I was feeling totally hopeless and trapped, even before I went home and found an email from Jason.

Macy,

I've been wanting to get in touch with you, but I haven't been sure what to say. I don't know if your mom told you, but I came on the Fourth because my grandmother had a stroke, and she's been deteriorating ever since. We're very close, as you know, but even so dealing with this, and the very real possibility that she may not make it, has been harder for me than I expected. I was disappointed to hear that you quit the info desk, and while I have a few ideas on the subject, I'd like to know, in your own words, what it was that precipitated that decision.

That's not really why I'm writing, however. I guess with everything that's happening in my own family right now I feel like I've had some added insight into how things must have been for you in the last couple of years. I think I was hard on you about the info desk earlier this summer, and for that I apologize. I know I suggested that we be on a break until I return, but I hope that whatever happens we can at least stay in contact, and stay friends. I hope you'll write back. I'd really like to hear from you.

I had read it twice, but it still didn't really make sense. I'd thought that quitting the info desk would be the final proof he needed that I would never be the girl for him. Now, though, with the prospect of loss hovering over him, he seemed to think the opposite. If anyone understood, I could see him reasoning, with that even, cool logic, it was me. Right?

"No," I said aloud. My mind was spinning. A week and a half earlier it had seemed like my life had changed for good. That *I* had changed it. But now it was all slipping away. I was back to being my mother's daughter, and with this, it seemed maybe I could be Jason's girlfriend, too. If I didn't take action, somehow, by the fall everything that had happened with Wish, and with Wes, would be smoothed over, forgotten, no more than a dream. So that night, after I'd wiped the counters down and put away the leftovers, I picked up my yoga mat, told my mother I'd be back by eight, and broke her rules, driving off to Sweetbud Road.

I pulled in to the still signless road, and dodged the hole unthinkingly, glancing at the heart in hand as I passed it. I was looking at everything, surprised that it didn't seem all that different until I realized it had only been about ten days since I'd last been there.

First I pulled into Wes's driveway, but his truck was gone, the house dark. I walked around the side of the house to his workshop. There were more pieces than ever grouped in the yard: I saw angels, a few large whirligigs, and one piece that was medium sized, barely begun, with only the frame of a stick figure with some brackets attached to the back.

On my way to Kristy's, I slowed down in front of Delia's house, peering through the front window. I could see Pete walking with Avery in his arms, rocking her, and Delia beyond him, stirring something on the stove as Lucy sat at her feet, stacking blocks on top of each other. I knew she would have been happy to see me, but instead I just watched them for a second, feeling sort of sad. It was as if everything had closed up and grown over my absence, like I'd never been there at all.

When I pulled in the driveway of the doublewide, I could see the light of the TV through the window. As I got out of my car and started up the steps, Bert came out of the front door. He was in khakis and a collared golf shirt that looked to be polyester, and he reeked of cologne. I actually smelled him before I saw him.

"Hey," I said. I was trying not to wince. "You look nice."

He smiled, obviously pleased. "Got a date," he said, hooking his fingers in his pockets and leaning back on his heels. "Going out to dinner."

"That's great," I said. "Who's the girl?"

"Her name's Lisa Jo. I met her at the Armageddon social. She's, like, an expert on the Big Buzz. Last summer, she went out west with her dad and recorded evidence of it."

"Really." A female Bert. I couldn't even imagine.

"Yup." He hopped off the step and started down the walk. "See you later."

"Bye," I said, watching as he cut through the garden, down the winding path that led back to his house. "Have fun."

I pulled open the doublewide door and called out a hello,

then stepped inside. There was no answer, and I glanced down the hallway to Kristy's room: the door was open, the light off. Looking the other way, I saw only Monica sitting on the couch, staring at the TV.

"Hey," I said again, and she turned her head slightly, finally seeing me. "Where's Kristy?"

"Out," she replied.

"With Baxter?" She nodded. "Oh," I said, crossing the room and sitting down on the ottoman in front of Stella's chair. "I thought maybe she'd be in tonight."

"Nope."

It was just too damn ironic that, in desperately seeking conversation, I'd ended up with, of all people, Monica. What was even sadder was that I stayed where I was, making various stabs at it anyway.

"So," I said, as she flipped channels, "what's been going on?"

"Nothing." She paused on a rap video, then moved on. "You?"

"I've been grounded," I said, a bit too eagerly. "I mean, I still am grounded, technically. I'm not supposed to be here . . . but I got this email from my boyfriend, and it kind of flipped me out. It's just . . . I feel like everything's changing, you know?"

"Mmm-hmm," she said sympathetically.

"It's just weird," I said, wondering why I was telling her all this, and yet fully unable to stop, "I don't know what to do."

She took in a breath, and for a second I thought I might actually get a full sentence. But then she sighed and said, "Uh-huh."

Clearly, this was not what I needed. So I said my good-byes, leaving Monica still flipping channels, and drove back into town. And there, at a traffic light by the Lakeview Mall, I finally found what I was looking for.

Wes. He was across the way, facing me, and I flicked my lights at him. When the light changed, he pulled into the lot in front of Milton's Market while I turned around and doubled back to meet him.

"I thought you were grounded," he said, as I got out of my car and walked over to where he was standing in front of the truck. I couldn't believe how happy I was to see him.

"I am," I said. "I'm at yoga."

He looked at me, raising his eyebrows, and I felt myself smile, suddenly feeling reassured. Of course I wouldn't go back to Jason. Of course I wasn't the same girl again. It had just taken seeing Wes to remind me.

"Okay, so I'm not at yoga," I said. I shook my head. "God, this night has just been . . . I don't know. Weird. I just needed to get out. Too much to think about."

He nodded, running a hand through his hair. "I know the feeling."

"So what are you doing?" I asked. "Working?"

"Um," he said, glancing at the truck, "not really. I took the night off. I have a bunch of stuff I have to get done."

I looked at my watch, then said, "I'm have another hour before I'm due home. You want company?"

"Um," he said again. I noticed this, for some reason. In fact, as I stood there, I noticed that he was jumpy, nervous even. "Better not. I've got to meet with this client at seven-thirty. You'd be late."

"Oh." I tucked a piece of hair behind my ear, and neither of us said anything for a minute, a silence more awkward than any

I'd ever felt between us. Something's going on, I thought, and immediately I flashed back to that night at the hospital, when I'd cried. Maybe it had been too much, and had freaked him out. We'd only talked on the phone since then, hadn't seen each other. For all I knew, this change had happened ages ago, and I was only just catching up with it now.

"It's just," he said, as I turned my head, watching a car pass by, "just this thing I have to do. You wouldn't want to come."

I felt my body reacting, my posture straightening, as I shifted into the defensive mode I knew so well. "Yeah, I should go anyway," I said.

"Well, hang out for a second," he said. "What's been going on?"

"Not much." I looked at my watch. "God, I'm gonna go. It's stupid for me to even be risking this, with everything that's happened. And I have this email from Jason to answer."

"Jason?" He looked surprised. "Really."

I nodded, flipping my car keys in my hand. "I don't know, he's having some problems, we're in touch. He wants to get back together, I think."

"Is that what you want?"

"I don't know," I said, even though I knew it wasn't. "Maybe."

He was looking at me now: I had his full attention. Which was why I turned my back and started walking to my car.

"Macy," he said, "hold on a second."

"I really have to go," I told him. "I'll see you around."

"Wait." I was still walking, but I could hear him coming up behind me, knew he'd put his hand on my shoulder even before he did. "Are you okay?"

"Yes," I said, and started walking again. "I'm fine." Even when I got to my car and opened the door, he hadn't moved, stayed there as I drove away. I would have thought this would make me feel better, for once getting to be the one to leave and not the one left behind. But it didn't. Not at all.

I was almost all the way home when I turned around.

But he was gone. I sat at the light for a second, the big time and temperature sign at Willow Bank blinking above me: 7:24, 78 degrees. I kept looking from the red stoplight to the numbers, then back again, and all of a sudden I knew where to go.

Call it a gut feeling, but all the way to the World of Waffles I was sure that somehow, I could fix this. Maybe I'd just been too sensitive. He had a lot on his mind. It probably had nothing to do with me. But he *had* been acting so weird, checking his watch. That I knew I hadn't imagined. But regardless, he needed to know why I'd been so cold to him, how important he was to me. Maybe that would freak him out, too. But it was the Truth. And we'd always held to that.

As soon as I saw his truck parked in the lot, I felt myself relax. I can do this, I thought, as I pulled in two spaces down and cut my engine, then pushed my door open. The air was full of that sweet, doughy smell, and as I started toward the front door, I reminded myself that this, too, was proof that I had changed. Once, I would have just let Wes go. But I was different now.

I was different all the way across the parking lot, to the edge of the curb, almost to the door. But then I saw him, sitting in the same booth against the window. He wasn't alone.

Gotcha, I thought, and it was weird that it felt exactly the same way, a sudden shock, a jump of the heart, like your entire system shuts down, and then, as you stand there gasping, somehow reboots. Somehow.

I hadn't heard a lot about Becky, but I recognized her with just one look. Like Wes had said, she was skinny, angular, with a short haircut, the ends of which barely touched her collarbone. She had on a thin black tank top, a rosary necklace, and dark red lipstick, which had already stained the rim of the coffee mug she was holding between her hands. Wes was sitting opposite her, talking, and she was looking at him intently, her gaze steady, as if what he was saying was the most important thing in the world. And probably it was. Maybe he was telling her his deepest secrets. Or asking her the question I'd been waiting for. I'd never know.

I got back in my car, starting the engine, then drove off. It wasn't until I pulled onto the highway that it all really sunk in, how temporary our friendship had been. We'd been on our breaks, after all, but it wasn't our relationships that were on pause: it was us. Now we were both in motion again, moving ahead. So what if there were questions left unanswered. Life went on. We knew that better than anyone.

Chapter Eighteen

For weeks, my mother had been concerned about me. Now, it was my turn to really worry.

My mother had always worked hard. But I'd never seen her like this. Maybe it was just that I was up close now, for six or seven hours each day, where I could hear the constant string of phone conversations, the clattering of her answering emails, and watch the constant stream of contractors, realtors, and salespeople coming in and out of her office. It was now July twenty-third, which meant the townhouse opening and the gala celebrating it were a little over two weeks away. Everyone else seemed to think things were going well, but my mother wasn't happy with the presales. Or the marble tubs that had been installed so far. Or several of her contractors, who, at least in her view, cared more about little things like sleeping and the occasional Sunday off than getting everything done exactly right, ahead of schedule. I'd been aware for awhile of how tired she looked, and how she hardly ever seemed to smile. But all of a sudden, I began to see that things were worse than I'd realized.

Maybe I should have noticed earlier, but I'd been distracted with my own problems. After what happened with Wes, though, I'd stopped resisting my punishment. It was weird how, with things pretty much done between us, I could so easily go back to the life I'd had before. I found myself forgetting the girl I'd become, who'd been, if not fearless, not as afraid.

My life was quiet, organized, and silent. My mother's however, was fast and frenetic. She never seemed to sleep, and she was losing weight, the dark circles under her eyes clearly visible, despite her always careful application of concealer. More and more I found myself watching her, worrying about the toll her stress was taking on her body. Sometimes you had signs: sometimes you didn't. But I kept a close eye anyway.

"Mom," I said one day, as I stood in her open door, the chicken salad sandwich I'd ordered for her in my hand. It was now two-thirty, which meant it had been sitting on the corner of my desk, the mayonnaise in it certainly courting food poisoning, for almost three hours. "You have to eat. Now."

"Oh, honey, I will," she said, picking up some pink message slips and flipping through them. "Bring it in, I'll get to it as soon as I finish this."

I came in just as she started talking on the phone again, clicking away at her keyboard. Arranging her sandwich on a paper plate, I listened as she talked with the chef she'd hired for the gala, who called himself Rathka. He'd come highly recommended, but so far he and my mother had butted heads repeatedly, about his erratic schedule (he never seemed to answer the phone), the expensive china dishes he insisted she rent (because only they allowed the full culinary experience), and the menu, about which he'd so far declined to give specifics.

"What I mean," my mother was saying as I poured her a Diet Coke, putting it next to her sandwich, "is that because I am inviting seventy-five people, and because this is a most important event, I'd like to have a bit more of a concrete idea of what we'll be eating."

I folded a napkin, sliding it under the edge of her paper plate, then nudged both closer to her elbow. Only when they bumped it did she look up at me, mouthing a thank-you. But then she only took a sip of the Diet Coke, ignoring the sandwich altogether.

"Yes, I understand there will be lamb," she said, rolling her eyes. Lately it seemed like my mother was battling with everyone. "But lamb does not a full menu make. . . . It means, I need more details." There was a pause. "I understand that you're an artiste, Rathka. But I am a businesswoman. And I need some idea of what I'm paying for."

I went back to my desk and sat down, swiveling in my chair, and punched a few keys, calling up my own email account. While working for my mother kept me busier than the info desk ever had, there was the occasional bit of downtime. It was then that I always seemed to find myself staring at another email from Jason.

The night I'd seen Wes, I'd come home to find Jason's message still on my screen. While my first thought was to just delete and ignore it, I reconsidered. So I sat down, my fingers poised over the keyboard. Being pushed back to this life was one thing. Now at least I felt like I was choosing it. And it wasn't like I had other options, anyway.

I wrote to Jason that I hated the info desk, that I just felt like it wasn't the job for me, and I probably should have quit right away instead of staying. I told him how his other email, announcing our break, had hurt me, and how I wasn't sure how

I felt about us getting back together at the end of the summer, or ever. But I also told him I was sorry about his grandmother, and that if he needed to talk, I was here. It was the least I could do, I figured. I wasn't going to turn my back on someone in their moment of weakness.

So now we were in contact, if you could call it that. Our emails were short and to the point: he talked about Brain Camp, how it was stimulating but a lot of work, and I wrote about my mother and how stressed out she was. I didn't worry so much about what he thought of what I wrote, what he might read between the lines. I didn't race to answer him either, sometimes letting a day or two go before I replied, letting the words come at their own pace. When they did, I'd just type them up and hit Send, trying not to overthink. He always wrote back faster than I did, and had even started hinting about us seeing each other the day he got back, the seventh, which was also the day of the gala. The more I pulled back, the more he seemed to move forward. I wondered if it was really because he cared about me, or if now I was just another challenge.

I still thought about Wes a lot. It had been about two weeks now, and we hadn't talked. The first few days afterwards he tried to call me on my cell phone, but when I saw his number pop up on the screen I just slid it aside, letting it ring, and eventually turned it off entirely. I knew what he'd think: we'd just been friends, after all, and we'd always talked about Becky and Jason before, so why not now? I didn't know the answer to this, just as I didn't know why it had bothered me so much to see him with Becky. She'd come back to him, just like Jason had come back to me, and I knew he was probably happy about that. I should have been happy, too, but I just wasn't.

Occasionally I heard from Kristy, who had in this interim gone from smitten with Baxter to positively lovesick. "Oh, Macy," she'd sigh in my ear, sounding so wistful and happy I could have hated her, if I hadn't thought she so deserved it. "He's just extraordinary. Truly extraordinary."

I kept waiting for her to bring up Becky, and her and Wes being back together, but she never did, knowing, probably, that it was a sore subject. She did, however, say that Wes had been asking about me, and she wondered if something had happened between us. "Is that what he said?" I asked her.

"No," she'd replied, switching the phone to her other ear. "It's Wes. He never says anything."

Once he had, I thought. Once he'd said a lot, to me. "It's nothing," I told her. "We just, you know, don't have that much in common." And maybe this was true, after all.

It was a Friday, which was supposed to be a good thing. For me, though, and the concrete guy in my mother's office, things were just going from bad to worse.

". . . and I will not be paying any overtime for a job that was guaranteed to be done over a week ago!" I could hear my mother say. This was the fourth meeting she'd had with a subcontractor today, and they'd all gone pretty much the same way. As in, not well.

"The weather," the concrete guy inside said, "was—"

"The weather," my mother shot back, interrupting him, "is something that you, as a professional who deals with it as a factor in all jobs, should take into consideration when submitting a bid for work. This is summer. It rains!"

My mother's voice, so brittle and shrill these days, sent a chill down my spine. I could only imagine how the concrete guy felt.

There was a bit more back and forth, and then their voices dropped, which meant this meeting was almost over. Sure enough, a second later the door opened, and the concrete guy, heavyset and irritated-looking, mumbled past my desk and slammed out of the office, the windows rattling in his wake.

My phone buzzed, and I picked it up. "Macy," my mother said. She sounded exhausted. "Could you bring me a water, please?"

I reached into the small fridge beside my desk to get one, then pushed out my chair and walked to her door. For once, my mother was not on the phone or staring at the computer screen. Instead, she was sitting back in her desk chair, looking out the window at the sign across the street advertising the townhouses. There was a truck parked in front of it, so you could see only the last part: AVAILABLE AUGUST 8TH. SIGN UP FOR YOURS NOW!

I twisted the cap off the water, then slid it across the desk to her. I watched her take a sip, closing her eyes, then said, "You okay?"

"I'm fine," she said, automatically, unthinkingly. "It's always like this at the end of a project. It was like this with the houses, and the apartments. It doesn't matter if it's fifty million-dollar townhouses or one spec house. Everything always gets crazy at the end. You just have to keep going, regardless of how awful it gets. So that's what I do." She sipped at her water again. "Even on days like this, when I'm sure it's going to kill me."

"Mom," I said. "Don't even say that."

She smiled again, a tired smile, the only smile I ever saw from her lately. "It's just an expression," she said, but I still felt uneasy. "I'm fine."

For the rest of the afternoon, I busied myself with the gala guest list. At four forty-five, I sat back in my chair, grateful I only had fourteen minutes and counting before I got to escape. Then, though, two things happened. The phone rang, and my sister walked in.

"Wildflower Ridge Sales," I said, waving at her as she shut the door behind her and walked up to my desk.

"Meez Queensh pleeze es Raffka," the voice on the other end said. Rathka, besides having an accent that made him almost completely incomprehensible, always seemed to talk with his mouth pressed right up to the receiver.

"Right, hold please." I hit the button, then looked up at Caroline, who was standing in front of me, hands clasped together, her face expectant. "Hey," I said. "What's up?"

She took a breath to answer, but then my mother opened her office door, sticking her head out. "Is line one for me?" she asked, then saw my sister. "Caroline, hello. When did you get here?"

My sister looked at her, then back at me. Clearly, she was working up to something. She took in another breath, smiled, then said, "It's done."

There was a second or two of silence as my mother and I processed this. On the phone in front of me, the red light was blinking.

"It's done," my mother repeated slowly.

Caroline was still looking at us, expectant.

"The beach house," I said finally. "Right?"

"Yes!" Caroline clapped her hands, three times fast, like this was a game show and I'd won the showcase showdown. "It's done! And it's fabulous. Fabulous! You have to come and see it. Right now."

"Now?" My mother glanced at the clock, then back at my blinking phone. "But it's—"

"Friday. Quitting time. The weekend." Caroline, clearly, had thought this through. "I've gassed up my car and bought sandwiches so we won't even have to stop for dinner. If we leave in the next half hour, we might even get there for the last of the sunset."

My mother put her hand on my desk. I watched her fingers curl around the edge. "Caroline," she said slowly, "I'm sure it's just wonderful. But I can't get away this weekend. There's just too much work to do."

It took Caroline a second to react to this. "It's just one night," she said after a minute. "You can come back first thing tomorrow."

"I have a meeting in the morning with my superintendents. We're on a very tight schedule. I can't get away."

Caroline lowered her hands to her sides. "But you've been saying that all summer."

"That's because it's been true all summer. It's just a bad time." My mother looked at the phone again, that blinking light, still so insistent. "Who is that holding?"

"Rathka," I said quietly.

"I should take it. It's probably important." She started back to her office, then turned and looked at my sister, who was just standing there, like she was in shock. I felt a pang of pity, thinking of her buying sandwiches, stocking a cooler, how excited she must have been to show us the house. "Honey," my mother said, pausing in the doorway, "I know how much you've put into this, and I so appreciate everything you've done."

I wasn't sure that she did, though. That either of us did. For the past few weeks, my sister had been in constant transit between the beach house and her own, stopping during each trip to give us an update. My mother and I, concerned with our own problems, had given what attention we could, but neither of us was ever as involved as she would have liked us to be.

Now, she stood in the doorway, biting her lip. I'd never thought I had that much in common with my sister, but now, watching her, I felt some sense of solidarity. Caroline, in the last few weeks, had engineered an amazing transformation, one she wanted more than anything to share with us, but especially my mother.

"Mom," Caroline said now, "you're going to love it. Just take twelve hours off and come and see. Please."

My mother sighed. "I'm sure I will. And I'll get there, okay? Just not today."

"Fine," Caroline said, in a voice that made it clear it really wasn't. She walked over and sat down in one of the chairs by the window, crossing one leg over the other. My mother was edging into her office, as if that red light was pulling her closer, when my sister said, "I guess it was kind of spur of the moment, thinking we could do this today. I mean, since we're going next Sunday anyway."

"Next Sunday," my mother repeated. She seemed confused. "What's happening then?"

Caroline was looking at her, and I had a bad feeling. Really bad. "We're going to the beach house for the week," I said quickly, looking from her to my mother, then back at Caroline. "On the eighth. Right?"

I was waiting for Caroline to agree. Instead, my mother said, "Next Sunday? The day after the party? That's impossible.

The phase will have just opened. When did you decide this?"

"I didn't," Caroline said, finally speaking. Her voice was level, even. "*We* did. Weeks ago."

My mother looked at me. "But that's impossible," she said, running a hand through her hair. "I wouldn't have agreed to that, it's too soon. The sales will have just started, and we have a meeting that Monday on breaking ground for the next phase. . . . I have to be here."

"I can't believe this," my sister said, shaking her head. "I can't believe you."

"Caroline, you have to understand," my mother told her. "This is important."

"No!" my sister screamed, the word suddenly just filling the room. "This is *work*, and for you, it's never done. You promised me we'd take this vacation, and I've killed myself getting ready on time so we could have this week together as a family. You said you'd be done, but you're never done. All this summer it's been about these stupid townhouses, and two days after they open, you're breaking ground for something else? God! You'll do *anything* to avoid it."

"Avoid what?" my mother said.

"The past," Caroline said. "Our past. I'm tired of acting like nothing ever happened, of pretending he was never here, of not seeing his pictures in the house, or his things. Just because you're not able to let yourself grieve."

"*Don't*," my mother said, her voice low, "talk to me about grief. You have no idea."

"I do, though." Caroline's voice caught, and she swallowed. "I'm not trying to hide that I'm sad. I'm not trying to forget. You hide here behind all these plans for houses and townhouses because they're new and perfect and don't remind you of anything."

"Stop it," my mother said.

"And look at Macy," Caroline continued, ignoring this. "Do you even know what you're doing to her?"

My mother looked at me, and I shrank back, trying to stay out of this. "Macy is fine," my mother said.

"No, she's not. God, you *always* say that, but she's not." Caroline looked at me, as if she wanted me to jump in, but I just sat there. "Have you even been paying the least bit of attention to what's going on with her? She's been miserable since Dad died, pushing herself so hard to please you. And then, this summer, she finally finds some friends and something she likes to do. But then one tiny slipup, and you take it all away from her."

"That has nothing to do with what we're talking about," my mother said.

"It has everything to do with it," Caroline shot back. "She was finally getting over what happened. Couldn't you see the change in her? I could, and I was barely here. She was *different*."

"Exactly," my mother said. "She was—"

"Happy," Caroline finished for her. "She was starting to live her life again, and it scared you. Just like me redoing the beach house scares you. You think you're so strong because you never talk about Dad. Anyone can hide. Facing up to things, working through them, *that's* what makes you strong."

"I've given everything I have to support this family," my mother replied, biting off the words. "And for you, it's still not enough."

"I'm not asking for everything you have." Caroline put her hands to her face, breathing in, then lowered them. "I'm asking you to allow me, and Macy, and especially yourself to remember Dad—"

My mother exhaled loudly, shaking her head.

"—and I'm asking you for one week of your time to begin doing it." Caroline looked at me, then back at my mother. "That's all."

The pause that followed this was long enough that I started to think maybe, just maybe, my mother was going to agree. She was just standing there, arms crossed over her chest, looking out the front window of the model home at the houses across the street.

"I have to be here," she said finally. "I can't just leave."

"It's one week," Caroline said. "It's not forever."

"I can't leave," my mother repeated. "I'm sorry." And she walked back into her office, stiffly, and shut the door behind her. I listened for the familiar noises—the squeak of her chair rollers, the phone being picked up so she could deal with Rathka, the keyboard clacking—but heard nothing. It was like she'd just disappeared.

My sister, gulping back tears, turned and pushed the front door open. "Caroline," I said, but she was already outside, walking down the front steps.

I thought about going after her. I wanted to be able to say something that would make everything okay, but I had no idea what that might be. *It's not forever*, she'd said, but to my mother, it might as well have been. She had made her choice, and this was it, where she felt safe, in a world she could, for the most part, control.

My sister was in her car now, wiping her eyes: I watched her as she cranked the engine, then drove away from the curb. As she moved away, I could see the sign across the street in full view now, and I read the rest of it. NEW PHASES COMING SOON! it said. And then, as if it was easy, or a good thing, always: COME CHANGE WITH US.

My mother was still in her office, silent, when the clock hit five and I stood up to leave. I thought about knocking at her door, even asking if she was okay, but instead I just gathered up my things and slipped out the front door, shutting it behind me hard enough so that she'd hear it and know I was gone.

As I came up our front walk, I saw the box on the front porch: small, square, parked in the direct center of our welcome mat. Waterville, Maine, I thought, even before I got close enough to check the return address. I picked it up and took it inside with me.

The house was quiet, cool, as I went into the kitchen, put the box on the counter, then found the scissors and cut it open.

Inside, there were two pictures: the first was of a belt loop sporting a huge, cluttered key ring that looked like it weighed about a hundred pounds. Then in the second picture, there was the same belt loop, but now attached to it was a square plastic box that looked sort of like a tape measure. Along one side, though, was a series of tabs, each a different color. *Frustrated with your old, clunky key chain?* asked the bright print below. *Get rid of it! Get organized. Get the EZ-Key!*

Apparently, with the EZ-Key, you could color code each of your keys, then attach them to a retracting cord, so that you only had to pull them out, unlock whatever needed unlocking, and zip! they shot right back into place. It was a good idea, really, I thought as I turned the box in my hand, rereading its breathless copy, but then they all were, at least on the surface.

About an hour later, as I was sliding some chicken breasts into the oven, my mother called.

"Macy," she said, "I need you to get me a phone number."

"Okay," I said, starting toward her office. "Let me just get your phone book."

"No, I think you know it. It's for that woman, Delia. The woman you worked for."

"Delia?" I said.

"Yes."

I just stood there for a second, waiting for her to offer an explanation. When she didn't, I said, "Why . . .?"

"Because," she said, "Rathka has just quit, and every other catering company is already booked for next Saturday or on vacation. This is a last resort."

"Rathka quit?" I asked, incredulous.

"Macy," she said. "The number, please."

I knew there was no way Delia would do it: she hadn't booked any jobs since Avery had been born, and it was way short notice. But with the way my mother's day had been going, I figured it was better not to point this out. "It's 555-7823," I said.

"Thank you," she said. "I'll be home soon." And then there was a click, and she was gone.

Chapter Nineteen

My sister stayed away for a full week, completely and totally incommunicado. She stopped answering her cell phone and ignored all emails, and when we finally got through on her home phone, it was always Wally who answered, his voice stiff and forced enough that it was immediately clear not only that he had been coached to say she was out but that she was standing right there behind him as he did so.

"She'll get over it," my mother kept saying, each time I relayed my thwarted efforts to reach her. "She will."

My mother wasn't worried, even if I was. There were other, bigger concerns on her mind now. And they all had to do with the gala reception.

It had started with Rathka quitting, but that was only the beginning. In the six days since, it seemed like everything that could go wrong had done just that. When the landscapers came to work on the yard, one of their riding mowers went haywire, ripping up huge clumps of grass and taking out a few shrubs in the process. They did their best to fix it, but the topography remained uneven. Just crossing from the garage to the steps felt like walking over little mountains and valleys. Half of the invitations we'd mailed came back due to some postal error, which meant I had to drive around one hot afternoon, hand delivering them to mailbox after mailbox. The next day, the string quartet cancelled, as three of the four had come down with food poisoning at an outdoor wedding.

The night before the party, however, my mother's luck seemed to be changing. The guys from the party rental place arrived early to assemble the tent. We stood and watched as they put it up and set up the chairs and tables beneath it, both of us braced for some sort of crisis. But everything went according to plan.

"Wonderful," she said to the tent guy, handing him his check. "I wasn't even sure we'd need a tent, but it just makes everything look that much nicer."

"And also," he told her, "if it rains, you're covered."

She just looked at him. "It is *not*," she said, firmly, as if there was no room for negotiation, "going to rain."

The only other good news my mother had gotten was that Delia, to my surprise, had agreed to take the gala job. It wouldn't be lamb on fine china, my mother had sighed, but she'd be glad for anything at this point, even if it was chicken on a stick and meatballs.

"Everyone loves meatballs," I'd told her, but she'd just looked at me before moving on to the next crisis at hand.

In a way, I was kind of grateful for all the various crises, if only because they kept me so busy. I didn't have time to worry about things, such as the awkwardness of seeing Wes after all this time, or handling Jason, who was now planning to drop by to say hello at some point during the evening. I'd just deal with it when it happened, I told myself, and that would be soon enough.

Now, as the tent guys drove off, I heard a car pull into the driveway. I glanced around the side of the house to see my sister getting out of a truck with a long, wide bed, which was packed with what I first assumed was metal patio furniture or some sort of construction refuse from the beach house. She parked and got out just as another car, which I recognized as belonging to one of my mother's salesmen, pulled up behind her.

"What on *earth* has she got there?" my mother asked me as we walked around the side of the house, and suddenly I realized it was Wes's stuff. Six pieces, at least, although they were stacked in such a way it was hard to tell. By the time we got up to the truck, Caroline had the tailgate down and she and the salesman were pulling a few pieces out, leaning them against the back bumper. I could see a big angel with a barbed-wire halo, as well as a whirligig that had been out at his house the last day I'd been there. It was made up of a series of bicycle wheels—from big ones to the tiny training kind—welded to a twisted piece of rebar.

"Caroline," my mother called out, her voice forced and cheery. "Hello."

Caroline didn't reply at first, but the salesman waved as they continued pulling pieces out and putting them in the driveway: a smaller angel with a stained-glass halo, another whirligig fashioned out of hubcaps and interlocking gears.

"We can just set them up on the grass," she said to the salesman. "Anywhere's fine, really."

"Caroline?" my mother said, as he began pulling the angel onto the lawn, dragging it over the bumpy terrain. I could tell she was concerned, but also trying to be careful to avoid another snit. In fact, she didn't say anything else, even as the angel dug up more grass in a path behind itself.

"Don't worry," Caroline said finally, wiping a hand across

her face. She was in shorts and a T-shirt, her hair pulled back in a ponytail. "I'm only stopping for a second. I need to take some shots of these and email them to Wally so we can decide which to take to the mountain house, and which I should just bring home with me."

"Well," my mother said, as Caroline and the salesman began to pull the larger angel onto the front lawn, positioning it for a second before going back to grab one of the smaller ones, "that's fine. Just fine."

None of us said anything for a few minutes as the pieces were assembled on the lawn. People kept driving past the house, then slowing, staring. My mother kept offering up her Good Neighbor wave and smile, but I could tell she wasn't happy.

By the time Caroline and the salesman were done, there were seven pieces on the lawn: two big angels, two small, a large square piece, and two sculptures, one with the hubcaps and another made out of gears and wheels of various sizes. The salesman stepped back, wiping a hand over his face. "You sure you don't want me to stick around to help you put them back in?"

"No, it's okay," Caroline said to him. "I'll get one of the neighbor kids to help or something. I just wasn't sure anyone would be here. But thanks."

"No problem," he said cheerfully. "Anything to help the cause. Deborah, I'll see you tomorrow."

"Right," my mother replied, nodding. "See you then."

As he left, my sister moved around the front yard, adjusting the pieces this way or that. After a second she looked down at the grass, as if just noticing the state it was in, then said, "What's wrong with the lawn?"

I shook my head, glancing at my mother.

"Nothing," my mother said evenly, as she walked up to the larger angel and peered at it more closely. "Well. These are certainly interesting. Where did you get them?"

"Macy's friend Wes," Caroline told her, wiping a smudge off one of the bicycle wheels. To me she said, "You know, he's really something."

"Yeah," I said, looking at the angel with the barbed-wire halo. Away from the farmer's market, and Wes's workshop, the pieces seemed that much more impressive. Even my mother noticed. I could tell by the way she was still studying the angel's face. "I know."

"Wes?" my mother said. "The boy who drove you home that night?"

"Didn't Macy tell you he was an artist?" Caroline said.

My mother glanced at me, but I looked away. Both of us knew it wouldn't have mattered, at the time. "No," she said quietly. "She didn't."

"Oh, he's fantastic," Caroline said, pushing a piece of hair out of her face. "I've been out at his studio for hours, looking at his pieces. Do you know he learned to weld in reform school?"

My mother was still watching me. She said, "You don't say."

"It's just the coolest story." Caroline squatted down, pushing one of the tiny wheels to make it spin. "They have professors from the university do volunteer outreach at the Myers School, and one of the heads of the art department came in and taught a class. He was so impressed with Wes he's been having him take college level art classes for the last two years. He showed at the university gallery a couple of months ago."

"He did?" I said. "He never told me that."

"Oh," Caroline said, "he didn't tell me either. His aunt was there, I can't remember her name—"

"Delia," I said.

"Right!" She started back toward the truck. "So anyway, we got to talking while he was loading up the truck. She also said he's had offers from several art schools for college, but he's not even sure he wants to go. As it is, his stuff is selling in a few galleries and garden art places so well he's on back order. And he was a winner of the Emblem Prize last year."

"What does that mean?" I asked.

"It's a state arts award," my mother said to me, looking down at the small angel near her feet, whose halo was decorated with small interlocking wrenches. "The governor's committee gives them out."

"It means," Caroline said, "that he's amazing."

"Wow," I said. I couldn't believe he hadn't told me all this, but then again, I'd never asked. Quiet but incredible, Delia had said.

Caroline said, "When I took those other pieces I bought and set them up in my yard, the women in my neighborhood went nuts." She adjusted the square piece, which, I now realized, was made up of what looked like an old bedframe. "I told him I'd probably have offers for twice what I paid for this stuff once I get it home. Not that I'm selling, of course."

"Really," my mother said, looking at the square piece, her head tilted to the side. Wes had removed the legs of the frame, leaving just the boxy middle part, then put shiny chrome along the inside. It tilted backwards on two outstretched pieces of pipe, so if you stood right in front of it, it looked like a big picture frame, with whatever was behind it the image inside. The way Caroline had set it up, it framed the front of the house perfectly: the red front door, the holly bushes on either side of the steps, then a set of windows.

"I love this," she said, as we all stood looking at it. "It's a new series he's been working on. I bought three of them. I just think it's amazing what it says, something about permanence, you know, and impermanence."

"Really," my mother said again.

"Absolutely," Caroline told her, in her art major voice, and I felt a rush suddenly of how much I missed Wes, wishing he was there to exchange a look with me, a bemused smile, raising his eyebrows. He'd acted like he'd never heard any of it before, ever, which I knew now hadn't been true. "An empty frame, in which the picture is always changing, makes a statement about how time is always passing. It doesn't really stop, even in a single image. It just feels that way."

It was early evening, the sun not even down yet, but as we stood there, the streetlight behind us buzzed, then flickered on. Instantly, I saw our shadows cast across the empty space behind the frame: my mother's tall and thin; Caroline's, her hands on her hips, elbows at right angles. And then there was me, falling between them. I put a hand to my face, then let it drop back to my side, watching my shadow mimic me.

"I should go ahead and get my pictures," Caroline said, starting toward the truck. "Before it gets totally dark."

As she walked to the truck, another car slowed down in front of the house, the horn beeping. The passenger side window rolled down and a woman I vaguely recognized as one of the realtors my mother did business with leaned across the front seat. "Deborah, how brilliant!"

My mother walked a little closer to the curb. "I'm sorry?" she said.

"Those pieces!" the woman replied, waving toward them. She had on a big clunky wooden bracelet that kept sliding up and down her arm with every gesture. "What a great tie-in to the finish of the construction phase, using building materials from the townhouses to make decorations! How smart of you!"

"Oh, no," my mother said, "it's not—"

"I'll see you tomorrow!" the woman said, not even listening. "Just brilliant!" And then she drove off, beeping the horn again, while my mother just stood there, watching her go.

Caroline was walking across the grass with her camera now, bending down to center the bigger angel in the shot. "You know," she said, looking down at her feet, "I don't care what you say. Something is wrong with the yard. I noticed it as soon as I pulled up. It's like . . . uneven, or something."

"We had a little problem," I told her, as she lifted the camera to her eye. A second later, the shutter snapped. "We've had a few, actually."

I was waiting for my mother to deny this, or at least smooth it over, but when I turned to look at her I saw she wasn't even really listening. Instead, she was facing the street, where, as often happened at this time of night, people were starting to pass by on after-dinner walks, pushing strollers or leading dogs, and kids were circling on their bikes, racing past, then doubling back, then back again. Tonight, though, something was different: everyone was looking at our yard, at the sculptures, some people just standing on the sidewalk outright staring. My mother saw this, too.

"You know," she said to Caroline, carefully, "I'm wondering

if maybe these pieces would work well at the reception. They certainly add a bit of flair to the yard, at any rate."

Caroline took another picture, then stood up and started toward the wheel whirligig. "I was going to leave tonight," she said, not looking at my mother as she set up another shot. "I have plans."

For a second, I thought that was it. She was saying no, and there was nothing we could do about it. My mother knew this, too, I could tell by the way she stepped back, nodding her head. "Of course," she said. "I understand completely."

For a second none of us said anything, and I wondered if, in the end, this is how all disputes are settled, with a shared silence as things become equal. You take something from me, I take something from you. We all want balance, one way or another.

"But," Caroline said, "I suppose I could stick around. It's just one night, right?"

"Yes," my mother said, as Caroline lifted the camera to her eye. "It's just one night."

So Caroline stayed, first taking pictures until dark, then going inside, where she and my mother circled each other warily but politely, until we all went to bed. As usual, I couldn't sleep, and after an hour or so of tossing and turning I climbed out onto my rooftop and stared down at Wes's work on the grass before me. The sculptures looked so out of place to me there, as if they'd been dropped from the sky.

I dozed until about three A.M., then woke up to feel a breeze blowing through my open window. Regardless of my mother's insistence, the weather was clearly changing. Sitting up, I pushed aside my curtain, looking out over the roof to the lawn.

All of the sculptures had parts that were now spinning madly, whistling, buzzing, calling. The noise was loud enough to drown out everything. I couldn't believe I'd even been able to sleep through it. I lay back down and listened for another hour or so, waiting for it to stop, for the wind to die back down, but it never did. If anything it grew louder, then louder still, and I thought I'd never get to sleep again. But somehow, I did.

Macy. Wake up.

I sat up, fast, my father's voice still in my head. It's a dream, I told myself, but in those first moments of waking confusion, I wasn't sure.

The last time I'd heard those words, that way, it had been winter. Cold, the trees bare. Now, a summer breeze, strong but sweet smelling, was blowing. A dream, I thought, and slid back down to put my cheek against my pillow, closing my eyes. But also like the last time, about three minutes later something made me get up.

I looked out the window, at first not believing my eyes. But after I blinked once, then twice, to make sure I was really awake, there was no denying that Wes was standing in my front yard, the truck parked at the curb behind him. It was seven A.M. and he was just looking at all his pieces, at their movement, and then, as I shifted, leaning in closer to my screen, at me.

For a second, we just stared at each other. Then I walked to my bureau, pulled on a T-shirt and a pair of shorts, slipped down the staircase quietly, and went outside.

The wind and the whirligigs moving made everything feel in motion. The mulch that the landscapers had laid around the beds was now scattered across the grass and the street, and small cyclones of flower petals and grass clippings were swirling here and there in smaller gusts. In the midst of all of it was Wes, and now me, standing still, with the length of the walk between us.

"What are you doing here?" I asked him. I had to raise my voice, almost yell, but the wind seemed to pick it up and carry it away almost instantly. Somehow, though, he heard me.

"I was dropping something off," he said. "I didn't think anyone would be up."

"I wasn't," I said. "I mean, not until just now."

"I tried to call you," he said now, taking a step toward me. I did the same. "After that night. Why didn't you answer?"

Another big gust blew over us. I could feel my shorts flapping around my legs. What is going on, I thought, glancing around.

"I don't know," I said, pushing my hair out of my eyes. "I just . . . it just seemed like everything had changed."

"Changed," he said, taking another step toward me. "You mean, on the Fourth? With us?"

"No," I said, and he looked surprised, hurt even, but it passed quickly, and I wondered if I'd been wrong, and it hadn't been there ever, at all. "Not that night. The night I saw you. You were so—"

I trailed off, not knowing what word to use. I wasn't used to this, having a chance to explain a good-bye or an ending.

But Wes was waiting. For whatever word came next.

"It was weird," I said finally, knowing this didn't do it justice, but I had to say something. "You were weird. And I just thought that it had been too much, or something."

"What had been too much?"

"That night. Me being so upset at the hospital," I said. He looked confused, like I wasn't making sense. "Us. Like we were too much. You were so strange, like you didn't want to face me—"

"It wasn't like that," he said. "It was just—"

"I followed you," I told him. "To say I was sorry. I went to the Waffle House, and I saw you. With Becky."

"You saw me," he repeated. "That night, after we talked outside Milton's?"

"It just made it clear," I told him. "But even before, we were so awkward, talking, and it just seemed like maybe everything on the Fourth had been too much for you, and I felt embarrassed."

"That's why you said that about Jason," he said. "About getting back together. And then you saw me, and—"

I just shook my head, letting him know he didn't have to explain to me. "It doesn't matter," I said. "It's fine."

"Fine," he repeated, and I wondered why it was I kept coming back to this, again and again, a word that you said when someone asked how you were but didn't really care to know the truth.

Something blew up behind me, hitting my leg, and I glanced down: it was a bit of white fabric, blown loose from someone's backyard or clothesline. A second later it took flight again, rising up and over the bushes beside me. "Look," I said, "We knew Jason and Becky would be back, the break would end. This isn't a surprise, it's what's supposed to happen. It's what we wanted. Right?"

"Is it?" he asked. "Is it what you want?"

Whether he intended it to be or not, this was the final question, the last Truth. If I said what I really thought, I was opening myself up for a hurt bigger than I could even imagine. I didn't have it in me. We'd changed and altered so many rules, but it was this one, the only one when we'd started, that I would break.

"Yes," I said.

I waited for him to react, to say something, anything, wondering what would happen now that the game was over. Instead, his eyes shifted slowly, from my face to above my head. Confused, I looked up, only to see the sky was swirling with white.

It was like snow, almost, but as the pieces began falling, blowing across me, I saw they were made of the same white, stiff fabric as the piece that had blown onto me earlier. But it wasn't until I heard a yelp from behind the house that everything clicked together.

"The tent!" my mother was shrieking. "Oh, my God!"

I turned back to look at Wes, but he was walking toward his truck. I just stood there, watching, as he got behind the wheel and started to drive away. So I'd won. But it didn't feel like it. Not at all.

We had a shredded tent. A yardful of flowers missing their petals. And now, rumbling in the distance, thunder.

"Uh-oh," Caroline said under her breath, nudging me, and I felt myself start, coming to. I was so out of it, even as I went through the motions, doing my best to soothe my mother's frayed nerves. When the tent people said no, they didn't have another, and all their crews were booked, so we'd just have to do our best with what we had, I'd patted her hand, insisting no one would notice the tent at all. When the wind kept blowing, knocking over the chairs and tables as quickly as we could set them up, I nodded agreement to Caroline's idea of doing away with them altogether and allowing, in her words, more of a "milling around sort of thing." And when my mother, minutes earlier, had stepped off the driveway of the model townhouse to cut the red ribbon stretched across there and broken the heel of her shoe, I'd stepped forward instantly, offering up my own while everyone chuckled. Through it all, I felt strangely detached, as if it was all happening at a distance, far enough that whatever the outcome, it wouldn't affect me at all.

Now, my mother was smiling for the cameras and shaking hands with her superintendents with the utmost composure as mean-looking dark clouds began to scoot against the sky. She seemed just fine, until we got into the car and she shut her door behind her.

"What in the world is going on?" she shrieked. "I started planning this weeks ago. This is not what's supposed to happen!"

Her voice filled the car, sounding loud in my ears, and as she began driving, the familiar scenery of the neighborhood whizzing by, I had a flash of Wes and me in the yard earlier, when I'd said something so similar to him about how we would leave things: *It's what's supposed to happen.* It made sense then, but now I was wondering.

As we took a corner there was another big crash of thunder overhead, and we all jumped. My sister leaned forward, peering out the windshield. "You know," she said, "we should probably have a rain plan."

"It's not going to rain," my mother told her flatly.

"Can't you hear that thunder?"

"It's just thunder," she said, pressing the accelerator down further as we exceeded, by a good twenty miles, the Wildflower Ridge Good Neighbor Speed Limit. "That doesn't mean it's going to rain."

Caroline just looked at her. "Mom. Please."

As we zoomed up the driveway, the wind was still blowing, and every once in a while a little piece of white tent sheeting would flutter past. My mother and Caroline were already going inside by the time I got out of the car, my mind still tangled with all these thoughts. By the time I caught up with them in the kitchen, they were bustling around, laying out the brochures and leaflets that would be arranged outside, getting the last of the things ready for the party. As soon as she saw me, my mother thrust a pile of folders, brochures, old newspapers, and several of my sister's home decorating magazines into my arms.

"Macy, please, take these and put them somewhere. Anywhere. And check the powder room to make sure the towels are straight and there's enough hand soap, and—" She paused for a second, glancing around wildly, her eyes finally settling on the countertop by the phone, where EZ-Key had been since I'd opened it the day before, "do something with that, *please*, and come back here so you can help me do something with the dining room. Okay?"

I nodded, still feeling out of it, but I did as she asked. The folders I put in her office, the newspapers in recycling, the magazines outside my sister's bedroom door. When the EZ-Key was the last thing left, I went into my room, then sat down on my bed with it in my hands.

Downstairs, I could hear my sister doing last minute vacuuming, my mother in my shoes clacking and re-clacking across the floor. I knew they needed me, but there was a part of me that just wanted to lie back in my bed, close my eyes, and find myself waking up again, to this morning, to another chance. Maybe I'd still go downstairs and across the lawn to Wes, but what I'd say, I knew now, would be different. He'd always told the truth. I should have done the same.

And this was it: Wes was my friend, absolutely, but regardless of what I'd led him to believe, the night I'd seen him with Becky I'd felt more than what a friend should. It was about time I admitted it. In fact, on some level, I'd known all along, which was what had almost sent me back to Jason, back to this neat, orderly life that I hoped would protect me from getting hurt again. And here, in this world, it was entirely possible to pretend that none of my summer with Wes, and Wish, had ever happened.

But it *had* happened. I had followed Delia's van that night, I had told Wes my Truths, I had stepped into his arms, showing him my raw, broken heart. I could pretend otherwise, pushing it out of sight and hopefully out of mind. But if something was really important, fate made sure it somehow came back to you and gave you another chance. I'd gotten one reaching out to grab Kristy's hand as she pulled me into the ambulance; another during the trip to the hospital that ended with seeing Avery born. Events conspired to bring you back to where you'd been. It was what you did then that made all the difference: it was all about potential.

I stood up and pulled my chair over to the closet, then climbed up to put away the EZ box. I was about to step down when I saw the shopping bag I'd put up there all those weeks ago. This whole day I'd felt like something was different. Which was probably why I pushed the box back and finally grabbed the bag off the shelf.

"I can't believe this," my mother muttered to herself, bemoaning the rumbling thunder as she passed my half-open door. "It's like we're cursed or something."

I sat down on my bed, then reached into the bag, pulling out the package. It was heavy in my hands as I shifted it into my lap, my fingers already loosening the wrapping paper.

"Honestly," she called out, over another thunderclap, "how are you supposed to plan for a day like this?"

The paper was coming off now, wrinkling, ripping, and even though I knew there was something familiar in the shape that was emerging, I couldn't place it.

"The lawn, the catering, the tent," my mother said, passing by again. "What happens now?"

I just sat there, looking at my gift, feeling my heart beating loud in my chest, then lifted my hand and pressed it over the one on the sculpture in my lap. A lot of things were beginning to make sense, while others were more confusing than ever. All I knew was that this heart in hand was mine. I'd wanted a sign, and all this time it had been so close by, waiting for me to be ready to find it.

My mother's last question was still echoing in my head as outside my window there was the biggest thunderclap yet. It shook the house, the windowpanes, the very earth, it felt like. And then, just like that, it was pouring. She'd gotten her answer. And so had I.

Chapter Twenty

When I came downstairs, all hell was breaking loose.

I'd put my heart in hand on my bedside table next to my angel, then stood up, sure now of what I had to do. As I came into the kitchen, though, I found my mother and sister in a frenzy of furniture rearranging, pushing chairs and couches up against walls in an attempt to somehow open up space for seventy-five people in our dining room, foyer, and living room.

"Macy," Caroline said to me, rushing past carrying an end table, "do something about the stools."

"Stools?" I asked.

"The island stools," my mother shrieked as she passed going the other direction, dragging a settee. "Put them against the wall. Or in my office. Do something with them! Just get them out of here!" Her voice was loud, wavering, crazy sounding, and for a second I just looked at her. But only for a second. Then I did exactly as I was told.

I'd seen my mother under pressure. I'd seen her grieving. But I'd never seen her look as out of control as she did just then, and it scared me. I turned and looked at Caroline, who just shook her head and went back to pushing one of the recliners against the den wall. There was no way a person could carry this much stress for much longer, I thought. Eventually, something had to give.

"Mom," I said to her as she passed by again, reaching out my hand to touch hers. "Are you okay?"

"Macy, not now!" she snapped. I pulled my hand back: now, even that was too much. "Please, honey," she said, shaking her head. "Not now."

For the next twenty minutes, I could see the tension building, in her neck, her features, the shaking timbre of her voice as one bad thing after another kept happening. When the phone wouldn't stop ringing. When the superintendent called to report that one of the windows in the model townhouse was leaking from all the rain. When the lights flickered, went out, then flickered back on again, still not seeming too steady. Each time, I watched my mother react, her body tensing, her voice rising, her eyes moving wildly across the room, scanning for one thing or another. Whenever she caught me watching her, I'd quickly look away.

"I'm worried about Mom," I said to Caroline as we tried to push the huge, oak-framed couch in the living room a foot or so backwards. Even with both our weights, it wasn't even budging. "I don't know how I can help her."

"You can't," she told me. "It's not worth even trying."

"Caroline." I stopped pushing. "God."

She pushed her hair out of her face with the back of her hand. "Macy," she said. "There's nothing you can do."

Just then, I heard the front door open and someone's heels clack into the foyer.

"Good God," Kristy said. "What the hell is going on here?"

I let my arms go slack, grateful for an excuse to do so, and turned around. There she was, standing in the foyer, carrying a stack of foil-covered pans. Monica was beside her, holding a cooler with a couple of cutting boards balanced on top. Bringing up the rear, carrying several long loaves of French bread under each arm, was Delia.

"We're having," I said to Kristy as the lights flickered again, "a little bit of a crisis."

There was a rattle, then a clank, as Bert appeared in the door, forcing Delia to step aside as he pulled one of the banged-up stainless-steel carts over the threshold. Outside, the rain was still coming down sideways.

"Crisis?" Delia asked. "What kind?"

Then in the powder room to her right, there was shriek, a crash, and everyone fell silent, the only sound the rain pelting the windows. Then the door opened, and my mother emerged.

Her cheeks were flushed from all the exertion of moving things, her lipstick smeared in one corner. She was still wearing my shoes, which were markedly too small for her, and there was some sort of dirt stain on the hem of her skirt. She looked tired. Beaten down. Or maybe even just beaten. And in her hand was the decorative soap dish from the powder room, which was now in two pieces.

It was just a soap dish, innocuous enough that I couldn't even remember when we'd gotten it. But my mother, staring at it in her open palm, was for some reason close to tears. I felt something rise up in my chest, and realized I was afraid. Terrified. I was used to seeing my mother many ways, but never weak. It made me feel small enough to disappear.

"Mom?" Caroline asked. "Are you—"

But my mother didn't seem to hear her, or even notice that any of us were there. Instead, she started down the hallway to the kitchen, taking slow, deliberate steps. She reached up, wiping her eyes, as she turned the corner toward her office, not looking back at any of us. A second later, I heard the door shut with a click.

"Oh, my God," I said.

"It's just a soap dish," Kristy offered helpfully. "I bet she can get another one."

Beside me, I could see Caroline already turning to follow, assuming, of course, that she would be the one to handle this. But I'd been waiting for a chance to talk to my mother for too long, always finding myself thwarted in one way or another, by my fears or her own. It was time to try again.

So as Caroline started down the hallway, I put my hand on her arm. She looked up at me, surprised. "Let me," I said, and then I went to my mother.

When I pushed the door open, she was standing behind her desk, her back to me. And she was crying, her shoulders shaking. The sound of it immediately brought a lump to my throat, and I wanted to turn and run. But instead, I took a deep breath and stepped inside.

She didn't turn around. I wasn't even sure she knew I was there. But as I stood watching her, I realized how truly hard it was, really, to see someone you love change right before your eyes. Not only is it scary, it throws your balance off as well. This was how my mother felt, I realized, over the weeks I worked at Wish, as she began to not recognize me in small ways, day after day. It was no wonder she'd reacted by pulling me closer, forcibly narrowing my world back to fit inside her own. Even now, as I finally saw this as the truth it was, a part of me was wishing my mother would stand up straight, take command, be back in control. But all I'd wanted when she was tugging me closer was to be able to prove to her that the changes in me were good ones, ones she'd understand if she only gave them a chance. I had that chance now. And while it was scary, I was going to take it.

I crossed the room, coming up behind her. I had so many things I wanted to tell her. I just didn't know where to begin.

Finally she turned around, one hand moving to her face, and for a second we just stood there, staring at each other. A million sentences kept starting in my head, then trailing off. This was the hard part, I thought. Whatever was said next started everything, so it had to be strong enough to carry the rest that would follow.

She took a breath. "I'm—"

But I didn't let her finish. Instead, I took one step forward and slid my arms around her neck. She stiffened, at first, surprised, but I didn't pull back, moving in even more and burying my face in her shoulder. At first I didn't feel her own arms sliding around me, her body moving in to enclose mine. I could feel her breath in my hair, her heart against my chest. After all this time, it could have been awkward, all elbows and hipbones. But it wasn't. It was perfect.

And as I held her, I kept thinking back to that night at the clearing, and what I'd told Wes. *For once, I'd just let her know exactly how I feel, without thinking first.* Finally, I had.

Somewhere in the midst of all this, down the hallway, I could hear Caroline's voice. She was in the kitchen, explaining our crisis to Delia, detailing every little thing that had gone wrong. As she did so, my mother and I held tight, leaning into each other. It was like that part of the roller coaster where the *click-clack-click* stops as you reach the top of the hill, and you know for sure that the uphill part is finally behind you, and any minute you'll begin that wild rush to the end.

I was ready. And I think she was, too. But if she wasn't, I could get her through. The first step is always the hardest.

"Okay," I heard Delia say. "Here's what we're going to do. . . ."

"Ho-ly shit," Kristy said, shaking her head. "Now that's some rain."

"Kristy," Delia said in her warning voice.

Caroline sighed. "No, she's right," she said. "It really is."

"Mmm-hmm," Monica added.

It was, indeed, still raining. Hard. So hard, in fact, that the lights had continued to flicker, although that could have been attributable to the wind, which was, yes, still blowing. Hard. A few minutes earlier, on the TV, our local weather girl, Lorna McPhail, had stood there in front of her Doppler map, eyes wide, as she explained that while a shower or two had been in the forecast, no one had expected this sort of incident.

"*Incident?*" Caroline had said as Lorna turned back to her map. "This isn't an incident. This is the end of the world."

"Nah," Bert told her as he passed behind her with a trayful of wineglasses, "the end of the world would be *much* worse than this."

Caroline looked at him. "You think?"

"Oh yeah," he said. "Absolutely."

Now, it was seven sharp, and our first arrivals were still sitting in their cars, optimistically waiting for a break in the torrential downpour. In a minute, they'd get out, come up the walk, and step inside, where everything was ready. The canapés were warming in the oven, the bar was stocked with ice and beverages, the cake that said in red icing WILDFLOWER RIDGE–A NEW PHASE BEGINS! was displayed on the table, encircled by flowers and stacks of brightly colored napkins. Plus, the whole house smelled like meatballs. And everyone loves meatballs.

After Caroline detailed our situation, I'd listened to Delia do what she did best: move into action. Within fifteen minutes, several of the tables and chairs we'd rented had been brought inside and assembled throughout the house ("bistro-style," she'd called it), then topped with thick vanilla-scented candles she'd had stashed in the van from a bridal shower weeks ago. The lights were dimmed in case they went out entirely—while making everything feel somehow cozy—and she'd put Bert and Monica to work doubling up on baking appetizers, reasoning that if people were well fed, they'd hardly notice that they barely had room to turn around. Caroline was sent to find a soap dish, and Kristy was stationed by the door with a tray of full wineglasses to offer up the minute people stepped inside (slightly buzzed people, Delia reasoned, would notice less as well).

Meanwhile, my mother and I were sitting on the edge of her desk, the Kleenex box between us, looking out at the rain.

"I wanted this party to be perfect," she said, dabbing at her eyes.

"No such thing," I told her.

She smiled ruefully, tossing a tissue into the garbage can. "It's a total disaster," she said with a sigh.

For a second, neither of us said anything.

"Well, in a way it's good," I said finally, remembering what

Delia had said to me, at that first party, all those weeks ago. "We know where we stand. Now things can only get better. Right?"

She didn't look convinced. But that was okay. So she didn't fully get it yet. But I had a feeling she would. And if not, there was more than enough time, now that this had finally begun, for me to explain it to her.

When we came out into the kitchen a few minutes later, Delia was laying out crab cakes. She took one look at my mother and insisted that she go upstairs and take a hot shower and a few deep breaths. To my surprise, my mother went with no argument, disappearing for a full twenty minutes. When she came back down, hair damp and wearing fresh clothes, she looked more relaxed than I'd seen her in weeks. There is a certain relief in things getting as bad as they could be. Maybe this second time around my mother was beginning to see that.

"What did you say to her?" my sister asked me, as we watched her come down the stairs.

"Nothing, really," I said. I felt her looking at me, but this was partially true. Or true enough.

Kristy was at the front door, tray in hand, as my mother passed her. "Wine?" she offered.

My mother paused, about to demur politely, but instead she took a deep breath. "What is that wonderful smell?"

"Meatballs," I said. "You want one?"

Again, I expected a no. But instead, she reached for a wineglass, took a sip, and nodded at me. "Yes," she said. "I would love one."

Now, as she stood with all of us in the front window, there was one last thing I was wondering about. I'd held off as long as

I could, hoping someone would offer an explanation, but finally there was nothing to do but ask outright. "So," I said, still looking out at the cars, "where's Wes?"

I saw Monica and Kristy exchange a look. Then Kristy said, "He had to run some pieces down to the coast this morning. But he said he'd stop by on his way back, to see if we needed him."

"Oh," I said. "Right."

An awkward silence followed this, during which I, and everyone else, just stared out at the rain. Gradually, though, I became aware of someone sighing heavily. Then clearing her throat. Repeatedly.

"Are you okay?" Bert asked Kristy.

She nodded, letting loose with another vehement *a-hem*. I glanced over at her, only to find her staring at me. "What?" I said.

"What?" she repeated. Clearly, she was annoyed. "What do you mean, *what*?"

"I mean," I said, somewhat confused, "what's the problem?"

She rolled her eyes. Beside her, Monica said, "Donneven."

"Kristy." Delia shook her head. "This isn't the time or the place, okay?"

"The time or the place for what?" Caroline asked.

"There is never," Kristy said adamantly, "a time or place for true love. It happens accidentally, in a heartbeat, in a single flashing, throbbing moment."

"Throbbing?" my mother said, leaning forward and looking at me. "Who's throbbing?"

"Macy and Wes," Kristy told her.

"We are *not*," I said indignantly.

"Kristy," Delia said helplessly. "Please God I'm begging you, not now."

"Wait a second, wait a second." Caroline held her hands up. "Kristy. Explain."

"Yes, Kristy," my mother said, but she was looking at me. Not really mad as much as confused. Join the club, I thought. "Explain."

Bert said, "This ought to be good."

Kristy ignored him, tucking a piece of hair behind her ear. "Wes wants to be with Macy. And Macy, whether she'll admit it or not, wants to be with Wes. And yet they're not together, which is not only unjust, but really, when you think about it, tragical."

"That's not a word," Bert pointed out.

"It is now," she said. "How else can you explain a situation where Wes, a truly extraordinary boy, would be sent packing in favor of some brainiac loser who severed ties with Macy because she didn't take her job at the library seriously enough and, even *worse*, because she dared to say she loved him?"

"Why," I said, feeling as embarrassed while this was broadcast as I had been the first time she'd stated it aloud, "do we have to keep talking about this?"

"Because it's tragical!" Kristy said.

"Jason decided on the break because you told him you loved him?" my mother asked me.

"No," I said. "Yes. Not exactly. It's a long story."

"I'll tell you what it is," Kristy said. "It's *wrong.* You should be with Wes, Macy. The whole time you guys were hanging out, talking about how you were both with other people, it was so obvious to everyone. It was even obvious to Wes. You were the only one who couldn't see it, just like you can't see it now."

"Mmm-hmm," Monica said, picking some lint off her apron.

"Wes never felt that way," I told her. I was fully aware that my mother—and Caroline, not to mention everyone else—was listening, but somehow I didn't care. Too much had happened this night already. "He was always going back to Becky, just like I was going back to Jason."

"That's not true," she said.

"It is true. He's been back with her. For weeks," I told her.

"No," she said, shaking her head.

"But I saw them together. At the World of Waffles. They were—"

"Breaking up," she finished for me. "That was the night he saw you at Milton's, right, and he said he had an appointment?"

I nodded, still confused.

"He was on his way to break up with her." She paused for a second, as if she could see this sinking in, all finally coming together. "He wants to be with *you*, Macy. Now if it was me, I would have told you that night, but he's not like that. He wanted to be free, totally in the clear, before he let you know how he feels. He's just been waiting for you, Macy."

"No," I said.

"*Yes*. Now, I've been telling him to just come over here and tell you, and ask you if you feel the same way," she said. "But he's not like that. He has to do it in his own way. In his own time."

Like the final question, I thought. He wasn't waiting to torture me, or because he didn't know it. He just wanted to get it right. Whatever that means.

Everyone was looking at me. Once, I thought, my life was private. Now the entire world was into my business, if not my heart. But, I thought, looking across their expectant faces, this wasn't really the whole world. Just mine.

"He came over today," I said slowly, all of this sinking in. "This morning."

"So what happened?" Kristy asked.

I glanced at my mother, waiting for her to realize I'd broken her rules. Instead, she was just looking at me, her head slightly cocked to the side, as if she was seeing something in me she hadn't before.

"Nothing," I said. "I mean, he just asked me if this, the way things are now, was what I wanted."

"And what did you say?"

"I said it was," I told her.

"Macy!" Kristy smacked her hand to her forehead. "God! What were you *thinking*?"

"I didn't know," I told her. Then, more softly, to myself, I said, "It's so unfair."

Kristy shook her head. "It's tragical."

"It's time," Delia said, nodding at the window. The rain had let up some, finally, and people were now starting to emerge from their cars, shutting doors and unfolding umbrellas. Regardless of everything else, the show had to go on. "Let's get to work."

Everyone started to move away from the window, toward their various tasks: Kristy picked up her tray of wineglasses, Bert and Delia headed toward the kitchen, and my mother moved to the mirror in the foyer, taking one last look at her face. Only Monica stayed where she was, staring out the window as I tried, hard, to comprehend everything that had just happened.

"I can't believe this," I said softly. "It's too late."

"It's never too late," she said.

For a second, I was sure I'd imagined it. After a summer of monotone, one-word answers or no answers at all, here, from Monica, was a complete sentence.

"But it is," I told her, turning to look at her. "I don't think I'd even know what to do if I did have another chance. I mean, what could I . . ."

She shook her head. "It's just one of those things," she said. Her voice was surprisingly level and clear. "You know, that just happen. You don't think or plan. You just do it."

There was something familiar about this, but it took me a second to realize where I'd heard it before. Then I remembered: it was what I'd said to her that night at the party, when I'd been trying to explain why I was holding Wes's hand.

"Monica!" Kristy yelled from the living room. "There's a tray of cheesepuffs in here with your name on it. Where are you?"

Monica turned from the window, starting across the foyer with her trademark slow shuffle. "Wait," I said, and she looked over her shoulder, back at me. I didn't know what to say. I was still in shock that she'd spoken at all, and wondered what other surprises she might have up her sleeve. "Thanks for that. I mean, I appreciate it."

She nodded. "Um-hmm," she said, and then she turned her back and walked away.

Chapter Twenty-One

I'd catered enough jobs to know the signs of a good party. You had to have plenty of good food, for one. A crowd that was relaxed and laughing a lot, for another. But then there was that other thing, the indefinable buzz of people talking and eating and communing, a palpable energy that makes little things like shredded tents or pouring rain or even the end of the world hardly noticeable. An hour in, my mother's party had all of these things, in spades. There was no question it was a success.

"Great party, Deborah!"

"Love the bistro idea!"

"These meatballs are divine!"

The compliments kept coming. My mother accepted each one gratefully, nodding and smiling as she moved among her guests. For the first time, it seemed to me that she was actually enjoying herself, not focusing on getting literature to every person or talking up the next phase, but instead just mingling with people, wineglass in hand. Every once in a while she'd pass behind me and I'd feel her hand on my back or my arm, but when I turned around to see if she needed me to do something, she'd have moved on, instead just glancing back over her shoulder to smile at me as she moved through the crowd.

My mother was okay. I was okay, too. Or I would be, eventually. I knew one night wouldn't change everything between us, and that there was a lot—an entire year and a half's worth, actually—for us to discuss. For now, though, I just tried to focus on the moment, as much as I could. Which was working fine, until I saw Jason.

He'd just come in and was standing in the foyer, in his rain jacket, looking around for me. "Macy," he called out, and then he started over to me. I didn't move, just stood there as he got closer, until he was right in front of me. "Hi."

"Hi," I said. I took a second to look at him: the clean-cut haircut, the conservative polo shirt tucked into his khakis. He looked just the same as he had the day he left, and I wondered if I did, too. "How are you?"

"Good."

There was a burst of laughter from a group of people nearby, and we both turned at the sound of it, letting it fill the silence that followed. Finally he said, "It's really good to see you."

"You, too."

He was just standing there, looking at me, and I felt hopelessly awkward, not sure what to say. He stepped a bit closer, lowering his head nearer to mine, and said, "Can we talk somewhere?"

I nodded. "Sure."

As we walked down the hallway to the kitchen, I was dimly aware that we were being watched. Sure that it was Kristy, glaring, or Monica, staring, I turned my head and was surprised to see my mother, standing by the buffet, her eyes following me as I passed. Jason glanced over and, seeing her, lifted his hand and waved. She nodded, smiling slightly, but kept her eyes on me, steady, until I rounded the corner and couldn't see her anymore.

Once in the kitchen, I saw the back door was open. In all the commotion, I'd hadn't even noticed the rain stopping. As we stepped outside, everything was dripping and kind of cool, but the sky had cleared. A few people were outside smoking, others clumped in groups talking, their voices rising and falling. Jason and I found a spot on the stairs, away from everyone, and I leaned back, feeling the dampness of the rail against my legs.

"So," Jason said, glancing around. "This is quite a party."

"You have no idea," I told him. "It's been crazy." Over his head, I could see into the kitchen, where Delia was sliding another pan of crab cakes into the oven. Monica was leaning against the island, examining a split end, with her trademark bored expression.

"Crazy?" Jason said. "How?"

I took a breath, thinking I would try to explain, then stopped myself. Too much to tell, I thought. "Just a lot of disasters," I said finally. "But it's all okay now."

My sister stepped through the door to the deck. She was talking loudly, and a group of people were trailing along behind her, clutching drinks and canapés in their hands. ". . . represents a real dichotomy of art and salvage," she was saying in her Art History Major voice as she passed us on the stairs. "These pieces are really compelling. Now, as you'll see in this first one, the angel is symbolic of the accessibility and limits of religion."

Jason and I stepped back as her group followed along behind her, nodding and murmuring as their lesson began. When they disappeared around the side of the house, he said, "Did she make those or something?"

I smiled. "No," I said. "She's just a big fan."

He leaned back, peering around the house at the angel, which Caroline and her people were now encircling. "They are interesting," he said, "but I don't know about symbolic. They just seem like yard art to me."

"Well, they are," I said. "Sort of. But they also have meaning, in their own way. At least Caroline thinks so."

He looked at the angel again. "I don't think the medium works well for the message," he said. "It's sort of distracting, actually. I mean, regardless of the loftiness of the vision, in the end it's just junk, right?"

I just looked at him, not sure what to say to this. "Well," I said. "It guess it depends on how you look at it."

He smiled at me. "Macy," he said, in a tone that for some reason made something prick at the back of my neck, "junk is junk."

I felt myself take a breath. He doesn't know, I told myself. He has no idea, he's just making conversation. "So," I said, "you wanted to talk about something?"

"Oh. Right. Yes, I did."

I stood there, waiting. Inside, the kitchen was empty now except for Bert, who was traying up a pan of meatballs, popping the occasional one in his mouth. He looked up, saw me watching him, and smiled, sort of embarrassed. I smiled back, and Jason turned his head, looking behind him.

"Sorry," I said. "You were saying?"

He looked down at his hands. "I just," he began, then stopped, as if he'd thought of another, better way to phrase this thought. "I know I handled things badly at the beginning of the summer, suggesting that break. But I'd really like for us to begin a conversation about our relationship and what, if we do decide to continue it, each of us would like to see it evolve into in the coming year."

I was listening. I really was. But even so, my mind kept picking up other things: the laughter from inside, the damp coolness of the air on the back of my neck, my sister's voice still talking about form and function and contrast.

"Well," I said. "I don't know, really."

"That's okay," Jason replied, nodding, as if this conversation was going exactly how he'd expected it to. "I'm not entirely sure either. But I think that's where this dialogue should begin, really. With how we each feel, and what limits we feel need to be put in place before we make another commitment."

". . . a real sense of perspective," Caroline was saying, "with the artist making a clear commentary on the events that happen within the frame, and how the frame affects them."

"What I was thinking," Jason continued, apparently not as distracted by this as I was, "was that we could each draw up a list of what we really want in a relationship. What we expect, what's important. And then, at a predetermined time, we'll sit down and go through them, seeing what corresponds."

"A list," I said.

"Yes," he said, "a list. That way, I figure, we'll have a written record of what we've agreed upon as our goals for our relationship. So if problems arise, we'll be able to consult the lists, see which issue it corresponds to, and work out a solution from there."

I could still hear my sister talking, but her voice was fading as she led her group around the house. I said, "But what if that doesn't work?"

Jason blinked at me. Then he said, "Why wouldn't it?"

"Because," I said.

He just looked at me. "Because . . ."

"Because," I repeated, as a breeze blew over us, "sometimes things just happen. That aren't expected. Or on the list."

"Such as?" he asked.

"I don't know," I said, frustrated. "That's the point. It would be out of the blue, taking us by surprise. Something we might not be prepared for."

"But we will be prepared," he said, confused. "We'll have the list."

I rolled my eyes. "Jason," I said.

"Macy, I'm sorry." He stepped back, looking at me. "I just don't understand what you're trying to say."

And then it hit me: he didn't. He had no idea. And this thought was so ludicrous, so completely unreal, that I knew it just had to be true. For Jason, there was no unexpected, no surprises. His whole life was outlined carefully, in lists and sublists, just like the ones I'd helped him go through all those weeks ago.

"It's just . . ." I said, then stopped, shaking my head.

"It's just what?" He was waiting, genuinely wanting to know. "Explain it to me."

But I couldn't. I'd had to learn it my own way, and so had my mother. Jason would eventually, as well. No one could tell you: you just had to go through it on your own. If you were lucky, you came out on the other side and understood. If you didn't, you kept getting thrust back, retracing those steps, until you finally got it right.

"Macy?" he said. "Please. Explain it to me."

I took in a breath, trying to figure out a way to say there was just no way, but then, over his head, coming into the kitchen through the side door, I saw Wes. And I let out that breath and just looked at him.

He was running a hand through his hair, glancing around at the people grouped in the living room and on the other side of the island. As I watched, Delia came bustling in, carrying a trayful of empty glasses. She put it down, kissing his cheek, and they talked for a second, both of them surveying the party. He said something, and she shrugged, gesturing toward the living room. *You sure?* I saw him ask and she nodded, then squeezed his arm and turned to the oven door, pulling it open. Then he glanced outside, and saw me. And Jason. I tried to keep my eyes on him, willing him to just stay there for another minute, but he turned around and went out the side door, and I watched it fall shut behind him.

"Macy?" Caroline came around the side of the house. "Can you come here a second?"

"Macy," Jason asked. "What—"

"Hold on," I told him. I started across the deck, dodging around groups of people, and went down the other steps, coming out right by the side door. I could see Wes at the end of the driveway.

"Do you know anything about this?" Caroline asked. For a second I thought she meant Wes, until I turned around to see her and her group standing in front of a sculpture.

"What about it?" I asked, distracted. I'd lost sight of him now.

"It's just," she said, looking up at it, "I've never seen it before. It's not one of mine."

"Macy?" Jason came up behind me. "I really think we should—"

But I wasn't listening. Not to him. Not to Caroline, who was still circling around the sculpture, making her Art Major noises.

Not to the sounds of the party floating through the window. All I could hear was the slight tinkling noise of the sculpture as it moved, this new angel. She was standing with her feet apart, her hands clasped at her chest. Her eyes were sea glass, circled with washers, her mouth a key, turned upwards. Her halo was circled with tiny hearts in hands. But most striking, most different, were the things that arched up over her head, made of thin aluminum, cut with strong peaks at the top, sweeping curves at the bottom, lined with tiny bells, which made the chiming noise I was hearing. That we could all hear.

"I don't get it," Caroline said, bemused. "She's the only one with wings. Why is that?"

There were so many questions in life. You couldn't ever have all the answers. But I knew this one.

"It's so she can fly," I said. And then I started to run.

I'd thought it might be like my dreams. But it wasn't. Running came back to me, as easily as anything else that had once been everything to you. The first few steps were hard; it took me a second to catch my breath, but then I found my pace, and everything fell away, until there was nothing but me and what lay ahead, growing closer every second. Wes.

By the time I reached him, I was breathless. Red-faced. And my heart was thumping hard enough in my chest that at first, it was all I could hear. He turned around just as I got to him, looking surprised, and for a second neither of us said anything as I struggled to catch my breath.

"Macy," he said. I could tell he was shocked by my running, by the very fact that I was standing there in front of him, gasping for air. "What—"

"I'm sorry." I put my hand up, palm facing him, and took another deep breath. "But there's been a change."

He blinked at me. "A change," he repeated.

I nodded. "In the rules."

It took him a second: he had no idea what I was talking about. Then, slowly, his face relaxed. "Ah," he said. "The rules."

"Yes."

"I wasn't notified," he pointed out.

"Well, it was pretty recent," I said.

"As in . . ."

"As in, effective right now."

Wes ran a hand through his hair and I saw the heart and hand slip into view, then disappear again. I had so much to tell him, I didn't even know where to start. Or maybe I did.

"Macy," he said softly, looking at me closely. "You don't have to—"

I shook my head. "The change," I said. "Ask me about the change."

He leaned back on his heels, sliding his hands into his pockets. "Okay," he said, after a second. "What's the change?"

"It's been decided," I told him, taking another breath, "that there's another step to winning the game. And that is that in order for me to really win, I have to answer the question you passed on, that night in the truck. Only then is it final."

"The question I passed on," he repeated.

I nodded. "That's the rule."

I knew, in the silence that followed, that anything could happen here. It might be too late: again, I might have missed my chance. But I would at least know I tried, that I took my heart and extended my hand, whatever the outcome.

"Okay," he said. He took a breath. "What would you do, if you could do anything?"

I took a step toward him, closing the space between us. "This," I said. And then I kissed him.

Kissed him. There, in the middle of the street, as the world went on around us. Behind me, I knew Jason was still waiting for an explanation, my sister was still lecturing, and that angel still had her eyes skyward, waiting to fly. As for me, I was just trying to get it right, whatever that meant. But now I finally felt I was on my way. Everyone had a forever, but given a choice, this would be mine. The one that began in this moment, with Wes, in a kiss that took my breath away, then gave it back—leaving me astounded, amazed, and most of all, alive.

Chapter Twenty-Two

"Macy. Wake up."

I rolled over, pulling my pillow over my face. "No," I said, my voice muffled. "Another hour."

"No way." I felt fingers flicking my bare feet. "Hurry up. I'll be outside."

Still half asleep, I heard him leave the room, then, a second later, the screen door slammed shut behind him. For a second I just lay there, so tempted to let sleep pull me in and under, back to dreaming. But then I pushed the pillow off my face and sat up in bed, looking out the window beside me. The sky was clear and blue, the waves crashing close in. Another nice day.

I got up, then pulled on my shorts and jog bra and my T-shirt, rolling the elastic off my wrist and using it to tie my hair up in a ponytail. I was still yawning as I crossed my bedroom and stepped out into the main part of the house, where my sister was sitting at the table, flipping through a magazine.

"You know what I've been thinking," she said, not even looking up, as if we'd been talking and were just picking up where we'd left off, "is that we could really use a chiminea here."

"A what?" I said, bending down to grab my shoes off the floor.

"A chiminea." She turned a page of her magazine, propping

her chin in her hands. "It's an outside chimney, very primal, really makes a statement. What do you think?"

I just smiled, sliding the screen door open. "Sounds great," I said. "Just great."

I stepped out onto the porch, taking in the day's first breath of cool, salty air. My mother, who was sitting in her Adirondack chair, coffee mug on the table beside her, turned around and looked at me.

"Good morning," she said, as I bent down and kissed her cheek. "Such dedication."

"Not me," I told her. "I wanted to sleep in."

She smiled, then picked up her coffee mug, taking the folder from underneath it and spreading it out on her legs. "Have fun," she said.

"You, too."

I stretched my arms over my head as I started down the stairs to the beach, squinting in the already bright sun. Now that the house was done, we spent most weekends here. At the beginning, it had been hard to walk through the door, and I'd cried a lot the first few times, missing my dad. But it was easier now. Even with all the new fabrics and floorings, everything he loved about the beach house—the moose, the fishing poles by the door, his beloved grill—was still there, which made it feel like he was, too.

There were other changes as well. My mother did come down on the weekends, but she always brought some work and her laptop, and her cell phone still rang constantly, although we were training her to let the voicemail pick up once in a while. As for me, I was running again, but now I didn't pay attention to times or distance, instead focusing on how it felt just to be in motion, knowing it wasn't about the finish line but how I got there that mattered.

And my mother and I were talking more, although it hadn't been easy at first. The trips to the beach had helped. While we sometimes had Wes with us, or Kristy, I'd come to appreciate the rides we took alone as well. During the long stretches of quiet two-lane highway, with the sun setting in the distance, it was somehow easier to say things aloud, and regardless of what was said, we just kept moving toward that horizon.

Caroline came down most weekends as well, Wally in tow, and puttered around the house examining her handiwork and musing about other changes she might make. Lately, though, she'd turned her attention to the house two lots down, which had recently gone on the market. It was a fixer-upper, just in need of a little TLC, she told us, as she spread out pictures for us to peruse, and she and Wally had been talking about buying a place at the beach. So many Befores, but I knew my sister. She could always see the After. Of all of us, she was the best at that.

Now, I walked over the dunes, the wind whipping around me. When I looked back at the house, I saw Caroline was out on the porch now, sitting on the new bench, most likely already picturing that chiminea. She and my mom waved, and I waved back, then turned my attention to the short stretch of beach I had to cover to catch up with that figure in the distance. As I started to run, feeling my feet get under me. I listened for the voice I knew so well, the one I always heard at the beginning.

Good girl, Macy! You're doing great! You know the first few steps are the hardest part!

They were. Sometimes I felt so out of sync, it was all I could do not to quit after a few strides. But I kept on, as I did now. I had to, to get to the next part, this part, where I finally caught up with Wes, my shadow aligning itself with his, and he turned to look at me, pushing his hair out of his eyes.

"Nice form," he said.

"Likewise."

We ran for a second in silence. Up ahead, all I could see was beach and sky.

"You ready?" he asked.

I nodded. "Go ahead. It's your turn."

"Okay," he said. "Let's see. . . ."

We'd start slow, the way we always did, because the run, and the game, could go on for awhile. Maybe even forever.

That was the thing. You just never knew. Forever was so many different things. It was always changing, it was what everything was really all about. It was twenty minutes, or a hundred years, or just this instant, or any instant I wished would last and last. But there was only one truth about forever that really mattered, and that was this: it was happening. Right then, as I ran with Wes into that bright sun, and every moment afterwards. Look, there. Now. Now. Now.

LOCK AND KEY

To Leigh Feldman, for seeing me through
this time, every time

and to Jay,
always waiting on the other side

Chapter One

“And finally,” Jamie said as he pushed the door open, “we come to the main event. Your room.”

I was braced for pink. Ruffles or quilting, or maybe even appliqué. Which was probably kind of unfair, but then again, I didn’t know my sister anymore, much less her decorating style. With total strangers, it had always been my policy to expect the worst. Usually they—and those that you knew best, for that matter—did not disappoint.

Instead, the first thing I saw was green. A large, high window, on the other side of which were tall trees separating the huge backyard from that of the house that backed up to it. Everything was big about where my sister and her husband, Jamie, lived—from the homes to the cars to the stone fence you saw first thing when you pulled into the neighborhood itself, made up of boulders that looked too enormous to ever be moved. It was like Stonehenge, but suburban. So weird.

It was only as I thought this that I realized we were all still standing there in the hallway, backed up like a traffic jam. At some point Jamie, who had been leading this little tour, had stepped aside, leaving me in the doorway. Clearly, they wanted me to step in first. So I did.

The room was, yes, big, with cream-colored walls. There

were three other windows beneath the big one I'd first seen, although they each were covered with thin venetian blinds. To the right, I saw a double bed with a yellow comforter and matching pillows, a white blanket folded over the foot. There was a small desk, too, a chair tucked under it. The ceiling slanted on either side, meeting in a flat strip in the middle, where there was a square skylight, also covered with a venetian blind—a little square one, clearly custom made to fit. It was so matchy-matchy and odd that for a moment, I found myself just staring up at it, as if this was actually the weirdest thing about that day.

"So, you've got your own bathroom," Jamie said, stepping around me, his feet making soft thuds on the carpet, which was of course spotless. In fact, the whole room smelled like paint and new carpet, just like the rest of the house. I wondered how long ago they had moved in—a month, six months? "Right through this door. And the closet is in here, too. Weird, right? Ours is the same way. When we were building, Cora claimed it meant she would get ready faster. A theory that has yet to be proved out, I might add."

Then he smiled at me, and again I tried to force a smile back. Who was this odd creature, my brother-in-law—a term that seemed oddly fitting, considering the circumstances—in his mountain-bike T-shirt, jeans, and funky expensive sneakers, cracking jokes in an obvious effort to ease the tension of an incredibly awkward situation? I had no idea, other than he had to be the very last person I would have expected to end up with my sister, who was so uptight she wasn't even pretending to smile at his attempts. At least I was trying.

Not Cora. She was just standing in the doorway, barely over the threshold, arms crossed over her chest. She had on a sleeveless sweater—even though it was mid-October, the house was beyond cozy, almost hot—and I could see the definition of her biceps and triceps, every muscle seemingly tensed, the same way they had been when she'd walked into the meeting room at Poplar House two hours earlier. Then, too, it seemed like Jamie had done all the talking, both to Shayna, the head counselor, and to me while Cora remained quiet. Still, every now and again, I could feel her eyes on me, steady, as if she was studying my features, committing me to memory, or maybe just trying to figure out if there was any part of me she recognized at all.

So Cora had a husband, I'd thought, staring at them as we'd sat across from each other, Shayna shuffling papers between us. I wondered if they'd had a fancy wedding, with her in a big white dress, or if they'd just eloped after she'd told him she had no family to speak of. Left to her own devices, this was the story I was sure she preferred—that she'd just sprouted, all on her own, neither connected nor indebted to anyone else at all.

"Thermostat's out in the hallway if you need to adjust it," Jamie was saying now. "Personally, I like a bit of a chill to the air, but your sister prefers it to be sweltering. So even if you turn it down, she'll most likely jack it back up within moments."

Again he smiled, and I did the same. God, this was exhausting. I felt Cora shift in the doorway, but again she didn't say anything.

"Oh!" Jamie said, clapping his hands. "Almost forgot.

The best part." He walked over to the window in the center of the wall, reaching down beneath the blind. It wasn't until he was stepping back and it was opening that I realized it was, in fact, a door. Within moments, I smelled cold air. "Come check this out."

I fought the urge to look back at Cora again as I took a step, then one more, feeling my feet sink into the carpet, following him over the threshold onto a small balcony. He was standing by the railing, and I joined him, both of us looking down at the backyard. When I'd first seen it from the kitchen, I'd noticed just the basics: grass, a shed, the big patio with a grill at one end. Now, though, I could see there were rocks laid out in the grass in an oval shape, obviously deliberately, and again, I thought of Stonehenge. What was it with these rich people, a druid fixation?

"It's gonna be a pond," Jamie told me as if I'd said this out loud.

"A pond?" I said.

"Total ecosystem," he said. "Thirty-by-twenty and lined, all natural, with a waterfall. And fish. Cool, huh?"

Again, I felt him look at me, expectant. "Yeah," I said, because I was a guest here. "Sounds great."

He laughed. "Hear that, Cor? *She* doesn't think I'm crazy."

I looked down at the circle again, then back at my sister. She'd come into the room, although not that far, and still had her arms crossed over her chest as she stood there, watching us. For a moment, our eyes met, and I wondered how on earth I'd ended up here, the last place I knew either one of us wanted me to be. Then she opened her mouth to speak for the first time since we'd pulled up in the driveway and all this, whatever it was, began.

"It's cold," she said. "You should come inside."

* * *

Before one o'clock that afternoon, when she showed up to claim me, I hadn't seen my sister in ten years. I didn't know where she lived, what she was doing, or even who she was. I didn't care, either. There had been a time when Cora was part of my life, but that time was over, simple as that. Or so I'd thought, until the Honeycutts showed up one random Tuesday and everything changed.

The Honeycutts owned the little yellow farmhouse where my mom and I had been living for about a year. Before that, we'd had an apartment at the Lakeview Chalets, the run-down complex just behind the mall. There, we'd shared a one-bedroom, our only window looking out over the back entrance to the J&K Cafeteria, where there was always at least one employee in a hairnet sitting outside smoking, perched on an overturned milk crate. Running alongside the complex was a stream that you didn't even notice until there was a big rain and it rose, overflowing its nonexistent banks and flooding everything, which happened at least two or three times a year. Since we were on the top floor, we were spared the water itself, but the smell of the mildew from the lower apartments permeated everything, and God only knew what kind of mold was in the walls. Suffice to say I had a cold for two years straight. That was the first thing I noticed about the yellow house: I could breathe there.

It was different in other ways, too. Like the fact that

it was a *house*, and not an apartment in a complex or over someone's garage. I'd grown used to the sound of neighbors on the other side of a wall, but the yellow house sat in the center of a big field, framed by two oak trees. There was another house off to the left, but it was visible only by flashes of roof you glimpsed through the trees—for all intents and purposes, we were alone. Which was just the way we liked it.

My mom wasn't much of a people person. In certain situations—say, if you were buying, for instance—she could be very friendly. And if you put her within five hundred feet of a man who would treat her like shit, she'd find him and be making nice before you could stop her, and I knew, because I had tried. But interacting with the majority of the population (cashiers, school administrators, bosses, ex-boyfriends) was not something she engaged in unless absolutely necessary, and then, with great reluctance.

Which was why it was lucky that she had me. For as long as I could remember, I'd been the buffer system. The go-between, my mother's ambassador to the world. Whenever we pulled up at the store and she needed a Diet Coke but was too hungover to go in herself, or she spied a neighbor coming who wanted to complain about her late-night banging around *again*, or the Jehovah's Witnesses came to the door, it was always the same. "Ruby," she'd say, in her tired voice, pressing either her glass or her hand to her forehead. "Talk to the people, would you?"

And I would. I'd chat with the girl behind the counter as I waited for my change, nod as the neighbor again threatened to call the super, ignored the proffered literature as I firmly shut the door in the Jehovah's faces. I was the first line of defense, always ready with an explanation or a bit of spin. "She's at the bank right now," I'd tell the landlord, even as she snored on the couch on the other side of the half-closed door. "She's just outside, talking to a delivery," I'd assure her boss so he'd release her bags for the day to me, while she smoked a much-needed cigarette in the freight area and tried to calm her shaking hands. And finally, the biggest lie of all: "Of course she's still living here. She's just working a lot," which is what I'd told the sheriff that day when I'd been called out of fourth period and found him waiting for me. That time, though, all the spin in the world didn't work. I talked to the people, just like she'd always asked, but they weren't listening.

That first day, though, when my mom and I pulled up in front of the yellow house, things were okay. Sure, we'd left our apartment with the usual drama—owing back rent, the super lurking around watching us so carefully that we had to pack the car over a series of days, adding a few things each time we went to the store or to work. I'd gotten used to this, though, the same way I'd adjusted to us rarely if ever having a phone, and if we did, having it listed under another name. Ditto with my school paperwork, which my mom often filled out with a fake address, as she was convinced that creditors and old landlords would track us down that way. For a long time, I thought this was the way everyone lived. When I got old enough to realize otherwise, it was already a habit, and anything else would have felt strange.

Inside, the yellow house was sort of odd. The kitchen was the biggest room, and everything was lined up against one wall: cabinets, appliances, shelves. Against another wall was a huge propane heater, which in cold weather worked hard to heat the whole house, whooshing to life with a heavy sigh. The only bathroom was off the kitchen, poking out with no insulated walls—my mom said it must have been added on; there'd probably been an outhouse, initially—which made for some cold mornings until you got the hot water blasting and the steam heated things up. The living room was small, the walls covered with dark fake-wood paneling. Even at high noon, you needed a light on to see your hand in front of your face. My mother, of course, loved the dimness and usually pulled the shades shut, as well. I'd come home to find her on the couch, cigarette dangling from one hand, the glow from the TV flashing across her face in bursts. Outside, the sun might be shining, the entire world bright, but in our house, it could always be late night, my mother's favorite time of day.

In the old one-bedroom apartment, I was accustomed to sometimes being awoken from a dead sleep, her lips close to my ear as she asked me to move out onto the couch, please, honey. As I went, groggy and discombobulated, I'd do my best not to notice whoever slipped back in the door behind her. At the yellow house, though, I got my own room. It was small, with a tiny closet and only one window, as well as orange carpet and those same dark walls, but I had a door to shut, and it was all mine. It made me feel like we'd stay longer than a couple of months, that things would be better here. In the end, though, only one of these things turned out to be true.

I first met the Honeycutts three days after we moved in.

It was early afternoon, and we were getting ready to leave for work when a green pickup truck came up the driveway. A man was driving, a woman in the passenger seat beside him.

"Mom," I called out to my mother, who was in the bedroom getting dressed. "Someone's here."

She sighed, sounding annoyed. My mother was at her worst just before going to work, petulant like a child. "Who is it?"

"I don't know," I said, watching as the couple—he in jeans and a denim work shirt, she wearing slacks and a printed top—started to make their way to the house. "But they're about to knock on the door."

"Oh, Ruby." She sighed again. "Just talk to them, would you?"

The first thing I noticed about the Honeycutts was that they were instantly friendly, the kind of people my mother couldn't *stand*. They were both beaming when I opened the door, and when they saw me, they smiled even wider.

"Well, look at you!" the woman said as if I'd done something precious just by existing. She herself resembled a gnome, with her small features and halo of white curls, like something made to put on a shelf. "Hello there!"

I nodded, my standard response to all door knockers. Unnecessary verbals only encouraged them, or so I'd learned. "Can I help you?"

The man blinked. "Ronnie Honeycutt," he said, extending his hand. "This is my wife, Alice. And you are?"

I glanced in the direction of my mother's room. Although usually she banged around a lot while getting ready—

drawers slamming, grumbling to herself—now, of course, she was dead silent. Looking back at the couple, I decided they probably weren't Jehovah's but were definitely peddling something. "Sorry," I said, beginning my patented firm shut of the door, "but we're not—"

"Oh, honey, it's okay!" Alice said. She looked at her husband. "Stranger danger," she explained. "They teach it in school."

"Stranger what?" Ronnie said.

"We're your landlords," she told me. "We just dropped by to say hello and make sure you got moved in all right."

Landlords, I thought. That was even worse than Witnesses. Instinctively, I eased the door shut a bit more, wedging my foot against it. "We're fine," I told them.

"Is your mom around?" Ronnie asked as Alice shifted her weight, trying to see into the kitchen behind me.

I adjusted myself accordingly, blocking her view, before saying, "Actually, she's—"

"Right here," I heard my mother say, and then she was crossing the living room toward us, pulling her hair back with one hand. She had on jeans, her boots, and a white tank top, and despite the fact that she'd just woken up about twenty minutes earlier, I had to admit she looked pretty good. Once my mother had been a great beauty, and occasionally you could still get a glimpse of the girl she had been—if the light was right, or she'd had a decent night's sleep, or, like me, you were just wistful enough to look for it.

She smiled at me, then eased a hand over my shoulder as she came to the door and offered them her other one. "Ruby

Cooper," she said. "And this is my daughter. Her name's Ruby, as well."

"Well, isn't that something!" Alice Honeycutt said. "And she looks just like you."

"That's what they say," my mom replied, and I felt her hand move down the back of my head, smoothing my red hair, which we did have in common, although hers was now streaked with an early gray. We also shared our pale skin—the redhead curse or gift, depending on how you looked at it—as well as our tall, wiry frames. I'd been told more than once that from a distance, we could almost be identical, and although I knew this was meant as a compliment, I didn't always take it that way.

I knew that my mother's sudden reaching out for me was just an act, making nice for the landlords, in order to buy some bargaining time or leverage later. Still, though, I noticed how easy it was for me to fold into her hip, resting my head against her. Like some part of me I couldn't even control had been waiting for this chance all along and hadn't even known it.

"It's our standard practice to just drop by and check in on folks," Ronnie was saying now, as my mother idly twisted a piece of my hair through her fingers. "I know the rental agency handles the paperwork, but we like to say hello face-to-face."

"Well, that's awfully nice of you," my mom said. She dropped my hair, letting her hand fall onto the doorknob so casually you almost would think she wasn't aware of it, or the inch or so she shut it just after, narrowing even farther the space between us and them. "But as Ruby was saying, I'm actually going to work right now. So . . ."

"Oh, of course!" Alice said. "Well, you all just let us know if there's anything you need. Ronnie, give Ruby our number."

We all watched as he pulled a scrap of paper and a pen out of his shirt pocket, writing down the digits slowly. "Here you go," he said, handing it over. "Don't hesitate to call."

"Oh, I won't," my mom said. "Thanks so much."

After a few more pleasantries, the Honeycutts finally left the porch, Ronnie's arm locked around his wife's shoulders. He deposited her in the truck first, shutting the door securely behind her, before going around to get behind the wheel. Then he backed out of the driveway with the utmost caution, doing what I counted to be at least an eight-point turn to avoid driving on the grass.

By then, though, my mother had long left the door and returned to her room, discarding their number in an ashtray along the way. "'Hello face-to-face' my ass," she said as a drawer banged. "Checking up is more like it. Busybodies."

She was right, of course. The Honeycutts were always dropping by unexpectedly with some small, seemingly unnecessary domestic project: replacing the garden hose we never used, cutting back the crepe myrtles in the fall, or installing a birdbath in the front yard. They were over so much, I grew to recognize the distinct rattle of their truck muffler as it came up the driveway. As for my mom, her niceties had clearly ended with that first day. Thereafter, if they came to the door, she ignored their knocks, not even flinching when Alice's face appeared in the tiny crack the living-room window shade didn't cover, white and ghostly with the bright light behind it, peering in.

It was because the Honeycutts saw my mother so rarely that it took almost two months for them to realize she was gone. In fact, if the dryer hadn't busted, I believed they might have never found out, and I could have stayed in the yellow house all the way until the end. Sure, I was behind on the rent and the power was close to getting cut off. But I would have handled all that one way or another, just like I had everything else. The fact was, I was doing just fine on my own, or at least as well as I'd ever done with my mom. Which wasn't saying much, I know. Still, in a weird way, I was proud of myself. Like I'd finally proven that I didn't need her, either.

As it was, though, the dryer *did* die, with a pop and a burning smell, late one October night while I was making macaroni and cheese in the microwave. I had no option but to stretch a clothesline across the kitchen in front of the space heater I'd been using since the propane ran out, hang everything up—jeans, shirts, and socks—and hope for the best. The next morning, my stuff was barely dry, so I pulled on the least damp of it and left the rest, figuring I'd deal with it that evening when I got home from work. But then Ronnie and Alice showed up to replace some supposedly broken front-porch slats. When they saw the clothesline, they came inside, and then they found everything else.

It wasn't until the day they took me to Poplar House that I actually saw the report that the person from social services had filed that day. When Shayna, the director, read it out loud, it was clear to me that whoever had written it had embellished, for some reason needing to make it sound worse than it actually was.

Minor child is apparently living without running water or heat in rental home abandoned by parent. Kitchen area was found to be filthy and overrun with vermin. Heat is non-functioning. Evidence of drug and alcohol use was discovered. Minor child appears to have been living alone for some time.

First of all, I had running water. Just not in the kitchen, where the pipes had busted. This was why the dishes tended to pile up, as it was hard to truck in water from the bathroom just to wash a few plates. As for the "vermin," we'd always had roaches; they'd just grown a bit more in number with the lack of sink water, although I'd been spraying them on a regular basis. And I did have a heater; it just wasn't on. The drug and alcohol stuff—which I took to mean the bottles on the coffee table and the roach in one of the ashtrays—I couldn't exactly deny, but it hardly seemed grounds for uprooting a person from their entire life with no notice.

The entire time Shayna was reading the report aloud, her voice flat and toneless, I still thought that I could talk my way out of this. That if I explained myself correctly, with the proper detail and emphasis, they'd just let me go home. After all, I had only seven months before I turned eighteen, when all of this would be a moot point anyway. But the minute I opened my mouth to start in about topic one, the water thing, she stopped me.

"Ruby," she said, "where is your mother?"

It was only then that I began to realize what would later seem obvious. That it didn't matter what I said, how carefully I crafted my arguments, even if I used every tool of evasion and persuasion I'd mastered over the years. There was only one thing that really counted, now and always, and this was it.

"I don't know," I said. "She's just gone."

* * *

After the tour, the pond reveal, and a few more awkward moments, Jamie and Cora finally left me alone to go downstairs and start dinner. It was barely five thirty, but already it was getting dark outside, the last of the light sinking behind the trees. I imagined the phone ringing in the empty yellow house as Richard, my mother's boss at Commercial Courier, realized we were not just late but blowing off our shift. Later, the phone would probably ring again, followed by a car rolling up the drive, pausing by the front window. They'd wait for a few moments for me to come out, maybe even send someone to bang on the door. When I didn't, they'd turn around hastily, spitting out the Honeycutts' neat grass and the mud beneath it from behind their back wheels.

And then what? The night would pass, without me there, the house settling into itself in the dark and quiet. I wondered if the Honeycutts had already been in to clean things up, or if my clothes were still stretched across the kitchen, ghostlike. Sitting there, in this strange place, it was like I could feel the house pulling me back to it, a visceral tug on my heart, the same way that, in the early days of the fall, I'd hoped it would do to my mom. But she hadn't come back, either. And now, if she did, I wouldn't be there.

Thinking this, I felt my stomach clench, a sudden panic

settling over me, and stood up, walking to the balcony door and pushing it open, then stepping outside into the cold air. It was almost fully dark now, lights coming on in the nearby houses as people came home and settled in for the night in the places they called home. But standing there, with Cora's huge house rising up behind me and that vast yard beneath, I felt so small, as if to someone looking up I'd be unrecognizable, already lost.

Back inside, I opened up the duffel that had been delivered to me at Poplar House; Jamie had brought it up from the car. It was a cheap bag, some promo my mom had gotten through work, the last thing I would have used to pack up my worldly possessions, not that this was what was in it anyway. Instead, it was mostly clothes I never wore—the good stuff had all been on the clothesline—as well as a few textbooks, a hairbrush, and two packs of cotton underwear I'd never seen in my life, courtesy of the state. I tried to imagine some person I'd never met before going through my room, picking these things for me. How ballsy it was to just assume you could know, with one glance, the things another person could not live without. As if it was the same for everyone, that simple.

There was only one thing I really needed, and I knew enough to keep it close at all times. I reached up, running my finger down the thin silver chain around my neck until my fingers hit the familiar shape there at its center. All day long I'd been pressing it against my chest as I traced the outline I knew by heart: the rounded top, the smooth edge on one side, the series of jagged bumps on the other. The night before, as I'd stood in the bathroom at Poplar House, it had been all that was familiar, the one thing I focused on as I faced the mirror. I could not look at the dark hollows under my eyes, or the strange surroundings and how strange I felt in them. Instead, like now, I'd just lifted it up gently, reassured to see that the outline of that key remained on my skin, the one that fit the door to everything I'd left behind.

* * *

By the time Jamie called up the stairs that dinner was ready, I'd decided to leave that night. It just made sense—there was no need to contaminate their pristine home any further, or the pretty bed in my room. Once everyone was asleep, I'd just grab my stuff, slip out the back door, and be on a main road within a few minutes. The first pay phone I found, I'd call one of my friends to come get me. I knew I couldn't stay at the yellow house—it would be the obvious place anyone would come looking—but at least if I got there, I could pick through my stuff for the things I needed. I wasn't stupid. I knew things had already changed, irrevocably and totally. But at least I could walk through the rooms and say good-bye, as well as try to leave some message behind, in case anyone came looking for me.

Then it was just a matter of laying low. After a few days of searching and paperwork, Cora and Jamie would write me off as unsaveable, getting their brownie points for trying *and* escaping relatively unscathed. That was what most people wanted anyway.

Now, I walked into the bathroom, my hairbrush in hand. I knew I looked rough, the result of two pretty much sleepless nights and then this long day, but the lighting in the bathroom, clearly designed to be flattering, made me look better than I knew I actually did, which was unsettling. Mirrors, if nothing else, were supposed to be honest. I turned off the lights and brushed my hair in the dark.

Just before I left my room, I glanced down at my watch, noting the time: 5:45. If Cora and Jamie were asleep by, say, midnight at the latest, that meant I only had to endure six hours and fifteen minutes more. Knowing this gave me a sense of calm, of control, as well as the fortitude I needed to go downstairs to dinner and whatever else was waiting for me.

Even with this wary attitude, however, I could never have been prepared for what I found at the bottom of the stairs. There, in the dark entryway, just before the arch that led into the kitchen, I stepped in something wet. And, judging by the splash against my ankle, cold.

"Whoa," I said, drawing my foot back and looking around me. Whatever the liquid was had now spread, propelled by my shoe, and I froze, so as not to send it any farther. Barely a half hour in, and already I'd managed to violate Cora's perfect palace. I was looking around me, wondering what I could possibly find to wipe it up with—the tapestry on the nearby wall? something in the umbrella stand?—when the light clicked on over my head.

"Hey," Jamie said, wiping his hands on a dishtowel. "I thought I heard something. Come on in, we're just about—" Suddenly, he stopped talking, having spotted the puddle and my proximity to it. "Oh, shit," he said.

"I'm sorry," I told him.

"Quick," he said, cutting me off and tossing me the dishtowel. "Get it up, would you? Before she—"

I caught the towel and was about to bend over when I realized it was too late. Cora was now standing in the archway behind him, peering around his shoulder. "Jamie," she said, and he jumped, startled. "Is that—?"

"No," he said flatly. "It's not."

My sister, clearly not convinced, stepped around him and walked over for a closer look. "It is," she said, turning back to look at her husband, who had slunk back farther into the kitchen. "It's pee."

"Cor—"

"It's pee, *again*," she said, whirling around to face him. "Isn't this why we put in that dog door?"

Dog? I thought, although I supposed this was a relief, considering I'd been worried I was about to find out something really disturbing about my brother-in-law. "You have a dog?" I asked. Cora sighed in response.

"Mastery of a dog door takes time," Jamie told her, grabbing a roll of paper towels off a nearby counter and walking over to us. Cora stepped aside as he ripped off a few sheets, then squatted down, tossing them over the puddle and adjacent splashes. "You know that expression. You can't teach an old dog new tricks."

Cora shook her head, then walked back into the kitchen without further comment. Jamie, still down on the floor, ripped off a few more paper towels and then dabbed at my shoe, glancing up at me. "Sorry about that," he said. "It's an issue."

I nodded, not sure what to say to this. So I just folded the dishtowel and followed him into the kitchen, where he tossed the paper towels into a stainless-steel trash can. Cora was by the windows that looked out over the deck, setting the wide, white table there. I watched as she folded cloth napkins, setting one by each of three plates, before laying out silverware: fork, knife, spoon. There were also place-mats, water glasses, and a big glass pitcher with sliced lemons floating in it. Like the rest of the house, it looked like something out of a magazine, too perfect to even be real.

Just as I thought this, I heard a loud, rattling sound. It was like a noise your grandfather would make, once he passed out in his recliner after dinner, but it was coming from behind me, in the laundry room. When I turned around, I saw the dog.

Actually first, I saw everything else: the large bed, covered in what looked like sheepskin, the pile of toys—plastic rings, fake newspapers, rope bones—and, most noticeable of all, a stuffed orange chicken, sitting upright. Only once I'd processed all these accoutrements did I actually make out the dog itself, which was small, black and white, and lying on its back, eyes closed and feet in the air, snoring. Loudly.

"That's Roscoe," Jamie said to me as he pulled open the fridge. "Normally, he'd be up and greeting you. But our dog walker came for the first time today, and I think it wore him out. In fact, that's probably why he had that accident in the foyer. He's exhausted."

"What would be *out* of the ordinary," Cora said, "is if he actually went outside."

From the laundry room, I heard Roscoe let out another loud snore. It sounded like his nasal passages were exploding.

"Let's just eat," Cora said. Then she pulled out a chair and sat down.

I waited for Jamie to take his place at the head of the table before claiming the other chair. It wasn't until I was seated and got a whiff of the pot of spaghetti sauce to my left that I realized I was starving. Jamie picked up Cora's plate, putting it over his own, then served her some spaghetti, sauce, and salad before passing it back to her. Then he gestured for mine, and did the same before filling his own plate. It was all so formal, and *normal,* that I felt strangely nervous, so much so that I found myself watching my sister, picking up my fork only when she did. Which was so weird, considering how long it had been since I'd taken any cues from Cora. Still, there had been a time when she had taught me everything, so maybe, like so much else, this was just instinct.

"So tomorrow," Jamie said, his voice loud and cheerful, "we're going to get you registered for school. Cora's got a meeting, so I'll be taking you over to my old stomping ground."

I glanced up. "I'm not going to Jackson?"

"Out of district," Cora replied, spearing a cucumber with her fork. "And even if we got an exception, the commute is too long."

"But it's mid-semester," I said. I had a flash of my locker, the bio project I'd just dropped off the week before, all of it, like my stuff in the yellow house, just abandoned. I swallowed, taking a breath. "I can't just leave everything."

"It's okay," Jamie said. "We'll get it all settled tomorrow."

"I don't mind a long bus ride," I said, ashamed at how tight my voice sounded, betraying the lump that had risen in my throat. So ridiculous that after everything that had happened, I was crying about *school*. "I can get up early, I'm used to it."

"Ruby." Cora leveled her eyes at me. "This is for the best. Perkins Day is an excellent school."

"Perkins Day?" I said. "Are you *serious*?"

"What's wrong with the Day?" Jamie asked.

"Everything," I told him. He looked surprised, then hurt. Great. Now I was alienating the one person who I actually had on my side in this house. "It's not a bad school," I told him. "It's just . . . I won't fit in with anyone there."

This was a massive understatement. For the last two years, I'd gone to Jackson High, the biggest high school in the county. Overcrowded, underfunded, and with half your classes in trailers, just surviving a year there was considered a badge of honor, especially if you were like me and did not exactly run with the most academic of crowds. After I'd moved around so much with my mom, Jackson was the first place I'd spent consecutive years in a long time, so even if it was a total shithole, it was still familiar. Unlike Perkins Day, the elite private school known for its lacrosse team, stellar SAT scores, and the fact that the student parking lot featured more luxury automobiles than a European car dealership. The only contact we ever had with Perkins Day kids was when they felt like slumming at parties. Even then, often their girls stayed in the car, engine running and radio on, cigarettes dangling out the window, too good to even come inside.

Just as I thought this, Jamie suddenly pushed his chair

back, jumping to his feet. "Roscoe!" he said. "Hold on! The dog door!"

But it was too late. Roscoe, having at some point roused himself from his bed, was already lifting his leg against the dishwasher. I tried to get a better look at him but only caught a fleeting glimpse before Jamie bolted across the floor, grabbing him in midstream, and then carried him, still dripping, and chucked him out the small flap at the bottom of the French doors facing us. Then he looked at Cora and, seeing her stony expression, stepped outside himself, the door falling shut with a click behind him.

Cora put a hand to her head, closing her eyes, and I wondered if I should say something. Before I could, though, she pushed back her chair and walked over to pick up the roll of paper towels, then disappeared behind the kitchen island, where I could hear her cleaning up what Roscoe had left behind.

I knew I should probably offer to help. But sitting alone at the table, I was still bent out of shape about the idea of me at Perkins Day. Like all it would take was dropping me in a fancy house and a fancy school and somehow I'd just be fixed, the same way Cora had clearly fixed herself when she'd left me and my mom behind all those years ago. But we were not the same, not then and especially not now.

I felt my stomach clench, and I reached up, pressing my fingers over the key around my neck. As I did so, I caught a glimpse of my watch, the overhead light glinting off the face, and felt myself relax. *Five hours, fifteen minutes,* I thought. Then I picked up my fork and finished my dinner.

* * *

Six hours and fifty long minutes later, I was beginning to worry that my brother-in-law—the Nicest Guy in the World and Lover of Incontinent Creatures—was also an insomniac. Figuring they were the early-to-bed types, I'd gone up to my room to "go to sleep" at nine thirty. Sure enough, I heard Cora come up about forty minutes later, padding past my bedroom to her own, which was at the opposite end of the floor. Her light cut off at eleven, at which point I started counting down, waiting for Jamie to join her. He didn't. In fact, if anything, there were more lights on downstairs now than there had been earlier, slanting across the backyard, even as the houses around us went dark, one by one.

Now I'd been sitting there for almost four hours. I didn't want to turn a light on, since I was supposed to be long asleep, so I'd spent the time lying on the bed, my hands clasped on my stomach, staring at the ceiling and wondering what the hell Jamie was doing. Truth be told, it wasn't that different from the nights a few weeks back, when the power had been cut off temporarily at the yellow house. At least there, though, I could smoke a bowl or drink a few beers to keep things interesting. Here, there was nothing but the dark, the heat cutting off and on at what—after timing them—I'd decided were random intervals, and coming up with possible explanations for the weird, shimmering light that was visible at the far end of the backyard. I was just narrowing it down to either aliens or some sort of celestial neo-suburban phenomenon when suddenly, the windows downstairs went dark. Finally, Jamie was coming to bed.

I sat up, brushing my hair back with my fingers, and

listened. Unlike the yellow house, which was so small and thin-walled you could hear someone rolling over in a bed two rooms away, Cora's palace was hard to monitor in terms of activity and movement. I walked over to my door, easing it open slightly. Distantly, I heard footsteps and a door opening and shutting. Perfect. He was in.

Reaching down, I grabbed my bag, then slowly drew the door open, stepping out into the hallway and sticking close to the wall until I got to the stairs. Downstairs in the foyer I got my first lucky break in days: the alarm wasn't set. Thank God.

I reached for the knob, then eased the door open, sliding my hand with the bag through first. I was just about to step over the threshold when I heard the whistling.

It was cheery, and a tune I recognized—some jingle from a commercial. Detergent, maybe. I looked around me, wondering what kind of company I would have on a subdivision street at one thirty in the morning. Soon enough, I got my answer.

"Good boy, Roscoe! Good boy!"

I froze. It was Jamie. Now I could see him, coming up the other side of the street with Roscoe, who had just lifted his leg on a mailbox, walking in front of him on a leash. *Shit,* I thought, wondering whether he was far enough away not to see if I bolted in the opposite direction, dodging the streetlights. After a quick calculation, I decided to go around the house instead.

I could hear him whistling again as I vaulted off the front steps, then ran through the grass, dodging a sprinkler spigot and heading for the backyard. There, I headed for that light I'd been studying earlier, now hoping that it *was* aliens, or some kind of black hole, anything to get me away.

Instead, I found a fence. I tossed my bag over and was wondering what my chances were of following, not to mention what I'd find there, when I heard a thwacking noise from behind me. When I turned around, I saw Roscoe emerging from his dog door.

At first, he was just sniffing the patio, his nose low to the ground, going in circles. But then he suddenly stopped, his nose in the air. *Uh-oh,* I thought. I was already reaching up, grabbing the top of the fence and scrambling to try and pull myself over, when he started yapping and shot like a bullet right toward me.

Say what you will about little dogs, but they can *move.* In mere seconds, he'd covered the huge yard between us and was at my feet, barking up at me as I dangled from the fence, my triceps and biceps already burning. "Shhh," I hissed at him, but of course this only made him bark more. Behind us, in the house, a light came on, and I could see Jamie in the kitchen window, looking out.

I tried to pull myself up farther, working to get more leverage. I managed to get one elbow over, hoisting myself up enough to see that the source of the light I'd been watching was not otherworldly at all, but a swimming pool. It was big and lit up and, I noticed, occupied, a figure cutting through the water doing laps.

Meanwhile, Roscoe was still yapping, and my bag was already in this strange person's yard, meaning I had little choice but to join it or risk being busted by Jamie. Straining,

I pulled myself up so I was hanging over the fence, and tried to throw a leg to the other side. No luck.

"Roscoe?" I heard Jamie call out from the patio. "Whatcha got there, boy?"

I turned my head, looking back at him, wondering if he could see me. I figured I had about five seconds, if Roscoe didn't shut up, before he headed out to see what his dog had treed. Or fenced. Another fifteen while he crossed the yard, then maybe a full minute before he'd put it all together.

"Hello?"

I was so busy doing all these calculations that I hadn't noticed that the person who'd been swimming laps had, at some point, stopped. Not only that, but he was now at the edge of the pool, looking up at me. It was hard to make out his features, but whoever it was was clearly male and sounded awfully friendly, considering the circumstances.

"Hi," I muttered back.

"Roscoe?" Jamie called out again, and this time, without even turning around, I could hear he was moving, coming closer. Unless I had a burst of superhuman strength or a black hole opened up and swallowed me whole, I needed a Plan B, and fast.

"Do you—?" the guy in the pool said, raising his voice to be heard over Roscoe, who was still barking.

"No," I told him as I relaxed my grip. His face disappeared as I slid down my side of the fence, landing on my feet with mere seconds to spare before Jamie ducked under the small row of trees at the edge of the yard and saw me.

"Ruby?" he said. "What are you doing out here?"

He looked so concerned that for a moment, I actually felt a pang of guilt. Like I'd let him down or something. Which was just ridiculous; we didn't even know each other. "Nothing," I said.

"Is everything okay?" He looked up at the fence, then back at me, as Roscoe, who'd finally shut up, sniffed around his feet, making snorting noises.

"Yeah," I said. I was making it a point to speak slowly. Calmly. Tone was everything. "I was just . . ."

Truth was, at that moment, I didn't know what I was planning to say. I was just hoping for some plausible excuse to pop out of my mouth, which, considering my luck so far, was admittedly kind of a long shot. Still, I was going to go for it. But before I could even open my mouth, there was a thunk from the other side of the fence, and a face appeared above us. It was the guy from the pool, who, in this better light, I could now see was about my age. His hair was blond and wet, and there was a towel around his neck.

"Jamie," he said. "Hey. What's up?"

Jamie looked up at him. "Hey," he replied. To me he said, "So . . . you met Nate?"

I shot a glance at the guy. *Oh, well,* I thought. *It's better than what I had planned.* "Yeah." I nodded. "I was just—"

"She came to tell me my music was too loud," the guy—Nate?—told Jamie. Unlike me, he didn't seem to be straining in the least, holding himself over the top of the fence. I wondered if he was standing on something. To me he added, "Sorry about that. I crank it up so I can hear it under the water."

"Right," I said. "I just . . . I couldn't sleep."

At my feet, Roscoe suddenly coughed, hacking up something. We all looked at him, and then Jamie said slowly, "Well . . . it's late. We've got an early day tomorrow, so . . ."

"Yeah. I should get to bed, too," Nate said, reaching down to pull up one edge of his towel and wiping it across his face. He had to be on a deck chair or something, I thought. No one has that kind of upper-body strength. "Nice meeting you, Ruby."

"You, too," I replied.

He waved at Jamie, then dropped out of sight. Jamie looked at me for a moment, as if still trying to decipher what had happened. I tried not to flinch as he continued to study my face, only relaxing once he'd slid his hands in his pockets and started across the lawn, Roscoe tagging along at his heels.

I'd just reached the line of trees, following him, when I heard a *"Pssst!"* from behind me. When I turned around, Nate had pushed open part of the fence and was passing my bag through. "Might need this," he said.

Like I was supposed to be grateful. *Unbelievable,* I thought as I walked over, picking up the bag.

"So what's it to?"

I glanced up at him. He had his hand on the gate and had pulled on a dark-colored T-shirt, and his hair was starting to dry now, sticking up slightly. In the flickering light from the nearby pool I could finally make out his face enough to see that he was kind of cute, but in a rich-boy way, all jocky and smooth edges, not my type at all. "What?" I said.

"The key." He pointed to my neck. "What's it to?"

Jamie was going into the house now, leaving the door open for me behind him. I reached up, twining my fingers around the chain hanging there. "Nothing," I told him.

I shifted my bag behind me, keeping it in my shadow as I headed across the lawn to the back door. *So close,* I thought. *A shorter fence, a fatter dog, and everything would be different.* But wasn't that always the way. It's never something huge that changes everything, but instead the tiniest of details, irrevocably tweaking the balance of the universe while you're busy focusing on the big picture.

When I got to the house, there was no sign of Jamie or Roscoe. Still, I figured it wasn't worth risking bringing my bag inside, and since the balcony was too high to toss it up, I decided to just stow it someplace and come back down for it in a couple of hours when the coast was clear. So I stuck it beside the grill, then slipped inside just as the shimmering lights from Nate's pool cut off, leaving everything dark between his house and ours.

I didn't see Jamie again as I climbed the stairs to my room. If I had, I wasn't sure what I would have said to him. Maybe he had fallen for my flimsy excuse, aided and abetted by a pool boy who happened to be in the right place at what, for me anyway, turned out to be the wrong time. It was possible he was just that gullible. Unlike my sister, who knew from disappearing and could spot a lie, even a good one, a mile off. She also probably would have happily provided the boost I needed up and over that fence, or at least pointed the way to the gate, if only to be rid of me once and for all.

I waited a full hour to slip back downstairs. When I eased open my door, though, there was my bag, sitting right there at my feet. It seemed impossible I hadn't heard Jamie leave it there, but he had. For some reason, seeing it made me feel the worst I had all day, ashamed in a way I couldn't even explain as I reached down, pulling it inside with me.

Chapter Two

My mom hated to work. Far from a model employee, she had never had a job, at least in my recollection, that she actually enjoyed. Instead, in our house, work was a four-letter word, the official end of good times, something to be dreaded and bitched about and, whenever possible, avoided.

Things might have been different if she was qualified for a glamorous occupation like travel agent or fashion designer. Instead, due to choices she'd made, as well as a few circumstances beyond her control, she'd always had low-level, minimum-wage, benefits-only-if-you're-really-lucky kinds of jobs: waitress, retail, telemarketer, temp. Which was why, when she got hired on at Commercial Courier, it seemed like such a good thing. Sure, it wasn't glamorous. But at least it was different.

Commercial Courier called itself an "all-purpose delivery service," but their primary business came from lost luggage. They had a small office at the airport where bags that had been routed to the wrong city or put onto the wrong plane would eventually end up, at which point one of their couriers would deliver them to their proper destination, whether it be a hotel or the bag owner's home.

Before Commercial, my mom had been working as a receptionist in an insurance office, a job she hated because it required the two things she hated above all else: getting up early and dealing with people. When her bosses let her go after six months, she'd spent a couple of weeks sleeping in and grumbling before finally hauling out the classifieds, where she spotted the ad for Commercial. DELIVERY DRIVERS NEEDED, it said. WORK INDEPENDENTLY, DAYS OR NIGHTS. She never would have called any job perfect, but just at a glance, it seemed pretty close. So she called and set up an interview. Two days later, she had a job.

Or, *we* did. The truth was, my mom was not a very good navigator. I'd suspected she was slightly dyslexic, as she was always mixing up her right and left, something that definitely would have been a problem for a job that relied almost entirely on following written driving directions. Luckily, though, her shift didn't start until five p.m., which meant that I could ride along with her, an arrangement that I'd assumed at first would only last for the initial few days, until she got the hang of things. Instead, we became coworkers, eight hours a day, five days a week, just her and me in her banged-up Subaru, reuniting people with their possessions.

Our night always started at the airport. Once the bags were stacked and packed in the car, she'd hand over the sheet of addresses and directions, and we'd set off, hitting the nearby hotels first before venturing farther to neighborhoods and individual homes.

People had one of two reactions when we arrived with their lost luggage. Either they were really happy and grateful, or chose to literally blame the messenger, taking out their ire at the entire airline industry on us. The best tactic, we learned, was empathy. "Don't I know it," my mom would say, holding her clipboard for the person's signature as they ranted on about having to buy new toiletries or clothes in a strange city. "It's an outrage." Usually, this was enough, since it was often more than the airlines had offered up, but occasionally someone would go above and beyond, being a total asshole, at which point my mom would just drop the bag at their feet, turn and walk back to the car, ignoring whatever they shouted after her. "It's karma," she'd say to me as we pulled away. "Watch. I bet we're here again before we know it."

Hotels were better, because we only had to deal with the bellmen or front-desk staff. They'd offer us some kind of perk for fitting them in early on our route, and we became regulars at all the hotel bars, grabbing a quick burger between deliveries.

By the end of the shift, the highways had usually cleared, and we were often the only car cresting silent hills in dark subdivisions. That late, people often didn't want to be bothered by us ringing the bell, so they'd leave a note on their front door asking us to drop the bag on the porch, or tell us, when we called to confirm the delivery, to just pop the trunk of their car and leave it in there. These were always the weirdest trips for me, when it was midnight or even later, and we pulled up to a dark house, trying to be quiet. Like a robbery in reverse, creeping around to leave something rather than take it.

Still, there was also was something reassuring about working for Commercial, almost hopeful. Like things that were lost could be found again. As we drove away, I always tried to imagine what it would be like to open your door to find something you had given up on. Maybe it had seen places you never had, been rerouted and passed through so many strange hands, but still somehow found its way back to you, all before the day even began.

* * *

I'd expected to sleep the same way I had at Poplar House—barely and badly—but instead woke with a start the next morning when Jamie knocked on my door, saying we'd be leaving in an hour. I'd been so out of it that at first I wasn't even sure where I was. Once I made out the skylight over my head, though, with its little venetian blind, it all came back to me: Cora's. My near-escape. And now, Perkins Day. Just three days earlier, I'd been managing as best I could at the yellow house, working for Commercial, and going to Jackson. Now, here, everything had changed again. But I was kind of getting used to that now.

When my mom first took off, I didn't think it was for good. I figured she was just out on one of her escapades, which usually lasted only as long as it took her to run out of money or welcome, a few days at most. The first couple of times she'd done this, I'd been so worried, then overwhelmingly relieved when she returned, peppering her with questions about where she'd been, which irritated her no end. "I just needed some space, okay?" she'd tell me, annoyed, before stalking off to her room to sleep—something that, by the looks of it, she hadn't done much of during the time she'd been gone.

It took me another couple of her disappearances—each a few days longer than the last—before I realized that this was exactly how I *shouldn't* react, making a big deal of it. Instead, I adopted a more blasé attitude, like I hadn't even really noticed she'd been gone. My mother had always been about independence—hers, mine, and ours. She was a lot of things, but clingy had never been one of them. By taking off, I decided, she was teaching me about taking care of myself. Only a weak person needed someone else around all the time. With every disappearance, she was proving herself stronger; it was up to me, in how I behaved, to do the same.

After two weeks with no word from her, though, I'd finally forced myself to go into her room and look through her stuff. Sure enough, her emergency stash—three hundred bucks in cash, last I'd checked—was gone, as were her saving-bonds certificates, her makeup, and, most telling, her bathing suit and favorite summer robe. Wherever she was headed, it was warm.

I had no idea when she'd really left, since we hadn't exactly been getting along. We hadn't exactly *not* been, either. But that fall, the hands-off approach we'd both cultivated had spilled over from just a few days here and there to all the time. Also, she'd stopped going to work—sleeping when I left for school in the morning, sleeping when I returned and headed out to Commercial, and usually out once I returned after all the deliveries were done—so it wasn't like we had a lot of chances to talk. Plus, the rare occasions she was home and awake, she wasn't alone.

Most times, when I saw her boyfriend Warner's beat-up old Cadillac in the driveway, I'd park and then walk around to my bedroom window, which I kept unlocked, and let myself in that way. It meant I had to brush my teeth with bottled water, and made washing my face out of the question, but these were small prices to pay to avoid Warner, who filled the house with pipe smoke and always seemed to be sweating out whatever he'd drunk the day before. He'd park himself on the couch, beer in hand, his eyes silently following me whenever I did have to cross in front of him. He'd never done anything I could point to specifically, but I believed this was due not to innocence but to lack of opportunity. I did not intend to provide him with one.

My mother, however, loved Warner, or so she said. They'd met at Halloran's, the small bar just down the street from the yellow house where she went sometimes to drink beer and sing karaoke. Unlike my mother's other boyfriends, Warner wasn't the meaty, rough-around-the-edges type. Instead, in his standard outfit of dark pants, cheap shirt, deck shoes, hat with captain's insignia, he looked like he'd just stepped off a boat, albeit not necessarily a nice one. I wasn't sure whether he had a nautical past and was pining for it, or was hoping for one still ahead. Either way, he liked to drink and seemed to have some money from somewhere, so for my mom he was perfect.

These days, when I thought about my mom, I sometimes pictured her on the water. Maybe she and Warner had gotten that old Cadillac all the way to Florida, like they'd always talked about doing, and were now on the deck of some boat, bobbing on the open sea. This was at least a prettier picture than the one I actually suspected, the little bit of denial I allowed myself. It wasn't like I had a lot of time for fantasies anyway.

When she left, it was mid-August, and I still had nine months before I turned eighteen and could live alone legally. I knew I had a challenge ahead of me. But I was a smart girl, and I thought I could handle it. My plan was to keep the job at Commercial until Robert, the owner, caught on to my mom's absence, at which point I'd have to find something else. As far as the bills went, because our names were identical I could access my mom's account for whatever paychecks—which were direct-deposited—I *was* able to earn. I figured I was good, at least for the time being. As long as I kept out of trouble at school, the one thing that I knew for sure would blow my cover, no one had to know anything was different.

And who knew? It could even have worked out if the dryer hadn't broken. But while my short-term plans might have changed, the long-term goal remained the same as it had been for as long as I could remember: to be free. No longer dependent or a dependent, subject to the whim or whimsy of my mother, the system, or anyone else, the albatross always weighing down someone's neck. It didn't really matter whether I served out the time at the yellow house or in Cora's world. Once I turned eighteen, I could cut myself off from everyone and finally get what I wanted, which was to be on my own, once and for all.

Now I did the best I could with my appearance, considering I was stuck with the same pair of jeans I'd had on for two days and a sweater I hadn't worn in years. Still, I thought, tugging down the hem of the sweater, which was about two sizes too small, it wasn't like I cared about impressing the people at Perkins Day. Even my best stuff would be their worst.

I grabbed my backpack off the bed, then started down the hall. Cora and Jamie's bedroom door was slightly ajar, and as I got closer, I could hear a soft, tinny beeping, too quiet to be an alarm clock but similar in sound and tone. As I passed, I glanced inside and saw my sister lying on her back, a thermometer poking out of her mouth. After a moment, she pulled it out, squinting at it as the beeping stopped.

I wondered if she was sick. Cora had always been like the canary in the coalmine, the first to catch anything. My mother said this was because she worried too much, that anxiety affected the immune system. She herself, she claimed, hadn't "had a cold in fifteen years," although I ventured to think this was because her own system was pickled rather than calm. At any rate, my memories of growing up with Cora were always colored with her various ailments: ear infections, allergies, tonsillitis, unexplained rashes and fevers. If my mother was right and it was stress related, I was sure I could blame myself for this latest malady, whatever it was.

Down in the kitchen, I found Jamie sitting at the island, a laptop open in front of him, a cell phone pressed to his ear. When he saw me, he smiled, then covered it with one hand. "Hey," he said. "I'll be off in a sec. There's cereal and stuff on the table—help yourself."

I glanced over, expecting to see a single box and some milk. Instead, there were several different boxes, most of them unopened, as well as a plate of muffins, a pitcher of orange juice, and a big glass bowl of fruit salad. "Coffee?" I asked, and he nodded, gesturing toward the opposite counter, where I saw a pot, some mugs laid out in front of it.

". . . yeah, but that's just the point," Jamie was saying as he cocked his head to one side, typing something on the keyboard. "If we're serious about considering this offer, we need to at least set some parameters for the negotiations. It's important."

I walked over to the coffeepot, picking up a mug and filling it. On Jamie's laptop, I could see the familiar front page of UMe.com, the networking site that it seemed like everyone from your favorite band to your grandmother had gotten on in the last year or so. I had a page myself, although due to the fact that I didn't have regular access to a computer, I hadn't checked it in a while.

"But that's just the point," Jamie said, clicking onto another page. "They say they want to preserve the integrity and the basic intention, but they've got corporate mindsets. Look, just talk to Glen, see what he says. No, not this morning, I've got something going. I'll be in by noon, though. Okay. Later."

There was a beep, and he put down the phone, picking up a muffin from beside him and taking a bite just as there was a *ping!* on the screen, the familiar sound of a new message in the UMe inbox. "You have a UMe page?" I asked him as I sat down at the table with my coffee. My sweater rode up again, and I gave it another tug.

He looked at me for a second. "Uh . . . yeah. I do." He nodded at my mug. "You're not eating?"

"I don't like breakfast," I told him.

"That's crazy talk." He pushed back his chair, walking over to grab two bowls out of a nearby cabinet, then stopped at the fridge, pulling it open and getting out some milk. "When I was a kid," he said, coming over and plopping everything onto the table beside me, "my mom fixed us eggs or pancakes every morning. With sausage or bacon, and toast. You gotta have it. It's brain food."

I looked at him over my coffee cup as he grabbed one of the cereal boxes, ripping it open and filling a bowl. Then he added milk, filling it practically to the top, and plopped it on a plate before adding a muffin and a heaping serving of fruit salad. I was about to say something about being impressed with his appetite when he pushed the whole thing across to me. "Oh, no," I said. "I can't—"

"You don't have to eat it all," he said, shaking cereal into his own bowl. "Just some. You'll need it, trust me."

I shot him a wary look, then put down my mug, picking up the spoon and taking a bite. Across the table, his own mouth full of muffin, he grinned at me. "Good, right?"

I nodded just as there was another *ping!* from the laptop, followed immediately by one more. Jamie didn't seem to notice, instead spearing a piece of pineapple with his fork. "So," he said, "big day today."

"I guess," I said, taking another bite of cereal. I hated to admit it, but now I was starving and had to work not to shovel the food in nonstop. I couldn't remember the last time I'd had breakfast.

"I know a new school is tough," he told me as there were

three more pings in quick succession. God, he was popular. "My dad was in the military. Eight schools in twelve years. It sucked. I was always the new kid."

"So how long did you go to Perkins Day?" I asked, figuring maybe a short stint would explain him actually liking it.

Ping. Ping. "I started as a junior. Best two years of my life."

"Really."

He raised an eyebrow at me, picking up a glass and helping himself to some orange juice. "You know," he said, "I understand it's not what you're used to. But it's also not as bad you think."

I withheld comment as four more messages hit his page, followed by a thwacking noise behind me. I turned around just in time to see Roscoe wriggling through his dog door.

"Hey, buddy," Jamie said to him as he trotted past us to his water bowl, "how's the outside world?"

Roscoe's only response was a prolonged period of slurping, his tags banging against the bowl. Now that I finally had a real chance to study him, I saw he was kind of cute, if you liked little dogs, which I did not. He had to be under twenty pounds, and was stocky, black with a white belly and feet, his ears poking straight up. Plus he had one of those pug noses, all smooshed up, which I supposed explained the adenoidal sounds I'd already come to see as his trademark. Once he was done drinking, he burped, then headed over toward us, stopping en route to lick up some stray muffin crumbs.

As I watched Roscoe, Jamie's laptop kept pinging: he had to have gotten at least twenty messages in the last five minutes. "Should you . . . check that or something?" I asked.

"Check what?"

"Your page," I said, nodding at the laptop. "You keep getting messages."

"Nah, it can wait." His face suddenly brightened. "Hey, sleepyhead! You're running late."

"Somebody kept hitting the snooze bar," my sister grumbled as she came in, hair wet and dressed in black pants and a white blouse, her feet bare.

"The same somebody," Jamie said, getting to his feet and meeting her at the island, "who was down here a full half hour ahead of you."

Cora rolled her eyes, kissing him on the cheek and pouring herself a cup of coffee. Then she bent down, mug in her hand, to pet Roscoe, who was circling her feet. "You guys should get going soon," she said. "There'll be traffic."

"Back roads," Jamie said confidently as I pushed back my chair, tugging down my sweater again before carrying my now empty bowl and plate to the sink. "I used to be able to get to the Day in ten minutes flat, including any necessary stoplights."

"That was ten years ago," Cora told him. "Times have changed."

"Not that much," he said.

His laptop pinged again, but Cora, like him, didn't seem to notice. Instead, she was watching me as I bent down, sliding my plate into the dishwasher. "Do you . . . ?" she said, then stopped. When I glanced up at her, she said, "Maybe you should borrow something of mine to wear."

"I'm fine," I said.

She bit her lip, looking right at the strip of exposed

stomach between the hem of my sweater and the buckle on my jeans I'd been trying to cover all morning. "Just come on," she said.

We climbed the stairs silently, her leading the way up and into her room, which was enormous, the walls a pale, cool blue. I was not surprised to see that it was neat as a pin, the bed made with pillows arranged so precisely you just knew there was a diagram in a nearby drawer somewhere. Like my room, there were also lots of windows and a skylight, as well as a much bigger balcony that led down to a series of decks below.

Cora crossed the room, taking a sip from the mug in her hands as she headed into the bathroom. We went past the shower, double sinks, and sunken bath into a room beyond, which turned out not to be a room at all but a closet. A *huge* closet, with racks of clothes on two walls and floor-to-ceiling shelves on the other. From what I could tell, Jamie's things—jeans, a couple of suits, and lots of T-shirts and sneakers—took up a fraction of the space. The rest was all Cora's. I watched from the doorway as she walked over to one rack, pushing some stuff aside.

"You probably need a shirt and a sweater, right?" she said, studying a few cardigans. "You have a jacket, I'm assuming."

"Cora."

She pulled out a sweater, examining it. "Yes?"

"Why am I here?"

Maybe it was the confined space, or this extended period without Jamie to buffer us. But whatever the reason, this question had just somehow emerged, as unexpected to me as I knew it was to her. Now that it was out, though, I was surprised how much I wanted to hear the answer.

She dropped her hand from the rack, then turned to face me. "Because you're a minor," she said, "and your mother abandoned you."

"I'm almost eighteen," I told her. "And I was doing just fine on my own."

"Fine," she repeated, her expression flat. Looking at her, I was reminded how really different we were, me a redhead with pale, freckled skin, such a contrast to her black hair and blue eyes. I was taller, with my mother's thin frame, while she was a couple of inches shorter and curvier. "You call that *fine*?"

"You don't know," I said. "You weren't there."

"I know what I read in the report," she replied. "I know what the social worker told me. Are you saying those accounts were inaccurate?"

"Yes," I said.

"So you weren't living without heat or water in a filthy house."

"Nope."

She narrowed her eyes at me. "Where's Mom, Ruby?"

I swallowed, then turned my head as I reached up, pressing the key around my neck into my skin. "I don't care," I said.

"Neither do I," she replied. "But the fact of the matter is, she's gone and you can't be by yourself. Does that answer your question?"

I didn't say anything, and she turned back to the clothes, pushing through them. "I told you, I don't need to borrow anything," I said. My voice sounded high and tight.

"Ruby, come on," she said, sounding tired. She pulled a black sweater off a hanger, tossing it over her shoulder before moving over to another shelf and grabbing a green T-shirt. Then she walked over, pushing them both at me as she passed. "And hurry. It takes at least fifteen minutes to get there."

Then she walked back through the bathroom, leaving me behind. For a moment, I just stood there, taking in the neat rows of clothes, how her shirts were all folded just so, stacked by color. As I looked down at the clothes she'd given me, I told myself I didn't care what the people at Perkins Day thought about me or my stupid sweater. Everything was just temporary anyway. Me being there, or here. Or anywhere, for that matter.

A moment later, though, when Jamie yelled up that it was time to go, I suddenly found myself pulling on Cora's T-shirt, which was clearly expensive and fit me perfectly, and then her sweater, soft and warm, over it. On my way downstairs, in clothes that weren't mine, to go to a school I'd never claim, I stopped and looked at myself in the bathroom mirror. You couldn't see the key around my neck: it hung too low under both collars. But if I leaned in close, I could make it out, buried deep beneath. Out of sight, hard to recognize, but still able to be found, even if I was the only one to ever look for it.

* * *

Cora was right. We got stuck in traffic. After hitting every red light between the house and Perkins Day, we finally pulled into the parking lot just as a bell was ringing.

All the visitor spaces were taken, so Jamie swung his car—a sporty little Audi with all-leather interior—into one in the student lot. I looked to my left—sure enough, parked there was a Mercedes sedan that looked brand-new. On our other side was another Audi, this one a bright red convertible.

My stomach, which had for most of the ride been pretty much working on rejecting my breakfast, now turned in on itself with an audible clench. According to the dashboard clock, it was 8:10, which meant that in a run-down classroom about twenty miles away, Mr. Barrett-Hahn, my homeroom teacher, was beginning his slow, flat-toned read of the day's announcements. This would be roundly ignored by my classmates, who five minutes from now would shuffle out, voices rising, to fight their way through a corridor designed for a student body a fraction the size of the current one to first period. I wondered if my English teacher, Ms. Valhalla—she of the high-waisted jeans and endless array of oversized polo shirts—knew what had happened to me, or if she just assumed I'd dropped out, like a fair amount of her students did during the course of a year. We'd been just about to start *Wuthering Heights,* a novel she'd promised would be a vast improvement over *David Copperfield,* which she'd dragged us through like a death march for the last few weeks. I'd been wondering if this was just talk or the truth. Now I'd never know.

"Ready to face the firing squad?"

I jumped, suddenly jerked back to the present and Jamie, who'd pulled his keys from the ignition and was now just sitting there expectantly, hand on the door handle.

"Oops. Bad choice of words," he said. "Sorry."

He pushed his door open and, feeling my stomach twist again, I forced myself to do the same. As soon as I stepped out of the car, I heard another bell sound.

"Office is this way," Jamie said as we started walking along the line of cars. He pointed to a covered walkway to our right, beyond which was a big green space, more buildings visible on the other side. "That's the quad," he said. "Classrooms are all around it. Auditorium and gym are those two big buildings you see over there. And the caf is here, closest to us. Or at least it used to be. It's been a while since I had a sloppy joe here."

We stepped up on a curb, heading toward a long, flat building with a bunch of windows. I'd just followed him, ducking under an overhang, when I heard a familiar *rat-a-tat-tat* sound. At first, I couldn't place it, but then I turned and saw an old model Toyota bumping into the parking lot, engine backfiring. My mom's car did the same thing, usually at stoplights or when I was trying to quietly drop a bag off at someone's house late at night.

The Toyota, which was white with a sagging bumper, zoomed past us, brake lights flashing as it entered the student parking lot and whipped into a space. I heard a door slam and then footsteps slapping across the pavement. A moment later, a black girl with long braids emerged, running, a backpack over one shoulder. She had a cell phone pressed to one ear and seemed to be carrying on a spirited conversation, even as she jumped the curb, went under the covered walkway, and began to sprint across the green.

"Ah, tardiness. Brings back memories," Jamie said.

"I thought you could get here in ten minutes."

"I could. But there were usually only five until the bell."

As we reached the front entrance and he pulled the glass door open for me, I was aware not of the stale mix of mildew and disinfectant Jackson was famous for but a clean, fresh-paint smell. It was actually very similar to Cora's house, which was a little unsettling.

"Mr. Hunter!" A man in a suit was standing just inside. As soon as he saw us, he strode right over, extending his hand. "The prodigal student returns home. How's life in the big leagues?"

"Big," Jamie said, smiling. They shook hands. "Mr. Thackray, this is my sister-in-law, Ruby Cooper. Ruby, this is Principal Thackray."

"Nice to meet you," Mr. Thackray said. His hand was large and cool, totally enveloping mine. "Welcome to Perkins Day."

I nodded, noting that my mouth had gone bone-dry. My experience with principals—and teachers and landlords and policemen—being as it was, this wasn't surprising. Even without a transgression, that same fight-or-flight instinct set in.

"Let's go ahead and get you settled in, shall we?" Mr. Thackray said, leading the way down the hallway and around the corner to a large office. Inside, he took a seat behind a big wooden desk, while Jamie and I sat in the two chairs opposite. Through the window behind him, I could see a huge expanse of soccer fields lined with bleachers. There was a guy on a riding mower driving slowly down one side, his breath visible in the cold air.

Mr. Thackray turned around, looking out the window, as well. "Looks good, doesn't it? All we're missing is a plaque honoring our generous benefactor."

"No need for that," Jamie said, running a hand through his hair. He sat back, crossing one leg over the other. In his sneakers, jeans, and zip-up hoodie, he didn't look ten years out of high school. Two or three, sure. But not ten.

"Can you believe this guy?" Mr. Thackray said to me, shaking his head. "Donates an entirely new soccer complex and won't even let us give him credit."

I looked at Jamie. "You did that?"

"It's not that big a deal," he said, looking embarrassed.

"Yes, it is," Mr. Thackray said. "Which is why I wish you'd reconsider and let us make your involvement public. Plus, it's a great story. Our students waste more time on UMe.com than any other site, and its owner donates some of the proceeds from that procrastination back into education. It's priceless!"

"Soccer," Jamie said, "isn't exactly education."

"Sports are crucial to student development," Mr. Thackray said. "It counts."

I turned my head, looking at my brother-in-law, suddenly remembering all those pings in his UMe inbox. *You could say that*, he'd said, when I'd asked if he had a page. Clearly, this was an understatement.

". . . grab a few forms, and we'll get a schedule set up for you," Mr. Thackray was saying. "Sound good?"

I realized, a beat too late, he'd been talking to me. "Yeah," I said. Then I swallowed. "I mean, yes."

He nodded, pushing back his chair and getting to his

feet. As he left the room, Jamie sat back, examining the tread of one sneaker. Outside, the guy on the mower had finished one side of the field and was now moving slowly up the other.

"Do you . . . ?" I said to Jamie. He glanced up at me. "You own UMe?"

He let his foot drop. "Well . . . not exactly. It's me and a few other guys."

"But he said you were the owner," I pointed out.

Jamie sighed. "I started it up originally," he said. "When I was just out of college. But now I'm in more of an overseeing position."

I just looked at him.

"CEO," he admitted. "Which is really just a big word, or a really small acronym, actually, for overseer."

"I can't believe Cora didn't tell me," I said.

"Ah, you know Cora." He smiled. "Unless you work eighty hours a week saving the world like she does, she's tough to impress."

I looked out at the guy on the mower again, watching as he puttered past. "Cora saves the world?"

"She tries to," he said. "Hasn't she told you about her work? Down at the public defender's office?"

I shook my head. In fact, I hadn't even known Cora had gone to law school until the day before, when the social worker at Poplar House had asked her what she did for a living. The last I knew, she'd been about to graduate from college, and that was five years ago. And we only knew that because, somehow, an announcement of the ceremony had made its way to us. It was on thick paper, a card with her name on it tucked inside. I remembered studying the envelope, wondering why it had turned up after all this time with no contact. When I'd asked my mom, she'd just shrugged, saying the school sent them out automatically. Which made sense, since by then, Cora had made it clear she wanted no part of us in her new life, and we'd been more than happy to oblige.

"Well," Jamie said as a palpable awkwardness settled over us, and I wondered what exactly he knew about our family, if perhaps my very existence had come as a surprise. Talk about baggage. "I guess you two have a lot of catching up to do, huh?"

I looked down at my hands, not saying anything. A moment later, Mr. Thackray walked back in, a sheaf of papers in his hand, and started talking about transcripts and credit hours, and this exchange was quickly forgotten. Later, though, I wished I had spoken up, or at least tried to explain that once I knew Cora better than anyone. But that was a long time ago, back when she wasn't trying to save the whole world. Only me.

* * *

When I was a kid, my mom used to sing to me. It was always at bedtime, when she'd come in to say good night. She'd sit on the edge of my bed, brushing my hair back with her fingers, her breath sweet smelling (a "civilized glass" or two of wine was her norm then) as she kissed my forehead and told me she'd see me in the morning. When she tried to leave, I'd protest, and beg for a song. Usually, if she wasn't in too bad a mood, she'd oblige.

Back then, I'd thought my mother made up all the songs

she sang to me, which was why it was so weird the first time I heard one of them on the radio. It was like discovering that some part of you wasn't yours at all, and it made me wonder what else I couldn't claim. But that was later. At the time, there were only the songs, and they were still all ours, no one else's.

My mother's songs fell into three categories: love songs, sad songs, or sad love songs. Not for her the uplifting ending. Instead, I fell asleep to "Frankie and Johnny" and a love affair gone very wrong, "Don't Think Twice It's All Right" and a bad breakup, and "Wasted Time" and someone looking back, full of regret. But it was "Angel from Montgomery," the Bonnie Raitt version, that made me think of her most, then and now.

It had everything my mother liked in a song—heartbreak, disillusionment, and death—all told in the voice of an old woman, now alone, looking back over all the things she'd had and lost. Not that I knew this; to me they were just words set to a pretty melody and sung by a voice I loved. It was only later, when I'd lie in a different bed, hearing her sing late into the night through the wall, that they kept me awake worrying. Funny how a beautiful song could tell such an ugly story. It seemed unfair, like a trick.

If you asked her, my mother would say that nothing in her life turned out the way she planned it. She was *supposed* to go to college and then marry her high-school sweetheart, Ronald Brown, the tailback for the football team, but his parents decided they were getting too serious and made him break up with her, right before Christmas of her junior year. Heartbroken, she'd allowed her friends to drag her to a party where she knew absolutely no one and ended up stuck talking to a guy who was in his freshman year at Middletown Tech, studying to be an engineer. In a kitchen cluttered with beer bottles, he'd talked to her about suspension bridges and skyscrapers, "the miracle of buildings," all of which bored her to tears. Which never explained, at least to me, why she ended up agreeing to go out with him, then sleeping with him, thereby producing my sister, who was born nine months later.

So at eighteen, while her classmates graduated, my mom was at home with an infant daughter and a new husband. Still, if the photo albums are any indication, those early years weren't so bad. There are tons of pictures of Cora: in a sunsuit, holding a shovel, riding a tricycle up a front walk. My parents appear as well, although not as often, and rarely together. Every once in a while, though, there's a shot of them—my mom looking young and gorgeous with her long red hair and pale skin, my dad, dark-haired with those bright blue eyes, his arm thrown over her shoulder or around her waist.

Because there was a ten-year gap between Cora and me, I'd always wondered if I was a mistake, or maybe a last-gasp attempt to save a marriage that was already going downhill. Whatever the reason, my dad left when I was five and my sister fifteen. We were living in an actual house in an actual neighborhood then, and we came home from the pool one afternoon to find my mom sitting on the couch, glass in hand. By themselves, neither of these things were noteworthy. Back then, she didn't work, and while she usually waited until my dad got home to pour herself a drink, occasionally she started without him. The thing that we did notice, though, right off, was that there was music playing, and my mom was singing along. For the first time, it wasn't soothing or pretty to me. Instead, I felt nervous, unsettled, as if the cumulative weight of all those sad songs was hitting me at once. From then on, her singing was always a bad sign.

I had vague memories of seeing my dad after the divorce. He'd take us for breakfast on the weekends or a dinner during the week. He never came inside or up to the door to get us, instead just pulling up to the mailbox and sitting there behind the wheel, looking straight ahead. As if he was waiting not for us but for anyone, like a stranger could have slid in beside him and it would have been fine. Maybe it was because of this distance that whenever I tried to remember him now, it was hard to picture him. There were a couple of memories, like of him reading to me, and watching him grilling steaks on the patio. But even with these few things, it was as if even when he was around, he was already distant, a kind of ghost.

I don't remember how or why the visits ceased. I couldn't recall an argument or incident. It was like they happened, and then they didn't. In sixth grade, due to a family-tree project, I went through a period where the mystery of his disappearance was all I could think about, and eventually I did manage to get out of my mom that he'd moved out of state, to Illinois. He'd kept in touch for a little while, but after remarrying and a couple of changes of address he'd vanished, leaving no way for her to collect child support, or any support. Beyond that, whenever I bugged her about it, she made it clear it was not a subject she wanted to discuss. With my mom, when someone was gone, they were gone. She didn't waste another minute thinking about them, and neither should you.

When my dad left, my mom slowly began to withdraw from my daily routine—waking me up in the morning, getting me ready for school, walking me to the bus stop, telling me to brush my teeth—and Cora stepped in to take her place. This, too, was never decided officially or announced. It just happened, the same way my mom just happened to start sleeping more and smiling less and singing late at night, her voice wavering and haunting and always finding a way to reach my ears, even when I rolled myself against the wall tight and tried to think of something, anything else.

Cora became my one constant, the single thing I could depend on to be there and to remain relatively unchanged, day in and day out. At night in our shared room, I'd often have to lie awake listening to her breathing for a long time before I could fall asleep myself.

"Shhh," I remembered her saying as we stood in our nightgowns in our bedroom. She'd press her ear against the door, and I'd watch her face, cautious, as she listened to my mom moving around downstairs. From what she heard—a lighter clicking open, then shut, cubes rattling in a glass, the phone being picked up or put down—she always gauged whether it was safe for us to venture out to brush our teeth or eat something when my mom had forgotten about dinner. If my mom was sleeping, Cora would hold my hand as we tiptoed past her to the kitchen. There I'd hold an old acrylic tray while she quickly piled it with cereal and milk—or, my favorite, English-muffin pizzas she made in the toaster oven, moving stealthily around the kitchen as my mother's breath rose and fell in the next room. When things went well, we'd get back upstairs without her stirring. When they didn't, she'd jerk awake, sitting up with creases on her face, her voice thick as she said, "What are you two doing?"

"It's okay," Cora would say. "We're just getting something to eat."

Sometimes, if she'd been out deeply enough, this was enough. More often, though, I'd hear the couch springs squeak, her feet hitting the hardwood floor, and it was then that Cora always stopped whatever she was in the midst of—sandwich making, picking through my mom's purse for lunch money, pushing the wine bottle, open and sweaty, farther back on the counter—and do the one thing I associated with her more than anything else. As my mother approached, annoyed and usually spoiling for a fight, my sister would always step in front of me. Back then, she was at least a head taller, and I remembered this so well, the sudden shift in my perspective, the view going from something scary to something not. Of course, I knew my mother was still coming toward me, but it was always Cora I kept my eyes on: her dark hair, the sharp angles of her shoulder blades, the way, when things were really bad, she'd reach her hand back to find mine, closing her fingers around it. Then she'd just stand there, as my mother appeared, ready to take the brunt of whatever came next, like the bow of a boat crashing right into a huge wave and breaking it into nothing but water.

Because of this, it was Cora who got the bulk of the stinging slaps, the two-hand pushes that sent her stumbling backward, the sudden, rough tugs on the arm that left red twisty welts and, later, bruises in the shape of fingertips. The transgressions were always hard to understand, and therefore even more difficult to avoid: we were up when we shouldn't have been, we were making too much noise, we provided the wrong answers to questions that seemed to have no right ones. When it was over, my mother would shake her head and leave us, returning to the couch or her bedroom, and I'd always look at Cora, waiting for her to decide what we should do next. More often than not, she'd just leave the room herself, wiping her eyes, and I'd fall in behind her, not talking but sticking very close, feeling safer if she was not just between me and my mom, but between me and the world in general.

Later, I'd develop my own system for dealing with my mom, learning to gauge her mood by the number of glasses or bottles already on the table when I came home, or the inflection in her tone when she said the two syllables that made up my name. I took a few knocks as well, although this became more rare when I hit middle school. But it was always the singing that was the greatest indicator, the one thing that made me hesitate outside a door frame, hanging back from the light. As beautiful as her voice sounded, working its way along the melodies I knew by heart, I knew there was a potential ugliness underneath.

By then, Cora was gone. A great student, she'd spent high school working shifts at Exclamation Taco! for college money and studying nonstop, to better her chances of receiving any one of the several scholarships she'd applied for. My sister was nothing if not driven and had always balanced the chaos that was our lives with a strict personal focus on order and organization. While the rest of the house was constantly dusty and in disarray, Cora's side of our shared room was neat as a pin, everything folded and in its place. Her books were alphabetized, her shoes lined up in a row, her bed always made, the pillow at a perfect right angle to the wall. Sometimes, sitting on my own bed, I'd look across and be amazed at the contrast: it was like a before-and-after shot, or a reverse mirror image, the best becoming the worst, and back again.

In the end, she received a partial scholarship to the U, the state university one town over, and applied for student loans to cover the rest. During the spring and summer of senior year, after she'd gotten her acceptance, there was a weird shift in the house. I could feel it. My sister, who'd spent most of the last year avoiding my mother entirely—going from school to work to bed and back again—suddenly seemed to loosen up, grow lighter. People came to pick her up on weekend nights, their voices rising up to our open windows as she got into their cars and sped away. Girls with easy, friendly voices called asking for Cora, who'd then take the phone into the bathroom where, even through the door, I could hear her voice sounded different speaking back to them.

Meanwhile my mother grew quieter, not saying anything as Cora brought home boxes to pack for school or cleaned out her side of the room. Instead, she just sat on the side porch during those long summer twilights, smoking cigarettes and staring off into the side yard. We never talked about Cora leaving, but as the day grew closer, that shift in the air was more and more palpable, until it was as if I could see my sister extracting herself from us, twisting loose and breaking free, minute by minute. Sometimes at night, I'd wake up with a start, looking over at her sleeping form across the room and feel reassured only fleetingly, knowing that the day would come soon when there would be nothing there at all.

The day she moved out, I woke up with a sore throat. It was a Saturday morning, and I helped her carry her boxes and a couple of suitcases downstairs. My mother stayed in the kitchen, chain-smoking and silent, not watching as we carted out my sister's few possessions, loading them into the trunk of a Jetta that belonged to a girl named Leslie whom I'd never met before that day and never saw again.

"Well," Cora had said, when she pushed the hatchback shut, "I guess that's everything."

I looked up at the house, where I could see my mom through the front window, moving through the kitchen to the den, then back again. And even with everything that had happened, I remember thinking that of course she wouldn't let Cora just go with no good-bye. But as the time passed, she got no closer to the door or to us, and after a while, even when I looked hard, I couldn't see her at all.

Cora, for her part, was just standing there, staring up at the house, her hands in her pockets, and I wondered if she was waiting, too. But then she dropped her hands, letting out a breath. "I'll be back in a sec," she said, and Leslie nodded. Then we both watched her slowly go up the walk and into the house.

She didn't stay long—maybe a minute, or even two. And when she came out, her face looked no different. "I'll call you tonight," she said to me. Then she stepped forward, pulling me into a tight hug. I remembered thinking, as she drove away, that my throat was so sore I'd surely be totally sick within hours. But I wasn't. By the next morning it was gone.

Cora called that first night, as promised, and the following weekend, checking in and asking how I was doing. Both times I could hear chatter in the background, voices and music, as she reported that she liked her roommate and her classes, that everything was going well. When she asked how I was, I wanted to tell her how much I missed her, and that my mom had been drinking a lot since she'd left. Since we'd hardly discussed this aloud face-to-face, though, bringing it up over the phone seemed impossible.

She never asked to speak to my mother, and my mom never once picked up when she called. It was as if their relationship had been a business arrangement, bound by contract, and now that contract had expired. At least that was the way I looked at it, until we moved a few weeks later and my sister stopped calling altogether. Then I realized that deep down in the fine print, my name had been on it as well.

For a long time, I blamed myself for Cora cutting ties with us. Maybe because I hadn't told her I wanted to keep in touch, she didn't know or something. Then I thought that maybe she couldn't find our new number. But whenever I asked my mom about this, she just sighed, shaking her head. "She's got her own life now, she doesn't need us anymore," she explained, reaching out to ruffle my hair. "It's just you and me now, baby. Just you and me."

Looking back, it seemed like it should have been harder to lose someone, or have them lose you, especially when they were in the same state, only a few towns over. It would have been so easy to drive to the U and find her dorm, walk up to her door, and announce ourselves. Instead, as the time passed and it became clear Cora wanted nothing to do with me and my mother, it made sense to wipe our hands of her, as well. This, like the alliance between me and my sister all those years ago, was never officially decided. It just happened.

It wasn't like it was so shocking, anyway. My sister had made a break for it, gotten over the wall and escaped. It was what we both wanted. Which was why I understood, even appreciated, why she didn't want to return for a day or even an hour. It wasn't worth the risk.

There were so many times during those years, though, as we moved from one house to another, that I would find myself thinking about my sister. Usually it was late at night, when I couldn't sleep, and I'd try to picture her in her dorm room forty-odd miles and a world away. I wondered if she was happy, what it was like out there. And if maybe, just maybe, she ever thought of me.

Chapter Three

"Ruby, welcome. Come join us, there's a free seat right over here."

I could feel everyone in the room watching me as I followed the outstretched finger of the teacher, a slight, blonde woman who looked barely out of college, to the end of a long table where there was an empty chair.

According to my new schedule, this was Literature in Practice with an M. Conyers. Back at Jackson, the classes all had basic names: English, Geometry, World History. If you weren't one of the few golden children, anointed early for the AP–Ivy League fast track, you made your choices with the minimal and usually disinterested help of one of the three guidance counselors allotted for the entire class. Here, though, Mr. Thackray had spent a full hour consulting my transcript, reading descriptions aloud from the thick course catalog, and conferring with me about my interests and goals. Maybe it was for Jamie's benefit—he was super donor, after all—but somehow, I doubted it. Clearly, they did things differently here.

Once I sat down, I read over my list of classes, separated into neat blocks—Intro to Calculus, Global Cultures and Practices, Drawing: Life and Form—twice, figuring that would give people adequate time to stare at me before moving on to something else. Sure enough, by the time I lifted my head a couple of minutes later to turn my attention to the teacher, a cursory check revealed everyone else was pretty much doing the same.

"As you know," she was saying, walking over to a table in front of a large dry-erase board and hopping up onto it, "we'll be doing several assignments over the course of the rest of the year. You'll have your research project on the novel of your choosing, and we'll also be reading a series of memoirs and oral histories."

I took a minute, now that I felt a bit more comfortable, to look around the room. It was large, with three big windows on one side that looked out onto the common green, some new-looking computers in the back of the room, and instead of desks, a series of tables, arranged in three rows. The class itself was small—twelve or fourteen people, tops. To my left, there was a girl with long, strawberry-blonde hair, twisted into one of those effortlessly perfect knots, a pencil sticking through it. She was pretty, in that cheerleader/student-council president/future nuclear physicist kind of way, and sitting with her posture ramrod straight, a Jump Java cup centered on the table in front of her. To my right, there was a huge backpack—about fourteen key chains hanging off of it—that was blocking my view of whoever was on the other side.

Ms. Conyers hopped off her desk and walked around it, pulling out a drawer. With her jeans, simple oxford shirt, and red clogs, she looked about twelve, which I figured had to make it difficult to keep control in her classroom. Then again, this didn't seem like an especially challenging group.

Even the row of guys at the back table—pumped-up jock types, slumped over or leaning back in their chairs—looked more sleepy than rowdy.

"So today," she said, shutting the desk drawer, "you're going to begin your own oral history project. Although it isn't exactly a history, as much as a compilation."

She started walking down the aisle between the tables, and I saw now she had a small plastic bowl in her hand, which she offered to a heavyset girl with a ponytail. The girl reached in, pulling out a slip of paper, and Ms. Conyers told her to read what was on it out loud. The girl squinted at it. "Advice," she said.

"Advice," Ms. Conyers repeated, moving on to the next person, a guy in glasses, holding out the bowl to him. "What is advice?"

No one said anything for a moment, during which time she kept distributing slips of paper, one person at a time. Finally the blonde to my left said, "Wisdom. Given by others."

"Good, Heather," Ms. Conyers said to her, holding the bowl out to a skinny girl in a turtleneck. "What's another definition?"

Silence. More people had their slips now, and a slight murmur became audible as they began to discuss them. Finally a guy in the back said in a flat voice, "The last thing you want to get from some people."

"Nice," Ms. Conyers said. By now, she'd gotten to me, and smiled as I reached into the bowl, grabbing the first slip I touched. I pulled it back, not opening it as she moved past the huge backpack to whoever was on the other side. "What else?"

"Sometimes," the girl who'd picked the word said, "you go looking for it when you can't make a decision on your own."

"Exactly," Ms. Conyers said, moving down the row of boys in the back. As she passed one—a guy with shaggy hair who was slumped over his books, his eyes closed—she nudged him, and he jerked to attention, looking around until she pointed at the bowl and he reached in for a slip. "So for instance, if I was going to give Jake here some advice, it would be what?"

"Get a haircut," someone said, and everyone laughed.

"Or," Ms. Conyers said, "get a good night's sleep, because napping in class is *not* cool."

"Sorry," Jake mumbled, and his buddy, sitting beside him in a Butter Biscuit baseball hat, punched him in the arm.

"The point," Ms. Conyers continued, "is that no word has one specific definition. Maybe in the dictionary, but not in real life. So the purpose of this exercise will be to take your word and figure out what it means. Not just to you but to the people around you: your friends, your family, coworkers, teammates. In the end, by compiling their responses, you'll have your own understanding of the term, in all its myriad meanings."

Everyone was talking now, so I looked down at my slip, slowly unfolding it. FAMILY, it said, in simple block print. *Great,* I thought. *The last thing I have, or care about. This must be—*

"Some kind of *joke,*" I heard someone say. I glanced over, just as the backpack suddenly slid to one side. "What'd you get?"

I blinked, surprised to see the girl with the braids from

the parking lot who'd been running and talking on her cell phone. Up close, I could see she had deep green eyes, and her nose was pierced, a single diamond stud. She pushed the backpack onto the floor, where it landed with a loud *thunk*, then turned her attention back to me. "Hello?" she said. "Do you speak?"

"Family," I told her, then pushed the slip toward her, as if she might need visual confirmation. She glanced at it and sighed. "What about you?"

"Money," she said, her voice flat. She rolled her eyes. "Of course the one person in this whole place who doesn't have it has to write about it. It would just be too *easy* for everyone else."

She said this loudly enough that Ms. Conyers, who was making her way back to her desk, looked over. "What's the matter, Olivia? Don't like your term?"

"Oh, I like the term," the girl said. "Just not the assignment."

Ms. Conyers smiled, hardly bothered, and moved on, while Olivia crumpled up her slip, stuffing it in her pocket. "You want to trade?" I asked her.

She looked over at my FAMILY again. "Nah," she said, sounding tired. "That I know too much about."

Lucky you, I thought as Ms. Conyers reassumed her position on her desk, a slim book in her hands. "Moving on," she said, "to our reading selection for today. Who wants to start us off on last night's reading of *David Copperfield*?"

Thirty minutes later, after what felt like some major literary déjà-vu, the bell finally rang, everyone suddenly pushing back chairs, gathering up their stuff, and talking at once. As I reached down, grabbing my own backpack off the floor, I couldn't help but notice that, like me, it looked out of place here—all ratty and old, still stuffed with notebooks full of what was now, in this setting, mostly useless information. I'd known that morning I should probably toss everything out, but instead I'd just brought it all with me, even though it meant flipping past endless pages of notes on *David Copperfield* to take even more of the same. Now, I slid the FAMILY slip inside my notebook, then let the cover fall shut.

"You went to Jackson?"

I looked up at Olivia, who was now standing beside the table, cell phone in hand, having just hoisted her own huge backpack over one shoulder. At first, I was confused, wondering if my cheap bag made my past that obvious, but then I remembered the JACKSON SPIRIT! sticker on my notebook, which had been slapped there by some overexcited member of the pep club during study hall. "Uh, yeah," I told her. "I do. I mean . . . I did."

"Until when?"

"A couple of days ago."

She cocked her head to the side, studying my face while processing this information. In the meantime, distantly through the receiver end of her phone, I heard another phone ringing, a call she'd clearly made but had not yet completed. "Me, too," she said, pointing at the coat she had on, which now that I looked more closely, was a Jackson letter jacket.

"Really," I said.

She nodded. "Up until last year. You don't look familiar,

though." Distantly, I heard a click. *"Hello?"* someone said, and she put her phone to her ear.

"It's a big place."

"No kidding." She looked at me for a minute longer, even as whoever was on the other end of the line kept saying hello. "It's a lot different from here."

"Seems like it." I shoved my notebook into my bag.

"Oh, you have *no* idea. You want some advice?"

As it turned out, this was a rhetorical question.

"Don't trust the natives," Olivia said. Then she smiled, like this was a joke, or maybe not, before putting her phone to her ear, our conversation clearly over as she began another one and turned toward the door. "Laney. Hey. What's up? Just between classes. . . . Yeah, no kidding. Well, obviously can't sit around waiting for you to call *me*. . . ."

I pulled my bag over my shoulder, following her out to the hallway, which was now bustling and busy, although at the same time hardly crowded, at least in terms of what I was used to. No one was bumping me, either by accident or on purpose, and if anyone did grab my ass, it would be pretty easy to figure out who it was. According to my schedule, I had Spanish in Conversation next, which was in building C. I figured that since this was my one day I could claim ignorance on all counts, there was no point in rushing, so I took my time as I walked along, following the crowd outside.

Just past the door, on the edge of the quad, there was a huge U-shaped sculpture made of some kind of chrome that caught the sunlight winking off it in little sparks and making everything seem really bright. Because of this effect, it was kind of hard at first to make out the people grouped around it, some sitting, some standing, which was why, when I first heard my name, I had no idea where it was coming from.

"Ruby!"

I stopped, turning around. As my eyes adjusted, I could see the people at the sculpture and immediately identified them as the same kind of crowd that, at Jackson, hung out on the low wall just outside the main office: the see-and-be-seens, the top of the food chain, the group that you didn't join without an express invitation. Not my kind of people. And while it was kind of unfortunate that the one person I knew outside of Perkins Day was one of them, it wasn't all that surprising, either.

Nate was standing on the edge of the green; when he saw me spot him, he lifted a hand, smiling. "So," he said as a short guy wearing a baseball hat skittered between us. "Attempted any great escapes lately?"

I glanced at him, then at his friends—which included the blonde Jump Java girl from my English class, I now noticed—who were talking amongst themselves a few feet behind him. *Ha-ha,* I thought. Moments ago, I'd been invisible, or as invisible as you can be when you're the lone new person at a school where everyone has probably known each other since birth. Now, though, I was suddenly aware that people were staring at me—and not just Nate's assembled friends, either. Even the people passing us were glancing over, and I wondered how many people had already heard this story, or would before day's end. "Funny," I said, and turned away from him.

"I'm only kidding around," he called out. I ignored this,

continuing on. A moment later he jogged up beside me, planting himself in my path. "Hey," he said. "Sorry. I was just . . . it was just a joke."

I just looked at him. In broad daylight, he looked even more like a jock than the night before—in jeans, a T-shirt with collared shirt over it, rope necklace around his neck, and thick flip-flops on his feet, even though it was way past beach season. His hair, as I'd noticed last night, was that white kind of blond, like he'd spent the summer in the sun, his eyes a bright blue. *Too perfect,* I thought. The truth was, if this was the first time I'd laid eyes on him, I might have felt a little bad about discounting him as a thick jock with a narrow mind-set and an even tinier IQ. As this was our second meeting, though, it was a little easier.

"Let me make it up to you," he said, nodding at my schedule, which I still had in my hand. "You need directions?"

"Nope," I said, pulling my bag higher up on my shoulder.

I expected him to look surprised—I couldn't imagine he got turned down much for anything—but instead he just shrugged. "All right," he said. "I guess I'll just see you around. Or tomorrow morning, anyway."

There was a burst of laughter from beside me as two girls sharing a pair of earphones attached to an iPod brushed past. "What's happening tomorrow morning?"

Nate raised his eyebrows. "The carpool," he said, like I was supposed to have any idea what he was talking about. "Jamie said you needed a ride to school."

"With you?"

He stepped back, putting a hand over his chest. "Careful,"

he said, all serious. "You're going to hurt my feelings."

I just looked at him. "I don't need a ride."

"Jamie seems to think you do."

"I don't."

"Suit yourself," he said, shrugging again. Mr. Easygoing. "I'll come by around seven thirty. If you don't come out, I'll move on. No biggie."

No biggie, I thought. *Who talks like that?* He flashed me another million-dollar smile and turned to leave, sliding his hands into his pockets as he loped back, casual as ever, to his crop of well-manicured friends.

The first warning bell rang just as started toward what I hoped—but was in no way sure—was Building C. *Don't trust the natives,* Olivia had told me, but I was already a step ahead of her: I didn't trust anyone. Not for directions, not for rides, and not for advice, either. Sure, it sucked to be lost, but I'd long ago realized I preferred it to depending on anyone else to get me where I needed to go. That was the thing about being alone, in theory or in principle. Whatever happened—good, bad, or anywhere in between—it was always, if nothing else, all your own.

* * *

After school, I was supposed to take a bus home. Instead, I walked out of Perkins Day's stone gates and a half mile down the road to the Quik Zip, where I bought myself a Zip Coke, then settled inside the phone booth. I held the sticky receiver away from my ear as I dropped in a few coins, then dialed a number I knew by heart.

"Hello?"

"Hey, it's me," I said. Then, too late, I added, "Ruby."

I listened as Marshall took in a breath, then let it out. "Ah," he said finally. "Mystery solved."

"I was a mystery?" I asked.

"You were something," he replied. "You okay?"

This was unexpected, as was the lump that rose up in my throat as I heard it. I swallowed, then said, "Yeah. I'm fine."

Marshall was eighteen and had graduated from Jackson the year before, although we hadn't known each other until he moved in with Rogerson, the guy who sold all my friends their pot. At first, Marshall didn't make much of an impression—just a tall, skinny guy who was always passing through or in the kitchen when we went over there to get bags. I'd never even talked to him until one day I went over by myself and Rogerson wasn't around, so it was just the two of us.

Rogerson was all business and little conversation. You knocked, you came in, got what you needed, and got out. I was expecting pretty much the same with Marshall, and at first he didn't disappoint, barely speaking as I followed him to the living room and watched him measure out the bag. I paid him and was just about to get to my feet when he reached over to a nearby cabinet, pulling open a drawer and taking out a small ceramic bowl. "You want some?" he asked.

"Sure," I replied, and then he handed it over, along with a lighter. I could feel him watching me, his dark eyes narrowed, as I lit it, took some in, and passed it back.

The pot was good, better than the stuff we bought, and I felt it almost instantly, the room and my brain slowly taking on a heavy, rolling haze. Suddenly, everything seemed that much more fascinating, from the pattern on the couch beneath me to Marshall himself, sitting back in his chair, his hands folded behind his head. After a few minutes, I realized we'd stopped passing the bowl back and forth and were just sitting there in silence, for how long I had no idea.

"You know what we need," he said suddenly, his voice low and flat.

"What's that?" My own tongue felt thick, my entire mouth dry.

"Slurpees," he said. "Come on."

I'd been afraid he would ask me to drive, which was completely out of the question, but instead, once outside, he led the way down a path that cut across a nearby field dotted with power lines, emerging a block down from a convenience store. We didn't talk the entire way there, or when we were in the store itself. It was not until we were leaving, in fact, each of us sucking away at our Slurpees—which were cold and sweet and perfect—that he finally spoke.

"Good stuff," he said, glancing over at me.

I nodded. "It's *fantastic*."

Hearing this, he smiled, which was unnerving simply because it was something I'd never seen before. Even stranger, as we started back across the path, he reached behind him, grabbing my hand, and then held it, walking a little bit ahead, the whole way home. I will never forget that, my Slurpee cold on my teeth and Marshall's palm warm against mine as we walked in the late-afternoon sunshine, those power lines rising up and casting long shadows all around us.

When he stopped walking and kissed me a few minutes later, it was like time had stopped, with the air, my heart, and the world all so still. And it was this I remembered every other time I was with Marshall. Maybe it was the setting, us alone in that field, or because it was the first time. I didn't know yet that this was all either of us was capable of: moments together that were great but also fleeting.

Marshall was not my boyfriend. On the other hand, he wasn't just a friend either. Instead, our relationship was elastic, stretching between those two extremes depending on who else was around, how much either of us had had to drink, and other varying factors. This was exactly what I wanted, as commitments had never really been my thing. And it wasn't like it was hard, either. The only trick was never giving more than you were willing to lose. With Marshall and me, it was like a game called I Could Care Less. I talked to a guy at a party; he disappeared with some girl at the next one. He didn't return my calls; I'd stay away for a while, making him wonder what I was up to. And so on.

We'd been doing this for so long that really, it came naturally. But now, I was so surprised by how nice it was to hear his voice, something familiar in all this newness, that I found myself breaking my own rule, offering up more than I'd planned.

"Yeah, so, I've just been, you know, dealing with some family stuff," I said, easing back against the booth wall behind me. "I moved in with my sister, and—"

"Hang on a sec, okay?" he said, and then I heard his hand cover the receiver, muffling it. Then he was saying something, his words impossible to make out before I heard him come back on. "Sorry," he said, then coughed. "What were you saying?"

And just like that, it was over. Even missing him was fleeting, like everything else.

"Nothing," I told him. "I should go. I'll catch up with you later, okay?"

"Yeah. See you around."

I hung up, leaving my hand on the receiver as I reached into my pocket, pulling out some more change. Then I took a breath and put it back to my ear, dropped in a few coins, and called someone I knew would be more than happy to talk.

"Ruby?" Peyton said as soon as she heard my voice. "Oh my God. What *happened* to you?"

"Well," I said.

But she was already continuing, her voice coming out in a gush. "I mean, I was waiting for you in the courtyard, just like always, and you never showed up! So I'm like, she must be mad at me or something, but then Aaron said the cops had pulled you out of class, and nobody knew why. And then I went by your house, and it was all dark, and—"

"Everything's fine," I said, cutting her off more out of a time concern than rudeness. Peyton was always summarizing, even when you knew the story as well as she did. "It's just a family thing. I'm staying with my sister for a while."

"Well," she said, "it's all *anyone* is talking about, just so you know. You should hear the rumors."

"Yeah?"

"It's terrible!" she said, sounding truly aghast. "They have you doing everything from committing murder to teen prostitution."

"I've been gone for two days," I said.

"Of course, I've been sticking up for you," she added quickly. "I told them there was no way you'd ever sleep with guys for money. I mean, come on."

This was typical Peyton. Defending my honor vigorously, while not realizing that she was implying that I might be capable of murder. "Well," I said, "I appreciate it."

"No problem." I could hear voices behind her; from the sound of it, she was at the clearing a ways down from school, where we always hung out after final bell. "So, like, what's the real story, though? Is it your mom?"

"Something like that," I told her. "Like I said, it's not a big deal."

Peyton was my closest friend at Jackson, but like everyone else, she had no idea my mom had taken off. She'd actually never even met her, which was no accident; as a rule, I preferred to keep my private life just that, private. This was especially important with someone like Peyton, whose family was pretty much perfect. Rich and functional, they lived in a big house in the Arbors, where up until the year before, she'd been the ideal daughter, pulling straight As and lettering in field hockey. During the summer, though, she'd started dating my friend Aaron, who was a harmless but dedicated pothead. In the fall, she'd gotten busted with a joint at school and was asked to leave St. Micheline's, the Catholic school she'd been attending. Her parents, of course, were none too pleased, and hoped Peyton's newfound rebellion was a just a phase that would end when she and Aaron broke up. After a few weeks, they did, but by that point, she and I were already friends.

Peyton was, in a word, cute. Short and curvy, she was

also incredibly naive, which was alternately annoying and endearing. Sometimes I felt more like a big sister to her than a friend—I was always having to rescue her from weird guys at parties, or hold her head when she puked, or explain again how to work the various expensive electronics her parents were always buying her—but she was fun to hang out with, had a car, and never complained about having to come all the way out to pick me up, even though it was on the way to nowhere. Or back.

"So the thing is," I said to her now, "I need a favor."

"Name it," she replied.

"I'm over here by Perkins Day, and I need a ride," I told her. "Can you come get me?"

"At Perkins Day?"

"Near there. Just down the street."

There was a pause, during which time I heard laughter behind her. "God, Ruby . . . I wish I could. But I'm supposed to be home in an hour."

"It's not that far," I said.

"I know. But you know how my mom's been lately." Since the last time Peyton had come home smelling like beer, her parents had instituted a strict accountability program involving constant tracking, elaborate sniff tests, and surprise room searches. "Hey, did you try Marshall? I bet he can—"

"No," I said, shaking my head. Peyton had never quite gotten Marshall's and my arrangement; an incurable romantic, to her, every story was a love story. "It's fine, don't worry about it."

There was another pause, and again, I could hear what

was happening around her: laughter, someone's radio playing, a car engine starting up. It was true what I'd said: it wasn't that far from there to here, only fifteen miles or so. But at that moment, it suddenly seemed like a long way.

"You sure?" she asked. "Because I could ask someone here."

I swallowed, leaning back against the side of the booth. On the opposite side, above the phone, someone had written WHERE DO YOU SLEEP? in thick black marker. Scratched underneath, less legibly, was a reply: WITH YOUR MAMA. I reached up, rubbing my face with my hand. It wasn't like I'd expected anyone to come rescue me, anyway. "Nah," I said. "That's all right. I'll figure out something."

"All right," she said. A car horn beeped in the background. "Give me your sister's number, though. I'll call you tonight, we can catch up."

"I'm still getting settled," I told her. "I'll give you a call in a few days."

"Okay," she said easily. "And hey, Ruby."

"What?"

"I'm glad you're not a hooker or a murderer."

"Yeah," I said. "Me, too."

I hung up the phone, then stepped out of the booth to finish off my Coke and contemplate my next move. The parking lot, which had been mostly empty when I first got there, had filled up with Perkins Day students. Clearly, this was some sort of off-site hangout, with people sitting on the hoods and bumpers of their expensive cars, slumming at the Quick Zip. Scanning the crowd, I spotted Nate off to the right, arms crossed over his chest, leaning against the driver's-side door of a black SUV. A dark-haired girl in a ponytail and a cropped blue jacket was with him, telling some story and gesturing wildly, the Zip Coke in her hand waving back and forth as she spoke. Nate, of course, was smiling as he listened, the epitome of the Nicest Guy in the World.

Then something occurred to me. I glanced at my watch. It was just before four, which meant I had a little over an hour before I'd be late enough for anyone to notice. It was enough time to do what I had to do, if I got going soon. All I needed was a little help, and if I worked things right, maybe I wouldn't even have to ask for it.

As I hitched my backpack over my shoulder and started toward the road, I made it a point not to look at the Perkins Day contingent, even as I passed right in front of them. Instead, I just kept my focus forward, on the big intersection that lay ahead. It was a long walk home, and even farther to where I really needed to be, making this a serious gamble, especially considering how I'd acted earlier. But part of being nice was forgiveness—or so I'd heard—so I rolled the dice anyway.

Two blocks down the road, I heard a car horn, then an engine slowing behind me. I waited until the second beep before arranging my face to look surprised, and turned around. Sure enough, there was Nate.

"Let me guess," he said. He was leaning across the passenger seat, one hand on the wheel, looking up at me. "You don't need a ride."

"Nope," I told him. "Thanks, though."

"This is a major road," he pointed out. "There's not even a sidewalk."

"Who are you, the safety monitor?"

He made a face at me. "So you'd prefer to just walk the six miles home."

"It's not six miles," I said.

"You're right. It's six point two," he replied as a red Ford beeped angrily behind him, then zoomed past. "I run it every Friday. So I know."

"Why are you so hell-bent on driving me somewhere?" I asked.

"I'm chivalrous," he said.

Yeah, right, I thought. *That's one word for it.* "Chivalry's dead."

"And you will be, too, if you keep walking along here." He sighed. "Get in."

And it was just that easy.

* * *

Inside, Nate's car was dark, the interior immaculate, and still smelled new. Even so, there was an air freshener hanging from the rearview. The logo on it said REST ASSURED EXECUTIVE SERVICES: WE WORRY SO YOU DON'T HAVE TO.

"It's my dad's company," he explained when he saw me looking at it. "We work to make life simpler in these complicated times."

I raised my eyebrows. "That sounds like something right off a brochure."

"Because it is," he said. "But I have to say it if anybody asks what we do."

"And what if they want an actual answer?"

"Then," he said, glancing behind him as he switched lanes, "I tell them we do everything from picking up mail to walking dogs to getting your dry-cleaning to frosting cupcakes for your kid's school party."

I considered this. "Doesn't sound as good."

"I know. Hence the rule."

I sat back in my seat, looking out the window at the buildings and cars blurring past. Okay, fine. So he wasn't terrible company. Still, I wasn't here to make friends.

"So look," he said, "about earlier, and that joke I made."

"It's fine," I told him. "Don't worry about it."

He glanced over at me. "What were you doing, though? I mean, on the fence. If you don't mind my asking."

I did mind. I was also pretty much at his mercy at this point, so I said, "Wasn't it obvious?"

"Yeah, I suppose it was," he said. "I think I was just, you know, surprised."

"At what?"

"I don't know." He shrugged. "Just seems like most people would be trying to break *into* that house, not escape it. Considering how cool Cora and Jamie are, I mean."

"Well," I said. "I guess I'm not most people."

I felt him look at me as I turned my head, looking out the window again. My knowledge of this part of town was fairly limited, but from what I could tell, we were getting close to Wildflower Ridge, Jamie and Cora's neighborhood, which meant it was time to change the subject. "So anyway," I said, shooting for casual, "I do appreciate the ride."

"No problem," he said. "It's not like we aren't going to the same place."

"Actually . . ." I paused, then waited for him to look over

at me. When he did, I said, "If you could just drop me off by a bus stop, that'd be great."

"Bus stop?" he said. "Where are you going?"

"Oh, just to a friend's house. I have to pick something up."

We were coming up to a big intersection now. Nate slowed, easing up behind a VW bug with a flower appliqué on the back bumper. "Well," he said, "where is it?"

"Oh, it's kind of far," I said quickly. "Believe me, you don't want to have to go there."

The light changed, and traffic started moving forward. *This is it,* I thought. *Either he takes the bait, or he doesn't.* It was four fifteen.

"Yeah, but the bus will take you ages," he said after a moment.

"Look, I'll be fine," I said, shaking my head. "Just drop me off up here, by the mall."

The thing about negotiations, not to mention manipulation, is you can't go too far in any direction. Refusing once is good, twice usually okay, but a third is risky. You never know when the other person will just stop playing and you end up with nothing.

I felt him glance over at me again, and I made a point of acting like I didn't notice, couldn't see him wavering. *Come on,* I thought. *Come on.*

"Really, it's cool," he said finally, as the entrance to the highway appeared over the next hill. "Just tell me where to go."

* * *

"Man," Nate said as he bumped up the driveway to the yellow house, avoiding holes and a sizable stack of water-logged newspapers. Up ahead, I could already see my mom's Subaru, parked just where I'd left it, gas needle on empty, that last day Peyton had picked me up for school. "Who lives here again?"

"Just this girl I know," I said.

As far as I was concerned, this entire endeavor would be quick and painless. Get in, get what I needed, and get out, hopefully with as little explanation as necessary. Then Nate would take me back to Cora's, and this would all be over. Simple as that.

But then, just as we passed the bedroom window, I saw the curtain move.

It was very quick, so quick I wondered if I'd seen anything at all—just a shift of the fabric an inch to the left, then back again. The exact way it would have to for someone to peer out and yet still not be seen.

I wasn't sure what I'd been expecting to find here. Maybe the Honeycutts, in the midst of some project. Or the house empty, cleaned out as if we'd never been here at all. This possibility, though, had never crossed my mind.

Which was why Nate hadn't even finished parking when I pushed open my door and got out. "Hey. Do you want—?" I heard him call after me, but I ignored him, instead taking the steps two at time and arriving at the front door breathless, my fingers already fumbling for the key around my neck. Once I put it in the lock, the knob, familiar in my hand, turned with a soft click. And then I was in.

"Mom?" I called out, my voice bouncing off all the hard surfaces back at me. I walked into the kitchen, where I could see the clothesline was still strung from one wall to the other, my jeans and shirts now stiff and mildewy as I pushed past them. "Hello?"

In the living room, there was a row of beer bottles on the coffee table, and the blanket we usually kept folded over one arm of the sofa was instead balled into one corner. I felt my heart jump. I would have folded it back. Wouldn't I?

I kept moving, pushing open my bedroom door and flicking on the single bulb overhead. This did look just like I'd left it, save for my closet door being left open, I assumed by whoever packed up the clothes that had been brought to me at Poplar House. I turned, crossing back into the living room and walking over to the other bedroom door, which was shut. Then I put my hand on the knob and closed my eyes.

It wasn't like making a wish or trying to dream something into being real. But in that moment, I tried to remember all the times I'd come home and walked to this same door, easing it open to see my mom curled up in her bed, hair spilling over the pillowcase, already reaching a hand to shield her eyes from the light behind me. This image was so clear in my mind that when I first pushed open the door, I was almost sure I did see a glimpse of red, some bit of movement, and my heart jumped into my throat, betraying in one instant all the emotions I'd denied to myself and everyone else in the last week. Then, though, just as quickly, something shifted. The objects and room itself fell into place: bed, dark walls . . . and that window, where I now remembered the bit of broken pane, half-taped up, where a breeze still could inch in, ruffling the curtain. I'd been mistaken. But even so, I stayed where I was, as if by doing so the room would, in the next moment, suddenly be anything but empty.

"Ruby?"

Nate's voice was low, tentative. I swallowed, thinking how stupid I was, thinking that my mom might have actually come back, when I knew full well that everything she needed she'd taken with her. "I'll be done in a sec," I said to him, hating how my voice was shaking.

"Are you . . . ?" He paused. "Are you okay?"

I nodded, all business. "Yeah. I just have to grab something."

I heard him shift his weight, taking a step, although toward me or away, I wasn't sure, and not knowing this was enough to make me turn around. He was standing in the doorway to the kitchen, the front door open behind him, turning his head slowly, taking it all in. I felt a surge of shame; I'd been so stupid to bring him here. Like I, of all people, didn't know better than to lead a total stranger directly to the point where they could hurt me most, knowing how easily they'd be able to find their way back to it.

"This place," Nate said, looking at the bottles on the table, a lone cobweb stretching across the room between us, "it's, like—"

Suddenly there was a gust of wind outside, and a few leaves blew in the open door, skittering in across the kitchen floor. I felt so shaken, unsettled, that my voice was sharp as I said, "Just wait in the car. All right?"

He looked at me for a second. "Yeah," he said. "Sure thing." Then he stepped outside, pulling the door shut behind him.

Stop it, I told myself, feeling tears pricking my eyes, so stupid. I looked around the room, trying to clear my head and concentrate on what I should take with me, but everything was blurring, and I felt a sob work its way up my throat. I put my hand over my mouth, my shoulders shaking, and forced my feet to move.

Think, think, I kept saying in my head as I walked back to the kitchen and began pulling stuff off the clothesline. Everything was stiff and smelly, and the more I took down the more I could see of the rest of the kitchen: the pots and pans piled in the sink, the buckets I'd used to collect water from the bathroom, the clothesline, now sagging over my head. *I was doing just fine,* I'd told Cora, and at the time, I'd believed it. But now, standing there with my stiff clothes in my arms, the smell of rotting food filling my nostrils, I wasn't so sure anymore.

I reached up, wiping my eyes, and looked back out at Nate, who was sitting behind the wheel of his car, a cell phone to his ear. God only knew what he was thinking. I looked down at my clothes, knowing I couldn't bring them with me, even though they, the few things in the next room, and that beat-up, broken-down Subaru were all I really had. As I dropped them onto the table, I told myself I'd come back for them and everything else, just as soon as I got settled. It was such an easy promise to make. So easy that I could almost imagine another person saying the same thing to themselves as they walked out that door, believing it, too. Almost.

* * *

I was not looking forward to the ride home, as God only knew what Nate would say to me, or how I would dodge the questions he would inevitably ask. So I decided, as I locked the door behind me, to go with a route I knew well: complete and total denial. I'd act like nothing out of the ordinary had happened, as if this trip was exactly what I had expected it to be. If I was convincing enough, he'd have no choice but to see it the same way.

I was all casual as I walked back to the car, playing my part. When I got in, though, I realized it wasn't even necessary. He still had the phone clamped to his ear and didn't even glance at me as he shifted into reverse, backing away from the house.

While he was distracted, I took one last look at that window into my mom's room. Talk about denial; even from a distance and in motion, I could tell there was no one inside. There's something just obvious about emptiness, even when you try to convince yourself otherwise.

"It's not a problem," Nate said suddenly, and I glanced over at him. He had his eyes on the road, his mouth a thin line as he listened to whoever was speaking. "Look, I can be there in ten minutes. Maybe even less than that. Then I'll just grab it from her, and—"

Whoever it was cut him off, their voice rising enough that I could hear it, though not make out specific words. Nate reached up, rubbing a hand over his face. "I'll be there in ten minutes," he said, hitting the gas as we turned back onto the main road. "No . . ." He trailed off. "I just had to run this errand for school. Yeah. Yes. Okay."

He flipped the phone shut, dropping it with a clank into the console between our seats. "Problem?" I said.

"Nah," he said. "Just my dad. He's a little . . . controlling about the business."

"You forgot to frost some cupcakes?"

He glanced over at me, as if surprised I was capable of humor. "Something like that," he said. "I have to make a stop on the way home. If you don't mind."

"It's your car," I said with a shrug.

As we merged onto the highway, the phone rang again. Nate grabbed it, glancing at the display, then flipped it open. "Hello? Yes. I'm on the way. On the highway. Ten minutes. Sure. Okay. Bye."

This time, he didn't put the phone down, instead just keeping it in his hand. After a moment, he said, "It's just the two of us, you know. Living together, working together. It can get . . . kind of intense."

"I know," I said.

Maybe it was because my mother was on my mind, but this came out before I even realized it, an unconscious, immediate reaction. It was also the last thing I wanted to be talking about, especially with Nate, but of course then he said, "Yeah?"

I shrugged. "I used to work with my mom. I mean, for a while anyway."

"Really?" I nodded. "What'd you do?"

"Delivered lost luggage for the airlines."

He raised his eyebrows, either surprised or impressed. "People really do that?"

"What, you think they just get teleported to you or something?"

"No," he said slowly, shooting me a look. "I just mean . . . it's one of those things you know gets done. You just don't actually think of someone doing it."

"Well," I said, "I am that someone. Or was, anyway."

We were taking an exit now, circling around to a stoplight. As we pulled up to it, Nate said, "So what happened?"

"With what?"

"The luggage delivery. Why did you quit?"

This time, I knew enough not to answer, only evade. "Just moved on," I said. "That's all."

Thankfully, he did not pursue this further, instead just putting on his blinker and turning into the front entrance of the Vista Mall, a sprawling complex of stores and restaurants. The parking lot was packed as we zipped down a row of cars, then another before pulling up behind an old green Chevy Tahoe. The back door was open, revealing an extremely cluttered backseat piled with boxes and milk crates, which were in turn filled with various envelopes and packing materials. A woman with red hair coiled into a messy bun wearing a fuzzy pink sweater and holding a to-go coffee cup in one hand was bent over them, her back to us.

Nate rolled down his window. "Harriet," he called out.

She didn't hear him as she picked up a crate, shoving it farther back. An empty coffee cup popped out and started to roll away, but she grabbed it, stuffing it in another box.

"Harriet," Nate repeated. Again, no answer as she bent deeper over a crate.

"You're going to have to be louder," I told him as he was barely speaking above a normal tone of voice.

"I know," he said. Then he took a breath, wincing slightly, and put his hand on the horn.

He only did it once, and it was quick: *beep!* Still, the woman literally jumped in the air. Completely vertical, feet off the ground, coffee spilling out of the cup backward, splattering the pavement. Then she whirled around, her free hand to her chest, and goggled at us.

"Sorry," Nate called out. "But you weren't—"

"What are you doing?" she asked him. "Are you *trying* to give me a nervous attack?"

"No." He pushed open his door, quickly climbing out and walking over to her. "Here, let me get that. It's these three? Or the crates, too?"

"All of them," the woman—Harriet?—said, clearly still flustered as she leaned against the Tahoe's bumper, flapping a hand in front of her face. As Nate began to load the boxes into the back of his car, I noticed she was rather pretty, and had on a chunky silver necklace with matching earrings, as well as several rings. "He knows I'm a nervous person," she said to me, gesturing at Nate with her cup. "And yet he beeps. He *beeps*!"

"It was an accident," Nate told her, returning for the last box. "I'm sorry."

Harriet sighed, leaning back against the bumper again and closing her eyes. "No," she said, "it's me. I'm just under this massive deadline, and I'm way behind, and I just knew I wasn't going to get to the shipping place before they closed—"

"—which is why you have us," Nate finished for her, shutting his own back door with a bang. "I'm taking them over right now. No worries."

"They all need to go Ground, not Next Day," she told him. "I can't afford Next Day."

"I know."

"And be sure you get the tracking information, because they're promised by the end of the week, and there's been bad weather out West. . . ."

"Done," Nate told her, pulling his door open.

Harriet considered this as she stood there clutching her coffee cup. "Did you drop off that stuff at the cleaners yesterday?"

"Ready on Thursday," Nate told her.

"What about the bank deposit?" she asked.

"Dad did it this morning. Receipt is in the envelope in your mailbox."

"Did he remember to—"

"—lock it back? Yes. The key is where you said to leave it. Anything else?"

Harriet drew in a breath, as if about to ask another question, then slowly let it out. "No," she said slowly. "At least not right at this moment."

Nate slid behind the wheel. "I'll e-mail you all the tracking info as soon as I get home. Okay?"

"All right," she said, although she sounded uncertain as he cranked the engine. "Thanks."

"No problem. Call if you need us."

She nodded but was still standing by her bumper, gripping her cup and looking uncertain, as we pulled away. I waited until we'd turned onto the main road again before saying, "That's resting assured?"

"No," Nate said, his voice tired. "That's Harriet."

By the time we pulled up to Cora's, it was five thirty. Only a little over an hour had passed since he'd picked me up, and yet it felt like so much longer. As I gathered up my stuff, pushing the door open, his phone rang again; he glanced at the display, then back at me. "Dad's getting nervous," he said. "I better go. I'll see you tomorrow morning?"

I looked over at him, again taking in his solid good looks and friendly expression. Fine, so he was a nice guy, and maybe not entirely the dim jock that I'd pegged him as at first glance. Plus, he had helped me out, not once but twice, and maybe to him this meant my previous feelings about a carpool would no longer be an issue. But I could not so easily forget Peyton earlier on the other end of that pay-phone line, how quickly she had turned me down at the one moment I'd really needed her.

"Thanks for the ride," I said.

Nate nodded, flipping his phone open, and I shut the door between us. I wasn't sure whether he had noticed I hadn't answered his question, or if he'd even care. Either way, by the time I was halfway down the walk, he was gone.

* * *

Earlier that morning, after we'd set up my schedule, Jamie headed off to work and Mr. Thackray started to walk me off to my English class. We were about halfway there when I suddenly heard Jamie calling after us.

"Hold up!"

I turned around, looking down the hallway, which was rapidly filling with people streaming out of their first class, and spotted him bobbing through the crowd. When he reached us, slightly out of breath, he smiled and held his hand out to me, gesturing for me to do the same.

My first instinct was to hesitate, wondering what else he could possibly offer me. But when I opened up my hand, palm flat, and he dropped a key into it, it seemed ridiculous to have expected anything else.

"In case you beat us home," he said. "Have a good day!"

At the time, I'd nodded, closing my hand around the key and slipping it into my pocket, where I'd totally forgotten about it until now, as I walked up to the front door of the house and pulled it out. It was small and on a single silver fob, with the words WILDFLOWER RIDGE engraved on the other side. Weird how it had been there all day, and I hadn't even felt it or noticed. The one around my neck I was always aware of, both its weight and presence, but maybe that was because it was closer to me, where it couldn't be missed.

Cora's door swung open almost soundlessly, revealing the big, airy foyer. Like at the yellow house, everything was still and quiet, but in a different way. Not untouched or forgotten, but more expectant. As if even a house knew the difference between someone simply stepping out for while and being gone for good.

I shut the door behind me. From the foyer, I could see

into the living room, where the sun was already beginning to sink in the sky, disappearing behind the trees, casting that special kind of warm light you only get right before sunset.

I was still just standing there watching this, when I heard a tippity-tapping noise coming from my left. I glanced over; it was Roscoe, making his way through the kitchen. When he saw me, his ears perked up straight on his head. Then he sat down and just stared at me.

I stayed where I was, wondering if he was going to start barking at me again, which after starting a new school and breaking into my old house was going to be the last thing I could take today. Thankfully, he didn't. Instead, he just began to lick himself, loudly. I figured this signaled it was safe to continue on to the kitchen, which I did, giving him a wide berth as I passed.

On the island, there was a sticky note, and even though it had been years since I'd seen it, I immediately recognized my sister's super neat handwriting, each letter so perfect you had to wonder if she'd done a rough draft first. *J,* it said, *Lasagna is in the fridge, put it in (350) as soon as you get home. See you by seven at the latest. Love, me.*

I picked the note up off the counter, reading it again. If nothing else, this made it clear to me that my sister had, in fact, finally gotten everything she wanted. Not just the things that made up the life she'd no doubt dreamed of—the house, the job, the security—all those nights in our shared room, but someone to share it with. To come home to and have dinner with, to leave a note for. Such simple, stupid things, and yet in the end, they were the true proof of a real life.

Which was why, after she'd worked so hard to get here, it had to really suck to suddenly have me drop back in at the very moment she'd started to think she'd left the old life behind for good. *Oh, well,* I thought. The least I could do was put in the lasagna.

I walked over to the oven and preheated it, then found the pan in the fridge and put it on the counter. I was pulling off the Saran wrap when I felt something against my leg. Looking down, I saw Roscoe had at some point crossed the room and was now sitting between my feet, looking up at me.

My first thought was that he had peed on the floor and was waiting for me to yell at him. But then I realized he was shaking, bouncing back and forth slightly from one of my ankles to the other. "What?" I asked him, and in response he burrowed down farther, pressing himself more tightly against me. All the while, he kept his big bug eyes on me, as if pleading, but for what, I had no idea.

Great, I thought. Just what I needed: the dog dies on my watch, thereby officially cementing my status as a complete blight on the household. I sighed, then stepped carefully around Roscoe to the phone, picking it up and dialing Jamie's cell-phone number, which was at the top of a list posted nearby. Before I was even done, Roscoe had shuffled across the floor, resituating himself at my feet, the shaking now going at full force. I kept my eyes on him as the phone rang twice, and then, thankfully, Jamie picked up.

"Something's wrong with the dog," I reported.

"Ruby?" he said. "Is that you?"

"Yes." I swallowed, looking down at Roscoe again, who in turn scooted closer, pressing his face into my calf. "I'm sorry to bother you, but he's just acting really . . . sick. Or something. I didn't know what to do."

"Sick? Is he throwing up?"

"No."

"Does he have the runs?"

I made a face. "No," I said. "At least, I don't think so. I just came home and Cora had left this note about the lasagna, so I put it in and—"

"Oh," he said slowly. "Okay. It's all right, you can relax. He's not sick."

"He's not?"

"Nope. He's just scared."

"Of lasagna?"

"Of the oven." He sighed. "We don't really understand it. I think it may have something to do with this incident involving some Tater Tots and the smoke detector."

I looked down at Roscoe, who was still in full-on tremulous mode. You had to wonder how such a thing affected a little dog like that—it couldn't be good for his nervous system. "So," I said as he stared up at me, clearly terrified, "how do you make it stop?"

"You can't," he said. "He'll do it the entire time the oven's on. Sometimes he goes and hides under a bed or the sofa. The best thing is to just act normal. If he drives you too crazy, just shut him in the laundry room."

"Oh," I said as the dog rearranged himself, wedging himself between my shoe and the cabinet behind me. "Okay."

"Look, I'm breaking up," he said, "but I'll be home soon. Just—"

There was a buzz, and then he was gone, dropping off

altogether. I hung up, replacing the phone carefully on its base. I wasn't sure what "soon" meant, but I hoped it meant he was only a few blocks away, as I was not much of an animal person. Still, looking down at Roscoe trembling against my leg, it seemed kind of mean to just shut him up in a small space, considering the state he was in.

"Just relax, okay?" I said, untangling myself from around him and walking to the foyer to my bag. For a moment he stayed where he was, but then he started to follow me. The last thing I wanted was any kind of company, so I started up the stairs at a quick clip, hoping he'd get the message and stay behind. Surprisingly, it worked; when I got to the top of the stairs and looked down, he was still in the foyer. Staring up at me looking pitiful, but still there.

Up in my room, I washed my face, then slid Cora's sweater off and lay back across the bed. I don't know how long I was there, staring out the windows at the last of the sunset, before Roscoe came into the room. He was moving slowly, almost sideways, like a crab. When he saw that I'd noticed him, his ears went flat on his head, as if he was expecting to be ejected but couldn't help taking a shot anyway.

For a moment, we just looked at each other. Then, tentatively, he came closer, then a bit closer still, until finally he was wedged between my feet, with the bed behind him. When he started shaking again, his tags jingling softly, I rolled my eyes. I wanted to tell him to cut it out, that we all had our problems, that I was the last person he should come looking to for solace. But instead, I surprised myself by saying none of this as I sat up, reaching a hand down to his head. The moment I touched him, he was still.

Chapter Four

At first, it just a rumbling, punctuated by the occasional shout: the kind of thing that you're aware of, distantly, and yet can still manage to ignore. Right as my clock flipped over to 8:00, though, the real noise began.

I sat up in bed, startled, as the room suddenly filled with the clanking of metal hitting rock. It wasn't until I got up and went out on my balcony and saw the backhoe that it all started to make sense.

"Jamie!"

I glanced to my right, where I could see my sister, in her pajamas, standing on her own balcony. She was clutching the railing, looking down at her husband, who was on the back lawn looking entirely too awake, a mug of coffee in his hands and Roscoe at his feet. When he looked up and saw her, he grinned. "Great, right?" he said. "You can really visualize it now!"

Most of Cora's response to this was lost in the ensuing din as the backhoe dug once more into the lawn, scooping up more earth from within Jamie's circle of rocks and swinging to the side to dump it on the already sizable pile there. As it moved back, gears grinding, to go in again, I just caught the end, when she was saying, ". . . Saturday morning, when some people might want to *sleep*."

"Honey, it's the pond, though," Jamie replied, as if he had heard every word. "We talked about this. Remember?"

Cora just looked at him, running a hand through her hair, which was sticking up on one side. Then, without further comment, she went inside. Jamie watched her go, his face quizzical. "Hey!" he shouted when he saw me. The backhoe dug down again, with an even louder clank. "Pretty cool, don't you think? If we're lucky, we'll have it lined by tonight."

I nodded, watching as the machine dumped another load of dirt onto the pile. Jamie was right, you could really picture it now: there was a big difference between a theoretical pond and a huge hole in the ground. Still, it was hard to imagine what he wanted—a total ecosystem, a real body of water, with fish and everything—seeming at home in the middle of such a flat, square yard. Even with the best landscaping, it would still look as if it had fallen from the sky.

Back inside, I flopped back into bed, although sleeping was clearly no longer an option. Hard to believe that the previous Saturday, I'd been at the yellow house, waking up on the couch with our old moldy afghan curled around me. Fast-forward a week, and here I was at Cora's. My basic needs were certainly being met—running water, heat, food—but it was still strange to be here. Everything felt so temporary, including me, that I hadn't even unpacked yet—my bag was still right by the bed, where I was living out of it like I was on a vacation, about to check out at any moment. Sure, it meant the little bit of stuff I had was that much more wrinkled, but rolling over every morning and seeing all my worldly possessions right there beside me made me feel somewhat in control of my situation. Which I needed, considering that everything else seemed completely out of my hands.

* * *

"The bus?" Jamie said that first night, when he mentioned Nate picking me up and I told him I'd prefer alternate transportation. "Are you serious?"

"There isn't a Perkins Day bus in the morning," Cora said from across the table. "They only run in the afternoon, to accommodate after-school activities."

"Then I'll take the city bus," I said.

"And go to all that trouble?" Jamie asked. "Nate's going to Perkins anyway. And he offered."

"He was just being nice," I said. "He doesn't really want to drive me."

"Of course he does," Jamie said, grabbing another roll from the basket between us. "He's a prince. And we're chipping in for gas. It's all taken care of."

"The bus is fine," I said again.

Cora, across the table, narrowed her eyes at me. "What's really going on here?" she asked. "You don't like Nate or something?"

I picked up my fork, spearing a piece of asparagus. "Look," I said, trying to keep my voice cool, collected, "it just seems like a big hassle. If I ride the bus, I can leave when I want, and not be at the mercy of someone else."

"No, you'll be at the mercy of the bus schedule, which is *much* worse," Jamie said. He thought for a second. "Maybe we should just get you a car. Then you can drive yourself."

"We're not buying another car," Cora said flatly.

"She's seventeen," Jamie pointed out. "She'll need to go places."

"Then she'll ride the bus. Or ride with Nate. Or borrow yours."

"Mine?"

Cora just looked at him, then turned her attention to me. "If you want to do the bus, fine. But if it makes you late, you have to do the carpool. All right?"

I nodded. Then, after dinner, I went online and printed out four different bus schedules, circling the ones I could catch from the closest stop and still make first bell. Sure, it meant getting up earlier and walking a few blocks. But it would be worth it.

Or so I thought, until I accidentally hit the snooze bar a few extra times the next morning and didn't get downstairs until 7:20. I was planning to grab a muffin and hit the road, running if necessary, but of course Cora was waiting for me.

"First bell in thirty minutes," she said, not looking up from the paper, which she had spread out in front of her. She licked a finger, turning a page. "There's no way."

So ten minutes later, I was out by the mailbox cursing myself, muffin in hand, when Nate pulled up. "Hey," he said, reaching across to push the door open. "You changed your mind."

That was just the thing, though. I hadn't. If anything, I was more determined than ever to not make friends, and this just made it harder. Still, it wasn't like I had a choice, so I got in, easing the door shut behind me and putting my muffin in my lap.

"No eating in the car."

The voice was flat, toneless, and came from behind me. As I slowly turned my head, I saw the source: a short kid wearing a peacoat and some serious orthodontia, sitting in the backseat with a book open in his lap.

"What?" I said.

He leaned forward, his braces—and attached headgear—catching the sunlight coming through the windshield. His hair was sticking up. "No eating in the car," he repeated, robotlike. Then he pointed at my muffin. "It's a rule."

I looked at Nate, then back at the kid. "Who are you?"

"Who are *you*?"

"This is Ruby," Nate said.

"Is she your new girlfriend?" the kid asked.

"No," Nate and I said in unison. I felt my face flush.

The kid sat back. "Then no eating. Girlfriends are the only exception to carpool rules."

"Gervais, pipe down," Nate said.

Gervais picked up his book, flipping a page. I looked at Nate, who was now pulling out onto the main road, and said, "So . . . where do you take him? The middle school?"

"Wrong," Gervais said. His voice was very nasal and annoying, like a goose honking.

"He's a senior," Nate told me.

"A senior?"

"What are you, deaf?" Gervais asked.

Nate shot him a look in the rearview. "Gervais is accelerated," he said, changing lanes. "He goes to Perkins in the morning, and afternoons he takes classes at the U."

"Oh," I said. I glanced back at Gervais again, but he ignored me, now immersed in his book, which was big and thick, clearly a text of some kind. "So . . . do you pick up anyone else?"

"We used to pick up Heather," Gervais said, his eyes still on his book, "when she and Nate were together. She got to eat in the car. Pop-Tarts, usually. Blueberry flavor."

Beside me, Nate cleared his throat, glancing out the window.

"But then, a couple of weeks ago," Gervais continued in the same flat monotone, turning a page, "she dumped Nate. It was big news. He didn't even see it coming."

I looked at Nate, who exhaled loudly. We drove on for another block, and then he said, "No. We don't pick up anyone else."

Thankfully, this was it for conversation. When we pulled into the parking lot five minutes later, Gervais scrambled out first, hoisting his huge backpack over his skinny shoulders and taking off toward the green without a word to either of us.

I'd planned to follow him, also going my own way, but before I could, Nate fell into step beside me. It was clear this just came so easily to him, our continuing companionship assumed without question. I had no idea what that must be like.

"So look," he said, "about Gervais."

"He's charming," I told him.

"That's one word for it. Really, though, he's not—"

He trailed off suddenly, as a green BMW whizzed past us, going down a couple of rows and whipping into a space. A moment later, the driver's-side door opened, and the blonde from my English class—in a white cable sweater, sunglasses parked on her head—emerged, pulling an overstuffed tote bag behind her. She bumped the door shut with her hip, then started toward the main building, fluffing her hair with her fingers as she walked. Nate watched her for a moment, then coughed, stuffing his hands in his pockets.

"Really what?" I said.

"What's that?" he asked.

Ahead of us, the blonde—who I had now figured out was the infamous, blueberry Pop-Tart–eating Heather—was crossing to a locker, dropping her bag at her feet. "Nothing," I said. "See you around."

"Yeah," he replied, nodding, clearly distracted as I quickened my pace, finally able to put some space between us. "See you."

He was still watching her as I walked away. Which was kind of pathetic but also not my problem, especially since from now on I'd be sticking to my original plan and catching the bus, and everything would be fine.

Or so I thought until the next day, when I again overslept, missing my bus window entirely. At first, I was completely annoyed with myself, but then, in the shower, I decided that maybe it wasn't so bad. After all, the ride was a short one. At least distance-wise.

"What kind of shampoo is that?" Gervais demanded from the backseat as soon as I got in the car, my hair still damp.

I turned back and looked at him. "I don't know," I said. "Why?"

"It stinks," he told me. "You smell like trees."

"Trees?"

"Gervais," Nate said. "Watch it."

"I'm just saying," Gervais grumbled, flopping back against the seat. I turned around, fixing my gaze on him. For a moment, he stared back, insolent, his eyes seemingly huge behind his glasses. But as I kept on, steady, unwavering, he finally caved and turned to stare out the window. *Twelve-year-olds*, I thought. *So easy to break*.

When I turned back to face forward, Nate was watching me. "What?" I said.

"Nothing," he replied. "Just admiring your technique."

At school, Gervais did his normal scramble-and-disappearing act, and again Nate walked with me across the parking lot. This time, I was not only aware of him beside me—which was still just so odd, frankly—but also the ensuing reactions from the people gathered around their cars, or ahead of us at the lockers: stares, raised eyebrows, entirely too much attention. It was unsettling, not to mention distracting.

When I'd started at Perkins, I'd instinctively gone into New School Mode, a system I'd perfected over the years when my mom and I were always moving. Simply put, it was this: come in quietly, fly under the radar, get in and out each day with as little interaction as possible. Because Perkins Day was so small, though, I was realizing it was inevitable that I'd attract some attention, just because I was new. Add in the fact that someone had figured out my connection to Jamie—"Hey, UMe!" someone had yelled as I walked in the hall a couple of days earlier—and staying anonymous was that much more difficult.

Nate deciding we were friends, though, made it almost

impossible. Even by my second day, I'd figured out he was one of the most popular guys at Perkins, which made me interesting (at least to these people, anyway) simply by standing next to him. Maybe some girls would have liked this, but I was not one of them.

Now, I looked over at him, annoyed, as a group of cheerleaders standing in a huddle by a shiny VW tittered in our wake. He didn't notice, too busy watching that same green BMW, which was parked a couple of rows over. I could see Heather behind the wheel, her Jump Java cup in one hand. Jake Bristol, the sleeper from my English class, was leaning in to talk to her, his arms resting on her open window.

This was not my problem. And yet, as with Gervais, when I saw bad behavior, I just couldn't help myself. Plus, if he was going to insist on walking with me, he almost deserved it.

"You know," I said to him. "Pining isn't attractive. On anyone."

He glanced over at me. "What?"

I nodded at Heather and Jake, who were still talking. "The worst thing you can do if you miss or need someone," I said, "is let them know it."

"I don't miss her," he said.

Yeah, right. "Okay," I replied, shrugging. "All I'm saying is that even if you do want her back, you should act like you don't. No one likes someone who's all weak and pitiful and needy. It's basic relationship 101."

"Relationship 101," he repeated, skeptical. "And this is a course you teach?"

"It's only advice," I told him. "Ignore it if you want."

Really, I assumed he'd do just that. The next morning, though, as he again fell into step beside me—clearly, this was a habit now—and we began crossing the parking lot, Heather's car once again came into view. Even I noticed it, and her, by now. But Nate, I saw, did not. Or at least didn't act like it. Instead, he glanced over at me and then just kept walking.

As the week went on—and my losses to the snooze bar continued—I found myself succumbing to the carpool and, subsequently, our walk together into school itself, audience and all. Resistance was futile, and Nate and I were becoming friends, or something like it. At least as far as he was concerned.

Which was just crazy, because we had absolutely nothing in common. Here I was, a loner to the core, burnout personified, with a train wreck of a home life. And in the other corner? Nate, the good son, popular guy, and all around nice, wholesome boy. Not to mention—as I found out over the next week—student body vice president, homecoming king, community liaison, champion volunteerer. His name just kept coming up, in event after event listed in the flat monotone of the guy who delivered the announcements each morning over the intercom. Going to the senior class trip fund-raiser? Contact Nate Cross. Pitching in to help with the annual campus cleanup? Talk to Nate. Need a study buddy for upcoming midterms? Nate Cross is your man.

He was not my man, however, although as the week—not to mention the staring I'd first noticed in the parking lot—continued, it was clear some people wanted to think otherwise. It was obvious Heather and Nate's breakup had been huge news, at least judging by the fact that weeks later, I was still hearing about their relationship: how they'd dated since he'd moved from Arizona freshman year, been junior prom king and queen, had plans to go off to the U for college in the fall together. For all these facts, though, the cause of their breakup remained unclear. Without even trying, I'd heard so many different theories—He cheated with some girl at the beach! She wanted to date other guys!—that it was obvious no one really knew the truth.

Still, it did explain why they were all so interested in me. The hot popular guy starts showing up with new girl at school, right on the heels of breakup with longtime love. It's the next chapter, or so it seems, so of course people would make their assumptions. And in another school, or another town, this was probably the case. But not here.

As for Perkins Day itself, it *was* a total culture shift, with everything from the teachers (who actually seemed happy to be there) to the library (big, with all working, state-of-the-art computers) to the cafeteria (with salad bar and smoothie station) completely different from what I'd been used to. Also, the small class size made slacking off pretty much a non-option, and as a result, I was getting my ass kicked academically. I'd never been the perfect student by a long shot, but at Jackson I'd still managed to pull solid Bs, even with working nights and my quasi-extracurricular activities. Now, without transportation or friends to distract me, I had all the time in the world to study, and yet I was still struggling, big-time. I kept telling myself it didn't matter, that I'd probably only be there until I could raise the money to take off, so there wasn't any real point in killing myself to keep up. But then, I'd find myself sitting in my room with nothing to do, and pull out the books and get to work, if only for the distraction.

The mentality at Perkins was different, as well. For instance, at Jackson at lunch, due to the cramped cafeteria, lack of coveted picnic tables, and general angst, there was always some kind of drama going on. Fistfights, yelling, little scuffles breaking out and settling down just as quickly, lasting hardly long enough for you to turn your head and notice them. At Perkins, everyone coexisted peacefully in the caf and on the green, and the most heated anything ever got was when someone at the HELP table got a little too fired up about some issue and it burst into a full-fledged debate, but even those were usually civil.

The HELP table itself was another thing I just didn't get. Every day at lunch, just as the period began, some group would set up shop at one of the tables right by the caf entrance, hanging up a sign and laying out brochures to rally support for whatever cause they were promoting. So far, in the time I'd been there, I'd seen everything from people collecting signatures for famine relief to asking for spare change to buy a new flat-screen TV for the local children's hospital. Every day there was something new, some other cause that needed our help and attention RIGHT NOW SO PLEASE SIGN UP or GIVE or LEND A HAND—IT'S THE LEAST YOU CAN DO!

It wasn't like I was a cruel or heartless person. I believed in charity as much as anyone else. But after everything I'd been through the last few months, I just couldn't wrap my mind around reaching out to others. My mother had taught me too well to look out for number one, and right now, in this strange world, this seemed smarter than ever. Still, every time I passed the HELP table, taking in that day's cause—Upcoming AIDS walk! Buy a cookie, it benefits early literacy! Save the Animals!—I felt strangely unsettled by all this want, not to mention the assumed and steady outpouring of help in return, which seemed to come as instinctively to the people here as keeping to myself did to me.

One person who clearly was a giver was Heather Wainwright, who always seemed to be at the HELP table, regardless of the cause. I'd seen her lecturing a group of girls with smoothies on the plight of the Tibetans, selling cupcakes for cancer research, and signing up volunteers to help clean up the stretch of highway Perkins Day sponsored, and she seemed equally passionate about all of them. This was yet another reason, at least in my mind, that whatever rumors were circulating about Nate and me couldn't have been more off the mark. Clearly, I wasn't his type, by a long shot.

Of course, if I had wanted to make friends with people more like me, I could have. The burnout contingent at Perkins Day was less scruffy than their Jackson counterparts but still easily recognizable, hanging out by the far end of the quad near the art building in a spot everyone called the Smokestack. At Jackson, the stoners and the art freaks were two distinct groups, but at Perkins, they had comingled, either because of the reduced population or the fact that there was safety in numbers. So alongside the guys in the rumpled Phish T-shirts, Hackey-sacking in their flip-flops, you also had girls in dresses from the vintage shop and combat boots, sporting multicolored hair and tattoos. The population of the Smokestack usually showed up about halfway through lunch, trickling in from the path that led to the lower soccer fields, which were farthest away from the rest of the school. Once they arrived, they could be seen furtively trading Visine bottles and scarfing down food from the vending machine, stoner behavior so classic and obvious I was continually surprised the administration didn't swoop in and bust them en masse.

It would have been so easy to walk over and join them, but even after a few lunches spent with only my sandwich, I still hadn't done so. Maybe because I wouldn't be there long, anyway—it wasn't like there was much point in making friends. Or maybe it was something else. Like the fact that I had a second chance now, an opportunity, whether I'd first welcomed it or not, to do things differently. It seemed stupid to not at least try to take it. It wasn't like the old way had been working for me so well, anyway.

Still, there was one person at Perkins Day that, if pressed, I could imagine hanging out with. Maybe because she was the only one less interested in making friends than I was.

By now, I'd figured out a few things about Olivia Davis, my seatmate and fellow Jackson survivor. Number one: she was *always* on the phone. The minute the bell rang, she had it out and open, quick as a gunslinger, one finger already dialing. She kept it clamped to her ear as she walked between classes and all through lunch, which she also spent alone, eating a sandwich she brought from home and talking the entire time. From the few snippets I overheard before our class started and just after it ended, she was mostly talking to friends, although occasionally she'd affect an annoyed, flat tone that screamed parental conversation. Usually, though, she was all noisy chatter, discussing the same things, in fact, that I heard from everyone else in the hallways or around me in my classrooms—school, parties, stress—except that her conversations were one-sided, her voice the only one I could hear.

It was also clear that Olivia was at Perkins Day under protest, and a vocal one at that. I had strong opinions about our classmates and their lifestyles but kept these thoughts to myself. Olivia practiced no such discretion.

"Yeah, right," she'd say under her breath as Heather Wainwright began a long analysis of the symbolism of poverty in *David Copperfield*. "Like *you* know from poverty. In your BMW and million-dollar mansion."

"Ah, yes," she'd murmur as one of the back-row jocks, prodded by Ms. Conyers to contribute, equated his experience not making starter with a character's struggle, "tell us about your pain. We're *riveted*."

Sometimes she didn't say anything but still made her point by sighing loudly, shaking her head, and throwing why-me-Lord? looks up at the ceiling. At first, her tortuous endurance of second period was funny to me, but after a while, it got kind of annoying, not to mention distracting. Finally, on Friday, after she'd literally tossed her hands up as one of our classmates struggled to define "blue collar," I couldn't help myself.

"If you hate this place so much," I said, "why are you here?"

She turned her head slowly, as if seeing me for the first time. "Excuse me?" she said.

I shrugged. "It's not like it's cheap. Seems like a waste of money is all I'm saying."

Olivia adjusted herself in her seat, as if perhaps a change of position might help her to understand why the hell I was talking to her. "I'm sorry," she said, "but do we know each other?"

"It's just a question," I said.

Ms. Conyers, up at the front of the room, was saying something about the status quo. I flipped a few pages in my notebook, feeling Olivia watching me. After a moment, I looked up and met her gaze, letting her know she didn't intimidate me.

"Why are *you* here?" she asked.

"No choice in the matter," I told her.

"Me neither," she replied. I nodded. This was enough, as far as I was concerned. But then she continued. "I was doing just fine at Jackson. It was my dad that wanted me here and made me apply for a scholarship. Better education, better teachers. Better class of friends, all that. You happy now?"

"Never said I wasn't," I told her. "You're the one moaning and groaning over there."

Olivia raised her eyebrows. Clearly, I'd surprised her, and I had a feeling this wasn't so easy to do. "What's your name again?"

"Ruby," I told her. "Ruby Cooper."

"Huh," she said, like this answered some other question, as well. The next time I saw her, though, in the quad between classes, she didn't just brush by, ignoring me in favor of whoever was talking in her ear. She didn't speak to me, either. But I did get a moment of eye contact, some acknowledgment, although of what I wasn't sure, and still couldn't say.

* * *

Now, lying on my bed Saturday morning, I heard a crash from outside, followed by more beeping. I got up and walked to the window, looking down at the yard. The hole was even bigger now, the red clay and exposed rock a marked contrast to the even green grass on either side of it. Jamie was still on the patio with the dog, although now he had his hands in his pockets and was rocking back on his heels as he watched the machine dig down again. It was hard to remember what the yard had looked like even twelve hours before, undisturbed and pristine. Like it takes so little not only to change something, but to make you forget the way it once was, as well.

Downstairs in the kitchen, the noise was even louder, vibrations rattling the glass in the French doors. I could see that Cora, now dressed, her hair damp from the shower, had joined Jamie outside. He was explaining something to her, gesturing expansively as she nodded, looking less than enthusiastic.

I got myself some cereal, figuring if I didn't, someone would give me another breakfast lecture, then picked up a section of the newspaper from the island. I was on my way to sit down when there was a bang behind me and Roscoe popped through the dog door.

When he saw me, his ears perked up and he pattered over, sniffing around my feet. I stepped over him, walking to the table, but of course he followed me, the way he'd taken to doing ever since the night of the lasagna trauma. Despite my best efforts to dissuade him, the dog liked me.

"You know," Jamie had said the day before, watching as Roscoe stared up at me with his big bug eyes during dinner, "it's pretty amazing, actually. He doesn't bond with just anyone."

"I'm not really a dog person," I said.

"Well, he's not just a dog," Jamie replied. "He's Roscoe."

This, however, was little comfort at times like this, when I just wanted to read my horoscope in peace and instead had to deal with Roscoe attending to his daily toilette—heavy on the slurping—at my feet. "Hey," I said, nudging him with the toe of my shoe. "Cut it out."

He looked up at me. One of his big eyes was running, which seemed to be a constant condition. After a moment, he went back to what he was doing.

"You're up," I heard Cora say from behind me as she came in the patio door. "Let me guess. Couldn't sleep."

"Something like that," I said.

She poured herself a cup of coffee, then walked over to the table. "Me," she said with a sigh as she sat down, dropping a hand to pat Roscoe's head, "I wanted a pool. Something we could swim in."

I glanced up at her, then out at the backhoe, which was swinging down into the hole. "Ponds are nice, though," I said. "You'll have fish."

She sighed. "So typical. He's already won you over."

I shrugged, turning a page. "I don't take sides."

I felt her look at me as I said this, her eyes staying on

me as I scanned the movie listings. Then she picked up her mug, taking another big sip, before saying, "So. I think we need to talk about a few things."

Just as she said this, the backhoe rattled to a stop, making everything suddenly seem very quiet. I folded the paper, pushing it aside. "Okay," I said. "Go ahead."

Cora looked down at her hands, twining her fingers through the handle of her cup. Then she raised her gaze, making a point of looking me straight in the eye as she said, "I think it's safe to say that this . . . situation was unexpected for both of us. It's going to take a bit of adjustment."

I took another bite of cereal, then looked at Roscoe, who was lying at Cora's feet now, his head propped up on his paws, legs spread out flat behind him like a frog. "Clearly," I said.

"The most important things," she continued, sitting back, "at least to Jamie and me, are to get you settled in here and at school. Routine is the first step to normalcy."

"I'm not a toddler," I told her. "I don't need a schedule."

"I'm just saying we should deal with one thing at a time," she said. "Obviously, it won't all run smoothly. But it's important to acknowledge that while we may make mistakes, in the long run, we may also learn from them."

I raised my eyebrows. Maybe I was still in survival mode, but this sounded awfully touchy-feely to me, like a direct quote from some book like *Handling Your Troubled Teen*. Turned out, I wasn't so far off.

"I also think," Cora continued, "that we should set you up to see a therapist. You're in a period of transition, and talking to someone can really—"

"No," I said.

She looked up at me. "No?"

"I don't need to talk to anyone," I told her. "I'm fine."

"Ruby," she said. "This isn't just me. Shayna at Poplar House really felt you would benefit from some discussion about your adjustment."

"Shayna at Poplar House knew me for thirty-six hours," I said. "She's hardly an expert. And sitting around talking about the past isn't going to change anything. There's no point to it."

Cora picked up her coffee cup, taking a sip. "Actually," she said, her voice stiff, "some people find therapy to be very helpful."

Some people, I thought, watching her as she took another slow sip. *Right*.

"All I'm saying," I said, "is that you don't need to go to a lot of trouble. Especially since this is temporary, and all."

"Temporary?" she asked. "How do you mean?"

I shrugged. "I'm eighteen in a few months."

"Meaning what?"

"Meaning I'm a legal adult," I told her. "I can live on my own."

She sat back. "Ah, yes," she said. "Because that was working out *so* well for you before."

"Look," I said as the backhoe started up again outside, startling Roscoe, who had nodded off, "you should be happy. You'll only be stuck with me for a little while and then I'll be out of your hair."

For a moment, she just blinked at me. Then she said, "To go where? Back to that house? Or will you get your own apartment, Ruby, with all the money at your disposal?"

I felt my face flush. "You don't—"

"Or maybe," she continued, loudly and dramatically, as if there was an audience there to appreciate it, "you'll just go and move back in with Mom, wherever she is. Because she probably has a great place with a cute guest room all set up and waiting for you. Is that your plan?"

The backhoe was rumbling again, scooping, digging deeper.

"You don't know anything about me," I said to her. "Not a thing."

"And whose fault is that?" she asked.

I opened my mouth, ready to answer this; it was a no-brainer, after all. Who had left and never returned? Stopped calling, stopped caring? Managed to forget, once she was free and past it, the life that she'd left behind, the one I'd still been living? But even as the words formed on my lips, I found myself staring at my sister, who was looking at me so defiantly that I found myself hesitating. Here, in the face of the one truth I knew by heart.

"Look," I said, taking another bite, "all I'm saying is that you shouldn't have to turn your whole life upside down. Or Jamie's, either. Go on as you were. It's not like I'm a baby you suddenly have to raise or something."

Her expression changed, the flat, angry look giving way to something else, something not exactly softer, but more distant. Like she was backing away, even while staying in the same place. She looked down at her coffee cup, then cleared her throat. "Right," she said curtly. "Of course not."

She pushed her chair up, getting to her feet, and I

watched her walk to the coffeemaker and pour herself another cup. A moment later, with her back still to me, she said, "You will need some new clothes, though. At least a few things."

"Oh," I said, looking down at my jeans, which I'd washed twice in three days, and the faded T-shirt I'd worn my last day at Jackson. "I'm okay."

Cora picked up her purse. "I've got an appointment this morning, and Jamie has to be here," she said, taking out a few bills and bringing them over to me. "But you can walk to the new mall. There's a greenway path. He can show you where it is."

"You don't have to—"

"Ruby. Please." Her voice was tired. "Just take it."

I looked at the money, then at her. "Okay," I said. "Thanks."

She nodded but didn't say anything, instead just turning around and walking out of the room, her purse under her arm. Roscoe lifted his head, watching her go, then turned his attention to me, watching as I unfolded the money. It was two hundred bucks. *Not bad*, I thought. Still, I waited another moment, until I was sure she'd gone upstairs, before pocketing it.

The door rattled beside me as Jamie came in, empty coffee mug dangling from one finger. "Morning!" he said, clearly on a pond high as he walked to the island, grabbing a muffin out of the box on the table on his way. Roscoe jumped up, following him. "So, did you guys get your shopping day all planned out? And FYI, there's no just browsing with her. She *insists* on a plan of attack."

"We're not going shopping," I said.

"You aren't?" He turned around. "I thought that was the plan. Girls' day out, lunch and all that."

I shrugged. "She said she has an appointment."

"Oh." He looked at me for a moment. "So . . . where'd she go?"

"Upstairs, I think."

He nodded, then glanced back out at the backhoe, which was backing up—*beep beep*. Then he looked at me again before starting out of the room, and a moment later, I heard the steady thump of him climbing the stairs. Roscoe, who had followed him as far as the doorway, stopped, looking back at me.

"Go ahead," I told him. "Nothing to see here."

Of course, he didn't agree with this. Instead, as Cora's and Jamie's voices drifted down from upstairs—discussing me, I was sure—he came closer, tags jingling, and plopped down at my feet again. Funny how in a place this big, it was so hard to just be alone.

* * *

An hour and a half later, dressed and ready with Cora's money in my pocket, I headed outside to ask Jamie for directions to the shortcut to the mall. I found him at the far end of the yard, beyond the now sizable and deep hole, talking to a man by Nate's fence.

At first, I assumed it was one of the guys from the digging company, several of whom had been milling around ever since the backhoe had arrived. Once I got closer, though, it became apparent that whoever this guy was, he didn't drive machinery for a living.

He was tall, with salt-and-pepper gray hair and tanned skin, and had on faded jeans, leather loafers, and what I was pretty sure was a cashmere sweater, a pair of expensive-looking sunglasses tucked into his collar. As he and Jamie talked, he was spinning his car keys around one finger, then folding them into his palm, again and again. *Spin, clank, spin, clank*.

". . . figured you were digging to China," the man was saying as I came into earshot. "Or for oil, maybe."

"Nope, just putting in a pond," Jamie said.

"A pond?"

"Yeah." Jamie slid his hands into his pockets, glancing over at the hole again. "Organic to the landscaping and the neighborhood. No chemicals, all natural."

"Sounds expensive," the man said.

"Not really. I mean, the initial setup isn't cheap, but it's an investment. Over time, it'll really add to the yard."

"Well," the man said, flicking his keys again, "if you're looking for an investment, we should sit down and talk. I've got some things cooking that might interest you, really up-and-coming ideas. In fact—"

"Ruby, hey," Jamie said, cutting him off as he spotted me. He slid an arm over my shoulder, saying, "Blake, this is Ruby, Cora's sister. She's staying with us for a while. Ruby, this is Blake Cross. Nate's dad."

"Nice to meet you," Mr. Cross said, extending his hand. He had a firm handshake, the kind I imagined they must teach in business school: two pumps, with solid eye contact the entire time. "I was just trying to convince your brother-in-law it's a better thing to put money in a good idea than the ground. Don't you agree?"

"Um," I said as Jamie shot me a sympathetic smile. "I don't know."

"Of course you do! It's basic logic," Mr. Cross said. Then he laughed, flicking his keys again, and looked at Jamie, who was watching the backhoe again.

"So," I said to Jamie, "Cora said you could tell me how to get to the mall?"

"The mall?" Jamie asked. "Oh, the greenway. Sure. It's just down the street, to the right. Stones by the entrance."

"Can't miss it," Mr. Cross said. "Just look for all the people not from this neighborhood traipsing through."

"Blake," Jamie said, "it's a community greenway. It's open to everyone."

"Then why put it in a private, gated neighborhood?" Mr. Cross asked. "Look, I'm as community oriented as the next person. But there's a reason we chose to live here, right? Because it's exclusive. Open up a part of it to just anyone and you lose that."

"Not necessarily," Jamie said.

"Come on," Mr. Cross said. "I mean, what'd you spend on your place here?"

"You know," Jamie said, obviously uncomfortable, "that's not really—"

"A million—or close to it, right?" Mr. Cross continued, over him. Jamie sighed, looking over at the backhoe again. "And for that price, you should get what you want, whether it be a sense of security, like-minded neighbors, exclusivity—"

"Or a pond," I said, just as the backhoe banged down again, then began to back up with a series of beeps.

"What's that?" Mr. Cross asked, cupping a hand over his ear.

"Nothing," I said. Jamie looked over at me, smiling. "It was nice to meet you."

He nodded, then turned his attention back to Jamie as I said my good-byes and started across the yard. On my way, I stopped at the edge of the hole, looking down into it. It was deep, and wide across, much more substantial than what I'd pictured based on Jamie's description. A lot can change between planning something and actually doing it. But maybe all that really matters is that anything is different at all.

Chapter Five

Maybe it was my talk with Cora, or just the crazy week I'd had. Whatever the reason, once I got to the mall, I found myself heading to the bus stop. Two transfers and forty minutes later, I was at Marshall's.

He lived in Sandpiper Arms, an apartment complex just through the woods from Jackson that was best known for its cheap rent and the fact that its units were pre-furnished. They were also painted an array of pastel colors, candy pinks and sky blues, bright, shiny yellows. Marshall's was lime green, which wasn't so bad, except for some reason going there always made me want a Sprite.

When I first knocked on the door, nobody answered. After two more knocks, I was about to pull out my bus schedule and start plotting my ride home, but then the door swung open, and Rogerson peered out at me.

"Hey," I said. He blinked, then ran a hand through his thick dreadlock-like hair, squinting in the sun. "Is Marshall here?"

"Bedroom," he replied, dropping his hand from the door and shuffling back to his own room. I didn't know much about Rogerson, other than the pot thing and that he and Marshall worked together in the kitchen at Sopas, a Mexican joint in town. I'd heard rumors about him spending some time in jail—something about assault—but he wasn't the most talkative person and pretty much kept to himself, so who knew what was really true.

I stepped inside, shutting the door behind me. It took a minute for my eyes to adjust: Marshall and Rogerson, like my mother, preferred things dim. Maybe it was a late-shift thing, this aversion to daylight in general, and morning specifically. The room smelled like stale smoke as I moved forward, down the narrow hallway, passing the small kitchen, where pizza boxes and abandoned soda bottles crowded the island. In the living room, some guy was stretched out across the sofa, a pillow resting on his face: I could see a swath of belly, pale and ghostly, sticking out from under his T-shirt, which had ridden up slightly. Across the room, the TV was on, showing bass fishing on mute.

Marshall's door was closed, but not all the way. "Yeah?" he said, after I knocked.

"It's me," I replied. Then he coughed, which I took as permission to enter and pushed it open.

He was sitting at the pre-fab desk, shirtless, the window cracked open beside him, rolling a cigarette. His skin, freckled and pale, seemed to almost glow in the bit of light the window allowed, and, this being Marshall, you could clearly make out his collarbones and ribs. The boy was skinny, but unfortunately for me, I liked skinny boys.

"There she is," he said, turning to face me. "Long time no see."

I smiled, then cleared a space for myself across from him on the unmade bed and sat down. The room itself was a mess of clothes, shoes, and magazines, things strewn all over the place. One thing that stuck out was a box of candy, one of those samplers, on the bureau top, still wrapped in plastic. "What's that?" I asked. "You somebody's Valentine?"

He picked up the cigarette, sticking it into his mouth, and I instantly regretted asking this. It wasn't like I cared who else he saw, if anybody. "It's October."

"Could be belated," I said with a shrug.

"My mom sent it. You want to open it?" I shook my head, then watched as he sat back, exhaling smoke up into the air. "So what's going on?"

I shrugged. "Not much. I'm actually looking for Peyton. You seen her?"

"Not lately." A phone rang in the other room, then abruptly stopped. "But I've been working a lot, haven't been around much. I'm about to take off—have to work lunch today."

"Right," I said, nodding. I sat back, looking around me, as a silence fell over us. Suddenly I felt stupid for coming here, even with my lame excuse. "Well, I should go, too. I've got a ton of stuff to do."

"Yeah?" he said slowly, leaning forward, elbows on his knees, closer to me. "Like what?"

I shrugged, starting to push myself to my feet. "Nothing that would interest you."

"No?" he asked, stopping me by moving a little closer, his knees bumping mine. "Try me."

"Shopping," I said.

He raised his eyebrows. "No kidding," he said. "One week at Perkins Day and you're already fashion-conscious."

"How'd you know I was at Perkins Day?" I asked.

Marshall shrugged, pulling back a bit. "Someone was talking about it," he said.

"Really."

"Yeah." He looked at me for a moment, then slid his hands out, moving them up my thighs to my waist. Then he ducked his head down, resting it in my lap, and I smoothed my hands over his hair, running it through my fingers. As I felt him relax into me, another silence fell, but this one I was grateful for. After all, with me and Marshall, it had never been about words or conversation, where there was too much to be risked or lost. Here, though, in the quiet, pressed against each other, this felt familiar to me. And it was nice to let someone get close again, even if it was just for a little while.

It was only later, when I was curled up under his blankets, half asleep, that I was reminded of everything that had happened since the last time I'd been there. Marshall was getting ready for work, digging around for his belt, when he laid something cool on my shoulder. Reaching up, I found the key to Cora's house, still on its silver fob, which must have slipped out of my pocket at some point. "Better hang on to that," he said, his back to me as he bent over his shoes. "If you want to get home."

As I sat up, closing it in my hand, I wanted to tell him that Cora's house wasn't home, that I wasn't even sure what that word meant anymore. But I knew he didn't really care, and anyway he was already pulling on a Sopas T-shirt, getting ready to leave. So instead, I began collecting my own clothes, all business, just like him. I didn't necessarily have to get out first, but I wasn't about to be left behind.

* * *

I'd never been much of a shopper, mostly because, like sky-diving or playing polo, it wasn't really within my realm of possibility. Before my mom needed me for Commercial, I'd had a couple of jobs of my own—working at greasy fast-food joints, ringing up shampoo and paper towels at discount drugstores—but all that money I'd tried to put away. Even then I'd had a feeling that someday I would need it for something more than sweaters and lipsticks. Sure enough, once my mom had taken off, I'd pretty much cleared out my savings, and now I was back at zero, just when I needed money most.

Which was why it felt so stupid to even be buying clothes, especially with two hundred bucks I'd scored by doing absolutely nothing. On the flip side, though, I couldn't keep wearing the same four things forever. Plus, Cora was already pissed at me; making her think I'd just pocketed her money would only make things worse. So I forced myself through the narrow aisles of store after store, loud music blasting overhead as I scoured clearance racks for bargains.

It wasn't like I could have fit in at Perkins on my budget, even if I wanted to. Which, of course, I didn't. Still, in the time I'd been there, I'd noticed the irony in what all the girls were wearing, which was basically expensive clothes made to look cheap. Two-hundred-dollar jeans with rips and patches, Lanoler cashmere sweaters tied sloppily around their waists, high-end T-shirts specifically weathered and faded to look old and worn. My old stuff at the yellow house, mildew aside, would have been perfect; as it was, I was forced to buy not only new stuff but cheap new stuff, and the difference was obvious. Clearly, you had to spend a lot of money to properly look like you were slumming.

Still, after an hour and a half, I'd vastly increased my working wardrobe, buying two new pairs of jeans, a sweater, a hoodie, and some actual cheap T-shirts that, mercifully, were five for twenty bucks. Still, seeing my cash dwindle made me very nervous. In fact, I felt slightly sick as I started down the airy center of the mall toward the exit, which was probably why I noticed the HELP WANTED sign ahead right away. Stuck to the side of one of the many merchandise carts arranged to be unavoidable, it was like a beacon, pulling me toward it, step-by-step.

As I got closer, I saw it was on a jewelry stall, which appeared to be unmanned, although there were signs of someone having just left: a Jumbo Smoothie cup sweating with condensation was sitting on the register, and there was a stick of incense burning, the smoke wafting in long curlicues up toward the high, bright glass atrium-like ceiling above. The jewelry itself was basic but pretty, with rows and rows of silver-and-turquoise earrings, a large display of beaded necklaces, and several square boxes filled with rings of all sizes. I reached forward, drawing out a thick one with a red stone, holding it up in front of me and turning it in the light.

"Oh! Wait! Hello!"

I jumped, startled, then immediately put the ring back just as the redheaded woman from whom Nate had been picking up the boxes that day—Harriet—came bustling up, a Jump Java cup in one hand, out of breath but talking anyway.

"Sorry!" she gasped, planting it beside the smoothie cup on the register. "I've been trying to kick my caffeine habit—" here she paused, sucking in a big, and much needed, by the sound of it, breath—"by switching to smoothies. Healthy, right? But then the headache hit and I could feel myself crashing and I just had to run down for a fix." She took another big breath, now fanning her flushed face with one hand. "But I'm here now. Finally."

I just looked at her, not exactly sure what to say, especially considering she was still kind of wheezing. Now that I was seeing her up close, I figured she was in her mid-thirties, maybe a little older, although her freckles, hair, and outfit—low-slung jeans, suede clogs, and Namaste T-shirt—made it hard to pinpoint exactly.

"Wait," she said, putting her coffee on the register and pointing at me, a bunch of bangles sliding down her hand. "Do I know you? Have you bought stuff here before?"

I shook my head. "I was with Nate the other day," I said. "When he came to pick up those things from you."

She snapped her fingers, the bangles clanging again. "Right. With the beeping. God! I'm still recovering from that."

I smiled, then looked down at the display again. "Do you make all this yourself?"

"Yep, I'm a one-woman operation. To my detriment, at times." She hopped up on a stool by the register, picking up her coffee again. "I just made those ones with the red stones, on the second row. People think redheads can't wear red, but they're wrong. One of the first fallacies of my life. And I believed it for *years*. Sad, right?"

I glanced over at her, wondering if she'd been able to tell from a distance that this, in fact, was the one I'd been looking at. I nodded, peering down at it again.

"I love *your* necklace," she said suddenly. When I glanced over to see her leaning forward slightly, studying it, instinctively my hand rose to touch it.

"It's just a key," I said.

"Maybe." She took another sip of her coffee. "But it's the contrast that's interesting. Hard copper key, paired with such a delicate chain. You'd think it would be awkward or bulky. But it's not. It works."

I looked down at my necklace, remembering the day that—fed up with always losing my house key in a pocket or my backpack—I'd gone looking for a chain thin enough to thread through the top hole but still strong enough to hold it. At the time, I hadn't been thinking about anything but managing to keep it close to me, although now, looking in one of the mirrors opposite, I could see what she was talking about. It was kind of pretty and unusual, after all.

"Excuse me," a guy with a beard and sandals standing behind a nearby vitamin kiosk called out to her. "But is that a coffee you're drinking?"

Harriet widened her eyes at me. "No," she called out over her shoulder cheerily. "It's herbal tea."

"Are you lying?"

"Would I lie to you?"

"Yes," he said.

She sighed. "Fine, fine. It's coffee. But organic free-trade coffee."

"The bet," he said, "was to give up all caffeine. You owe me ten bucks."

"Fine. Add it to my tab," she replied. To me she added, "God, I *always* lose. You'd think I'd learn to stop betting."

I wasn't sure what to say to this, so I looked over the necklaces for another moment before saying, "So . . . are you still hiring?"

"No," she replied. "Sorry."

I glanced at the sign. "But—"

"Okay, *maybe* I am," she said. Behind her, the vitamin guy coughed loudly. She looked at him, then said reluctantly, "Yes. I'm hiring."

"All right," I said slowly.

"But the thing is," she said, picking up a nearby feather duster and busily running it across a display of bracelets, "I hardly have any hours to offer. And what I *can* give you is erratic, because you'd have to work around my schedule, which varies wildly. Some times I might need you a lot, others hardly at all."

"That's fine," I said.

She put the duster down, narrowing her eyes at me. "This is boring work," she warned me. "Lots of sitting in one place while everyone passes you by. It's like solitary confinement."

"It is not," Vitamin Guy said. "For God's sake."

"I can handle it," I told her as she shot him a look.

"It's like I said, I'm a one-woman operation," she added. "I just put up that sign. . . . I don't know why I put it up. I mean, I'm doing okay on my own."

There was pointed cough from the vitamin kiosk. She turned, looking at the guy there. "Do you need some water or something?"

"Nope," he replied. "*I'm* fine."

For a moment they just stared at each other, with me between them. Clearly, something was going on here, and my life was complicated enough. "You know, forget it," I said. "Thanks anyway."

I stepped back from the kiosk, hoisting my bags farther up my wrist. Just as I began to walk away, though, I heard another cough, followed by the loudest sigh yet.

"You have retail experience?" she called out.

I turned back. "Counter work," I said. "And I've cashiered."

"What was your last job?"

"I delivered lost luggage for the airlines."

She'd been about to fire off another question, but hearing this, she stopped, eyes widening. "Really."

I nodded, and she looked at me for a moment longer, during which time I wondered if I actually wanted to work for someone who seemed so reluctant to hire me. Before I could begin to consider this, though, she said, "Look, I'll be honest with you. I don't delegate well. So this might not work out."

"Okay," I said.

Still, I could feel her wavering. Like something balanced on the edge, that could go either way.

"Jesus," Vitamin Guy said finally. "Will you tell the girl yes already?"

"Fine," she said, throwing up her hands like she'd lost another bet, a big one. "We'll give it a try. But only a try."

"Sounds good," I told her. Vitamin Guy smiled at me.

She still looked wary, though, as she stuck out her hand. "I'm Harriet."

"Ruby," I said. And with that, I was hired.

* * *

Harriet was not lying. She was a total control freak, something that became more than clear over the next two hours, as she walked me through an in-depth orientation, followed by an intricate register tutorial. Only after I'd endured both of these things—as well as a pop quiz on what I'd learned—and had her shadow me while I waited on four separate customers did she finally decide to leave me alone while she went for another coffee.

"I'll just be right here," she said, pointing to the Jump Java outpost, which was less than five hundred feet away. "If you scream, I'll hear you."

"I won't scream," I assured her.

She hardly looked convinced, however, as she walked away, checking back on me twice before I stopped counting.

Once she was gone, I tried to both relax and remember everything I'd just been taught. I was busy dusting the displays when the vitamin guy walked over.

"So," he said. "Ready to quit yet?"

"She is a little intense," I agreed. "How do her other employees deal with it?"

"They don't," he said. "I mean, she doesn't have any others. Or she hasn't. You're the first."

This, I had to admit, explained a lot. "Really."

He nodded, solemn. "She's needed help forever, so this is a big step for her. Huge, in fact," he said. Then he reached into his pocket, pulling out a handful of small pill packs. "I'm Reggie, by the way. Want some free B-complexes?"

I eyed them, then shook my head. "Ruby. And um, no thanks."

"Suit yourself," he said. "Yo, Nate! How those shark-cartilage supplements treating you? Changed your life yet?"

I turned around. Sure enough, there was Nate, walking toward us, carrying a box in his hands. "Not yet," he said, shifting to slapping hands with Reggie. "But I only just started them."

"You got to keep them up, man," Reggie said. "Every day, twice a day. Those aches and pains will be gone. It's miraculous."

Nate nodded, then looked at me. "Hey," he said.

"Hi."

"She works for Harriet," Reggie said, nudging him.

"No way," Nate said, incredulous. "Harriet actually hired someone?"

"Why is that so surprising?" I said. "She had a HELP WANTED sign up."

"For the last six months," Nate said, putting his box down on the stool behind me.

"And tons of people have applied," Reggie added. "Of course she had a reason for rejecting every one of them. Too perky, bad haircut, possible allergies to the incense . . ."

"She hired you, though," I said to Nate. "Right?"

"Only under duress," he replied, pulling some papers out of the box.

"Which is why," Reggie said, popping a B-complex, "it's so huge that she agreed to take you on."

"No kidding," Nate said. "It is pretty astounding. Maybe it's a redhead thing?"

"Like does speak to like," Reggie agreed. "Or perhaps our Harriet has finally realized how close she is to a stress-related breakdown. I mean, have you seen how much coffee she's been drinking?"

"I thought she switched to smoothies. You guys made a bet, right?"

"Already caved," Reggie said. "She owes me, like, a thousand bucks now."

"What are you guys doing?" Harriet demanded as she walked up, another large coffee in hand. "I finally hire someone and you're already distracting her?"

"I was just offering her some B-complexes," Reggie said. "I figured she'll need them."

"Funny," she grumbled, walking over to take the paper Nate was holding out to her.

"You know," he said to her as she scanned it, "personally, I think it's a great thing you finally admitted you needed help. It's the first step toward healing."

"I'm a small-business owner," she told him. "Working a lot is part of the job. Just ask your dad."

"I would," Nate said. "But I never see him. He's always working."

She just looked at him, then grabbed a pen from the register, signing the bottom of the paper and handing it back to him. "Do you want a check today, or can you bill me?"

"We can send a bill," he said, folding the paper and sliding it into his pocket. "Although you know my dad's pushing his new auto-draft feature these days."

"What's that?"

"We bill you, then take it directly out of your account. Draft it and forget it, no worries," Nate explained. "Want to sign up? I've got the forms in the car. It'll make your life even easier."

"No," Harriet said with a shudder. "I'm already nervous enough just letting you mail stuff."

Nate shot me a told-you-so look. "Well, just keep it in mind," he told her. "You need anything else right now?"

"Nothing you can help me with," Harriet replied, sighing. "I mean, I still have to teach Ruby so much. Like how to organize the displays, the setup and closing schedule, the right way to organize stock alphabetically by size and stone . . ."

"Well," Nate said, "I'm sure that's doable."

"Not to mention," she continued, "the process for the weekly changing of the padlock code on the cash box, alternating the incense so we don't run out of any one kind too quickly, and our emergency-response plan."

"Your what?" Reggie asked.

"Our emergency-response plan," Harriet said.

He just looked at her.

"What, you don't have a system in place as to how to react if there's a terrorist attack on the mall? Or a tornado?

What if you have to vacate the stall quickly and efficiently?"

Reggie, eyes wide, shook his head slowly. "Do you sleep at night?" he asked her.

"No," Harriet said. "Why?"

Nate stepped up beside me, his voice low in my ear. "Good luck," he said. "You're going to need it."

I nodded, and then he was gone, waving at Harriet and Reggie as he went. I turned back to the display, bracing myself for the terrorism-preparedness tutorial, but instead she picked up her coffee, taking another thoughtful sip. "So," she said, "you and Nate are friends?"

"Neighbors," I told her. She raised her eyebrows, and I added, "I mean, we just met this week. We ride to school together."

"Ah." She put the coffee back on the register. "He's a good kid. We joke around a lot, but I really like him."

I knew I was supposed to chime in here, agree with her that he was nice, say I liked him, too. But if anyone could understand why I didn't do this, I figured it had to be Harriet. She didn't delegate well in her professional life; I had the same reluctance, albeit more personal. Left to my own devices, I'd be a one-woman operation, as well. Unfortunately, though, with Nate the damage was already done. If I'd never tried to take off that first night, if I'd gotten a ride from someone else, we'd still really just be neighbors, with no ties to each other whatsoever. But now here I was, too far gone to be a stranger, not ready to be friends, the little acquaintance we had made still managing to be, somehow, too much.

* * *

When I got back to Cora's house later that evening, the driveway was packed with cars and the front door was open, bright light spilling out onto the steps and down the walk. As I came closer, I could see people milling around in the kitchen, and there was music coming from the backyard.

I waited until the coast was clear before entering the foyer, easing the door shut behind me. Then, bags in hand, I quickly climbed the stairs, stopping only when I was at the top to look down on the scene below. The kitchen was full of people gathered around the island and table, the French doors thrown open as others milled back and forth from the backyard. There was food laid out on the counters, something that smelled great—my stomach grumbled, reminding me I'd skipped lunch—and several coolers filled with ice and drinks were lined up on the patio. Clearly, this wasn't an impromptu event, something decided at the last minute. Then again, me being here hadn't exactly been a part of Cora and Jamie's plan, either.

Just as I thought this, I heard voices from my right. Looking over, I saw Cora's bedroom door was open. Inside, two women, their backs to me, were gathered around the entrance to her bathroom. One was petite and blonde, wearing jeans and a sweatshirt, her hair in a ponytail. The other was taller, in a black dress and boots, a glass of red wine in one hand.

". . . okay, you know?" the blonde was saying. "You know the minute you stop thinking about it, it'll happen."

"Denise," the brunette said. She shook her head, taking a sip of her wine. "That's not helpful. You're making it sound like it's her fault or something."

"That's not what I meant!" Denise said. "All I'm saying is that you have plenty of time. I mean, it seems like just yesterday when we were all so *relieved* to get our periods when we were late. Remember?"

The brunette shot her a look. "The point is," she said, turning back to whoever they were speaking to, "that you're doing everything right: charting your cycle, taking your temperature, all that. So it's really frustrating when it doesn't happen when you want it to. But you've only just started this whole process, and there are a lot of ways to get pregnant these days. You know?"

I was moving away from the door, having realized this conversation was more than private, even before both women stepped back and I saw my sister walk out of her bathroom, nodding and wiping her eyes. Before she could see me, I flattened myself against the wall by the stairs, holding my breath as I tried to process this information. Cora wanted a *baby*? Clearly, her job and marital status weren't the only things that had changed in the years we'd been apart.

I could hear them still talking, their voices growing louder as they came toward the door. Just before they got to me, I pushed myself back up on the landing, as if I was just coming up the stairs, almost colliding with the blonde in the process.

"Oh!" She gasped, her hand flying up to her chest. "You scared me . . . I didn't see you there."

I glanced past them at Cora, who was watching me

with a guarded expression, as if wondering what, if anything, I'd heard. Closer up, I could see her eyes were red-rimmed, despite the makeup she'd clearly just reapplied in an effort to make it seem otherwise. "This is Ruby," she said. "My sister. Ruby, this is Denise and Charlotte."

"Hi," I said. They were both studying me intently, and I wondered how much of our story they'd actually been told.

"It's so nice to meet you!" Denise said, breaking into a big smile. "I can see the family resemblance, I have to say!"

Charlotte rolled her eyes. "Excuse Denise," she said to me. "She feels like she always has to say something, even when it's completely inane."

"How is that inane?" Denise asked.

"Because they don't look a thing alike?" Charlotte replied.

Denise looked at me again. "Maybe not hair color," she said. "Or complexion. But in the face, around the eyes . . . you can't see that?"

"No," Charlotte told her, taking another sip of her wine. After swallowing, she added, "No offense, of course."

"None taken," Cora said, steering them both out of the doorway and down the stairs. "Now go eat, you guys. Jamie bought enough barbecue to feed an army, and it's getting cold."

"You coming?" Charlotte asked her as Denise started down to the foyer, her ponytail bobbing with each step.

"In a minute."

Cora and I both stood there, watching them as they

made their way downstairs, already bickering about something else as they disappeared into the kitchen. "They were my suitemates in college," she said to me. "The first week I thought they hated each other. Turned out it was the opposite. They've been best friends since they were five."

"Really," I said, peering down into the kitchen, where I could now see Charlotte and Denise working their way through the crowd, saying hello as they went.

"You know what they say. Opposites attract."

I nodded, and for a moment we both just looked down at the party. I could see Jamie now, out in the backyard, standing by a stretch of darkness that I assumed was the pond.

"So," Cora said suddenly, "how was the mall?"

"Good," I said. Then, as it was clear she was waiting for more detail, I added, "I got some good stuff. And a job, actually."

"A job?"

I nodded. "At this jewelry place."

"Ruby, I don't know." She crossed her arms over her chest, leaning back against the rail behind her. "I think you should just be focusing on school for the time being."

"It's only fifteen hours a week, if that," I told her. "And I'm used to working."

"I'm sure you are," she said. "But Perkins Day is more rigorous, academically, than you're used to. I saw your transcripts. If you want to go to college, you really need to make your grades and your applications the number one priority."

College? I thought. "I can do both," I said.

"You don't have to, though. That's just the point." She shook her head. "When I was in high school, I was working thirty-hour weeks—I had no choice. You do."

"This isn't thirty hours," I said.

She narrowed her eyes at me, making it clear I just wasn't getting what she was saying. "Ruby, we want to do this for you, okay? You don't have to make things harder than they have to be just to prove a point."

I opened my mouth, ready to tell her that I'd never asked her to worry about my future, or make it her problem. That I was practically eighteen, as well as being completely capable of making my own decisions about what I could and could not handle. And that being in my life for less than a week didn't make her my mother or guardian, regardless of what it said on any piece of paper.

But just as I drew in a breath to say all this, I looked again at her red eyes and stopped myself. It had been a long day for both of us, and going further into this would only make it longer.

"Fine," I said. "We'll talk about it. Later, though. All right?"

Cora looked surprised. She clearly had not been expecting me to agree, even with provisions. "Fine," she said. She swallowed, then glanced back down at the party. "So, there's food downstairs, if you haven't eaten. Sorry I didn't mention the party before—everything's been kind of crazy."

"It's okay," I said.

She looked at me for another moment. "Right," she said slowly, finally. "Well, I should get back downstairs. Just . . . come down whenever."

I nodded, and then she stepped past me and started down the stairs. Halfway down, she looked back up at me, and I knew she was still wondering what exactly had precipitated this sudden acquiescence. I couldn't tell her, of course, what I'd overheard. It wasn't my business, then or now. But as I started to my room, I kept thinking about what Denise had said, and the resemblance she claimed to be able to see. Maybe my sister and I shared more than we thought. We were both waiting and wishing for something we couldn't completely control: I wanted to be alone, and she the total opposite. It was weird, really, to have something so contrary in common. But at least it was something.

* * *

". . . all I can say is, acupuncture works. What? No, it doesn't hurt. At all."

". . . so that was it. I decided that night, no more blind dates. I don't care if he *is* a doctor."

". . . only thirty thousand miles and the original warranty. I mean, it's such a steal!"

I'd been walking through the party for a little more than twenty minutes, nodding at people who nodded at me and picking at my second plate of barbecue, coleslaw, and potato salad. Even though Jamie and Cora's friends seemed nice enough, I was more than happy not to have to talk to anyone, until I heard one voice that cut through all the others.

"Roscoe!"

Jamie was standing at the back of the yard, past the far end of the pond, peering into the dark. As I walked over to him, I got my first up-close look at the pond, which I was surprised to see was already filled with water, a hose dangling in from one side. In the dark it seemed even bigger, and I couldn't tell how deep it was: it looked like it went down forever.

"What's going on?" I asked when I reached him.

"Roscoe's vanished," he said. "He tends to do this. He's not fond of crowds. It's not at the level of the smoke detector, but it's still a problem."

I looked into the dark, then slowly turned back to the pond. "He can swim, right?"

Jamie's eyes widened. "Shit," he said. "I didn't even think about that."

"I'm sure he's not in there," I told him, feeling bad for even suggesting it as he walked to the pond's edge, peering down into it, a worried look on his face. "In fact—"

Then we both heard it: a distinct yap, high-pitched and definitely not obscured by water. It was coming from the fence. "Thank God," Jamie said, turning back in that direction. "Roscoe! Here, boy!"

There was another series of barks, but no Roscoe. "Looks like he might have to be brought in by force," Jamie said with a sigh. "Let me just—"

"I'll get him," I said.

"You sure?"

"Yeah. Go back to the party."

He smiled at me. "All right. Thanks."

I nodded, then put my plate down by a nearby tree as he walked away. Behind me, the party was still going strong, but the voices and music diminished as I walked to the end of the yard, toward the little clump of trees that ran alongside the fence. Not even a week earlier, I'd been running across this same expanse, my thoughts only of getting away. Now, here I was, working to bring back the one thing that had stopped me. Stupid dog.

"Roscoe," I called out as I ducked under the first tree, leaves brushing across my head. "Roscoe!"

No reply. I stopped where I was, letting my eyes adjust to the sudden darkness, then turned back to look at the house. The pond, stretching in between, looked even more vast from here, the lights from the patio shimmering slightly in its surface. Nearer now, I heard another bark. This time it sounded more like a yelp, actually.

"Roscoe," I said, hoping he'd reply again, Marco Polo–style. When he didn't, I took a few more steps toward the fence, repeating his name. It wasn't until I reached it that I heard some frantic scratching from the other side. "Roscoe?"

When I heard him yap repeatedly, I quickened my pace, moving down to where I thought the gate was, running my hand down the fence. Finally, I felt a hinge, and a couple of feet later, a gap. Very small, almost tiny. But still big enough for a little dog, if he tried hard enough, to wriggle through.

When I crouched down, the first thing I saw was Mr. Cross, standing with his hands on his hips by the pool. "All right," he said, looking around him. "I know you're here, I saw what you did to the garbage. Get out and show yourself."

Uh-oh, I thought. Sure enough, I spotted Roscoe cowering behind a potted plant. Mr. Cross clearly hadn't yet seen him, though, as he turned, scanning the yard again. "You have to come out sometime," he said, bending down and looking under a nearby chaise lounge. "And when you do, you'll be sorry."

As if in response, Roscoe yelped, and Mr. Cross spun, spotting him instantly. "Hey," he said. "Get over here!"

Roscoe, though, was not as stupid as I thought. Rather than obeying this order, he took off like a shot, right toward the fence and me. Mr. Cross scrambled to grab him as he passed, missing once, then getting him by one back leg and slowly pulling him back.

"Not so fast," he said, his voice low, as Roscoe struggled to free himself, his tags clanking loudly. Mr. Cross yanked him closer, his hand closing tightly over the dog's narrow neck. "You and I, we have some—"

"Roscoe!"

I yelled so loudly, I surprised myself. But not as much as Mr. Cross, who immediately released the dog, then stood up and took a step back. Our eyes met as Roscoe darted toward me, wriggling through the fence and between my legs, and for a moment, we just looked at each other.

"Hi there," he called out, his voice all friendly-neighbor-like, now. "Sounds like quite a party over there."

I didn't say anything, just stepped back from the fence, putting more space between us.

"He gets into our garbage," he called out, shrugging in a what-can-you-do? kind of way. "Jamie and I have discussed it. It's a problem."

I knew I should respond in some way; I was just standing there like a zombie. But all I could see in my mind was his hand over Roscoe's neck, those fingers stretching.

"Just tell Jamie and Cora to try to keep him on that side, all right?" Mr. Cross said. Then he flashed me that same white-toothed smile. "Good fences make good neighbors, and all that."

Now I did nod, then stepped back, pulling the gate shut. The last glimpse I had of Mr. Cross was of him standing by the pool, hands in his pockets, smiling at me, his face rippled with the lights from beneath the water.

I turned to walk back to our yard, trying to process what I'd just seen and why exactly it had creeped me out so much. I still wasn't sure, even as I came up on Roscoe, who was sniffing along the edge of the pond. But I scooped him up under my arm and carried him the rest of the way, anyway.

* * *

As we got closer to the house, I heard the music. At first, it was just a guitar, strumming, but then another instrument came in, more melodic. "All right," someone said over the strumming. "Here's an old favorite."

I put Roscoe on the ground, then stepped closer to the assembled crowd. As a guy in a leather jacket standing in front of me shifted to the left, I saw it was Jamie who had spoken. He was sitting on one of the kitchen chairs, playing a guitar, a beer at his feet, a guy with a banjo nodding beside him as they went into an acoustic version of Led Zeppelin's "Misty Mountain Hop." His voice, I realized, was not bad, and his playing was actually pretty impressive. So strange how my brother-in-law kept surprising me: his incredible career, his passion for ponds, and now, this music. All things I might never have known had I found that gate the first night.

"Having fun?"

I turned around to see Denise, Cora's friend, standing beside me. "Yeah," I said. "It's a big party."

"They always are," she said cheerfully, taking a sip of the beer in her hand. "That's what happens when you're overwhelmingly social. You accumulate a lot of people."

"Jamie does seem kind of magnetic that way."

"Oh, I meant Cora," she replied as the song wrapped up, the crowd breaking into spontaneous applause. "But he is, too, you're right."

"Cora?" I asked.

She looked at me, clearly surprised. "Well . . . yeah," she said. "You know how she is. Total den-mother type, always taking someone under her wing. Drop her in a roomful of strangers, and she'll know everyone in ten minutes. Or less."

"Really," I said.

"Oh, yeah," she replied. "She's just really good with people, you know? Empathetic. I personally couldn't have survived my last breakup without her. Or any of my breakups, really."

I considered this as Denise took another sip of her beer, nodding to a guy in a baseball cap as he pushed past us. "I guess I don't really know that side of her," I said. "I mean, we've been out of touch for a while."

"I know," she said. Then she quickly added, "I mean, she talked about you a lot in college."

"She did?"

"Oh, yeah. Like, all the time," she said, emphatic. "She really—"

"Denise!" someone yelled, and she turned, looking over the shoulder of the guy beside us. "I need to get that number from you, remember?"

"Right," she said, then smiled at me apologetically. "One sec. I'll be right back. . . ."

I nodded as she walked away, wondering what she'd been about to say. Thinking this, I scanned the crowd until I spotted Cora standing just outside the kitchen door with Charlotte. She was smiling, looking much happier than the last time I'd seen her. At some point she'd pulled her hair back, making her look even younger, and she had on a soft-looking sweater, a glass of wine in her hand. Here I'd just assumed all these people were here because of Jamie, but of course my sister could have changed in the years we'd been apart. *She has her own life now,* my mom had told me again and again. This was it, and I wondered what that must be like, to actually get to start again, forget the world you knew before and leave everything behind. Maybe it had even been easy.

Easy. I had a flash of myself, just a week earlier, coming home from a long night at Commercial to the darkness of the yellow house. How much had I thought about it—my home or my school or anything from before—in the last few days? Not as much as I should have. All this time, I'd been so angry Cora had forgotten me, just wiped our shared slate clean, but now I was doing the same thing. Where *was* my mother? Was it really this easy, once you escaped, to just not care?

I suddenly felt tired, overwhelmed, everything that had happened in the last week hitting me at once. I stepped back from the crowd, slipping inside. As I climbed the stairs, I was glad for the enclosed space of my room, even if it, too, was temporary like everything else.

I just need to sleep, I told myself, kicking off my shoes and sinking down onto the bed. I closed my eyes, trying to shut out the singing, doing all I could to push myself into the darkness and stay there until morning.

When I woke up, I wasn't sure how long I'd been asleep, hours or just minutes. My mouth was dry, my arm cramped from where I'd been lying on it. As I rolled over, stretching out, my only thought was to go back to the dream I'd been having, which I couldn't remember, other than it had been good, in that distant, hopeful way unreal things can be. I was closing my eyes, trying to will myself back, when I heard some laughter and clapping from outside. The party was still going on.

When I went out onto my balcony, I saw the crowd had dwindled to about twenty people or so. The banjo player was gone, and just Jamie remained, plucking a few notes as people chatted around him.

"It's getting late," Charlotte, who'd put on a sweater over her dress, said. She stifled a yawn with her hand. "Some of us have to be up early tomorrow."

"It's Sunday," Denise, sitting beside her, said. "Who doesn't sleep in on Sunday?"

"One last song," Jamie said. He glanced around, looking behind him to a place I couldn't see from my vantage point. "What do you think?" he said. "One song?"

"Come on," Denise pleaded. "Just one."

Jamie smiled, then began to play. It was cold outside, at least to me, and I turned back to my room, feeling a yawn of my own rising up, ready to go back to bed. But then I realized there was something familiar about what he was playing; it was like it was tugging at some part of me, faint but persistent, a melody I thought was mine alone.

"'I am an old woman, named after my mother. . . .'"

The voice was strong and clear, and also familiar, but in a distant way. Similar to the one I knew, and yet different—prettier and not as harsh around the edges.

"'My old man is another child that's grown old. . . .'"

It was Cora. Cora, her voice pure and beautiful as it worked its way along the notes we'd both heard so many times, the song more than any other that made me think of my mother. I thought of how strange I'd felt earlier, thinking we'd both just forgotten everything. But this was scary, too, to be so suddenly connected, prompting a stream of memories—us in our nightgowns, her reaching out for me, listening to her breathing, steady and soothing, from across a dark room—rushing back too fast to stop.

I felt a lump rise in my throat, raw and throbbing, but even as the tears came I wasn't sure who I was crying for. Cora, my mom, or maybe, just me.

Chapter Six

I could not prove it scientifically. But I was pretty sure Gervais Miller was the most annoying person on the planet.

First, there was the voice. Flat and nasal with no inflection, it came from the backseat, offering up pronouncements and observations. "Your hair's matted in the back," he'd tell me, when I hadn't had adequate time with the blow-dryer. Or when I pulled a shirt last-minute from the laundry: "You stink like dryer sheets." Attempts to ignore him by pretending to study only resulted in a running commentary on my academic prowess, or lack thereof. "Intro to Calculus? What are you, stupid?" or "Is that a *B* on that paper?" And so on.

I wanted to punch him. Daily. But of course I couldn't, for two reasons. First, he was just a kid. Second, between his braces and his headgear, there was really no way to get at him and really make an impact. (The fact that I'd actually thought about it enough to draw this conclusion probably should have worried me. It did not.)

When it all got to be too much, I'd just turn around and shoot him the evil eye, which usually did the trick. He'd quiet down for the rest of the ride, maybe even the next day, as well. In time, though, his obnoxiousness would return, often even stronger than before.

In my more rational moments, I tried to feel empathy for Gervais. It had to be hard to be a prodigy, supersmart but so much younger than everyone else at school. Whenever I saw him in the halls, he was always alone, backpack over both shoulders, walking in his weird, leaning-forward way, as if powering up to head-butt someone in the chest.

Being a kid, though, Gervais also lacked maturity, which meant that he found things like burps and farts *hysterical*, and even funnier when they were his own. Put him in a small, enclosed space with two people every morning, and there was no end to the potential for hilarity. Suffice it to say, we always knew what he'd had for breakfast, and even though it was nearing winter, I often kept my window open, and Nate did the same.

On the Monday after Cora's party, though, when I got into the car at seven thirty, something just felt different. A moment later, I realized why: the backseat was empty.

"Where's Gervais?" I asked.

"Doctor's appointment," Nate said.

I nodded, then I settled into my seat to enjoy the ride. My relief must have been palpable, because a moment later Nate said, "You know, he's not so bad."

"Are you joking?" I asked him.

"I mean," he said, "I'll admit he's not the easiest person to be around."

"Please." I rolled my eyes. "He's *horrible*."

"Come on."

"He stinks," I said, holding up a finger. Then, adding another, I said, "And he's rude. And his burps could wake the dead. And if he says one more thing about my books or my classes I'm going to—"

It was at about this point that I realized Nate was looking at me like I was crazy. So I shut up, and we just drove in silence.

"You know," he said after a moment, "it's a shame you feel that way. Because I think he likes you."

I just looked at him. "Did you not hear him tell me I was fat the other day?"

"He didn't say you were *fat,*" Nate replied. "He said you looked a little rotund."

"How is that different?"

"You know," he said, "I think you're forgetting Gervais is twelve."

"I assure you I am not."

"And," he continued, "boys at twelve aren't exactly slick with the ladies."

"'Slick with the ladies'?" I said. "Are *you* twelve?"

He switched lanes, then slowed for a light. "He teases you," he said slowly, as if I was stupid, "*because* he likes you."

"Gervais does not like me," I said, louder this time.

"Whatever." The light changed. "But he never talked to Heather when she rode with us."

"He didn't?"

"Nope. He just sat back there, passing gas, without comment."

"Nice," I said.

"It really was." Nate downshifted as we slowed for a red light. "All I'm saying is that maybe he just wants to be friends but doesn't exactly know how to do it. So he says you smell like trees or calls you rotund. That's what kids do."

I rolled my eyes, looking out the window. "Why," I said, "would Gervais want to be friends with me?"

"Why wouldn't he?"

"Because I'm not a friendly person?" I said.

"You're not?"

"Are you saying you think I am?"

"I wouldn't say you're unfriendly."

"I would," I said.

"Really."

I nodded.

"Huh. Interesting."

The light changed, and we moved forward.

"Interesting," I said, "meaning what?"

He shrugged, switching lanes. "Just that I don't see you that way. I mean, you're reserved, maybe. Guarded, definitely. But not unfriendly."

"Maybe you just don't know me," I said.

"Maybe," he agreed. "But unfriendly is usually one of those things you pick up on right away. You know, like B.O. There's no hiding it if it's there."

I considered this as we approached another light. "So when we met that first night," I said, "by the fence, you thought I was friendly?"

"I didn't think you weren't," he said.

"I wasn't very nice to you."

"You were jumping a fence. I didn't take it personally."

"I didn't even thank you for covering for me."

"So?"

"So I should have. Or at least not been such a bitch to you the next day."

Nate shrugged, putting on his blinker. "It's not a big deal."

"It is, though," I said. "You don't have to be so nice to everyone, you know."

"Ah," he said, "but that's the thing. I do. I'm compulsively friendly."

Of course he was. And I'd noticed it first thing that night by the fence, because it, too, was something you couldn't hide. Maybe I could have tried to explain myself more to Nate, that there was a reason I was this way, but he was already reaching forward, turning on the radio and flipping to WCOM, the local community station he listened to in the mornings. The DJ, some girl named Annabel, was announcing the time and temperature. Then she put on a song, something peppy with a bouncy beat. Nate turned it up, and we let it play all the way to school.

When we got out of the car, we walked together to the green, and then I peeled off to my locker, just like always, while he headed to the academic building. After I'd stuffed in a few books and taken out a couple of others, I shut the door, hoisting my bag back over my shoulder. Across the green, I could see Nate approaching his first-period class. Jake Bristol and two other guys were standing around outside. As he walked up, Jake reached out a hand for a high five, while the other two stepped back, waving him through. I was late myself, with other things to think about. But I stayed there and watched as Nate laughed and stepped through the door, and they all fell in, following along behind him, before I turned and walked away.

* * *

"All right, people," Ms. Conyers said, clapping her hands. "Let's get serious. You've got fifteen minutes. Start asking questions."

The room got noisy, then noisier, as people left their seats and began to move around the room, notebooks in hand. After slogging my way through an extensive test on *David Copperfield* (ten IDs, two essays), all I wanted to do was collapse. Instead, to get us started on our "oral definition" projects, we were supposed to interview our classmates, getting their opinions on what our terms meant. This was good; I figured I needed all the help I could get, considering the way I defined my own family kept changing.

It had been almost two weeks since I'd come to Cora's, and I was slowly getting adjusted. It wasn't like things were perfect, but we had fallen into a routine, as well as an understanding. For my part, I'd accepted that leaving, at least right now, was not in my best interest. So I'd unpacked my bag, finally unloading my few possessions into the big, empty drawers and closet. I wasn't ready to spread out farther into the house itself—I took my backpack upstairs with me as soon as I came home and stood by the dryer as my clothes finished, then folded them right away. It was a big place. God only knew how much could get lost there.

It was weird to be living in such sudden largess, especially after the yellow house. Instead of stretching a pack of pasta over a few days and scraping together change for groceries, I had access to a fully packed pantry, as well as a freezer stocked with just about every entrée imaginable. And that wasn't even counting the "pocket money" Jamie was always trying to give me: twenty bucks for lunch here, another forty in case I needed school supplies there. Maybe someone else would have accepted all this easily, but I was still so wary, unsure of what would be expected of me in return, that at first I refused it. Over time, though, he wore me down and I gave in, although spending it was another matter entirely. I just felt better with it stashed away. After all, you never knew when something, or everything, might change.

Cora had compromised, as well. After much discussion—and some helpful lobbying from Jamie—it was decided I could work for Harriet through the holidays, at which point we'd "reconvene on the subject" and "evaluate its impact on my grades and school performance." As part of the deal, I also had to agree to attend at least one therapy session, an idea I was not at all crazy about. I needed the money, though, so I'd bitten my tongue and acquiesced. Then we'd reached across the kitchen island, shaking on it, her hand small and cool, her strong grip surprising me more than it probably should have.

I'd been thinking about my mother a lot, even more than when she'd first left, which was weird. Like it took a while to really miss her, or let myself do so. Sometimes at night, I dreamed about her; afterward, I always woke up with the feeling that she'd just passed through the room, convinced I could smell lingering smoke or her perfume in the air. Other times, when I was half asleep, I was sure I could feel her sitting on the side of my bed, one hand stroking my hair, the way she'd sometimes done late at night or early in the morning. Back then, I'd always been irritated, wishing she'd go to sleep herself or leave me alone. Now, even when my conscious mind told me it was just a dream, I remained still, wanting it to last.

When I woke up, I always tried to keep this image in my head, but it never stayed. Instead, there was only how she'd looked the last time I'd seen her, the day before she'd left. I'd come home from school to find her both awake and alone, for once. By then, things hadn't been good for a while, and I'd expected her to look bleary, the way she always did after a few beers, or sad or annoyed. But instead, as she turned her head, her expression had been one of surprise, and I remembered thinking maybe she'd forgotten about me, or hadn't been expecting me to return. Like it was me who was leaving, and I just didn't know it yet.

In daylight, I was more factual, wondering if she'd made it to Florida, or if she was still with Warner. Mostly, though, I wondered if she had tried to call the yellow house, made any effort to try and locate me. I wasn't sure I even wanted to talk to her or see her, nor did I know if I ever would. But it was important to simply be sought, even if you didn't ever want to be found.

What is family? I'd written in my notebook that first day, and as I opened it up now I saw the rest of the page was blank, except for the definition I'd gotten from the dictionary: *a set of relations, esp. parents and children.* Eight words, and one was an abbreviation. If only it was really that easy.

Now Ms. Conyers called out for everyone to get to work,

so I turned to Olivia, figuring I'd hit her up first. She hardly looked like she was in the mood for conversation, though, sitting slumped in her chair. Her eyes were red, a tissue clutched in one hand as she pulled the Jackson High letter jacket she always wore more tightly around herself.

"Remember," Ms. Conyers was saying, "you're not just asking what your term means literally, but what it means to the person you're speaking with. Don't be afraid to get personal."

Considering Olivia was hardly open on a *good* day, I decided maybe I should take a different tack. My only other option, though, was Heather Wainwright, on my other side, who was also looking around for someone to talk to, and I wasn't sure I wanted to go there.

"Well? Are we doing this or not?"

I turned back to Olivia. She was still sitting facing forward, as if she hadn't spoken at all. "Oh," I said, then shot a pointed look at the tissue in her hand. In response, she crumpled it up smaller, tucking it down deeper between her fingers. "All right. What does family mean to you?"

She sighed, reaching up to rub her nose. All around us, I could hear people chattering, but she was silent. Finally she said, "Do you know Micah Sullivan?"

"Who?"

"Micah Sullivan," she repeated. "Senior? On the football team? Hangs out with Rob Dufresne?"

It wasn't until I'd heard this last name that I realized she was talking about Jackson. Rob Dufresne had sat across from me in bio sophomore year. "Micah," I said, trying to think. Already, my classmates at Jackson were a big blur, their faces all running together. "Is he really short?"

"No," she snapped. I shrugged, picking up my pen. Then she said, "Okay, so he's not as *tall* as some people."

"Drives a blue truck?"

Now she looked at me. "Yeah," she said slowly. "That's him."

"I know of him."

"Did you ever see him with a girl? At school?"

I thought for another moment, but all I could see was Rob Dufresne going dead pale as we contemplated our frog dissection. "Not that I remember," I said. "But like you said, it's a big place."

She considered this for a moment. Then, turning to face me, she said, "So you never saw him all over some field-hockey player, a blonde with a tattoo on her lower back. Minda or Marcy or something like that?"

I shook my head. She looked at me for a long moment, as if not sure whether to trust me, then faced forward again, pulling her jacket more tightly around her. "Family," she announced. "They're the people in your life you don't get to pick. The ones that are given to you, as opposed to those you get to choose."

Since my mind was still on Micah and the field-hockey player, I had to scramble to write this down. "Okay," I said. "What else?"

"You're bound to them by blood," she continued, her voice flat. "Which, you know, gives you that much more in common. Diseases, genetics, hair, and eye color. It's like, they're part of your blueprint. If something's wrong with you, you can usually trace it back to them."

I nodded and kept writing.

"But," she said, "even though you're stuck with them, at the same time, they're also stuck with you. So that's why they always get the front rows at christenings and funerals. Because they're the ones that are there, you know, from the beginning to the end. Like it or not."

Like it or not, I wrote. Then I looked at these words and all the others I'd scribbled down. It wasn't much. But it was a start. "Okay," I said. "Let's do yours."

Just then, though, the bell rang, triggering the usual cacophony of chairs being banged around, backpacks zipping, and voices rising. Ms. Conyers was saying something about having at least four definitions by the next day, not that I could really hear her over all the noise. Olivia had already grabbed her phone, flipping it open and calling someone on speed dial. As I put my notebook away, I watched her stuff the tissue in her pocket, then run a hand over her braids as she got to her feet.

"It's Melissa," I told her as she turned to walk away.

She stopped, then looked at me, slowly lowering her phone from her ear. "What?"

"The blonde with the back tattoo. Her name is Melissa West," I said, picking up my bag. "She's a sophomore, a total skank. And she plays soccer, not field hockey."

People were moving past us now, en route to the door, but Olivia stayed where she was, not even seeming to notice as Heather Wainwright passed by, glancing at her red eyes before moving on.

"Melissa West," she repeated.

I nodded.

"Thanks."

"You're welcome," I told her. Then she put her phone back to her ear slowly, and walked away.

* * *

When I came out of school that afternoon after final bell, Jamie was waiting for me.

He was leaning against his car, which was parked right outside the main entrance, his arms folded over his chest. As soon as I saw him, I stopped walking, hanging back as people streamed past me on either side, talking and laughing. Maybe I was just being paranoid, but the last time someone had showed up unexpectedly for me at school, it hadn't been to deliver good news.

In fact, it wasn't until after I'd begun to mentally list the various offenses for which I *could* be busted that I realized there really weren't any. All I'd done lately was go to school, go to work, and study. I hadn't even been out on a weekend night. Still, I stayed where I was, hesitant out of force of habit or something else, until the crowd cleared and he spotted me.

"Hey," he called out, raising his hand. I waved back, then pulled my bag more tightly over my shoulder as I started toward him. "You working today?"

I shook my head. "No."

"Good. I need to talk to you about something."

He stepped away from the car, pulling the passenger door open for me. Once in, I forced myself to take a breath as I watched him round the front bumper, then get in and join me. He didn't crank the engine, though, just sat there instead.

Suddenly, it hit me. He was going to tell me I had to leave. Of course. The very minute I allowed myself to relax, they would decide they'd had enough of me. Even worse, as I thought this, I felt my breath catch, suddenly realizing how much I didn't want it to happen.

"The thing is . . ." Jamie said, and now I could hear my heart in my ears. "It's about college."

This last word—*college*—landed in my ears with a clunk. It was like he'd said *Minnesota* or *fried chicken*, that unexpected. "College," I repeated.

"You are a senior," he said as I sat there, still blinking, trying to decide if I should be relieved or more nervous. "And while you haven't exactly had the best semester—not your fault, of course—you did take the SATs last year, and your scores weren't bad. I was just in talking to the guidance office. Even though it's already November, they think that if we really hustle, we can still make the application deadlines."

"You went to the guidance office?" I asked.

"Yeah," he said. I must have looked surprised, because then he added, "I know, I know. This is more Cora's department. But she's in court all week, and besides, we decided that maybe . . ."

I glanced over at him as he trailed off, leaving this unfinished. "You decided maybe what?"

He looked embarrassed. "That it was better for me to bring this up with you. You know, since Cor was kind of tough on you about your job at first, and the therapy thing. She's tired of being the bad guy."

An image of a cartoon character twirling a mustache as

they tied someone to the train tracks immediately popped into my head. "Look," I said, "school isn't really part of my plans."

"Why not?"

I probably should have had an answer to this, but the truth was that I'd never actually been asked it before. Everyone else assumed the same thing that I had from day one: girls like me just didn't go further than high school, if they even got that far. "It's just . . ." I said, stalling. "It's not really been a priority."

Jamie nodded slowly. "It's not too late, though."

"I think it is."

"But if it isn't?" he asked. "Look, Ruby. I get that this is your choice. But the thing is, the spring is a long way away. A lot could change between now and then. Even your mind."

I didn't say anything. The student parking lot was almost empty now, except for a couple of girls with field-hockey sticks and duffel bags sitting on the curb.

"How's this," he said. "Just make a deal with me and agree to apply. That way, you're not ruling anything out. Come spring, you still decide what happens next. You just have more options."

"You're assuming I'll get in somewhere. That's a big assumption."

"I've seen your transcripts. You're not a bad student."

"I'm no brain, either."

"Neither was I," he said. "In fact, in the interest of full disclosure, I'll tell you I wasn't into the idea of higher education, either. After high school, I wanted to take my guitar and move to New York to play in coffeehouses and get a record deal."

"You did?"

"Yup." He smiled, running his hand over the steering wheel. "However, my parents weren't having it. I was going to college, like it or not. So I ended up at the U, planning to leave as soon as I could. The first class I took was coding for computers."

"And the rest is history," I said.

"Nah." He shook his head. "The rest is now."

I eased my grip on my bag, letting it rest on the floorboard between my feet. The truth was, I liked Jamie. So much that I wished I could just be honest with him and say the real reason that even applying scared me: it was one more connection at a time when I wanted to be doing the total opposite. Yes, I'd decided to stay here as long as I had to, but only because really, I'd had no choice. If I went to college—at least this way, with him and Cora backing me—I'd be in debt, both literally and figuratively, at the one time when all I wanted was to be free and clear, owing no one anything at all.

Sitting there, though, I knew I couldn't tell him this. So instead, I said, "So I guess you never have regrets. Wish you'd gone to New York, like you wanted."

Jamie sat back, leaning his head on the seat behind him. "Sometimes I do. Like on a day like today, when I'm dealing with this new advertising campaign, which is making me nuts. Or when everyone in the office is whining and I think my head's going to explode. But it's only in moments. And anyway, if I hadn't gone to the U, I wouldn't have met your sister. So that would have changed everything."

"Right," I said. "How did you guys meet, anyway?"

"Talk about being the bad guy." He chuckled, looking down at the steering wheel, then explained, "She doesn't exactly come across that well in the story."

I had to admit I was intrigued now. "Why not?"

"Because she yelled at me," he said flatly. I raised my eyebrows. "Okay, she'd say she didn't yell, that she was just being assertive. But her voice *was* raised. That's indisputable."

"Why was she yelling at you?"

"Because I was playing guitar outside on the dorm steps one night. Cor's not exactly pleasant when you get between her and her sleep, you know?" I actually didn't but nodded, anyway. "So there I was, first week of classes freshman year, strumming away on a nice late summer night, and suddenly this girl just opens up her window and lets me have it."

"Really."

"Oh, yeah. She just went ballistic. Kept saying it was so inconsiderate, keeping people up with my noise. That's what she called it. Noise. I mean, here I was, thinking I was an artiste, you know?" He laughed again, shaking his head.

I said, "You're awfully good-natured about it, considering."

"Yeah, well," he said. "That was just that first night. I didn't know her yet."

I didn't say anything, instead just looked down at my backpack strap, running it through my fingers.

"My point is," Jamie continued, "not everything's perfect, especially at the beginning. And it's all right to have a little bit of regret every once in a while. It's when you feel it all the time and can't do anything about it . . . that's when you get into trouble."

Over on the curb, the girls with the field-hockey sticks were laughing at something, their voices muffled by my window. "Like," I said, "say, not applying to college, and then wishing you had?"

He smiled. "Okay, fine. So subtlety is not my strong suit. Do we have a deal or what?"

"This isn't a deal," I pointed out. "It's just me agreeing to what you want."

"Not true," he replied. "You get something in return."

"Right," I said. "A chance. An opportunity I wouldn't have otherwise."

"And something else, too."

"What's that?"

"Just wait," he said, reaching forward to crank the engine. "You'll see."

* * *

"A fish?" I said. "Are you serious?"

"Totally!" Jamie grinned. "What more could you want?"

I figured it was best not to answer this, and instead turned my attention back to the round tank between us, which was filled with white koi swimming back and forth. In rows all around us were more tanks, also filled with fish I'd never heard of before: comets, shubunkin, mosquito fish, as well as many other colors of koi, some solid, some speckled with black or red.

"I'm going to go find someone to test my water, make sure it's all balanced," he said, pulling a small plastic container out of his jacket pocket. "Take your time, all right? Pick a good one."

A good one, I thought, looking back down at the fish in the tank beneath me. Like you could tell with a glance, somehow judge their temperament or hardiness. I'd never had a fish—or any pet, for that matter—but from what I'd heard they could die at the drop of a hat, even when kept in a safe, clean tank. Who knew what could happen outside, in a pond open to the elements and everything else?

"Do you need help with the fish?"

I turned around, prepared to say no, only to be startled to see Heather Wainwright standing behind me. She had on jeans and a DONOVAN LANDSCAPING T-shirt, a sweater tied around her waist, and seemed equally surprised by the sight of me.

"Hey," she said. "It's Ruby, right?"

"Yeah. I'm, um, just looking."

"That's cool." She stepped up to the tank, next to me, dropping a hand down into the water: as she did so, the fish immediately swam toward her, circling her fingers. She glanced up at me and said, "They get crazy when they think you're going to feed them. They're like begging dogs, practically."

"Really."

"Yep." She pulled her hand out and wiped it on her jeans. I had to admit, I was surprised to see she worked at a place like this. For some reason, I would have pegged her as the retail type, more at home in a mall. No, I realized a beat later. That was me. Weird. "The goldfish aren't quite as aggressive. But the koi are prettier. So it's a tradeoff."

"My brother-in-law just built a pond," I told her as she bent down and adjusted a valve on the side of the tank. "He's obsessed with it."

"They are pretty awesome," she said. "How big did he go?"

"Big." I glanced over at the greenhouses, where Jamie had headed. "He should be back soon. I'm supposed to be picking a fish."

"Just one?"

"It's my personal fish," I told her, and she laughed. Never in a million years would I have imagined myself here, by a fish tank, with Heather Wainwright. Then again, I wasn't supposed to be here with anyone, period. What I'd noticed, though, was that more and more lately, when I tried to picture where I *did* belong, I couldn't. At first, it had been easy to place myself in my former life, sitting at a desk at Jackson, or in my old bedroom. But now it was like I was already losing my old life at the yellow house, without this one feeling real, either. I was just stuck somewhere in the middle, vague and undefined.

"So you're friends with Nate," Heather said after a moment, adjusting the valve again. "Right?"

I glanced over at her. The whole school had noticed, or so it seemed; it only made sense she would have, as well. "We're neighbors," I told her. "My sister lives behind him."

She reached up to tuck a stray piece of hair behind her ear. "I guess you've heard we used to go out," she said.

"Yeah?" I said.

She nodded. "We broke up this fall. It was big news for a while there." She sighed, touching her hand to the water again. "Then Rachel Webster got pregnant. Which I wasn't happy about, of course. But it did make people stop talking about us, at least for a little while."

"Perkins Day is a small school," I said.

"Tell me about it." She sat back, wiping her hand on her jeans, then looked over at me. "So . . . how's he doing these days?"

"Nate?" I asked.

She nodded.

"I don't know," I said. "Fine, I guess. Like I said, we're not that close."

She considered this as we both watched the fish circling, first one way, then another. "Yeah," she said finally. "He's hard to know, I guess."

This hadn't been what I meant, actually, not at all. If anything, in my mind, Nate was too easy to read, all part of that friendly thing. But saying this seemed odd at that moment, so I just stayed quiet.

"Anyway," Heather continued a beat later, "I just . . . I'm glad you and Nate are friends. He's a really good guy."

I had to admit this was not what I was expecting—it wasn't exactly ex-girlfriend behavior. Then again, she was the queen of compassion, if her time logged at the HELP table was any indication. Of course Nate would fall in love with a *nice* girl. What else did I expect?

"Nate has a lot of friends," I told her now. "I doubt one more makes that much of a difference."

Heather studied my face for a moment. "Maybe not," she said finally. "But you never know, right?"

What? I thought, but then I felt a hand clap my shoulder; Jamie was behind me. "So the water's good," he said. "You find the perfect one yet?"

"How do you even pick?" I asked Heather.

"Just go on instinct," she replied. "Whichever one speaks to you."

Jamie nodded sagely. "There you go," he said to me. "Let the fish speak."

"There's also the issue of who runs from the net," Heather added. "That often makes the decision for you."

In the end, it was a mix of both these things—me pointing and Heather swooping in—that got me my fish. I went with a small white koi, which looked panicked as I held it in its plastic bag, circling again and again as Jamie picked out a total of twenty shubunkins and comets. He also got several more koi, although no other white ones, so I could always find mine in the crowd.

"What are you going to name it?" he asked me as Heather shot oxygen from a canister into the bags for the ride home.

"Let's just see if it survives first," I said.

"Of course it will," he replied as if there was no question.

Heather rang us up, then carried the bags out to the car, where she carefully arranged them in a series of cardboard boxes in the backseat.

"You will need to acclimate them slowly," she explained as the fish swam around and around in their bags, their faces popping up, then disappearing. "Put the bags in the water for about fifteen minutes so they can get adjusted to the temperature. Then open the bags and let a little bit of your pond water in to mix with what they're in. Give it another fifteen minutes or so, and then you can let them go."

"So the key is to ease them into it," Jamie said.

"It's a big shock to their systems, leaving the tank," Heather replied, shutting the back door. "But they usually do fine in the end. It's herons and waterbirds you really need to worry about. One swoop, and they can do some serious damage."

"Thanks for all your help," Jamie told her as he slid back behind the wheel.

"No problem," she said. "See you at school, Ruby."

"Yeah," I said. "See you."

As Jamie began backing out, he glanced over at me. "Friend of yours?"

"No," I said. "We just have a class together."

He nodded, not saying anything else as we pulled out into traffic. It was rush hour, and we didn't talk as we hit mostly red lights heading toward home. Because my fish was alone, in a small bag, I was holding it in my lap, and I could feel it darting from one side to the other. *It's a big shock to their systems,* Heather had said. I lifted the bag up to eye level, looking at my fish again. Who knew if it—or anything—would survive the week, or even the night.

Still, when we got back to Cora's, I went with Jamie to the backyard, then crouched by the pond, easing my bag into it and watching it bob there for those fifteen minutes before letting in that little bit of water, just as I was told. When I finally went to release the koi, it was almost totally dark outside. But even so, I could see my fish, white and bright, as it made its way past the opening into the vast body of water that lay beyond. I expected it to hesitate, or even turn back, but it didn't. It just swam, quick enough to blur, before diving down to the bottom, out of sight.

* * *

When Jamie first called up the stairs to me, I was sure I'd heard wrong.

"Ruby! One of your friends is here to see you!"

Instinctively, I looked at the clock—it was 5:45, on a random Tuesday—then out the window over at Nate's house. His pool lights were on, and I wondered if he'd come over for some reason. But surely, Jamie would've identified him by name.

"Okay," I replied, pushing my chair back and walking out into the hallway. "But who is—?"

By then, though, I'd already looked down into the foyer and gotten the answer as I spotted Peyton, who was standing there patting Roscoe as Jamie looked on. When she glanced up and saw me, her face broke into a wide smile. "Hey!" she said, with her trademark enthusiasm. "I found you!"

I nodded. I knew I should have been happy to see her—as unlike Nate or Heather, she actually *was* my friend—but instead I felt strangely uneasy. After all, I'd never even invited her into the yellow house, always providing excuses about my mom needing her sleep or it being a bad time—keeping the personal, well, personal. But now here she was, already in.

"Hey," I said when I reached the foyer. "What's going on?"

"Are you surprised?" she asked, giggling. "You would

not believe what I went through to track you down. I was like Nancy Drew or something!"

Beside her, Jamie smiled, and I forced myself to do the same, even as I noticed two things: that she reeked of smoke and that her eyes were awfully red, her mascara pooled beneath them. Peyton had always been bad with Visine, and clearly this had not changed. Plus, even though she was dressed as cute as ever—hair pulled back into two low ponytails, wearing jeans and red shirt with an apple on it, a sweater tied loosely around her waist—she had always been the kind of person who, when high, looked it, despite her best efforts. "How did you find me?" I asked her.

"Well," she said, holding her hands, palms facing out and up to set the scene, "it was like this. You'd told me you were living in Wildflower Ridge, so—"

"I did?" I asked, trying to think back.

"Sure. On the phone that day, remember?" she said. "So I figure, it can't be that big of a neighborhood, right? But then, of course, I get over here and it's freaking *huge*."

I glanced at Jamie, who was following this story, a mild smile on his face. Clueless, or so I hoped.

"Anyway," Peyton continued, "I'm driving around, getting myself totally lost, and then I finally just pull over on the side of the road, giving up. And right then, then I see this, like, totally hot guy walking a dog down the sidewalk. So I rolled down my window and asked him if he knew you."

Even before she continued, I had a feeling what was coming next.

"And he did!" she said, clapping her hands. "So he pointed me this way. Very nice guy, by the way. His name was—"

"Nate," I finished for her.

"Yeah!" She laughed again, too loudly, and I got another whiff of smoke, even stronger this time. Like I hadn't spent ages teaching her about the masking ability of breath mints. "And here I am. It all worked out in the end."

"Clearly," I said, just as I heard the door that led from the garage to the kitchen open then shut.

"Hello?" Cora called out. Roscoe, ears perked, trotted toward the sound of her voice. "Where is everybody?"

"We're in here," Jamie replied. A moment later, she appeared in the entrance to the foyer in her work clothes, the mail in one hand. "This is Ruby's friend Peyton. This is Cora."

"You're Ruby's sister?" Peyton asked. "That's so cool!"

Cora gave her the once-over—subtly, I noticed—then extended her hand. "Nice to meet you."

"You, too," Peyton replied, pumping it eagerly. "Really nice."

My sister was smiling politely. Her expression barely changed, only enough to make it more than clear to me that she had seen—and probably smelled—what Jamie had not. Like Peyton's mom, she didn't miss much. "Well," she said. "I guess we should think about dinner?"

"Right," Jamie said. "Peyton, can you stay?"

"Oh," Peyton said, "actually—"

"She can't," I finished for her. "So, um, I'm going to go ahead and give her the tour, if that's all right."

"Sure, sure," Jamie said. Beside him, Cora was studying Peyton, her eyes narrowed, as I nodded for her to follow me into the kitchen. "Be sure to show her the pond!"

"Pond?" Peyton said, but by then I was already tugging her onto the deck, the door swinging shut behind us. I waited until we were a few feet away from the house before stopping and turning to face her.

"What are you *doing*?" I asked.

She raised her eyebrows. "What do you mean?"

"Peyton, you're blinded. And my sister could totally tell."

"Oh, she could not," she said easily, waving her hand. "I used Visine."

I rolled my eyes, not even bothering to address this. "You shouldn't have come here."

For a moment, she looked hurt, then pouty. "And you should have called me," she replied. "You said you were going to. Remember?"

Cora and Jamie were by the island in the kitchen now, looking out at us. "I'm still getting settled in," I told her, but she turned, ignoring this as she walked over to the pond. In her ponytails and in profile, she looked like a little kid. "Look, this is complicated, okay?"

"For me, too," she said, peering down into the water. As I stepped up beside her I saw it was too dark to see anything, but you could hear the pump going, the distant waterfall. "I mean, a lot's happened since you left, Ruby."

I glanced back inside. Jamie was gone, but Cora remained, and she was looking right at me. "Like what?"

Peyton glanced over at me, then shrugged. "I just . . ."

she said softly. "I wanted to talk to you. That's all."

"About what?"

She took in a breath, then let it out just as Roscoe popped through the dog door and began to trot toward us. "Nothing," she said, turning back to the water. "I mean, I miss you. We used to hang out every day, and then you just disappear. It's weird."

"I know," I said. "And believe me, I'd go back to the way things were in a minute if I could. But it's just not an option. This is my life now. At least for a little while."

She considered this as she looked at the pond, then turned slightly, taking in the house rising up behind us. "It is different," she said.

"Yeah," I agreed. "It is."

In the end, Peyton stayed for less than an hour, just long enough to get a tour, catch me up on the latest Jackson gossip, and turn down two more invitations to stay for dinner from Jamie, who seemed beside himself with the fact that I actually had a real, live friend. Cora, however, had a different take, or so I found out later, when I was folding clothes and looked up to see her standing in my bedroom doorway.

"So," she said, "tell me about Peyton."

I focused on pairing up socks as I said, "Not much to tell."

"Have you two been friends a long time?"

I shrugged. "A year or so. Why?"

"No reason." She leaned against the doorjamb, watching as I moved on to jeans. "She just seemed . . . sort of scattered, I guess. Not exactly your type."

It was tempting to point out that Cora herself wasn't exactly in a position to claim to know me that well. But I held my tongue, still folding.

"Anyway," she continued, "in the future, though, if you could let us know when you were having people over, I'd appreciate it."

Like I'd had so many people showing up—all one of them!—that this was suddenly a problem. "I didn't know she was coming," I told her. "I forgot she even knew where I was staying."

She nodded. "Well, just keep it in mind. For next time."

Next time, I thought. *Whatever.* "Sure," I said aloud.

I kept folding, waiting for her to say something else. To go further, insinuating more, pulling me into an argument I didn't deserve, much less want to have. But instead, she just stepped back out of the doorway and started down the hall to her own room. A moment later, she called out for me to sleep well, and I responded in kind, these nicer last words delivered like an afterthought to find themselves, somewhere, in the space between us.

Chapter Seven

Usually I worked for Harriet from three thirty till seven, during which time she was supposed to take off to eat a late lunch and run errands. Invariably, however, she ended up sticking around for most of my shift, her purse in hand as she fretted and puttered, unable to actually leave.

"I'm sorry," she'd say, reaching past me to adjust a necklace display I'd already straightened twice. "It's just . . . I like things a certain way, you know?"

I knew. Harriet had built her business from the ground up, starting straight out of art school, and the process had been difficult, involving struggle, the occasional compromise of artistic integrity, and a near brush with bankruptcy. Still, she'd soldiered on, just her against the world. Which was why, I figured, it was so hard for her to adjust to the fact that now there were two of us.

Still, sometimes her neurosis was so annoying—following along behind me, checking and redoing each thing I did, taking over every task so I sometimes spent entire shifts doing nothing at all—that I wondered why she'd bothered to hire me. One day, when she had literally let me do nothing but dust for hours, I finally asked her.

"Truth?" she said. I nodded. "I'm overwhelmed. My orders are backed up, I'm constantly behind in my books, and

I'm completely exhausted. If it wasn't for caffeine, I'd be dead right now."

"Then let me help you."

"I'm *trying*." She took a sip from her ever-present coffee cup. "But it's hard. Like I said, I've always been a one-woman operation. That way, I'm responsible for everything, good and bad. And I'm afraid if I relinquish any control . . ."

I waited for her to finish. When she didn't, I said, "You'll lose everything."

Her eyes widened. "Yes!" she said. "How did you know?"

Like I was going to go there. "Lucky guess," I said instead.

"This business is the only thing I've ever had that was all mine," she said. "I'm scared to death something will happen to it."

"Yeah," I said as she took another gulp of coffee, "but accepting help doesn't have to mean giving up control."

It occurred to me, saying this, that I should take my own advice. Thinking back over the last few weeks, however—staying at Cora's, my college deal with Jamie—I realized maybe I already had.

Harriet was so obsessed with her business that, from what I could tell, she had no personal life whatsoever. During the day, she worked at the kiosk; at night, she went straight home, where she stayed up into the early hours making more pieces. Maybe this was how she wanted it. But there were clearly others who would welcome a change.

Like Reggie from Vitamin Me, for example. When he was going for food, he always stopped to see if she needed anything. If things were slow, he'd drift over to the open space between our two stalls to shoot the breeze. When

Harriet said she was tired, he instantly offered up B-complexes; if she sneezed, he was like a quick draw with the echinacea. One day after he'd brought her an herbal tea and some ginkgo biloba—she'd been complaining she couldn't remember anything anymore—she said, "He's just so nice. I don't know why he goes to so much trouble."

"Because he likes you," I said.

She jerked her head, surprised, and looked at me. "What?"

"He likes you," I repeated. To me, this was a no-brainer, as obvious as daylight. "You know that."

"Reggie?" she'd said, her surprised tone making it clear she did not. "No, no. We're just friends."

"The man gave you ginkgo," I pointed out. "Friends don't do that."

"Of course they do."

"Harriet, come on."

"I don't even know what you're talking about. I mean, we're friends, but the idea of something more is just . . ." she said, continuing to thumb through the receipts. Then, suddenly, she looked up at me, then over at Reggie, who was helping some woman with some protein powder. "Oh my God. Do you really think?"

"Yes," I said flatly, eyeing the ginkgo, which he'd piled neatly on the register with a note. Signed with a smiley face. "I do."

"Well, that's just ridiculous," she said, her face flushing.

"Why? Reggie's nice."

"I don't have time for a relationship," she said, picking up her coffee and taking a gulp. The ginkgo she now eyed warily, like it was a time bomb, not a supplement. "It's almost Christmas. That's my busiest time of the year."

"It doesn't have to be one or the other."

"There's just no way," she said flatly, shaking her head.

"Why not?"

"Because it won't work." She banged open the register drawer, sliding in the receipts. "Right now, I can only focus on myself and this business. Everything else is a distraction."

I was about to tell her this didn't have to be true, necessarily. That she and Reggie already had a relationship: they were friends, and she could just see how it went from there. But really, I had to respect where she was coming from, even if in this case I didn't agree with it. After all, I'd been determined to be a one-woman operation, as well, although lately this had been harder than you'd think. I'd found this out firsthand a few days earlier, when I was in the kitchen with Cora, minding my own business, and suddenly found myself swept up in Jamie's holiday plans.

"Wait," Cora said, looking down at the shirt on the table in front of her. "What is this for again?"

"Our Christmas card!" Jamie said, reaching into the bag he was holding to pull out another shirt—also a denim button-up, identical to hers—and handing it to me. "Remember how I said I wanted to do a photo this year?"

"You want us to wear matching shirts?" Cora asked as he took out yet one more, holding it up against his chest. "Seriously?"

"Yeah," Jamie said. "It's gonna be great. Oh, and wait. I forgot the best part!"

He turned, jogging out of the room into the foyer.

Cora and I just stared at each other across the table.

"Matching shirts?" I said.

"Don't panic," she said, although her own expression was hardly calm. She looked down at her shirt again. "At least, not yet."

"Check it out," Jamie said, coming back into the room. He had something behind his back, which he now presented to us, with a flourish. "For Roscoe!"

It was—yes—a denim shirt. Dog sized. With a red bow tie sewn on. Maybe I should have been grateful mine didn't have one of these, but frankly, at that moment, I was too horrified.

"Jamie," Cora said as he bent down beneath the table. I could hear banging around, along with some snuffling, as I assumed he attempted to wrangle Roscoe, who'd been dead asleep, into his outfit. "I'm all for a Christmas card. But do you really think we need to match?"

"In my family, we *always* wore matching outfits," he said, his voice muffled from the underside of the table. "My mom used to make sweaters for all of us in the same colors. Then we'd pose, you know, by the stairs or the fireplace or whatever, for our card. So this is a continuation of the tradition."

I looked at Cora. *"Do something,"* I mouthed, and she nodded, holding up her hand.

"You know," she said as Jamie finally emerged from the table holding Roscoe, who looked none too happy and was already gnawing at the bow tie, "I just wonder if maybe a regular shot would work. Or maybe just one of Roscoe?"

Jamie's face fell. "You don't want to do a card with all of us?"

"Well," she said, glancing at me, "I just . . . I guess it's just not something we're used to. Me and Ruby, I mean. Things were different at our house. You know."

This, of course, was the understatement of the century. I had a few memories of Christmas when my parents were still together, but when my dad left, he pretty much took my mom's yuletide spirit with him. After that, I'd learned to dread the holidays. There was always too much drinking, not enough money, and with school out I was stuck with my mom, and only my mom, for weeks on end. No one was happier to see the New Year come than I was.

"But," Jamie said now, looking down at Roscoe, who had completely spit-soaked the bow tie and had now moved on to chewing the shirt's sleeve, "that's one reason I really wanted to do this."

"What is?"

"You," he said. "For you. I mean, and Ruby, too, of course. Because, you know, you missed out all those years."

I turned to Cora again, waiting for her to go to bat for us once more. Instead, she was just looking at her husband, and I could have sworn she was tearing up. Shit.

"You know what?" she said as Roscoe coughed up some bow tie. "You're absolutely right."

"What?" I said.

"It'll be fun," she told me. "And you look good in blue."

This was little comfort, though, a week later, when I found myself posing by the pond, Roscoe perched in my lap, as Jamie fiddled with his tripod and self-timer. Cora, beside me in her shirt, kept shooting me apologetic looks, which I was studiously ignoring. "You have to understand," she said under her breath as Roscoe tried to lick my face. "He's just like this. The house, and the security, this whole life. . . . He's always wanted to give me what I didn't have. It's really sweet, actually."

"Here we go!" Jamie said, running over to take his place on Cora's other side. "Get ready. One, two . . ."

At three, the camera clicked, then clicked again. Never in a million years I thought, when I saw the pictures later, stacked up next to their blank envelopes on the island. HAPPY HOLIDAYS FROM THE HUNTERS! it said, and looking at the shot, you could almost think I was one of them. Blue shirt and all.

I wasn't the only one being forced out of my comfort zone. About a week later, I was at my locker before first bell when I felt someone step up beside me. I turned, assuming it was Nate—the only person I ever really talked to at school on a regular basis—but was surprised to see Olivia Davis standing there instead.

"You were right," she said. No hello or how are you. Then again, she didn't have her phone to her ear, either, so maybe this was progress.

"About what?"

She bit her lip, looking off to the side for a moment as a couple of soccer players blew past, talking loudly. "Her name is Melissa. The girl my boyfriend was cheating with."

"Oh," I said. I shut my locker door slowly. "Right."

"It's been going on for weeks, and nobody told me," she

continued, sounding disgusted. "All the friends I have there, and everyone I talk to regularly . . . yet somehow, it just doesn't come up. I mean, come on."

I wasn't sure what to say to this. "I'm sorry," I told her. "That sucks."

Olivia shrugged, still looking across the hallway. "It's fine. Better I know than not, right?"

"Definitely," I agreed.

"Anyway," she said, her tone suddenly brisk, all business, "I just wanted to say, you know, thanks. For the tip."

"No problem."

Her phone rang, the sound already familiar to me, trilling from her pocket. She pulled it out, glancing at it, but didn't open it. "I don't like owing people things," she told me. "So you just let me know how we get even here, all right?"

"You don't owe me anything," I said as her phone rang again. "I just gave you a name."

"Still. It counts." Her phone rang once more, and now she did flip it open, putting it to her ear. "One sec," she said, then covered the receiver. "Anyway, keep it in mind."

I nodded, and then she was turning, walking away, already into her next conversation. So Olivia didn't like owing people. Neither did I. In fact, I didn't like people period, unless they gave me a reason to think otherwise. Or at least, that was the way I had been, not so long ago. But lately, I was beginning to think it was not just my setting that had changed.

Later that week, Nate and I were getting out of the car before school, Gervais having already taken off at his usual breakneck pace. By this point, we weren't attracting as much attention—there was another Rachel Webster, I supposed, providing grist for the gossip mill—although we still got a few looks. "So anyway," he was telling me, "then I said that I thought maybe, just maybe, she could hire me and my dad to get her house in order. I mean, you should see it. There's stuff piled up all over the place—mail and newspapers and laundry. God. *Piles* of laundry."

"Harriet?" I said. "Really? She's so organized at work."

"That's work, though," he replied. "I mean—"

"Nate!"

He stopped walking and turned to look over at a nearby red truck, a guy in a leather jacket and sunglasses standing next to it. "Robbie," he said. "What's up?"

"You tell me," the guy called back. "Coach said you've quit the team for good now. And you had that U scholarship in the bag, man. What gives?"

Nate glanced at me, then pulled his bag farther up his shoulder. "I'm just too busy," he said as the guy came closer. "You know how it is."

"Yeah, but come on," the guy replied. "We need you! Where's your senior loyalty?"

I heard Nate say something but couldn't make it out as I kept walking. This clearly had nothing to do with me. I was about halfway to the green when I glanced behind me. Already, Nate was backing away from the guy in the leather jacket, their conversation wrapping up.

I only had a short walk left to the green. The same one I would have been taking alone, all this time, if left to my own devices. But as I stepped up onto the curb, I had a flash of Olivia, her reluctant expression as she stood by my locker, wanting to be square, not owing me or anyone anything. It was a weird feeling, knowing you were indebted, if not connected. Even stranger, though, was being aware of this, not liking it, and yet still finding yourself digging in deeper, anyway. Like, for instance, consciously slowing your steps so it still looked accidental for someone to catch up from behind, a little out of breath, and walk with you the rest of the way.

* * *

The picture was of a group of people standing on a wide front porch. By their appearance—sideburns and loud prints on the men, printed flowy dresses and long hair on the women—I guessed it was taken sometime in the seventies. In the back, people were standing in haphazard rows; in the front, children were plopped down, sitting cross-legged. One boy had his tongue sticking out, while two little girls in front wore flowers in their hair. In the center, there was a girl in a white dress sitting in a chair, two elderly women on each side of her.

There had to be fifty people in all, some resembling each other, others looking like no one else around them. While a few were staring right into the camera with fixed smiles on their faces, others were laughing, looking off to one side or the other or at each other, as if not even aware a picture was being taken. It was easy to imagine the photographer giving up on trying to get the shot and instead just snapping the shutter, hoping for the best.

I'd found the photo on the island when I came downstairs, and I picked it up, carrying it over to the table to look at while I ate my breakfast. By the time Jamie came down twenty minutes later, I should have long moved on to the paper and my horoscope, but I was still studying it.

"Ah," he said, heading straight to the coffeemaker. "You found the ad. What do you think?"

"This is an ad?" I asked. "For what?"

He walked over to the island. "Actually," he said, digging around under some papers, "that's not the ad. This is."

He slid another piece of paper in front of me. At the top was the picture I'd been looking at, with the words IT'S ABOUT FAMILY in thick typewriter-style block print beneath it. Below that was another picture, taken in the present day, of a bunch of twenty-somethings gathered on what looked like the end zone of a football field. They were in T-shirts and jeans, some with arms around each other, others with hands lifted in the air, clearly celebrating something. IT'S ABOUT FRIENDS, it said underneath. Finally, a third picture, which was of a computer screen, filled with tiny square shots of smiling faces. Looking more closely, I could see they were same ones as in the other pictures, cut out and cropped down, then lined up end to end. Underneath, it said, IT'S ABOUT CONNECTING: UME.COM.

"The idea," Jamie explained over my shoulder, "is that while life is getting so individualistic—we all have our own phones, our own e-mail accounts, our own everything—we continue to use those things to reach out to each other. Friends, family . . . they're all part of communities we make and depend on. And UMe helps you do that."

"Wow," I said.

"Thousands spent on an advertising agency," he said,

reaching for the cereal box between us, "hours wasted in endless meetings, and a major print run about to drop any minute. And all you can say is 'wow'?"

"It's better than 'it sucks,'" Cora said, entering the kitchen with Roscoe at her heels. "Right?"

"Your sister," Jamie told me in a low voice, "does not like the campaign."

"I never said that," Cora told him, pulling the fridge open and taking out a container of waffles as Roscoe headed my way, sniffing the floor. "I only said that I thought your family might not like being featured, circa nineteen seventy-six, in magazines and bus shelters nationwide."

I looked back at the top picture, then at Jamie. "This is your family?"

"Yep," he said.

"And that's not even all of them," Cora added, sticking some waffles into the toaster oven. "Can you even believe that? They're not a family. They're a tribe."

"My grandmother was one of six children," Jamie explained.

"Ah," I said.

"You should have seen it when we got married," Cora said. "I felt like I'd crashed my own wedding. I didn't know *anybody*."

It took a beat for the awkwardness following this statement to hit, but when it did, we all felt it. Jamie glanced up at me, but I focused on finishing the bite of cereal I'd just taken, chewing carefully as Cora flushed and turned her attention to the toaster oven. Maybe it would have been easier to actually *acknowledge* the weirdness that was our estrangement and the fact that my mom and I hadn't even known Cora had gotten married, much less been invited to the wedding. But of course, we didn't. Instead we just sat there, until suddenly the smoke detector went off, breaking the silence.

"Shit," Jamie said, jumping up as ear-piercing beeping filled the room. Immediately I looked at Roscoe, whose ears had gone flat on his head. "What's burning?"

"It's this stupid toaster oven," Cora said, pulling it open and waving her hand back and forth in front of it. "It always does this. Roscoe, honey, it's okay—"

But it was too late. The dog was already bolting out of the room, in full flight mode, the way he'd taken to doing the last week or so. For some reason, Roscoe's appliance anxiety had been increasing, spurred on not only by the oven but anything in the kitchen that beeped or had the potential to do so. The smoke detector, though, remained his biggest fear. Which, I figured, meant that right about now he was probably up in my bathroom closet, his favorite hiding place of late, shaking among my shoes and waiting for the danger to pass.

Jamie grabbed the broom, reaching it up to hit the detector's reset button, and finally the beeping stopped. As he got down and came back to the table, Cora followed him, sliding into a chair with her waffle, which she then nibbled at halfheartedly.

"It may be time to call a professional," she said after a moment.

"I'm not putting the dog on antidepressants," Jamie told her, picking up the paper and scanning the front page. "I don't care how relaxed Denise's dachshund is now."

"Lola is a Maltese," Cora said, "and it wouldn't necessarily mean that. Maybe there's some training we can do, something that will help him."

"We can't keep coddling him, though," Jamie said. "You know what the books say. Every time you pick him up or soothe him when he's freaking out like that, you're reinforcing the behavior."

"So you'd prefer we just stand by and let him be traumatized?"

"Of course not," Jamie said.

Cora put down her waffle, wiping her mouth with a napkin. "Then I just think that there's got to be a way to acknowledge his fear and at the same time—"

"Cora." Jamie put down the paper. "He's a dog, not a child. This isn't a self-esteem issue. It's Pavlovian. Okay?"

Cora just looked at him for a moment. Then she pushed back her chair, getting to her feet, and walked to the island, dropping her plate into the sink with a loud clank.

As she left the room, Jamie sighed, running a hand over his face as I pulled the family picture back toward me. Again, I found myself studying it: the varied faces, some smiling, some not, the gentle regalness of the elderly women, who were staring right into the camera. Across the table, Jamie was just sitting there, looking out at the pond.

"I do like the ad, you know," I said to him finally. "It's cool."

"Thanks," he said, distracted.

"Are you in this picture?" I asked him.

He glanced over at it as he pushed his chair out and got

to his feet. "Nah. Before my time. I didn't come along for a few more years. That's my mom, though, in the white dress. It was her wedding day."

As he left the room, I looked down at the picture again, and at the girl in the center, noticing how serene and happy she looked surrounded by all those people. I couldn't imagine what it would be like to be one of so many, to have not just parents and siblings but cousins and aunts and uncles, an entire tribe to claim as your own. Maybe you would feel lost in the crowd. Or sheltered by it. Whatever the case, one thing was for sure: like it or not, you'd never be alone.

* * *

Fifteen minutes later I was standing in the warmth of the foyer, waiting for Nate to pull up at the mailbox, when the phone rang.

"Cora?" the caller said, skipping a hello.

"No," I said. "This is—"

"Oh, Ruby, hi!" The voice was a woman's, entirely perky. "It's Denise, Cora's old roommate—from the party?"

"Right. Hi," I said, turning my head as Cora came down the stairs, briefcase in her hand.

"So how's life?" Denise asked. "School okay? It's gotta be a big adjustment, starting at a new place. But Cora did say it's not the first time you've switched schools. Personally, I lived in the same place my whole entire life, which is really not much better, actually, because—"

"Here's Cora," I said, holding the phone out as she got to the bottom step.

"Hello?" Cora said as she took it from me. "Oh, hey.

Yeah. At nine." She reached up, tucking a piece of hair behind her ear. "I will."

I walked over to the window by the door, looking for Nate. He was usually right on time, and when he wasn't, it was often because Gervais—who had trouble waking up in the morning and was often dragged to the car by his mother—held things up.

"No, I'm all right," Cora was saying. She'd gone down the hallway, but only a few steps. "Things are just kind of tense. I'll call you after, okay? Thanks for remembering. Yeah. Bye."

There was a beep as she hung up. When I glanced back at her, she said, "Look. About earlier, and what I said about the wedding. . . . I didn't mean to make you feel uncomfortable."

"It's fine," I said just as the phone rang again. She looked down at it, then answered.

"Charlotte, hey. Can I call you back? I'm kind of in the middle of—Yeah. Nine a.m. Well, hopefully." She nodded. "I know. Positivity. I'll let you know how it goes. Okay. Bye."

This time, as she hung up, she sighed, then sat down on the bottom step, laying the phone beside her. When she saw me watching her she said, "I have a doctor's appointment this morning."

"Oh," I said. "Is everything—are you all right?"

"I don't know," she replied. Then she quickly added, "I mean, I'm fine, health-wise. I'm not sick or anything."

I nodded, not sure what to say.

"It's just . . ." She smoothed her skirt with both hands.

"We've been trying to get pregnant for a while, and it's just not happening. So we're meeting with a specialist."

"Oh," I said again.

"It's all right," she said quickly. "Lots of people have problems like this. I just thought you should know, in case you ever have to take a message from a doctor's office or something. I didn't want you to worry."

I nodded, turning back to the window. This would be a great time for Nate to show up, I thought. But of course he didn't. Stupid Gervais. And then I heard Cora draw in a breath.

"And like I was saying, about earlier," she said. "About the wedding. I just . . . I didn't want you to feel like I was . . ."

"It's fine," I said again.

". . . still mad about that. Because I'm not."

It took me a moment to process this, like the sentence fell apart between us and I had to string the words back together. "Mad?" I said finally. "About what?"

"You and Mom not coming," she said. She sighed. "Look, we don't have to talk about this. It's ancient history. But this morning, when I said that thing about the wedding, you just looked so uncomfortable, and I knew you probably felt bad. So I thought maybe it would be better to just clear the air. Like I said, I'm not mad anymore."

"You didn't invite us to your wedding," I said.

Now she looked surprised. "Yes," she said slowly. "I did."

"Well, then the invitation must have gotten lost in the mail, because—"

"I brought it to Mom, Ruby," she said.

"No, you didn't." I swallowed, taking a breath. "You . . . you haven't seen Mom in years."

"That's not true," she said simply, as if I'd told her the wrong time, something that innocuous. "I brought the invitation to her personally, at the place she was working at the time. I wanted you there."

Cars were passing by the mailbox, and I knew any moment one of them would be Nate's, and I'd have to leave. But right then, I couldn't even move. I was flattened against the window, as if someone had knocked the wind out of me. "No," I said again. "You disappeared. You went to college, and you were gone. We never heard from you."

She looked down at her skirt. Then, quietly, she said, "That's not true."

"It is. I was there." But even to me, I sounded unsure, at the one time I wanted—needed—to be absolutely positive. "If you'd ever tried to reach us—"

"Of *course* I tried to reach you," she said. "I mean, the time I spent tracking you down alone was—"

Suddenly, she stopped talking. Mid-sentence, mid-breath. In the silence that followed, a red BMW drove past, then a blue minivan. Normal people, off to their normal lives. "Wait," she said after a moment. "You do know about all that, don't you? You have to. There's no way she could have—"

"I have to go," I said, but when I reached down for the doorknob and twisted it, I heard her get to her feet and come up behind me.

"Ruby, look at me," she said, but I stayed where I was,

facing the small crack in the door, feeling cold air coming through. "All I wanted was to find you. The entire time I was in college, and after. . . . I was trying to get you out of there."

Now, of course, Nate did pull up to the curb. Perfect timing. "You left that day, for school," I said, turning to face her. "You never came back. You didn't call or write or show up for holidays—"

"Is that what you really think?" she demanded.

"That's what I know."

"Well, you're wrong," she said. "Think about it. All those moves, all those houses. A different school every time. The jobs she could never hold, the phone that was rarely hooked up, and then never in her real name. Did you ever wonder why she put down fake addresses on all your school stuff? Do you think that was some kind of accident? Do you have any idea how hard she made it for me to find you?"

"You didn't try," I said, and now my voice was cracking, loud and shaky, rising up into the huge space above us.

"I did," Cora said. Distantly, from outside, I heard a beep: Nate, getting impatient. "For years I did. Even when she told me to stop, that you wanted nothing to do with me. Even when you ignored my letters and messages—"

My throat was dry, hard, as I tried to swallow.

"—I still kept coming back, reaching out, all the way up to the wedding. She swore she would give you the invitation, give you the choice to come or not. By that time I had threatened to get the courts involved so I could see you, which was the last thing she wanted, so she promised me. She *promised* me, Ruby. But she couldn't do it. She upped and moved you away again instead. She was so afraid of being alone, of you leaving, too, that she never gave you the chance. Until this year, when she knew that you'd be turning eighteen, and you could, and most likely would. So what did she do?"

"Stop it," I said.

"She left you," she finished. "Left you alone, in that filthy house, before you could do the same to her."

I felt something rising in my throat—a sob, a scream—and bit it back, tears filling my eyes, and I hated myself for crying, showing any weakness here. "You don't know what you're talking about," I said.

"I do, though." And now her voice was soft. Sad. Like she felt sorry for me, which was the most shameful thing of all. "That's the thing. I do."

Nate beeped again, louder and longer this time. "I have to go," I said, yanking the door open.

"Wait," Cora said. "Don't just—"

But I ran outside, pulling the door shut behind me. I didn't want to talk anymore. I didn't want anything, except a moment of peace and quiet to be alone and try to figure what exactly had just happened. All those years there were so many things I couldn't rely on, but this, the story of what had happened to my family, had always been a given, understood. Now, though, I wasn't so sure. What do you do when you only have two people in your life, neither of whom you've ever been able to fully trust, and yet you have to believe one of them?

I heard the door open again. "Ruby," Cora called out. "Just wait a second. We can't leave it like this."

But this, too, wasn't true. Leaving was easy. It was everything else that was so damned hard.

* * *

I'd only just gotten my door shut and seat belt on when it started.

"What's wrong with *you*? You look like crap."

I ignored Gervais, instead keeping my eyes fixed straight ahead. Still, I could feel Nate looking at me, concerned, so I said, "I'm fine. Let's just go." It took him another moment, but then he was finally hitting the gas and we were pulling away.

For the first few blocks, I just tried to breathe. *It's not true,* I kept thinking, and yet in the next beat it was all coming back: those moves and new schools, and the paperwork we always fudged—addresses, phone—because of bad landlords or creditors. The phones that were never hooked up, that graduation announcement my mom had said was just sent out automatically. *Just you and me, baby. Just you and me.*

I swallowed, keeping my eyes on the back of the bus in front of us, which was covered with an ad reading IT'S A FESTIVAL OF SALADS! I narrowed my focus to just these five words, holding them in the center of my vision, even as there was a loud, ripping burp from behind me.

"Gervais." Nate hit his window button. As it went down he said, "What did we just spend a half hour talking about with your mom?"

"I don't know," Gervais replied, giggling.

"Then let me refresh your memory," Nate said. "The burping and farting and rudeness stops right now. Or else."

"Or else what?"

We pulled up to a red light, and Nate turned around, then leaned back between our seats. Suddenly, he was so close to me that even in my distracted state I couldn't help but breathe in the scent of the USWIM sweatshirt he had on: a mix of clean and chlorine, the smell of water. "Or else," he said, his voice sounding very un-Nate-like, stern and serious, "you go back to riding with the McClellans."

"No way!" Gervais said. "The McClellans are *first-graders*. Plus, I'd have to walk from the lower school."

Nate shrugged. "So get up earlier."

"I'm *not* getting up earlier," Gervais squawked. "It's already too early!"

"Then quit being such a pain in the ass," Nate told him, turning back around as the light changed.

A moment later I felt Nate glance at me. I knew he was probably expecting a thank-you, since he'd clearly gone to Mrs. Miller that morning to talk about Gervais because of what I'd said, trying to make things better. But I was so tired, suddenly, of being everyone's charity case. I never asked anyone to help me. If you felt compelled to anyway, that was your problem, not mine.

When we pulled into the lot five minutes later, for the first time I beat Gervais out of the car, pushing my door open before we were even at a full stop. I was already a row of cars away when Nate yelled after me. "Ruby," he said. "Wait up."

But I didn't, not this time. I just kept going, walking faster. By the time I reached the green, the first bell hadn't yet rung, and people were everywhere, pressing on all sides.

When I saw the door to the bathroom, I just headed straight for it.

Inside, there were girls at the sinks checking their make-up and talking on the phone, but the stalls were all empty as I walked past them, sliding into the one by the wall and locking the door. Then I leaned against it, closing my eyes.

All those years I'd given up Cora for lost, hated her for leaving me. What if I had been wrong? What if, somehow, my mother had managed to keep her away, the only other person I'd ever had? And if she had, why?

She left you, Cora had said, and it was these three words, then and now, that I heard most clearly of all, slicing through the roaring in my head like someone speaking right into my ear. I didn't want this to make sense, for her to be right in any way. But even I could not deny the logic of it. My mother had been abandoned by a husband and one daughter; she'd had enough of being left. So she'd done what she had to do to make sure it didn't happen again. And this, above all else, I could understand. It was the same thing I'd been planning to do myself.

The bell rang overhead, and the bathroom slowly cleared out, the door banging open and shut as people headed off to class. Then, finally, it was quiet, the hallways empty, the only sound the flapping of the flag out on the green, which I could hear from the high half-open windows that ran along the nearby wall.

When I was sure I was alone, I left the stall and walked over to the sinks, dropping my bag at my feet. In the mirror overhead, I realized Gervais had been right: I looked terrible, my face blotchy and red. I reached down, watching my fingers as they picked up the key at my neck, then closed themselves tightly around it.

"I told you, I had to get a pass and sign out," I heard a voice say suddenly from outside. "Because this place is like a prison, okay? Look, just hold tight. I'll be there as soon as I can."

I looked outside, just in time to see Olivia passing by, phone to her ear, walking down the breezeway to the parking lot. As soon as I saw her take her keys out of her backpack, I grabbed my bag and bolted.

I caught up with her by a row of lockers just as she was folding her phone into her back pocket. "Hey," I called out, my voice bouncing off the empty corridor all around us. "Where are you going?"

When she turned around and saw me, her expression was wary, at best. Then again, with my blotchy face, not to mention being completely out of breath, I couldn't exactly blame her. "I have to go pick up my cousin. Why?"

I came closer, taking a breath. "I need a ride."

"Where?"

"Anywhere."

She raised her eyebrows. "I'm going to Jackson, then home. Nowhere else. I have to be back here by third."

"That's fine," I told her. "Perfect, in fact."

"You have a pass?"

I shook my head.

"So you want me to just take you off campus anyway, risking my ass, even though it's totally against the rules."

"Yes," I said.

She shook her head, no deal.

"But we'll be square," I added. "You won't owe me anymore."

"This is way more than what I owe you," she said. She studied my face for a moment, and I stood there, waiting for her verdict. She was right, this was probably stupid of me. But I was tired of playing it smart. Tired of everything.

"All right," she said finally. "But I'm not taking you from here. Get yourself to the Quik Zip, and I'll pick you up."

"Done," I told her, pulling my bag over my shoulder. "See you there."

Chapter Eight

When I slid into Olivia's front seat ten minutes later, my foot immediately hit something, then crunched it flat. Looking down, I saw it was a popcorn tub, the kind you buy at the movies, and it wasn't alone: there were at least four more rolling across the floorboards.

"I work at the Vista Ten," she explained, her engine puttering as she switched into reverse. "It pays crap, but we get all the free popcorn we can eat."

"Right," I said. Now that I thought of it, that did explain the butter smell.

We pulled out onto the main road, then merged into traffic and headed for the highway. I'd spent so much time riding with Jamie and Nate that I'd almost forgotten what it was like to be in a regular car, i.e., one that was not new and loaded with every possible gadget and extra. Olivia's Toyota was battered, the fabric of the seats nubby, with several stains visible, and there was one of those prisms hanging on a cord dangling from the rearview. It reminded me of my mother's Subaru, the thought of which gave me a pang I quickly pushed away, focusing instead on the entrance to the highway, rising up in the distance.

"So what's the deal?" Olivia asked as we merged into traffic, her muffler rattling.

"With what?"

"You."

"No deal," I said, sitting back and propping my feet on the dashboard.

She eyed my feet pointedly. I dropped them back down again. "So you just decided to cut school for the hell of it," she said.

"Pretty much."

We were getting closer, passing another exit. The one to Jackson was next. "You know," she said, "you can't just show up and hang out on campus. They're not as organized as Perkins, but they *will* kick you off."

"I'm not going to campus," I told her.

When we came over the hill five minutes later and Jackson came into view—big, sprawling, trailers lined up behind—I felt myself relax. After so many weeks of being out of place, it was nice to finally see something familiar. Olivia pulled up in front, where there was a row of faded plastic benches. Sitting on the last one was a heavyset black girl with short hair and glasses. When she saw us, she slowly got to her feet and began to shuffle in our direction.

"Oh, look at this," Olivia said loudly, rolling down her window. "Seems like *someone* should have listened to someone else who said maybe running a mile wasn't such a smart idea."

"It's not because of the running," the girl grumbled, pulling open the back door and sliding gingerly onto the seat. "I think I have the flu."

"All the books say you should start slow," Olivia continued. "But not you. You have to sprint the first day."

"Just shut up and give me some Advil, would you please?"

Olivia rolled her eyes, then reached across me and popped the glove compartment. She pulled out a bottle of pills, then chucked it over her shoulder. "This is Laney, by the way," Olivia said, banging the glove compartment shut again. "She thinks she can run a marathon."

"It's a five-K," Laney said. "And some support would be nice."

"I'm supportive," Olivia told her, turning around in her seat. "I support you so much that I'm the only one telling you this isn't a good idea. That maybe, just maybe, you could hurt yourself."

Laney just looked at her as she downed two Advils, then popped the cap back on. "Pain is part of running," she said. "That's why it's an endurance sport."

"You don't know anything about endurance!" Olivia turned to me. "One night she sees that crazy woman Kiki Sparks in one of those infomercials, talking about caterpillars and butterflies and potential and setting fitness goals. Next think you know, she thinks she's Lance Armstrong."

"Lance Armstrong is a cyclist," Laney pointed out, wincing as she shifted her weight. "That's not even a valid analogy."

Olivia harrumphed but withheld further comment as we pulled forward out of the turnaround. As she put on her blinker to turn left, I said, "Do you mind going the other way? It's not far."

"There's nothing up there but woods," she said.

"It'll only take a minute."

I saw her glance back at Laney in the rearview, but then

she was turning, slowly, the engine chugging as we headed up the hill. The parking lots gave way to more parking lots, which then turned into scrub brush. About half a mile later, I told her to slow down.

"This is good," I said as we came up on the clearing. Sure enough, there were two cars parked there, and I could see Aaron, Peyton's ex—a chubby guy with a baby face he tried to counter by dressing in all black and scowling a lot—sitting on one of them, smoking a cigarette. "Thanks for the ride."

Olivia looked over at them, then back at me. "You want to get out here?"

"Yeah," I said.

She was clearly skeptical. "How are you planning to get back?"

"I'll find a way," I said. I got out of the car and picked up my bag. She was still watching me, so I added, "Look, don't worry."

"I'm not worried," she said. "I don't even know you."

Still, she kept her eyes on me while Laney opened the back door and slid out slowly, taking her time as she made her way into the front seat. As she pulled the door shut, Olivia said, "You know, I can take you home, if you want. I mean, I'm missing third by now, anyway, thanks to Laney."

I shook my head. "No, I'm good. I'll see you at school, okay?"

She nodded slowly as I patted the roof of the car, then turned around and headed for the clearing. Aaron squinted at me, then sat up straighter. "Hey, Ruby," he called out as I approached. "Welcome back."

"Thanks," I said, hopping up on the hood beside him. Olivia had stayed where I left her, watching me from behind the wheel, but now she moved forward, turning around in the dead end, her engine put-putting. The prism hanging from her rearview caught the light for a moment, throwing sparks, and then she was sliding past, over the hill and out of sight. "It's good to be here."

* * *

I'd actually come looking for Peyton, who had a free second period and often skipped third to boot, spending both at the clearing. But Aaron, whose schedule was flexible due to a recent expulsion, claimed he hadn't seen her, so I settled in to wait. That had been a couple of hours ago.

"Hey."

I felt something nudge my foot. Then again, harder. When I opened my eyes, Aaron was holding out a joint, the tip smoldering. I tried to focus on it, but it kept blurring, slightly to one side, then the other. "I'm okay," I said.

"Oh, yeah," he said flatly, putting it to his own lips and taking a big drag. In his black shirt and jeans, his white skin seemed so pale, almost glowing. "You're just fine."

I leaned back, then felt my head bonk hard against something behind me. Turning slightly, I saw thick treads, sloping metal, and I could smell rubber. It took me another minute, though, to realize I was sitting against a car. There was grass beneath me and trees all around; looking up, I could see a bright blue sky. I was still at the clearing, although how I got on the ground I wasn't exactly sure.

This was because I was also drunk, the result of the pint of vodka we'd shared soon after I'd arrived. That I remembered at least partially—him pulling out the bottle from his pocket, along with a couple of orange-juice cartons someone had nicked from the cafeteria during breakfast. We'd poured some of each into an empty Zip cup, then shook them up, cocktail style, and toasted each other in his front seat, the radio blasting. And repeat, until the orange juice was gone. Then we'd switched to straight shots, each burning a little less as they went down.

"Damn," he'd said, wiping his mouth as he passed the bottle back to me. The wind had been blowing, all the trees swaying, and everything felt distant and close all at once, just right. "Since when are you such a lush, Cooper?"

"Always," I remembered telling him. "It's in my genes."

Now he took another deep drag, sputtering slightly as he held it in. My head felt heavy, fluid, as he exhaled, the smoke blowing across me. I closed my eyes, trying to lose myself in it. That morning, all I'd wanted was to feel oblivious, block out everything I'd heard about my mom from Cora. And for a while, sitting with him and singing along to the radio, I had. Now, though, I could feel it hovering again, crouching just out of sight.

"Hey," I said, forcing my eyes open and turning my head. "Let me get a hit off that."

He held it out. As I took it, my fingers fumbled and it fell to the ground between us, disappearing into the grass. "Shit," I said, digging around until I felt heat—pricking, sudden—against my skin. As I came up with it, I had to concentrate on guiding it to my mouth slowly, easing my lips around it before pulling in a big drag.

The smoke was thick, sinking down into my lungs, and

feeling it I sat back again, my head hitting the fender behind me. God, this was good. Just floating and distant, every worry receding like a wave rushing out and then pulling back, wiping the sand clean behind it. I had a flash of myself, walking through these same woods not so long ago, feeling this same way: loose and easy, everything still ahead. Then I hadn't been alone, either. I'd been with Marshall.

Marshall. I opened my eyes, squinting down at my watch until it came into focus. That was what I needed right now—just any kind of closeness, even if it was only for a little while. Sandpiper Arms was only a short walk from here, via a path through the woods; we'd done it tons of times.

"Where you going?" Aaron asked, his voice heavy as I pushed myself to my feet, stumbling slightly before regaining my footing. "I thought we were hanging out."

"I'll be back," I told him, and started for the path.

By the time I reached the bottom of Marshall's stairs, I felt slightly more coherent, although I was sweating from the walk, and I could feel a headache setting in. I took a moment to smooth down my hair and make myself slightly more presentable, then pushed on up to the door and knocked hard. A moment later, the door creaked open, and Rogerson peered out at me.

"Hey," I said. My voice sounded low, liquidy. "Is Marshall home?"

"Uh," he replied, looking over his shoulder. "I don't know."

"It's cool if he's not," I told him. "I can wait in his room."

He looked at me for a long moment, during which I felt myself sway, slightly. Then he stepped aside.

The apartment was dark, as usual, as I moved down the hallway to the living room. "You know," Rogerson said from behind me, his voice flat, "he probably won't be back for a while."

But at that point, I didn't care. All I wanted was to collapse onto the bed, pulling the sheets around me, and sleep, finally able to block out everything that had happened since I'd woken up in my own room that morning. Just to be someplace safe, someplace I knew, with someone, anyone, familiar nearby.

When I pushed open the door, the first thing I saw was that Whitman's sampler. It caught my eye even before I recognized Peyton, who was sitting beside it, a chocolate in her hand. I watched, frozen, as she reached it out to Marshall, who was lying beside her, hands folded over his chest, and dropped it into his open mouth. This was just the simplest gesture, taking mere seconds, but at the same time there was something so intimate about it—the way his lips closed over her fingers, how she giggled, her cheeks pink, before drawing them back—that I felt sick, even before Marshall turned his head and saw me.

I don't know what I was expecting him to do or say, if anything. To be surprised, or sorry, or even sad. In the end, though, his expression said it all: I Could Care Less.

"Oh, *shit*," Peyton gasped. "Ruby, I'm so—"

"Oh my God," I said, stumbling backward out of the door frame. I put my hand to my mouth as I turned, bumping the wall as I ran back down the hallway to the front door. Vaguely, I could hear her calling after me, but I ignored this as I burst out into the daylight again, gripping the banister as I ran down to the parking lot.

"Ruby, wait," Peyton was yelling, her own steps loud on the stairs as she followed me. "Jesus! Just let me explain!"

"Explain?" I said, whirling to face her. "How in the world do you explain this?"

She stopped by the banister, hand to her heart, to catch her breath. "I tried to tell you," she gasped. "That night, at your house. But it was so hard, and then you kept saying how things had changed, anyway, so—"

Suddenly, something clicked in my brain, and I had a flash of her that night, in the foyer with Roscoe and Jamie, then of Marshall handing me back my key that last time I'd seen him. *You told me you lived in Wildflower Ridge,* she'd said, but I was sure I hadn't. I was right. He had.

"That's why you came over?" I asked. "To tell me you were sleeping with my boyfriend?"

"You never called him that!" she shot back, pointing at me. "Not even once. You just said you had a *thing,* an *arrangement.* I thought I was being nice, wanting to tell you."

"I don't need you to be nice to me," I snapped.

"Of course you don't," she replied. At the top of the stairs, I could see Rogerson just past the open door, looking down at us. We were making a scene, the last thing he wanted. "You don't need anything. Not a boyfriend, not a friend. You were always so clear about that. And that's what you got. So why are you surprised now?"

I just stood there, looking at her. My head was spinning, my mouth dry, and all I could think about was that I wanted to go someplace safe, someplace I could be alone and okay, and that this was impossible. My old life had changed and my new one was still in progress, altering by the second. There was nothing, *nothing* to depend on. And why *was* I surprised?

I walked away from her, back to the path, but as I entered the woods I was having trouble keeping on it, roots catching my feet, branches scratching me from all sides. I was so tired—of this day, of everything—even as it all came rushing back: Cora's face in the foyer that morning, Olivia's prism glinting in the sun, stepping into the familiar dimness of the apartment, so sure of what I was there for.

As I stumbled again, I started to catch myself, then stopped, instead just letting my body go limp, hitting knees first, then elbows, in the leaves. Up ahead, I could see the edge of the clearing, and Aaron looking at me, but it suddenly felt right, even perfect, to be alone. So as I lay back on the ground, the sky already spinning above me, I tried to focus again on the idea of that wave I'd thought of earlier, wiping everything clean, blue and big and wide enough to suck me in. Maybe it was a wish, or a dream. Either way, it was so real that at some point, I could actually feel it. Like a presence coming closer, with arms that closed around me, lifting me up with a scent that filled my senses: clean and pure, a touch of chlorine. The smell of water.

* * *

The first thing I saw when I opened my eyes was Roscoe.

He was sitting on the empty seat beside me, right in front of the steering wheel, facing forward, panting. As I tried to focus, I suddenly smelled dog breath—ugh—and my stomach twisted. *Shit,* I thought, bolting forward, my hand fumbling for the door handle. Just in time, though,

I saw the Double Burger bag positioned between my feet. I'd only barely grabbed it and put it to my lips before I was puking up something hot and burning that I could feel all the way to my ears.

My hands were shaking as I eased the bag onto the floor, then sat back, my heart thumping in my chest. I was freezing, even though I was now wearing a USWIM sweatshirt that looked awfully familiar. Looking outside, I saw we were parked in some kind of strip mall—I could see a dry-cleaner and a video store—and I had no idea how I'd gotten here. In fact the only thing familiar, other than the dog, was the air freshener hanging from the rearview, which said: WE WORRY SO YOU DON'T HAVE TO.

Oh my God, I thought as these things all suddenly collided. I looked down at the sweatshirt again, breathing in that water smell, distant and close all at once. Nate.

Suddenly, Roscoe let out a yap, which was amplified by the small space around us. He leaped up on the driver's-side window, nails tap-tapping, his nub of a tail wriggling around wildly. I was wondering whether I was going to puke again when I heard a pop and felt a rush of fresh air from behind me.

Immediately, Roscoe bounded into the backseat, his tags jingling. It took me considerably longer to turn myself around—God, my head was pounding—and focus enough to see Nate, at the back of his car, easing in a pile of dry-cleaning. When he looked up and saw me, he said, "Hey, you're conscious. Good."

Good? I thought, but then he was slamming the back door shut (ouch) before walking around to pull open the driver's-side door and get in behind the wheel. As he slid his keys into the ignition, he glanced over at the bag at my feet. "How you doing there? Need another one yet?"

"Another one?" I said. My voice was dry, almost cracking on the words. "This . . . this isn't the first?"

He shot me a sympathetic look. "No," he said. "It isn't."

As if to punctuate this, my stomach rolled threateningly as he began to back out of the space. I tried to calm it, as Roscoe climbed up between our two seats, sticking his head forward and closing his eyes while Nate rolled down his window, letting in some fresh air.

"What time is it?" I asked, trying to keep my voice level, if only to control the nausea.

"Almost five," Nate replied.

"Are you serious?"

"What time did you think it was?"

Honestly, I didn't even know. I'd lost track of time on the walk back to the clearing when everything went fluid. "What—?" I said, then stopped, realizing I wasn't even sure what I was about to ask. Or even where to begin. "What is Roscoe doing here?"

Nate glanced back at the dog, who was still riding high, his ears blowing back in the wind. "He had a four o'clock vet appointment," he said. "Cora and Jamie both had to work, so they hired me to take him. When I went to pick him up and you weren't at home, I figured I'd better go looking for you."

"Oh," I said. I looked at Roscoe, who immediately took this as an invitation to start licking my face. I pushed him away, moving closer to the window. "But how did you—?"

"Olivia," he said. I blinked, a flash of her driving away popping into my head. "That's her name, right? The girl with the braids?"

I nodded slowly, still trying to piece this together. "You know Olivia?"

"No," he said. "She just came up to me before fourth period and said she'd left you in the woods—at your request, she was very clear on that—and thought I should know."

"Why would you need to know?"

He shrugged. "I guess she thought you might need a friend."

Hearing this, I felt my face flush, suddenly embarrassed. Like I was so desperate and needing to be rescued that people—strangers—were actually convening to discuss it. My worst nightmare. "I was with my friends," I said. "Actually."

"Yeah?" he asked, glancing over at me. "Well, then, they must be the invisible kind. Because when I got there, you were alone."

What? I thought. That couldn't be true. Aaron had been right there in the clearing, and he'd seen me lie down. Now that I thought about it, though, it had been midday then; it was late afternoon now. If Nate was telling the truth, how long had I been there, alone and passed out? *Are you surprised?* I heard Peyton say again in my head, and a shiver ran over me. I wrapped my arms around myself, looking out the window. The buildings were blurring past, but I tried to find just one I could recognize, as if I could somehow locate myself that way.

"Look," Nate said, "what happened today is over. It doesn't matter, okay? We'll get you home, and everything will be fine."

Hearing this, I felt my eyes well up unexpectedly with hot tears. It was bad to be embarrassed, hard to be ashamed. But pitied? That was the worst of all. Of course Nate would think this could all be so easily resolved. It was how things happened in his world, where he was a friendly guy and worried so you didn't have to as he went about living his life of helpful errands and good deeds. Unlike me, so dirty and used up and broken. I had a flash of Marshall looking over his shoulder at me, and my head pounded harder.

"Hey," Nate said now, as if he could hear me thinking this, slipping further and further down this slope. "It's okay."

"It's not," I said, keeping my eyes fixed on the window. "You couldn't even understand."

"Try me."

"No." I swallowed, pulling my arms tighter around myself. "It's not your problem."

"Ruby, come on. We're friends."

"Stop saying that," I said.

"Why?"

"Because it's not true," I said, now turning to face him. "We don't even know each other. You just live behind me and give me a ride to school. Why do you think that makes us somehow something?"

"Fine," he said, holding up his hands. "We're not friends."

And now I was a bitch. We rode in silence for a block, Roscoe panting between us. "Look," I said, "I appreciate what you did. What you've done. But the thing is . . . my life isn't like yours, okay? I'm messed up."

"Everybody's messed up," he said quietly.

"Not like me," I told him. I thought of Olivia in English class, throwing up her hands: *Tell us about your pain. We're riveted!* "Do you even know why I came to live with Cora and Jamie?"

He glanced over at me. "No," he said.

"Because my mom abandoned me." My voice felt tight, but I took a breath and kept going. "A couple of months ago, she packed up and took off while I was at school. I was living alone for weeks until my landlords busted me and turned me in to social services. Who then called Cora, who I hadn't seen in ten years, since *she* took off for school and never contacted me again."

"I'm sorry." This response was automatic, so easy.

"That's not why I'm telling you." I sighed, shaking my head. "Do you remember that house I brought you to that day? It wasn't a friend's. It was—"

"Yours," he finished for me. "I know."

I looked over at him, surprised. "You knew?"

"You had the key around your neck," he said quietly, glancing at it. "It was kind of obvious."

I blinked, feeling ashamed all over again. Here at least I thought I'd managed to hide something from Nate that day, kept a part of me a secret, at least until I was ready to reveal it. But I'd been wide open, exposed, all along.

We were coming up on Wildflower Ridge now, and as Nate began to slow down, Roscoe jumped onto my seat, clambering across me to press his muzzle against the window. Without thinking, I reached up to deposit him back where he'd come from, but as soon as I touched him he sank backward, settling into my lap as if this was the most natural thing in the world. For one of us, anyway.

When Nate pulled up in front of Cora's, I could see the kitchen lights were on, and both her and Jamie's cars were in the driveway, even though it was early for either of them to be home, much less both. Not a good sign. I reached up, smoothing my hair out of my face, and tried to ready myself before pushing open the door.

"You can tell them he got his shots and the vet said everything's fine," Nate said, reaching into the backseat for Roscoe's leash. Seeing it, the dog leaped up again, moving closer, and he clipped it on his collar. "And if they want to pursue behavioral training for the anxiety thing, she has a couple of names she can give them."

"Right," I said. He handed the leash to me, and I took it, picking up my bag with the other hand as I slowly slid out of the car. Roscoe, of course, followed with total eagerness, stretching the leash taut as he pulled me to the house. "Thanks."

Nate nodded, not saying anything, and I shut the door. Just as I started up the walk, though, I heard the whirring of a window lowering. When I turned around, he said, "Hey, and for what it's worth? Friends don't leave you alone in the woods. Friends are the ones who come and take you out."

I just looked at him. At my feet, Roscoe was straining at his leash, wanting to go home.

"At least," Nate said, "that's been my experience. I'll see you, okay?"

I nodded, and then his window slid back up, and he was pulling away.

As I watched him go, Roscoe was still tugging, trying to pull me closer to the house. My instinct was to do the total opposite, even though by now I'd left, and been left, enough times to know that neither of them was good, or easy, or even preferable. Still, it wasn't until we started up the walk to those waiting bright lights that I realized this—coming back—was the hardest of all.

* * *

"Where the hell have you been?"

It was Cora I was braced for, Cora I was expecting to be waiting when I pushed open the door. Instead, the first thing I saw was Jamie. And he was *pissed*.

"Jamie," I heard Cora say. She was at the end of the hall, standing in the doorway to the kitchen. Roscoe, who had bolted the minute I dropped his leash, was already circling her feet, sniffling wildly. "At least let her get inside."

"Do you have any idea how worried we've been?" Jamie demanded.

"I'm sorry," I said.

"Do you even *care*?" he said.

I looked down the hallway at my sister, who had picked Roscoe up and was now watching me. Her eyes were red, a tissue in her hand, and as I realized she, like Jamie, was still in the clothes she'd had on that morning, I suddenly remembered their doctor's appointment.

"Are you *drunk*?" Jamie said. I looked at the mirror by the stairs, finally seeing myself: I looked terrible—in Nate's baggy sweatshirt—and clearly, I stank of booze and who knew what else. I looked tired and faded and so familiar, suddenly, that I had to turn away, sinking down onto the bottom stair behind me. "This is what you do, after we take you in, put you in a great school, give you everything you need? You just run off and get *wasted*?"

I shook my head, a lump rising in my throat. It had been such a long, terrible day that it felt like years ago, entire lifetimes, since I'd been in this same place arguing with Cora that morning.

"We gave you the benefit of the doubt," Jamie was saying. "We gave you *everything*. And this is how you thank us?"

"Jamie," Cora said again, louder this time. "Stop it."

"We don't need this," he said, coming closer. I pulled my knees to my chest, trying to make myself smaller. I deserved this, I knew it, and I just wanted it to be over. "Your sister, who *fought* to bring you here, even when you were stupid and resisted? *She* doesn't need this."

I felt tears fill my eyes, blurring everything again, and this time I was glad, grateful for it. But even so, I covered my face with my hand, just to make sure.

"I mean," Jamie continued, his voice bouncing off the walls, rising up to the high ceiling above us, "what kind of person just takes off, disappears, no phone call, not even caring that someone might be wondering where they are? Who *does* that?"

In the silence following this, no one said a word. But I knew the answer.

More than anyone in that room, I was aware of exactly the sort of person who did such a thing. What I hadn't realized until that very moment, though, was that it wasn't just my mother who was guilty of all these offenses. I'd told myself that everything I'd done in the weeks before and since she left was to make sure I would never be like her. But it was too late. All I had to do was look at the way I'd reacted to what Cora had told me that morning—taking off, getting wasted, letting myself be left alone in a strange place—to know I already was.

It was almost a relief, this specific truth. I wanted to say it out loud—to him, to Cora, to Nate, to everyone—so they would know not to keep trying to save me or make me better somehow. What was the point, when the pattern was already repeating? It was too late.

But as I dropped my hand from my eyes to say this to Jamie, I realized I couldn't see him anymore. My view was blocked by my sister, who had moved to stand between us, one hand stretched out behind her, toward me. Seeing her, I remembered a thousand nights in another house: the two of us together, another part of a pattern, just one I'd thought had long ago been broken, never to be repeated.

Perhaps I was just like my mother. But looking up at Cora's hand, I had to wonder whether it was possible that this wasn't already decided for me, and if maybe, just maybe, this was my one last chance to try and prove it. There was no way to know. There never is. But I reached out and took it anyway.

Chapter Nine

When I came down the next morning, Jamie was out by the pond. From the kitchen, I could see his breath coming out in puffs as he crouched by its edge, his coffee mug on the ground by his feet. It was what he did every morning, rain or shine, even when it was freezing, the grass still shiny with frost all around him. Just a few minutes spent checking on the state of the small world he'd created, making sure it had all made it through to another day.

It was getting colder now, and the fish were staying low. Pretty soon, they'd disappear entirely beneath the leaves and rocks on the bottom to endure the long winter. "You don't take them in?" I'd asked him, when he'd first mentioned this.

Jamie shook his head. "It's more natural this way," he explained. "When the water freezes, they go deep, and stay there until the spring."

"They don't die?"

"Hope not," he said, adjusting a clump of lilies. "Ideally, they just kind of . . . go dormant. They can't handle the cold, so they don't try. And then when it warms up, they'll get active again."

At the time, this had seemed so strange to me, as well as yet another reason not to get attached to my fish. Now, though, I could see the appeal of just disappearing, then laying low and waiting until the environment was more friendly to emerge. If only that was an option for me.

"He's not going to come to you," Cora said now from where she was sitting at the island, flipping through a magazine. The clothes I'd been wearing the night before were already washed and folded on the island beside her, one thing easily fixed. "If you want to talk to him, you have to take the first step."

"I can't," I said, remembering how angry he'd been the night before. "He hates me."

"No," she said, turning a page. "He's just disappointed in you."

I looked back out at Jamie, who was now leaning over the waterfall, examining the rocks. "With him, that seems even worse."

She looked up, giving me a sympathetic smile. "I know."

The first thing I'd done when I woke up that morning—after acknowledging my pounding, relentless headache—was try to piece together the events from the day before. My argument with Cora I remembered, as well as my ride to school and to Jackson. Once I got to the clearing, though, it got fuzzy.

Certain things, however, were crystal clear. Like how strange it was not only to see Jamie angry, but to see him angry at me. Or catching that glimpse of my mother's face, distorted with mine, staring back from the mirror. And finally how, after I took her hand, Cora led me silently up the stairs to my room, where she'd stripped off my clothes and stood outside the shower while I numbly washed my hair and myself, before helping me into my pajamas and my bed. I'd wanted to say something to her, but every time I tried she just shook her head. The last thing I recalled before falling asleep was her sitting on the edge of my mattress, a dark form with the light coming in the window behind her. How long she stayed, I had no idea, although I vaguely remembered opening my eyes more than once and being surprised to find her still there.

Now the door behind me opened, and Jamie came in, Roscoe tagging along at his feet. I looked up at him, but he brushed past, not making eye contact, to put his mug in the sink. "So," Cora said slowly, "I think maybe we all should—"

"I've got to go into the office," he said, grabbing his phone and keys off the counter. "I told John I'd meet him to go over those changes to the campaign."

"Jamie," she said, looking over at me.

"I'll see you later," he said, then kissed the top of her head and left the room, Roscoe following. A moment later, I heard the front door shut behind him.

I swallowed, looking outside again. From anyone else, this would be hardly an insult, if even noticeable. But even I knew Jamie well enough to understand it as the serious snub it was.

Cora came over, sliding into the chair opposite mine. "Hey," she said, keeping her eyes on me until I finally turned to face her. "It's okay. You guys will work this out. He's just hurt right now."

"I didn't mean to hurt him," I said as a lump rose in my throat. I was suddenly embarrassed, although whether by the fact I was crying, or crying in front of Cora was hard to say.

"I know." She reached over, sliding her hand onto mine. "But you have to understand, this is all new to him. In his family, everyone talks about everything. People don't take off; they don't come home drunk. He's not like us."

Like us. Funny how up until recently—like maybe even the night before—I hadn't been convinced there was an us here at all. So maybe things *could* change. "I'm sorry," I said to her. "I really am."

She nodded, then sat back, dropping her hand. "I appreciate that. But the fact is, we did trust you, and you betrayed that trust. So there have to be some consequences."

Here it comes, I thought. I sat back, picking up my water bottle, and braced myself.

"First," she began, "no going out on weeknights. Weekends, only for work, for the foreseeable future. We strongly considered making you give up your job, but we've decided to let you keep it through the holidays, with the provision that we revisit the issue in January. If we find out that you skipped school again, the job goes. No discussion."

"All right," I said. It wasn't like I was in any position to argue.

Cora swallowed, then looked at me for a long moment. "I know a lot happened yesterday. It was emotional for both of us. But you doing drugs or drinking . . . that's unacceptable. It's a violation of the agreement we arranged so you could come here, and if the courts ever found out, you'd have to go back to Poplar House. It *cannot* happen again."

I had a flash of the one night I'd stayed there: the scratchy pajamas, the narrow bed, the house director reading over the sheriff's report while I sat in front of her, silent. I swallowed, then said, "It's not going to."

"This is serious, Ruby," she said. "I mean, when I saw you come in like that last night, I just . . ."

"I know," I said.

". . . it's too familiar," she finished. Then she looked at me, hard. "For both of us. You're better than that. You know it."

"It was stupid of me," I said. "I just . . . When you told me that about Mom, I just kind of freaked."

She looked down at the salt shaker between us, sliding it sideways, then back again. "Look, the bottom line is, she lied to both of us. Which shouldn't really be all that surprising. That said, though, I wish I could have made it easier for you, Ruby. I really do. There's a lot I'd do different, given the chance."

I didn't want to ask. Luckily, I didn't have to.

"I've thought about it so much since I left, how I could have tried harder to keep in touch," she said, smoothing back a few curls with her hand. "Maybe I could have found a way to take you with me, rent an apartment or something."

"Cora. You were only eighteen."

"I know. But I also knew Mom was unstable, even then. And things only got worse," she said. "I shouldn't have trusted her to let you get in touch with me, either. There were steps I could have taken, things I could have done. I mean, now, at work, I deal every day with these kids from messed-up families, and I'm so much better equipped to handle it. To handle taking care of you, too. But if I'd only known then—"

"Stop," I said. "It's over. Done. It doesn't matter now."

She bit her lip. "I want to believe that," she said. "I really do."

I looked at my sister, remembering how I'd always followed her around so much as a kid, clinging to her more and more as my mom pulled away. What a weird feeling to find myself back here, dependent on her again. Just as I thought this, something occurred to me. "Cora?"

"Yeah?"

"Do you remember that day you left for school?"

She nodded.

"Before you left, you went back in and spoke to Mom. What did you say to her?"

She exhaled, sitting back in her chair. "Wow," she said. "I haven't thought about that in years."

I wasn't sure why I'd asked her this, or if it was even important. "She never mentioned it," I said. "I just always wondered."

Cora was quiet for a moment, and I wondered if she was even going to answer me at all. But then she said, "I told her that if I found out she ever hit you, I would call the police. And that I was coming back for you as soon as I could, to get you out of there." She reached up, tucking a piece of hair behind her ear. "I believed that, Ruby. I really did. I wanted to take care of you."

"It's all right," I told her.

"It's not," she continued, over me. "But now, here, I have the chance to make up for it. Late, yes, but I do. I know you don't want to be here, and that it's far from ideal, but . . . I want to help you. But you have to let me. Okay?"

This sounded so passive, so easy, although I knew it wasn't. As I thought this, though, I had a flash of Peyton again, standing at the bottom of that stairway. *Why are you surprised?* she'd said, and for all the wrongness of the situation, I knew she was right. You get what you give, but also what you're willing to take. The night before, I'd offered up my hand. Now, if I held on, there was no telling what it was possible to receive in return.

For a moment we just sat there, the quiet of the kitchen all around us. Finally I said, "Do you think Mom's okay?"

"I don't know," she replied. And then, more softly, "I hope so."

Maybe to anyone else, her saying this would have seemed strange. But to me, it made perfect sense, as this was the pull of my mother: then, now, always. For all the coldness, her bad behavior, the slights and outright abuse, we were still tied to her. It was like those songs I'd heard as a child, each so familiar, and all mine. When I got older and realized the words were sad, the stories tragic, it didn't make me love them any less. By then, they were already part of me, woven into my consciousness and memory. I couldn't cut them away any more easily than I could my mother herself. And neither could Cora. This was what we had in common—what made us this us.

After outlining the last few terms of my punishment (mandatory checking-in after school, agreeing to therapy, at least for a little while), Cora squeezed my shoulder, then left the room, Roscoe rousing himself from where he'd been planted in the doorway to follow her upstairs. I sat in the quiet of the kitchen for a moment, then I went out to the pond.

The fish were down deep, but after crouching over the water for a few minutes, I could make out my white one, circling by some moss-covered rocks. I'd just pushed myself to my feet when I heard the bang of a door slamming. When I turned, expecting to see Cora, no one was there, and I realized the sound had come from Nate's house. Sure enough, a moment later I saw a blond head bob past on the other side of the fence, then disappear.

Like the night before, when I'd been poised with Roscoe at the top of the walk, my first instinct was to go back inside. Avoid, deny, at least while it was still an option. But Nate had taken me out of those woods. For my own twisted reasons, I might not have wanted to believe this made us friends. But now, if nothing else, we were something.

I went inside, picked up his sweatshirt from the counter, then took in a breath and started across the grass to the fence. The gate was slightly ajar, and I could see Nate through the open door to the nearby pool house, leaning over a table. I slid through the gate, then walked around the pool to come up behind him. He was opening up a stack of small bags, then lining them up one by one.

"Let me guess," I said. "They're for cupcakes."

He jumped, startled, then turned around. "You're not far off, actually," he said when he saw me. "They're gift bags."

I stepped in behind him, then walked around to the other side of the table. The room itself, meant to be some kind of cabana, was mostly empty and clearly used for the business; a rack on wheels held a bunch of dry-cleaning, and I recognized some of Harriet's milk-crate storage system piled against a wall. There was also a full box of WE WORRY SO YOU DON'T HAVE TO air fresheners by the door, giving the room a piney scent that bordered on medicinal.

I watched quietly as Nate continued to open bags until the entire table was covered. Then he reached beneath it for a box and began pulling plastic-wrapped objects out of it, dropping one in each bag. *Clunk, clunk, clunk.*

"So," I said as he worked his way down the line, "about yesterday."

"You look like you feel better."

"Define better."

"Well," he said, glancing at me, "you're upright. And conscious."

"Kind of sad when that's an improvement," I said.

"But it is an improvement," he replied. "Right?"

I made a face. Positivity anytime was hard for me to take, but in the morning with a hangover, almost impossible. "So," I said, holding out the sweatshirt, "I wanted to bring this back to you. I figured you were probably missing it."

"Thanks," he said, taking it and laying it on a chair behind him. "It is my favorite."

"It does have that feel," I replied. "Well worn and all that."

"True," he said, going back to the bags. "But it also reflects my personal life philosophy."

I looked at the sweatshirt again. "'You swim' is a philosophy?"

He shrugged. "Better than 'you sink,' right?"

Hard to argue with that. "I guess."

"Plus there's the fact," he said, "that wearing that sweatshirt is the closest I might get to the U now."

"I thought you had a scholarship," I said, remembering the guy who'd called out to him in the parking lot.

"I did," he said, going back to dropping things into the bags. "But that was before I quit swim team. Now I've got to get in strictly on my grades, which frankly are not as good as my swimming."

I considered this as he moved down the next row, still adding things to the bags. "So why did you quit?"

"I don't know." He shrugged. "I was really into it when I lived in Arizona, but here . . . it just wasn't that fun anymore. Plus my dad needed me for the business."

"Still, seems like a big decision, giving it up entirely," I said.

"Not really," he replied. He reached down, picking up another box. "So, was it bad when you came in last night?"

"Yeah," I said, somewhat surprised by the sudden change in subject. "Jamie was really pissed off."

"Jamie was?"

"I know. It was bizarre." I swallowed, taking a breath. "Anyway, I just wanted to say . . . that I appreciate what you did. Even if, you know, it didn't seem like it at the time."

"You weren't exactly grateful," he agreed. *Clunk, clunk, clunk.*

"I was a bitch. And I'm sorry." I said this quickly, probably too quickly, and felt him look up at me again. *So embarrassing,* I thought, redirecting my attention to the bag in front of me. "What are you putting in there, anyway?"

"Little chocolate houses," he replied.

"What?"

"Yeah," he said, tossing one to me. "See for yourself. You can keep it, if you want."

Sure enough, it was a tiny house. There were even windows and a door. "Kind of strange, isn't it?" I said.

"Not really. This client's a builder. I think they're for some open house or something."

I slid the house into my pocket as he dropped the box, which was now almost empty, and pulled out another one, which was full of brochures, a picture of a woman's smiling face taking up most of the front. QUEEN HOMES, it said. LET US BUILD YOUR CASTLE! Nate started sliding one into each bag, working his way down the line. After watching him for a moment, I reached across, taking a handful myself and starting on the ones closest to me.

"You know," he said, after we'd worked in silence for a moment, "I wasn't trying to embarrass you by showing up yesterday. I just thought you might need help."

"Clearly, I did," I said, glad to have the bags to concentrate on. There was something soothing, orderly, to dropping in the brochures, each in its place. "If you hadn't come, who knows what would have happened."

Nate didn't speculate as to this, which I had to admit I appreciated. Instead, he said, "Can I ask you something?"

I looked up at him, then slid another brochure in. "Sure."

"What was it really like, living on your own?"

I'd assumed this would be a question about yesterday, like why I'd done it, or a request for further explanation of my twisted theories on friendship. This, however, was completely unexpected. Which was probably why I answered it honestly. "It wasn't bad at first," I said. "In fact, it was kind of a relief. Living with my mom had never been easy, especially at the end."

He nodded, then dropped the box onto the floor and pulled out another one, this one filled with magnets emblazoned with the Queen Homes logo. He held it out to me and I took a handful, then began working my way up the line. "But then," I said, "it got harder. I was having trouble keeping up with bills, and the power kept getting turned off. . . ." I was wondering if I should go on, but when I glanced up, he was watching me intently, so I continued. "I don't know. There was more to it than I thought, I guess."

"That's true for a lot of things," he said.

I looked up at him again. "Yeah," I said, watching him continue to drop in magnets, one by one. "It is."

"Nate!" I heard a voice call from outside. Over his shoulder, I could see his dad, standing in the door to the main house, his phone to his ear. "Do you have those bags ready yet?"

"Yeah," he called over his shoulder, reaching down to pull out another box. "Just one sec."

"They need them now," Mr. Cross said. "We told them ten at the latest. Let's move!"

Nate reached into the new box, which was full of individually wrapped votive candles in all different colors, and began distributing them at warp speed. I grabbed a handful, doing the same. "Thanks," he said as we raced through the rows. "We're kind of under the gun here."

"No problem," I told him. "And anyway, I owe you."

"You don't," he said.

"Come on. You saved my ass yesterday. Literally."

"Well," he said, dropping in one last candle, "then you'll get me back."

"How?"

"Somehow," he said, looking at me. "We've got time, right?"

"Nate!" Mr. Cross called out, his tone clearly disputing this. "What the hell are you doing in there?"

"I'm coming," Nate said, picking up the empty boxes and beginning to stack the bags into them. I reached to help, but he shook his head. "It's cool, I've got it. Thanks, anyway."

"You sure?"

"Nate!"

He glanced over his shoulder at his dad, still standing in the doorway, then at me. "Yeah. I'm good. Thanks again for your help."

I nodded, then stepped back from the table as he shoved the last of the bags into a box, stacking it onto the other one. As he headed for the door, I fell in behind him. "Finally," Mr. Cross said as we came out onto the patio. "I mean, how hard is it—" He stopped, suddenly, seeing me. "Oh," he said, his face and tone softening. "I didn't realize you had company."

"This is Ruby," Nate said, bringing the box over to him.

"Of course," Mr. Cross said, smiling at me. I tried to reciprocate, even though I suddenly felt uneasy, remembering that night I'd seen him in this same place with Roscoe. "How's that brother-in-law of yours doing? There's some buzz he might be going public soon with his company. Any truth to that?"

"Um," I said. "I don't know."

"We should go," Nate said to him. "If they want us there by ten."

"Right." Still, Mr. Cross stayed where he was, smiling at me, as I started around the pool to the gate. I could see Nate behind him in the house. He was watching me as well, but when I raised my hand to wave, he stepped down a hallway, out of sight. "Take care," Mr. Cross said, raising his hand to me. He thought I'd been waving at him. "Don't be a stranger."

I nodded, still feeling unsettled as I got to the fence and pushed my way through. Crossing the yard, I remembered the house Nate had given me, and reached down to pull it out and look at it again. It was so perfect, pristine, wrapped away in plastic and tied with a pretty bow. But there was something so eerie about it, as well—although what, I couldn't say—that I found myself putting it away again.

* * *

"Okay," I said, uncapping my pen. "What does family mean to you?"

"Not speaking," Harriet replied instantly.

"Not speaking?" Reggie said.

"Yeah."

He was just staring at her.

"What? What were you going to say?"

"I don't know," he said. "Comfort, maybe? History? The beginning of life?"

"Well, that's you," she told him. "For me, family means the silent treatment. At any given moment, someone is always not speaking to someone else."

"Really," I said.

"We're passive-aggressive people," she explained, taking a sip of her coffee. "Silence is our weapon of choice. Right now, for instance, I'm not speaking to two of my sisters and one brother."

"How many kids are in your family?" I asked.

"Seven total."

"That," Reggie said, "is just plain sad."

"Tell me about it," Harriet said. "I never got enough time in the bathroom."

"I meant the silence thing," Reggie told her.

"Oh." Harriet hopped up on the stool by the register, crossing her legs. "Well, maybe so. But it certainly cuts down the phone bill."

He shot her a disapproving look. "That is not funny. Communication is crucial."

"Maybe at your house," she replied. "At mine, silence is golden. And common."

"To me," Reggie said, picking up a bottle of Vitamin A and moving it thoughtfully from one hand to the other, "family is, like, the wellspring of human energy. The place where all life begins."

Harriet studied him over her coffee cup. "What do your parents do, again?"

"My father sells insurance. Mom teaches first grade."

"So suburban!"

"Isn't it, though?" He smiled. "I'm the black sheep, believe it or not."

"Me, too!" Harriet said. "I was supposed to go to med school. My dad's a surgeon. When I dropped out to do the jewelry-design thing, they freaked. Didn't speak to me for months."

"That must have been awful," he said.

She considered this. "Not really. I think it was kind of good for me, actually. My family is so big, and everyone always has an opinion, whether you want to hear it or not. I'd never done anything all on my own before, without their help or input. It was liberating."

Liberating, I wrote down. Reggie said, "You know, this explains a *lot*."

No kidding, I thought.

"What's that supposed to mean?" Harriet asked.

"Nothing," he told her. "So what makes you give up the silent treatment? When do you decide to talk again?"

Harriet considered this as she took a sip of coffee. "Huh," she said. "I guess when someone else does something worse. Then you need people on your side, so you make up with one person, just as you're getting pissed off at another."

"So it's an endless cycle," I said.

"I guess." She took another sip. "Coming together, falling apart. Isn't that what families are all about?"

"No," Reggie says. "Only yours."

They both burst out laughing, as if this was the funniest thing ever. I looked down at my notebook, where all I had written was *not speaking, comfort, wellspring,* and *liberating.* This project was going to take a while.

"Incoming," Harriet said suddenly, nodding toward a guy and girl my age who were approaching, deep in conversation.

". . . wrong with a Persian cat sweatshirt?" said the guy, who was sort of chubby, with what looked like a home-done haircut.

"Nothing, if she's eighty-seven and her name is Nana," the girl replied. She had long curly hair, held back at the nape of her neck, and was wearing cowboy boots, a bright red dress, and a cropped puffy parka with mittens hanging from the cuffs. "I mean, think about it. What kind of message are you trying to send here?"

"I don't know," the guy said as they got closer. "I mean, I like her, so . . ."

"Then you don't buy her a sweatshirt," the girl said flatly. "You buy her jewelry. Come on."

I put down the feather duster I was holding, standing up straighter as they came up to the cart, the girl already eyeing the rows of thin silver hoops on display. "Hi," I said to the guy, who, up close, looked even younger and dorkier. His T-shirt—which said ARMAGEDDON EXPO '06: ARE YOU READY FOR THE END?—didn't help matters. "Can I help you?"

"We need something that screams romance," the girl said, plucking a ring out and quickly examining it before putting it back. As she leaned into the row of lights overhead, I noticed that her face was dotted with faint scars. "A ring is too serious, I think. But earrings don't say enough."

"Earrings don't say anything," the guy mumbled, sniffing the incense. He sneezed, then added, "They're inanimate objects."

"And you are hopeless," she told him, moving down to the necklaces. "What about yours?"

Startled, I glanced back at the girl, who was looking right at me. "What?"

She nodded at my neck. "Your necklace. Do you sell those here?"

"Um," I said, my hand reaching up to it, "not really. But we do have some similar chains, and charms that you can—"

"I like the idea of the key, though," the girl said, coming around the cart. "It's different. And you can read it so many ways."

"You want me to give her a key?" the guy asked.

"I want you to give her a *possibility*," she told him, looking at my necklace again. "And that's what a key represents. An open door, a chance. You know?"

I'd never really thought about my key this way. But in the interest of a sale, I said, "Well, yeah. Absolutely. I mean, you could buy a chain here, then get a key to put on it."

"Exactly!" the girl said, pointing a finger at the nearby KEY-OSK, which sold keys and key accessories of all kinds. "It's perfect."

"You'll want a somewhat thick one," I told her. "But not too thick. You need it to be strong and delicate at the same time."

The girl nodded. "That's it," she said. "Just what I had in mind."

Ten minutes and fifteen dollars later, I watched them as they walked away, bag in hand, over to the KEY-OSK cart, where the girl explained what she wanted. I watched the saleswoman as she pulled out a small collection of keys, sliding them across for them to examine.

"Nice job," Harriet said, coming up beside me. "You salvaged the sale, even if we didn't have exactly what she was looking for."

"It was her idea," I said. "I just went with it."

"Still. It worked, right?"

I glanced over again at KEY-OSK, where the girl in the parka was picking up a small key as her friend and the saleswoman looked on. People were passing between us, hustling and bustling, but still I craned my neck, watching with Harriet as she slid it over the clasp, carefully, then down onto our chain. It dangled there for a second, spinning slightly, before she closed her hand around it, making it disappear.

* * *

I'd just stepped off the greenway, later that afternoon, when I saw the bird.

At first, it was just a shadow, passing overhead, temporarily blotting out the light. Only when it cleared the trees and reached the open sky did I see it in full. It was *huge,* long and gray, with an immense wingspan, so big it seemed impossible for it to be airborne.

For a moment, I just stood there, watching its shadow move down the street. It was only when I started walking again that it hit me.

It's herons and waterbirds you really need to worry about, Heather had said. *One swoop, and they can do some serious damage.*

No way, I thought, but at the same time I found myself picking up the pace as Cora's house came into view, breaking into a jog, then a run. It was cold out—the air was stinging my lungs, and I knew I had to look crazy, but I kept going, my breath ragged in my chest as I cut across the neighbor's lawn, then alongside Cora's garage to the side yard.

The bird was impossible to miss, standing in the shallow end, its wings slightly raised as if it had only just landed there. Distantly, I realized that it was beautiful, caught with the sun setting in the distance, its elegant form reflected in the pond's surface. But then it dipped its massive beak down into the water.

"Stop!" I yelled, my voice carrying and carrying far. "Stop it!"

The bird jerked, its wings spreading out a little farther, so it looked like it was hovering. But it stayed where it was.

For a long moment, nothing happened. The bird stood there, wings outstretched, with me only a short distance away, my heart thumping in my ears. I could hear cars passing on the street, a door slamming somewhere a few yards over. But all around us, it was nothing but still.

At any moment, I knew the bird could reach down and pluck up a fish, maybe even my fish. For all I knew I was already too late to save anything.

"Get out!" I screamed, louder this time, as I moved closer. "Now! *Get out now!*"

At first, it didn't move. But then, almost imperceptibly at first, it began to lift up, then a little farther, and farther still. I was so close to it as it moved over me, its enormous wings spread out, pumping higher and higher into the night sky, so amazing and surreal, like something you could only imagine. And maybe I would have thought it was only a dream, if Jamie hadn't seen it, too.

I didn't even realize he was standing right behind me, his hands in his pockets, and his face upturned, until I turned to watch as the bird soared over us, still rising.

"It was a heron," I told him, forgetting our silence. I was gasping, my breath uneven. "It was in the pond."

He nodded. "I know."

I swallowed, crossing my arms over my chest. My heart was still pounding, so hard I wondered if he could hear it. "I'm sorry for what I did," I said. "I'm so, so sorry."

For a moment, he was quiet. "Okay," he said finally. Then he reached a hand up, resting it on my shoulder, and together, we watched the bird soar over the roofline into the sky.

Chapter Ten

"You want buttered, or not?"

"Either is fine," I said.

Olivia eyed me over the counter, then walked over to the butter dispenser, sticking the bag of popcorn she was holding underneath it and giving it a couple of quick smacks with her hand. "Then you are officially my favorite kind of customer," she said. "As well as unlike ninety-nine percent of the moviegoing population."

"Really."

"Most people," she said, turning the bag and shaking it slightly, then adding a bit more, "have very strong views on their butter preference. Some want none—the popcorn must be dry, or they freak out. Others want it sopping to the point they can feel it through the bag."

I made a face. "Yuck."

She shrugged. "I don't judge. Unless you're one of those totally anal-retentive types that wants it in specific layers, which takes ages. Then I hate you."

I smiled, taking the popcorn as she slid it across to me. "Thanks," I said, reaching for my wallet. "What do I—?"

"Don't worry about it," she said, waving me off.

"You sure?"

"If you'd asked for butter layers, I would have charged you. But that was easy. Come on."

She came out from behind the counter, and I followed her across the lobby of the Vista 10—which was mostly empty except for some kids playing video games by the restrooms—to the box office door. She pulled it open, ducking inside, then flipped the sign in the window to OPEN before clearing a bunch of papers from a nearby stool for me to sit down. "You sure?" I said, glancing around. "Your boss won't mind?"

"My dad's the manager," she said. "Plus I'm working Saturday morning, the kiddie shift, against my will. The girl who was supposed to be here flaked out on him. I can do what I want."

"The kiddie—?" I began, then stopped when I saw a woman approaching with about five elementary school–aged children, some running ahead in front, others dragging along behind. One kid had a handheld video game and wasn't even looking where he was going, yet still managed to navigate the curb without tripping, which was kind of impressive. The woman, who appeared to be in her mid-forties and was wearing a long green sweater and carrying a huge purse, stopped in front of the window, squinting up.

"Mom," one of the kids, a girl with ponytails, said, tugging on her arm. "I want Smarties."

"No candy," the woman murmured, still staring up at the movie listings.

"But you promised!" the girl said, her voice verging on a whine. One of the other kids, a younger boy, was now on her other side, tugging as well. I watched the woman reach out to him absently, brushing her hand over the top of his head as he latched himself around her leg.

"Yes!" the kid with the handheld yelled, jumping up and down. "I made level five with the cherries!"

Olivia shot me a look, then pushed down the button by her microphone, leaning into it. "Can I help you?" she asked.

"Yes," the woman said, still staring up, "I need . . . five children and one adult for *Pretzel Dog Two.*"

Olivia punched this into her register. "That'll be thirty-six dollars."

"Thirty-six?" the woman said, finally looking at us. The girl was tugging her arm again. "With the child's price? Are you sure?"

"Yes."

"Well, that's crazy. It's just a movie!"

"Don't I know it," Olivia told her, hitting the ticket button a few times. She put her hand on the tickets as the woman reached into her huge purse, digging around for a few minutes before finally coming up with two twenties. Then Olivia slid them across, along with her change. "Enjoy the show."

The woman grumbled, hoisting her bag up her shoulder, then moved into the theater, the kids trailing along behind her. Olivia sighed, sitting back and stretching her arms over her head as two minivans pulled into the lot in front of us in quick succession.

"Don't I know it," I said, remembering my mom with

her clipboard, on so many front stoops. "My mom used to say that."

"Empathy works," Olivia replied. "And it's not like she's wrong. I mean, it *is* expensive. But we make the bulk of our money on concessions, and she's sneaking in food for all those rug rats. So it all comes out even, really."

I looked over my shoulder back into the lobby, where the woman was now leading her brood to a theater. "You think?"

"Did you see that purse? Please." She reached over, taking a piece of popcorn from my bag, which I hadn't even touched. Apparently she'd noticed, next saying, "What? Too much butter?"

I shook my head, looking down at it. "No, it's fine."

"I was about to say. Don't get picky on me now."

The minivans were deboarding now, people emptying car seats and sliding open back doors. Olivia sighed, checking her watch. "I didn't really come here for the popcorn," I said. "I wanted . . . I just wanted to thank you."

"You already did," she said.

"No," I corrected her, "I *tried*—twice—but you wouldn't let me. Which, frankly, I just don't understand."

She reached for the popcorn again, taking out a handful. "Honestly," she said as another pack of parents and kids approached, "it's not that complicated. You did something for me, I did something for you. We're even. Let it go already."

This was easier said than done, though, something I considered as she sold a bunch of tickets, endured more kvetching about the prices, and directed one woman with a very unhappy toddler in the direction of the bathroom. By the time things had calmed down, fifteen minutes had passed, and I'd worked my way halfway through the popcorn bag.

"Look," I said, "all I'm saying is that I just . . . I want you to know I'm not like that."

"Like what?" she said, arranging some bills in the register.

"Like someone who ditches school to get drunk. I was just having a really bad day, and—"

"Ruby." Her voice was sharp, getting my attention. "You don't have to explain, okay? I get it."

"You do?"

"Switching schools totally sucked for me," she said, sitting back in her chair. "I missed everything about my life at Jackson. I still do—so much so that even now, after a year, I haven't really bothered to get settled at Perkins. I don't even have any friends there."

"Me neither," I said.

"Yes, you do," she said. "You have Nate Cross."

"We're not really friends," I told her.

She raised her eyebrows. "The boy drove fifteen miles to pick you up out of the woods."

"Only because you told him to," I said.

"No," she said pointedly. "All I did was let him know where you were."

"Same thing."

"Actually, it isn't," she said, reaching over and taking another piece of popcorn. "There's a big difference between information and action. I gave him the facts, mostly because I felt responsible about leaving you there with that loser in the first place. But going there? That was all him. So I hope you were sufficiently grateful."

"I wasn't," I said quietly.

"No?" She seemed genuinely surprised. "Well . . ." she said, drawing the word out. "Why not?"

I looked down at my popcorn, already feeling that butter-and-salt hangover beginning to hit. "I'm not very good at accepting help," I said. "It's an issue."

"I can understand that," she said.

"Yeah?"

She shrugged. "It's not the easiest thing for me, either, especially when I think I don't need it."

"Exactly."

"But," she continued, not letting me off the hook, "you *were* passed out in the woods. I mean, you clearly needed help, so you're lucky he realized it, even if you didn't."

There was a big crowd approaching now, lots of kids and parents. We could see them coming at us from across the parking lot like a wide, very disorganized wave.

"I want to try to make it up to him," I said to Olivia. "To change, you know? But it's not so easy to do."

"Yeah," she said, taking another handful of popcorn and tossing it into her mouth as the crowd closed in. "Don't I know it."

* * *

Everyone has their weak spot. The one thing that, despite your best efforts, will always bring you to your knees, regardless of how strong you are otherwise. For some people, it's love. Others, money or alcohol. Mine was even worse: calculus.

I was convinced it was the reason I would not go to college. Not my checkered background, or that I was getting my applications together months after everyone else, or even the fact that up until recently, I hadn't even been sure I wanted to go at all. Instead, in my mind, it would all come down to one class and its respective rules and theorems, dragging down my GPA and me with it.

I always started studying with the best of intentions, telling myself that today just might be the day it all fell into place, and everything would be different. More often than not, though, after a couple of pages of practice problems, I'd find myself spiraling into an all-out depression. When it was really bad, I'd put my head down on my book and contemplate alternate options for my future.

"Whoa," I heard a voice say. It was muffled slightly by my hair, and my arm, which I locked around my head in an effort to keep my brain from seeping out. "You okay?"

I lifted myself up, expecting to see Jamie. Instead, it was Nate, standing in the kitchen doorway, a stack of drycleaning over one shoulder. Roscoe was at his feet, sniffing excitedly.

"No," I told him as he turned and walked out to the foyer, opening the closet there. With Jamie hard at work on the new ad campaign, and Cora backlogged in cases, they'd been outsourcing more and more of their errands to Rest Assured, although this Saturday morning was the first time Nate had shown up when I was home. Now I heard some banging around as he hung up the cleaning. "I was just thinking about my future."

"That bad, huh?" he said, crouching down to pet Roscoe, who leaped up, licking his face.

"Only if I fail calculus," I said. "Which seems increasingly likely."

"Nonsense." He stood up, wiping his hands on his jeans, and came over, leaning against the counter. "How could that happen, when you personally know the best calc tutor in town?"

"You?" I raised my eyebrows. "Really?"

"Oh God, no," he said, shuddering. "I'm good at a lot of things, but not that. I barely passed myself."

"You did pass, though."

"Yeah. But only because of Gervais."

Immediately, he popped into my head, small and foul smelling. "No thanks," I said. "I'm not that desperate."

"Didn't look that way when I came in." He walked over, pulling out a chair and sitting down opposite me, then drew my book over to him, flipping a page and wincing at it. "God, just looking at this stuff freaks me out. I mean, how basic is the power rule? And yet why can I still not understand it?"

I just looked at him. "The what?"

He shot me a look. "You need Gervais," he said, pushing the book at me. "And quickly."

"That is just what I *don't* need," I said, sitting back and pulling my leg to my chest. "Can you imagine actually asking Gervais for a favor? Not to mention owing him anything. He'd make my life a living hell."

"Oh, right," Nate said, nodding. "I forgot. You have that thing."

"What thing?"

"The indebtedness thing," he said. "You have to be self-sufficient, can't stand owing anyone. Right?"

"Well," I said. Put that way, it didn't sound like something you wanted to agree to, necessarily. "If you mean that I don't like being dependent on people, then yes. That is true."

"But," he said, reaching down to pat Roscoe, who had settled at his feet, "you *do* owe me."

Again, this did not seem to be something I wanted to second, at least not immediately. "What's your point?"

He shrugged. "Only that, you know, I have a lot of errands to run today. Tons of cupcakes to ice."

"And . . ."

"And I could use a little help," he said. "If you felt like, you know, paying me back."

"Do these errands involve Gervais?" I asked.

"No."

I thought for a second. "Okay," I said, shutting my book. "I'm in."

* * *

"Now," he said, as I followed him up the front steps of a small brick house that had a flag with a watermelon flying off the front, "before we go in, I should warn you about the smell."

"The smell?" I asked, but then he was unlocking the door and pushing it open, transforming this from a question to an all-out exclamation. *Oh my God,* I thought as the odor hit me from all sides. It was like a fog; even as you walked right through it, it just kept going.

"Don't worry," Nate said over his shoulder, continuing through the living room, past a couch covered with a brightly colored quilt to a sunny kitchen area beyond. "You get used to it after a minute or two. Soon, you won't even notice it."

"What *is* it?"

Then, though, as I waited in the entryway—Nate had disappeared into the kitchen—I got my answer. It started with just an odd feeling, which escalated to creepy as I realized I was being watched.

As soon as I spotted the cat on the stairs—a fat tabby, with green eyes—observing me with a bored expression, I noticed the gray one under the coatrack to my right, followed by a black one curled up on the back of the couch and a long-haired white one stretched out across the Oriental rug in front of it. They were everywhere.

I found Nate on an enclosed back porch where five carriers were lined up on a table. Each one had a Polaroid of a cat taped to it, a name written in clean block lettering beneath: RAZZY. CESAR. BLU. MARGIE. LYLE.

"So this is a shelter or something?" I asked.

"Sabrina takes in cats that can't get placed," he said, picking up two of the carriers and carrying them into the living room. "You know, ones that are sick or older. The unwanted and abandoned, as it were." He grabbed one of the Polaroids, of a thin gray cat—RAZZY, apparently—then glanced around the room. "You see this guy anywhere?"

We both looked around the room, where there were several cats but no gray ones. "Better hit upstairs," Nate said. "Can you look around for the others? Just go by the pictures on the carriers."

He left the room, jogging up the stairs. A moment later, I heard him whistling, the ceiling creaking as he moved around above. I looked at the row of carriers and the Polaroids attached, then spotted one of them, a black cat with yellow eyes—LYLE—watching me from a nearby chair. As I picked up the carrier, the picture flipped up, exposing a Post-it that was stuck to the back.

Lyle will be getting a checkup and blood drawn to monitor how he's responding to the cancer drugs. If Dr. Loomis feels they are not making a difference, please tell him to call me on my cell phone to discuss if there is further action to take, or whether I should just focus on keeping him comfortable.

"Poor guy," I said, positioning the carrier in front of him, the door open. "Hop in, okay?"

He didn't. Even worse, when I went to nudge him forward, he reached out, swiping at me, his claws scraping across my skin.

I dropped the carrier, which hit the floor, the open door banging against it. Looking down at my hand, I could already see the scratches, beads of blood rising up in places. "You little shit," I said. He just stared back at me, as if he'd never moved at all.

"Oh, man," Nate said, coming around the corner carrying two cats, one under each arm. "You went after Lyle?"

"You said to get them," I told him.

"I said to *look*," he said. "Not try to wrangle. Especially that one—he's trouble. Let me see."

He reached over, taking my hand and peering down at it to examine the scratches. His palm was warm against the underside of my wrist, and as he leaned over it I could see the range of color in his hair falling across his forehead, which went from white blond to a more yellow, all the way to almost brown.

"Sorry," he said. "I should have warned you."

"I'm okay. It's just a little scrape."

He glanced up at me, and I felt my face flush, suddenly even more aware of how close we were to each other. Over his shoulder, Lyle was watching, the pupils of his yellow eyes widening, then narrowing again.

In the end, it took Nate a full twenty minutes to get Lyle in the carrier and to the car, where I was waiting with the others. When he finally slid behind the wheel, I saw his hands were covered with scratches.

"I hope you get combat pay," I said as he started the engine.

"I don't scar, at least," he replied. "And anyway, you can't really blame the guy. It's not like he's ever been given a reason to like the vet."

I just looked at him as we pulled away from the curb. From behind us, someone was already yowling. "You know," I said, "I just can't get behind that kind of attitude."

Nate raised his eyebrows, amused. "You can't what?"

"The whole positive spin—the "oh, it's not the cat's fault

he mauled me" thing. I mean, how do you do that?"

"What's the alternative?" he asked. "Hating all creatures?"

"No," I said, shooting him a look. "But you don't have to give everyone the benefit of the doubt."

"You don't have to assume the worst about everyone, either. The world isn't always out to get you."

"In your opinion," I added.

"Look," he said, "the point is there's no way to be a hundred percent sure about anyone or anything. So you're left with a choice. Either hope for the best, or just expect the worst."

"If you expect the worst, you're never disappointed," I pointed out.

"Yeah, but who lives like that?"

I shrugged. "People who don't get mauled by psycho cats."

"Ah, but you *did,*" he said, pointing at me. "So clearly, you aren't that kind of person. Even if you want to be."

After the group vet appointment—during which Lyle scratched the vet, the vet tech, and some poor woman minding her own business in the waiting room—we went back to Sabrina's and re-released the cats to their natural habitat. From there, we hit the dry-cleaners (where we collected tons of suits and dress shirts), the pharmacy (shocking how many people were taking antidepressants, not that I was judging), and One World—the organic grocery store—where we picked up a special order of a wheat-, eggs-, and gluten-free cake, the top of which read HAPPY FORTIETH, MARLA!

"Forty years without wheat or eggs?" I said as we carried it up the front steps of a big house with columns in the front. "That's got to suck."

"She doesn't eat meat, either," he told me, pulling out a ring of keys and flipping through them. When he found the one he was looking for, he stuck it in the lock, pushing the door open. "Or anything processed. Even her shampoo is organic."

"You buy her shampoo?"

"We buy everything. She's always traveling. Kitchen's this way."

I followed him through the house, which was huge and immensely cluttered. There was mail piled on the island, recycling stacked by the back door, and the light on the answering machine was blinking nonstop, the way it does when the memory is packed.

"You know," I said, "for someone so strict about her diet, I'd expect her to be more anal about her house."

"She used to be, before the divorce," Nate said, taking the cake from me and sliding it into the fridge. "Since then, it's gone kind of downhill."

"That explains the Xanax," I said as he took a bottle out of the pharmacy bag, sticking it on the counter.

"You think?"

I turned to the fridge, a portion of which was covered with pictures of various Hollywood actresses dressed in bikinis. On a piece of paper above them, in black marker, was written THINK BEFORE YOU SNACK! "Yes," I said. "She must be really intense."

"Probably is," Nate said, glancing over at the fridge. "I've never met her."

"Really?"

"Sure," he said. "That's kind of the whole point of the business. They don't have to meet us. If we're doing our job right, their stuff just gets done."

"Still," I said, "you have to admit, you're privy to a lot. I mean, look at how much we know about her just from this kitchen."

"Maybe. But you can't really *know* anyone just from their house or their stuff. It's just a tiny part of who they are." He grabbed his keys off the counter. "Come on. We've got four more places to hit before we can quit for the day."

I had to admit it was hard work, or at least harder than it looked. In a way, though, I liked it. Maybe because it reminded me of Commercial, driving up to houses and leaving things, although in this case we got to go inside, and often picked things up, as well. Plus there was something interesting about these little glimpses you got into people's lives: their coat closet, their garage, what cartoons they had on their fridge. Like no matter how different everyone seemed, there were some things that everyone had in common.

Our last stop was a high-rise apartment building with a clean, sleek lobby. As I followed Nate across it, carrying the last of the dry-cleaning, I could hear both our footsteps, amplified all around us.

"So what's the story here?" I asked him as we got into the elevator. I pulled the dry-cleaning tag where I could see it. "Who's P. Collins?"

"A mystery," he said.

"Yeah? How so?"

"You'll see."

On the seventh floor, we stepped out into a long hall lined with identical doors. Nate walked down about halfway, then pulled out his keys and opened the door in front of him. "Go ahead," he said.

When I stepped in, the first thing I was aware of was the stillness. Not just a sense of something being empty, but almost hollow, even though the apartment was fully furnished with sleek, contemporary furniture. In fact, it looked like something out of a magazine, that perfect.

"Wow," I said as Nate took the cleaning from me, disappearing into a bedroom that was off to the right. I walked over to a row of windows that looked out over the entire town, and for miles farther; it was like being on top of the world. "This is amazing."

"It is," he said, coming back into the room. "Which is why it's so weird that whoever it belongs to is never here."

"They must be," I said. "They have dry-cleaning."

"That's the only thing, though," he said. "And it's just a duvet cover. We pick it up about every month or so."

I walked into the kitchen, looking around. The fridge was bare, the counters spotless except for one bottle cap, turned upside down. "Aha," I said. "They drink root beer."

"That's mine," Nate said. "I left it there last time as an experiment, just to see if anyone moved it or threw it away."

"And it's still here?"

"Weird, right?" He walked back over to the windows, pulling open a glass door. Immediately I could smell fresh air blowing in. "I figure it's got to be a rental, or some company-owned kind of deal. For visiting executives or something."

I went into the living room, scanning a low bookcase by the couch. There were a few novels, a guide to traveling in Mexico, a couple of architectural-design books. "I don't know," I said. "I bet someone lives here."

"Well, if they do, I feel for them," he said, leaning into the open door. "They don't even have any pictures up."

"Pictures?"

"You know, of family or friends. Some proof of a life, you know?"

I thought of my own room back at Cora's—the blank walls, how I'd only barely unpacked. What would someone think, coming in and seeing my stuff? A few clothes, some books. Not much to go on.

Nate had gone outside, and was now on the small terrace, looking out into the distance. When I came to stand next to him, he looked down at my hand, still crisscrossed with scratches. "Oh, I totally forgot," he said, reaching into his pocket and pulling out a small tube. "I got something at One World for that."

BOYD'S BALM, it said in red letters. As he uncapped it, I said, "What is this, exactly?"

"It's like natural Neosporin," he explained. When I gave him a doubtful look, he added, "Marla swears by it."

"Oh, well. Then by all means." He gestured for me to stick out my hand. When I did, he squeezed some on, then began to rub it in, carefully. It burned a bit at first, then turned cold, but not in a bad way. Again, with us so close to each other, my first instinct was to pull back, like I had before. But instead, I made myself stay where I was and relax as his hand moved over mine.

"Done," he said after a moment, when it was all rubbed in. "You'll be healed by tomorrow."

"That's optimistic."

"Well, you can expect your hand to fall off, if you want," he said. "But personally, I just can't subscribe to that way of thinking."

I smiled despite myself. Looking up at his face, the sun just behind him, I thought of that first night, when he'd leaned over the fence. Then it had been impossible to make out his features, but here, all was clear, in the bright light of day. He wasn't really at all what I'd assumed or expected, and I wondered if I'd surprised him, too.

Later, after he dropped me off, I came in to find Cora at the stove, peering down into a big pot as she stirred something. "Hey," she called out as Roscoe ran to greet me, jumping up. "I didn't think you were working today."

"I wasn't," I said.

"Then where were you?"

"Everywhere," I said, yawning. She looked up at me, quizzical, and I wondered why I didn't just tell her the truth. But there was something about that day that I wanted to keep to myself, if just for a little while longer. "Do you need help with dinner?"

"Nah, I'm good. We'll be eating in about a half hour, though, okay?"

I nodded, then headed up to my room. After dropping my bag onto the floor, I went out onto my balcony, looking across the yard and the pond to Nate's house. Sure enough, a minute later I saw him carrying some things into the pool house, still working.

Back inside, I kicked off my shoes and climbed onto the bed, stretching out and closing my eyes. I was just about to drift off when I heard a jingle of tags and looked over to see Roscoe in the doorway to my room. *Cora must have turned on the oven,* I thought, waiting for him to move past me to my closet, where he normally huddled until the danger had passed. Instead, he came to the side of the bed, then sat down, peering up at me.

I looked at him for a second, then sighed. "All right," I said, patting the bed. "Come on."

He didn't hesitate, instantly leaping up, then doing a couple of quick spins before settling down beside me, his head resting on my stomach. As I began to pet him, I looked down at the scratches Lyle had given me, smoothing my fingers across them and feeling the slight rises there as I remembered Nate doing the same. I kept doing this, in fact, for the rest of the night—during dinner, before bed—tracing them the way I once had the key around my neck, as if I needed to memorize them. And maybe I did, because Nate was right: By the next morning, they were gone.

Chapter Eleven

"All I'm saying," Olivia said, picking up her smoothie and taking a sip, "is that to the casual observer, it looks like something is going on."

"Well, the casual observer is mistaken," I said. "And even if there was, it wouldn't be anyone's business, anyway."

"Oh, right. Because *so* many people are interested. All one of me."

"You're asking, aren't you?"

She made a face at me, then picked up her phone, opening it and hitting a few buttons. The truth was, Olivia and I had never officially become friends. But clearly, somewhere between that ride and the day in the box office, it had happened. There was no other explanation for why she now felt so completely comfortable getting into my personal life.

"Nothing is going on with me and Nate," I said to her, for the second time since we'd sat down for lunch. This was something else I never would have expected, us eating together—much less being so used to it that I barely noticed as she reached over, pinching a chip out of my bag. "We're just friends."

"A little while ago," she said, popping the chip into her mouth, "you weren't even willing to admit to that."

"So?"

"So," she said as the phone suddenly rang, "who knows what you'll be copping to a week or two from now? You might be engaged before you're willing to admit it."

"We are not," I said firmly, "going to be engaged. Jesus."

"Never say never," she said with a shrug. Her phone rang again. "Anything's possible."

"Do you even see him here?"

"No," she said. "But I do see him over at the sculpture, *looking* over here."

I turned my head. Sure enough, Nate was behind us, talking to Jake Bristol. When he saw us watching him, he waved. I did the same, then turned back to Olivia, who was regarding me expressionlessly, her phone still ringing.

"Are you going to answer that?" I asked.

"Am I allowed to?"

"Are you saying I make the rules now?"

"No," she said flatly. "But I certainly don't want to be rude and inconsiderate, carrying on two conversations at once." This was, in fact, exactly what I'd said, when I got sick of her constantly interrupting me to take calls. Which, now that I thought of it, was very friend-like as well, in its own way. "Unless, of course, you feel differently now?"

"Just make it stop ringing, please," I said.

She sighed, as if it was just such a hardship, then flipped open her phone, putting it to her ear. "Hey. No, just eating lunch with Ruby. What? Yes, she did say that," she said, eyeing me. "I don't know, she's fickle. I'm not even trying to understand."

I rolled my eyes, then looked over my shoulder at Nate again. He was still talking to Jake and didn't see me this time, but as I scanned the rest of the courtyard, I did spot someone staring right at me. Gervais.

He was alone, sitting at the base of a tree, his backpack beside him, a milk carton in one hand. He was also chewing slowly, while keeping his eyes steady on me. Which was kind of creepy, I had to admit. Then again, Gervais had been acting sort of strange lately. Or stranger.

By this point, I'd gotten so used to his annoying car behavior that I hardly even noticed it anymore. In fact, as Nate and I had gotten closer, Gervais had almost become an afterthought. Which was probably why, at least at first, I didn't realize when he suddenly began to change. But Nate did.

"How can you not have noticed he's combing his hair now?" he'd asked me a couple of mornings earlier, after Gervais had already taken off and we were walking across the parking lot. "*And* he's lost the headgear?"

"Because unlike some people," I said, "I don't spend a lot of time looking at Gervais?"

"Still, it's kind of hard to miss," he replied. "He looks like a totally different person."

"*Looks* being the operative word."

"He smells better, too," Nate added. "He's cut down considerably on the toxic emissions."

"Why are we talking about this again?" I asked him.

"I don't know," he said, shrugging. "When someone starts to change, and it's obvious, it's sort of natural to wonder why. Right?"

I wasn't wondering about Gervais, though. In fact, even if he got a total makeover and suddenly smelled like petunias,

I couldn't have cared less. Now, though, as I looked across the green at him, I had to admit that Nate was right—he did look different. The hair was combed, not to mention less greasy, and without the headgear his face looked completely changed. When he saw me looking at him, he flinched, then immediately ducked his head, sucking down the rest of his carton of milk. *So weird,* I thought.

". . . no, I don't," Olivia was saying now as she took another sip of her smoothie. "Because shoes are not going to make you run faster, Laney. That's all hype. What? Well, of course they're going to tell you that. They get paid on commission!"

"Who does?" Nate said, sliding onto the bench beside me. Olivia, listening to Laney, raised her eyebrows at me.

"No idea," I told him. "As you'll notice, she's not talking to me. She's on the phone."

"Ah, right," he said. "You know, that's really kind of rude."

"Isn't it?"

Olivia ignored us, picking up my chip bag and helping herself again. Then she offered it to Nate, who took a handful out, popping them into his mouth. "Those are mine," I pointed out.

"Yeah?" Nate said. "They're good."

He smiled, then bumped me with his knee. Across the table, Olivia was still talking to Laney about shoes, her voice shifting in and out of lecture mode. Sitting there with them, it was almost hard to remember when I first came to Perkins, so determined to be a one-woman operation to the end. But that was the thing about taking help and giving it, or so I was learning: there was no such thing as really getting even. Instead, this connection, once opened, remained ongoing over time.

* * *

At noon on Thanksgiving Day I was positioned in the foyer, ready to perform my assigned duty as door-opener and coat-taker. Just as the first car slowed and began to park in front of the house, though, I realized there was a hole in my sweater.

I took the stairs two at a time to my room, heading into the bathroom to my closet. When I pulled the door open, I jumped, startled. Cora was inside, sitting on the floor with Roscoe in her lap.

"Don't say it," she said, putting a hand up. "I know this looks crazy."

"What are you doing?"

She sighed. "I just needed to take a time-out. A few deep breaths. A moment for myself."

"In my closet," I said, clarifying.

"I came to get Roscoe. You know how he gets when the oven is on." She shot me a look. "But then, once I was in here, I began to understand why he likes it so much. It's very soothing, actually."

For the first time, Cora and Jamie were hosting Thanksgiving dinner, which meant that within moments, we'd be invaded by no less than fifteen Hunters. Personally, I was kind of curious to meet this extended tribe, but Cora, like Roscoe, was a nervous wreck.

"You were the one who suggested it," Jamie had said to her the week before as she sat at the kitchen table in full stress mode, surrounded by cookbooks and copies of

Cooking Light. "I never would have asked you to do this."

"I was just being polite!" she said. "I didn't think your mother would actually take me up on it."

"They want to see the house."

"Then they should come for drinks. Or appetizers. Or dessert. Something simple. Not on a major holiday, when I'm expected to provide a full meal!"

"All you have to do is the turkey and the desserts," Jamie told her. "They're bringing everything else."

Cora glared at him. "The turkey," she said, her voice flat, "is the center of the whole thing. If I screw it up, the entire holiday is ruined."

"Oh, that's not true," Jamie said. Then he looked at me, but I stayed quiet, knowing better than to get involved in this. "It's a turkey. How hard can it be?"

This question had been answered the night before, when Cora went to pick up the bird she'd ordered, which weighed twenty-two pounds. It took all three of us just to get it inside, and then it wouldn't even fit in the fridge.

"Disaster," Cora announced once we'd wrestled it onto the island. "Complete and total disaster."

"It's going to be fine," Jamie told her, confident as always. "Just relax."

Eventually, he had managed to get it into the fridge, although it meant removing just about everything else. As a result, the countertops were lined not only with all the stuff Cora had bought for the meal, but also all the condiments, breads, and cans of soda and bottled water— everything that didn't absolutely have to be refrigerated. Luckily, we'd been able to arrange to use Nate's oven for overflow—he and his dad were going to be gone all day, getting double time from clients who needed things done for their own dinners—as nothing else could fit in ours while the turkey was cooking. Still, all of this had only made Cora more crabby, to the point that I'd finally taken a loaf of bread, some peanut butter, and jelly into the enormous dining room, where I could fix myself sandwiches and eat in peace.

"You know," Jamie had said the night before, as Cora rattled around the kitchen beyond the doorway, "I think this is actually going to be a really good thing for us."

I looked at my sister, who was standing by the stove, examining a slotted spoon as if not exactly sure what to do with it. "Yeah?"

He nodded. "This is just what this house needs—a real holiday. It gives a place a sense of fullness, of family, you know?" He sighed, almost wistful. "And anyway, I've always loved Thanksgiving. Even before it was our anniversary."

"Wait," I said. "You guys got married on Thanksgiving?"

He shook his head. "June tenth. But we got together on Turkey Day. It was our first anniversary, you know, before the wedding one. It was, like, our first real date."

"Who dates on a major holiday?"

"Well, it wasn't exactly planned," he said, pulling the bread toward him and taking out a few slices. "I was supposed to go home for Thanksgiving that year. I was pumped for it, because, you know, I'm all about an eating holiday."

"Right," I said, taking a bite of my own sandwich.

"But then," he continued, "the night before, I ate some weird squid at this sushi place and got food poisoning. Seriously bad news. I was up sick all night, and the next day I was completely incapacitated. So I had to stay in the dorm, alone, for Thanksgiving. Isn't that the saddest thing you ever heard?"

"No?" I said.

"Of course it is!" He sighed. "So there I am, dehydrated, miserable. I went to take a shower and felt so weak I had to stop and rest on the way back in the hallway. I'm sitting there, fading in and out of consciousness, and then the door across from me opens up, and there's the girl that yelled at me the first week of classes. Alone for the holiday, too, fixing English-muffin pizzas in a contraband toaster oven."

I looked in at my sister, who was now consulting a cookbook, her finger marking the page, and suddenly remembered those same pizzas—English muffin, some cheap spaghetti sauce, cheese—that she'd made for me, hundreds of times.

He picked up the knife out of the jelly jar. "At first, she looked alarmed—I was kind of green, apparently. So she asked me if I was okay, and when I said I wasn't sure, she came out and felt my forehead, and she told me to come in and lie down in her room. Then she walked over to the only open convenience store—which was, like, miles away—bought me a six-pack of Gatorade, and came back and shared her pizzas with me."

"Wow," I said.

"I know." He shook his head, flipping a piece of bread over. "We spent the whole weekend together in her room, watching movies and eating toasted things. She took care of me. It was the best Thanksgiving of my life."

I glanced back at Cora again, remembering what Denise

had said about her that night at the party. Funny how it was so hard to picture my sister as a caretaker, considering that had been what she was to me, once. And now again.

"Which is not to say," Jamie added, "that other Thanksgivings can't be equally good, or even better in their own way. That's why I'm excited about this year. I mean, I love this house, but it's never totally felt like home to me. But tomorrow, when everyone's here, gathered around the table, and reading their thankful lists, it will."

I was listening to this, but still thinking about Cora and those pizzas so intently that I didn't really hear the last part. At least intially. "Thankful lists?"

"Sure," he said, pulling another piece of bread out and bringing the peanut butter closer to him. "Oh, that's right. You guys didn't do those, either, did you?"

"Um, no," I said. "I don't even know what that is."

"Just what it sounds like," he said, scooping out a glop of peanut butter and putting it on his bread. "You make a list of everything you're thankful for. For Thanksgiving. And then you share it with everyone over dinner. It's great!"

"Is this optional?" I asked.

"What?" He put down the knife with a clank. "You don't want to do it?"

"I just don't know . . . I'm not sure what I'd say," I said. He looked so surprised I wondered if he was hurt, so I added, "Off the top of my head, I mean."

"Well, that's the great thing, though," he said, going back to spreading the peanut butter. "You don't have to do it at the moment. You can write up your list whenever you want."

I nodded, as if this was actually my one hesitation. "Right."

"Don't worry," he said. "You'll do great. I know it."

You had to admire Jamie's optimism. For him, anything was possible: a pond in the middle of the suburbs, a wayward sister-in-law going to college, a house becoming a home, and thankful lists for everyone. Sure, there was no guarantee any of these things would actually happen as he envisioned. But maybe that wasn't the point. It was the planning that counted, whether it ever came to fruition or not.

Now, as Cora and I sat in the closet, we heard the doorbell ring downstairs. Roscoe perked up his ears, then yelped, the sound bouncing around the small space.

"That's me," I said, pulling off my sweater and grabbing another one off a nearby hanger. "I'll just—"

I felt a hand clamp around my leg, jerking me off balance. "Let Jamie get it," she said. "Just hang out here with me for a second. Okay?"

"You want me to get in there?"

"No." She reached over to rub Roscoe's ears before adding, more quietly, "I mean, only if you want to."

I crouched down, and she scooted over as I crawled in, moving aside my boots so I could sit down.

"See?" she said. "It's nice in here."

"Okay," I told her. "I will say it. You're acting crazy."

"Can you blame me?" She leaned back with a thud against the wall. "Any minute now, the house will be crawling with people who are expecting the perfect family Thanksgiving. And who's in charge? Me, the last person who is equipped to produce it."

"That's not true," I said.

"How do you figure? I've never done Thanksgiving before."

"You made pizzas that year, for Jamie," I pointed out.

"What, you mean back in college?" she asked.

I nodded.

"Okay, that is so *not* the same thing."

"It was a meal, and it counts," I told her. "Plus, he said it was the best Thanksgiving of his life."

She smiled, leaning her head back and looking up at the clothes. "Well, that's Jamie, though. If it was just him, I wouldn't be worried. But we're talking about his entire family here. They make me nervous."

"Why?"

"Because they're all just so well adjusted," she said, shuddering. "It makes our family look like a pack of wolves."

I just looked at her. "Cora. It's one day."

"It's Thanksgiving."

"Which is," I said, "just one day."

She pulled Roscoe closer to her. "And that's not even including the whole baby thing. These people are so fertile, it's ridiculous. You just know they're all wondering why we've been married five years and haven't yet delivered another member into the tribe."

"I'm sure that's not true," I said. "And even if it is, it's none of their business, and you're fully entitled to tell them so if they start in on you."

"They won't," she said glumly. "They're too nice. That's what so unsettling about all this. They all get along, they love me, they'll eat the turkey even if it's charred *and* raw.

No one's going to be drunk and passed out in the sweet potatoes."

"Mom never passed out in food," I said.

"That you remember."

I rolled my eyes. We hadn't talked about my mom much since the day Cora had laid down my punishment, but she also wasn't as taboo a topic as before. It wasn't like we agreed wholeheartedly now on our shared, or unshared, past. But at the same time, we weren't split into opposing camps—her attacking, me defending—either.

"I'm just saying," she said, "it's a lot of pressure, being part of something like this."

"Like what?"

"A real family," she said. "On the one hand, a big dinner and everyone at the table is the kind of thing I always wanted. But at the same time, I just feel . . . out of place, I guess."

"It's your house," I pointed out.

"True." She sighed again. "Maybe I'm just being hormonal. This medication I'm taking might be good for my ovaries, but it's making me crazy."

I made a face. Being privy to the reproductive drama was one thing, but specific details, in all honesty, made me kind of queasy. A few days before, I'd gone light-headed when she'd only just mentioned the word *uterus*.

The doorbell rang again. The promise of visitors clearly won out over the fear of the oven, as Roscoe wriggled loose, taking off and disappearing around the corner.

"Traitor," Cora muttered.

"Okay. Enough." I got out of the closet, brushing myself

off, then turned around to face her. "This is happening. So you need to go downstairs, face your fears, and make the best of it, and everything will be okay."

She narrowed her eyes at me. "When did you suddenly become so positive?"

"Just get out of there."

A sigh, and then she emerged, getting to her feet and adjusting her skirt. I shut the closet door, and for a moment we both stood there, in front of the full-length mirror, staring at our reflections. Finally I said, "Remember Thanksgiving at our house?"

"No," she said softly. "Not really."

"Me neither," I said. "Let's go."

* * *

It wasn't so much that I was positive. I just wasn't fully subscribing to such a negative way of thinking anymore.

That morning, when Cora had been in serious food-prep freak-out mode—covered in flour, occasionally bursting into tears, waving a spoon at anyone who came too close—all I'd wanted was a reason to escape the house. Luckily, I got a good one.

"Hey," Nate said from the kitchen as I eased in through his sliding-glass door, carrying the four pies stacked on two cookie sheets. "For me? You shouldn't have."

"If you even as much as nip off a piece of crust," I warned him, carrying them carefully to the stove, "Cora will eviscerate you. With an eggbeater, most likely."

"Wow," he said, recoiling slightly. "That's graphic."

"Consider yourself warned." I put the pies down. "Okay to go ahead and preheat?"

"Sure. It's all yours."

I pushed the proper buttons to set the oven, then turned and leaned against it, watching him as he flipped through a thick stack of papers, jotting notes here and there. "Big day, huh?"

"Huge," he said, glancing up at me. "Half our clients are out of town and need their houses or animals checked on, the other half have relatives visiting and need twice as much stuff done as usual. Plus there are those who ordered their entire dinners and want them delivered."

"Sounds crazy," I said.

"It isn't," he replied, jotting something else down. "It just requires military precision."

"Nate?" I heard his dad call out from down a hallway. "What time is the Chambells' pickup?"

"Eleven," Nate said. "I'm leaving in ten minutes."

"Make it five. You don't know how backed up they'll be. Do you have all the keys you need?"

"Yes." Nate reached over to a drawer by the sink, pulling out a key ring and dropping it on the island, where it landed with a clank.

"Double-check," Mr. Cross said. "I don't want to have to come back here if you end up stuck somewhere."

Nate nodded, making another note as a door slammed shut in another part of the house.

"He sounds stressed," I said.

"It's his first big holiday since we started the business," he said. "He signed up a lot of new people just for today. But he'll relax once we get out there and start getting things done."

Maybe this was true. Still, I could hear Mr. Cross muttering to himself in the distance, the noise not unlike that my own mother would make, banging around before she reluctantly headed off to work. "So when, in the midst of all this, do *you* get to eat Thanksgiving dinner?"

"We don't," he said. "Unless hitting the drive-through at Double Burger with someone else's turkey and potatoes in the backseat counts."

"That," I said, "is just plain sad."

"I'm not much for holidays," he said with a shrug.

"Really."

He raised his eyebrows. "Why is that surprising?"

"I don't know," I said. "I guess I just expected someone who was, you know, so friendly and social to be a big fan of the whole family-gathering thing. I mean, Jamie is."

"Yeah?"

I nodded. "In fact, I'm supposed to be making up my thankful list as we speak."

"Your what?"

"Exactly," I said, pointing at him. "Apparently, it's a list of the things you're thankful for, to be read aloud at dinner. Which is something we never did. Ever."

He flipped through the pages again. "Neither did we. I mean, back when we *were* a we."

I could hear Mr. Cross talking now, his voice bouncing down the hall. He sounded much more cheerful than before, and I figured he had to be talking to a customer. "When did your parents split, anyway?"

Nate nodded, picking up the key ring and flipping through it. "When I was ten. You?"

"Five," I said as the oven beeped behind me. Instantly, I thought of Roscoe, huddling in my closet. "My dad's pretty much been out of the picture ever since."

"My mom lives in Phoenix," he said, sliding a key off the ring. "I moved out there with her after the divorce. But then she got remarried and had my stepsisters, and it was too much to handle."

"What was?"

"Me," he said. "I was in middle school, mouthing off, a pain in her ass, and she just wanted to do the baby thing. So year before last, she kicked me out and sent me back here." I must have looked surprised, because he said, "What? You're not the only one with a checkered past, you know."

"I just never imagined you checkered," I told him. Which was a massive understatement, actually. "Not even close."

"I hide it well," he said easily. Then he smiled at me. "Don't you need to put in those pies?"

"Oh. Right."

I turned around, opening the oven and sliding them onto the rack, side by side. As I stood back up, he said, "So what's on your thankful list?"

"I haven't exactly gotten it down yet," I said, easing the oven shut. "Though, actually, you being checkered might make the top five."

"Really," he said.

"Oh, yeah. I thought I was the only misfit in the neighborhood."

"Not by a long shot." He leaned back against the counter behind him, crossing his arms over his chest. "What else?"

"Well," I said slowly, picking up the key he'd taken off

the ring, "to be honest, I have a lot to choose from. A lot of good things have happened since I came here."

"I believe it," he said.

"Like," I said slowly, "I'm very thankful for heat and running water these days."

"As we should all be."

"And I've been really lucky with the people I've met," I said. "I mean, Cora and Jamie, of course, for taking me in. Harriet, for giving me my job. And Olivia, for helping me out that day, and just, you know, being a friend."

He narrowed his eyes at me. "Uh-huh."

"And," I continued, shifting the key in my hand, "there's always Gervais."

"Gervais," he repeated, his voice flat.

"He's almost totally stopped burping. I mean, it's like a miracle. And if I can't be thankful for that, what can I be thankful for?"

"Gee," Nate said, cocking his head to the side, "I don't know."

"There *might* be something else," I said slowly, turning the key in my palm, end over end. "But it's escaping me right now."

He stepped closer to me, his arm brushing, then staying against mine as he reached out, taking the key from my palm and sliding it back onto the table. "Well," he said, "maybe it'll come to you later."

"Maybe," I said.

"Nate?" Mr. Cross called out. He was closer now, and Nate immediately stepped back, putting space between us just before he stuck his head around the corner. He glanced at me, giving a curt nod instead of a hello, then said, "What happened to five minutes?"

"I'm leaving right now," Nate told him.

"Then let's go," Mr. Cross said, ducking back out. A nearby door slammed and I heard his car start up, the engine rumbling.

"I better hit it," Nate said, grabbing up the stack of papers and the key ring. "Enjoy your dinner."

"You, too," I said. He squeezed my shoulder as he passed behind me, quickening his steps as he headed out into the hallway. Then the door banged behind him, and the house was quiet.

I checked on the pies again, then washed my hands and left the kitchen, turning off the light behind me. As I walked to the door that led out onto the patio, I saw another one at the end of the hallway. It was open just enough to make out a bed, the same USWIM sweatshirt Nate had lent me that day folded on top of it.

I don't know what I was expecting, as it wasn't like I'd been in a lot of guys' rooms. A mess, maybe. Some pinup in a bikini on the wall. Perhaps a shot of Heather in a frame, a mirror lined with ticket stubs and sports ribbons, stacks of CDs and magazines. Instead, as I pushed the door open, I saw none of these things. In fact, even full of furniture, it felt . . . empty.

There was a bed, made, and a bureau with a bowlful of change on it, as well as a couple of root beer bottle caps. His backpack was thrown over the chair of a nearby desk, where a laptop was plugged in, the battery light blinking. But there were no framed pictures, and none of the bits and pieces I'd expected, like Marla's fridge collage, or even Sabrina's tons of cats. If anything, it looked more like the last apartment he'd taken me to, almost sterile, with few if any clues as to who slept, lived, and breathed there.

I stood looking for a moment, surprised, before backing out and returning the door to exactly how it had been. All the way back home, though, I kept thinking about his room, trying to figure out what it was about it that was so unsettling. It wasn't until I got back to Cora's that I realized the reason: it looked just like mine. Hardly lived in, barely touched. Like it, too, belonged to someone who had just gotten there and still wasn't sure how long they'd be sticking around.

* * *

"Can I have your attention, please. Hello?"

At first, the plinking noise was barely audible. But as people began to quiet down, and then quieted those around them, it became louder, until finally it was all you could hear.

"Thanks," Jamie said, putting down the fork he'd been using to tap his wineglass. "First, I want to thank all of you for coming. It means a lot to us to have you here for our first holiday meal in our new place."

"Hear, hear!" someone in the back said, and there was a pattering of applause. The Hunters were effusive people, or so I'd noticed while letting them in and taking their coats. His mom, Elinor, was soft-spoken with a kind face; his dad, Roger, had grabbed me in a big hug, ruffling my hair like I was ten. All three of his sisters shared Jamie's dark coloring and outspokenness, whether it was about the pond (which they admired, loudly) or the recent elections (about which they disagreed, also loudly, albeit good-naturedly). And then there were children, and brothers-in-law, various uncles and cousins—so many names and relationships to remember that I'd already decided to give up trying and was just smiling a lot, hoping that compensated. It would have to.

"And now that we have you here," Jamie continued, "there's something else we'd like to share with you."

Standing at the entrance to the foyer, I was behind him, with the perfect view of his audience as he said this. The response was two-pronged: first, hopeful expressions—raised eyebrows, mouths falling open, hands to chests—followed by everyone looking at Cora at once. *Oh, shit,* I thought.

My sister turned pink instantly, then pointedly took a sip from the wineglass in her hand before forcing a smile. By then, Jamie had realized his mistake.

"It's about UMe," he said quickly, and everyone slowly directed their attention back to him. "Our new advertising campaign. It rolls out officially tomorrow, all over the country. But you get to see it here first."

Jamie reached behind a chair, pulling out a square piece of cardboard with the ad I'd seen blown up on it. I looked at Cora again, but she'd disappeared into the kitchen, her glass abandoned on a bookcase.

"I hope you like it," Jamie said, holding the picture up in front of him. "And, um, won't want to sue."

I slipped through the foyer, missing the Hunters' initial reactions, although I did hear some gasps and shrieks, followed by more applause, as I entered the kitchen where

Cora was sliding rolls into the oven, her back to me. She didn't turn around as she said, "Told you."

I glanced behind me, wondering how on earth she could have known for sure it was me. "He felt horrible," I said. "You could tell."

"I know." She shut the oven, tossing a potholder onto the island. From the living room, I could hear people talking over one another, their voices excited. Cora glanced over at the noise. "Sounds like they like it."

"Did he really think they wouldn't?"

She shrugged. "People are weird about family stuff, you know?"

"Really?" I said as I slid onto a stool by the island. "I wouldn't know a thing about that."

"Me either," she agreed. "Our family is perfect."

We both laughed at this, although not nearly loudly enough to drown out the merriment from the next room. Then Cora turned back to the oven, peering in through the glass door. "So," I said, "speaking of family. What does it mean to you?"

She looked at me over her shoulder, one eyebrow raised. "Why do you ask?"

"It's a project for school. I'm supposed to ask everybody."

"Oh." Then she was quiet for a moment, her back still to me. "What are people saying?"

"So far, different things," I told her. "I haven't made a lot of headway, to be honest."

She moved down to the stove, lifting up a lid on a pot and examining the contents. "Well, I'm sure my definition is probably similar to yours. It would have to be, right?"

"I guess," I said. "But then again, you have another family now."

We both looked into the living room. From my angle, I could see Jamie had put the blown-up ad on the coffee table, and everyone else was gathered around. "I guess I do," she said. "But maybe that's part of it, you know? That you're not supposed to have just one."

"Meaning what?"

"Well," she said, adjusting a pot lid, "I have my family of origin, which is you and Mom. And then Jamie's family, my family of marriage. And hopefully, I'll have another family, as well. Our family, that we make. Me and Jamie."

Now I felt bad, bringing this up so soon after Jamie's gaffe. "You will," I said.

She turned around, crossing her arms over her chest. "I hope so. But that's just the thing, right? Family isn't something that's supposed to be static or set. People marry in, divorce out. They're born, they die. It's always evolving, turning into something else. Even that picture of Jamie's family was only the true representation for that one day. By the next, something had probably changed. It had to."

In the living room, I heard a burst of laughter. "That's a good definition," I said.

"Yeah?"

I nodded. "The best yet."

Later, when the kitchen had filled up with people looking for more wine, and children chasing Roscoe, I looked across all the chaos at Cora, thinking that of course you would assume our definitions would be similar, since we had come from the same place. But this wasn't actually true.

We all have one idea of what the color blue is, but pressed to describe it specifically, there are so many ways: the ocean, lapis lazuli, the sky, someone's eyes. Our definitions were as different as we were ourselves.

I looked into the living room, where Jamie's mom was now alone on the couch, the ad spread out on the table in front of her. When I joined her, she immediately scooted over, and for a moment we both studied the ad in silence.

"Must be kind of weird," I said finally. "Knowing this is going to be out there for the whole world to see."

"I suppose." She smiled. Of all of them, to me she looked the most like Jamie. "At the same time, I doubt anyone would recognize me. It was a long time ago."

I looked down at the picture, finding her in the center in her white dress. "Who were these women?" I asked, pointing at the elderly women on each side of her.

"Ah." She leaned forward, a little closer. "My great-aunts. That's Carol on the far left, and Jeannette, next to her. Then Alice on my other side."

"Was this at your house?"

"My parents'. In Cape Cod," she said. "It's so funny. I look at all those children in the front row, and they're all parents themselves now. And all my aunts have passed, of course. But everyone still looks so familiar, even as they were then. Like it was just yesterday."

"You have a big family," I told her.

"True," she agreed. "And there are times I've wished otherwise, if only because the more people you have, the more likely someone won't get along with someone else. The potential for conflict is always there."

"That happens in small families, too, though," I said.

"Yes," she said, looking at me. "It certainly does."

"Do you know who all these people are, still?" I asked.

"Oh, yes," she said. "Every one."

We were both quiet for a moment, looking at all those faces. Then Elinor said, "Want me to prove it?"

I looked up at her. "Yeah," I said. "Sure."

She smiled, pulling the photo a little closer, and I wondered if I should ask her, too, the question for my project, get her definition. But as she ran a finger slowly across the faces, identifying each one, it occurred to me that maybe this was her answer. All those names, strung together like beads on a chain. Coming together, splitting apart, but still and always, a family.

* * *

Despite Cora's concerns, when dinner did hit a snag, it wasn't her fault. It was mine.

"Hey," Jamie said as we cleared the table, having told Cora to stay put and relax. "Where are the pies?"

"Whoops," I said. With all the time in the closet, not to mention the chaos of turkey for eighteen, I'd forgotten all about the ones over at Nate's.

"Whoops," Jamie repeated. "As in, whoops the dog ate them?"

"No," I said. "They're still next door."

"Oh." He glanced into the dining room, biting his lip. "Well, we've got cookies and cake, too. I wonder if—"

"She'll notice," I said, answering this question for him. "I'll go get them."

It had been bustling and noisy at our house for so long

that I was actually looking forward to the quiet of Nate's house. When I stepped inside, all I could hear was the whirring of the heating system and my own footsteps.

Luckily, I'd set the timer, so the pies weren't burned, although they were not exactly warm, either. I was just starting to arrange them back on the cookie sheets when I heard a thud from the other side of the wall.

It was solid and sudden, something hitting hard, and startled me enough that I dropped one of the pies onto the stove, where it hit a burner, rattling loudly. Then there was a crash, followed by the sound of muffled voices. Someone was in the garage.

I put down the pies, then stepped out into the hallway, listening again. I could still hear someone talking as I moved to the doorway that led to the garage, sliding my hand around the knob and carefully pulling it open. The first thing I saw was Nate.

He was squatting down next to a utility shelf that by the looks of it had been leaning against the garage wall up until very recently. Now, though, it was lying sideways across the concrete floor, with what I assumed were its contents—a couple of paint cans, some car-cleaning supplies, and a glass bowl, now broken—spilled all around it. Just as I moved forward to see if he needed help, I realized he wasn't alone.

". . . *specifically* said you should check the keys before you left," Mr. Cross was saying. I heard him before I saw him, now coming into view, his phone clamped to his ear, one hand covering the receiver. "One thing. *One thing* I ask you to be sure of, and you can't even get that right. Do you even know how much this could cost me? The Chambells are half our business in a good week, easily. Jesus!"

"I'm sorry," Nate said, his head ducked down as he grabbed the paint cans, stacking them. "I'll just get it now and go straight there."

"It's too late," Mr. Cross said, snapping his phone shut. "You screwed up. *Again*. And now I'm going to have to deal with this personally if we're going to have any hope of saving the account, which will put us even more behind."

"You don't. I'll talk to them," Nate told him. "I'll tell them it was my fault—"

Mr. Cross shook his head. "No," he said, his voice clenched. "Because that, Nate, is admitting incompetence. It's bad enough I can't count on you to get a single goddamned thing right, *ever*, but I'll be damned if I'm going to have you blabbing about it to the clients like you're proud of it."

"I'm not," Nate said, his voice low.

"You're not what?" Mr. Cross demanded, stepping closer and kicking a bottle of Windex for emphasis. It hit the nearby lawnmower with a bang as he said, louder, "*Not what*, Nate?"

I watched as Nate, still hurriedly picking things up, drew in a breath. I felt so bad for him, and somehow guilty for being there. Like this was bad enough without me witnessing it. His voice was even quieter, hard to make out, as he said, "Not proud of it."

Mr. Cross just stared at him for a moment. Then he shook his head and said, "You know what? You just disgust me. I can't even look at your face right now."

He turned, then crossed the garage toward me, and I quickly moved down the hallway, ducking into a bathroom.

There, in the dark, I leaned back against the sink, listening to my own heart beat, hard, as he moved around the kitchen, banging drawers open and shut. Finally, after what seemed like forever, I heard him leave. I waited a full minute or two after hearing a car pull away before I emerged, and even then I was still shaken.

The kitchen looked the same, hardly touched, my pies right where I'd left them. Past the patio and over the fence, Cora's house, too, was unchanged, the lights all bright downstairs. I knew they were waiting for the pies and for me, and for a moment I wished I could just go and join them, stepping out of this house, and what had just happened here, entirely. At one time, this might have even come naturally. But now, I opened the garage door and went to find Nate.

He was down on the floor, picking up glass shards and tossing them into a nearby trash can, and I just stood there and watched him for a second. Then I took my hand off the door behind me, letting it drop shut.

Immediately, he looked up at me. "Hey," he said, his voice casual. *I hide it well,* I heard him say in my head. "What happened to dinner? You decide to go AWOL rather than do your thankful list?"

"No," I said. "I, um, forgot about the pies, so I had to come get them. I didn't think anyone was here."

Just like that, his face changed, and I knew he knew—either by this last sentence, or the look on my face—that I'd been there. "Oh," he said, this one word flat, toneless. "Right."

I came closer and, after a moment, bent down beside him

and started to pick up pieces of glass. The air felt strange all around me, like just after or before a thunderstorm when the very ions have been shifted, resettled. I knew that feeling. I hadn't experienced it in a while, but I knew it.

"So," I said carefully, my voice low, "what just happened here?"

"Nothing." Now he glanced at me, but only for a second. "It's fine."

"That looked like more than nothing."

"It's just my dad blowing off steam. No big deal. The shelf took the brunt of it."

I swallowed, taking in a breath. Out on the street, beyond the open garage door, an older couple in windsuits walked by, arms swinging in tandem. "So . . . does he do that a lot?"

"Pull down shelves?" he asked, brushing his hands off over the trash can.

"Talk to you like that."

"Nah," he said.

I watched him as he stood, shaking his hair out of his face. "You know," I said slowly, "my mom used to slap us around sometimes. When we were younger. Cora more than me, but I still caught it occasionally."

"Yeah?" He wasn't looking at me.

"You never knew when to expect it. I hated that."

Nate was quiet for a moment. Then he said, "Look, my dad's just . . . he's got a temper. Always has. He blows up, he throws stuff. It's all hot air."

"Has he ever hit you, though?"

He shrugged. "A couple of times when he's really lost it. It's rare, though."

I watched as he reached down, picking up the shelf and pushing it back up against the wall. "Still," I said, "it sounds like he's awfully hard on you. That stuff about you disgusting him—"

"Please," he replied, stacking the paint cans on the bottom shelf. "That's nothing. You should have heard him at my swim meets. He was the only parent to get banned from the deck entirely, for life. Not that it stopped him. He just yelled from behind the fence."

I thought back to that day in the parking lot, the guy who had called after him. "Is that why you quit?"

"One reason." He picked up the Windex. "Look, like I said, it's no big deal. I'm fine."

Fine. I'd thought the same thing. "Does your mom know about this?"

"She's aware that he's a disciplinarian," he said, drawing out this last word in such a way that it was clear he'd heard it a lot, said in a certain way. "She tends to be a bit selective in how she processes information. And anyway, in her mind, when she sent me back here, that was just what I needed."

"Nobody needs that," I said.

"Maybe not. But it's what I've got."

He headed for the door, pulling it open. I followed him inside, watching as he went to the island, picking up the key that I'd been holding earlier. I could remember so clearly turning it in my palm, the way he'd taken it from me—putting it back on the island but not on the ring—and suddenly

I felt culpable, even more a part of this than I already was.

"You could tell someone, you know," I said as he slid it into his pocket. "Even if he's not always hitting you, it's not right."

"What, and get put into social services? Or shipped off to live with my mom, who doesn't want me there? No thanks."

"So you have thought about it," I said.

"Heather did. A lot," he said, reaching up to rub his face. "It freaked her out. But she just didn't understand. My mom kicked me out, and at least he took me in. It's not like I have a lot of options here."

I thought of Heather, that day at the pond place. *I'm glad you and Nate are friends,* she'd said. "She was worried about you," I said.

"I'm fine." I couldn't help notice each time he said this. "At this point, I've only got six months until graduation. After that, I'm coaching a swim camp up north, and as long as I get into school somewhere, I'm gone."

"Gone," I repeated.

"Yeah," he said. "To college, or wherever. Anyplace but here."

"Free and clear."

"Exactly." He looked up at me, and I thought of us standing in this same spot earlier as he took that key from my hand. I'd felt so close to something then—something that, back at the yellow house or even in my first days at Cora's, I never would have imagined. "I mean, you stayed with your mom, stuck it out even though it was bad. You understand, right?"

I did. But it was more than that. Sure, being free and clear had been just what I'd wanted, so recently that it should have been easy to agree with it. But if it was still true, I wouldn't have even been there. I'd have left when I'd had the chance earlier, staying out of this, of everything.

But I hadn't. Because I wasn't the same girl who'd run to that fence the first night, thinking only of jumping over it and getting away. Somewhere, something had changed.

I could have stood there and told him this, and more. Like how glad I was, now, that the Honeycutts had turned me in, because in doing so they'd brought me here to Cora and Jamie and all the things I was thankful for, including him. And how even when you felt like you had no options or didn't need anyone, you could be wrong. But after all he'd just told me, to say this seemed foolish, if not impossible. Six months wasn't that long. And I'd been left behind enough.

You understand, right? he'd said. There was only one answer.

"Yeah," I said. "Of course I do."

Chapter Twelve

"There you are! Thank God!"

It was the day after Thanksgiving, the biggest shopping day of the year, and the mall was opening at six a.m. for door-buster specials. Harriet, however, insisted I had to be there at five thirty to get ready. This seemed a little extreme to me, but still I'd managed to rouse myself in the dark and stumble into the shower, then pour myself a big cup of coffee, which I sucked down as I walked along the greenway, a flashlight in my other hand. When I got to the mall itself, people were already lined up outside the main entrance, bundled up in parkas, waiting.

Inside, all the stores I passed were bustling—employees loading up stock, chattering excitedly—everyone in serious preparation mode, bracing for the crowds. When I got to Harriet's kiosk, it was clear she had already been there for a while: there were two Jump Java cups already on the register, a third clamped in her hand. Needless to say, she was pumped.

"Hurry, hurry," she called out to me now, waving her arms back and forth as if she could move me closer faster, by sheer force of will. "We don't have much time!"

Slightly alarmed, I looked over at Reggie, who was sitting at the Vitamin Me kiosk, a cup with a tea bag poking out of it in one hand. He took a sleepy sip, waving at me as I passed.

"You had to be here early, too?" I asked him. I couldn't imagine someone actually wanting some shark cartilage for Christmas.

He shrugged. "I don't mind it. I kind of like the bustle."

Then he smiled and looked at Harriet, who was maniacally lighting another incense stick. *Yeah*, I thought. *The bustle.*

"Okay," Harriet said, pulling me to stand next to her in front of the cart as she took another gulp of coffee. "Let's do a check and double check. We've got the low-dollar stuff on the bottom, higher on the top. Rings by the register for impulse buyers, incense burning for ambience, plenty of ones in the register. Do you remember the disaster plan?"

"Grab the cashbox and the precious gems, do a headcount, proceed to the food court exit," I recited.

"Good," she said with a curt nod. "I don't think we'll need it, but on a day like this you never know."

I glanced over at Reggie, who just shook his head, stifling a yawn.

"You know," Harriet continued, studying the kiosk, "as I'm looking at this now, I think maybe we should switch the earrings and bracelets. They don't look right. In fact—"

"Harriet. They're great. We're ready," I told her.

She sighed. "I don't know," she said. "I still feel like I'm missing something."

"Could it be, maybe, the true meaning of the holiday season?" Reggie called out from his kiosk. "In which we focus on goodwill and peace on earth, and not on making as much money as possible?"

"No," Harriet said. Then she snapped her fingers, the sound loud, right by my ear. "Hold on!" she said. "I can't believe I almost forgot."

She bent down beneath the register, pulling out the plastic bin where she kept all her stock. As she picked through the dozens of small plastic bags, finally pulling one out and opening it, I looked at my watch. It was 5:51. When I looked back at Harriet, she was fastening a clasp around her neck, her back to me.

"Okay," she said. "I made these a couple of weeks back, just fooling around, but now I'm wondering if I should put them out. What do you think?"

When she turned around, the first thing I saw was the key. It was silver and delicate, dotted with red stones, and hung from a braided silver chain around her neck. Instantly, I was aware of my own key, which was bulkier and not nearly as beautiful.But even so, seeing this one, I understood why I'd gotten so many comments on it. There was something striking about a single key. It was like a question waiting to be answered, a whole missing a half. Useless on its own, needing something else to be truly defined.

Harriet raised her eyebrows. "Well?"

"It's—"

"You hate it, don't you," she decided, before I could even finish. "You think it's tacky and derivative."

"It's not," I said quickly. "It's beautiful. Really striking."

"Yeah?" She turned to the mirror, reaching up to touch

the key, running her finger over it. "It kind of is, isn't it? Unique, at any rate. You think they'll sell?"

"You made more?"

She nodded, reaching into the box again. As she laid more bags out on the counter, I counted at least twenty, none of them the same: some keys were smaller, some bigger, some plain, others covered in gemstones. "I got inspired," she explained as I examined them one by one. "It was kind of manic, actually."

"You should definitely put them out," I told her. "Like, right now."

In record time, we'd slapped on price tags and organized a display. I was just putting the last necklace on the rack when the clock hit six and the doors opened. At first, the sound was distant, but then, like a wave, it got louder and louder as people spilled into sight, filling the long, wide corridor between us. "It's on," Harriet said. "Here we go."

We sold the first key necklace twenty minutes later, the second, a half hour after that. If I hadn't been there to see it myself, I never would have believed it, but every single customer who came by paused to look at them. Not everyone bought, but clearly they drew people's attention. Over and over again.

The day passed in a blur of people, noise, and the Christmas music overhead, which I only heard in bits and pieces, whenever the din briefly died down. Harriet kept drinking coffee, the key necklaces kept selling, and my feet began to ache, my voice getting hoarse from talking. The zinc lozenges Reggie offered up around one o'clock helped, but not much.

Still, I was grateful for the day and the chaos, if only because it kept my mind off what had happened the day before with Nate. All that evening, after I'd taken the pies back and watched them get devoured, then helped Cora load the dishwasher before collapsing onto my bed, I'd kept going over and over it in my head. It was all so unsettling: not only what I'd seen and heard, but how I'd responded afterward.

I never would have thought of myself as someone who would want to help or save anybody. In fact, this was the one thing that bugged me so much about Nate in the first place. And yet, I was surprised, even disappointed, that at that crucial moment—*You understand, right?*—I'd been so quick to step back and let the issue drop, when, as his friend, I should have come closer. It wasn't just unsettling, even. It was shameful.

At three o'clock, the crowds were still thick, and despite the lozenges, I'd almost totally lost my voice. "Go," Harriet said, taking a sip of her umpteenth coffee. "You've done more than enough for one day."

"Are you sure?" I asked.

"Yes," she replied, smiling at a young woman in a long red coat who was buying one of the last key necklaces. She handed over the bag, then watched the woman disappear into the crowd. "That's fifteen we've sold today," she said, shaking her head. "Can you even believe it? I'm going to have to go home and stay up all night making more. Not that I'm complaining, of course."

"I told you," I said. "They're beautiful."

"Well, I have you to thank for them. Yours was the

inspiration." She picked up one trimmed with green stones. "In fact, you should take one. It's the least I can do."

"Oh, no. You don't have to."

"I want to." She gestured at the rack. "Or I can make you one special, if you prefer."

I looked at them, then down at my own necklace. "Maybe later," I said. "I'm good for now."

Outside, the air was crisp, cool, and as I headed toward the greenway and home, I reached up, running my hand over my own necklace. The truth was, lately I'd been thinking about taking it off. It seemed kind of ridiculous to be carrying around a key to a house that was no longer mine. And anyway, it wasn't like I could go back, even if I wanted to. More than once, I'd even gone so far as to reach up to undo the clasp before stopping myself.

On that first night, when Nate and I had met, he had asked me, *What's it to?* and I'd told him, nothing. In truth, though, then and now, the key wasn't just to that lock at the yellow house. It was to me, and the life I'd had before. Maybe I'd even begun to forget it a bit over the last few weeks, and this was why it was easier to imagine myself without it. But now, after what had happened the night before, I was thinking maybe having a reminder wasn't such a bad idea. So for now, it would stay where it was.

* * *

After everything that had happened on Thanksgiving, I'd thought things might be a little awkward for the ride on the first day back at school. And they were. Just not in the way I was expecting.

"Hey," Nate said as I slid into the front seat. "How's it going?"

He was smiling, looking the same as always. Like nothing out of the ordinary had happened. But then to him, I supposed that it hadn't. "Good," I said, fastening my seat belt. "You?"

"Miserable," he announced cheerfully. "I've got two papers and a presentation due today. I was up until two last night."

"Really," I said, although actually, I knew this, as I'd been awake until about the same time, and I could see the lights from his room—two small squares, off to the right—breaking up the dark that stretched between our two houses. "I've got a calculus test that I have to pass. Which means, almost certainly, that I won't."

As soon as I said this, I expected Gervais to chime in from the backseat, agreeing with this, as it was the perfect setup to slam me. When I turned around, though, he was just sitting there, quiet and unobtrusive, the same way he had been for the last couple of weeks. As if to compensate for his silence, though, I was seeing him more and more. At least once a week, I caught him watching me at lunch, the way he had that one day, and whenever I passed him in the hallways he was always giving me these looks I couldn't figure out.

"What?" he said now, as I realized I was still looking strangely at him.

"Nothing," I replied, and turned back.

Nate reached for the radio, cranking it up, and then we

were turning out into traffic. Everything actually felt okay, wholly unchanged, and I realized maybe I'd overreacted, thinking they would have. The bottom line was, I knew something I hadn't the week before, and we were friends—at least for another six months or so. I didn't have to get all wrought up about what was going on with his dad; I'd never wanted anyone to get involved with me and my domestic drama. Maybe what we had now, in the end, was best—to be close but not too close, the perfect middle ground.

Half a block from school, Nate pulled into the Quik Zip for gas. As he got out to pump it, I sat back in my seat, opening the calc book in my lap. About half a page in, though, I heard a noise from behind me.

By this point, I was well acquainted with Gervais's various percussions, but this wasn't one I was used to. It was more like an intake, a sudden drawing in of breath. The first one I ignored; the second, barely noted. By the third, though, I was starting to think he might be having an attack of some sort, so I turned around.

"What are you doing?" I asked him.

"Nothing," he said, instantly defensive. But then, he did it again. "The thing is—"

He was interrupted by Nate opening his door and sliding back behind the wheel. "Why is it," he said to me, "that whenever I'm in a hurry I always get the slowest gas pump in the world?"

I glanced at Gervais, who had hurriedly gone back to his book, his head ducked down. "Probably the same reason you hit every red light when you're late."

"And lose your keys," he added, cranking the engine.

"Maybe it's the universe conspiring against you."

"I have had a run of bad luck lately," he agreed.

"Yeah?"

He glanced over at me. "Well, maybe not all bad."

Hearing this, I had a flash of us in the kitchen that day, his hand brushing against mine as he reached for the key lying in my palm. As Nate turned back to the road, I suddenly did feel awkward, in just the way I'd thought I would. Talk about bad luck. Maybe this wouldn't be so easy after all.

* * *

For me, December was all about work. Working for Harriet, working on my applications, working on calculus. And when I wasn't doing any of these things, I was tagging along with Nate on his job.

Logically, I knew the only way to stay in that middle ground with Nate was to let space build up between us. But it wasn't so easy to stop something once it had started, or so I was learning. One day you were all about protecting yourself and keeping things simple. The next thing you know, you're buying macaroons.

"Belgian macaroons," Nate corrected me, pulling two boxes off the shelf. "That's key."

"Why?"

"Because a macaroon you can buy anywhere," he replied. "But these, you can only find here at Spice and Thyme, which means they are gourmet and expensive, and therefore suitable for corporate gift-giving."

I looked down at the box in my hand. "Twelve bucks is a lot for ten macaroons," I said. Nate raised his eyebrows. "*Belgian* macaroons, I mean."

"Not to Scotch Design Inc.," he said, continuing to add boxes to the cart between us. "In fact, this is the very low end of their holiday buying. Just wait until we get to the nut-and-cheese-straw towers. *That's* impressive."

I glanced at my watch. "I might not make it there. My break is only a half hour. If I'm even a minute late, Harriet starts to have palpitations."

"Maybe," he said, adding a final box, "you should buy her some Belgian macaroons. For ten bucks, they might cure her of that entirely."

"I somehow doubt the solution is that easy. Or inexpensive."

Nate moved back to the head of the cart, nudging it forward past the chocolates into the jelly-bean section. Spice and Thyme was one of those huge gourmet food stores designed to feel small and cozy, with narrow aisles, dim lighting, and stuff stacked up everywhere you turned. Personally, it made me feel claustrophobic, especially during Christmas, when it was twice as crowded as usual. Nate, however, hardly seemed bothered, deftly maneuvering his cart around a group of senior citizens studying the jelly beans before taking the corner to boxed shortbreads.

"I don't know," he said, glancing at the list in his hand before beginning to pull down tins decorated with the face of a brawny Scotsman playing a bagpipe. "I think that what Harriet needs might be simpler than she thinks."

"Total organization of her house, courtesy of Rest Assured?" I asked.

"No," he said. "Reggie."

"Ah," I said as the senior citizens passed us again, squeezing by the cart. "So you noticed, too."

"Please." He rolled his eyes. "It's kind of flagrant. What does she think all that ginkgo's about?"

"That's what I said," I told him. "But when I suggested it to her, she was shocked by the idea. *Shocked*."

"Really," he said, pulling the cart forward again. "Then she must be more distracted than we even realize. Which, honestly, I'm not quite sure is possible."

We jerked to a stop suddenly, narrowly missing a collision with two women pushing a cart entirely full of wine. After some dirty looks and a lot of clanking, they claimed their right of way and moved on. I said, "She said she was too busy for a relationship."

"Everyone's busy," Nate said.

"I know. I think she's really just scared."

He glanced over at me. "Scared? Of Reggie? What, she thinks he might force her to give up caffeine for real or something?"

"No," I said.

"Of what, then?" he asked.

I paused, only just now realizing that the subject was hitting a little close to home. "You know, getting hurt. Putting herself out there, opening up to someone."

"Yeah," he said, adding some cheese straws to the cart, "but risk is just part of relationships. Sometimes they work, sometimes they don't."

I picked up a box of cheese straws, examining it. "Yeah," I said. "But it's not all about chance, either."

"Meaning what?" he asked, taking the box from me and adding it to the rest.

"Just that, if you know ahead of time that there might an issue that dooms everything—like, say, you're incredibly controlling and independent, like Harriet—maybe it's better to acknowledge that and not waste your time. Or someone else's."

I looked over at Nate, who I now realized was watching me. He said, "So being independent dooms relationships? Since when?"

"That was just one example," I said. "It can be anything."

He gave me a weird look, which was kind of annoying, considering he'd brought this up in the first place. And anyway, what did he want me to do, just come out and admit it would never work between us because it was too hard to care about anyone, much less someone I had to worry about? It was time to get back to the theoretical, and quickly. "All I'm saying is that Harriet won't even trust me with the cashbox. So maybe it's a lot to ask for her to give over her whole life to someone."

"I don't think Reggie wants her life," Nate said, nudging the cart forward again. "Just a date."

"Still," I said, "one can lead to the other. And maybe, to her, that's too much risk."

I felt him look at me again, but I made a point of checking my watch. It was almost time to go. "Yeah," he said. "Maybe."

Ten minutes later—and one minute late—I arrived back at Harriet's, where, true to form, she was waiting for me. "Am I glad to see you," she said. "I was starting to get nervous. I think we're about to have a big rush. I can just kind of feel it."

I looked down the middle of the mall, which was busy but not packed, and then the other way at the food court, which looked much the same. "Well, I'm here now," I said, sticking my purse in the cabinet under the register. As I did, I remembered the thing I'd bought for her, pulling it out. "Here," I said, tossing it over. "For you."

"Really?" She caught it, then turned the box in her hand. "Macaroons! I love these."

"They're Belgian," I said.

"All right," she replied, tearing them open. "Even better."

* * *

"Come on, Laney! Pick up the pace!"

I looked at Olivia, then in the direction she was yelling, the distant end of the mall parking lot. All I could see were a few cars and a Double Burger wrapper being kicked around by the breeze. "What are you doing, again?"

"Don't even ask," she told me. This was the same thing she'd said when I'd come across her, ten minutes earlier, sitting on the curb outside the Vista 10 box office on this unseasonably warm Saturday, a book open in her lap. "All I can say is it's not my choice."

"Not your—" I said, but then this sentence, and my concentration, were interrupted by a *thump-thump* noise. This time when I turned, I saw Laney, wearing a purple tracksuit, rounding the distant corner of Meyer's Department Store at a very slow jog, headed our way.

"Finally," Olivia said, pulling a digital kitchen timer out from beneath her book and getting to her feet. "You're going to have to go faster than that if you want me to sit out here for another lap!" she yelled, cupping her hands around her mouth. "You understand?"

Laney ignored her, or just didn't hear, keeping her gaze straight as she kept on, *thump-thump, thump-thump.* As she got closer I saw her expression was serious, her face flushed, although she did give me a nod as she passed.

Olivia consulted the stopwatch. "Eight minutes," she called out as Laney continued on toward the other end of the mall. "That's a sixteen-minute mile. Also known as *slow.*"

"Still training for the five-K, huh?" I asked as a mall security guard rolled by, glancing at us.

"Oh, she's beyond training now," Olivia replied, sitting down on the curb again and setting the timer beside her. "She's focused, living and breathing the run. And yes, that *is* a direct quote."

"You're supportive," I said.

"No, I'm realistic," she replied. "She's been training for two months now, and her times aren't improving. At all. If she insists on doing this, she's just going to embarrass herself."

"Still," I said, looking at Laney again, who was still plodding along. "You have to admit, it's kind of impressive."

Olivia harrumphed. "What is? Total denial?"

"Total commitment," I said. "You know, the idea of discovering something that, for all intents and purposes, goes against your abilities, and yet still deciding to do it anyway. That takes guts, you know?"

She considered this as the security guard passed by, going the other way. "If she's so gutsy, though, why is it that she usually quits at about the two-mile mark, then calls me to come pick her up?"

"She does that?" I asked.

"Only about every other time. Oh, wait. Is that not supportive, though?"

I sat back, ignoring this, planting my hands on the pavement behind me. It wasn't like I was some expert on the meaning of being supportive. Was it being loyal even against your better judgment? Or, like Olivia, was it making your displeasure known from the start, even when someone didn't want to hear it? I'd been thinking about this more and more since Nate's and my discussion at Spice and Thyme. Maybe he was someone who lived in the moment, easily able to compartmentalize one part of his life from another. But to me, the Nate I was spending more and more time with was still the same one who was going home to a bad situation with his dad and who planned to get out as soon as he could—both of these were reasons I should have kept away, or at least kept my distance. Yet if anything, I kept moving closer, which just made no sense at all.

Now, I looked over at Olivia, who was squinting into the distance, the timer still counting down in her lap. "Do you remember," I asked, "how you said that when you first came from Jackson, it was hard for you, and that's why you never bothered to talk to anyone or make friends?"

"Yeah," she said, sounding a bit wary. "Why?"

"So why did you, then?" I asked, looking at her. "I mean, with me. What changed?"

She considered this as a minivan drove by, pulling up on the other side of the box office. "I don't know," she said. "I guess it was just that we had something in common."

"Jackson."

"Yeah, that. But also, not being like everyone else at Perkins. You know, having some part that's different, and yet shared. I mean, with me it's my family, my economic standing. You, well, you're a lush and a delinquent—"

"Hey," I said. "That was just one day."

"I know, I'm just kidding," she said, waving me off with her hand. "But neither of us exactly fit the mold there."

"Right."

She sat back, brushing her braids away from her face. "My point is, there are a lot of people in the world. No one ever sees everything the same way you do; it just doesn't happen. So when you find one person who gets a couple of things, especially if they're important ones . . . you might as well hold on to them. You know?"

I looked down at the stopwatch sitting on the curb between us. "Nicely put," I said. "And all in less than two minutes."

"Conciseness is underrated," she said easily. Then she looked over my shoulder, suddenly raising her hand to wave to someone behind me. When I turned, I was surprised to see Gervais, in his peacoat standing in front of the box office. Seeing me, his face flushed, and he hurriedly grabbed his ticket from under the glass and darted inside.

"You know Gervais?" I asked her.

"Who, extra salt, double-lic whip? Sure. He's a regular." I just looked at her. "That's his concession order," she explained. "Large popcorn, no butter, extra salt, and two packs of licorice whips. He hits at least one movie a week. The boy likes film. How do you know him?"

"We ride to school together," I said. So Gervais had a life outside of carpool. It wasn't like it should have been surprising, but for some reason, it was.

Just then, I heard a buzzing: her phone. She pulled it out of her pocket, looked at the screen, then sighed. Laney. "I'd say I told you so," she said. "But it's not like I get any satisfaction from this."

I watched as she flipped it open, hitting the TALK button and saying she'd be there in a minute. Then she picked up her book and got to her feet, brushing herself off. "Still," I said, "you have to get something, though."

"From what? "

"From this." I gestured around me. "I mean, you are out here timing her. So you can't be totally opposed to what she's doing."

"No, I am." She pulled her keys out of her pocket, shoving the book under her arm. "But I'm also a sucker. Clearly."

"You are not," I said.

"Well, then, I don't know the reason," she said. "Other than she's my cousin, and she asked, so I'm here. I try not to go deeper than that. I'll see you around, okay?"

I nodded, and then she was walking away, across the lot to her car. Watching her, I kept thinking of what she'd said earlier about having things in common, and then of Nate and me in his garage on Thanksgiving, when I'd told him about my mom and our history. Clearly, sharing something could take you a long way, or at least to a different place than you'd planned. Like a friendship or a family, or even just alone on a curb on a Saturday, trying to get your bearings as best you can.

* * *

It wasn't just me that was feeling out of sorts. Even the weather was weird.

"You have to admit," Harriet said, shaking her head as we stepped out into the employee parking lot later that night, "this is very strange. When has it ever been seventy-seven degrees a week before Christmas?"

"It's global warming," Reggie told her. "The ice caps are melting."

"I was thinking more along the lines of the apocalypse," she said.

He sighed. "Of course you were."

"Seriously, though, who wants to Christmas-shop when it feels like summer?" she asked as we started across the lot. "This *cannot* be good for sales."

"Do you ever think about anything but business?" Reggie said.

"The apocalypse," she told him. "And occasionally coffee."

"You know," he said, "I'm aware that you're kidding, but that's still really—"

"Good night," I called out as I peeled off toward the greenway. They both waved, still bickering. This, however, was not strange in the least; it was the way I always left them.

Often, Harriet gave me a ride home, as she hated me taking the greenway in the dark, but as the weather had grown oddly warm I'd been insisting on walking instead, just to make the most of the unseasonable weather while it lasted. On my way back to Cora's, I passed several bicyclists, two runners, and a pack of kids on scooters, all with the same idea. Weirdest of all, though, was what I saw at home when I walked in the front door: Jamie, at the bottom of the stairs, wearing his bathing suit and swim fins, a towel thrown over his shoulder. It might not have been a sign of the apocalypse, but it seemed pretty close.

At first, it was clear that I'd surprised him: he jumped, flustered, before quickly recovering and striking a casual pose. "Hey," he said, like he hung out in swimgear in the foyer every day. "How was work?"

"What are you—?" I began, then stopped as Cora appeared at the top of the stairs, a pair of shorts pulled over her own suit.

"Oh," she said, stopping suddenly, her face flushing. "Hi."

"Hi," I said slowly. "What's going on?"

They exchanged a guilty look. Then Cora sighed and said, "We're going pool jumping."

"You're what?"

"It's seventy-five degrees! In December!" Jamie said. "We have to. We can't help ourselves."

I looked up at my sister again. "It is pretty nice out," she said.

"But the neighborhood pool doesn't even have water in it," I said.

"That's why we're going to Blake's," Jamie told me. "You want to come?"

"You're sneaking into Nate's pool?"

Cora bit her lip as Jamie said, "Well, technically, it's not really sneaking. I mean, we're neighbors. And it's right there, heated, with nobody using it."

"Do you have permission?" I asked.

He looked up at Cora, who squirmed on the step. "No," she said. "But I saw Blake earlier and he said he and Nate were taking off for an overnight business thing. So . . ."

". . . you're just going to jump their fence and their pool," I finished for her.

Silence. Then Jamie said, "It's seventy-five degrees! In December! Do you know what this means?"

"The apocalypse?" I asked.

"What?" he said. "No. God. Why would you—"

"She's right, you know," Cora said, coming down the stairs. "We're not exactly setting a good example."

"It was your idea," Jamie pointed out. Cora flushed again. "Your sister," he said to me, "is a serious pool jumper. In college, she was always the first to go over the fence."

"Really," I said, turning to look at her.

"Well," she replied, as if about to justify this. Then she just said, "You know, it's seventy-five degrees. In December."

Jamie grabbed her hand, grinning. "That's my girl," he said, then pointed at me. "You coming?"

"I don't have a bathing suit," I told him.

"In my closet, bottom right-hand drawer," Cora said. "Help yourself."

I just shook my head, incredulous, as they started through the kitchen. Cora was laughing, Jamie's flippers slapping the floor, and then they were outside, the door swinging shut behind them.

I wasn't going to go and certainly didn't plan to swim. But after sitting on my bed in the quiet for a few moments, I did go find a suit of Cora's, pull on some sweatpants over it, and head downstairs, crossing the yard to where I could hear splashing just beyond the fence.

"There she is," Jamie said as I slipped through. He was in the shallow end, next to Roscoe, who was on the deck, barking excitedly, while Cora was underwater, swimming down deep, her hair streaming out behind her. "Couldn't resist, huh?"

"I don't think I'm coming in," I said, walking over and sitting down on the edge, my knees pulled to my chest. "I'll just watch."

"Ah, that's no fun," he said. Then, with Roscoe still barking, he dove under, disappearing. As he swam the length of the pool, the dog ran alongside, following him.

I looked over at Cora, who was now bobbing in the deep end, brushing her hair back from her face. "You know," I said, "I never would have figured you for a lawbreaker."

She made a face at me. "It's not exactly a felony. And besides, Blake owes us."

"Really? Why?" I asked, but she didn't hear me, or chose not to answer, instead diving under again to join Jamie, who was circling along the bottom.

As they emerged a moment later, laughing and splashing each other, I kicked off my shoes, then rolled up my sweatpants and dunked my feet in the water. It was warm, even more so than the air, and I leaned back on my palms, turning my face up to the sky. I hadn't been swimming since the last time we'd lived in a complex with a pool, around ninth grade. In the summer, I would spend hours there, staying in until my mom had to come get me when dark was falling.

Jamie and Cora stayed in for about a half hour, dunking each other and playing Marco Polo. By the time they climbed out, it was past ten, and even Roscoe—who'd been barking nonstop—was exhausted. "See," Jamie said as they toweled off, "one dip, no harm done."

"It is nice," I agreed, moving my feet through the water.

"You coming back with us?" Cora asked as they walked behind me, heading for the fence.

"In a minute. I think I'll hang out a little while longer."

"Might as well make the most of it," Jamie said as Roscoe trotted behind him. "After all, it won't be like this forever."

Then they were gone, through the fence, where I could hear their voices fading as they crossed the yard. I waited until it had been quiet for a few minutes before slipping off my sweatpants. Then, with one last quick look around me to make sure I was alone, I jumped in.

It was startling, at first, being back in a pool after so long not swimming. Just as quickly, though, all the instinct came back, and before I knew it I was moving steadily to the other side, the water filling my ears. I don't know how many laps I'd done, back and forth, only that I had hit such a rhythm that at first, I didn't even notice when a light clicked on in the house. By the time the second one came on, it was too late.

I froze, sinking down below the pool's edge, as a figure

moved through the now-bright living room. After it crossed back once, then again, I heard a door slide open. *Shit,* I thought, then panicked, taking a deep breath and submerging myself.

Which, as it turned out, was not the smartest move, as became apparent when I looked up through the shifting blue water above to see Nate staring down at me. By that time, my lungs were about to explode, so I had no choice but to show myself.

"Well, well," he said as I sputtered to the surface. "What's this all about?"

I swam to the edge, just to do something, then ran a hand over my face. "Um," I said. "Actually—"

"Cora and Jamie were pool jumping, huh?" he said. I just looked at him, confused, until he pulled one flipper, then another, from behind his back. "They're not exactly slick about it," he said, dropping them on the deck beside his feet. "These were right there on that chair. Last time they left a swimming noodle."

"Oh," I said. "Yeah. I guess we're busted."

"No big deal." He crouched down by me, dipping his hand in the water. "It's good someone's getting some use out of this thing. My dad's always complaining about how much it costs to heat it."

"You don't swim at all anymore?"

"Not really," he said.

"You must miss it, though."

He shrugged. "Sometimes. It was a good escape. Until, you know, it wasn't."

I thought of what he'd said, about his dad getting banned but still yelling from the fence. "You should come in," I said. "It's really warm."

"Nah, I'm okay." He sat on a nearby chair. "You go ahead, though."

I bobbed there for a second, neither of us talking. Finally I said, "So I thought you were out of town on a business thing."

"Change of plans," he said. "It was decided I should come home early."

"Decided," I repeated.

He looked up, then gave me a tired smile. "It's been a long day, let's just say that."

I'll bet, I thought. Out loud, I said, "All the more reason to take a dip. I mean, it's December. Seventy-five degrees. You know you want to."

I honestly didn't think he'd agree with this; I was just talking. But then he nodded slowly, and pushed himself to his feet. "All right," he said. "I'll be back in a sec."

As he disappeared inside, it occurred to me that maybe this was not the smartest idea. After all, I was trying to keep my distance and now, with this invitation, had narrowed the space we were in considerably. Before I could figure out how to change this, though—or even if I wanted to—he was coming back outside, now in trunks, and walking across the patio. Needless to say, this was distracting. That first night, I hadn't really seen him shirtless, and now I could focus on little else. All the more reason, I realized, to backtrack, but before I could he was stretching his arms overhead and diving in, hitting the water with barely a splash and disappearing below.

You swim, I thought, having a flash of that sweatshirt as he came to the surface, then closer toward me with a breaststroke that looked effortless. When he emerged, shaking his head and sending droplets flying, I said, “Nice form.”

“Thanks,” he said, bobbing in front of me. “Years of training.”

Suddenly, I was so aware of how close we were to each other, with only the water between us. I looked down: beneath the surface my skin looked so pale, almost blue, my necklace lying across it. When I glanced up again, he was looking at it, too, and after meeting my gaze for a second he reached over, catching it in one hand to lie flat on his palm.

“How many of those key necklaces do you think Harriet has sold since Thanksgiving?” he asked.

“I don’t know,” I said. “A lot.”

“I saw a girl at Jump Java today wearing one. It was so weird.”

“I’ll be sure to tell Harriet you said that,” I said. “She’ll be overjoyed.”

“I don’t mean it like that.” He turned his palm, letting the key fall loose, and it slowly floated back down to rest against me again. “It’s just that I associate them with you, and this one. You know? It was the first thing I noticed about you that night we met.”

“Even before I was jumping the fence?”

“Okay.” He smiled. “Maybe the second.”

All around us, the neighborhood was quiet, the sky

spread out wide and sprinkled with stars overhead. I could feel him right there in front of me, and I thought of what Jamie had said earlier: *It won't be like this forever.* That was true, and also the reason I should have climbed out right then, as well as why I knew I would stay.

He was still watching me, both of us bobbing, and I could feel the water around me, pressing in, pulling back. Then, slowly, Nate was moving closer, leaning in, and despite all I'd told myself, and all I wanted to believe I was and wasn't capable of, I stayed where I was as he kissed me. His lips were warm, his skin wet, and when he drew back, I felt myself shiver, unaccustomed to anyone being so close, and yet still not ready for him to pull away.

"Are you cold?" he asked.

I was about to shake my head, say it wasn't that at all, but before I could, I felt his hand close over mine. "Don't worry," he said, "it's warmer the deeper you go." Then, to prove it, he went under, and I took a deep breath, the biggest I could, and let him pull me down with him.

* * *

I already knew Jamie liked holidays. There were the matching blue shirts, for one thing, not to mention the thankful lists. But even armed with this knowledge, I still was not fully prepared for how he approached Christmas.

"Just stand still, okay?" Cora said, making a face as she stuffed the pillow farther up under his jacket. "Stop wriggling around."

"I can't," Jamie replied. "This long underwear is a lot itchier than I thought it would be."

"I told you to just wear your boxer shorts."

"Santa doesn't wear boxers!" he said, his voice rising slightly as she yanked the wide black belt of his costume tight over the pillow, holding it in place. "If I'm going to do this, I want to be authentic about it."

"I seriously doubt," Cora said, pushing herself to her feet, "that the Santa police do an underwear check. Now where's your beard?"

"On the bed," he told her. Then he saw me. "Hey, Ruby! So what do you think? Pretty great, right?"

This wasn't exactly the first word that had come to mind at seeing him in a full-on Santa outfit: red suit, black boots, and big white wig, which to me looked itchier than any underwear could ever be. But in the interest of family, I decided to play along.

"Yeah," I agreed as Cora reached over his head, fastening his beard. "Are you going to a party or something?"

"No," he said. Cora stepped back, hands on her hips, examining her work. "It's Christmas Eve."

"Right," I said slowly. "So this is for . . ."

"Walking around the neighborhood!" he finished for me. I just looked at Cora, who simply shook her head. "My dad always dressed up like Santa on Christmas Eve," he explained. "It was a family tradition."

"Which we did not have a lot of," Cora added. "And Jamie knows that, which is why he's made it a personal mission to make up for it now."

Jamie looked from her to me, then back at her again. Even in the full costume, wig and all, he still looked so boyish, like *Santa: The Early Days*. "I know, it's a little over the top," he said. "It's just . . . we always made a big deal of Christmas at my house. I guess it's kind of rubbed off on me."

Even without the Santa outfit, this was an understatement. All month long, Jamie had thrown himself into getting ready for Christmas: stringing up an elaborate light show out front, putting Advent calendars in practically every room, dragging home the biggest tree he could find, which we then decorated with a mix of brand-new ornaments and homemade ones from Hunter holidays past. Between all this and working at the mall, I'd frankly been over the holidays weeks ago. But as with most things involving Jamie, I'd gone along anyway, allowing myself to be dragged to the neighborhood tree-lighting ceremony, watching the Charlie Brown Christmas special over and over again, even holding Roscoe down while Jamie outfitted him in an elaborate harness of jingle bells.

"Here," he said now, reaching behind him to the bed to pick up a red elf's hat. "For you."

"Me?"

"Yeah. So we'll match, when we go out."

I looked at Cora again, but this time she avoided my eyes, busily putting away her blusher, which she'd used to give Jamie his festive red cheeks. "Where," I said slowly, "are we going?"

"To hand out gifts in the neighborhood," he said, like this was obvious. "They're all in the foyer, ready to go. Come on!"

He brushed past me, his own hat in hand, and bounded down the stairs, his boots thumping on the carpet. I narrowed my eyes at Cora until she finally turned to face me.

"I'm sorry," she said, looking like she meant it. "But I did it last year."

And that was how I ended up out in Wildflower Ridge, at eight o'clock on Christmas Eve, with Jamie in his Santa suit, and Roscoe in his jingle bells, spreading good cheer. Or, looking at it another way, walking in the cold—which had returned with a vengeance—and interrupting people from their own family celebrations while scaring the occasional motorist.

After the first couple of houses, we worked out a system: I rang the bell, then let Jamie stay front and center, hanging back with Roscoe until the door was opened, and pitching in when needed to help hand out the gifts, which were mostly stuffed animals and boxes of mini candy canes. Aside from a few weird looks—and some people who were clearly home but chose to ignore us—people seemed happy to see us, especially the kids, and after about an hour and three blocks, our stuff was mostly gone.

"We've got enough for maybe two more stops," Jamie said as we stood on the corner by Nate's house, having paused for Roscoe, bells jingling, to relieve himself against a mailbox. "So which ones do you think? You want to take something to Nate?"

I looked over at the Cross house, dark except for a couple of lights in the back. "I don't know," I said. "He might not be your target audience. Maybe we should go a little younger."

"I'll do that," he said, reaching into his almost-empty sack. "But you go ahead and bring him some candy canes. I'll meet you back here. All right?"

"Okay," I said, handing over Roscoe's leash. He took it,

then tossed his sack over his shoulder—the Santa police would have approved—and started across the street to a house with brightly lit snowflakes on either side of the front steps.

I slid the box of candy canes in my pocket, then headed up Nate's walk, taking a deep breath of cool air. The truth was, I'd thought about getting him a Christmas gift. I had even picked out more than one before stopping myself, not sure even after that night in the pool that I was ready or able to make such a grand gesture. But in the days since, I'd also realized that with Nate, everything just came so easily, as easily as letting him take my hand and pull me beneath the surface. Maybe it was impossible for someone to share everything with you, but I was beginning to think what we had was enough. And anyway, it was Christmas, a time above all for hope, or so I'd been told. He'd given me so much, and now, here, I was finally ready to reciprocate. So I stepped up to the door and rang the bell.

The moment he opened the door, I knew something was wrong. It was just the look on his face—surprised, even alarmed—followed immediately by the way he eased the door a bit more shut, the same move I'd once mastered with the Jehovah's and landlords. "Ruby," he said, his voice low. "Hey. What are you doing here?"

Right that moment, I heard his dad: loud, bellowing, barely muffled from behind a nearby wall. I swallowed, then said, "Jamie was just handing out stuff, for Christmas—"

"It's not a good time," he said as there was a bang, or a thud, discernible. "I'll call you a little later, okay?"

"Are you all right?" I asked him.

"I'm fine."

"Nate—"

"I am. But I've got to go," he said, easing the door closed a bit more. I could barely see him now. "I'll talk to you tomorrow."

I didn't get a chance to answer this, as the door was already shutting with an audible click. I just stood there, my mouth dry, wondering what I should do. *I'm fine,* he'd said. I reached out, putting my hand on the knob and turning it. Here I was, finally ready to let him in, and it was me locked out.

"Hey!" Jamie called from behind me. I turned. He and Roscoe were across the street, coming closer. "Are they there?"

Say something, I thought, but even as I tried to form the words, any words, I remembered that day in the garage, how he'd asked me to keep this quiet. *You understand.* Did I want to be the Honeycutts, stepping in and ruining everything, even if I thought it was for the best? Jamie was coming up the walk, Roscoe pulling ahead. I had to decide, now.

"They're not home," I said, stepping off the porch. The box of candy canes was still in my pocket, and I slid my fingers in, cupping them around it. It felt almost like a hand, resting in mine. "Let's just go."

Chapter Thirteen

I was up until way late, but not waiting for Santa. Instead, I lay on my bed, watching the lights from Nate's pool dance across the trees, the same way I had that first night. More than once, I thought about sneaking over again to find him and see if he was okay. But then I'd remember him shutting the door in my face, the click of the latch catching, and stay where I was.

The next morning, I got a new backpack, some CDs, a few books, and a laptop. Cora got her period.

"I'm fine, I'm fine," she sputtered when, shortly after we'd opened gifts, I found her sitting on her bed, crying. "Really."

"Honey." Jamie came over, sitting beside her and sliding his arm over her shoulder. "It's okay."

"I know." Her voice was still choked as she reached up, wiping her eyes with the back of her hand. "It's just, I really had a feeling it had happened this month. Which I know is so stupid . . ."

"You're not stupid," Jamie said softly, smoothing a hand over her head.

". . . but I just started thinking how great it would be to find out today and be able to tell you guys, and how it would be the best gift ever—" She drew in a long, shaky breath, her eyes welling up again. "But it didn't happen. I'm not pregnant. Again."

"Cora."

"I know," she said, waving her hand. "It's Christmas, we have a wonderful life, roof over our head, things so many people want. But I want this. And no matter what I do, I can't get it. It just . . ." She trailed off, wiping her eyes again. This time, Jamie didn't say anything.

"Sucks," I finished for her.

"Yeah," she said, looking up at me. "It *sucks*."

I felt so helpless, the way I always did when I saw Cora upset about the baby issue. It was the one thing that could take her from zero to emotional in less than five minutes, the single tender spot in her substantial personal armor. The previous month she'd finally agreed to a little pharmaceutical help, via an ovulation drug, which made her hot and emotional, liable to be sweating or weeping or both at any given moment. Not a good mix, especially during the holidays. And now, it was all for nothing. It did suck.

"We'll just try again," Jamie was saying now. "It was just the first month. Maybe the second time will be the charm."

Cora nodded, but I could see she was hardly convinced as she reached up, running her finger over the gift I'd given her that morning: one of Harriet's key necklaces, a silver one lined with red stones. I'd been strangely nervous as she opened the box, worried she wouldn't like it, but the minute she slid it out into her hand, her eyes widening, I knew I'd scored. "It's beautiful," she said, looking up at me. "It's like yours!"

"Kind of," I said. "But not completely."

"I love it," she told me, reaching up immediately to put it on. She brushed her hair over her shoulders. "What do you think? Does it look good?"

It had, and did now, as she rested her head on Jamie's shoulder, curling into him. She still had one hand around the key. The necklace looked different on her than on me, but you could see some similarities. You just had to know where to look.

Just then, the doorbell rang. Roscoe, who'd been snoozing at the foot of the bed, perked up his ears and let out a yap. "Was that the door?" Jamie asked.

"It was," Cora said as Roscoe hopped down, bolting from the room. A moment later, we heard him barking from the foyer as the bell sounded again. "Who would show up on Christmas?"

"I'll find out," I said, although as I quickly got up, heading for the stairs, I was hoping I already knew. The bell rang again when I was halfway down, then once more as I approached the door. When I got to the door and looked through the peephole, though, Nate wasn't there. Nobody was. Then it chimed again—so weird—so I just opened it.

It was Gervais. Too short for the peephole, he was standing on the front step, in his glasses, peacoat, and scarf, with what looked like a brand-new scooter parked on the walk behind him. "Hi," he said.

I just looked at him. "Hey," I said slowly. "What are you—?"

"I have a proposition for you," he said, all business. "Can I come in?"

"Um," I said. Behind me, Roscoe had stopped barking but was still trying to nudge past me. "We're kind of busy, actually—"

"I know." He reached up, adjusting his glasses. "This will only take a minute."

I still didn't really want to let him in. But in the spirit of the holiday, I stepped aside. "Shouldn't you be with your family?" I asked as he shut the door behind him.

"We finished Christmas hours ago," he told me. "My dad already took down the tree."

"Oh." Now we were just standing there, together, in the foyer. "Well," I said, "we're still kind of doing things, so—"

"Do you think you'll be prepared for your next big calculus exam?"

I just looked at him. "What?"

"Your next exam. It's in March and counts for half your grade, right?"

"How do you know that?"

"Will you be prepared for it?"

Upstairs, I heard Cora laughing. A good sign. "Define prepared," I said.

"Scoring a ninety or higher."

"No," I said. Which was, sadly, the truth. Even with all my studying and preparation, calculus was still the one thing that could take me from zero to panicked in less than thirty seconds.

"Then you should let me help you," Gervais said.

"Help me?"

"I'm very good at calculus," he explained, pushing up his glasses. "Not only doing it, but explaining it. I'm tutoring two people in my class at the U right now. And that's college-level calc, not that easy-schmeezy kind you're doing."

Easy-schmeezy, I thought. He hadn't changed entirely. "You know," I said, "that's a very nice offer. But I think I'll be okay."

"It's not an offer," he said. "It's a proposition."

Suddenly, I had a flash of him in the car that day, drawing in his breath. Plus the staring at lunch in the green, and the weird way he'd acted at the Vista 10. *Oh, God,* I thought, finally getting it. Nate was right. He *liked* me. This was just what I needed. "You know," I said, reaching behind him for the door, "you're a nice kid, Gervais, but—"

"It's about Olivia," he said.

I stopped, mid-sentence, not sure I was hearing him right. "What?"

He coughed. Then blushed. "Olivia Davis," he said. "You're friends with her, aren't you?"

"Yes," I said slowly. "Why?"

"Because," he said. He coughed again. "I, um, like her. Kind of."

"You like *Olivia*?"

"Not like that," he said quickly. "I just . . ."

I waited. It seemed like a long time passed.

". . . I want to be her friend," he finished.

This was kind of sweet, I had to admit. Also surprising. Which brought me to my next question. "Why?"

"Because," he said as if it was simple, obvious. When it became clear this was not the case, he added, "She talks to me."

"She talks to you," I repeated.

He nodded. "Like, at the theater. And when she sees me in the hall at school, she always says hello. Nobody else does that. Plus, she likes the same movies I do."

I looked down at him, standing there before me in his heavy coat and glasses. Sure, he was annoying, but it did have to be hard for him. No matter how smart you were, there was a lot you couldn't learn from books. "Then just be friends with her," I said. "You don't need me for that."

"I do, though," he said. "I can't just go up and talk to her. But if I was, you know, helping you with your calculus at lunch or something, then I could just hang out with you guys."

"Gervais," I said slowly. "I think that's really sweet—"

"Don't say no," he pleaded.

"—but it's also deceptive."

He shook his head, adamant. "It's not, though! I don't like her that way. I just want to be friends."

"Still, it would be like I'm setting her up. And friends don't do that."

Never in a million years would I have thought I would be offering up a primer on friendship, much less to Gervais Miller. Even less likely? That I would feel sorry for him after I did so. But as he regarded me glumly, then stepped back to the door, I did.

"All right," he said, his voice flat. Defeated. "I understand."

I watched him as he turned the knob, pulling the door open. Once again, I found myself torn as to what to do, but this time, the stakes weren't so high. Maybe I couldn't do anything for Nate. But I could help someone.

"How about this," I said. He turned back to me slowly. "I'll hire you."

"Hire me?"

"As a tutor. I pay what everyone else pays, you do what you do. If it just so happens we meet during lunch and Olivia is there, then so be it. But she is not part of the deal. Understood?"

He nodded vigorously, his glasses bobbing slightly. "Yes."

"All right then," I said. "Merry Christmas."

"Merry Christmas," he replied, stepping outside and starting down the stairs. Halfway there, he turned back to me. "Oh. I'm twenty dollars an hour, by the way. For the tutoring."

Of course he was. I said, "Am I going to pass calculus?"

"It's guaranteed," he replied. "My method is proven."

I nodded, and then he continued down the steps, grabbing his helmet from his scooter and pulling it on. Maybe this was a big mistake, one among many. But sometimes, we all need a little help, whether we want to admit it or not.

* * *

"Come in, come in," Jamie said as yet another group came bustling in, their chatter rising up to the high ceiling of the foyer. "Welcome! Drinks are in the back, and there's tons of food. Here, let me take your coat. . . ."

I leaned back against the doorjamb of the laundry room, where I'd been hiding out with Roscoe ever since Jamie and Cora's post-Christmas, pre–New Year holiday open house began. Officially, it was my job to keep the ice bucket full and make sure the music was audible, but other than doing this on a most perfunctory level, I wasn't exactly mingling.

Now, though, as Jamie, with his arms full of coats, glanced around him, I knew I should show myself and offer to help him stow them upstairs. Instead, I slid down into a sitting position, my back to the dryer, nudging the door shut with my foot. Roscoe, who'd been exiled here for his own mental well-being, immediately hopped up from his bed and came over to join me.

It had been two days since Christmas, and I hadn't seen or talked to Nate. Once, this would have seemed impossible, considering our very proximity—not to mention how often we crossed paths, intentionally or otherwise. Maybe it was just that school was out, we weren't riding together, and we were both busy with our respective jobs, where things hadn't slowed down, even after Christmas. But even so, I had the distinct feeling he was avoiding me.

This was surprising, but even more shocking was the fact that it was bothering me so much. After all, this was what I'd wanted once—more space between us, less connection. Now that I had it, though, I felt more worried about him than ever.

Just then, the door opened. "One second, I just have to grab another roll of—" Cora was halfway inside, still talking to someone over her shoulder, when she stopped in mid-stride and sentence, seeing me and Roscoe on the floor. "Hey," she said slowly. "What's going on?"

"Nothing," I said. She shut the door as Roscoe got up, wagging his tail. "Just taking a breather."

"But not in the closet," she said.

"This was closer."

She reached over the washing machine, pulling down a

roll of paper towels. "Already a spill on the carpet," she said, tearing them open. "Happens every year."

"Sounds like it's going well otherwise, though," I said as some people passed by in the hallway outside, their voices bouncing off the walls.

"It is." She turned back to me, the towels in her arms. "You should come out, have some food. It's not that bad, I promise."

"I'm a little low on cheer," I told her.

She smiled. "You've been a real trooper, I have to say. Christmas with Jamie is like an endurance trial. My first year I almost had a total breakdown."

"It's just weird," I said. "I mean, last year . . ." I trailed off, realizing I didn't even remember what I'd done last year for the holidays. I had a vague recollection of delivering luggage, maybe a company party at Commercial. But like everything else from my old life, this was distant, faded. "I'm just tired, I guess."

"Just make an appearance," she said. "Then you can come back here, or hit the closet for the rest of the day. All right?"

I looked up at her, dubious, as she extended her hand to me. But then I let her pull me to my feet and followed her out into the hallway. Two steps later, as we entered the kitchen, we were ambushed.

"Cora! Hello!" I jumped, startled, as a petite woman in a flowing, all-white ensemble, her dark hair pulled back at her neck, suddenly appeared in front of us, a wineglass in one hand. "Happy holidays!"

"Happy holidays," Cora replied, leaning forward to

accept a kiss—and a shadow of a lipstick stain—on her cheek. "Barbara, this is my sister, Ruby. Ruby, this is Barbara Starr."

"You have a sister?" Barbara asked. She was wearing several multicolored beaded necklaces that swayed and clacked across her chest each time she moved, as she did now, turning to face me. "Why, I had no idea!"

"Ruby just came to live with us this year," Cora explained. To me, she said, "Barbara is an author. Best-selling, I might add."

"Oh, stop," Barbara replied, waving her hand. "You'll embarrass me."

"She was one of my very first clients," Cora added. "When I was working in a family law practice, just out of school."

"Really," I said.

"I got divorced," Barbara explained, taking a sip of her wine. "Which is never fun. But because of your sister, it was the *best* divorce I've ever had. And that's really saying something."

I looked at Cora, who shook her head almost imperceptibly, making it clear I should not ask what exactly this meant. Instead, she said, "Well, we should probably go check on the food, so . . ."

"Everything is just wonderful. I love the holidays!" Barbara said, sighing. Then she smiled at me and said, "Is the rest of your family here, as well? I'd just love to meet your mother."

"Um," I said, "actually—"

"We're not really in touch with our mom these days,"

Cora told her. "But we *are* lucky to have so many great friends like you here today. Would you like some more wine?"

"Oh," Barbara said, looking at her glass, then at us. "Well, yes. That would be lovely."

Cora eased the glass from her hand—still smiling, smiling—then passed it off to me, touching the small of my back with her other hand. As I took this cue, moving forward, I looked back at her. Barbara was talking again, her hands fluttering as she made some point, but my sister, even as she nodded, was watching me. Awfully smooth, I thought. But then again, she'd been away from my mom a lot longer than I had. Practice does make perfect, or close to it.

Glass in hand, I made my way through the crowd, which had grown considerably since the last time I'd checked the ice and music. Jamie was still in the foyer, answering the door and taking coats, when I finally reached the bar area to get the white wine.

"Macaroons!" I heard him say suddenly. "You shouldn't have."

I turned around. Sure enough, there was Nate, in jeans and a blue collared shirt, his hands in his pockets. His dad was beside him, shrugging off his jacket and smiling as Jamie admired his offering. "They're Belgian," Mr. Cross said. "*Very* expensive."

"I'll bet," Jamie replied, clapping Nate on the shoulder. "Now, let me get you a drink. What's your poison, Blake? We've got beer, Scotch, wine . . ."

He gestured toward the bar, and as they all turned, Nate's eyes met mine. Mr. Cross lifted a hand, waving at me, but I just picked up the glass, quickly folding myself back into the crowd.

When I returned to the spot where I'd left Cora and Barbara, however, they were both gone, a couple of Jamie's UMe.com employees—easily identified by their so-nerdy-they're-cool glasses, expensive jeans, and vintage T-shirts—in their place, jabbering about Macs. I turned slowly, scanning the crowd for Barbara. Instead, I came face-to-face with Nate.

"Hey," he said. "Merry Christmas."

I swallowed, then took in a breath. "Merry Christmas."

There was a pause, which then stretched to an awkward pause, even as someone laughed behind us.

"So I brought you a present," he said, reaching behind him and pulling out a wrapped parcel from his back pocket.

"Let me guess," I said. "Macaroons."

"No," he replied, making a face as he held it out to me. "Open it up."

I looked down at the gift, which was wrapped in red paper decorated with little Christmas trees, and thought of myself standing at his door that night, my own small offering in hand. "You know," I said, nodding to the glass of wine I was still holding, "I should probably—"

"Never delay opening a gift," Nate said, reaching to take the glass from me, putting it on a nearby counter. "Especially one that's already belated."

Emptyhanded, I had no choice but to take it from him, turning it over in my hands and running a finger under the tape. Two women passed by us, chattering excitedly, their heels clacking, as it fell open to reveal a T-shirt. On the front, in that same familiar block lettering: USWIM.

"Your personal philosophy," I said.

"Well," he said, "I looked for one that said 'If you expect the worst you'll never be disappointed,' but they were all out."

"I'll bet." I looked up at him. "This is really nice. Thank you."

"No problem." He leaned back against the wall behind him, smiling at me, and I had a flash of us in the pool together, how he'd grabbed my hand and pulled me under. The memory was so close, I could see every bit of it. But just as clearly, there was the other night, how his face had looked, retreating through the crack in that door. Two opposite images, one easing me closer, another pushing away. "So," he said, "how was your Christmas?"

"How was yours?" I replied, and while I didn't mean for there to be an edge in my voice, even I could hear it. So could he. His face immediately changed, the smile not disappearing, but seeming to stretch more thin. I cleared my throat, then looked down at the shirt again. "I mean, you had to expect I'd ask."

Nate nodded, glancing across the kitchen to the living room, where I could see his dad was talking to a stout woman in a red Christmas sweater. "It was fine," he said. "A little stressful, as you saw."

"A little?" I asked.

"It's not a big deal, okay?"

"Sure seemed that way."

"Well, it wasn't. And it's ancient history."

"It was three days ago," I pointed out.

"So the holidays suck. That's not exactly a news flash, is it?" He ducked his head, a shock of hair falling across his face as the same women passed back by in a cloud of perfumed hand soap, leaving the powder room. When they were gone, he said, "Look, I'm sorry I couldn't talk to you that night. But I'm here now. And I brought a gift. That's got to count for something, right?"

I looked back down at the shirt. *You swim*, I thought. Like he'd said, it was better than sinking. Maybe this was just part of staying afloat. "I don't have anything for you, though."

"Not even Belgian macaroons?"

I shook my head.

"That's all right. They're actually pretty overrated."

"Really."

He nodded, glancing over across the party again, then reached down, sliding his hand around my free one and tugging me a bit down the hallway, around the corner. There, out of sight, he leaned against the wall, gently looping his arms around my waist and pulling me closer. "Okay," he said, his voice low. "Let's try this again. Merry Christmas, Ruby."

I looked up at him, taking in the line of his chin, his eyes and long lashes, the way his fingers were already brushing a bit of my hair off my face, entwining themselves in the strands there. So nearby now, after the distance before. But he was here.

"Merry Christmas," I said, and it was this closeness I tried to concentrate on—not that it might be fleeting, a feeling I knew too well—as he leaned down and put his lips to mine, kissing me, as around the corner the party went on without us, noisy and continuous and completely unaware.

* * *

"Cora," I said as we pulled up outside the mall, "we really don't have to do this."

"We do," she replied, cutting the engine. "Like I said, desperate times call for desperate measures."

"That's just my point, though," I said as she pushed open her door to climb out and I reluctantly did the same. "I'm not desperate."

She just looked at me as I came around the back of the car, then hoisted her purse over one shoulder. "First," she said, "I gave you money for clothes. You bought four things."

"Seven, actually," I pointed out.

"Then," she continued, ignoring this, "for Christmas, I gave you gift cards, with which you bought nothing."

"I don't need anything!"

"And so really, you have given me no choice but to take you shopping by force." She sighed, then reached up, dropping her sunglasses down from their perch on her head to cover her eyes. "Do you even realize how happy the average teenage girl would be in your shoes? I have a credit card. We're at the mall. I want to buy you things. It's like adolescent nirvana."

"Well," I said as we passed two moms pushing strollers, "I guess I'm not the average teenage girl."

She looked over at me as we approached the entrance. "Of course you're not," she said more quietly. "Look, I know this is kind of weird for you. But we have the money, and it's something Jamie and I want to do."

"It's not weird," I told her. "Just unnecessary."

"You know," she said as the automatic doors to Esther Prine, the upscale department store, slid open in front of us, "it's okay to accept things from people. It doesn't make you weak or helpless, even if that is how Mom felt about it."

This was a bit too reminiscent of the ground I'd been forced to cover during my first (and hopefully only) therapy session a few weeks earlier, so instead of responding, I stepped inside. As always, I was temporarily blinded by the gleaming white tile of the store, as well as the polished-to-a-high-sheen jewelry cases. To our left, a guy in a tuxedo was playing Pachelbel by the escalators. It was always kind of odd to be talking about my mother, anyway, but in this setting, it bordered on surreal.

"It's not about Mom," I said as Cora gestured for me to follow her up to the next floor. "Or not just about her. It's a big change. I'm not used to . . . We didn't have much these last few years."

"I know," she replied. "But that's just what I'm saying. In some ways, that was a choice, too. There were things Mom could have done to make things easier for you and for herself."

"Like get in touch with you," I said.

"Yes." She cleared her throat, looking out over cosmetics as we rose up higher, then higher. "But it goes even further back than that. Like with Dad, and the money he tried to give her. But she was so stubborn and angry, she wouldn't take it."

"Wait," I said as we finally reached the top, and she stepped off into Juniors. "I thought Dad never gave her any money. That he dodged her for child support, just disappeared."

Cora shook her head. "Maybe he did later, once he moved to Illinois. But those early years, right after he moved out? He tried to do the right thing. I remember."

Maybe this shouldn't have surprised me. After all, by now I knew my mom had kept so much secret, tweaking her history and my own. Cora was not what I'd been led to believe, so why would my father be, either? Thinking this, though, something else occurred to me. Something that also didn't belong in the polished world of Esther Prine, and yet I had to bring it in, anyway.

"Cora," I said as she drifted over to a table of sweaters, running her hand over them, "do you know where Dad is?"

In the pause that followed, I saw my entire life changing again, twisted and shifting and different. But then she turned around to face me. "No," she said softly as a salesgirl drifted past, pushing a rack of flimsy dresses. "I've thought about looking for him, though, many times. Mostly because Jamie's been really insistent about it, how easy it would be. But I guess I'm sort of afraid still."

I nodded. This, if nothing else, I could understand. There were so many levels to the unknown, from safe to dangerous to outright nebulous, scariest of all.

"You never know, though," she said. "Maybe we can do it together. Strength in numbers and all that."

"Maybe," I said.

She smiled at me, a bit tentatively, then looked back

at the sweaters. "Okay, now—down to business. We're not leaving here until you have at least two new outfits. And a jacket. And new shoes."

"Cora."

"No arguments." She hoisted her purse over her shoulder, then pushed on into Juniors, disappearing between two racks of jeans. After a moment, all I could see was her head bobbing in and out of the displays, her expression caught in the occasional mirror, focused and determined. At first, I stayed where I was, out in the open aisle as the salegirl passed by once more, smiling at me. But then I looked for Cora again and couldn't spot her right away, which was enough to make me force myself forward, in after her.

Chapter Fourteen

"Wow," Nate said. "You look great."

This was exactly the kind of reaction I'd been hoping to avoid, especially considering Cora had assured me repeatedly that my new clothes did not necessarily look that, well, new. Apparently she was wrong.

"It's just a jacket," I told him, pulling my seat belt over my shoulder. As I did so, I glanced at Gervais, who was studying me, as well. "What?"

"Nothing," he said, shrinking back a little bit in his seat.

I sighed, shaking my head, then looked over at Nate, who was just sitting behind the wheel, a half smile on his face. "So what's the occasion for the makeover? Got a hot date for Valentine's or something?"

"Nope," I said, and he laughed, shifting into gear and pulling away from the curb. As we came up to the stop sign at the end of the street, though, he reached over, squeezing my knee, and kept his hand there as we turned onto the next street.

It was February now, which meant Nate and I had been doing whatever it was we were doing—dating, making out, spending most of our free time together—for over a month. And I had to admit, I was happy about it, at least most of the time. But regardless of how well we were getting to know each other, there was always the issue with his dad, the one part of himself he still held back and kept from me. It was only a single thing, but somehow it counted for a lot. Like even when things were as good as they could be, they could only be good enough.

Such as Valentine's Day, which was less than twenty-four hours away. Normally, I'd be happy to have a boyfriend (or something close to it) on the very day you're made to be *very* aware when you don't. But even as Nate hinted at his big plans for us—which, by the sound of it, were secret, detailed, and still in development—I couldn't completely just relax and enjoy it. Rest Assured had run a special promotion for gift baskets and flower delivery for its customers, and the response had been overwhelming. As a result, they were booked fully for that day, just like on Thanksgiving, and I'd not forgotten how that had turned out.

"It's going to be fine," Nate had assured me the night before, out by the pond, when I'd brought this up. We'd taken to meeting there sometimes in the evening, between our respective homework and work schedules, if only for a few moments. "I'll do deliveries all afternoon, be done by seven. Plenty of time for what I have in mind."

"Which is what?" I asked.

"You'll see." He reached over, brushing my hair back from my face. Behind him I could see the lights from the pool flickering over the fence, and even as he leaned in, kissing my temple, I was distracted, knowing that he was supposed to be over there, assembling gift baskets and that any moment his dad might wander out and find him gone. This must have been obvious, as after a moment he pulled back. "What's wrong?"

"Nothing."

"You look worried."

"I'm not."

"Look," he said, his expression serious, "if this is about my gift . . . just relax. I'm not expecting anything phenomenal. Just, you know, super great."

I just looked at him, regretting once again that in a moment of weakness a few days earlier, I'd confessed to Olivia—who then had of course told Nate—that I was stressing about finding the right thing for him for Valentine's. Her loyalty aside, though, the truth was that having dropped the ball at Christmas, it seemed especially important to deliver something good here, if not phenomenal.

"It's not about your gift," I told him.

"Then what is it?"

I shrugged, then looked past him again, over at the pool house. After a moment, he turned and glanced that way as well, then back at me, finally getting it. "It's fine, okay? I'm off the clock," he said. "All yours."

But that was just the thing. Even in these moments—sitting by the pond with his leg linked around mine, or riding in the car with his hand on my knee—I never felt like I had all of Nate, just enough to make me realize what was missing. Even stranger was that with anyone else I'd ever been with—especially Marshall—what I was given, as well as what I gave, had always been partial, and yet that had still been plenty.

Now, we pulled into the Perkins lot, and Gervais jumped

out, bolting for the building as always. As soon as the door shut behind him, Nate leaned across the console between us and kissed me. "You do look great," he said. "So what made you finally break down and spend those gift cards?"

"I didn't. Cora ambushed me and took me to Esther Prine. I was powerless to resist."

"Most girls I know would consider that wish fullfillment, not torture."

I sat back, shaking my head. "Why does everyone keep saying that? Who says just because I'm a girl I'm hardwired to want to spent a hundred and eighty bucks on jeans?"

Nate pulled away, holding up his hands. "Whoa there," he said. "Just making an observation."

"Well, don't." I looked down at my lap and those expensive jeans, not to mention the shoes I had on with them (suede, not on sale) and my jacket (soft leather, some label I'd never even heard of). Who was this person in these fancy clothes, at this expensive school, with a for-all-intents-and-purposes boyfriend who she was actually worried wasn't opening up to her enough emotionally? It was like I'd been brainwashed or something.

Nate was still watching me, not saying anything. "Sorry," I said finally. "It's just . . . I don't know. Everything feels overwhelming right now, for some reason."

"Overwhelming," he repeated.

It was times like these that I knew I should just come clean and tell him that I worried about him. Having the courage to do that was the part of me *I* was still holding back. And I was always aware of it, even as, like now, I did it once again.

"Plus," I said, sliding my knee so it rested against his, "there's this issue of your gift."

"My gift," he repeated, raising an eyebrow.

"It's just so all-encompassing," I said with a sigh, shaking my head. "Huge. And detailed . . . I mean, the flow charts and spread sheets alone are out of control."

"Yeah?" he said.

"I'll be lucky if I get it all in place by tonight, to be honest."

"Huh." He considered this. "Well. I have to admit, I'm intrigued."

"You should be."

He smiled, then reached over, running a hand over my jacket. "This is pretty cool," he said. "What's the inside look like?"

"The inside . . ." I said, just as he slid his hand over my shoulder, easing off one sleeve. "Ah, right. Well, it's equally impressive."

"Yeah? Let me see." He nudged it off over the other shoulder, and I shook my head. "You know, it is. This sweater is pretty nice, too. Who makes it?"

"No idea," I said.

I felt his hand go around my waist, then smoothly move up my back to the tag. "Lanoler," he read slowly, ducking his head down so his lips were on my collarbone. "Seems well made. Although it's hard to tell. Maybe if I just—"

I glanced outside the car, where people were walking past to the green, coffees in hand, backpacks over shoulders. "Nate," I said. "It's almost first bell."

"You're so conscientious," he said, his voice muffled by

my sweater, which he was still trying to ease off. "When did that happen?"

I sighed, then looked at the dashboard clock. We had five minutes before we'd be officially late. Not all the time we wanted, but maybe this, too, was too much to ask for. "Okay," I told him as he worked his way back around my neck, his lips moving up to my ear. "I'm all yours."

* * *

When I got home that afternoon, I saw Jamie seated at the island with his laptop. As he heard me approach, he quickly leaped up, grabbing a nearby loaf of bread and holding it in front of him as if struck by a sudden desire to make a sandwich.

I raised my eyebrows. "What are you doing?"

He exhaled loudly. "I thought you were Cora," he said, tossing the bread down. "Whew! You scared me. I've worked too hard on this for her to find out about it now."

As he sat back down, I saw that the island was covered with piles of CDs, some in their cases, others scattered all over the place. "So this is your Valentine's Day gift?"

"One of them," he said, opening a case and taking out a disk. "It'll be, like, the third or fourth wave."

"Wave?"

"That's my V-day technique," he explained, sliding the disk into the side of his laptop. I heard a whirring, then some clicks, and the screen flickered. "Multiple gifts, given in order of escalating greatness, over the entire day. So, you know, you begin with flowers, then move to chocolates, maybe some balloons. This'll come after that, but before the gourmet dinner. I'm still tweaking the order."

"Right," I said glumly, sitting down across from him and picking up a Bob Dylan CD.

He glanced over at me. "What's wrong? Don't tell me you don't like Valentine's Day. *Everyone* likes Valentine's Day."

I considered disputing this, but as he'd said the same thing about Thanksgiving, Christmas, and New Year's, I figured it wasn't worth the argument. "I'm just kind of stuck," I said. "I need to get something for someone. . . ."

"Nate," he said, hitting a couple of buttons on the laptop. I looked up at him. "Ruby, come on. We're not that *dense*, you know. Plus half the house does look out at the pond, even at night."

I bit my lip, turning the CD case in my hands. "Anyway," I said, "I want it to be, like, this great gift. But I can't come up with anything."

"Because you're overthinking it," he said. "The best gifts come from the heart, not a store."

"This from the man who buys in waves."

"I'm not buying this," he pointed out, nodding at the laptop. "I mean, I bought the CDs, yeah. But the idea is from the heart."

"And what's the idea?"

"All the songs Cora loves to sing, in one place," he said, sounding pleased with himself. "It wasn't easy, let me tell you. I wrote up a list, then found them online or at the record store. For the really obscure ones, I had to enlist this guy one of my employees knows from his Anger Management class who's some kind of music freak. But now I finally have them all. 'Wasted Time,' 'Frankie and Johnny,' 'Don't Think Twice, It's All Right' . . ."

"'Angel from Montgomery,'" I said quietly.

"Exactly!" He grinned. "Hey, you can probably help me, now that I think of it. Just take a look at the list, and see if I'm missing anything."

He pushed a piece of paper across to me, and I glanced down at it, reading over the familiar titles of the songs my mom had always sung to me, listed in block print. "No," I said finally. "This is pretty much all of them."

"Great." He hit another button, taking out the CD and putting it on the counter as I pushed out my chair, getting to my feet. "Where you headed?"

"Shopping," I said, pulling my bag over my shoulder. "I have to find something phenomenal."

"You will," he replied. "Just remember: the heart! Start there, and you can't go wrong."

I remained unconvinced, however, especially once I got to the mall, where there were hearts everywhere: shaped into balloons and cookies, personalized on T-shirts, filled with chocolate and held by fuzzy teddy bears. But even after going into a dozen stores, I still couldn't find anything for Nate.

"Personally," Harriet said as I slumped onto her stool an hour later for a much-needed rest, "I think this holiday is a total crock, completely manufactured by the greeting-card companies. If you really love someone, you should show it every day, not just one."

"And yet," Reggie said, from his kiosk, "you are not averse to running a two-for-one Valentine's Day special on bracelets and assorted rings."

"Of course not!" she said. "I'm a businesswoman. As

long as the holiday exists, I might as well profit from it."

Reggie rolled his eyes and went back to stacking daily multis. "I just want to get something good," I said. "Something that *means* something."

"Just try to forget about it for a while," she replied, adjusting a rack of pendants. "Then, out of nowhere, the perfect gift will just come to you."

I looked at my watch. "I have about twenty-six hours. Not exactly a lot of time for inspiration to strike."

"Oh." She took a sip of her coffee. "Well, then I'd get him some of those macaroons you bought me at Christmas. Those you can't go wrong with."

In the end, though, it didn't come to that, although what I did end up with was almost as pathetic: a gift card to PLUG, the music store. It wasn't phenomenal, not even decent, and as I left the mall feeling thoroughly defeated, all I could hope was that Harriet was right, and I'd come up with something better in the short time I had remaining.

The next morning, though, this still hadn't happened, a fact made even more obvious when I came down for breakfast and walked right into Jamie's first wave. Four dozen roses in varying colors were arranged in vases all around the kitchen, each tied with a big white bow. Cora was at the counter, reading the card off of one of them, her face flushed, as I helped myself to coffee.

"He *always* overdoes it on Valentine's," she said, although she looked kind of choked up as she tucked the card into her purse. "The first year we were married, he got me a new car."

"Really," I said.

"Yep. Totally overwhelmed me." She sighed, picking up her mug. "It was so sweet, but I felt terrible. All I'd gotten him was a gift card."

I swallowed. "I have to go."

What I needed, I decided as I headed down the walkway to Nate's car ten minutes later, was to just stop thinking about Valentine's Day altogether. Which seemed easy, at least until I opened the car door and found myself face-to-face with a huge basketful of candy and flowers.

"Sorry," Nate said from somewhere behind the tiny balloons that were poking out of the top of it. "We're a little cramped in here. Do you mind holding that in your lap?"

I picked up the basket, then slid into the seat, pulling the door shut behind me. The instant it was closed, the smell of roses was overpowering, and as I shifted in my seat I saw why: the entire back was piled with baskets of assorted sizes, stacked three deep. "Where's Gervais?" I asked.

"I'm here," I heard a muffled voice say. A huge bunch of baby's breath shifted to one side, revealing his face. "And I think I'm having an allergic reaction."

"Just hang in there for a few more minutes," Nate told him, opening his window as we pulled away from the curb. His phone rang, rattling the console, and I peered around the flowers in my lap to look at him as he grabbed it, putting it to his ear. "Yeah," he said, slowing for the next light. "I'm on my way to school right now, so in ten or so I'll start down the list. Lakeview first, then over to the office complex. Right. Okay. Bye."

"You're not going to school today?" I asked as he hung up.

"Duty calls," he said, shutting his phone. "My dad got

a little overambitious with the response to the special, so we're pretty booked. We'll be lucky to get it all done, even with the two of us going all day."

"Really," I said quietly.

"Don't worry," he said as his phone rang again. "I'll be done in plenty of time for our thing tonight."

But this wasn't what I was worried about, and I wondered if he knew it. It was hard to tell, since he was talking to his dad again as he pulled up in front of Perkins Day, and Gervais and I extracted ourselves to disembark. As he headed off, sneezing, I put the basket I'd been holding back on the seat, then stood by the open door, waiting for Nate to hang up. Even as he did, he was already shifting back into gear, moving on.

"I gotta go," he said to me, over the flowers. "But I'll see you tonight, okay? Seven, at the pond. Don't be late."

I nodded and shut the door. He already had his phone back to his ear as he pulled into traffic. As he drove off, all I could see were a bunch of heart-shaped balloons in the back window, bobbing and swaying, first to one side, then back again.

* * *

Jamie and Cora were out for dinner—in the midst of a wave, no doubt—so I was alone, sitting at the kitchen table, my stupid gift card in hand, when the clock over the stove flipped to seven o'clock.

I stood up, sliding it into my pocket, then ran a hand through my hair as I stepped out onto the patio, Roscoe rousing himself from his dog bed to follow along behind me. Outside, the air was cold, the lights from Nate's pool and house visible over the fence.

Call it a bad feeling. Or just the logical conclusion to an unavoidable situation. But I think I knew, even before that first fifteen minutes passed with no sign of him, that he wasn't just late, something was wrong. Before my fingers—even jammed into the pockets of my new jacket—began to get numb, before Roscoe abandoned me for the warmth of the house, before another set of lights came up from the opposite side, lighting up the trees briefly before cutting off and leaving me in darkness again. It was eight fifteen when I saw Cora appear in the patio doorway, cupping a hand over her eyes. A moment later, she stuck her head out.

"Are you okay?" she said. "It's freezing out there."

"How was dinner?" I asked her.

"Fantastic." She glanced behind her at Jamie, who was walking into the kitchen with one of those leftover containers shaped into a swan. "You should hear this CD he made for me. It's—"

"I'll be in soon," I told her. "Just a couple more minutes."

She nodded slowly. "Okay," she said. "Don't wait too long, though."

But I already had. And not just that hour and fifteen minutes, but every moment that had passed since Thanksgiving, when I should have told Nate I couldn't just stand by and worry about him. Instead, though, I had let months pass, pushing down my better instincts, and now, sitting out in the February chill, I was getting exactly what I deserved.

When I finally went inside, I tried to distract myself

with homework and TV, but instead I kept looking over at Nate's house, and his window, which I could see clearly from my own. Behind the shade, I could see a figure moving back and forth. After a little while, it stopped, suddenly so still that I wondered if it was really anyone at all.

It was over an hour later when the phone rang. Cora and Jamie were downstairs, eating wave-two chocolates out of the box and listening to her CD, their voices and the music drifting up to me. I didn't even look at the caller ID, lying back on my bed instead, but then Jamie was calling my name. I looked at the receiver for a minute, then hit the TALK button. "Hello?"

"I know you're probably pissed," Nate said. "But meet me outside, okay?"

I didn't say anything, not that it mattered. He'd hung up, the dial tone already buzzing in my ear.

Billie Holiday was playing as I went downstairs and back outside, retracing my steps across the grass, which felt stiff and ungiving beneath my feet. This time, I didn't sit, instead crossing my arms over my chest as Nate emerged from the shadows. He had one hand behind his back, a smile on his face.

"Okay," he said, before he'd even gotten to me, "I know that me being over two hours late was not *exactly* the surprise you were expecting. But today was crazy, I just now got home, and I'll make it up to you. I promise."

We were in the swath of darkness between the lights from his house and those of Cora's, so it was hard to make out all the details of his face. But even so, I could tell there was something off: a nervous quality, something almost jittery. "You've been home," I told him. "I saw your light was on."

"Yeah, but we had stuff to do," he said easily, although now he was slowing his steps. "I had to put things away, get the accounts all settled. And then, you know, I had to wrap this."

He pulled his hand out from behind his back, extending a small box to me, tied with a simple bow. "Nate," I said.

"Go ahead," he told me. "It won't make it all better. But it might help a little bit."

I took the box but didn't open it. Instead, I sat down on the bench, holding it between my knees, and a moment later he came and sat down beside me. Now closer, I could see his neck was flushed, the skin pink around his collar. "I know you've been home for a couple of hours," I said quietly. "What was going on over there?"

He slid one leg over the bench, turning to face me. "Nothing. Hey, we've got two hours left of Valentine's Day. So just open your gift, and let's make the most of it."

"I don't want a gift," I said, and my voice sounded harsher than I meant it to. "I want you to tell me what happened to you tonight."

"I got held up dealing with my dad," he replied. "That's all."

"That's all," I repeated.

"What else do you want me to say?"

"Do you understand how worried I've been about you? How I've sat over here all night, looking at your house, wondering if you're okay?"

"I'm fine," he said. "I'm here now. With you, on Valentine's Day, which is the only place I've wanted to be all day. And now that I *am* here, I can think of a million things I'd rather talk about than my dad."

I shook my head, looking out over the water.

"Like," he continued, putting his hands on either side of me, "my gift, for instance. Word on the street is that it's phenomenal."

"It's not," I said flatly. "It's a gift card, and it sucks."

He sat back slightly, studying my face. "Okay," he said slowly. "So maybe we shouldn't talk."

With this, I could feel him moving closer, and then his lips were on my ear, moving down my neck. Normally, this was enough to push everything away, at least temporarily, the sudden and indisputable closeness that made all other distance irrelevant. Tonight, though, was different. "Stop," I said, pulling back and raising my hands between us. "Okay? Just stop."

"What's wrong?"

"What's wrong?" I repeated. "Look, you can't just come here and tell me everything's fine and kiss me and just expect me to go along with it."

"So," he said slowly, "you're saying you don't want me to kiss you."

"I'm saying you can't have it both ways," I told him. "You can't act like you care about someone but not let them care about you."

"I'm not doing that."

"You are, though," I said. He looked away, shaking his head. "Look, when we first met, you practically made a practice of saving my ass. That night at the fence, coming to pick me up at Jackson—"

"That was different."

"Why? Because it was me, not you?" I asked. "What, you think just because you help people and make their lives easier that you're somehow better and don't need help yourself?"

"I don't."

"So it's just fine that your dad yells at you and pushes you around."

"What happens between me and my dad is private," he said. "It's a family thing."

"So was my living alone in that place you called a slum," I told him. "Are you saying you would have left me there if I had told you to? Or in the clearing that day?"

Nate immediately started to say something in response to this, then let out a breath instead.

Finally, I thought. *I'm getting through*.

"I don't understand," he said, "why these two things always have to be connected."

"What two things?" I said.

"Me and my dad, and me and everyone else." He shook his head. "They're not the same thing. Not even close."

It was that word—*always*—that did it, nudging a memory loose in my brain. Me and Heather, that day over the fish. *You never know*, she'd said, when I'd told her one more friend would hardly make a difference. The sad way he looked at her, all those mornings walking to the green, so many rumors, and maybe none of them true. "So that's why you and Heather broke up," I said slowly. "It wasn't that she couldn't take what was happening. It was not being able to help you."

Nate looked down at his hands, not saying anything. Here I'd thought Heather and I were so different. But we, too, had something in common, all along.

"Just tell someone what's going on," I said. "Your mom, or—"

"I can't," he said. "There's no point. Don't you understand that?"

This was the same thing he'd asked me, all those weeks ago, and I'd told him yes. But now, here, we differed. Nate might not have thought that whatever was happening with his dad affected anything else, but I knew, deep in my heart, that this wasn't true. My mother, wherever she was, still lingered with me: in the way I carried myself, the things that scared me, and the way I'd reacted the last time I'd been faced with this question. Which was why this time, my answer had to be no.

But first, I lifted my hand, putting it on his chest, right over where I'd noticed his skin was flushed earlier. He closed his eyes, leaning into my palm, and I could feel him, warm, as I slowly pushed his shirt aside. Again, call it a bad feeling, a hunch, or whatever—but there, on his shoulder, the skin was not just pink but red and discolored, a broad bruise just beginning to rise. "Oh, Jesus," I said, my voice catching. "Nate."

He moved closer, covering my hand with his, squeezing it, and then he was kissing me again, sudden and intense, as if trying to push down these words and everything that had prompted them. It was so hungry and so good that I was almost able to forget all that had led up to it. But not quite.

"No," I said, pulling back. He stayed where he was, his mouth inches from mine, but I shook my head. "I can't."

"Ruby," he said. Even as I heard this, though, breaking my heart, I could see his shirt, still pushed aside, the reason undeniable.

"Only if you let me help you," I said. "You have to let me in."

He pulled back, shaking his head. Over his shoulder, I could see the lights of the pool flickering—otherworldy, alien. "And if I don't?" he said.

I swallowed, hard. "Then no," I told him. "Then go."

For a moment, I thought he wouldn't. That this, finally, more than all the words, would be what changed his mind. But then he was pushing himself to his feet, his shirt sliding back, space now between us, everything reverting to how it had been before. *You don't have to make it so hard,* I wanted to say, but there was a time I hadn't believed this, either. Who was I to tell anyone how to be saved? Only the girl who had tried every way not to be.

"Nate," I called out, but he was already walking away, his head ducked, back toward the trees. I sat there, watching him as he folded into them, disappearing.

A lump rose in my throat as I stood up. The gift he'd brought was still on the bench, and I picked it up, examining the rose-colored paper, the neatly tied bow. So pretty on the surface, it almost didn't matter what was inside.

When I went back in the house, I tried to keep my face

composed, thinking only of getting up to my room, where I could be alone. But just as I started up the stairs, Cora came out of the living room, where her CD was still playing—Janis Joplin now—the chocolate box in her hands. "Hey, do you want—?" she said, then stopped suddenly. "Are you all right?"

I started to say yes, of course, but before I could, my eyes filled with tears. As I turned to the wall and sucked down a breath, trying to steady myself, I felt her come closer. "Hey," she said, smoothing my hair gently off my shoulder. "What's wrong?"

I swallowed, reaching up to wipe my eyes. "Nothing."

"Tell me."

Two words, said so easily. But even as I thought this, I heard myself doing it. "I just don't know," I said, my voice sounding bumpy, not like mine, "how you help someone who doesn't want your help. What do you do when you can't do anything?"

She was quiet for a moment, and in that silence I was bracing myself, knowing the next question would be harder, pulling me deeper. "Oh, Ruby," she said instead, "I know. I know it's hard."

More tears were coming now, my vision blurring. "I—"

"I should have known this CD would remind you of all that," she said. "Of course it would—that was stupid of me. But Mom's not your responsibility anymore, okay? We can't do anything for her. So we have to take care of each other, all right?"

My mother. Of course she would think that was what

I was talking about. What else could there be? What other loss would I ever face comparable to it? None. None at all.

Cora was behind me, still talking. Through my tears, I could hear her saying it was all going to be okay, and I knew she believed this. But I was sure of something, too: it's a lot easier to be lost than found. It's the reason we're always searching, and rarely discovered—so many locks, not enough keys.

Chapter Fifteen

"So as you can see," Harriet said, moving down the kiosk with a wave of her hand, "I work mostly in silver, using gemstones as accents. Occasionally I've done things with gold, but I find it's less inspiring to me."

"Right," the reporter replied, scribbling this down as her photographer, a tall guy with a mustache, repositioned one of the key necklaces on the rack before taking another shot. "And how long have you been in business at this location?"

"Six years." As the woman wrote this down, Harriet, a nervous expression on her face, glanced over at Vitamin Me, where I was standing with Reggie. I flashed her a thumbs-up, and she nodded, then turned back to the reporter.

"She's doing great," Reggie said, continuing work on his pyramid of omega-3 bottles, the centerpiece of his GET FISH, GET FIT display. "I don't know why she was so nervous."

"Because she's Harriet," I told him. "She always nervous."

He sighed, adding another bottle to the stack. "It's the caffeine. If she'd give it up, her whole life would change. I'm convinced of it."

The truth was, Harriet's life *was* changing, though coffee had nothing to do with it. Instead, it was the KeyChains—as she'd taken to calling them since Christmas—which were now outselling everything else we carried, sparking somewhat of a local phenomenon. Suddenly we had shoppers coming from several towns over, seeking them out, not to mention multiple phone calls from people in other states, asking if we did mail order (yes) or had a Web site (in the works, up any day). When she wasn't fielding calls or requests, Harriet was busy making more keys, adding shapes and sizes and different gems, as well as experimenting with expanding the line to bracelets and rings. The more she made, the more she sold. These days, it seemed like every girl at my school was wearing one, which was kind of weird, to say the least.

This reporter was from the style section of the local paper, and Harriet had been getting ready all week, making new pieces and working both of us overtime to make sure the kiosk looked perfect. Now, Reggie and I watched as—at the reporter's prompting—she posed beside it, a KeyChain studded with rhinestones around her neck, smiling for the camera.

"Look at her," I said. "She's a superstar."

"That she is," Reggie replied, adding another bottle to his stack. "But it's not because she's suddenly famous. Harriet's always been special."

He said this so easily, so matter-of-factly, that it kind of broke my heart. "You know," I said to him as he opened another box, "you could tell her that. How you feel, I mean."

"Oh, I have," he replied.

"You have? When?"

"Over Christmas." He picked up a bottle of shark-cartilage capsules, examining it, then set it aside. "We went down to Garfield's one night after closing, for drinks. I had a couple of margaritas, and the next thing I knew . . . it was all out."

"And?"

"Total bust," he said, sighing. "She said she's not in a relationship place right now."

"A relationship place?" I repeated.

"That's what she said." He emptied the box, folding it. "The KeyChains are selling so well, she's got to focus on her career, maybe expanding to her own store someday. Eye on the ball, and all that."

"Reggie," I said softly. "That sucks."

"It's okay," he replied. "I've known Harriet a long time. She's not much for attachments."

I looked over at Harriet again. She was laughing, her face flushed, as the photographer took another picture. "She doesn't know what she's missing."

"That's very nice of you to say," Reggie replied, as if I'd complimented his shirt. "But sometimes, we just have to be happy with what people can offer us. Even if it's not what we want, at least it's something. You know?"

I nodded, even though it was exactly what I didn't believe, at least not since Nate and I had argued on Valentine's Day. The space I'd once claimed to want between us was now not just present, but vast. Whatever it was we'd had—something, nothing, anything—it was over.

As a result, so was my involvement in the carpool, which I'd decided to opt out of after a couple of very silent and very awkward rides. In the end, I'd dug out my old bus schedules, set my alarm, and decided to take advantage of the fact that my calculus teacher, Ms. Gooden, was an early bird who offered hands-on help before first bell. Then I asked Gervais to pass this information along to Nate, which he did. If Nate was surprised, he didn't show it. But then again, he wasn't letting on much these days, to me or anyone.

I still had the gift he'd given me, if only because I couldn't figure out a way to return it that wasn't totally awkward. So it sat, wrapped and bow intact, on my dresser, until I finally stuffed it into a drawer. You would think it would bother me, not knowing what was inside, but it didn't, really. Maybe I'd just figured out there were some things you were better off not knowing.

As for Nate himself, from what I could tell, he was always working. Like most seniors in spring semester—i.e., those who hadn't transferred from other schools with not-so-great grades they desperately needed to keep up in order to have any chance at college acceptance—he had a pretty light schedule, as well as a lot of leeway for activities. While most people spent this time lolling on the green between classes or taking long coffee runs to Jump Java, whenever I saw Nate, either in the neighborhood or at school, he seemed to be in constant motion, often loaded down with boxes, his phone pressed to his ear as he moved to and from his car. I figured Rest Assured had to be picking up, business-wise, although his work seemed even more ironic to me than ever. All that helping, saving, taking care. As if these were the only two options, when you had that kind of home life: either caring about yourself and no one else, like I had, or only about the rest of the world, as he did now.

I'd been thinking about this lately every time I passed

the HELP table, where Heather Wainwright was set up as usual, accepting donations or petition signatures. Ever since Thanksgiving, I'd sort of held it against her that she'd broken up with Nate, thinking she'd abandoned him, but now, for obvious reasons, I was seeing things differently. So much so that more than once, I'd found myself pausing and taking a moment to look over whatever cause she was lobbying for. Usually, she was busy talking to other people and just smiled at me, telling me to let her know if I had any questions. One day, though, as I perused some literature about saving the coastline, it was just the two of us.

"It's a good cause," she said as I flipped past some pages illustrating various stages of sand erosion. "We can't just take our beaches for granted."

"Right," I said. "I guess not."

She sat back, twirling a pen in her hand. Finally, after a moment, she said, "So . . . how's Nate doing?"

I shut the brochure. "I wouldn't really know," I said. "We're kind of on the outs these days."

"Oh," she said. "Sorry."

"No, it's okay," I said. "It's just . . . it got hard. You know?"

I wasn't expecting her to respond to this, really. But then she put her pen down. "His dad," she said, clarifying. I nodded, and she smiled sadly, shaking her head. "Well, I hate to tell you, but if you think keeping your distance makes it easier not to worry . . . it doesn't. Not really."

"Yeah," I said, looking down at the brochure again. "I'm kind of getting that."

"For me, the worst was just watching him change, you know?" She sighed, brushing her hair back from her face.

"Like with quitting swim team. That was his entire world. But in the end, he gave it up, because of this."

"He gave you up, too," I said. "Right?"

"Yeah." She sighed. "I guess so."

Across the green, there was a sudden burst of laughter, and we both looked in its direction. As it ended, she said, "Look, for what it's worth, I think I could have tried harder. To stick by him, or force the issue. I kind of wish I had."

"You do?"

"I think he would have done it for me," she said. "And that's been the hardest part of all of this, really. That maybe I failed him, or myself, somehow. You know?"

I nodded. "Yeah," I said. "I do."

"So," a dark-haired girl with a ponytail said to Heather, sliding into the empty seat beside her. "I just spent, like, a half hour working on Mr. Thackray, and he's finally agreed to let us plug our fund-raiser again this afternoon during announcements. I'm thinking we should write some new copy, though, to really make an impact, like . . ."

I started to move down the table, our conversation clearly over. "Take care, Ruby," Heather called after me.

"You, too," I told her. As she turned back to the girl, who was still talking, I reached into my pocket, pulling out the few dollars' change from my lunch and stuffing it into the SAVE OUR BEACHES! jar. It wasn't much, in the grand scheme of things. But it made me feel somewhat better, nonetheless.

Also slightly encouraging was the fact that while I hadn't been of help to Nate, I didn't have to look far to find someone who *had* benefited from my actions. Not now that Gervais was front and center, at my picnic table, every weekday from 12:05 to 1:15.

"Again," he said to me, pointing at the book with his pencil, "remember the power rule. It's the key to everything you're trying to do here."

I sighed, trying to clear my head. The truth was, Gervais was a good tutor. Already, I understood tons more than I had before he'd begun working with me, stuff even my early-morning help sessions couldn't make sense of. But there were still distractions. Initially, it had been me worrying about how he'd interact with Olivia, whether he'd act so goopy or lovesick she'd immediately suspect something, and rightfully blame me. As it turned out, though, this wasn't an issue at all. If anything, I was a third wheel now.

"The power rule," Olivia recited, flipping her phone open. "The derivative of any given variable (x) to the exponent (n) is equal to product of the exponent and the variable to the (n–1) power."

I just looked at her. "Exactly right," Gervais said, beaming. "See? Olivia gets it."

Of course she did. Olivia was apparently a whiz at calculus, something she had neglected to mention the entire time we'd been sharing our lunch hour. Now that Gervais had joined us, though, they were in math heaven. That is, when they weren't talking about one of the other myriad, inexplicable things they had in common, including but not limited to a love of movies, the pros and cons of various college majors, and, of course, picking on me.

"What exactly is going on with you two?" I'd asked her

recently after one of Gervais's visits, which I had spent alternately struggling with the power rule and sitting by, open-mouthed, as they riffed on the minute details of a recent sci-fi blockbuster, down to the extra scenes after the credits.

"What do you mean?" she asked. We were crossing the green. "He's a nice kid."

"Look, I have to be honest," I told her. "He likes you."

"I know."

She said this so simply, so matter-of-factly, that I almost stopped walking. "You know?"

"Sure. I mean, it's kind of obvious, right?" she said. "He was always hanging around the theater when I was working. Not exactly slick."

"He wants to be friends with you," I told her. "He asked me to help him do it."

"Did you?"

"No," I said. "But I did tell him he could help me with my calculus at lunch. And that you might, you know, be there."

I kind of spit this last part out, as I was already bracing myself for her reaction. To my surprise, though, she seemed hardly bothered. "Like I said," she said with a shrug, "he's a nice kid. And it's got to be tough for him here, you know?"

Ah, I thought, remembering back to what she'd said to me about having things in common. Who knew Gervais would count, too? "Yeah," I said. "I guess you're right."

"Plus," she continued, "he knows nothing is going to happen between us."

"Are you *sure* he knows that?"

Now she stopped walking, narrowing her eyes at me. "What?" she said. "Do you think I'm not capable of being clear?"

I shook my head. "No. You are."

"That's right." She started walking again. "We both know the limits of this relationship. It's understood. And as long as we're both comfortable with that, nobody gets hurt. It's basic."

Basic, I thought. *Just like the power rule.*

Calculus aside, I had surprised myself by not only keeping up my end of the deal I'd made with Jamie but actually feeling slightly confident as I sent off my applications back at the end of January. Because of ongoing worries about my GPA, I'd done all I could to strengthen the rest of my material, from my essays to my recommendations. In the end, I'd applied to three schools: the U, Cora's alma mater and one town over; a smaller, more artsy college in the mountains called Slater-Kearns; and one long shot, Defriese University, in D.C. According to Mrs. Pureza, my guidance counselor, all three were known to take a second look at "unique" students like myself. Which meant I might actually have a chance, a thought that at times scared the hell out of me. I'd been looking ahead to the future for so long, practically my entire life. Now that it was close, though, I found myself hesitant, not so sure I was ready.

There was still a lot of the year to go, though, which I reminded myself was a good thing whenever I surveyed what I had done so far on my English project. One day, in a burst of organization I'd hoped would lead to inspiration, I'd spread out everything I had on the desk in my room: stacks of notes, Post-its with quotes stuck up on the wall above, the books I'd used as research—pages marked—piled on either side. Lately, after dinner or when I wasn't working, I'd sit down and go through it bit by bit waiting for that spark.

So far, no luck. In fact, the only thing that ever made me feel somewhat close was the picture of Jamie's family, which I'd taken from the kitchen and tacked up on the wall, right at eye level. I'd spent hours, it felt like, sitting there looking over each individual face, as if one of them might suddenly have what I was searching for. *What is family?* For me, right then, it was one person who'd left me, and two I would have to leave soon. Maybe this was an answer. But it wasn't the right one. Of that, I was sure.

Now, I heard Harriet call my name, jerking me back to the mall, and the present. When I looked up, she was waving me over to the kiosk, where she was standing with the reporter.

"This is my assistant, Ruby Cooper," she said to the reporter as I walked up. "She had on that necklace the day I hired her, and it was my inspiration."

As both the photographer and the reporter immediately turned their attention to my key, I fought not to reach up and cover it, digging my hands into my pockets instead. "Interesting," the reporter said, making a note on her pad. "And what was *your* inspiration, Ruby? What compelled you to start wearing your key like that?"

Talk about being put on the spot. "I . . . I don't know," I said. "I guess I just got tired of always losing it."

The reporter wrote this down, then glanced at the photographer, who was still snapping some shots of the necklaces. "I think that ought to do it," she said to Harriet. "Thanks for your time."

"Thank you," Harriet said. When they'd walked away, she whirled around to face me. "Oh my God. I was a nervous wreck. You think I did all right?"

"You were great," I told her.

"Better than," Reggie added. "Cool as a cuke."

Harriet sat down on her stool, wiping a hand over her face. "They said it will probably run on Sunday, which would be huge. Can you imagine if this gives us an even bigger boost? I can barely keep up with orders as it is."

This was typical Harriet. Even the good stuff meant worrying. "You'll do fine," Reggie said. "You have good help."

"Oh, I know," Harriet said, smiling at me. "It's just . . . a little overwhelming, is all. But I guess I can get Rest Assured to do more, too. Blake's been pushing me to do that anyway. You know, shipping, handling some of the Web site stuff, all that. . . ."

"Just try to enjoy this right now," Reggie told her. "It's a good thing."

I could understand where Harriet was coming from, though. Whenever something great happens, you're always kind of poised for the universe to correct itself. Good begets bad, something lost leads to found, and on and on. But even knowing this, I was surprised when I came home later that afternoon to find Cora and Jamie sitting at the kitchen table, the phone between them. As they both turned to look at me, right away I knew something was wrong.

"Ruby," Cora said. Her voice was soft. Sad. "It's about Mom."

* * *

My mother was not in Florida. She was not on a boat with Warner or soaking up sun or waiting tables in a beachside pancake joint. She was in a rehab clinic, where she'd ended up two weeks earlier after being found unconscious by a maid in the hotel where she'd been living in Tennessee.

At first, I was sure she was dead. So sure, in fact, that as Cora began to explain all this, I felt like my own heart stopped, only beating again once these few words—*hotel, unconscious, rehab, Tennessee*—unscrambled themselves in my mind. When she was done, the only thing I could say was, "She's okay?"

Cora glanced at Jamie, then back at me. "She's in treatment," she said. "She has a long way to go. But yes, she's okay."

It should have made me feel better now that I knew where she was, that she was safe. At the same time, the thought of her in a hospital, locked up, gave me a weird, shaky feeling in my stomach, and I made myself take in a breath. "Was she alone?" I asked.

"What?" Cora said.

"When they found her. Was she alone?"

She nodded. "Was . . . Should someone have been with her?"

Yes, I thought. *Me*. I felt a lump rise up in my throat, sudden and throbbing. "No," I said. "I mean, she had a boyfriend when she left."

She and Jamie exchanged another look, and I had a flash of the last time I'd come back to find them waiting for me in this same place. Then, I'd caught a glimpse of myself in the mirror and seen my mother, or at least some part of her—bedraggled, half-drunk, messed up. But at least someone had been expecting me. No one was picking up my mom from the side of the road, getting her home safe. It was probably only coincidence—a maid's schedule, one room, one day—that got her found in time.

And now she was found, no longer lost. Like a bag I'd given up for good suddenly reappearing in the middle of the night on my doorstep, packed for a journey I'd long ago forgotten. It was odd, considering I'd gotten accustomed to her being nowhere and anywhere, to finally know where my mother was. An exact location, pinpointed. Like she'd crossed over from my imagination, where I'd created a million lives for her, back into this one.

"So what . . ." I said, then swallowed. "What happens now?"

"Well," Cora replied, "the initial treatment program is ninety days. After that, she has some decisions to make. Ideally, she'd stay on, in some kind of supported environment. But it's really up to her."

"Did you talk to her?" I asked.

She shook her head. "No."

"Then how did you hear?"

"From her last landlords. The hospital couldn't find anyone to contact, so they ran a records search, their name came up, and they called us." She turned to Jamie. "What was their name? Huntington?"

"Honeycutt," I said. Already they'd popped into my head, Alice with her elfin looks, Ronnie in his sensible plaid. *Stranger danger!* she'd said that first day, but how weird that they were now the ones that led me back not only to Cora but to my mother, as well.

I felt my face get hot; suddenly, it was all too much. I looked around me, trying to calm down, but all I could see was this clean, lovely foyer, in this perfect neighborhood, all the things that had risen up in my mother's absence, settling into the space made when she left.

"Ruby," Jamie said. "It's all right, okay? Nothing's going to change. In fact, Cora wasn't even sure we should tell you, but—"

I looked at my sister, still seated, the phone in her hands. "But we did," she said, keeping her eyes steady on me. "That said, you have no obligation to her. You need to know that. What happens next with you and Mom, or even if anything does, is up to you."

As it turned out, though, this wasn't exactly true. We soon found out that the rehab place where my mother was staying—and which Cora and Jamie were paying for, although I didn't learn that until later—had a strong policy of patient-focused treatment. Simply put, this meant no outside contact with family or friends, at least not initially. No phone calls. No e-mails. If we sent letters, they'd be kept until a date to be decided later. "It's for the best," Cora told me, after explaining this. "If she's going to do this, she needs to do it on her own."

At that point, we didn't even know if my mom would stay in the program at all, as she hadn't exactly gone willingly. Once they resuscitated her at the hospital, the police found some outstanding bad-check warrants, so she'd had to choose: rehab or jail. I would have had more faith if she'd gone of her own accord. But at least she was there.

Nothing's going to change, Jamie had said that day, but I'd known even then this wasn't true. My mother had always been the point that I calibrated myself against. In knowing where she was, I could always locate myself, as well. These months she'd been gone, I felt like I'd been floating, loose and boundaryless, but now that I knew where she was, I kept waiting for a kind of certainty to kick in. It didn't. Instead, I was more unsure than ever, stuck between this new life and the one I'd left behind.

The fact that this had all happened so soon after Nate and I had fallen out of touch seemed ironic, to say the least. At the same time, though, I was beginning to wonder if this was just how it was supposed to be for me, like perhaps I wasn't capable of having that many people in my life at any one time. My mom turned up, Nate walked away, one door opening as another clicked shut.

As the days passed, I tried to forget about my mom, the way I'd managed to do before, but it was harder now. This was partly because she wasn't lost anymore, but there was also the fact that everywhere I went—school, work, just walking down the street—I saw people wearing Harriet's KeyChains, each one sparkling and pretty, a visible reminder of this, my new life. But the original was there as well—more jaded and rudimentary, functional rather than romantic. It fit not just the yellow house but another door, deep within my own heart. One that had been locked so tight for so long that I was afraid to even try it for fear of what might be on the other side.

Chapter Sixteen

"So basically," Olivia said, "you dig a hole and fill it with water, then throw in some fish."

"No," I said. "First, you have to install a pump system and a skimmer. And bring in rocks and plants, and do something to guard it against birds, who want to eat the fish. And that's not even counting all the water treatments and algae prevention."

She considered this as she leaned forward, peering down into the pond. "Well," she said, "to me, that seems like a lot of trouble. Especially for something you can't even swim in."

Olivia and I were taking a study break from working on our English projects, ostensibly so I could introduce to her to Jamie, who'd been out puttering around the pond, the way he always did on Saturday mornings. When we'd come out, though, he'd been called over to the fence by Mr. Cross, and now, fifteen minutes later, they were still deep in discussion. Judging by the way Jamie kept inching closer to us, bit by bit—as well as the fact that Nate's dad seemed to be doing all the talking—I had a feeling he was trying to extricate himself, although he'd had little luck thus far.

"Then again," Olivia said, sitting back down on the bench, "with a spread like this, you could have a pond *and* a pool, if you wanted."

"True," I agreed. "But it might be overkill."

"Not in this neighborhood," she said. "I mean, honestly. Did you see those boulders when you come in? What is this supposed to be, Stonehenge?"

I smiled. Over by the fence, Jamie took another step backward, nodding in that all-right-then-see-you-later kind of way. Mr. Cross, not getting the hint—or maybe just choosing not to—came closer, bridging the gap again.

"You know, he looks familiar," Olivia said, nodding toward them.

"That's Nate's dad," I told her.

"No, I meant your brother-in-law. I swear, I've seen him somewhere."

"He donated some soccer fields to Perkins," I told her.

"Maybe that's it," she said. Still, she kept her eyes on them as she said, "So Nate lives right there, huh?"

"I told you we were neighbors."

"Yeah, but I didn't realize he was right behind you, only a few feet away. Must make this stalemate—or breakup—you two are in the midst of that much harder."

"It's not a stalemate," I told her. "Or a breakup."

"So you just went from basically hanging out constantly, pretty much on the verge of dating, to not speaking and totally ignoring each other for no reason," she said. "Yeah. *That* makes sense."

"Do we have to talk about this?" I asked as Jamie took another definitive step backward from Mr. Cross, lifting his hand. Mr. Cross was still talking, although this time he stayed where he was.

"You know," Olivia said, "it's pretty rare to find someone

you actually *like* to be with in this world. There are a lot of annoying people out there."

"Really?"

She made a face at me. "My point is, clearly you two had something. So maybe you should think about going to a little trouble to work this out, whatever it is."

"Look," I said, "you said yourself that relationships only work when there's an understanding about the limits. We didn't have that. So now we don't have a relationship."

She considered this for a moment. "Nice," she said. "I especially like how you explained that without actually telling me anything."

"The bottom line is that I just get where you're coming from now, okay?" I said. "You don't want to waste your time on anything or anyone you don't believe in, and neither do I."

"You think that's how I am?" she asked.

"Are you saying it's not?"

Jamie was crossing the yard to us, finally free. He lifted a hand, waving hello. "I'm not saying anything," Olivia replied, leaning back again and shaking her head. "Nothing at all."

"Ladies," Jamie said, ever the happy host as he came up to the bench. "Enjoying the pond?"

"It's very nice," Olivia said politely. "I like the skimmer."

I just looked at her, but Jamie, of course, beamed. "Jamie, this is my friend Olivia," I said.

"Nice to meet you," he said, sticking out his hand.

They shook, and then he crouched down at the edge of the pond, reaching his hand down into the water. As he scooped some up, letting it run over his fingers, Olivia suddenly gasped. "Oh my God. I know where I know you from!" she said. "You're the UMe guy!"

Jamie looked at her, then at me. "Um," he said. "Yeah. I guess I am."

"You recognize him from UMe?" I asked.

"Hello, he's only on the new sign-in page, which I see, like, ten million times a day," she said. She shook her head, clearly still in shock. "Man, I can't believe this. And Ruby never even said anything."

"Well, you know," Jamie said, pushing himself back to his feet, "Ruby is not easily impressed."

Unlike Olivia, who now, as I watched, incredulous, began to actually gush. "Your site," she said to Jamie, putting a hand to her chest, "saved my *life* when I had to switch schools."

"Yeah?" Jamie said, obviously pleased.

"Totally. I spent every lunch in the library on my UMe page messaging with my old friends. And, of course, all night, too." She sighed, wistful. "It was, like, my only connection with them."

"You still had your phone," I pointed out.

"I can check my page on that, too!" To Jamie she said, "Nice application, by the way. Very user friendly."

"You think? We've had some complaints."

"Oh, please." Olivia flipped her hand. "It's easy. Now, the friends system? *That* needs work. I hate it."

"You do?" Jamie said. "Why?"

"Well," she said, "for starters, there's no way to search through them easily. So if you have a lot, and you want to reorganize, you have to just keep scrolling, which takes forever."

I thought of my own UMe.com page, untouched all these months. "How many friends do you have, anyway?" I asked her.

"A couple of thousand," she replied. I just looked at her. "What? Online, I'm popular."

"Obviously," I said.

Later, when Olivia had gone—taking with her a promotional UMe.Com messenger bag packed with UMe.com stickers and T-shirts—I found Jamie in the kitchen, marinating some chicken for dinner. As I came in, the phone began to ring: I went to grab it, but after glancing at the caller ID, he shook his head. "Just let the voice mail get it."

I looked at the display screen, which said CROSS, BLAKE. "You're screening Mr. Cross?"

"Yeah," he said with a sigh, dribbling some olive oil over the chicken and shaking the pan slightly. "I don't want to. But he's being really persistent about this investment thing, so . . ."

"What investment thing?"

He glanced up at me, as if not sure whether or not he wanted to expound on this. Then he said, "Well, you know. Blake's kind of a wheeler-dealer. He's always got some grand plan in the works."

I thought of Mr. Cross that morning, practically stalking Jamie in the yard. "And he wants to do a deal with you?"

"Sort of," he said, going over to the cabinet above the stove and opening it, then rummaging through the contents.

After a minute, he pulled out a tall bottle of vinegar. "He says he wants to expand his business and is looking for silent partners, but really I think he's just short on cash, like last time."

I watched him add a splash of vinegar, then bend down and sniff the chicken before adding more. "So this has happened before."

He nodded, capping the bottle. "Last year, a few months after we moved in. We had him over, you know, for a neighborly drink, and we got to talking. Next thing I know, I'm getting the whole epic saga about his hard financial luck—none of which was his fault, of course—and how he was about to turn it all around with this new venture. Which turned out to be the errand-running thing."

Roscoe came out of the laundry room, where he'd been enjoying one of his many daily naps. Seeing us, he yawned, then headed for the dog door, vaulting himself through it, and it shut with a *thwack* behind him.

"Did you see that?" Jamie said, smiling. "Change is possible!"

I nodded. "It is impressive."

We both watched Roscoe go out into the yard and lift his leg against a tree, relieving himself. Never had a simple act resulted in such pride. "Anyway," Jamie said, "in the end I gave him a check, bought in a bit to the business. It wasn't that much, really, but when your sister found out, she hit the roof."

"Cora did?"

"Oh, yeah," he said. "She's been off him from the start, for some reason. She claims it's because he always talks about money, but my uncle Ronald does that, too, and him she loves. So go figure."

I didn't have to, though. In fact, I was pretty sure I knew exactly why Cora didn't like Mr. Cross, even if she herself couldn't put her finger on it.

"Anyway," Jamie said, "now Blake's scrambling again, I guess. He's been hounding me about this new billing idea and the money ever since Thanksgiving, when I asked him about borrowing his oven. I keep putting him off, but man, he's tenacious. I guess he figures since I'm a sucker, he can pull me in again."

I had a flash of Olivia on the curb, using this same word. "You're not a sucker. You're just nice. You give people the benefit of the doubt."

"Usually to my detriment," he said as the phone rang again. We both looked at it: CROSS, BLAKE. The message light was already beeping. "However," he continued, "other times, people even surpass my expectations. Like you, for instance."

"Does this mean you're going to give me a check?" I asked.

"No," he said flatly. I smiled. "But I am proud of you, Ruby. You've come a long way."

Later, up in my room, I kept thinking about this, the idea of distance and accomplishment. The further you go, the more you have to be proud of. At the same time, in order to come a long way, you have to be behind to begin with. In the end, though, maybe it's not how you reach a place that matters. Just that you get there at all.

* * *

Middle-school girls, I had learned, moved in packs. If you saw them coming, the best thing to do was step aside and save yourself.

"Look, you guys! These are the ones I was telling you about!" a brown-haired girl wearing all pink, clearly the leader of this particular group, said as they swarmed the kiosk, going straight for the KeyChains. "Oh my God. My brother's girlfriend has this one, with the pink stones. Isn't it great?"

"I like the diamond one," a chubby blonde in what looked like leather pants said. "It's the prettiest."

"That's not a diamond," the girl in pink told her as their two friends—twins, by the look of their matching red hair and similar features—moved down to the bracelets. "Otherwise, it would be, like, a million dollars."

"It's diamonelle," Harriet corrected her, "and very reasonably priced at twenty-five."

"Personally," the brunette said, draping the pink-stoned one across her V-necked sweater, "I like the plain silver. It's classic, befitting my new, more streamlined, eco-chic look."

"Eco-chic?" I said.

"Environmentally friendly," the girl explained. "Green? You know, natural metals, non-conflict stones, minimal but with big impact? All the celebrities are doing it. Don't you read *Vogue*?"

"No," I told her.

She shrugged, taking off the necklace, then moved down the kiosk to her friends, who were now gathered around the rings, quickly dismantling the display I'd just spent a good twenty minutes organizing. "You would think," I said to Harriet as we watched them take rings on and off, "that they could at least try to put them back. Or pretend to."

"Oh, let them make a mess," she said. "It's not that big a deal cleaning it up."

"Says the person who doesn't have to do it."

She raised her eyebrows at me, walking over to take her coffee off the register. "Okay," she said slowly. "You're in a bad mood. What gives?"

"I'm sorry," I said as the girls finally moved on, leaving rings scattered across the counter behind them. I went over and began to put them away. "I think I'm just stressed or something."

"Well, it kind of makes sense," Harriet said, coming over to join me. She put an onyx ring back in place, a red one beside it. "You're in your final semester, waiting to hear about college, the future is wide open. But that doesn't necessarily have to get you all bent out of shape. You could look at it as, you know, a great opportunity to embrace stepping out of your comfort zone."

I stopped what I was doing, narrowing my eyes at her as she filled out another row of rings, calm as you please. "Excuse me?" I said.

"What?"

I just looked at her, waiting for her to catch the irony. She didn't. "Harriet," I said finally, "how long did you have that HELP WANTED sign up before you hired me?"

"Ah," she said, pointing at me, "but I *did* hire you, right?"

"And how long did it take you to leave me alone here, to run the kiosk myself?"

"Okay, so I was hesitant," she admitted. "However, I

think you'll agree that I now leave you fairly often with little trepidation."

I considered pointing out that the *fairly* and *little* spoke volumes. Instead I said, "What about Reggie?"

She wiped her hands on her pants, then moved down to the KeyChains, adjusting the pink one on the rack. "What about him?"

"He told me what happened at Christmas," I said. "What was it you said? That you weren't in a 'relationship place'? Is that anywhere near your comfort zone?"

"Reggie is my friend," she said, straightening a clasp. "If we took things further and it didn't work out, it would change everything."

"But you don't know it won't work out."

"I don't know it *will*, either."

"And that's reason enough to not even try," I said. She ignored me, moving down to the rings. "You didn't know that hiring me would work out. But you did it anyway. And if you hadn't—"

"—I'd be enjoying a quiet moment at my kiosk right now, without being analyzed," she said. "Wouldn't that be nice!"

"—you never would have made the KeyChains and seen them be so successful," I finished. "Or been able to enjoy my company, and this conversation, right now."

She made a face at me, then walked back over and hopped up on her stool, opening up the laptop she'd recently bought to keep up with her Web site stuff. "Look. I know in a perfect, utterly romantic world, I'd go out with

Reggie and we'd live happily ever after," she said, hitting the power button. "But sometimes you just have to follow your instincts, and mine say this would not be a good thing for me. All right?"

I nodded. Really, considering everything I'd just gone through, Harriet was someone I should be trying to emulate, not convince otherwise.

I moved back to the rings, reorganizing them the way I had originally, in order of size and color. I was just doing another quick pass with the duster when I heard Harriet say, "Huh. This is weird."

"What is?"

"I'm just checking into my account, and my balance is kind of off," she said. "I know I had a couple of debits out, but not for this much."

"Maybe the site's just delayed," I said.

"I knew I shouldn't have signed on for this new system with Blake. I just feel better when I sign every check myself, you know?" She sighed, then picked up her phone and dialed. After a moment, she closed it. "Voice mail. Of course. Do you know Nate's number, offhand?"

I shook my head. "No. I don't."

"Well, when you see him, tell him I need to talk to him. Like, soon. Okay?"

I wanted to tell her I wouldn't be seeing him, much less delivering messages. But she was already back on the computer, scrolling down.

Harriet wasn't the only one not resting assured, or so I found out when I got home and found Cora in the foyer, wiping up the floor with a paper towel. Roscoe, who usually could not be prevented from greeting me with a full body attack, was conspicuously absent.

"No way," I said, dropping my bag on the floor. "He's mastered the dog door."

"We lock it when we're not here," she told me, pushing herself to her feet. "Which is usually no problem, but someone didn't bother to show up to walk him today."

"Really?" I said. "Are you sure? Nate's usually really dependable."

"Well, not today," she replied. "Clearly."

It was weird. So much so that I wondered if maybe Nate had taken off or something, as that seemed to be the only explanation for him just blowing off things he usually did like clockwork. That night, though, his lights were on, just like always, as were the ones in the pool. It was only when I really looked closely, around midnight, that I saw something out of the ordinary: a figure cutting through the water. Moving back and forth, with steady strokes, dark against all that blue light. I watched him for a long time, but even when I finally turned out the light, he was still swimming.

Chapter Seventeen

That weekend, there was only one thing I should have been thinking about: calculus. The test that pretty much would decide the entire fate of both my GPA and my future was on Monday, and according to Gervais—whose method was proven—it was time to shift into what he called "Zen mode."

"I'm sorry?" I'd said the day before, Friday, when he'd announced this.

"It's part of my technique," he explained, taking a sip of his chocolate milk, one of two he drank each lunch period. "First, we did an overview of everything you were supposed to learn so far this year. Then, we homed in on your weaknesses therein, pinpointing and attacking them one by one. Now, we move into Zen mode."

"Meaning what?" I asked.

"Admitting that you are powerless over your fate, on this test and otherwise. You have to throw out everything that you've learned."

I just looked at him. Olivia, who was checking her UMe page on her phone, said, "Actually, that is a very basic part of Eastern cinema tradition. The warrior, once taught, must now, in the face of his greatest challenge, rely wholly on instinct."

"Why have I spent weeks studying if I'm now supposed to forget everything I've learned?" I said. "That's the stupidest thing I've ever heard."

Olivia shrugged. "The man says his method is proven."

Man? I thought.

Gervais said, "The idea isn't to forget everything. It's that by now, you should know all this well enough that you don't *have* to actively think about it. You see a problem, you know the solution. It's instinct."

I looked down at the practice sheet he'd given me, problems lined up across it. As usual, with just one glance I felt my heart sink, my brain going fuzzy around the edges. If this was my instinct talking, I didn't want to hear what it was saying.

"Zen mode," Gervais said. "Clear your head, accept the uncertainty, and the solutions appear. Just trust me."

I was not convinced, and even less so when he presented me with his instructions for my last weekend of studying. (Which, incidentally, were bullet-pointed and divided into headings and subheadings. The kid was nothing if not professional.) Saturday morning, I was supposed to do a final overview, followed in the afternoon by a short series of problems he'd selected that covered the formulas I had most trouble with. Sunday, the last full day before the test, I wasn't supposed to study at all. Which seemed, frankly, insane. Then again, if the goal was to forget everything by Monday morning, this did seem like the way to do it.

Early the next morning, I sat down on my bed and started my overview, trying to focus. More and more, though, I found myself distracted, thinking about Nate, as I had been pretty much nonstop—occasional calculus obsessions aside—since I'd seen him swimming a couple of nights earlier. In the end, both Harriet and Cora had heard from Mr. Cross, who was wildly apologetic, crediting Harriet's account and offering Cora a free week's worth of walks to compensate. But in the days since, whenever I'd seen Nate across the green or in the halls at school, I couldn't help but notice a change in him. Like even with the distance between us, something about him—in his face or the way he carried himself—was suddenly familiar in a way I hadn't felt before, although how, exactly, I couldn't say.

After two hours of studying, I felt so overwhelmed that I decided to take a break and quickly run over to get my paycheck from Harriet. As soon as I stepped off the greenway, I saw people everywhere—lined up on the curb that ran alongside the mall, gathered in the parking lot, crowded at the base of a stage set up by the movie theater.

"Welcome to the Vista Five-K!" a voice boomed from the stage as I worked my way toward the main entrance, stepping around kids and dogs and more runners stretching and chatting and jogging in place. "If you're participating in the race, please make your way to the start line. Ten minutes to start!"

The crowd shifted as people headed toward the banner—VISTA 5K: RUN FOR YOUR LIFE!—strung between the parking lot and the mall entrance. Following them, I kept an eye out for Olivia but didn't see her—just runners of all shapes and sizes, some in high-tech lycra bodysuits, others in gym shorts and ratty T-shirts.

Inside the mall, it was much quieter, with few shoppers

moving between stores. I could still hear the announcer's voice from outside, along with the booming bass of the music they were playing, even as I walked from the entrance down to the kiosk courtyard, where I found Harriet and Reggie standing at Vitamin Me.

"I'm not doing the fish oil," she was saying as I walked up. "I'm firm on that."

"Omega-threes are crucial!" Reggie told her. "It's like a wonder drug."

"I didn't agree to wonder drugs. I agreed to take a few things, on a trial basis. Nobody said anything about fish."

"Fine." Reggie picked up a bottle, shaking some capsules into a plastic bag. "But you're taking the zinc and the B-twelve. Those are deal breakers."

Harriet shook her head, taking another sip of coffee. Then she saw me. "I thought you might turn up," she said. "Forget vitamins. Money is crucial."

Reggie sighed. "That kind of attitude," he said, "is *precisely* why you need more omega-threes."

Harriet ignored this as she walked over to her register, popping it open and taking out my check. "Here," she said, handing it over to me. "Oh, and there's a little something extra in there for you, as well."

Sure enough, the amount was about three hundred bucks more than I was expecting. "Harriet," I said. "What is this?"

"Profit-sharing," she said, then added, "And a thank-you for all the work you've put in over the last months."

"You didn't have to do this," I said.

"I know. But I got to thinking the other day, after we

had that talk. You were right. The KeyChains, all that. I couldn't have done it without you. Literally."

"That's not why I said that," I told her.

"I know. But it made me think. About a lot of things."

She looked over at Reggie, who was still adding things to her bag. Now that I thought of it, she had been awfully receptive to that zinc. And what was that about a few things, on a trial basis? "Wait," I said, wagging my finger between his kiosk and ours. "What's going on here?"

"Absolutely nothing," she replied, shutting the register.

I raised my eyebrows.

"Fine. If you must know, we just had drinks last night after work, and he convinced me to try a few samples."

"Really."

"Okay, maybe there was a dinner invitation, too," she added.

"Harriet!" I said. "You changed your mind."

She sighed. Over at Vitamin Me, Reggie was folding the top of her bag over neatly, working the crease with his fingers. "I didn't mean to," she said. "Initially, I just went to tell him the same thing I said to you. That I was worried about it not working out, and what that would do to our friendship."

"And?"

"And," she said, sighing, "he said he totally understood, we had another drink, and I said yes to dinner anyway."

"What about the vitamins?"

"I don't know." She flipped her hand at me. "These things happen."

"Yeah," I said, looking over at Reggie again. He'd been

so patient, and eventually he, too, got what he wanted. Or at least a chance at it. "Don't I know it."

By the time I went to the bank, ran a couple of errands, and then doubled back around to the greenway, the Vista 5K was pretty much over. A few runners were still milling around, sipping paper cups of Gatorade, but the assembled crowd had thinned considerably, which was why I immediately spotted Olivia. She was leaning forward on the curb, looking down the mall at the few runners left that were slowly approaching the finish line.

"No Laney yet?" I asked.

She shook her head, not even turning to look at me. "I figure she's dropped out, but she has her phone. She should have called me."

"Thanks to everyone who came out for the Vista Five-K!" a man with a microphone bellowed from the grandstand. "Join us next year, when we'll run for our lives again!"

"She's probably collapsed somewhere," Olivia said. "God, I *knew* this was going to happen. I'll see you, okay?"

She was about halfway across the street when I looked down the mall again and saw something. Just a tiny figure at first, way off in the distance.

"Olivia," I called out, pointing. "Look."

She turned, her eyes following my finger. It was still hard to be sure, so for a moment we just stood there, watching together, as Laney came into sight. She was going so slowly, before finally coming to a complete stop, bending over with her hands on her knees. "Oh, man," Olivia said finally. "It's her."

I turned around, looking at the man on the stage, who

had put down his microphone and was talking to some woman with a clipboard. Nearby, another woman in a Vista 5K T-shirt was climbing a stepladder to the clock, reaching up behind it.

"Wait," I called out to her. "Someone's still coming."

The woman looked down at me, then squinted into the distance. "Sorry," she said. "The race is over."

Olivia, ignoring this, stepped forward, raising her hands to her mouth. "Laney!" she yelled. "You're almost done. Don't quit now!"

Her voice was raw, strained. I thought of that first day I'd found her here with her stopwatch, and all the complaining about the race since. Olivia was a lot of things. But I should have known a sucker wasn't one of them.

"Come on!" she yelled. She started clapping her hands, hard, the sound sharp and single in the quiet. "Let's go, Laney!" she yelled, her voice rising up over all of us. *"Come on!"*

Everyone was staring as she jumped up and down in the middle of the road, her claps echoing off the building behind us. Watching her, I thought of Harriet, doubtfully eyeing those vitamins as Reggie dropped them into the bag, one by one, and then of me with Nate on the bench by the pond the last time we'd been together. *And if I don't?* he'd asked, and I'd thought there could be only one answer, in that one moment. But now, I was beginning to wonder if you didn't always have to choose between turning away for good or rushing in deeper. In the moments that it really counts, maybe it's enough—more than enough, even—just to be there. Laney must have thought so. Because right then, she started running again.

When she finally finished a few minutes later, it was hard to tell if she was even aware that the crowds had thinned, the clock was off, and the announcer didn't even call her time. But I do know that it was Olivia she turned to look for first, Olivia she threw her arms around and hugged tight, as that banner flapped overhead. Watching them, I thought again of how we can't expect everybody to be there for us, all at once. So it's a lucky thing that really, all you need is someone.

* * *

Back home, I sat down with my calculus notes, determined to study, but within moments my mind wandered past the numbers and figures and across the room to the picture of Jamie's family, still up on the wall over my desk. It was the weirdest thing—I'd studied it a thousand times, in this same place, the same way. But suddenly, all at once, it just made sense.

What is family? They were the people who claimed you. In good, in bad, in parts or in whole, they were the ones who showed up, who stayed in there, regardless. It wasn't just about blood relations or shared chromosomes, but something wider, bigger. Cora was right—we had many families over time. Our family of origin, the family we created, as well as the groups you moved through while all of this was happening: friends, lovers, sometimes even strangers. None of them were perfect, and we couldn't expect them to be. You couldn't make any one person your world. The trick was to take what each could give you and build a world from it.

So my true family was not just my mom, lost or found;

my dad, gone from the start; and Cora, the only one who had really been there all along. It was Jamie, who took me in without question and gave me a future I once couldn't even imagine; Olivia, who did question, but also gave me answers; Harriet, who, like me, believed she needed no one and discovered otherwise. And then there was Nate.

Nate, who was a friend to me before I even knew what a friend was. Who picked me up, literally, over and over again, and never asked for anything in return except for my word and my understanding. I'd given him one but not the other, because at the time I thought I couldn't, and then proved myself right by doing exactly as my mother had, hurting to prevent from being hurt myself. Needing was so easy: it came naturally, like breathing. Being needed by someone else, though, that was the hard part. But as with giving help and accepting it, we had to do both to be made complete—like links overlapping to form a chain, or a lock finding the right key.

I pushed out my chair, and headed downstairs, through the kitchen and out into the yard. I knew this was crazy, but suddenly it seemed so crucial that I somehow tell Nate I was sorry, reach out to him and let him know that I was here.

When I got to the gate, I pulled it open, then peered in, looking for him. But it was Mr. Cross I saw a moment later, walking quickly through the living room, his phone to his ear. Immediately I stepped back, around the fence, hiding as he slid open the glass door and came out onto the patio.

"I told you, I've been out of town all day," he was saying as he crossed by the pool, over to the garage. "He was supposed to be doing pickups and check-ins. Did he come by and get the cleaning today?" He paused, letting out a breath. "Fine. I'll keep looking for him. If you see him, tell him I want him home. Now. Understood?"

As he went back inside, all I could hear, other than my breathing, was the bubbling of the nearby pump, pushing the water in and out, in and out. I thought of Nate swimming laps that night, his dark shadow moving beneath the trees, how long it had been since I'd seen him alone in the pool.

Mr. Cross was inside now, still looking as his pace quickened, moving faster, back and forth. Watching him, I had a flash of Nate at school the last time I'd seen him, suddenly realizing why his expression—distant, distracted—had been so familiar. It was the same one on my mother's face the last time I'd seen her, when I walked into a room and she turned, surprised.

And this was why, as Mr. Cross called his name again, I knew his searching was useless. There's just something obvious about emptiness, even when you try to convince yourself otherwise. Nate was gone.

Chapter Eighteen

"Here," Jamie said. "For luck."

I watched him as he slid his car keys across the table toward me. "Really?" I said. "Are you sure?"

"Positive," he replied. "It's a big day. You shouldn't have to start it on the bus."

"Wow," I said, slipping them into my pocket. "Thanks."

He sat down across from me, pouring himself his usual heaping bowl of cereal, which he then drowned with milk. "So," he said, "what's your state of mind. Confident? Nervous? Zen?"

I made a face at him. "I'm fine," I told him. "I just want to get it over with."

His phone, which was on vibrate, suddenly buzzed, skipping itself sideways across the table. Jamie glanced at the caller ID and groaned. "Jesus," he said, but answered anyway. Still, his voice was curt, not at all Jamie-like, as he said, "Yes?"

I pushed out my chair, taking my own bowl to the sink. As I passed him, I could hear a voice through the receiver, although the words were indistinguishable.

"Really," Jamie said, and now he sounded concerned. "When was the last time you saw him? Oh. Okay, hold on, I'll ask her." He moved the phone away from his ear. "Hey, have you talked to Nate lately? His dad's looking for him."

I knew it, I thought. Out loud, I said, "No."

"Did you see him this weekend?"

I shook my head. "Not since school on Friday."

"She hasn't seen him since Friday," Jamie repeated into the phone. "Yeah, absolutely. We'll definitely let you know if we do. Keep us posted, okay?"

I opened the dishwasher, concentrating on loading in my bowl and spoon as he hung up. "What's going on?" I asked.

"Nate's gone AWOL, apparently," he said. "Blake hasn't seen him since Friday night."

I stood up, shutting the dishwasher. "Has he called the police?"

"No," he said, taking a bite of cereal. "He thinks he probably just took off for the weekend with his friends—you know, senioritis or whatever. Can't have gone far, at any rate."

But I, of course, knew this wasn't necessarily true. You could get anywhere on foot, especially if you had money and time. And Nate hadn't had a fence to jump. He'd just walked out. Free and clear.

And I was too late. If I'd just gone over there that night I'd seen him swimming, or talked to him on Friday at school, maybe, just maybe, I might have been able to help. Now, even if I wanted to go after him, I didn't know where to start. He could be anywhere.

It was weirder than I'd expected, driving myself to school after so many long months of being dependent on someone else. Under any other circumstances, I probably would have enjoyed it, but instead it felt almost strange to be sitting in traffic in the quiet of Jamie's Audi, other cars on all sides of me. At one light, I glanced over to see a woman in a minivan looking at me, and I wondered if to her I was just a spoiled teenage girl in an expensive car, a backpack on the seat beside her, blinker on to turn in to an exclusive school. This was unnerving for some reason, so much so that I found myself staring back at her, hard, until she turned away.

Once at school, I started across the green, taking a deep breath and trying to clear my head. Because of my certainty that Nate had taken off—even before I knew it for sure—I'd actually ended up following Gervais's Zen-mode plan, if only because I'd been too distracted to study the night before. Now, though, calculus was the last thing on my mind, even as I approached my classroom and found him waiting outside the door for me.

"All right," he said. "Did you follow my pre-test instructions? Get at least eight hours sleep? Eat a protein-heavy breakfast?"

"Gervais," I said. "Not right now, okay?"

"Remember," he said, ignoring this, "take your time on the first sets, even if they seem easy. You need them to prime your brain, lay the groundwork for the harder stuff."

I nodded, not even bothering to respond this time.

"If you find yourself stumbling with the power rule, remember that acronym we talked about. And write it down on the test page, so you can have it right in front of you."

"I need to go," I said.

"And finally," he said as, inside, my teacher Ms. Gooden was picking up a stack of papers, shuffling them as she prepared to hand them out, "if you get stuck, just clear your head. Envision an empty room, and let your mind examine it. In time, you will find the answer."

He blurted out this last part, not very Zen at all, as he rushed to fit it in as the bell rang. Even in my distracted state, as I looked at him I realized I should be more grateful. Sure, we'd had a deal, and I had paid him his twenty bucks an hour when he invoiced me (which he did on a biweekly basis on preprinted letterhead, no joke). But showing up like this, for a last-minute primer? That was above the call of duty. Even for a multipronged, proven method like his.

"Thanks, Gervais," I said.

"Don't thank me," he replied. "Just go get that ninety. I don't want you messing up my success rate."

I nodded, then turned to go into my classroom, sliding into my seat. When I looked back out the door, he was still standing there, peering in at me. Jake Bristol, who was sitting beside me looking sleepy, leaned across the aisle, poking my shoulder. "What's up with you and Miller?" he asked. "You into jailbait or something?"

I just looked at him. Jerk. "No," I said. "We're friends."

Now, Ms. Gooden came down the aisle, smiling at me as she slid a test, facedown, onto the desk in front of me. She was tall and pretty, with blonde hair she wore long, twisting it back with a pencil when she got busy filling up the board with theorems. "Good luck," she said as I turned it over.

At first glance, I felt my heart sink, immediately overwhelmed. But then I remembered what Gervais had said, about taking my time and priming my brain, and picked up my pencil and began.

The first one was easy. The second, a little harder, but still manageable. It wasn't until I got to the bottom of the front page that I realized that somehow, I was actually doing this. Carefully moving from one to the next, following Gervais's advice, jotting the power rule down in the margin: *The derivative of any given variable (x) to the exponent (n) is equal to product of the exponent and the variable to the (n–1) power.* I could hear Olivia saying it in my head, just as I heard Gervais's voice again and again, telling me the next step, and then the one following, each time I found myself hesitating.

There were ten minutes left on the clock when I reached the last problem, and this one did give me pause, more than any of the others. Staring down at it, I could feel myself starting to panic, the worry rising up slowly from my gut, and this time, no voices were coming, no prompting to be heard. I glanced around me at the people on either side still scribbling, at Ms. Gooden, who was flipping through *Lucky* magazine, and finally at the clock, which let me know I had five minutes left. Then I closed my eyes.

An empty room, Gervais had said, and at first I tried to picture white walls, a wood floor, a generic anywhere. But as my mind began to settle, something else came slowly into view: a door swinging open, revealing a room I recognized. It wasn't one in the yellow house, though, or even Cora's, but instead one with high glass windows opposite, a bedroom to the side with a dry-cleaned duvet, sofas that had hardly been used. A room empty not in definition, but in feeling. And finally, as my mind's eye moved across all of these, I saw one last thing: a root-beer cap sitting square on a countertop, just where someone had left it to be found.

I opened my eyes, then looked back down at the one blank spot on my paper, the problem left unsolved. I still had three minutes as I quickly jotted down an answer, not thinking, just going on instinct. Then I brought my paper to the front of the room, handed it in, and pushed out the door onto the green, heading toward the parking lot. I could just barely hear the bell, distant and steady, as I drove away.

* * *

In a perfect world, I would have remembered not only where the apartment building was, what floor to take the elevator to, but also the exact number of the unit. Because this was my world, however, I found myself on the seventh floor, all those doors stretching out before me, and no idea where to begin. In the end, I walked halfway down the hallway and just started knocking.

If someone answered, I apologized. If they didn't, I moved on. At the sixth door, though, something else happened. No one opened it, but I heard a noise just inside. On instinct—call it Zen mode—I reached down and tried the knob. No key necessary. It swung right open.

The room was just as I'd pictured it earlier. Sofas undisturbed, counter clutter-free, the bottle cap just where it had been. The only difference was a USWIM sweatshirt hanging over the back of one of the island stools. I picked it up, putting it to my face as I breathed in the smell of chlorine, of water. Of Nate. And then, with it still lingering, I looked outside and found him.

He was standing on the balcony, hands on the rail, his back to me, even though it was cold, so cold I could feel the air seeping through the glass as I came closer. I reached for the door handle to pull it open, then stopped halfway, suddenly nervous. How do you even begin to return to someone, much less convince them to do the same for you? I had no idea. More than ever, though, right then I had to believe the answer would just come to me. So I pulled the door open.

When Nate turned around, I could tell I'd startled him. His face was surprised, only relaxing slightly when he saw it was me. By then, I'd already noticed the marks on his cheek and chin, red turning to blue. There comes a point when things are undeniable and can't be hidden any longer. Even from yourself.

"Ruby," he said. "What are you doing here?"

I opened my mouth to say something in response to this. Anything, just a word, even if it wasn't the perfect one. But as nothing came, I looked at the landscape spread out behind him, wide and vast on either side. It wasn't empty, not at all, but maybe this could inspire you as well, because right then, I knew just what to say, or at least a good place to start, even if only because it was what Cora had said to me back when all this began.

"It's cold," I said, holding out my hand to him. "You should come inside."

Chapter Nineteen

Nate did come in. Getting him to come back with me, though, was harder.

In fact, we'd sat on the couch in that apartment for more than two hours, going over everything that had happened, before he finally agreed to at least talk to someone. This part, at least, I didn't even have to think about. I'd picked up his phone and dialed a number, and by the time we got back to my house, Cora was already waiting.

They sat at the kitchen table, me hanging back against the island, as Nate told her everything. About how when he'd first moved back, living with his dad had been okay—occasionally, he had money problems and issues with creditors, but when he took out his stress on Nate it was infrequent. Since the fall, though, when Rest Assured began to struggle, things had been getting worse, culminating in the months since Christmas, when a bunch of loans had come due. Nate said he had always planned to stick it out, but after a particularly bad fight a few nights earlier—the end result of which were the bruises on his face—he'd had enough.

Cora was amazing that day. She did everything—from just listening, her face serious, to asking careful questions, to calling up her contacts at the social-services division to answer Nate's questions about what his options were. In the end, it was she who dialed his mom in Arizona, her voice calm and professional as she explained the situation, then nodded supportively as she handed the receiver over to Nate to do the rest.

By that night, a plane ticket was booked, a temporary living arrangement set. Nate would spend the rest of the school year in Arizona, followed by working the swim-camp job in Pennsylvania he'd already set up through the summer. Come fall, he'd head off to the U, where he'd recently gotten in early admission, albeit without his scholarship due to quitting swim team midyear. Still, it was his hope that the coach might be open to letting him try for alternate, or at least participate in practices. It wasn't exactly what he'd planned, but it was something.

Mr. Cross was not happy when he found out about all this. In fact, at first he insisted that Nate return home, threatening to get the police involved if he didn't. It wasn't until Cora informed him that Nate had more than enough cause to press charges against him that he acquiesced, although even then he made his displeasure known with repeated phone calls, as well as making it as difficult as he could for Nate to collect his stuff and move in with us for the few days before he left town.

I did my best to distract Nate from all this, dragging him to movies at the Vista 10 (where we got free popcorn and admission, thanks to Olivia), hanging out with Roscoe, and taking extended coffee trips to Jump Java. He didn't go back to Perkins, as Cora had arranged for him to finish the little bit of work he had left via correspondence or online, and every afternoon as I came up the front walk, I was nervous, calling out to him the minute I stepped in the door. I finally understood what Jamie and Cora had gone through with me those first few weeks, if only from the relief I felt every time I heard his voice responding.

All the while, though, I knew he soon wouldn't be there. But I never talked to him about this. He had enough to worry about, and what mattered most was that I was just there for him, however he needed me to be. Still, the morning of his flight, when I came downstairs to find him in the foyer, his bags at his feet, I felt that same twist in my stomach.

I wasn't the only one upset. Cora sniffled through the entire good-bye, hugging him repeatedly, a tissue clutched in her hand. "Now, I'll call you tonight, just to make sure you're getting settled in," she told him. "And don't worry about things on this end. It's all handled."

"Okay," Nate said. "Thanks again. For everything."

"Don't be a stranger, all right?" Jamie told him, giving him a bear hug and a back slap. "You're family now."

Family, I thought as we pulled out of the driveway. The neighborhood was still asleep, houses dark as we drove out past those big stone pillars, and I remembered how I'd felt, coming in all those months ago, with everything so new and different.

"Are you nervous?" I asked Nate as we pulled out onto the main road.

"Not really," he replied, sitting back. "It's all kind of surreal, actually."

"It'll hit you eventually," I told him. "Probably at the exact moment it's too late to come back."

He smiled. "But I am coming back," he said. "I just have to survive Arizona and my mother first."

"You think it'll be that bad?"

"I have no idea. It isn't like she chose for me to come there. She's only doing this because she has to."

I nodded, slowing for a light. "Well, you never know. She might surprise you," I said. He did not look convinced, so I added, "Either way, don't decide to pack it in the first night, or jump any fences. Give it a few days."

"Right," he said slowly, looking over at me. "Any other advice?"

I switched lanes, merging onto the highway. It was so early, we had all the lanes to ourselves. "Well," I said, "if there's some annoying neighbor who tries to make nice with you, don't be a total jerk to them."

"Because you might need them later," he said. "To take you out of the woods, or something."

"Exactly."

I felt him look at me but didn't say anything as we came up to the airport exit. As I took it, circling around, I could see a plane overhead—just a sliver of white, heading up, up, up.

At the terminal, even at this early hour, there were a fair amount of people, heading off, arriving home. The sun was coming up now, the sky streaked with pink overhead as we unloaded his stuff, piling it on the curb beside him. "All right," I said. "Got everything?"

"Think so," he said. "Thanks for the ride."

"Well, I did kind of owe you," I said, and he smiled. "But there is one more thing, actually."

"What's that?"

"Even if you do make tons of new friends," I told him, "try not to forget where you came from, okay?"

He looked down at me. "I seriously doubt that could happen."

"You'd be surprised," I told him. "New place, new life. It's not hard to do."

"I think," he said, "that I'll have plenty to remind me."

I hoped this was true. Even if it wasn't, all I could do was hand over what I could, with the hope of something in return. But of course, this was easier said than done. Ever since Christmas, I'd been trying to come up with the perfect gift for Nate, something phenomenal that might come close to all he'd given me. Once again, I thought I had nothing to offer. But then I looked down and realized I was wrong.

The clasp of my necklace was stubborn at first, and as I took the key to the yellow house off and put it into my pocket, I noticed how worn it was. Especially in comparison to the bright, shiny new one to Jamie and Cora's, which I slid onto the chain in its place. Then I took Nate's hand, turning it upward, and pressed the necklace, with Cora's key on it, into his palm.

"Well," I said, "just in case."

He nodded, wrapping his hand around the necklace, and my hand, as well. This time, I let my palm relax against his, feeling the warmth there and pressing back, before stepping in closer. Then I reached up, sliding my hand behind his neck and pulling him in for a kiss, closing that space between us once and for all.

In the weeks since, Nate and I had been in constant contact, both by phone and on UMe.com. My page, long inactive, was now not only up and running but full of extras, thanks to Olivia, who helped me set it up and tweaked it on a regular basis. So far, I'd only accrued a few friends—her, Nate, Gervais, as well as Jamie, who sent me more messages than anyone—although I had lots of photos, including a couple Nate had sent of him at his new job, lifeguarding at a pool near his mom's house. He was swimming every day now, working on his times and getting back into shape; he said it was slow progress, but he was seeing improvements, bit by bit. Sometimes at night in my room when I couldn't sleep, I imagined him in the pool, crossing its length again and again, stroke by even stroke.

In my favorite picture, though, he's not in the water but posing in front of a lifeguard stand. He's smiling, the sun bright behind him, and has a whistle around his neck. If you look really closely, you can see there's another, thinner chain behind, with something else dangling from it. It was hard to make it out, exactly. But I knew what it was.

Chapter Twenty

"Ruby? You about ready?"

I turned, looking over my shoulder at Cora, who was standing in the door to the kitchen, her purse over her shoulder. "Are we leaving?" I asked.

"As soon as Jamie finds the camcorder," she replied. "He's determined to capture every moment of this milestone."

"You have to document important family events!" I heard Jamie yell from somewhere behind her. "You'll thank me later."

Cora rolled her eyes. "Five minutes, whether he finds it or not. We don't want to be late. Okay?"

I nodded, and she ducked back inside, the door falling shut behind her, as I turned back to the pond. I'd been spending a lot of time out there lately, ever since the day a couple of months earlier when I'd come home from work to find her and Jamie huddled over something in the foyer.

"Jamie. Put it down."

"I'm not opening it. I'm just looking."

"Would you stop?"

I came up right behind them. "What are you guys doing?"

Cora jumped, startled. "Nothing," she said. "We were just—"

"You got a letter from the U," Jamie told me, holding up what I now saw was an envelope. "I brought it in about an hour ago. The anticipation has been *killing* us."

"It was killing Jamie," Cora said. "I was fine."

I walked over to where they were standing, taking the envelope from him. After all I'd heard and read about thick and thin letters, this one was, of course, neither. Not bulky, not slim, but right in the middle.

"It only takes a page to say no," Jamie told me as if I'd said this aloud. "It is only one word, after all."

"Jamie, for God's sake!" Cora swatted him. "Stop it."

I looked at the envelope again. "I'm going to take it outside," I said. "If that's okay."

Jamie opened his mouth to protest, but Cora put her hand over it. "That's fine," she said. "Good luck."

Then it was April. The grass had gone from that nubby, hard brown to a fresh green, and the trees were all budding, shedding pollen everywhere. A nice breeze was blowing as I walked out to the pond, the envelope dangling from my hand. I walked right up to the edge, where I could see my reflection, then tore it open.

I was just about to unfold the pages within when I saw something, out of the corner of my eye, moving quickly, so quickly I almost doubted it. I stepped closer, peering down into the murky depths, past the rocks and algae and budding irises, and there, sure enough, I saw a flash of white blurring past. There were others as well, gold and speckled and black, swimming low. But it was the white one, my fish, that I saw first. I took a deep breath and tore the letter open.

Dear Ms. Cooper, it began. *We are pleased to inform you . . .*

I turned around, looking back at the kitchen door where, unsurprisingly, Jamie and Cora were both standing, watching me. Jamie pushed it open, then stuck his head out. "Well?" he said.

"Good news," I said.

"Yeah?" Beside him, Cora put her hand to her mouth, her eyes widening.

I nodded. "And the fish are back. Come see."

Now, in mid-June, they were even more present, circling around the lilies and water grasses. Above them, in the water's surface, I could see my reflection: my hair loose, black gown, cap in one hand. Then a breeze blew across the yard, rustling the leaves overhead and sending everything rippling. Beside me, sitting on the grass, Roscoe closed his eyes.

As always, when I saw myself, it was weird to be without my necklace. Even now, I was still very aware of its absence, the sudden empty space where for so long I'd always seen something familiar. A few days earlier, though, I'd been digging through a drawer and come across the box Nate had given me for Valentine's Day. The next time we spoke, I mentioned this, and he told me to open it. When I did, I saw that once again he'd known what I needed, even before I did. Inside was a pair of key-shaped earrings—clearly Harriet's work—studded with red stones. I'd been wearing them every day since.

I looked across the yard, the trees swaying overhead, to Nate's house. I still called it that, a habit that I had yet to break, even though neither he nor his dad had lived there for a while. Mr. Cross had put it up for sale in May, just after a lawsuit was filed by several Rest Assured clients who had began to notice, and question, various discrepancies on their accounts. The last I'd heard, he was still in business, but just barely, and renting an apartment somewhere across town. The new owners of the house had small children and used the pool all the time. On warm afternoons, from my window, I could hear them laughing and splashing.

As for me, thanks to Gervais's method, I'd made a ninety-one on my calc test—guaranteeing my own spot at the U—and soon would be walking across the green at Perkins Day, taking my diploma from Mr. Thackray, officially a high-school graduate. In the lead up to the ceremony, I'd received endless paperwork and e-mails about getting tickets for family, and all the rules and regulations about how many we were allowed to reserve. In the end, I'd taken four, for Cora and Jamie, Reggie and Harriet. Not all family, but if there was one thing I'd learned over these last few months, it was that this was a flexible definition.

At least, that was the final thesis of my English project, which I'd handed in during the last week of classes. We'd each had to get up in front of the class and do a presentation that showcased our research and findings, and for mine, I'd brought in two pictures. The first was of Jamie's extended tribe, which I put up while I explained about the different definitions I'd gathered, and how they all related to one another. The second was more recent, from the eighteenth birthday party Cora had thrown me at the end of May. I'd told her not to make a fuss, but of course she'd ignored me, insisting that we had to do something, and that I should invite anyone I wanted to celebrate with me.

In the picture, we're all posing by the pond, one big group. I'm in the center, with Cora on one side, Olivia on the other. You can see Jamie, slightly blurred from running back into the shot after setting the timer on the camera—he's standing by Harriet, who is looking at me and smiling, and Reggie, who is of course looking at her. Next to them you can see Laney, smiling big, and then Gervais, the only one eating, a plate of cake in his hand. Like the first one, which I'd studied all these months, it is not a perfect picture, not even close. But in that moment, it was exactly what it was supposed to be.

It was also, like the one of Jamie's family, already changing, even if that day we hadn't known it yet. That came a couple of weeks later, when I was leaving for school one morning and found my sister sitting on her bed, crying.

"Cora?" I dropped my backpack, then came over to sit beside her. "What's wrong?"

She drew in a big, shuddering breath, shaking her head, clearly unable to answer. By then, though, I didn't need her to; I'd already seen the pregnancy-test box on the bedside table. "Oh, Cora," I said. "It's okay."

"I—I—" she said, sobbing through the words.

"What's going on?" Jamie, who had just come up the stairs, said as he came into the room. I nodded at the test box, and his face fell. "Oh," he said, taking a seat on her other side. "Honey. It's all right. We've got that appointment next week—we'll see what's going on—"

"I'm fine," Cora sputtered as I grabbed her some tissues. "I really am."

I reached over, taking her hand so I could put the tissues into it. She was still holding the test stick, so I took it from her as she drew in another breath. It wasn't until after I put it down on the bed beside me that I actually looked at it.

"Are you, though?" Jamie was saying, rubbing her shoulders. "Are you sure?"

I stared at the stick again, double-checking it. Then tripling. "Yeah," I said, holding it up, the plus sign more than clear as Cora dissolved in tears again. "She's positive."

She was also sick as a dog, morning and night, as well as so tired she couldn't stay up much past dinner. Not that I'd heard her complain, even once.

All of this had got me thinking, and a few days before my birthday, I'd sat down at my desk to write a letter, long overdue, to my own mother, who was still in rehab in Tennessee. I wasn't sure what I wanted to say, though, and after sitting there for a full hour, with nothing coming, I'd just photocopied my acceptance letter from the U and slid it inside the envelope. It wasn't closure, by any means, but it was progress. If nothing else, now we knew where to find each other, even if only time would tell if either of us would ever come looking.

"Got it! Let's go!" I heard Jamie yell from inside. Roscoe perked up his ears, and I watched him run, tags jingling, across the grass to the house.

It was only then, when I knew I was alone, at least for the moment, that I reached under my gown into the pocket of my dress. As I pulled out my key from the yellow house, which I'd kept on my bureau since the day Nate left, I traced the shape one last time before folding my hand tightly around it.

Behind me, Cora was calling again. My family was waiting. Looking down at the pond, all I could think was that it is an incredible thing, how a whole world can rise from what seems like nothing at all. I stepped closer to the edge, keeping my eyes on my reflection as I dropped the key into the water, where it landed with a splash. At first, the fish darted away, but as it began to sink they circled back, gathering around. Together, they followed it down, down, until it was gone.

TURN THE PAGE TO READ AN EXCERPT FROM SARAH DESSEN'S

ONCE AND FOR ALL

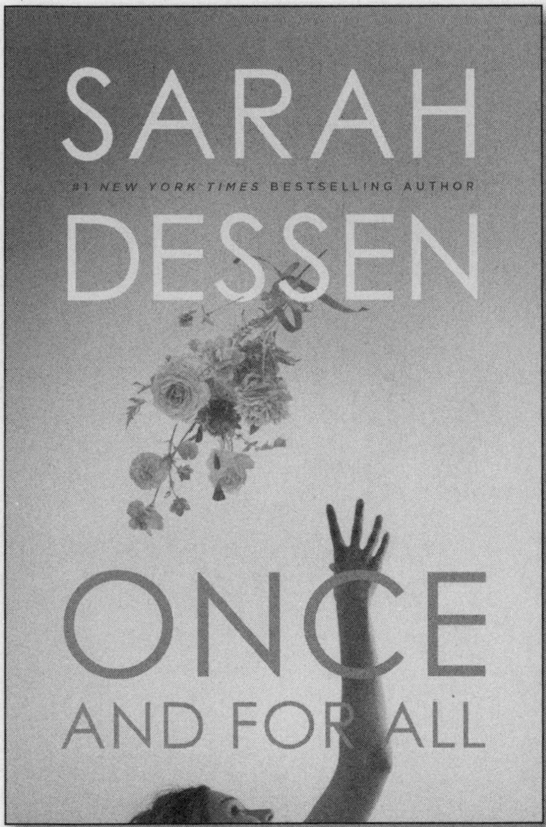

THE SAND WAS chilly on my feet as I stepped onto it that August night. With the music still audible from the patio, I hooked the straps of my shoes onto my thumb, then slid my phone into the pocket of my dress. Ahead, the beach was flat and dark, dotted with the lights from hotels and, farther along, houses. Thinking I'd only go a little way before I turned around, I started walking.

If he hadn't been wearing that white shirt, bright almost to the point of glowing, I might not have even seen him. But he was. The boy who had asked me to dance, standing by the water's edge. I couldn't miss him. No, more than that. I can never picture him in anything else.

The real surprise, though, was that he saw *me*. When you come across someone on the beach at night, contemplating the ocean, you don't exactly interrupt. It's one of those unwritten rules. So I'd just walked behind him, keeping my head down, when I heard him say, "All done for the night?"

It's funny, the details you remember from the things you cannot forget. The sand cool on my feet. The weight of my shoes, shifting as they swung in my hand. And again, that shirt bright in contrast to my own black dress, so dark I wondered later how he'd seen me at all.

We stood there a second, facing each other. His shirttails, now untucked, were ruffling in the wind. I'd never had this feeling before, that something big was about to happen, and there was nothing I had to do but wait for it. A beat. Then another. Finally, Ethan stepped back from me, away from the thrown brightness of the hotel and into the dimness of the beach beyond. The wind blew my hair, the straps of my shoes twisting around each other as he smiled at me, then gestured for me to join him there.

I didn't hesitate. So much of life is not being sure of anything. How I wished, later, I'd been able to savor them, those few steps and moments when for once, I just knew.

Behind us, I heard a swell of music, something easy and slow; it had to be deafening by the bonfire. Where we were, though, it was caught in the wind and carried, just distant enough to seem ghostlike. Or maybe that was the wrong word. Perhaps I wouldn't have used it at that moment, but only now.

Ethan walked out a little farther into the sand and water, the wind catching that white shirt, again sending the back billowing behind him. It was like he was glowing, more alive than anything I'd ever seen, when he turned back to me, holding out his hand. "Okay, I'll only ask once more, I promise. Want to dance?"

Could I hear the music, still? In my memory, the answer is yes. But in retrospect everything is perfect, as are all the other details of this night. At that moment, though, everything was brand-new, including the way I felt as I stepped forward, locking my fingers into his as he pulled me in closer. Me and Ethan, dancing in the dark at the end of the world. It was like I'd waited all my life to have something like this, and I knew even then, at the start, that it would be hard, so hard to lose. The big stuff always is.